The English Companion

The English Companion

An Idiosyncratic Guide
to England & Englishness
from A to Z

Godfrey Smith

Clarkson N. Potter, Inc./Publishers
DISTRIBUTED BY CROWN PUBLISHERS, INC., NEW YORK

Published in the United States by Clarkson N. Potter, Inc.
One Park Avenue, New York, New York 1001

Originally published in Great Britain in 1984
by Pavilion Books Ltd., 196 Shaftesbury Avenue,
London WC2H 8JL

Manufactured in the United States

Library of Congress Cataloging in Publication Data

Smith, Godfrey, 1926–
    The English companion.
    1. England—Social life and customs—20th
century—Dictionaries. 2. National
characteristics, English—Dictionaries.
    I. Title.
DA566.4.S555
1984   306′.0941   84-16036

    ISBN 0-517-55584-0

10 9 8 7 6 5 4 3 2 1

First American Edition

for Asa

Introduction

Companions nowadays take a capital initial letter. They have scholarly editors, and thousands of pages. They are designed to guide us through dauntingly complex landscapes: art, film, literature, science and theatre. Yet when the first, *The Oxford Companion to English Literature,* was originally discussed, it took a small 'c'. It was intended to be an unassuming friend who would stroll with the reader, pointing out an interesting tree here, a shrub there, a pleasing valley or refreshing stream. It would tell you a yarn or two on your journey, but would not chuck its weight about.

In putting together *The English Companion* I have tried to follow this modest first plan. It is an informal ramble through English things. It makes no pretensions to original thought, academic distinction, or comprehensive sweep. Indeed, not to put too fine a point on it, it is subjective, idiosyncratic, and, some would say, perversely capricious. Thus Auden is included but not Eliot, Winchester is discussed but not Canterbury, Fortnums but not Selfridges. There was of course no choice about this piecemeal policy: to attempt to deal exhaustively with English preoccupations would need a dozen volumes and defeat the object of the exercise, for if a companion cannot go unobtrusively where the reader goes, what is the use of it?

Nevertheless, I hope the subjects I have included will divert readers and perhaps even occasionally tell them something new; certainly I have learned a lot about my native country, and my fellow countrymen, in putting it together. The English are curiously neglected. Until George Orwell sat down to write on the English people, as his biographer Bernard Crick points out, there was really very little in the language on the theme apart from the orotund guff of Winston Churchill, Arthur Bryant, and A.L. Rowse. What we might call the Whitbread view of England – a smiling land full of wheatfields and wenches, gaffers and gumboots, cakes and ale – had its heyday in Edwardian England and lingered on between the wars. It can still be detected residually, but happily a new spirit of realism is abroad and the English now take themselves far less seriously than they did. Over and again in putting this book together I have been struck by the way in which words and ideas once taken quite literally and solemnly are now used increasingly in an ironic and mocking sense.

To take just one obvious example: it is increasingly hard in modern England to use the word gentleman four-square. It is introduced, if at all, in a flip way which seems to say: I'm using this word but of course you realise I'm not to be taken seriously when I do so. Are we then to assume that the national character is changing? Marginally and gradually, perhaps it is; but I think it is the *perception* of England which is changing. The world sees us differently; we see ourselves differently. Ancient stereotypes have been stood on their heads. England, once the richest country in the world, now ranks fifteenth in terms of real income, well behind Norway and Sweden, and roughly on a par with Austria. The English, once seen as the coldest fish in Europe, now show clear signs of becoming one of the randiest races on earth. On the other hand certain English attributes seem never to change: a daunting philistinism, a shaky grip on hygiene, an obsession with animals, a predilection for gambling, a gift with gardens, a passion for sport, an incomprehension of foreigners and a huge sense of humour.

There remains too the English preoccupation with class. I have argued under that heading in this companion that though class has been the English pox, increasingly what really preoccupies the English is not so much class as style. I may be wrong, but it does seem to me this is one way in which the texture of English life has changed most radically. The collapse of the old deference structure is in my mind one of the best developments in modern England, and though I have tried not to flinch at English failings, no reader will be left in much doubt where my affections really lie. I find England so overwhelmingly the best country in the world that it is really rather bad form to say how much. Nevertheless Arcadias are precarious places that must be perennially guarded and things could go very wrong in England very quickly. So perhaps it is not a bad idea to stop and take stock of our credit balance every now and then.

A final word: this is an English companion, not a British one. The Scots, the Welsh and the Irish have long been adept at blowing their own trumpets, and I admire them for it. In this book however, we are giving two cheers for England. I like to think that only an Englishman could have thought of giving just those two cheers.

Godfrey Smith
Malmesbury
Summer 1984

Bread and Butter Letter

Acknowledgements are notoriously the most boring part of any book, so in this *English Companion* I thought we would substitute the fine old English institution of the bread and butter letter.

My thanks are due first to Colin Webb, managing director of Pavilion Books. In my experience publishers are not usually good at coming up with irresistibly good ideas, but this book was totally Colin's; and he had no sooner outlined it than I had agreed to do it. I should like to thank too my agent Anne McDermid who suggested the lunch with Colin from which the idea sprang; it is just this kind of catalyst that a good agent should be.

Once again I am grateful to Oscar Turnill, that prince among editors, who has put this book, like so many others, through the fine mesh of his mill. Since even Oscar is not omniscient I shall not claim that he has obviated every error; but he has certainly taken out a great many while tightening up the bolts of my prose, and I would not dream of committing a book like this to the press unless it first had the benefit of his wisdom, humour and common sense. I am equally grateful to Judy Dauncey, who saw the book through to press at Pavilion Books, and to John Lawrence for his elegant drawings.

I should like to thank my wife, Mary Schoenfeld Smith, for much valuable research and for many suggestions throughout the writing. I am grateful to Judith Woolliams, who researched and typed for me so cheerfully in the country, and my daughter, Amanda Smith, who performed the same function so briskly in London.

When it comes to books I feel like Gerald Asher, who prefaces his last enchanting work on wine with the disarming disclaimer that if he tried to thank everybody who had helped him understand wine he would really have to tell the story of his life. And which reader is going to wait to hear his – or mine? Still, I cannot end without naming a few key titles.

First, of course, no one in his right mind would take on a book like this without the *Oxford English Dictionary* at his side. I also found the three volumes of the *Supplement* continuously useful, and my old friend Robert Burchfield, chief editor of the *OED,* sportingly let me see many galleys from his forthcoming and final volume.

The *Dictionary of National Biography* has been another stalwart friend, and where it presently runs out, in 1970, the three volumes of *Obituaries from The Times* have gallantly come to my rescue. I have looked into many other books of reference but should like to single out one that has proved as readable as it is reliable: the third edition of A.C. Ward's *Longman's Companion to Twentieth Century Literature*. I hope we may soon have a fourth edition, for the press of new writing never diminishes, and we need his light touch at our elbow to guide us through it.

Finally, there was hardly a town or a shop, a club or a sport, a society or a company discussed in this companion that did not give me unstinted help in seeing that my facts and figures were as up-to-date as they could be: and many supplied reams of fascinating material on their histories and quiddities too. I have tried to thank each individually; let me end by giving them one great heartfelt thank-you here. There is little kindness in the world, remarks Sidney Greenstreet as he topples dramatically down the stairs to his death in *The Mask of Dimitrios;* but there is much kindness yet in England; to that I can testify.

Glossary of Selected Abbreviations

BSA   Birmingham Small Arms

BTH   British Transport Hotel

CBE   Commander (of the order) of the British Empire

CBI   Confederation of British Industry

C.Lit   Companion of Literature

CPR   Canadian Pacific Railway

DFC   Distinguished Flying Cross

DSO   Distinguished Service Order

EEC   European Economic Community (Common Market)

FRSL   Fellow of the Royal Society of Literature

GLC   Greater London Council

GPO   General Post Office

ITN   Independent Television Network

ITV   Independent Television

MCC   Marylebone Cricket Club

NAAFI   Navy, Army and Air Force Institutes

OED   Oxford English Dictionary

RADA   Royal Academy of Dramatic Art

SAS   Special Air Service

SDP   Social Democratic Party

TUC   Trades Union Congress

*An asterisk within the text indicates a cross-reference to a separate subject heading.

Abroad Nothing conveys the ambivalence of the English quite so much as their attitude to being abroad. On the one hand, abroad is the place where the island race made their names and fortunes. It was as natural for your young Englishman to make his way abroad as it was for him to breathe. 'Go out and govern New South Wales!' exhorted Hilaire Belloc in a celebrated verse. On the other hand, foreigners were suspect, and all wogs began at Calais.

For the English writer the temptations of abroad were manifest. He needed no office or factory to make his living, the pound was strong and the Mediterranean sun beckoned him south. Besides, he could throw off abroad what seemed the repressive *moeurs* of his native land (Norman Douglas, D.H. Lawrence). There is a famous remark made by a celebrated actress on entering Somerset Maugham's* living room at the Villa Mauresque in the south of France. In the room were Noël Coward*, Godfrey Winn and Beverley Nichols. 'Why,' she exclaimed, 'this is fairyland!'

Interestingly, though, a new race of English writers have matured who cannot be doing with abroad, and will go there only when they must (Kingsley Amis*, Philip Larkin*). On balance, abroad has probably done the Englishman more good than harm, and the fact that some six hundred million now speak his lingo bears eloquent testimony to the peripatetic restlessness of his forebears; even as it makes him one of the world's worst linguists.

It must also be faced that in the eyes of the world the Englishman is at his worst abroad: with his buck teeth, baggy shorts, braying voice and dowdy memsahib he's a twerp at best, a thug at worst, and a pain in the arse at most times.

Accent   It is just over seventy years since Professor Henry Higgins first boasted to Colonel Pickering in Bernard Shaw's play *Pygmalion* that he could take a flower girl like Eliza Doolittle and in three months pass her off as a duchess (or get her a place as a shop assistant, which required – and requires – better English). Bernard Shaw had seized on the crashingly obvious point that no Englishman can open his mouth without being despised by some other Englishman.

The years since the claim was first made have seen remarkably little change in that basic proposition. Employers still speak the lingo of Winchester and New College (Oxford), or Shrewsbury and Peterhouse (Cambridge); the trade union leaders with the accents they learned in Ebbw Vale or Heckmondwike, Jarrow or Poplar. We are still two nations. Subtle changes, however, have complicated the old clean-cut divisions.

Certain varieties of upper-class inflection are now archaic. Mayfair cockney has almost gone, though it lingers on in the mouths of the surviving Mitford girls. Gaumont British newsreel gung-ho has given way to television *Newsnight* neutral. There is a middle English now that anyone with half an ear can acquire. It is the language of Robin Day (Oxford Union extra-clear) and Robert Kee (Anglo-Irish ascendancy), of Bernard Levin (with a dash of Christ's Hospital school still obtruding) and Ludovic Kennedy (though even here Eton, where Ludo did his three Rs, contributes some minor chords).

Meanwhile the young have acquired their own secret code: a kind of pop-culture cockney, into which they can switch from their parental accent and back at the drop of an aspirate. The lesson Higgins taught us has been well learned. Mrs Thatcher (with her duchess drawl) is perhaps his most striking disciple.

Acting   It is frankly amazing that there has been any good acting in England when one considers the eccentric and chaotic ragbag of talents that have made up the *soi-disant* profession. Through the gallimaufry of Hooray Henrys*, superannuated subalterns, peripatetic alcoholics, plum-faced actor-managers and (*pace* Noël Coward*) unrepentant Miss Worthingtons, there nevertheless always ran a thin thread of excellence: among the buffoons, the odd Olivier*, Gielgud, Richardson or Redgrave.

Today if you take a boat down the Thames* from Westminster Pier you will pass some of the best acting in the world on your starboard bow, and do so again a mile down to port: the National Theatre is on the south bank; the Royal Shakespeare now well entrenched in its new metropolitan headquarters at the Barbican. Meanwhile, the traditional West End theatre is deeply in the doldrums; financially unable and perhaps mentally unwilling to take risks with much more than one-set four-in-handers.

In any event, despite the drought in the West End, fringe theatre abounds, lunchtime theatre booms, student theatre escalates, and with the mushrooming of commercial radio and cable television, there seems plenty of scope for any aspirant English actor who can lay hands on an Equity card – by no means an easy trick, by the way.

The chances for the young actor outside London proliferate. To take just three towns at random: in Manchester the Royal Exchange theatre flourishes under a lively management; in Bath the Theatre Royal has recently been sparklingly refurbished and attracts metropolitan talents on their way into town; at Chichester the theatre festival thrives in what Olivier called its concrete hexagon.

Afters   There is no word for what an Englishman eats after his meat that does not make some other Englishman wince. The upper class say pudding (or 'pud') – a patent misnomer if what comes up is sorbet or grapes. Dessert, which all Americans use without bother, strikes English ears as pretentious, whereas sweet – which after all explains most nearly what it is – puts middle-class teeth on edge. So in many a trendy English bistro nowadays, the profiteroles and rum babas are improbably described as afters. It is a good old-fashioned working-class word, pressed into middle-class service to cover an absurd and quite unnecessary difficulty.

Aldershot   This ugly little Hampshire town has two claims to fame: firstly, it is the home of the British army*. The brainchild of Victoria's husband Albert, it has seen many generations of British soldiers knocked into shape. Though much of its old Victorian grandeur has gone, the officers' library, stocked with treatises on the art of war, and the garrison church, replete with the loot of empire, survive, while the Duke of Wellington's huge statue still gazes down on the drilling, the cussing, the boozing and the wenching. It is an artefact of empire, a sweatshop for the craft of arms, and a repository for spit and polish.

Secondly, however, it is the setting for a famous romance. One day in the 1939-45 war John Betjeman* was sitting in the canteen at the Ministry of Information, where he worked. Then he saw a young assistant manageress who was the very exemplar of an English rose. Smitten,

Betjeman asked someone her name. On hearing that she was a Miss Joan Hunter Dunn, he underwent a revelation not dissimilar to St Paul's on the road to Damascus.

The quintessentially English name at once unlocked a flood of images in his mind. He divined instantly that she would come from Aldershot, and that her people would be connected with the army. He was uncannily right: her family did live near there, and her father had been an army doctor. Betjeman, on hearing how near he had been, at once sat down and wrote *A Subaltern's Love Song,* with its celebrated opening couplet: 'Miss Joan Hunter Dunn, Miss Joan Hunter Dunn / Furnish'd and burnish'd by Aldershot sun' and its magnificent dénouement: 'We sat in the car-park till quarter past one / And now I'm engaged to Miss Joan Hunter Dunn.'

The scene of Second Lt Betjeman's proposal – if we may blur fact with fantasy for a moment – was nearby 'nine o'clock Camberley, heavy with bells / And mushroomy, pinewoody, evergreen smells'. Every Englishman knows that sandy terrain, the moss, heath, scrubland and conifers, by a kind of osmosis, even if he has not physically set foot in the place. Aldershot is embedded deep in our collective memory, and as James Morris observes in the opening volume of his trilogy on the British empire, *Heaven's Command*: 'When, at one o'clock precisely each day, the Aldershot time gun was fired electronically from the Royal Observatory at Greenwich, it was like a time-check for the entire Raj.'

Ale The English type of beer. Unlike most foreign beers, it is made by allowing the yeast to ferment at the top. It should mature naturally in its cask in the cellar of a pub. Unhappily the giant breweries have found it convenient to filter, pasteurise or chill their beer so that it no longer matures, but is stable or dead, and is then delivered to the glass by gas pressure from a cylinder of carbon dioxide.

It was antipathy to this dead but artificially fizzed beer which precipitated the Campaign for Real Ale (CAMRA). This is beer made from the traditional ingredients – malted barley, liquor (water) and yeast – matured in casks and delivered to the glass by any method that does not involve gas; generally by a simple suction hand pump, or drawn by gravity straight from the barrel. CAMRA, despite some recent internal political troubles, has been a great populist movement, and the nearest English male equivalent to women's lib.

For the English love of ale is true and deep. 'Good ale, the true and proper drink of Englishmen,' declared George Borrow; and every Englishman feels with the Boy in Shakespeare's *Henry V* at the battle:

'Would I were in a alehouse in London: I would give all my fame for a pot of ale and safety.' Yet the best single remark on the matter was made by Alfred, Lord Tennyson, then Poet Laureate, on the occasion of his visit to the International Exhibition of 1862. Having written an ode to be sung by a choir of four thousand at its opening he enquired: 'Is there anywhere in this damned place where we can get a decent bottle of Bass?'

Hence the innate thrall of the great real ale brewers to the Englishman, reverberating through his mind like a litany: Adnams of Southwold, Ruddles of Rutland, Theakston of Masham, Vaux of Sunderland, Thwaites of Blackburn, and the Laureate's favourite, four-square tipple, Bass of Burton.

Alma Mater Foster mother, the name given by the English middle class to their schools or universities, is now rather going out of use, though the actual cult of the alma mater still flourishes. It is probably strongest, by dint of sheer longevity, at Oxbridge and the older public schools, and is notoriously more prevalent among men than women. It is quite possible to meet men in England who have still not gone down from their old Oxbridge alma mater after a hundred and twenty terms; and a college appeal for funds to rebuild the stonework or endow new fellowships will meet with a response out of all proportion to numbers. An Oxford college, for example, with three hundred in residence at any one time and perhaps four thousand living old members, will have no difficulty at all in raising three or four million from them. Graham Greene perfectly caught the seamy underside of the alma mater cult in *England Made Me:* 'I see you were at the old place ... Those were the days eh?... I don't suppose you'd remember old Tester (six months for indecent assault). I try to keep up with them. Whose house were you in?' But see also under *Old Boy Network* and *Old School Tie.*

Ambition 'It is important in this world to be pushing,' said the great Benjamin Jowett, 'but it is fatal to seem so.' That really sums up the English position about ambition.

Amis, Kingsley (born 1922) 'A fair-haired young man came down staircase three and paused on the bottom step. Norman instantly pointed his right hand at him in the semblance of a pistol and uttered a short coughing bark to signify a shot... The young man's reaction was immediate. Clutching his chest in a rictus of agony, he threw one arm up against the archway and began slowly crumpling downwards, fingers scoring the stonework.' The future poet, novelist and critic Philip Larkin, an eighteen-year-old wartime undergraduate at St John's College, Oxford, had just met another – the future novelist, critic and poet Kingsley Amis. Amis's gift for mimicry was thus early noted and celebrated. He was to use it in his first published novel, *Lucky Jim*, when the ghastly Bertrand Welch is made to say 'you sam' when he means 'you see' and 'hostelram' when he means 'hostelry'. This curious verbal hallmark of the saloon-bar shitface was well established, but it had never been nailed in print.

Malcolm Bradbury has drawn parallels between Amis and Evelyn Waugh*, noting that each began as a Young Turk writing for his own generation and signalling a change in social values through what he calls 'a cleansing comic vision'. Perhaps; and both are Oxford-educated former Army officers with two wives apiece (in Amis's case perhaps we should add the pious caveat 'so far'). Each has a gifted writer as a son. Still, the parallels cannot be pushed too far. Waugh was no lover of jazz or science fiction; Amis is not noted for his views on painting or architecture. Waugh was a globe-trotter, travel-writer, and war correspondent; Amis likes it here. Still, Waugh in his sixty-two years and Amis in his sixty-two so far have each produced a body of vastly entertaining work in which the easy reading is made by hard writing. Yet Amis has the wider range: from picaresque comedy to sexual satire; from his primer on booze to scholarly essays on Jane Austen*, Tennyson, and Kipling; from a mordant evocation of geriatric horrors (*Ending Up*) to a loving pastiche of the thirties thriller (*The Riverside Villas Murder*).

Nor should we forget that Amis is a formidable critic (he rapped the chief editor of the *OED* over the knuckles for an inadequate definition of the Immelmann turn) and a skilful poet. In *Songs of Experience*, for example, he tells the story of a commercial traveller regaling a pub with accounts of his amatory conquests: 'He tried all colours, white and black and coffee / Though quite a few were chary, more were bold / Some took it like the host, some like a toffee / The two or three who wept were soon consoled.'

Anthony Burgess* has noted in the loosely grouped fifties writers, Amis, Osborne, and Braine, a common tendency to what he calls hypergamy: 'bedding a woman of a social class superior to one's own'. That was thirty years ago, though; and as Amis has himself moved across the political spectrum from communism to conservatism so his heroes have moved across the sexual spectrum from philandering to misogyny. Miscast as an Angry Young Man, Amis has grown more atrabilious with age; but the acid has precipitated some pearls. 'More will mean worse' elegantly crystallises his position and can be applied to virtually any aspect of the modern world he so distrusts and dislikes, except, oddly, his own work.

Anon   One of the most prolific and gifted writers the English language has ever known, he is responsible for the serene words of 'Greensleeves' and the ironic lines of 'Nice One Cyril'. He wrote 'My name is George Nathaniel Curzon' and 'Would you like to Sin with Elinor Glyn?' He it was at the Battle of Blenheim who composed the prayer: 'O God, if there is a God, save my soul if I have a soul.' He it was at the Battle of Bastogne during the Ardennes campaign in 1944 who summed it all up so magisterially: 'My dear fellow, the noise ... and the people!' He it was who described Oxford as the Latin Quarter of Morris Cowley and coined the hippie slogan 'Make love not war'. He dreamed up phrases like 'the eternal triangle' and 'the king over the water'. He devised some of the greatest advertising slogans: this is the age of the train, and whiter than white. He sometimes lays claim to lines which one could have sworn belong to Benjamin Disraeli or Oscar Wilde ('The Church of England is the Tory Party at prayer') and then proves to have clear title. In an increasingly sophisticated audio-visual world where everything is recorded and banked away on tapes, it seems hard to believe that he should continue to flourish. But he does. As he once remarked: the future is not what it was.

Apples   It is so self-evident to your Englishman that his apples are the best in the world that he considers it unnecessary to labour the point. The determined French campaign to flood England with Golden Delicious merely fortifies his resolution that there is no other fruit quite so clean, hard, sweet and true as the Cox's Orange Pippin.

Note that there are at least five hundred further varieties grown in our little island, which is just as well, for the Cox's, world-famous though its flavour remains, is a temperamental fruit that does not take kindly even to the English midlands, let alone north. Fortunately there are other varieties just about as good: notably the James Grieve, Ellison Orange, and Ribston Pippin.

Note again that in some subconscious mental process, the Englishman sees the apple as a symbol of wholesomeness, and even goodness. When something is amiss with his apples, it is amiss with the world too. During the sporadic alarms about police corruption, images of rotten apples spreading their disease through the whole barrel abound, and contrariwise.

'I said to Heart, how goes it?' proclaimed Belloc in one of his celebrated couplets. 'Heart replied / Right as a Ribston Pippin. But Heart lied.'

Aristocracy 'The stately homes of England' sang Noël Coward*, 'How beautiful they stand / To prove the upper classes have still the upper hand.' How right he was and is. Land is still the attribute which underwrites the survival of the English upper classes, and though there are poor peers (Earl Nelson of Trafalgar, descendant of the great admiral, is a police sergeant and likes to be called Pete Nelson) there are plenty of rich ones (the dukes of Westminster, Devonshire and Bedford are together probably worth about a billion pounds).

A survey of landed wealth undertaken on the telephone by the *Spectator* magazine not long ago revealed that one peer they rang was dead, another drunk, and a third could not remember whether he owned ten or a hundred thousand acres. This eccentricity, however, should not be taken *au pied de la lettre*. The English aristocracy were still hunting, shooting, wenching and wining in the shires while their French cousins were having their heads cut off. It is impossible to make any generalisation that will cover the whole class except to say that they are all exempt from jury service, a privilege they share with convicted felons, MPs, barristers, bankrupts and lunatics.

As aristos go, the English are probably a better bet than any other lot. They have the only communist in either House of Parliament (Lord Mitford). They have won the Nobel Prize for literature (Winston Churchill* and Bertrand Russell) and the VC (Lord de Lisle and Dudley). They have competed in the Olympic Games (Lord Burghley). They have founded new political movements (Lord Weymouth's Wessex party) and formed their own jazz bands (Humphrey Lyttelton).

Indeed, frankly they survive by offering the English unstinted and continuing entertainment these many centuries. It was Lord Home himself who told, in his autobiography, the story of the footnote to a ministerial brief that was inadvertently read out in the House of Lords: 'This is a rotten argument, but it should be good enough for their lordships on a hot summer afternoon.'

Army Insofar as the Englishman thinks about his army at all, he usually dwells on its follies and disasters: Dunkirk* and the Dardanelles, the fall of Singapore and the Charge of the Light Brigade. Yet the truth is that the real modes of war – long periods of boredom broken by hectic spells of chaos – suit the English soldier. Over the centuries he has cussed and plodded his way through well-nigh unbelievable hardships for king and country; and in a quiet way, done it uncommonly well.

'My Lord, we are dreadfully cut up; can you not relieve us for a little while?' asked General Halkett at Waterloo. 'Impossible,' returned the Duke of Wellington. 'Very well, my Lord, we'll stand till the last man falls.' And they did. Afterwards Wellington summed up: 'Our loss is immense particularly in that best of all Instruments, British Infantry.' In the Crimea, stricken with cholera, fever, bowel and lung disease, the British infantry fought their way uphill against vastly superior forces and hacked their way through Cossacks ten times their number. In 1914 they marched to the bloody slaughter singing self-deprecatory and often obscene songs. 'No other army,' wrote A.J.P. Taylor*, 'has ever gone to war proclaiming its own incompetence and reluctance to fight, and no army has fought better.' In the Second World War, led by General Slim, the unknown Fourteenth Army fought its way through the dysentery and monsoon of the Burmese jungle and smashed the apparently invincible Japanese.

Through all this the Poor Bloody Infantry (as it dubbed itself) has been led by some extremely eccentric officers: Gordon of Khartoum; Montgomery of Alamein; Orde Wingate, creator of the Chindits; David Stirling, creator of the SAS. They have doubled as Fellows of All Souls like Lawrence of Arabia and professors of classics like General Sir John Hackett. They have been poetry-lovers like Field Marshal Wavell, who published a best-selling anthology of verse at the height of the 1939-45 war; and music-lovers like Marine General Jeremy Moore, commander of land forces in the Falklands* conflict, whose previous qualifications for the job included an improbable stint as Purveyor of Music to the Royal Navy*. One thing all these officers had in common; not one of them could by any stretch of the imagination be called dull. Whether any of them would pass a modern selection board is a moot point. Most Englishmen would like to think so, but would not put too much money on it.

Arse One of the primal chasms that separate us from our American cousins is that which yawns between our terms for the human fundament. To Americans, it is the ass: a niminy-piminy word, blurred by being used equally for the donkey, and confusingly for the female pudenda or even sexual coition itself. To Englishmen it is the arse: a round, honest and unambiguous word which says what it means.

Infinitely proliferating among all schoolboys and soldiers, it is one of the key verbal bricks in the construction of contempt. 'This goddam place is the asshole of the universe,' says the drunken GI of London in the old wartime canard. 'Yus mate,' replies the Tommy, 'and you're just passing through it.' A vivid and precise index of spatial reference, it was used in the last war both for the pilot who weaved in his plane at the rear of the squadron and for the tail-gunner in a bomber – 'arse-end Charlie'. It is also powerfully employed in images of complacency; notably in Louis MacNeice's* great poem *Bagpipe Music*: 'Sit on your arse for fifty years and hang your hat on a pension.'

We must allow our American cousins, however, the development of the colourful phrase for somebody whose company we would rather do without – 'he's a pain in the ass'. The word has also been effectively disguised by one of those wits who seek perpetually to penetrate the gravitas of *The Times** letters page: a sober letter printed by that great newspaper purported to be from R. Supwards.

The temptation to rhyme arsehole with castle has given rise to some rich vernacular verse, notably the charming music-hall ditty: 'My name is fair Lily / I'm a whore in Piccadilly / My mother is another in the Strand / My father hawks his arsehole / Round the Elephant and Castle / Don't you think that as a family / We're grand?'

A further compound of infinite power is afforded by the coinage for one of the least popular sports known to the English, the 'arse-crawl', or more arcanely, for the unpleasant character defect known as 'arse-licking'. Such people, as far as your average Englishman is concerned, are best rewarded metaphorically, and if possible literally too, by that most salutary of all remedies, 'a good kick up the arse'.

Artists It came out only after the death of Sir Winston Churchill's wife Clementine that, at some point in 1955 or 1956, she had ordered the destruction of Graham Sutherland's portrait of her husband. There was some protest in artistic circles, but the great British public overwhelmingly endorsed her right to destroy a picture which had caused her husband distress. Nor was this the first time Clementine had exercised her right of personal veto against artists of whom she disapproved. She put her foot in 1917 through a sketch Sickert had done of Winston and she even persuaded President Roosevelt to destroy a charcoal sketch of her husband in the presidential museum. Thus does England deal with her artists.

'Remember I'm an artist,' says Gulley Jimson in Joyce Cary's *The Horse's Mouth*, 'and you know what that means in a court of law. Next worst to an actress.' Both Cary's trilogy and Somerset Maugham's *The Moon and Sixpence* are powerful accounts of the artist outside society, which is where the Englishman perceives him to be. 'The artist,' said Osbert Sitwell, 'like the idiot or clown, sits on the edge of the world, and a push may send him over it.' It must be allowed, on the other hand, that many English artists have seemed inspired by extreme states of the human condition: 'It sounds like angels shrieking with joy,' said the visionary English painter Stanley Spencer, taken as a boy by his elder brother to hear Bach's *St Anne Prelude and Fugue*, and images of the human scream occur over and over again in the bizarre and compelling *oeuvre* of Francis Bacon.

Perhaps James McNeill Whistler was right when he said there never was an art-loving nation. Still, among the non-lovers, the English have something larger than a walk-on part. Only taken unawares will the Englishman give his artists their grudging due: as when walking in a Paris street and finding young French artists at an exhibition in the Latin Quarter queuing to sign the visitor's book in homage to the miraculous line of Bradford-born David Hockney. After all, he reflects, if these Frogs see something in an *English* artist, he must be all right.

Ascot 'Everyone who should be heah is heah,' sing the gorgeously attired chorus in the Ascot scene from *My Fair Lady*. In fact a great many people who should not be theah are theah, according to that seasoned social commentator Nigel Dempster, gossip columnist of the *Daily Mail,* who after the 1983 meeting launched an impassioned onslaught in his newspaper against the phonies, the hustlers, the poseurs and the shysters who in his view were ruining a gracious and select English occasion. Yet there have always been outsiders at Ascot. A morning suit and a grey topper from Moss Bros can hide a multitude of sins, and if big business is more in evidence than it used to be it was always there somewhere; indeed, the occasion would perish without it. It is a quintessentially royal occasion, with the Queen* opening the jollities in style as she bowls down the straight mile in her open landau; it is hard indeed to believe, as a forest of gleaming toppers are doffed and an ocean of foaming curtsies made, that Queen Victoria was once booed as she rode down this course. Yet she was, early in her reign, for accusing one of her ladies-in-waiting, the umarried Lady Flora Hastings, of being pregnant when what she in fact had was inoperable cancer. All that is long forgotten, and if the preposterous Mrs Shilling always got mountains of gash publicity every Ascot from her increasingly gigantic and outrageous hats, it seemed a small price to pay for so much bubbly, lobster, strawberries and cream, and so many pretty women in their floppy Ascot hats. The racing is all right too. See also *Derby*.

Aston-Martin   Every Aston engine carries on a brass plate the name of the man who built its engine. If offered a new Aston, look for the signature of Frank Matthews or Bert Nash or Fred Waters; if it's not there it's not genuine. Put your £40,000 away again.

Test drivers say, however, that they have no need to look; they can tell which craftsman built the engine in the car they happen to be driving from the way it responds. This may be because Astons make just four cars a week. Each weighs nigh on two tons, and goes from rest to 60 mph in 5.2 seconds. Nor may you extend it to even half its top whack on an English road without breaking the law.

Not that you would need to do anything so vulgar; the true beauty of the Aston lies in its well-bred discretion; in its colossal reserves of pace and power. Even in these mad days, about half all Astons are sold to Englishmen; typically men of forty-five or so who run engineering businesses in the Midlands* or north and who understand its thorough-bred qualities.

It is the favoured transport of Prince Charles and was famously driven by James Bond. It is an exquisite piece of English folly, made with love. See also *Rolls-Royce*.

Auden, Wystan Hugh (1907-73)   Asked by his tutor at Oxford, Nevill Coghill, what he wanted to be, Auden replied simply: a poet. Ah, yes, returned Coghill, that is the right way to start reading English. 'You don't understand at all,' Auden reproved him. 'I mean a *great* poet.' He became just that. He is, indeed the greatest English poet of this century. (T.S. Eliot, even after he became a naturalised British subject remained inaccessible, as Auden never was.)

Distinctly odd in his everyday persona (he once replied, when reproved for burning a hole in his host's grand piano with a cigarette, that it wouldn't affect the sound), Auden was able to fashion miracles out of plain words. He was a an avowed homosexual ('Lay your sleeping head, my love / Human on my faithless arm' is deliberately ambiguous in its sexual pitch), a maverick Christian, a socialist of sorts, and an inspired teacher. His range is remarkable: from pure lyricism ('Earth, receive an honoured guest / William Yeats is laid to rest') to black comedy ('They laid her out on the table / The students began to laugh / And Mr Rose the surgeon / He cut Miss Gee in half'). He is at his most formidable when his unblinking and unsentimental gaze is focused on the everyday world: 'Happy Birthday, Johnny / Live beyond your income / Follow your own nose.' He described himself as a mid-Atlantic Goethe; and was not too far out.

Austen, Jane (1785-1817)   'It is a truth universally acknowledged that a single man in possession of a good fortune must be in want of a wife.' The first sentence of *Pride and Prejudice* is not only the best opening in English literature; it is also a perfect microcosm of the world Jane Austen inhabits. The elegant shape of the epigram precisely forecasts the graceful architecture of the novel; its worldly tone announces the rules by which the beguiling game will be played; and its delicious irony at once alerts the reader to the fun in store.

Jane Austen has been criticised for writing as if the worlds of power and politics, war and want did not exist; in fact she is simply obeying the first rule of any writer's school and staying firmly inside the ambit of what she knows. None of her characters is drawn from outside the ranks of the English country gentry into which she was born; no two men ever converse in her books without a woman present.

It was not only impractical for a woman of her time to talk politics; it would have been impolite, which was much worse. We are fortunate, however, in the change in public taste, which when she was born held it ill-bred for a woman to write, but thought it quite natural by the time she died. Still, in her own time she never put her name to her books, and the famous squeaking door in the house at Chawton was never oiled, so that she could hide her manuscripts from prying eyes.

Her fame rests on just six novels. *Pride and Prejudice* is the most accomplished; Benjamin Disraeli read it seventeen times; Winston Churchill*, laid low by illness when wartime prime minister, had his actress daughter Sarah read the whole book to him in bed. Jane has had a few detractors (notably Charlotte Brontë*) but her books caught on at once and have been best-sellers ever since. 'Let other pens dwell on guilt and misery,' she characteristically declared in *Mansfield Park*. No one understood better the delicate steps of the marital minuet; but she never married herself, though not for want of suitors. Some have seen her long silence from 1798 to 1809 as the consequence of some intense love affair. Perhaps she was simply discouraged by the early indifference of publishers to her genius. Still, she was to know fame in her lifetime.

'I think I may boast myself to be, with all possible vanity, the most unlearned and uninformed female who ever dared to be an authoress,' she confessed. She told her sister she thought *Pride and Prejudice* 'too light and bright and sparkling'. They are faults any writer should be glad to cultivate. Somerset Maugham paid her the fellow-writer's ultimate compliment: 'When you reach the bottom of a page you eagerly turn it in order to know what will happen next; nothing very much does and again you turn the page with the same eagerness.'

Australians While most Australians cordially dislike the English, the emotion is not reciprocated, if only because the English have not paused to think sufficiently long and clearly about their Antipodean cousins to take a view of them. The trouble with Englishmen or Poms, the Aussies claim, is that when they arrive down under they tend to whinge, swank and pong, three highly unattractive character faults if true. Australians who make the long trip to England on the other hand tend to be high achievers who thrive, rise and shine.

Ask an Englishman what the word Australian means to him, and he will think of entertainers like Rolf Harris and Barry Humphries, cricketers like Dennis Lillee and Greg Chappell, businessmen like Robert Holmes a' Court and Rupert Murdoch, and writers like Clive James and Germaine Greer. Clearly a good case could be made out against any Aussie on that list, but your average Englishman does not let a vague sense of the pervasive brashness that informs the sample congeal into a brooding race hatred.

Besides, much harmless amusement has been gained from collating the hideous Australian accent into a formal dialect called Strine ('Emma Chizzit' is not a newly discovered novel by Dickens but Strine for 'How much is it?'); and Englishmen nowadays will readily concede that it is an unpardonable canard to assume that all Aussies are descendants of the old convicts deported to penal servitude; they only sound as if they are.

Autumn The quick of the English year, autumn never short-changes us as spring does. The point is well made by Cyril Connolly*, apostle of autumn: 'Fallen leaves lying on grass in November sun bring more happiness than daffodils. Spring is a call to action, hence to disillusion, therefore is April called the cruellest month. Autumn is the mind's true spring.'

To all English politicians, publishers, schoolboys and soldiers autumn is the true start of the year; the time for new laws, new books, new terms, and new wars. When the crop is safely in, tanks may surely roll. The magnificent *Autumn Journal* of Louis MacNeice*, written in the false reprieve of 1938, perfectly catches the sense of foreboding mingled with the sweetness of the season: 'Today was a beautiful day, the sky was a brilliant / Blue for the first time for weeks and weeks / But posters flapping on the railings tell the fluttered / World that Hitler speaks, that Hitler speaks'.

Though the war is coming and the leaves are falling, the sap is rising. Connolly (what a debt we owe to our Anglo-Irish writers!) again expertly sums up: 'The creative moment of a writer comes with the autumn. The winter is the time for reading, revision, preparation of the soil; the spring for the thawing back to life; the summer is for the open air, for satiating the body with health and action, but from October to Christmas for the release of mental energy, the hard crown of the year.'

In the English country the trees put on a showbiz bezazz for us which only the North American fall can match: a dazzling spectrum from the terracotta of September through the gold and crimson of October to the deep purple of November. In these deep-freeze days, preparations for Yuletide pud and pies quicken. It is time for that weird English rite, the toasted crumpet*, made if possible on that indestructible English oddity, the open fire. It is the time for piss-ups and teach-ins, for launching new books and films on a generally uncaring world, for advertising bonanzas and winning football pools. It is a good moment for party conferences and a bad one for trade union militants as the chap on the shop floor begins to count the cost of Christmas.

It is the moment when the well-thumped football, tracing its sweet parabola in the rinsed sky, mirrors the soaring spirits of the young, and stirs the lees of forgotten delights in those who have hung up their boots. English air in autumn is ichor, and the buttered light, filtered through mist, gives the English that gift for allusion and ambiguity which their enemies call imprecision and deviousness. Autumn in England is not an incident. It is the quiddity of Englishness.

Baked Beans Though they now seem as English as HP sauce* they are a totally American invention, based on a traditional New England recipe, and were slow to catch on over here. Indeed they began life in England as a delicacy sold by Fortnum and Mason*. At first they were far too expensive for the working man: in 1911 a 16 oz. can cost nine old pence or about three per cent of the average wage then. Gradually as their cost came down (to five old pence a pound in 1939) baked beans became a staple of English working-class life. The piece of pork which used to flavour each tin was left out because it was hard to come by in the last war, but in their vegetarian guise baked beans still prevail and today the Englishman packs away more of the flatulent fodder than any other race on earth (no less than 13 lb. per person each year). Like so many grand old English institutions, baked beans have recently found a potent new source of respectability: as a staple of the internationally famed high fibre 'F-Plan' diet.

Balls In the sense of rubbish the word has been recorded for only a hundred years, while its logical concomitant, the 'balls-up', can be traced no further back than 1939, and 'balls-aching,' in the sense of boring, has not yet been dignified with an *OED* definition. In medieval English 'ball' was, among many other meanings, short for eyeball, with the result that generations of English schoolboys have been unable to take with the respect they deserve any lines of Shakespeare in which the ardent suitor rapturously claims that the image of his lady love is riding on his balls. In their straightforward slang sense of testicles one would have thought the word now had almost universal currency; it was not always so, and a BBC recording of a children's programme in which the young listeners are urged to throw their balls in the air is one of the most treasured in the entire archive. We must, however, grant to our American cousins the most memorable confusion over the handy monosyllable. Marilyn Monroe, after having been served matzo balls for Friday-night dinner for the third time at the house of her parents-in-law when married to Arthur Miller, inquired plaintively if there was not some other part of the matzo one could eat.

Bangers   'Give us a bash of the bangers and mash me muvver used to make' sang Peter Sellers famously if ungratefully to Sophia Loren. He was tired of the constant diet of canelloni and macaroni on which she was feeding him in the song, just as in reality English secretaries in New York grow weary of a steady diet of frankfurters and hamburgers and implore visitors from home to include in their luggage a pound of good old British sausages*. It is an English predilection, dating certainly from Roman times (the *salsicia,* which came fresh, dry, or smoked), and much fortified by the house of Hanover's residual weakness for the *Wurst* of their original homeland. Queen Victoria herself ordained that the royal banger was to be chopped, not minced, and that the sausage skins should be filled by hand through a funnel. George V always included well-grilled sausages in his breakfasts and his granddaughter's subjects currently put away six billion a year.

Barmaid   Whereas in America it has traditionally been a man who has been on the receiving end of the drinker's problems ('set 'em up Joe') in England women have served behind bars for centuries. The word barmaid therefore has an immediate connotation for every Englishman. He sees an amply-bosomed lady of uncertain years, her girth increased by many years of pulling pints of bitter; worldly, humorous, cynical and unshockable. Perhaps she is no better than she ought to be; but most of the saucy talk and amorous proposals she receives will be as the froth on the pints she pulls.

The greatest barmaid in English fiction is surely Rosie Driffield in Somerset Maugham's* *Cakes and Ale.* Nowhere in his *oeuvre* does the old crosspatch achieve such a marvellously rounded, human, fallible and female character as he does here. Rosie is the first wife of Edward Driffield, for whose portrait Thomas Hardy (see *Wessex*) undoubtedly sat. The narrator (a look-alike for Maugham himself) meets the Driffields by chance as a boy, and falls in love with Rosie. 'Her breasts were straight and firm and they stood out from the chest as though carved in marble. It was a body made for the act of love. In the light of the candle . . .' and so on.

This is the English barmaid at her most lovable and endearing. Quite different, but equally recognisable, is the hoity-toity barmaid so marvellously realised by Joyce Carey in Noël Coward's* film *Brief Encounter,* where her decorous dalliance with stationmaster Stanley Holloway forms a hilarious backdrop to the bourgeois agonisings of Trevor Howard and Celia Johnson. None of the quartet would quite convince nowadays, but the English barmaid lives on. Today, though, she is quite likely to be an Australian 'Sheila' doing her European grand tour and pulling a few pints on the side.

Bath A scoop of pure honey set in a green bowl, Bath was never intended for anything but pleasure, and has indulged its destiny with style. A stunningly cosmopolitan Roman city, it received visitors two thousand years ago from Chartres, Trier, and Metz; we know, because they left their names in the stone. The Romans saw at once the point of the magical hot springs that gush from the volcanic innards of the earth at the steady rate of a quarter of a million gallons a day and a constant temperature of 46.5 degrees. Over this they built a marvellously sophisticated palazzo for urban diversions: swimming pools, saunas, massage rooms, colonnades for gossip, shops and gyms, sculptures, mosaics and paintings. (The central heating system is far more advanced than anything built subsequently until modern times.) Few stories are more exciting than that of how Roman Bath or *Aquae Sulis* was rediscovered, and is still being unearthed.

From the time when the Romans went till the era when Queen Anne came to take the healing waters, more than a thousand dark years intervened. Then three ill-assorted men of genius – showman Richard (Beau) Nash, who drew up the rules for the conduct of polite society, entrepreneur Ralph Allen, who saw the value of the pale freestone despised since the Romans went, and architect John Wood, who used it to create a graceful and airy miracle of Palladian grandeur – combined to make Bath the focus of the age of elegance. Samuel Pepys took the waters here, and Jane Austen bought bonnets for the ballroom; Hester Thrale came here to escape the tyranny of Samuel Johnson*, and in our own era Cyril Connolly* took cover in Bath to escape the rigours of life in London.

It is still a small city, best seen on foot. With its international music festival, its royal agricultural show, its gorgeously refurbished Regency theatre in cobalt, white and gold, its arcades and crescents, it remains a Georgian city built on Roman foundations, still savouring the accreted delights of the slow centuries while folded into a time-warp in the Somerset hills. One last claim to fame: it is the one English city whose name no American can pronounce.

BBC At a casual glance the Englishman might well be forgiven for deciding that he has not had much of a look-in at the British Broadcasting Corporation, dominated as it has been by a succession of Scottish goers (John Reith, Alasdair Milne), Welsh wizards (Wynford Vaughan-Thomas, Huw Wheldon), and Irish leprechauns (Terry Wogan, Frank Delaney). Yet some doughty English names (Dimbleby, Day, Parkinson, Robinson) have surfaced amid all the Celtic fizz. The subject is so vast, the issues so enormous, that a couple of thoughts only in this ambit must suffice. Nobody wanted the BBC to be born; the press was hostile (for self-regarding reasons that proved invalid); people, it was urged, would cease to read and think.

Yet once under way, the titanic power of the medium was quickly seen, and it was a tall, (6 feet 6 inches), lean, dour, war-scarred, God-directed, thirty-four-year-old Aberdonian engineer who was given the first chance to aim that great gusher. John Reith had posted his letter of application in his club before looking up the man to whom he was applying (Sir William Noble) in *Who's Who*. Seeing Noble was a fellow Aberdonian, he retrieved his letter from the club post box, opened it, and added a footnote: 'I think you know my people . . .' In truth, no other applicant had Reith's Messianic vision, and though his sixteen-year reign could easily be criticised and was (announcers had to wear dinner jackets when giving the news), perhaps in retrospect it was better that the BBC should start bland but not bent.

Reith maintained his precarious independence during the General Strike of 1926 – but only just, and in effect took the government side. Again, with the coming of war there was an obvious clash of principle between telling the truth and needing to win. The BBC got over that huge hurdle bloody but unbowed and showed its independence in the Falklands* affair by having its camera crews and reporters in Buenos Aires throughout the hostilities.

Throughout the swinging sixties it had a necessary dose of liberalism under Hugh Carleton Greene, but fell foul of Harold Wilson who decided to teach it a lesson by moving Charles Hill, formerly the 'radio doctor', from being chairman of the ITA to chairman of the BBC. The BBC smiled through its tears.

The coming of independent broadcasting was a huge shot in the arm, giving the BBC a sparring partner after the years of monopolistic torpor, and forcing it to hone its skills till they were clearly world-class. Still, the charge of political bias remains. The right is convinced that the BBC is full of left-wing activists; the left, that it lost the last two elections because of broadcasting's right-wing bias. The problem is unlikely to go away, and the BBC still badly needs minders like Reith and Greene; though preferably not at the same time.

The battle will manifestly be fought first and foremost for the small square screen: what the Australian jokesmith Clive James arrestingly dubbed the crystal bucket. Increasingly it has become clear that whoever controls the cathode ray controls the hearts and minds of the people it purports to serve, but in truth sways. The opportunities offered by the gift of television to mankind are matched only by its dangers. This evident axiom has been firmly grasped by one or two of the principal television tribunes.

'The instinctive reaction of politicians to the dangers of television', wrote Robin Day in 1961, 'is to think in terms of restrictions, controls, limitations, when what is needed is freedom, diversity, and independence . . . During the next quarter of a century let us *distribute* the power of television, so that in 1984 it will not be an Orwellian instrument of mass hypnosis, but will have long been built into a broad and open platform of democratic opinion.'

So how has it all worked out? No mass *hypnosis* perhaps; though to the charge of mass *narcosis* there may not be such a ready answer. Manifestly there are pools of excellence in British television and Robin Day's own *Question Time* is one; but even here eternal vigilance is the customary price of liberty; and recently his team have had to tighten their grip on the selection of studio audiences to prevent the incursion of pressure groups. While anyone eccentric enough to think any other country's television better than British should be locked up in his hotel bedroom in New York, Zurich, Bombay or Tokyo until he sees the error of his ways, the heartbeat of excellence is uncertain.

The BBC is yielding audience share heavily to ITV at the time of writing; and in the face of ITN's clear lead in news and Granada's evident mastery in drama, now is the time for a drastic rethink at the Beeb. All our four channels, indeed, seem desperately in need of new names; nothing wears out *any* face like the unwinking glare of a television camera; and many of those now on view have been around far, far too long.

Beaverbrook (1879-1964) To English intellectuals, Max Aitken was evil incarnate: if not the devil himself, then assuredly one of his imps. Mischief was his business, gossip his pabulum, ink the ichor that flowed in his veins. We still know very little about the financial legerdemain that made him a millionaire before he was thirty; it may not stand too close scrutiny. He regarded himself as a political failure, though his part in the downfall of Asquith in 1916 was crucial. He was a trusted henchman of Churchill's in the Second World War, got the planes built, and could wheel and deal with the Russians on level, or rather equally twisting, terms. He fought all his life for imperial preference, not surely an infamous aim so much as an impractical one.

To push this cause, he bought the *Daily Express* from a Bovril tycoon for £17,000, and got the *Evening Standard* for nothing. It was a sweetener from Rothermere for diddling the dying Edward Hulton into thinking it was not Rothermere but Max who was buying his papers. Max proved a wizard at making popular newspapers. In this he was aided by master craftsmen like editors Blumenfeld and Christiansen, left-wing artists like Low and Vicky (who were given total freedom) and leftish writers like Michael Foot, Aneurin Bevan, Alan Taylor and Harold Nicolson, many of whom, against the run of the play, became lifelong buddies. The interaction between Beaverbrook and his acolytes provided Fleet Street with an unending stream of uproarious stories, for the little gnome with the Canadian accent and prayerbook vernacular was incapable of stringing two dull sentences together.

His speech at the great dinner given by Roy Thomson to celebrate his eighty-fifth birthday was an astonishing *tour de force.* He was dying – indeed had only two weeks to live – but got out of bed to make a titanic and cinematic exit. No Hollywood scriptwriter could have done it better. After reviewing his many apprenticeships – as financier, politician, newspaperman – he concluded that he would be starting a new apprenticeship 'some day soon'.

'He's a dear old bugger,' said one editor, puffing a cigar Beaverbrook had just given him, then added ruminatively, 'The accent is on the word bugger.' Now, though, some privately wish the old bugger were back.

Betjeman, Sir John (1906-84) It has been observed of Betjeman's work that it gives you the key to a lost past which you will instantly recognise *even if you were never there.* Few key words in the lumber room of every Englishman's mind (Ovaltine, Sturmey-Archer bicycles, Home and Colonial stores) are not memorably embedded in his *oeuvre.* His inimitable artifice has transmuted these folk memories into art.

His skill was a rare one: critical acclaim coupled with best-sellerdom. Every line is thumpingly clear: there are no tangled nets in Betjeman. Nevertheless the key is by no means always C major: darkness often obtrudes: and sometimes despair itself beats time to his music. There have been many essentially English poets before Betjeman and many who hymned England: none ever caught the charisma of the humdrum quite so expertly. Betjeman sees glints of the eternal in the ordinary. Open him anywhere, and his idiosyncratic magic leaps from the page: 'Oh! Fuller's angel-cake, Robertson's marmalade, / Liberty lampshades, come shine on us all.'

Betjeman is the apostle of childhood: 'Then what sardines in the half-lighted passages! / Locking of fingers in long hide and seek', but also the weed in need of an earth mother: 'You will protect me, my silken Myfanwy / Ringleader, tom-boy, and chum to the weak.' The condescending suggestion that Betjeman is a good bad poet is at once refuted by scores of marvellous lines that continue to chime in the mind: 'When Boris used to call in his Sedanca / When Teddy took me down to his estate / When my nose excited passion / When my clothes were in the fashion / When my beaux were never cross if I was late.'

Though Betjeman saw himself as a serious poet (and was right in his perception) the laughter is never too far away: 'At sundown on my tricycle / I tour the Borough's edge / And icy as an icicle / see bicycle on bicycle / Stacked waiting in the hedge.' He is, too, a trenchant chronicler of the sensual thrall: 'Oh whip the dogs away my Lord / They make me ill with lust / Bend bare knees down to pray my Lord / Teach sulky lips to say my Lord / That flaxen hair is lust.' Though he can sometimes tremble on the edge of sentiment ('Oh little body do not die') he is more often astringently hard-nosed ('Come friendly bombs and fall on Slough').

He was fortunate in his time (coeval of Auden*, taught by Eliot, protégé of Bowra) and in his destiny. He was champion of the Church of England*, vindicator of Victorian architecture, staunch defender of stations, follies and piers. He was besides a broadcaster of true class: funny, gentle, unexpected, and right. His disasters were, *sub specie aeternitatis,* all little ones. 'Fourth generation, John', his father reminded him in a homily on the family business, 'They'll look to you / They're artist craftsmen to their finger-tips . . . Go on creating beauty.'

That kind of beauty Betjeman was congenitally unable to conjure. Another kind, though, he could and did: 'Red hair she had and golden skin / Her sulky lips were shaped for sin / Her sturdy legs were flannel slack'd / The strongest legs in Pontefract.' A song of songs, which is Betjeman's!

Bird Another of those oscillating, many-faceted words that show the riotous growth of the language most vividly. As slang for a girl it was much in favour in the thirties, then seemed to falter and fail; but something or somebody brought it back into favour and by the sixties it was about as if it had never been away, and is now more worked than ever. Bird is doubly interesting because of the load it carries on one slim line: not only slang for a young female person, but also for a man, particularly a slightly odd one, as in 'queer bird' or 'old bird'; then again a much favoured term for a prison sentence – 'he's doing bird'; then again, imported from America, a term of derision in 'strictly for the birds'. As if these multifarious uses were not enough, it is still used for the thumbs down in the theatre, learnedly derived (though who remembers?) from *The Birds* of Aristophanes. First and foremost, though, it now conveys to any Englishman a piece of crumpet*.

Birmingham 'One has no great hopes from Birmingham. I always say there is something direful in the sound.' So thought Mrs Elton in Jane Austen's *Emma*. Others have found it more inspiring. When William Hutton, later historian of Birmingham, first went there in 1741, he found a vivacity he had never seen before: 'I had been among dreamers, but now I saw men awake.' What he was in fact seeing was the quick forge in which the Industrial Revolution was made. Many people have thrived in Birmingham, rightly dubbed the city of a thousand trades, but it proved especially fertile for a small clutch of men touched with genius: John Baskerville, the printer; Joseph Priestley, discoverer of oxygen; William Murdoch, inventor of gas lighting; James Watt, maker of the double action steam engine, and his partner, the industrialist Matthew Boulton, who provided to the edge of bankruptcy the capital Watt needed and, just as importantly, the moral support to save him from his own self-doubt.

The tone of Birmingham had long been free-thinking or dissenting, and its most famous son, Joseph Chamberlain, was a pillar of the Unitarian church. When he became mayor in 1873 he claimed that 'in twelve months' time, by God's help, the town shall not know itself'. He was as good as his word. By 1890 an American visitor was able to claim without hyperbole that Birmingham was the best governed city in the world. It gave England its first secondary school, its first children's court, its first municipal bank, and its first municipal orchestra. It was also to have the first workers' model village, Bournville, built by the Cadbury chocolate family, four miles outside town. It was at Birmingham in 1900 that the first performance of *The Dream of Gerontius* by Edward Elgar* was given, and here that J.R.R. Tolkien, creator of the Hobbits, was educated. As befits a city only forty minutes from Stratford, the library houses the largest Shakespeare collection outside America, with 50,000 items in ninety languages.

Birmingham has always been a risk city, and the very nature of the products it traditionally makes – a third of all Britain's cars, a quarter of all her exports – put her most in peril when the great recession of the seventies broke. By the spring of 1984 unemployment in this city of a million people was 90,000 and in some wards running at 30 per cent. Birmingham has reacted to the challenge with traditional vim. The National Exhibition Centre, a monument to civic enterprise, now houses some 80 per cent of the nation's exhibitions and a National Convention Centre is planned to complement it. Aston Science Park, designed to test the high-tech ideas of budding entrepreneurs and make them marketable, opened a year ago.

'Next week-end it is likely in the heart's funfair we shall pull / Strong enough on the handle to get back our money; or at any rate it is possible.' So wrote the poet Louis MacNeice*, who taught classics at Birmingham University from 1930 to 1936. At first he found the place a rude culture shock after Oxford; later, he was to make a group of good and gifted friends there: the writer Walter Allen; the poet Henry Reed; the BBC* producer R.D. Smith. MacNeice's early poems contain many lines redolent of his Birmingham years: 'Tonight is so coarse with chocolate / The wind blowing from Bournville.'

Today Cadbury's has had to rationalise the hundreds of chocolate lines it once made; the old BSA motorcycle factory at Small Heath has been bulldozed; the factory where the Austin Seven was made is now part of British Leyland and a fraction of its former self. New industries like British Telecom have taken their place; and new metals like titanium, zirconium, hanium, and niobium. Not for nothing are there now thirty Birminghams; twenty-two of them in American and one out in space – there is a Birmingham crater on the moon.

Black Pudding To southern eyes, there is something mysterious, even sinister, about the northerner's black pudding. What exactly *is* it, for a start? The answer does little to inspire your average southerner either. For the black pudding is no more than pig's blood, pearl barley, and diced pork fat stuffed into a sausage skin with marjoram, thyme, sage, spices, salt, pepper and onion. It sounds disgusting, but is in truth delicious. It was the traditional staple of Lancashire housewives on Monday washdays and still is. A rich crop of yarns has accreted round the curious artefact: that it was invented by a Lancashire wrestler (false); that its natural colour is white (true – it has to be dyed black); that it is eaten raw (false – it is cooked for two hours before it is sold); that a basket leaves Bury, capital city of the black pudding, for Harley Street where its therapeutic qualities are well understood (just possible). Beyond question, though, the black pudding is gaining ground south of the Wash, particularly at Christmas time, when people have time to contemplate those fried breakfasts of which it forms such a beguiling part. Though one of the oldest dishes in the world, and known throughout Europe (*boudin* in France, *sanquinacci* in Spain, *palten* in Russia, *Bludwurst* in Germany) there are still southerners in England who give it up overnight when they learn what's in it.

Blackberries These are the most common of all English fruit and to go blackberrying or brambling has been one of the most universal treats for English children over countless generations. The blackberry is perhaps the best example of a free fruit: delicious ripe and raw in summer, bottled as blackberry and apple jam or just bottled on its own. The time to pick blackberries is between the beginning of the school summer holidays and the end of September: no later, according to the old country superstition, or the devil will spit on them. Nowadays it is not exactly that the devil has done that, but that hedgerows grow daily more scant and regulated and the blackberries in them rarer and rarer. What was once the largesse of the countryside is becoming a scarce resource.

Blackpool The capital of the old working class. No other town in England glories quite so unashamedly in its plebeian pleasures. 'Blackpool,' says the town brochure, 'is fish and chips and football. Hot dogs and hamburgers and hotels. Juke boxes and jokes and jeans. Pubs and pints and piers and Punch and Judy.' But we have the picture; and it is hard to believe that eighteenth-century Blackpool was an upper-class resort. Gentlemen found on the beach when the ladies were bathing were fined a bottle of wine.

Not any more, though. The coming of the railway in 1846 changed all that, though it is interesting that Blackpool still needed entrepreneurs with vision to pull it out of various tight corners thereafter. Thus when the development plans nearly foundered in the 1840s for lack of capital, the situation was saved by the notion of cheap excursion trains from industrial Lancashire*. Trippers flooded in. They still do. Again in the 1870s the Central Pier was revivified when open-air dancing for the working classes was introduced; the gentry still promenaded on the

North Pier in the evenings.

In the 1890s the town got another shot in the arm when a group of businessmen took what many thought a reckless decision and built the Tower in imitation of the Eiffel in Paris. That iron monster still pays fat dividends, containing as it does the gigantic Tower Ballroom, the Circus, Aquarium, and Mighty Wurlitzer. In an audio-visual age, the Illuminations, with their 375,000 electric light bulbs and fifty miles of festoon, might seem unsophisticated fare. Not so: eight million people still come to see them.

The traditional Blackpool landlady, who according to northern mythology used to sleep two shifts of lodgers in the same bed, is giving way to the self-catering flat, and few will grieve. The many thousands of mill girls who used to invade Blackpool for their annual Wakes Week holidays may now be off to the Costa Brava on the backs of their blokes' bikes: but TV's *Hi De Hi* team has been playing the Opera House and comedian Les Dawson packing them in at the Grand. That's Entertainment – in Blackpool anyway.

Bloomsbury The four Stephen children moved to 46 Gordon Square, London WC1 in 1904. Their widowed father, Sir Leslie Stephen, editor of the *Dictionary of National Biography*, had died after a long and distressing illness and they were now orphans. Thoby Stephen, his eldest son, a massive, charming, masculine and humorous hero-figure, died suddenly and tragically of typhoid in 1907, but before he did so had acted as the vital link between his clever Cambridge friends – Lytton Strachey, Leonard Woolf, Clive Bell, Desmond Macarthy, all four to become distinguished writers – and his two beautiful sisters, Virginia and Vanessa. Thoby was 'At Home' each Thursday evening, and people dropped in from ten o'clock till midnight, were regaled with whisky, cocoa, and buns, and often stayed till two or three in the morning. When Vanessa married Clive Bell in 1907, Virginia and Adrian, the younger Stephen brother, moved to Bernard Shaw's old house at 29 Fitzroy Square, and these two addresses were to be the axes of the Bloomsbury Group. Virginia married Leonard on his return from Burma in 1912 ('I've got a confession to make,' she wrote to her friend Violet Dickinson. 'I'm going to marry Leonard Woolf. He's a penniless Jew. I'm more happy than anyone ever said was possible.')

The high summer of Bloomsbury spans the years 1907-1914, though in a sense it continued to spread its unplanned influence till well into the twenties. Stephen Spender*, who knew the Woolfs as a young left-wing poet between the wars, differentiated between the old Bloomsbury and the new; but essentially the properties of each were the same: a respect for truth, however embarassing the consequences; a love of beauty; a passion for ancient Greece; a distaste for material values (but at the same time a practical insistence on enough money to be independent – what Virginia Woolf called £500 year and a room of one's own); liberal, verging on socialist, politics; agnostic beliefs and pacifist principles; a reverence for France and in particular for French Impressionist painting; a high regard for personal relationships, coupled with a penchant for free love (Michael Holroyd's revelations about the Bloomsbury sexual merry-go-round when he published his two-volume life of Lytton Strachey in 1967 and 1968 caused a sensation).

Later key Bloomsberries (as they were called) were the novelist E.M. Forster, painters Roger Fry and Duncan Grant, and Maynard Keynes*. Most members of the Bloomsbury Group had been at one or other of two Cambridge colleges, King's and Trinity; many were members of the Apostles, an elite Cambridge secret society; and a number either were or became members of the Strachey and Stephen families. They have been criticised for their clannish aloofness and emotional aridity; but their achievements speak for themselves. They must have been daunting to know. It was their custom never to smile on being introduced; and once when Lytton's mother, Lady Strachey, came to tea with Vanessa at Gordon Square, Hans, the Stephens' dog, made a large mess on the floor. Neither lady mentioned it. The Bloomsbury revolt from Victorian values was not as thorough-going as all that.

The Boat Race Not the least of the frivolities spawned by the river Thames* the Boat Race, on the face of it the most boring and predictable of races, in the upshot seldom fails to provide some absurd drama. Both crews have sunk during the race, and in the 130th encounter in March 1984 Cambridge were effectively scuppered before the race began when their tiny cox rowed them in practice flat out into a moored German barge under Putney Bridge.

The race was rowed next day, the first of the 130 contests ever to be held on a Sunday. It was, as it turned out, the fastest ever, with both teams beating the fastest previous time and Oxford prevailing. So the score now stands at 68 Cambridge wins to 61 for Oxford, with the 1877 race standing as an equivocal 'dead heat to Oxford by five feet'.

Though Africa is no longer as it once was, a country of blacks ruled by blues, the Church of England have long swung together. The first race in 1829 could boast a future bishop of St Andrews, deans of Lincoln and Repton, and a prebendary of York in the Oxford boat; bishops of New

Zealand and Lichfield, a dean of Ely, and a chancellor of the Diocese of Manchester in the Cambridge boat.

Even twenty-five years ago, future bishops of Chichester, Gloucester and Lichfield were all rowing blues. Nowadays, however, your typical young man in the blue boat is more likely to be a scientist with a first degree already behind him in metallurgy or biochemistry. He is also likely to be six feet three and a little under fourteen stone. Again, though roughly a third of all rowing blues have been Etonians, the eighteen young men who took part in the 1984 boat race included seven born abroad: three Canadians, two Americans and two Australians. Yet even in 1984, one Etonian, R.C. Clay, was still gallantly making sure that Oxford were steady from stroke to bow by rowing at bow himself.

Book Collecting An archetypally English mania. Needless to say, there are eminent American collectors, and bibliomaniacs span the world from Mexico to Japan and Argentina to Iran. Yet no other nation can produce a book collector on quite the heroic scale of Sir Thomas Phillipps (1792-1872), who in fifty years amassed the greatest private library the world has ever seen, spending on it some £250,000 (add two noughts for inflation). Since 1886 – repeat, 1886 – Sotheby's have been slowly selling that vast treasure house at auction, have realised three million pounds so far, and have still not completed the gigantic task.

No other nation can produce a book forger (only a bibliomaniac after all, with his moral machinery out of kilter) on quite such a grand scale as Thomas Wise, who fooled the world of books with his prodigious skills for half a century, was given an honorary degree at Oxford, and died in 1937 without having ever been charged with an offence. Few other nations can produce such dedicated book loonies as the contemporary savant Bernard Levin, who has been advised that should he ever be rash enough to display on shelves the tons of books he has amassed even so far, he would assuredly bring the walls of his London apartment crashing about his ears.

The bibliomaniac is well answered by the English bookseller, since the day when Samuel Johnson's* father Michael set up his stall in Lichfield, a travelling question-and-answer man, prepared to try to help his customers in all sorts of unexpected ways. 'The phrase antiquarian bookseller scares me somewhat as I equate antique with expensive,' wrote Helene Hanff to Marks and Co. on 5 October 1949, so opening a riveting correspondence that was to last twenty years and become the raw material for a best-selling book, then play: *84 Charing Cross Road*. Scared or no, she sent off her first list, no one book to exceed five dollars, and got a letter back three weeks later with two-thirds of her problems solved, the rest being worked on.

It is the idiosyncratic spell of the mania that a collector will be far more concerned about the ache of missing a long-sought book than distressed about its price. Indeed the price is often only of the most academic interest, since the collector has no intention of selling. Occasionally, of course, he will get a glimpse of what his books are worth. Only the other day, a copy of Ian Fleming's first novel *Casino Royale* – signed to his secretary but no more antique than 1953 – was knocked down at Sotheby's for £2,500. On balance, we should reserve our pity not for the bibliomane but for his wife, who must find space to accommodate his ever-swelling plunder and tolerate his irrational forays in quest of new treasure. One of these unfortunate women has confessed to having sat knitting outside every bookshop in Europe.

Bournemouth 'A hundred years ago there was no Bournemouth,' wrote Brian Vesey-Fitzgerald in his 1949 history of Hampshire*. its story, he added, was 'a romance of big business, but it will never be history, unless it be the history of a ruined coast-line'. You would be lucky, he claimed, to hear a Hampshire voice in it, 'though you will hear plenty of Lancashire and Birmingham, for it is the ambition of most businessmen in the Midlands and north to settle here when they have made enough brass. . . It can be dismissed from any book about Hampshire.'

In Thomas Hardy's Wessex it is renamed Sandbourne: 'Like a fairy palace,' he says in *Tess of the D'Urbervilles,* 'suddenly created by the stroke of a wand, and allowed to get a little dusty.' He too, though, regrets the coastline on which it is built, with its prehistoric soil and ancient trackways: 'Not a sod having been turned there since the time of the Caesars.'

On the face of it, then, a boring and inimical place, over which hangs one fascinating question: how did it get there? In 1810 it was a tavern and a few cottages at the mouth of the Bourne, a haunt for smugglers and wildfowl hunters; but in that year a local landowner called Tregonwell built a villa there. It became the swanky Royal and Imperial Exeter Hotel, patronised by the empress of Austria and other royal nobs.

The year of the first royal visit is significant: 1888, when the railway arrived. Birmingham now lay only five comfortable hours' travel away. Seven miles of sand and two thousand acres of pines lent Bournemouth a luxuriant, balmy, feminine torpor: it is, concluded John Betjeman*, one of the few English towns it is safe to call 'she'. Doctors recommended it for convalescence. 'In no other town,' said a 1908 guide book, 'is the now familiar dress of a nurse so frequently seen.'

While the great, gritty cities of Manchester*, Bolton, Blackburn and Wigan declined between 1911 and 1951, languid, genteel towns like Bournemouth doubled their numbers. Nothing much seemed to happen there; though it was from Bournemouth in 1940 that the Labour Party conference sent word that they would back a Churchill government. The place riveted a young writer called Cyril Connolly* who painted a haunting picture of the Branksome Towers Hotel there in *The Unquiet Grave:* 'Steamy tropical atmosphere . . . led by chance to discover the hanging foot bridge over Alum Chine. Walking over the quivering planks I felt rooted, as in a nightmare . . . What a place to make away with oneself or some loved one!'

His book was published in 1944. Two years later the sadistic psychopath, Neville Heath, murdered twenty-one-year-old Doreen Marshall. Police discovered her body one hundred yards down the hill from the Branksome Towers Hotel.

Bread   One of the very few foods that was not rationed in the 1939-45 war. It may have been sad stuff, grey, grimy, coarse and bland; but at least you could eat as much of it as you liked to fill yourself up. When therefore bread was rationed in the austere imperatives of postwar Britain, it seemed to the British people the unkindest cut of all. Yet bread has made a dramatic comeback, and today will stand up to the best in the world, whether made as split tin, granary loaf, tin twist, notched brick or wholemeal cob. The Englishman has moreover become fond of a whole range of exotic breads introduced to him by the ethnic minorities who now share his country with him: Polish rye, German pumpernickel, French baguettes, Jewish chola plait, Irish barmbrack and Welsh bara brith. The upshot is that your average Englishman now has a range of breads at his disposal far richer than those on offer to his continental neighbours.

Bread and Butter Letter   A staple of middle-class life, the written thank-you for bed and board is slowly being transmuted to the bread and butter card, especially by the young and particularly if they can find a Victorian postcard. It is usually (but not always) written by female guest to female host and, if thanks for dinner, will praise food, booze, and company, usually in that order and not always quite seriously: 'Henry was not totally sober for two days afterwards'. (See page 8.)

Breakfast Though the English cannot truthfully be said to have invented breakfast, they certainly gave the world the English breakfast, that noble dish of eggs and bacon which Somerset Maugham* once said should be eaten four times a day when one was in England. The fact is that very few Englishmen – and fewer Englishwomen – have time for the full gubbins on working days, usually settling for the ubiquitous breakfast foods invented in America, and sometimes for no more than a cup of tea or coffee. Still, the memory of vast breakfasts taken from groaning sideboards in country houses haunts the collective subconscious of the English, most of whom have got no nearer to the grilled kidneys than the one-and-nines at an old Ealing* comedy.

Similarly, though few Englishmen have had much to do with kedgeree, faint resonances of the imperial Raj convince him that he has, and he will order it with confidence and indeed nostalgia on holiday and especially afloat. The English will to breakfast well is most graphically expressed by British Rail, who persist in serving up a monstrous meal with a garnish of sausages*, tomatoes, mushrooms, potatoes and fried bread added to the basic bacon and eggs at a price which seems to escalate weekly. Though it is manifestly the sort of meal that by rights should lay most folk out for the day, many Englishmen and their memsahibs seem to lash into it on trains and survive without evident dyspepsia.

It is a meal designed for silence, and is properly celebrated in gentlemen's clubs where a stand on the table holds the member's *Times** at the right angle as he meditatively tucks in. The improbable notion that an Englishman could be made to eat his breakfast and watch TV at the same time like an American led to the uncertain start of breakfast television here, as anyone with the slightest knowledge of English life could have confidently predicted.

Brighton Try as one may to stress the cultural and historical role of the place – the Prince Regent and the Pavilion, Thackeray and the Thrales, Pinky's patch in Graham Greene's great novel *Brighton Rock* – it still conveys one overwhelmingly powerful image to your average Englishman: the dirty weekend. The end of the road for Genevieve in a vastly successful Pinewood comedy, it is a town eminently suited to irregular sexual congress with its sugar-cake hotels, regency terraces, handy racecourse and raffish pier. The place seems positively to thrum with oysters and ozone. There is only one snag in this endearing cameo: the English increasingly fail to see anything improper in a weekend for two people who are not legally married to each other. The town has recently reacted to this new style by promoting the dirty weekend as a tourist attraction. But without the illicit flavouring it will never have quite the same tang.

The Brontës 'Her business is not half so much with the human heart as with the human eyes, mouth, hands, and feet,' wrote Charlotte Brontë (1816-1855) of Jane Austen*; 'what sees keenly, speaks aptly, moves flexibly, it suits her to study; but what throbs fast and full, though hidden, what the blood rushes through, what is the unseen seat of Life and the sentient target of death – this Miss Austen ignores. . . If this is heresy I cannot help it.'

Indeed not, for the difference between reading Jane and Charlotte is like that between taking a small sip of madeira and taking a large slug of brandy. What throbs fast and full is what the Brontës are about; three astonishingly gifted sisters whose father relieved his feelings by firing pistols from the back door, and whose brother Branwell was sacked from his job as a railway clerk because of culpable negligence, took to opium and died of consumption. Anne Brontë (1820-1849) wrote *Agnes Grey* and was well called by George Moore a sort of literary Cinderella; Charlotte Brontë wrote *Jane Eyre* and, said G.K. Chesterton, 'showed that abysses may exist inside a government and eternities inside a manufacturer'; Emily Brontë (1818-1848) wrote *Wuthering Heights*, which was, according to Dante Gabriel Rossetti, 'a fiend of a book, an incredible monster, combining all the stronger female tendencies. . . The action is laid in Hell – only it seems places and people have English names there.'

Yet the most striking verdict on the Brontës was made by Muriel Spark. In summing up Branwell she wrote: 'The Brontë son did not fulfil his early promise; his great misfortune was that he was a man. If he had been constrained as were his sisters, by the spirit of the times; if he had been compelled, for want of other outlet, to take up his pen or else burst, he might have been known today as rather more than the profligate brother of the Brontës.'

The three Brontë sisters lived a hundred years before Women's Lib was born and are paradoxically the best of all arguments for and against it. For, in the sense that they showed how a woman can equal in power and passion the mind of any man; against, in the sense that they showed how little the rules need matter to a woman with a mind of her own.

Bumf Short for bum-fodder, a word with an honourable pedigree stretching back now nearly a century, and meaning, first, lavatory paper, and more generally later any paper on which useless information is printed; nearly always government paper.

Bunter, Billy   In the safe enclosed world of Greyfriars School there are many more admirable characters than Bunter. Harry Wharton is more decent, Hurree Jamset Ram Singh more exotic, Linley more clever, Redwing more deserving, and Vernon-Smith more bent. Yet it is Bunter who has become an institution, with a triumphant entry to himself in the new *Supplement* to the *Oxford English Dictionary*. Bunter was fortunate in the artist who created his public image for generations of schoolboys – and schoolgirls. It was the prolific Charles Hamilton (Frank Richards) who gave him his lines ('I say you fellows, I'm expecting a postal order') but it was Leonard Shields who drew the check pattern on Bunter's bags, that ample cross-hatch against which boots were perennially thudding. Socially, Bunter was a snob who liked to claim that he lived at Bunter Towers (like many of his schoolmates who, if they did not have a pater and mater at the Towers, then certainly at the Grange or even Castle). Yet Bunter's people were not all that skint. His dad was a stockbroker, living at Bunter Villa in the lush suburbs, and making enough to support both Billy and his young brother Sammy at Greyfriars, not to mention Bessie at the nearby girls' school. Though a liar, a coward and a sneak, Bunter was an excellent cook, and indeed an essential cog in the Greyfriars mechanism. Hamilton created him from the less attractive character traits of three people he knew; but was told by one editor to whom he took an early Bunter story that he would never catch on. Yet Bunter lives on, immortalised in print, radio and television, and his name and exploits are celebrated wherever the English language is spoken. He is moreover brilliantly discussed by George Orwell* in one of his translucent essays; a distinction that not even Mr Quelch, the learned pedagogue whose misfortune it was to teach Bunter Latin, could rival. The Fat Owl of the Remove, as ever, gets the last laugh.

Burgess, Anthony (born 1917)   He is a hero to the Americans and an enigma to the English, who cannot decide where he fits in. He was the son of a chief cashier who was a gifted pub pianist, and a noted music hall singer called Beautiful Belle Burgess. He was educated at the Xaverian College, Manchester, and at Manchester University. Despite stints as lecturer, civil servant, schoolmaster, and colonial officer he had seen himself as a composer till he was thirty-eight (his Third Symphony in C has been performed and recorded).   When the doctors told him – quite wrongly – that he had a year to live, he wrote five novels in that year to leave his wife some money. He has now spun out thirty works of fiction, as well as film and television scripts, translations, musicals biographies and criticism. In a matter of weeks he recently turned out a book naming and assessing the ninety-nine best novels written in English since 1939. Modesty prevented him adding one of his own as a hundredth; but he was not always so modest. He was sacked from his job as literary critic on the *Yorkshire Post* for reviewing one of his own books, published under his pseudonym Joseph Kell. It was, he wrote, a dirty book in many ways; but he praised its 'gross richness'.

It is the comic spirit which fuels Burgess, but it is the Balzacian scale which inspires him, and the giant figures of history that enthral him: Napoleon, Beethoven, Jesus, Moses, Nero. Yet there is nothing portentous about his prose. 'He said it was artificial respiration,' says a woman in *Inside Mr Enderby*, the novel that got him fired, 'but now I find I am to have his child.' He found world fame when his novel *The Clockwork Orange* was filmed, but would like better than anything to see his projected film of Shakespeare's life become a reality. He invents private languages for his characters, and endlessly baffles his readers with new coinings (Orwell's *1984* was a *dystopia*, lightning becomes *levin*).

He remains hypnotically readable. The opening to his enormous novel *Earthly Powers* is written tongue-in-cheek, but is none the worse for that: 'It was the afternoon of my eighty-first birthday, and I was in bed with my catamite when Ali announced that the archbishop had come to see me.' Where should the English place this prodigiously fecund, colour-blind, lapsed Catholic, tax exile, writer-composer? Certainly among the top hundred writers in English since 1939; and some would put him very much higher than that.

Cad One of the most interesting words in the language. In its relatively short life – hardly more than a hundred years – it reversed its meaning and then gently expired for want of use. As first noted by the *OED* it was being used contemptuously of townsmen at Oxford in 1831 and within ten years to denote any vulgar or ill-bred fellow. In Compton Mackenzie's celebrated Edwardian Oxford novel *Sinister Street,* there is a scene in which the hero, Michael Fane, and some of his friends decide to rag the rooms of a fellow undergraduate called Smithers. What has Smithers done? Nothing; but he is a cad: a poor scholar, a carpenter's son with a cockney accent, and he is to be ragged for his general bearing and plebeian origin.

The irony, of course, lies in the fact that insofar as the word still means anything in England, it is Fane and his friends who are the cads, not Smithers. The word has subtly changed its meaning and certainly in inter-war years conveyed the idea of someone who knows how to behave but fails to do so; a gentleman, in short, who has given up his code.

The golden (or rather chromium) age of the cad was undoubtedly the thirties: epoch of the cocktail shaker, brothel-creeper, and silver cigarette case. The cad's weaknesses are girls, gin, and gee-gees, usually in that order. He often turns out to be rather a good man in a tight corner. Capel Maturin in Michael Arlen's story *The Ace of Cads,* for instance, has won the DSO and Bar, but has been cashiered from the Brigade of Guards for pouring wine in a restaurant over a conductor who persists in playing Mendelssohn's 'Spring Song' after being asked three times to desist.

The most thorough-going rotter in recent English fiction must be

Captain Edward Fox-Ingleby, hero of A.G. Macdonnell's *Autobiography of a Cad*. It is a sustained satire on the English upper class – or more specifically the Tory Party – the hard-faced men who had done well out of the war. Fox-Ingleby's especial hero is F.E. Smith, later Lord Birkenhead. That fits.

English cads, if not celebrated by Armenian writers like Michael Arlen, are best portrayed by Russian actors like George Sanders. As he remarked in his *Memoirs of a Professional Cad*: 'I was beastly but I was never coarse. I was a high class sort of heel.' Not even that could be truthfully said of the new wave of fictional heroes like Ian Fleming's* James Bond or Len Deighton's Harry Palmer. They have learned that the Queensberry rules don't work any more, that the glory and the girls go to the man who can best aim a swift kick to the crotch, as his adversaries assuredly will.

Besides, women are so fond of cads. In that immortal exchange in *Pygmalion,* Colonel Pickering gallantly tries to make sure Henry Higgins is a fit person to tutor Eliza Doolittle (see *Accent*). 'Are you a man of good character where women are concerned?' Higgins: 'Have you ever met a man of good character where women are concerned?' Precisely: we are all cads nowadays.

Cambridge The other place is quieter than Oxford*, and to some disinterested eyes more beautiful; it is also a little more serious. Good at economics (Marshall, Pigou, Keynes*) and Eng. Lit. (Leavis, Tillyard, Quiller-Couch) it would nevertheless be hard to imagine Cambridge nurturing a Max Beerbohm, a Lewis Carroll*, an Oscar Wilde, an Evelyn Waugh* or a Kenneth Tynan. Though Cambridge cannot boast one college like Christ Church at Oxford which has the portraits of a dozen sons who became prime minister, it can claim one laboratory, the Cavendish, which has nurtured a string of world-class physicists (Maxwell, Rayleigh, Thompson and Rutherford). Newton gave Cambridge a lead in mathematics it has never lost; and the recent unravelling of the double helix in Cambridge illustrates the place's pre-eminence in biological science as well. The novels of C.P.Snow, set as they are in the corridors of power, illustrate to perfection the slightly more bony texture of Cambridge life.

On the other hand, it must be said that the Foolights Club since the war has turned out a string of real goers, notably Peter Hall, Trevor Nunn, Jonathan Miller, Peter Cook, Alan Bennett and Clive James. Oxford, of course, can riposte with Kingsley Amis*, Richard Ingrams, Dudley Moore, Rowan Atkinson. . . but one can go on like this forever and prove nothing, except that Oxford and Cambridge are yoked together in an uneasy amalgam called Oxbridge, a matter for concern or celebration depending on your own alma mater*.

The degree of seriousness in the ancient rivalry between the two places may best be judged by Harold Wilson's account of how, as a young don at University College, Oxford, he was involved in the appointment of a new Master. The best man for the job was the distinguished academic lawyer A.L. Goodhart, but there were three possible drawbacks to his election: he was a Jew, an American, and a Cambridge man. 'We found the first point interesting,' Harold remembered, 'and the second amusing. But the third gave us a lot of trouble.' Goodhart, needless to say, was elected.

Carroll, Lewis (1832-98) By modern standards he was a snob (the only trouble with Margate, he remarked, was the commercial class of person one found there) and a prig (he ended his friendship with Ellen Terry when she went to live with a man not her husband). He was a useful mathematician, an original logician, a pioneer photographer and, of course, the author of *Alice's Adventures in Wonderland* and *Through the Looking-glass*. The occasion when the story was first told is precisely known: 4 July 1862, as Charles Lutwidge Dodgson, mathematics tutor at Christ Church, Oxford, and his friend Robinson Duckworth rowed the three little Liddell girls – Alice, Lorina and Edith – up to Godstowe under a cloudless blue sky, the river a watery mirror below, the drops tinkling from the oars. Dodgson in the story became the Dodo, Duckworth the Duck, the Prince and Princess of Wales (with whom the three little girls had just been playing croquet on the Deanery lawn) the King and Queen of Hearts. Was Lewis Carroll in love with Alice? Perhaps, but if he ever declared that love there is no record of it, and he wrote formally to her as Mrs Hargreaves twenty-five years later when raising the question of a facsimile edition of the Alice manuscript. (She sold the original at Sotheby's in 1928 for £15,400.)

Modern critics have read sinister depths into his penchant for little girls; if there were any truth in it, no word of complaint about it has survived. The Alice books were immediate best-sellers, and have remained so ever since. The *Adventures* are more widely quoted than any other book outside the Shakespeare canon and the Bible, and are applicable to virtually every human situation. Seen as the precursor of every modern movement from Surrealism to psychoanalysis, Carroll was in truth the master, not of nonsense, but of uncommon sense, which is not the same thing at all. 'I can't explain *myself*, I'm afraid sir,' said Alice, 'because I'm not myself, you see.' 'I don't see,' said the Caterpillar. But children did – and still do.

Cats The royal family cannot be doing with cats. There is not even a cat below stairs at Buckingham Palace, though there is no objection in principle to them being kept in the Royal Mews. During the Second World War, Churchill* and Roosevelt were famed cat-lovers, while Hitler and Mussolini were cat-haters, and we can all see what happened to them. In Britain there are some nine million cats, most of them shamelessly spoiled. Some cats have owners like historian A.L. Rowse, who talks to his over the transatlantic telephone. Others, like Marmaduke Ginger Bits, have been the subject of pitched battles about ownership in the courts with lawyers' bills of £10,000 resulting.

The ultimate accolade for the cat fanciers of England has been the preposterous success of the Andrew Lloyd Webber musical *Cats*, based on the T.S. Eliot poems, which at the time of writing has just entered its third year with no sign of a decline in takings. Investors who put cash into the unlikely project have already had their money back and returns of more than 100 per cent a year. The London show is now nearly £3 million in the black and productions are currently running in New York, Budapest, Vienna and Tokyo.

There is one London woman, known simply as the Cat Lady, who saves 1,000 stray cats a year. Five British cats were recently left £65,000 by their owner, a retired railway clerk. Until last year there was a cat in the ladies' loo at Paddington station who was so fat he could do little but waddle, so much money was put in his saucer at the loo. It cost £15 a week to feed him, and he had fan mail and Christmas cards from all over the world. There is, in short, no lunacy the island race will not encompass when it comes to cats. (See, for a general statement of principle on the whole issue, under *Pets*.)

Champagne It is a much-loved English tipple. The French ship more bubbly here than to any other country in the world; more even than to America. The island race put away ten million bottles a year; and it is the English taste for *brut* or dry champagne that has put it so firmly on the map. Bubbly was pricey till 1861 when wine-loving William Ewart Gladstone reduced the duty on each bottle to let it sell here at around five shillings a bottle. By 1869 the most popular music-hall song was 'Champagne Charlie'; the epithet lingers on to this day. Prominent Champagne Charlies ranged from the great swindler Horatio Bottomley (Pommery) to the great statesman Winston Churchill* (Pol Roger). On

Winston's death Madame Pol Roger ordained that a black border be put round the edge of their label: it remains to this day. 'Champagne certainly gives one werry gentlemanly ideas,' remarked Mr Jorrocks, 'but for a continuance, I don't know but I should prefer mild hale.' Hilaire Belloc is quoted at each general election with never diminishing effect: 'The accursed power which stands on Privilege (And goes with Women, and Champagne, and Bridge) Broke – and Democracy resumed her reign: (Which goes with Bridge, and Women, and Champagne).'

Charters and Caldicott Made their debut in 1938 when a classic Hitchcock thriller called *The Lady Vanishes* was released. They were two absurd, cricket-mad Englishmen hurrying back to England for the Test at Old Trafford when a little local difficulty with some Nazi bounders detains their train. Basil Radford and Naunton Wayne were such a hit as the immortal pair that they appeared as the same chaps in two more films, and a new BBC TV series based on their updated doings has now been written by playwright Keith Waterhouse.

Writer-director Sidney Gilliat, who dreamed up the characters, originally called them Charters and Spanswick – his gardener's name, common in Wiltshire. Edward Black, the producer, in a moment of pure inspiration, changed Spanswick to Caldicott. Gainsborough, the production company, kept 50 per cent of the rights in the characters, Gilliat and his partner Frank Launder the rest.

Like Holmes and Watson, Charters and Caldicott never address each other by their first names. Like Wooster* and Wimsey*, they are not quite so daft as they appear. In an allegorical scene, apt for 1938, Charters goes to apologise to the Nazis ambushing the train and is shot in the hand for his pains. A passenger called Todhunter is for surrender. Caldicott asks him for his gun: 'Pacifist eh? Won't work, old boy. Early Christians tried it and got thrown to the lions. Come on, hand it over.' Needless to say, he turns out to be a crack shot.

As *The Times* remarked in its obituary of Radford, he excelled at playing the Englishman of popular romantic convention, no great shakes as a thinker, but never losing his sense of values and, in the thick of fearful hazards, less dismayed by the likelihood of imminent capture than by the news that England had collapsed in the second innings. All Englishmen will trust that Radford and Wayne are now sitting in the Great Pavilion in the Sky, waiting for the celestial covers to come off as they sip a well-earned gin and nectar.

Cheese Even to this day some country shops in England offer just two kinds of cheese: mild or tasty. By this they intend the two great varieties of the most English of all cheeses, Cheddar: hard, clean, delicate and golden and for three centuries the simple, portable lunch of farm-workers, miners, builders and soldiers. It is the centrepiece of the ploughman's, still the most popular snack for the English drinker, and the perfect adjunct for the English apple.

Once made in virtually every county in England, and formerly a product of the farmhouse, English cheese has now effectively narrowed to nine varieties: Cheddar, Caerphilly, Cheshire, Derby, Gloucester, Lancashire, Leicester, Stilton and Wensleydale. Stilton has long been the king of cheeses, and can compete against the world for nobility and richness; however, with affluence and travel your average Englishman has been learning of continental enticements like Camembert and Dolce Latte.

To meet this challenge the English cheese industry has therefore evolved a new soft cheese that looks as if it comes from the Dordogne but in fact hails from Somerset. Mild, creamy and lightly veined, it was christened, in a moment of cloth-eared lunacy, Lymeswold. Despite this grisly handicap, Lymeswold may win its way in England; but not while they charge more for it than for Brie.

Cheltenham Laxative, diuretic and antacid, the waters of Cheltenham Spa are naturally alkaline and in this respect unique in England. The Duke of Wellington found them a natural antidote to liver disease brought on by military service, and so put the place on the map. With its caryatids, window boxes, hanging baskets of marigolds and lobelia, Victorian letter boxes, coloured granite lamp posts honouring Gordon of Khartoum, pharmacy with gilded pestle and mortar, and intricate Regency ironwork, Cheltenham still has much of the feel of a hill station at the height of the Raj. Its three public schools – Cheltenham College, Dean Close and Cheltenham Ladies' College – lend emphasis to the sense of elegant torpor. Festivals of music, literature and cricket seem well sited, and the swarms of dog collars at the Cheltenham Races suggest that the Irish priesthood know a good thing when they see one. However, as usual in England, there are subversive currents running beneath this bland surface. The spa is also the home of the country's worldwide electronic intelligence network, and the scene of a recent major spy scandal. Here too during the war a schoolboy at the college named Lindsay Anderson, son of a major general, was already reacting against the system into which he had been born, and was to make a string of films and plays (most notably *If ...*) which were the living and articulate antithesis of everything Cheltenham stands for.

Christmas This festival does not find the island race at its best. It has become the apotheosis of materialism. It focuses the minds of children not on what they can give but on what they can get. It is the moment no longer for the accomplishment of grace but the acquisition of gew-gaws. It is the time for the laying up of precisely those treasures on earth that the proponent of treasures in heaven so eloquently despised.

It is the high season for dyspepsia and cirrhosis. It throws together in confined spaces generations of diametrically opposed interests. It is the moment of the year for a torrent of fatalities and dismemberment on the roads. It is a trough of inanition some six weeks across in which no sensible decisions can be expected from anyone. It is the time for the proliferation on the television screen of the very worst that the human intellect can devise: an unending diet of pap and tripe, of tuneless tunes, and plotless plots, all whipped into a bland and saccharine cake mix of spurious goodwill. It is also the time for the Queen's annual broadcast, one of the low points in the royal year.

No other nation has made such a hash of the iridescent simplicities spun out by the revolutionary rabbi from Nazareth. What would the man who told the parable of the rich man and the eye of the needle say to Fortnums* in Christmas week? For the sickly maw of sentiment in which their celebration of the winter solstice wallows the English must thank Prince Albert, who brought the Christmas tree with him from Saxe Coburg-Gotha, and Charles Dickens* who wrapped it in tinsel.

Chuffed One of the curious English words which means two opposite things; here, pleased and displeased. Writers are still using it in both senses, but the first seems to be getting the better of the argument.

Church of England It has affected the destiny of the nation only once in recent times. Edward VIII abdicated in 1936 because there was no way the Church of England, of which he was head, could condone his marriage with Mrs Simpson, who had two divorced husbands still living. The issue was of no importance to his hundreds of millions of Hindu and Moslem subjects; it was not even a crucial matter to the Church of Scotland, which permitted divorce. It was an issue solely for the Established Church which at that time had some three million regular worshippers in England.

Twenty years later there was a faint but far less important reverberation of the same issue, when Princess Margaret wished to marry Group Captain Peter Townsend. It was left to a divorced prime minister, Anthony Eden, to tell her that she could not marry the divorced Townsend and maintain her royal prerogatives. Only in this role may the Church of England still be the Tory Party at prayer; otherwise its influence is fragmentary and inconclusive.

Indeed the sporting connection may be one of its strongest remaining traditions. We have already noted the powerful connection between the Boat Race* and the Bench of Bishops; and J.B. Priestley* remarked that it was difficult to know where the Church of England ended and the MCC began.

Churchill, Winston (1874-1965) He was a small (5 feet 6½ inch), pink-faced, sandy-haired bounder. When Clementine Hozier, his future wife, was introduced to him at a ball, her partner asked why she had been talking to 'that frightful fellow'. The Tories hated him because he had crossed the floor of the House and joined the Liberals on the issue of tariff reform; the working class hated him because he put in troops to break strikes.

When he entered the Commons as Prime Minister for the first time on 13 May 1940, he was cheered – but only by the Labour benches. His conduct of the war was bold, eccentric, and vigorous. Ellen Wilkinson noted that when Attlee took the Cabinet in Winston's absence, the work was expeditiously done in three hours. When Winston took it, the agenda was not even reached and the Cabinet went on till midnight: but everyone there knew they had been in the presence of history.

He made himself Minister of Defence and effectively ran the war with his chiefs of staff single-handed, heckling and harrying them unmercifully. His closest friends – Beaverbrook*, Bracken and Birkenhead – were known to his wife as the three terrible Bs. All were self-made men: adventurers and *arrivistes*. He badly misjudged the mood of the country in 1945 and could never understand why he had been thrown unceremoniously from office. None of this matters tuppence.

He was perfectly cast for his role in history and the fates saw to it that his exits and entrances were meticulously timed. The scope and sweep of his life were on a heroic scale. He held almost every great office of state open to a commoner. He not only led his nation to a triumphant victory in the Second World War; he also wrote a magisterial six-volume history of it. He witnessed the last charge of the British cavalry (Omdurman, 1898) and lived to congratulate President Kennedy on sending man into space.

When all the reservations are made, the final balance sheet is clear: the little bounder became the greatest Englishman of his time. Any Englishman who can recall the war at all will get the authentic frisson at hearing again a record of Winston delivering any of his magnificent wartime speeches: 'We shall fight on the beaches, we shall fight on the landing grounds, we shall fight in the fields and in the streets, we shall fight in the hills; we shall never surrender.'

He will remember too, with wry pleasure, that as Winston sat down to an ovation he is said to have turned to his neighbour and added: 'And if they do come we shall have to hit them over the head with bottles, because we have nothing else.'

Clanger To *drop a clanger* is to make a *faux pas*; but note again the superior strength of the Anglo-Saxon. Though so far traced back only to 1948 by the *Oxford English Dictionary*, it was certainly service slang in the 1939-45 war, and probably had its origin when some fitter or artificer dropped some tackle on the floor with a resounding crash. The onomatopoeia helps too.

Claret Originally from the French *clairet* and meaning any clear or light wine as opposed to a dark one, claret imperceptibly came to mean first red wine and then the red wines of Bordeaux. The trend is natural enough; the English ruled Bordeaux for three hundred years. One English king is buried there and two more who ruled it lie in French soil. Nine of the great estates of Bordeaux are English-owned today, including Latour, Léoville-Barton and, as one might have suspected, Smith-Haut-Lafitte.

Claret is for boys, said Samuel Johnson, and perhaps then it was: but as it has grown in complexity and authority it has become increasingly celebrated in England as the thinking man's tipple and a staple of Oxbridge novels (eg, C.P. Snow's *The Masters*). In English politics claret is indissolubly associated with Roy Jenkins, co-founder of the Social Democratic Party; so much so that Sir Geoffrey Howe, when Chancellor of the Exchequer, had only to mention a change in the claret duty during a budget speech to get the next laugh even before the inevitable sally about Roy's fancy followed.

With the formation of the Alliance between the SDP and the Liberals, an ingenious sobriquet has been coined to exemplify their balancing act between previously disparate forces in English politics: they are the party of *claret and chips.*

It must be faced, however, that there are formidable claret bores.

There is a well-authenticated story of a celebrated wine correspondent whose merest footfall could scatter the drinkers from the bar at the old Press Club. He never bought anyone a drink but bored everyone to distraction with his unending tales of great vintages and *premiers crus*. One day he announced to the cringing assembly: 'And tomorrow I am going to Bordeaux.' From the other end of the bar came the only possible response: 'Who's Doe?'

Class The English pox. But just as the incidence of pox in England has fallen virtually to zero, so has the prevalence of class. Indeed, we may say of class as we do of money and sex that it really matters very little unless one has too little or too much of it. Yet some Englishmen have seen England as soaked in class. Certainly Orwell*, who placed himself very precisely in the lower-upper middle class, saw it that way; but the world has moved on in the half century since he wrote his great political moralities and what he saw as distinctions in class are now being imperceptibly elided into varieties of style.

The first reason for this is economic. A miner now earns three times more in real terms than he did before the war. A factory worker earns twice as much and is now on level terms with a graduate schoolmaster or an executive officer in the civil service. A printer on piecework in Fleet Street may live in a council house and eat in a caff while earning an income ten times as high as a Wykehamist curate with a first in Greats. A video editor in television may be better off than many a managing director; still sending his children to the comprehensive as the MD ploddingly pays for school fees in instalments throughout his career.

Dress has also become almost, if not entirely, classless among the young. While the Sloane Ranger may still affect certain class indicators like Huskies and pearls, track-suits are the universal garb of the new chic professions – green goddesses, photographers, advertising men and record managers.

The old working class has dramatically shrunk. Whereas before the war some three quarters of the population did unskilled or semi-skilled manual jobs, the proportion is now much nearer a quarter, and sinking fast. With the rise of the combine harvester the fields are empty of farmworkers and the car plants will soon be innocent of human inhabitants except for the technicians who service the automated robots.

Even in the forties Orwell believed he could see the emergence of a new class: 'The technicians and the higher paid skilled workers, the airmen and the mechanics, the radio experts, film producers, popular journalists and industrial chemists. They are the indeterminate strata at which the older class distinctions are beginning to break down . . .'

It is this new class which surely has filled the ranks of the Alliance in politics, that curious amalgam of old-fashioned Liberals and new-style Social Democrats which has made such heavy inroads into the traditional Labour vote. They have indeed become the new middle class.

It is technically possible to slice up the English middle class into a dozen disparate layers if we use a carving knife as thin as Orwell's. For all practical purposes however it remains a simple three-tiered structure. The lower middle class, which as George Mikes once remarked is the only one in England nobody is proud of belonging to, still provides the country with the bulk of its talent and its genius (Dickens, Wells, Lloyd George, Asquith). The middle of the middle class is the hardest layer to identify but was neatly caught by Jilly Cooper when she labelled them the Weybridges, for that is the sort of town round which they typically cluster: the minor entrepreneurs, the solicitors, the engineers, architects and doctors.

The upper middle class is immediately identifiable: a small but enormously powerful group of civil service mandarins, large-scale farmers, managing directors and bright, youngish brigadiers. They will shade into the upper class by marriage and back again by divorce; but they are the most assured segment of English society, and noticeably nicer than their French, German or Italian equivalents. The upper class is discussed under *Aristocracy;* here note only their astonishing flair for survival and renewal; a trick worked by constant inter-marriage with brains and money from abroad: Argentinian tin heiresses, New York Jewish princesses, Rhodesian landowners. In the country they still hunt and shoot as if the world had never changed; in towns they tend to melt into the classless cauldron that now seethes in the capital. Here, anything goes: class is out; style is all.

Clerihew When Edmund Clerihew Bentley was a sixteen-year-old schoolboy at St Paul's, he jotted down in class one day these lines: 'Sir Humphrey Davy / Abominated gravy / He lived in the odium / Of having discovered Sodium.' Thus was the first clerihew born: the word is now in the *Oxford English Dictionary.* E.C. Bentley gave the world many delights in his life; his detective story *Trent's Last Case* remains an early classic of the genre. Nothing, however, that he ever did gave more pleasure than his clerihews.

One can argue about the best. Some give the laurels to: 'Sir Christopher Wren / Said, "I'm going to dine with some men / If anybody calls / Say I'm designing St Paul's".' Others prefer: 'The Art of biography /

is different from geography / Geography is about maps / But biography is about chaps.'

Many poets have had a go at the clerihew, not often with success. Auden* got close with: 'William Blake / Found Newton hard to take / And was not enormously taken / With Francis Bacon.' It is a minuscule art form to which anyone can aspire.

The subject matter can be literary: 'If I had been / Albertine / I'd have disparue / Too.' It can be political: 'President Charles de Gaulle / Staked his future on the poll / And having polled more nons than ouis / Went home to Colombey-les-deux-Eglises'.

They can be sporting: 'Sir Donald Bradman / Would have been a very glad man / If his Test average had been .06 more / Than 99.94' – a true summary of a great sporting record. They can also be subversive, as in: 'Mrs Mary Whitehouse / Caught sight of a lighthouse / It did not escape her detection / That erection.'

Clogs For many years the former prime minister Harold Wilson had to try to live down the charge that he had claimed to have gone to school barefoot. In truth he had said that when he was a boy growing up in Yorkshire, many children – though not Harold himself – had not possessed any shoes; they had worn clogs instead. This indeed was the normal working-class footwear in the industrial north till the age of affluence dawned after the last war; the old northern proverb, clogs to clogs in three generations, is self-explanatory. More recently a gifted northern artist called Bill Tidy introduced in *Private Eye** his cartoon characters The Cloggies, a team of down-to-earth northern clog dancers, to delight a new and well-shod generation.

Clubs By rights, they should all be gone by now. In an era when men and women, by law at least, have equal rights and chaps now go home to help with the babies and washing the dishes, the notion of a gentleman's club in the West End of London should be an anachronism. Nothing of the sort: the club flourishes; not least, perhaps, because it enshrines and perpetuates the old ways. If a thousand men are prepared to chip in three hundred a year each, with perhaps another couple of hundred each as entrance money, they can run an elegant town house far beyond their individual means, hire servants that have now vanished from private service, and enjoy the pleasure of each other's company over honest food and decent wine.

So at least runs the theory; in practice clubs differ dramatically in the quality and quantity of what they can offer. The old aristos' clubs still flourish: White's, where Randolph Churchill and Evelyn Waugh* once exchanged purple-faced insults and Aneurin Bevan was kicked in the arse by an enraged member; Pratt's, the private property of the Duke of Devonshire, where only sixteen can sit down at a time and all club servants are still called George; and Boodle's, the country gents' club in St James's where Dominic Medina MP, the arch-rotter in John Buchan's superlative thrillers, had ensconced himself as a member.

Meantime the literary and artistic clubs have met with mixed fortunes. The Garrick is immensely fashionable and with a twelve-year waiting list, while the equally elegant Savile, catering for very similar interests and tastes, has no waiting list at all. Possibly this has something to do with the Garrick's decision to admit women each night to dine as guests in the coffee room, while the hard core of members on their own sit down the long table in the middle. The struggle that some clubs have had to survive is seen in the amalgamation of four: The East India, founded in 1849 for officers of the East India Company on leave in London, the Devonshire, an old Liberal club whose fortunes seem to have declined with its party's, the Sports, and the Public Schools.

Perhaps membership of a London club does not have quite the cachet it once did, and the truth is that while the black ball still exists, some of those who have been excluded by it have been far more interesting and worthwhile than those who exercised its veto. One has to think no further than Bernard Levin, blackballed at the Garrick for being rude about the Lord Chief Justice, and George Brown, found *non persona grata* at the Savile.

The phenomenon of the club bore still exists in the best-regulated clubs, but the convention of the clubman swapping stories after dinner as a vehicle for the launch of a novel, so beloved of Somerset Maugham*, is mercifully giving way to fresher tricks. Yet the old image of the somnolent clubman asleep in the library still persists, most vividly captured recently by the cartoonist Michael Heath in a scene where one venerable clubman, reading *The Times*, glances up and remarks to his recumbent friend: 'Good Lord, Fenton, I had no idea you were dead!'

Coal Has a quasi-mystical role in English life. The country stands on a vast foundation of the hard, black carbonaceous rock, made from immense wodges of compressed peat: the fuel that fired the Industrial Revolution. It was to make a small group of landowners in England immeasurably rich (the idea that you owned the mineral rights *under* your land was refuted in France and continental Europe) and obliged many millions of Englishmen to live their working lives out of sight and savour of God's good air and light.

This gave the miners (or pitmen as they like to be called) a cachet they have never lost: an aura of glamour, danger, solidarity and bloody-mindedness that has marked them out from their workmates and from their countrymen. In the Second World War one young man in ten eligible for national service was directed down the mines: getting the coal was as important as that. Politically the miners have been since early days a bastion of the Labour movement; though Welsh magicians like Aneurin Bevan and Scottish firebrands like Willie Gallacher have not unnaturally seized the imagination, the Durham Miner's Gala each summer is one of the pinnacles of the English working-class year. No one mocks the miners with impunity in England to this day, and the miners' leaders – men like Joe Gormley and Arthur Scargill – whether loved or loathed, become perforce part of the fabric of English political life.

It is indeed not too much to say that he or she who mocks the miners in English politics is careless of his or her political life: such was certainly Edward Heath's experience in 1974 when, by opposing them, he ended his own government. Equally, one could argue that to placate them, as Wilson and Callaghan have done, did no more than prove who were the masters now.

No one who has ever been down an old pit is likely to forget its Stygian thrall: the seams so exhausted that sometimes the men worked in spaces only as high as the length of their own boots; the stalls for the ponies with names like Bounce, Bob, Prince and (improbably) Eton; the big drums in which they once kept the first aid for the horrendous accidents; the stretchers that ran along rails carrying injured men; the rivulets of black underground streams.

The gap between pit-owner and pit-worker was always stark and vast and probably best closed by the state taking over. The Sitwells, exquisite products of inherited plenty, could just hear the picks of the miners at work under their ancestral seat on still evenings near Scarborough. One of the greatest cartoons ever drawn by Vicky, lover and hater of English *moeurs,* showed a patrician Sir Alec Douglas-Home, professed intimate of the working man, gormlessly bagging grouse on his broad acres while below him, in cut-away relief, the miners hacked away, as ever, at the coal-face.

The central question remains: if mining is indeed one of the most hateful callings in the land, why are miners so keen to keep their jobs? Between the two wars they left the pits in droves to become schoolmasters or milkmen; anything but the pits. Perhaps the answer is encapsulated in the testimony of D.H. Lawrence: 'My father,' he wrote 'loved the pit. He was hurt badly more than once, but he would never stay away. He loved the contact, the intimacy... the curious dark intimacy of the mines, the naked sort of contact.' The pull of the pit is not totally amenable to rational analysis; but is best not totally ignored either.

Colour Supplement *The Sunday Times* printed its first colour section (as it was then called) on 4 February 1962. It was a spectacular flop. No one seemed to like it, least of all its progenitor, Roy Thomson, owner of *The Sunday Times* who had envisaged something rather like the funnies back home in Canada – coarse-grained, downmarket colour pages for women and children. What he got was a curious *mélange* of reportage in text and photographs about a new lifestyle. It was so different from what had been published in England before that it seemed almost surreal. Soon it had given birth to a new and pejorative term: colour supplement living. This was held by those who coined it to exemplify all that was worst about modern England: trendiness and gluttony, cynicism and materialism, a kind of glossy heartlessness. The case was most eloquently put by the art critic John Berger on BBC TV when he contrasted the lush colour ads for cars, clothes, food and booze with the photo essays in between of want and war, cruelty and disease.

It was touch and go for the first year whether *The Sunday Times* colour magazine would make it. About a million pounds was lost before the penny dropped. It occurred one day to just one advertising agency that here was a way of reaching three million AB readers, the top socio-economic group, in colour. They began to advertise, so did everybody else, and the drought of ads turned into a torrent. The *Observer* and *Telegraph,* who had been the first to mock the new colour medium, were obliged to follow suit.

The colour magazines, from being a liability, turned into the spearhead of new circulation drives. Series on the great middle-class preoccupations – education, health, houses, money, marriage – could more than offset the downward pull of a price rise. The magazines *were* mirrors of the swinging sixties, but they were also vehicles for the best photographers, writers and artists in the business. They still flourish, but inside the commercial constraints which again seem to justify John Berger's original strictures. Between the early disasters and the later bonanzas, they may have done their best work.

The colour supplement opened the eyes of the English by showing them new ways of spending their new wealth. Indeed, it showed them how to feel both wealthy and guilty at the same time: an unbeatable formula in England.

It failed by being irrevocably middle class: a term of abuse used by the English for those that made them what they are.

Conan Doyle, Sir Arthur (1859-1930)   We tend to forget all the other things he wrote and did. Sherlock Holmes and Dr Watson tower over the English imagination – and the world's – obscuring a mass of other work. There are the historical romances: *The Exploits of Brigadier Gerard*, for example; *Micah Clarke*, set during the Monmouth rebellion; *The White Company*, about the exploits of a band of medieval knights errant; *Uncle Bernac*, set during the French Revolution; and *Rodney Stone*, a novel about prize-fighting in Regency England.

There are the science fiction fantasies: *The Lost World*, in which Professor Challenger discovers an Amazon plateau inhabited by pre-historic beasts; *The Poison Belt*, about the coming destruction of human life; and *The Maracot Deep* in which a submarine finds Atlantis flourishing beneath the sea. There are the war reports, written out of a deep sense of patriotism: *The Great Boer War* (he had served in South Africa as a doctor); and his *History of the British Campaign in France and Flanders* in no fewer than six volumes. He also found time to write a polemic against Belgian colonialism (*The Crime of the Congo*) which was to bring him close to Roger Casement (who as a young British consular official had first drawn attention to the horrors), an allegiance which did not desert him when the Irish rebel – as he became – was tried and hanged for treason: Doyle subscribed most of the money for Casement's defence.

He used his detective skills, learned in his days as a medical student from Dr Jospeh Bell, his teacher at Edinburgh University, who sat for the portrait of Sherlock Holmes, to fight two *causes célèbres*: against the unjust convictions of George Edalji for cattle mutilation and of Oscar Slater for murder. Slater walked out of court a free man in 1928, nineteen years after he had been sentenced to death, with an *ex gratia* payment of £6,000.

It is hard to believe that such a shrewd and intelligent man as Conan Doyle could also espouse the cause of spiritualism and seriously claim in *The Strand Magazine* that some photographs, manifest fakes to modern eyes, proved the existence of fairies. Yet the spiritualism arose from a deep need to believe: he had lost his son Kingsley and his brother Innes in the First World War. He understood more about sex than most writers of his generation (he wrote a thesis on syphilis) and told his daughter that while he was not prepared to call himself a socialist, he thought he might well be one. (In fact he stood for parliament twice, unsuccessfully, in the Liberal Unionist cause. It was Roger Casement who subsequently converted him to the necessity of Home Rule.)

He was in every way a big man. He had played rugby for Blackheath (like Doctor Watson) in his youth; he played cricket with A.E.W. Mason, author of *The Four Feathers*, and with the young P.G. Wodehouse* on whom he remained a lasting influence. 'Don't you feel as you age, that the tragedy of life is that your early heroes lose their glamour?' wrote Plum. 'Now with Doyle I don't have this feeling. I still revere his work as much as ever. I used to think it swell, and I still think it swell.' He is not alone.

Concorde   The island race began work on Concorde in 1943, when the war was far from over (just as they had begun work on postwar reconstruction in 1940 when it looked lost). In view of the vast cost, they tried in 1960 to interest three other nations making a partnership: America, Germany and France. The Americans were working on quite different lines, envisaging a plane that would fly at three times the speed of sound, or 2,250 mph. The British opted for Mach 2.1 or 1,575 mph. Even at that daunting speed, they would have to cope with a temperature range from −45°C to 120°C; Concorde gets very hot as it cleaves through the sky. Mach 3 would have meant absorbing temperatures of up to 300°C. It could be done; but the Brits reckoned the development would take too long.

Besides, there was another clinching point: Mach 2 could dispatch Concorde across the Atlantic in 3 hours 20 minutes; Mach 3 would lop only 20 minutes off that time. So the Americans decided to go it alone. The Germans said they were not ready for such a vaulting venture just yet; but it turned out that the French were thinking on very similar lines to the British. A deal was struck in November 1962; and the improbable partnership began. Most of the Frenchmen on the project, being involved in international aviation, spoke English already. While the Brits generally commanded French at little more than schoolboy level, most learned enough during Concorde's building for technical discussion.

Odd social differences surfaced. At one meeting the British leader suggested to his French counterpart that they should call in Honorine and dictate a summary of what they had just agreed. 'D'accord,' replied the Frenchman, 'mais qui est Honorine?' She turned out to be his own secretary, whom he always addressed as Mademoiselle Dupont.

Concorde first flew on 2 March 1969, a shimmering white mirage that after all the high tech had come out looking like some gorgeous prehistoric bird. Then came the long years of proving and marketing.

Concorde flew to Alaska and Rio, to Saudi Arabia and Melbourne. It had plenty of enemies. In March 1971 the American Congress refused to vote further funds for their SST project. On 31 January 1973, the last day of their six-month option to buy Concorde, Pan-Am pulled out. TWA followed a few hours later. The two events were not directly related; the American airlines simply thought Concorde could not be economically viable.

In one sense they were right; but once the British government had written off all development costs and made a present of it to British Airways, Concorde proved one of their biggest money-spinners, with up to a hundred passengers paying £2,200 for the return trip to New York. Concorde customers have become a kind of exclusive jet-setter's club; one already has four hundred flights under his belt. Meanwhile the American airlines have been complaining about the unfair competition Concorde is offering them: handsome tribute indeed to the beautiful and improbable white bird the Brits and Frogs made together.

Connolly, Cyril (1903-74) 'Connolly was on the way to have become one of the outstanding day-dreamers of his generation had not a penchant for the visible world involved him in extravagance which could only be redeemed by a lifetime of literary effort for which in 1946 a grateful country rewarded him with the Legion of Honour.

'Arms: a nez purpure, impaled upon a grindstone proper between two duns rampant. Crest: a hack in his element, hobbled. Motto: filez sans payer.'

With this typical burst of comic self-denigration Connolly introduced himself in *Previous Convictions*, a 1963 collection of his work over the previous decade. It was not the first time he had given himself the treatment. 'I have always disliked myself at any given moment,' he wrote in the opening pages of *A Georgian Boyhood*, the coruscating coda to his writer's primer, *Enemies of Promise,* 'the sum of these moments is my life.'

It was published in the week of Munich, when Cyril was thirty-five, and was intended, he said, as a didactic inquiry into the problem of how to write a book which lasts ten years. It did; but roused one critic's censure because Cyril set to work after a now-celebrated lunch of omelette, Vichy water and peaches, though at that time in France where he was writing peaches were cheaper than potatoes.

Only son of upper-middle-class Anglo-Irish parents ('England = Grannie, Lodgings, School, Poverty, Middle Class; Ireland = Aunt Mab, Castles, Holidays, Riches, Upper Class'), scholar of Eton and Balliol, Cyril came to London with the heaviest of artistic burdens: a glittering reputation as wit, dandy, aesthete, iconoclast and, on the reverse of that polished coin, the obligation of promise to fulfil. How did he make out?

He wrote one minor novel, *The Rock Pool*, which he described as the centre part of a triptych on snobbery set by the Mediterranean, his spiritual watering-hole: 'I think I may claim to have created a young man as futile as any . . . The bars are closed, the hotel is empty, the nymphs have departed.' That famous elegaic chord recurs again more insistently in *The Condemned Playground*, an exhilarating collection of his critical essays from 1927 to 1944: 'It is closing time in the gardens of the West and from now on an artist will be judged only by the resonance of his solitude or the quality of his despair.'

Was it really closing time though? He was halfway through a decade of editing the literary magazine *Horizon*; on those 121 honourably battered booklets alone many literary men would gladly rest their reputations. He had moreover recently published his flawed masterpiece *The Unquiet Grave*: 'Approaching forty, I am about to heave my carcass of vanity, boredom, guilt, and remorse into another decade . . .' But we have had enough of Cyril's luxuriating self-pity. He was a critic of glittering intelligence, a travel-writer of rare quality, a parodist of undisputed dexterity and withal, an enchanting man. Case dismissed.

The Conservatives   While the Labour Party has long been an army of brilliant goers led by honest plodders (MacDonald, Attlee, Callaghan) the Conservative Party has long been an army of honest plodders led by brilliant goers (Disraeli, Macmillan, Thatcher). Few have seen the true nature of Conservatism more deeply than Disraeli, who nevertheless used it so effectively as a springboard to his own advantage.

'Conservatism', he wrote in *Coningsby*, 'discards Prescription, shrinks from Principle, disavows Progress; having rejected all respect for antiquity, it offers no redress for the present, and makes no preparation for the future.' To the twentieth-century Englishman, conservatism is dominated by the romantic vision of Winston Churchill*, the artful draughtsmanship of Rab Butler, the doomed interregnum of Anthony Eden, the surly logistics of Edward Heath, and, most recently, the steely imperatives of Margaret Thatcher. This last regime may well be the most radical turn the Conservative Party has ever made, and lead it to triumph or perdition.

There are those, some of them high in the Conservative Party, who would argue that Thatcherite conservatism precisely echoes every charge made by Disraeli in *Coningsby*, and is thus destined to fail. While they applaud her courage, her decision, and her skill, they deplore her inflexibility, her insensitivity, and her arrogance. There is, in short, for the first time in its long history, an opposition contained within the ranks of the parliamentary Conservative party able and strong enough to take instant power if called on. So far, Margaret Thatcher appears inviolate to such unscripted and previously unimaginable threats. She looks, that is, unassailable. She has adopted what looks uncommonly like a presidential, indeed well-nigh monarchical stance.·

'If Her Majesty stood for Parliament,' declares Alf Garnett in Johnny Speight's epochal television series *Till Death Do Us Part*, 'if the Tory Party had any sense and made her its leader instead of that grammar school twit Heath – us Tories, mate, would win every election we went in for.' She has; and so, for the time being at any rate, it looks as if they will.

Cotswolds   The case against the Cotswolds is easily made. It has been swamped by tourists and gentrified by rich Londoners. The indigenous denizens have been priced out of what has become a nightmare region of cottages with ersatz coach lamps and farmhouses with carports, wrought-iron gates and ornamental fountains. There is something in the charge, but just as there are still postmen and bus drivers in Beverly Hills, so there are still plenty of ordinary folk in the Cotswolds. The trouble is that the Cotswolds are so ludicrously beautiful – and now royally patronised – that the inhabitants do tend to take cover. This is not hard; for it is a curiously elusive place.

What exactly are the Cotswolds? It is easier to ask than to answer. Much of Gloucestershire is Cotswolds; some is not. Parts of Oxfordshire and even Berkshire are essentially part of that same magical blend of honey-coloured stone. Technically, there is a forty mile-long escarpment running from just north of Chipping Campden to a point southwest of Stroud. To the west, the land drops away steeply, yielding stunning views of the Severn valley and deep into Wales; eastward, the land slopes gently away through a tangle of small rivers to the Thames valley and Berkshire Downs. There are no big towns here and no industry to speak of till you get to Bristol in the south or Birmingham* in the north; but there is a whole treasure house of small towns whose names suggest enchantment and do not disappoint: Stow-on-the-Wold, Moreton in Marsh and Bourton on the Water. The Cotswolds are a thousand square miles of rolling hills and deep valleys, chuckling rivers, noble trees and – above all – exquisite houses.

The stone from which they are fashioned is a variety of limestone called oolite. It is composed of small, round grains of calcium like the roe of a fish. When the sun strikes it the stone looks golden; in other kinds of light it seems brown or cream or grey. It is used in the Cotswolds not just for the walls but also for the roofs, so that, clustered together, softened by moss or lichen, they blur into the landscape in a way seen nowhere else in the world. It is a piece of earth that has a fair claim to call itself the heart of England.

Cottage   Like so many other things, the cottage has worked its way right through English society: from the hovel for the starving to the hideaway for the lovesick: from the tied cottage for the farmworker to the weekend cottage for the advertising copywriter. While many have been ruined by additions quite out of keeping with their age, many have been lovingly restored, their inglenooks unblocked and their timber beams exposed again.

The charms of the English cottage are clear enough: made perforce from materials at hand, it followed the contours imposed by timber and stone and thus always looks beguilingly artless and resolutely rooted: there are ugly cottages in England but they are not many; and some, though tarted up, have a dream-like beauty unequalled anywhere in the world.

Besides, the remote chance of finding a cottage going for a song impels the affluent bourgeois still; and even now you can find people who will claim casually that they bought their place from an obliging farmer for a mere £400 a mere twelve years ago. Add two noughts for any cottage within a day's drive of London and you will be nearer the mark.

The central heating now thrums under many a thatch; but it is not all gain. Connoisseurs of the old English cottage will recall the yellow pool of light thrown by the oil lamp, the hiss of the logs in the fire, the voluptuous comfort of the feather bed, the draughty dash to the outside privy, and the creamy feel of the rainwater gathered in the water butt by the back door.

Council House   The heyday of the council house lasted some sixty years: from 1923, when the term is first noted by the *OED*, to 1983, when it became an issue at the general election. Inside that era the council house was the bastion and the symbol of the English working class. To the old, it was a sanctuary from the workhouse which might otherwise have been their fate; to the young, a springboard from which to escape to the semi-detached suburbs or indeed beyond.

Despite canards to the contrary, the council house was nearly always well kept by its tenants; the case against it was that it belonged to Big Brother and was administered by him. The Tories saw that selling council houses to tenants could be a huge vote-catcher: it turned the council estate into a new province of the property-owning democracy so beloved of Tory Central Office. The Labour Party did not see the danger till it was too late, and though this was by no means the only issue in 1983, it was a mighty powerful one.

If you want to see the case for the old council house, redbrick, raw-boned, repetitive and regulated though it may have been, take a look at a Victorian photograph of the inner-city slums where the homeless lived. If the sight of Rovers and Jaguars parked in council estates still causes a red mist to swim before some bourgeois eyes (Minis and Escorts are all right), a quick antidote is to consider countries like Cambodia, where power changed hands suddenly and the professors were put to work in the paddy fields. The council house has in truth been a staging post on the long road to peaceable change.

Countryside Even today, some 82 per cent of England is used for agriculture; a further 5 per cent for forestry. Thus England from the air still seems – and in some ways is – a green and pleasant land. On the other hand four English people in every five now live in a town. The countryside has thus been emptied of human habitation; but the umbilical cord is strong. Three English people in every four make at least one trip to the countryside every year. A third of all such trips are made to some specific place like a stately home; a further fifth to the coast; one in ten to a particular village; but one in four are making for nowhere particular at all. The random thrall of the English countryside draws them back.

Ironically, the traditional roles have been reversed; post-war controls have thwarted urban pollution while the cavalier use of agrochemicals has fouled the rural landscape. As landscape consultant Chris Baines graphically put it: 'Kingfishers and water-spiders thrive in Black Country canals. The once common frog has been evicted from the farming countryside and owes its survival almost entirely to the gnome-fringed garden pond.'

So far, some good; but the real threat to the English countryside must come from its gradual erosion by houses, factories, roads, quarries. This toll is currently running at the rate of 30,000 acres a year and will never be reversed. On the other hand, the number of English people actively concerned for the conservation of their countryside escalates with heartening speed: overnight stays in youth hostels quintupled in the seventies, and one acre in ten of England and Wales is now in a national park.

What may be lost for ever is the *unregulated* English countryside; the kind Rupert Brooke went to look for with his brother during the weekend of 2 August 1914, last Sunday of the old world at peace: 'I know the *heart* of England. It has a hedgy, warm, bountiful, dimpled air. Baby fields run up and down the little hills, and all the roads wiggle with pleasure. There's a spirit of rare homeliness about the houses and the countryside, earthy, uneccentric yet elusive, fresh, meadowy, gaily gentle. It is perpetually June in Warwickshire and always six o'clock of a warm afternoon...'

Covent Garden When the flower, fruit and vegetable market finally left WC2 for its new home south of the Thames, it left behind the piazza designed by Inigo Jones and the large, airy, elegant Georgian building in which the market had been housed. Various proposals were made for its future: helicopter landing pad, atomic shelter, giant ice rink. In the end the GLC decided to develop it into a new shopping centre, and allocated £4 million for the task.

It reopened in 1980 with forty-five shops, a pub, a wine bar, three restaurants and a patisserie. The question of what kind of shops had been hotly debated. Some wanted them just to cater for the local residents and workforce (3,000 and 37,000 people respectively) but Covent Garden has 300,000 people living or working within ten to fifteen minutes' walk and it was this much larger catchment area which became the planners' target.

Goods on sale in the new shops ranged from hand-made dolls to candle-holders, from rare newspapers to glass mirrors, from herbs and spices to pottery and ceramics. Some critics said the shops were too up-market; others too down. At any rate there was a mixture: if the fashion trade had had their way, they would have taken every shop.

Whether or not you like the new Covent Garden will much depend on whether you like instant oldness. However, there is one large slice of customers who clearly do like what they now find there. It already ranks as London's third most popular tourist shopping area – before King's Road.

Most English people, however, will not quickly forget the old Covent Garden, where debs were bought flowers and strawberries by their boyfriends after dancing the night away; even if they were not there themselves. They will not quickly forget Eliza Doolittle, arguably Covent Garden's most celebrated denizen, who was harmlessly selling flowers outside the Opera House when she first came to the attention of Professor Henry Higgins in Bernard Shaw's* enchanted fable, *Pygmallion*.

Though none of them will remember the old theatre's disasters (Charles Macklin, aged eighty-nine, was led off in 1789 after forgetting his lines in Shylock; Edmund Kean was carried off after a stroke during Othello in 1833), it would be a dull Englishman who knew nothing of its triumphs: premières for Benjamin Britten (*Billy Budd, Gloriana, A Midsummer Night's Dream*); for William Walton (*Troilus and Cressida*), and Michael Tippett (*The Midsummer Marriage*). Only Sheridan Morley struck a jarring note when he said that the people in dinner jackets at Covent Garden made him feel he had strayed into a convention of head waiters.

Coward, Sir Noël (1899-1973) 'Forty years ago,' wrote Kenneth Tynan, 'he was Slightly in *Peter Pan*, and you might say he has been wholly in *Peter Pan* ever since.' Yet the truth is that Tynan got somewhere nearer the mark when he noted that he had a face like an old boot – but an unmistakably hand-made boot. For though Coward had, by his own precise assessment, a talent to amuse, he was also as tough as old boots. He had to be. After the heady triumphs of his youth (he went on the stage at ten and had four plays on together in London at twenty-six) he had to face the doldrums in the forties and early fifties when the world found his work outmoded, irrelevant and precious.

It was the inspired idea of an American impresario to book him for a cabaret season at Las Vegas, of all places. He was paid $40,000 a week ('For that money,' he remarked, 'they can throw bottles at me if they so choose.') He was a *succès fou*, and never looked back. By the sixties he was being revived at the National Theatre in London and in theatres worldwide. He lived to see *Cowardy Custard*, his life story in words and music, at the Mermaid, and to be knighted just before he died in his sleep at his house on a Jamaican hill. It had been a happy life.

He had been the friend of Somerset Maugham*, Louis Mountbatten and the Queen Mum. Winston Churchill* and Franklin D. Roosevelt had sung his *Mad Dogs and Englishmen* after one of their great wartime parleys. ('Hindus and Argentines sleep firmly from twelve to one / But Englishmen detest a / Siesta'). He was manifestly homosexual, but totally discreet. He liked women, but had few illusions about them; some, he asserted, should be struck regularly – 'like gongs'.

He once wrote to Lawrence of Arabia, who at the time was rather ostentatiously disguising himself as Aircraftsman Ross, service number

338171: 'Dear 338171, May I call you 338?' He remarked during the war that if an Englishman told you he was a spy, it was a lie; if an American told you he was a spy it was true. He was indeed as English as the puddings he adored.

Cricket   Groucho Marx, taken by an English host to see his first cricket match, sat in rapt attention for half an hour. Finally his host turned and asked how he was enjoying himself. 'Fine,' said Groucho, 'when does it start?' Never, for the non-English-speaking world; for though the island race effortlessly exported soccer and rugger to more than a hundred countries, and even taught the Swiss to slalom, they have never persuaded any country outside the old perimeters of empire to take up cricket. French cricket of course exists, but a French cricketer would be an absurdity. What foreigner would be prepared to wait five days for a result which even then may never come? It is not so much a game as a code; not so much a contest as a dialogue; and was well called chess on grass.

'Capital game – smart sport – fine exercise – very,' says Mr Jingle in *The Pickwick Papers*. Dickens wrote beautifully about the game; but then so did Hazlitt and Meredith, Conan Doyle* (who once actually bowled W.G. Grace) and H.G. Wells (whose father, Joseph Wells, playing for Kent on 26 June 1862, took four Sussex wickets with four successive balls). No sport can remotely approach cricket in the profusion and excellence of its literature. It can boast one Nobel prizewinner (Samuel Beckett – who once turned out for Ireland) and, among contemporary writers, Harold Pinter and Tim Rice (both of whom have their own elevens). It can claim one of the best-known (if banal) of English poems ('There's a breathless hush in the Close tonight / Ten to make and the match to win') as well as one of the most beautiful ('For the field is full of shades as I near the shadowy coast / And a ghostly batsman plays to the bowling of a ghost / And I look through my tears on a soundless-clapping host / As the run-stealers flicker to and fro, to and fro . . .').

The game is not what it was; but then it never was. Politics – particularly the politics of race and colour – obtrude; but then half a century ago the political ties between Britain and Australia were tried to breaking point by the bodyline controversy. A TUC eleven recently defeated a CBI eleven at the height of an industrial dispute. Unlike soccer and rugger, hunting and shooting, cricket has no class connotation: every Englishman has played it at some time. Besides, it is in its essence a great leveller. 'Lord Frederick had royal blood in 'en, so 'twere said', as Francis Brett Young tells us, 'For his granmer were Nelly Gwynn, King Charles's fancy / But when Billy and him walked out to the pitch, side by side / You couldn't tell which were the farmer and which the gentleman / The pair on 'em looked that majestic. . .' A postwar prime minister (Alec Home) was president of the MCC, while his arch-enemy Harold Wilson, when President of the Board of Trade, turned out for the British delegation against the British Embassy during a lull in the trade talks with Russia (and was accused by the local press of indulging in lakeside orgies and pirouettes). Floodlit cricket, one-day cricket, and the advent of the helmet and visor (and hence the bouncer) have deprived cricket of its innate grace but have probably done it no inner harm. Despite all the *longueurs,* incidents, rows, feuds and threats, great cricket still suddenly flowers like a benison: Imran Khan, for example, will bowl a series of thrilling overs so lethal in their hostility as to be virtually unplayable; or Botham will hit one of his titanic centuries to rank with the greatest of all time. Besides, cricket flourishes at village level, the real heart of the game. 'It has been said of the unseen army of the dead,' wrote James Barrie, 'on their everlasting march, that when they are passing a rural cricket ground, the Englishman falls out of the ranks for a moment to look over the gate and smile.'

Croquet Ostensibly a gentle game invariably associated with sunlit days and level lawns in country rectories, it is in practice a handy vehicle for the exercise of the will to win: and can involve a whole spectrum of unexpected human frailties from gamesmanship through sharp practice to downright cheating. It is thus a fitting irony that the word croquet derives from the French word for a crook.

Crumpet In England the word now means two separate, though perhaps occasionally related, things. It is a soft, round cake with holes in the top, made from a yeast batter and if at all possible toasted in front of an open fire. In this context it is an indispensable part of the English autumn, or at least the Englishman's idealised perception of it. Sir John Masterman, Vice-Chancellor of Oxford University from 1957 to 1960, for example, memorably transfixed the crumpet experience in his autobiography *On the Chariot Wheel.*

Writing of his days as an undergraduate before the First World War (he went up to Worcester College in 1909) he recalled: 'The height of luxury was reached in the winter afternoons. There were no bathrooms, so we fetched boiling water in large tin cans from a tap by the kitchen and filled our tin baths which we put in front of our sitting-room fire. Lying in a tin bath, in front of a coal fire, drinking tea and eating well-buttered crumpets is an experience which few can have today.'

Few indeed. Seventy-five years on, crumpet to most young Englishmen is a collective form for young available female talent and sometimes for the female pudenda as well, as in the celebrated rugby song. 'One night in gay Paree / I paid five francs to see / a much-tattooed lady...' and so on till the denouement of the entertainment: 'And on her crumpet, on her crumpet, / Louis Armstrong played his trumpet.' We have thus come a long way from crumpet in front of the fire: or any rate what Sir John meant by it.

The crumpet has a near cousin in the more homely muffin. Though it still flourishes in America as the English muffin, it has been usurped by its sin-laden relation in the land of its birth. Hard to make at home, as even Mrs Beeton noted, it is no longer carried from door to door by the muffin man of Dickensian England.

Custard 'Food, glorious food, cold jelly and custard,' sing the hungry boys in Lionel Bart's musical *Oliver*. This is fair reporting, for most English children seem to like custard as much as some of them dislike rice pudding. Ironically, the word is a corruption of the French *croustade*, which means a dish prepared with crusts or a pasty and bears little relation indeed to what the English now mean by custard. Strictly, and certainly in the world of Mrs Beeton, a custard is a mixture of beaten eggs and milk sweetened and then baked.

For nearly a century and a half now, however, most English people have in truth been happy instead with the cornflour-based custard powder devised by the Victorian chemist Alfred Bird because his wife had a delicate stomach and could not take egg-based dishes. 'From 1837 to this very day,' pronounced Bird's in the *Daily Mail* on the accession of King George V in 1911, 'Bird's Custard has reigned supreme as the national family dish.' It was 'as welcome at every table as King George himself would be: it crowns every meal with success!'

The craze for custard with every pud is not one that the Brits have exported with any success; middle Europeans starting their restaurants in postwar England were mystified to be asked for custard with their lovingly presented *Apfel-strudel*. As the island race gradually grows more travelled and worldly, the national penchant for custard is giving way to a preference for cream, ice cream, yoghurt, or nothing at all with puds.

Still, custard remains a firm favourite with children, northerners, old-age pensioners and people who eat in caffs. Confusingly, custard powder is now sold in sachets to the French, who rather like it and call it *le pudding*.

Darts Though there have been attempts to trace darts back to archery, all we can say for sure is that the modern game began around the turn of the century. At first it was faced with a legal hurdle: in 1908 a Yorkshire landlord was hauled before the Leeds magistrates accused of running a game of chance in his pub. With a sense of histrionics worthy of Perry Mason, he rigged up a board in the courtroom and threw three darts into the double top – then did it again to show it was no fluke. The case was dismissed.

With the superseding of the old wooden barrel by the new aerodynamic tungsten body, darts began to attract sponsorship money and is now big business. It is a cheap, convenient game requiring both mental and physical skills, appealing to both sexes and all ages. It transcends social barriers, but is obviously played best in a pub* with a pint*. Indeed the dimensions of some of the world's best players, now displayed regularly on television, illustrate vividly how closely the two pleasures relate.

There are now some six and half million players in Britain, and that makes darts the most popular of all English games. Top player in the world at the time of writing is the Englishman Eric Bristow: with his strange grave face, preternaturally large eyes and supernatural skills quite possibly a time-traveller from some future, dart-sharp civilisation.

D-Day Most Englishmen heard of it first on the 8 o'clock news that heady morning of June 6 forty years ago; ironically the BBC then was merely relaying a German announcement; John Snagge's cool voice did not give the official British version till 9.32 a.m. It was probably the best single moment of the war; VE day was a blurred delight that in a sense stretched a week from the 1st of May, when the world heard that Hitler had killed himself, till May 8, when the European war untidily ended.

The south of England had been in effect a no-go area since February but no one knew exactly when the invasion would happen; not even Eisenhower knew himself till the day before; but when he said 'let's go' he was playing a gigantic hunch that worked. The weather to come would have prevented an invasion for the next fortnight, and might have scuppered it. All the clichés applied; and General Montgomery, commanding 21 Army Group, used them unsparingly. 'The time has come to deal the enemy a terrific blow,' he told his troops. 'Let us pray that the Lord Mighty in Battle go forth with our armies ... Good luck to each one of you. And good hunting on the mainland of Europe.' Winston Churchill went to the House of Commons at noon to give them the momentous news looking, wrote Harold Nicolson, then a National Labour MP, 'as white as a sheet'. Did he have some dreadful tidings for them? No; but he deliberately spun out the tension by dealing first with the fall of Rome.

Over the retrospect of the forty years two things become plain: the Germans, many marinated on the eastern front, had much the better of the fighting when on anything like level terms; but the Brits brilliantly won the battle of intelligence. They bamboozled the Germans so thoroughly into thinking the invasion would come much further east, in the Pas de Calais, that for weeks after the Normandy landings they continued to believe the real blow was still to fall up there and locked up their armour far from the real battle. Indeed it is now known that the entire German espionage system in Britain had been turned round and, for most of the war, was working a double-cross against its former masters. Perfidious Albion!

Few who took part in D-Day, the greatest armada ever mounted, and came away unscathed, had any regrets. For once the grandiose exhortation of Henry V sounded apt: '...and gentlemen in England now abed / Shall think themselves accurs'd they were not here.' One or two English gentlemen did, however, have other things on their mind that great morning. Evelyn Waugh*, on extended leave from his army duties (his superiors were frankly relieved to be rid of him) was finishing *Brideshead Revisited*. 'This morning at breakfast the waiter told me the Second Front had opened,' he noted in his diary. 'I sat down early to work and wrote a fine passage of Lord Marchmain's death agonies. Carolyn came to tell me the popular front was open. I sent for the priest to give Lord Marchmain the last sacraments . . . My only fear is lest the invasion upset my typist at St. Leonard's.'

Debrett The name by which everybody knows the great guide to the peerage, baronetage, and knightage of England, Ireland, Wales and Scotland which has been published under various guises for three centuries now but which was given its stamp of authority and truthfulness by John Debrett (1753-1822).

In the days of his predecessor John Almon, a Piccadilly bookseller, the guide had not been renowned for its accuracy; not to put too fine a point upon it, Almon would flatter certain peers whose origins were obscure, by suppressing their real provenance in favour of a splendid but fictional lineage. Debrett changed all that. He renamed the guide *Debrett's Correct Peerage*; and it flourished.

None of his children was interested in it, and after many vicissitudes it passed into the hands of Odhams who still publish it every year. One of the oddities in the task of continuously overhauling this great chronicle of the British nobility is that many of the collateral branches of the nobility have faded into obscurity.

They become bar tenders, night watchmen, cobblers and farm labourers. Nevertheless, most of them cooperate with *Debrett* in keeping the mighty work abreast with changes in their *curriculum vitae*. Just one example of this odd but endearing tendency: the present and ninth Earl Nelson of Trafalgar and of Merton is also forty-two-year-old Detective-Sergeant Peter Nelson of the Hertfordshire police force. Nevertheless his son and heir is duly listed by *Debrett*. His courtesy title: Viscount Merton.

Derby Day It is the great English lark; the one day of the year when the class strucure dissolves in a vast kaleidoscopic blur. The royals are there, and so are the gypsies; the rich arrive in helicopters and the trippers in trains; the clubmen charter private buses and the punters commandeer all the taxis. The bookies have a field day and so do the pickpockets. Men will wear anything from grey toppers to knotted hankies; women anything from Balenciaga to bikinis. Bollinger and Bass wash down the lobster and the whelks.

It is a horse race that was started as a bit of fun by some young aristos two centuries ago; it is still just that. It was said of Lord Rosebery that, by being prime minister, marrying a Rothschild and winning the Derby he had proved that you could improve your bank balance, run the country, and still study form. Though the racing can be spectacular, it is simply the pretext for a national rave-up.

Anyone who takes the Derby seriously is breaking the unwritten rule. When the gallant Emily Davison threw herself under the king's horse at the Derby in 1912 for her suffragette faith, she had unwittingly broken that rule: several clergymen declined to give her a Christian burial.

Dickens, Charles (1812-70)   We tend to think of audience ratings as an essentially twentieth-century device. Not so: Charles Dickens knew all about them. All his working life he enjoyed the challenge of the serial form: the rigour of the deadline and the need to pull something fresh out of the hat each week; the kick of swift reader-response and the chastening constraint of sales. He had been probably the fastest shorthand-writer ever to sit in the House of Commons; and he was to be one of the readiest novelists ever to spin out his own human comedy instead of the one he had previously been paid to report. He got the offer to write *Pickwick Papers* on 10 February 1836, accepted on 16 February, began writing on 18 February, and saw the first number published on 31 March. Understandably it took a few weeks for him to settle down; but once he did, he established a magical rapport with his audience he was never to lose. He did it by filling his books with a huge cast of people so real that they leap off the page at the reader; so real to Dickens himself that he was once found lurching about his study in alarming distress: he was writing a scene for the evil dwarf, Quilp. Characters and readers were thus equally alive to Dickens; and when he picked up his pen he switched on the current between them.

He had hankered after his own weekly magazine as early as 1845 ('price three halfpence, if possible, partly original, partly select, notices of books, notices of theatres ... cheerful views, sharp anatomisation of humbug, jolly good temper'). Five years later he became editor of *Household Words*, and remained the active editor of a periodical till his death twenty years later (after a quarrel with his publisher he launched his own magazine *All the Year Round* in 1859). As owner, editor, and writer, therefore, Dickens knew on a week-to-week basis exactly how what he had to offer was going down. If one of his writers contributed a weak serial, sales would melt away as relentlessly as a modern TV-rating. When that happened Dickens had both the generosity of mind and titanic vim to step in and pull the serial round. He ran, in effect, an early writers' workshop.

To do that, he had to have an exact and lively idea of what the common reader wanted. That is why there are few longueurs or obscurities in Dickens. 'He was successful,' concluded Leslie Stephen, 'beyond any English novelist, probably beyond any novelist that has ever lived, in exactly hitting off the precise tone of thought and feeling that would find favour with grocers.' Queen Victoria concurred. 'He had a large loving mind,' she wrote on his death, 'and the strongest sympathy with the poorest classes. He felt sure a better feeling, and much greater union of classes, would take place in time. And I pray earnestly it may.' Insofar as Victoria's prayer has been answered, Charles Dickens, pop writer *nonpareil*, must be given a bold credit line.

Dog Yet another of those common English words which seems to carry far too heavy a load of meanings for its small size. More, this plethora of definitions and contexts leads to all kinds of problems. Why for example should a 'dog's dinner' denote both anything highly ornate *and* a right mess? How can it come to mean both a worthless fellow and a gallant? 'What you dogs,' cried Dr Johnson* from his window, seeing his friends beneath, 'will you have sport?' Nor is it altogether archaic in that sense: 'In the old days with married women's stockings / Twisted round his bedpost he felt himself a gay / Dog but now his liver has begun to groan,' wrote Louis MacNeice* in 'The Libertine'. How do we pick our way among such disparate senses as a showbiz flop (American), feet and, on both sides of the Atlantic, a sausage? Then what about its use as the name of a star, a grappling iron, the tooth of a wheel, or the iron rest for burning wood in a fireplace? All this before we even consider its common-sense use as the name of a domestic animal. When did a 'dogsbody' cease to be a sailor's name for dried pease boiled in a cloth and become the universal English name for a general factotum? Not, according to the *OED*, till D.H. Lawrence used it thus in 1922. The transition is clear. A dogsbody was a junior midshipman; that most lowly of all naval officers. A wretch like this is so often 'in the doghouse' that he must occasionally need 'a hair of the dog' that bit him; after which he's 'like a dog with two tails'.

Perhaps it is just the sheer number of dogs in England which leads to all these meanings. There are some six million in the country, ranging from the lordly champions at Cruft's Dogs Show with exotic names like Grayco Hazlenut and Burtonswood Bossy Boots to the fourteen thousand anonymous mongrels given refuge each year by the Battersea Dogs Home. Only half the dogs in England have a licence, and it costs three and a half million pounds to collect the one million pounds revenue. But it is as pointless to expect common sense from the English where dogs are concerned as it is with cats*.

Domino Another multi-purpose word, with new meanings accreting on the ancient ones. It is (a) a monk's habit (b) the keys of a piano (c) a mistake in music (d) the light used to illumine the cyclorama or backdrop of a television studio or (e) most familiarly to English people, a piece of ivory, bone or wood marked with dots and used in a pub game for some two hundred years.

And there is the term *domino effect;* a phrase first coined during the Eisenhower era in the mid-fifties to encapsulate the theory that if any one country in south-east Asia fell to the communists, its neighbours would fall in line.

There is a further curious resonance about the word though: it was once used by soldiers when they received the final lash in a flogging and meant either the blow itself or, more commonly, the last in any series of things, pleasant or unpleasant. Of all the varieties of domino games – matadors, sebastopol, bergen, and so on – the best, according to *Hoyle's Games,* is the kind called bingo. Yet bingo is also the exclamation made by somebody winning the desolate game that has now stolen the name of bingo, and is a kind of lotto or, in serviceman's lingo, housey-housey. Do people now cry bingo as they would once have cried domino? The lineage seems insecure, and not for the first time, we must put the echo down to the deep reverberation of coincidence that runs right through the English language.

The Dorchester Hotel A child of the thirties. The old Dorchester House on whose site it was built had to come down for one good reason if no other: it had just four bathrooms. The new hotel aimed to compete with the best in the world: that now meant a bathroom with every bedroom, and there were to be two hundred and ninety of each; plus seventy sitting rooms and five suites. The swish new hotel had one curious feature, apt perhaps for the violent world into which it was born: it is so built that anybody who can pay can occupy as many rooms as he likes and go from one to the other without ever emerging into a corridor. Another oddity: each bedroom has a lining of compressed seaweed, the perfect non-conductor of sound.

The Dorchester opened its doors to the public on 20 April 1931. A single room cost thirty-two shillings and sixpence; lunch eight shillings and sixpence; dinner with dancing fifteen shillings and sixpence. The first big night there was the Speed Ball on 9 June 1931, organised by the Air League to celebrate Britain's holding at that point world speed records for land, sea and air. Famed thirties racing drivers Woolf Barnato and Kaye Don were there, air pioneers Sir Alan Cobham and Colonel

J.T.C. Moore-Brabazon, later Lord Brabazon – who held the first pilot's licence in Britain; and Sir Malcolm Campbell, who was to hold both land and water speed records.

Later that month the Dorchester was the elegant setting for the Famous Beauties Ball at which the debutante of the previous year, Margaret Whigham, (later Duchess of Argyll, renowned for quite a different sort of fastness) starred. General Eisenhower, finding Claridge's too lush for his taste (to be exact, too like 'a goddam fancy funeral parlour'), moved to the Dorchester during the war. Here his chauffeuse and lady love Kay Summersby did her best to make him feel less funereal. Here too the queen of thirties society hostesses, Lady Sybil Colefax, gave the last of her great Thursday dinner parties. She was by now, relatively speaking, poor; and guests got a discreet little bill some days after each party. But her friends were loyal, kept her secret, and paid up.

In 1976 the McAlpine family, who had built the Dorchester, sold it to an Arab consortium. The Arabs paid £9 million for it and also cleared a debt of £1.5 million. It was a bargain. They then spent another £10 million refurbishing it, installed master chef Anton Mosiman, and despite some grumbles about alien ownership, have made it one of the most elegant hostelries in the world. But lunch no longer costs eight-and-six.

Dover   Though to most Englishmen the unhappy inspiration for one of the most dire popular songs (Vera Lynn's) and one of the most banal poems (Alice Duer Miller's) the white cliffs of Dover have at least this to recommend them: they are the gateway to Abroad*.

Downing Street   Once the place where James Boswell lodged when first savouring the urban delights of London, and where Tobias Smollett attempted to set up a surgery, Downing Street has become justly celebrated, with No. 10 perhaps the most modest site for a head of government in the civilised world; while the matey proximity of the chancellor of the exchequer at No. 11 only adds to the suburban feel of the arrangement (when he was chancellor, Geoffrey Howe used to refer to the prime minister as Margaret-next-door). No. 10 has not quite recovered from the famous picture of the young Harold Wilson, all of eight and nearly hidden in his flat cap, hopefully posing outside as an earnest of his future plans. He was to occupy No. 10 just forty years on as prime minister himself.

Dunkirk It is nothing to do with victory or defeat, heroism or cowardice, though all four of course showed their faces there. It is to do with luck, and perhaps with knowing how to play your luck.

It is also a vivid example of war, not as some ordered gavotte between opposing armies, but what it really is; a dance to the music of chaos. On 23 May 1940 the German army to the south of the British army halted. Why they did so is still not clear. They had been mauled by the British armour. They did not realise the extent of the French collapse. They wanted to regroup for further battles. They probably did not even think Britain would fight on when France had gone. Whatever the reason, they let the British army off the hook.

Perfect June weather helped 338,226 allied troops get away; a third from the Dunkirk beaches, the rest from Dunkirk harbour. Of these 139,097 were French. Admiral Darlan sent an order to the French forces to let the British withdraw first. Churchill countermanded it: we would go *bras-dessus, bras-dessous.*

Most of these troops and their officers behaved very well. Some behaved very badly. Churchill told the Commons they should be careful not to assign to this deliverance the attributes of a victory. Wars, he said, are not won by evacuation. But there was a victory inside the deliverance, and it had been won by the Royal Air Force.

It was nothing like the stunning victory promulgated at the time; indeed it was the usual damn close-run thing. Still, the boys did well. Dunkirk showed the Brits neither as heroes nor poltroons; but certainly as game-players who know to give luck a chance.

Durham It makes Winchester* and Canterbury seem maelstroms. Perhaps the peninsular foundation on which cathedral and castle stand gives Durham this sense of singular tranquillity; perhaps it is to do with the immense perspective afforded by the enshrinement here of Cuthbert and Bede. Whatever the reason, Durham remains a medieval haven set in some of the most stunning and uncelebrated countryside in the land. It is a curiously tolerant place, able to accommodate both the celebrated Miners' Gala and the Rolls-Royce Car Rally. It can boast the oldest regatta in the country and a cluster of the best castles (Durham itself, Raby, Barnard and Bowes). It has one of the oldest regiments (the Durham Light Infantry) and its university did England a notable service when its inception ended the six-hundred-year monopoly of Oxbridge. Above all, it is a place where you can hear yourself think. The great knocker on the cathedral door symbolised sanctuary for miscreants over the centuries, and still does.

Ealing Studios   Though films were made in this quiet suburban backwater from the very beginning of the cinema (Will Barker, a pioneer of the industry, bought two houses facing Ealing Green in 1902, and was shooting on his first covered stage by 1907), the apogee of Ealing was the twenty-one-year-period (1938-59) when Sir Michael Balcon was in charge.

From first to last it was an archetypal cottage industry, turning out quiet, understated films about small groups of embattled people at odds with the big battalions. The typical Ealing film would take a sample of widely variegated human beings and follow their fortunes in the grip of some vast extraneous force; *Dunkirk* and *The Cruel Sea* are good examples. It specialised too in polished and urbane comedies like *Kind Hearts and Coronets* or *Passport to Pimlico*.

Sometimes accused of making nothing but comedies and war films, Ealing in fact essayed every genre except the musical (though some may rank *Champagne Charlie* as one) and the Western. The actor most closely associated with Ealing's golden years is Alec Guinness, who turned in performances in films like *The Ladykillers* and *The Lavender Hill Mob* which are masterpieces of understated irony.

Eventually sold to the BBC, Ealing is now used as television studios; a proper destiny for a company that had always excelled with ordinary people doing believable things against realistic backgrounds: what we now call the documentary style of film-making.

Elgar, Sir Edward (1857-1934)   When his First Symphony was played for the first time at a Hallé Concert in the Free Trade Hall, Manchester, on 3 December 1908, a nineteen-year-old youth called Neville Cardus was in the enraptured audience. 'No English symphony existed then, at least not big enough to make a show of comparison with a symphony by Beethoven or Brahms', he wrote much later, 'I cannot hope... to describe the pride taken in Elgar by young English students of that far-away epoch.'

The audience would not let the symphony proceed after the great slow movement until the composer had come out to acknowledge their ovation, and at the end of the work the orchestra rose as a man and cheered him to the echo. 'This was not only Elgar's first symphony', wrote his biographer Michael Kennedy, 'it was England's.'

There will be those who prefer the teasing conundrums set in the Enigma Variations, some who are moved by the mystical thrall of The Dream of Gerontius. Others again will opt for the brooding grandeur of the Cello concerto and there will be simpler spirits who still like to hear the stirring melody, albeit worn smooth with use, of the first Pomp and Circumstance March. ('Gosh man, I've got a tune in my head!' he wrote to his friend Jaeger.) Whichever work we choose as our own, Elgar speaks always of England, or more precisely, sets England to music.

Essentially a landscape artist painting in sound, he told his musicians to play the First 'like something you hear down by the river'. Frequently at odds with Edwardian England (he walked out of a Royal Academy dinner because he thought he had not been properly seated and resigned from the Athenaeum when Ramsay MacDonald was elected) he nevertheless caught perfectly its bitter-sweet flavour. When he was born, there was something in the jibe that England was a land without music; by the time he died his own work alone had made nonsense of the charge.

Elms   In country lore they are trees of ill-omen: timber for coffins, and too slow-burning to make good logs. Yet they have been integral to the English landscape these last eight thousand years; their outlines, as one tree-lover wrote, billowing like a cloud in a thunder storm. They are deeply woven into the poetry and prose of England, most notably perhaps in Tennyson's tremendous 'The moan of doves in immemorial elms / And murmuring of innumerable bees.'

The notion that elms could be afflicted by disease is not new; the first was noted as long ago as 1838 and was back again by 1927. Yet within ten years the great English elms had shrugged off the epidemic – though not before it had killed at least one in ten; maybe more. Then a new and far more deadly form of Dutch elm disease was identified in the sixties, killing 400,000 trees a year in America and Canada. It reached England before 1970, and by the end of the decade had killed no fewer than eleven million elms.

Nothing is sadder than those great gaunt skeletons straddling the landscape, leaving what had once been the inimitable verdure of the English countryside as bare as a battlefield. To this grievous loss there is no quick answer; but new trees are being planted to replace the dead giants: oak, beech, chestnut, lime, ash, poplar, sycamore, maple and willow. It would be comforting to believe that the most robust elms will in the end grow immune to the beetle that has laid them low; such optimism would be misplaced.

The English Language   Our greatest single national asset. Its capital value is unquantifiable. It is the first language in the world. It is the principal language of business and diplomacy. It has the richest literature and is the greatest treasury of fiction, poetry and drama. It is an exquisitely subtle and endlessly flexible tongue. It is crammed with idiom and slang. It is vastly hospitable to new words and fresh cultures. It is as earthy as it is elegant, as randy as it is fastidious. It is the language of the sea and the air, the international argot of all sea captains and airline pilots. It is the first language of sport and science. It is the language of computer software and hard rock. Any new young English or American writer has an immediate audience of 600 million; a young Armenian or Finn has no such luck. To this vast good fortune in life's lottery your average Englishman is totally impervious. He takes it as a matter of course that the world speaks English: what else would it speak?

Epsom   To Englishmen it means two things: its salts, culled from a local spring and only too effective in moving the bowels, and its racecourse. See also *Derby*.

Establishment   Earlier contexts can be found, but in precisely the sense now used, one man has the honour of having coined it. In the *Spectator* on 23 September 1955, Henry Fairlie wrote: 'By the Establishment I do not mean only the centres of official power – though they are certainly part of it – but rather the whole matrix of official and social relations within which power is exercised.' It very quickly took on a pejorative colouring it has never lost.

Eton 'I had got in on the first round, being put up by Knebworth but after they had left only the smell of Balkan Sobrani and Honey and Flowers remained to prove it was not a dream.' Thus Cyril Connolly* on his election to Pop, the unlegislated ruling body of Eton. Such was the prestige of Pop Connolly tells us, that some boys who failed to get in never recovered: 'One was rumoured to have procured his sister for the influential members.' In this privileged cocoon the outside world looked bleak, the future empty: 'I dreaded leaving ... early laurels weigh like lead and of many of the boys whom I knew at Eton, I can say that their lives are over.'

In an imaginary dialogue with his old school Connolly is chided for wasting his chances: 'You could have made lasting friendships with people who will govern the country – not flashy people, but those from whose lodges, in a Scotch deer-forest, great decisions are taken. You Bolshies keep on thinking the things we stand for – cricket, shooting, Ascot, Lords, the Guards, the House of Commons and the Empire are dead. But you all want to put your sons down for Eton.' How true: then, anyway.

Connolly was at Eton with George Orwell*, Anthony Powell, Henry Green, John Lehmann, Harold Acton and Alec Douglas-Home. Is a contemporary Etonian living among such future goers? Only time will tell. We shall argue under the Old Boy Network* that when Margaret Thatcher's new government took its place on the Front Bench of the Commons in 1983 it contained not a single Etonian. This was true: but only a few months later, one of the grammar school boys (Cecil Parkinson) got a girl into trouble and had to go. Who should take his place? Hey presto, Nicholas Ridley, Old Etonian! Meanwhile Hailsham still sits on the Woolsack in the Lords where Eton is always in strength. Yet it is now twenty years since the last Etonian was prime minister: how long will it be before the next?

Europe To an Englishman, still the Continent. Thus one of the great political debates of the last decade was whether or not we should go into *Europe;* the fact that we were for all other purposes already in it was ignored. To this day, *we* are in England; *they* are in Europe.

Fag This is one of the portmanteau words that mean different things both on either side of the Atlantic and, in England, to different layers of society. Thus while in America the word is a shortened form of *faggot* and means a homosexual, here it means variously a cigarette, a chore, or a junior boy who works for a senior boy in a public school. In this last sense it has had a good run for its money, surfacing at the opening of the nineteeth century and probably reaching its apogee (if that is the right word) in *Tom Brown's Schooldays,* published in 1857, and drawing a horrendous picture of cruelty practised by older boys on smaller ones.

While fags are no longer (one hopes) roasted on open fires as they were then, at Wellington as late as 1959 fags had to warm the lavatory seats by sitting on them first for their fagmasters. Still, if you must be a fag, it is no doubt better to have a cold bum than a burnt one. The theory of fagging was that however grand your own background, it did you no harm to black somebody else's boots and grill his sausages until you grew big enough to give the orders yourself.

In some schools now fagging is even being unionised with modest weekly payments to the long-suffering fag for the work he does. Certainly even in modern England it is possible to meet grown men who have still not got over their old fagging relationship. It may have involved beating, bullying, buggery and perhaps all three; but once you've been through all that with your fagmaster it stays with you for life.

The Falklands Conflict Does it belong in the annals of glory or the theatre of the absurd? To the average Englishman watching the British fleet majestically sail out of Portsmouth with ensigns fluttering and bands playing there could be only one answer: both. On millions of colour television sets, it looked like a weird signal picked up in a time warp from the world of 1940: perhaps even 1914. It was magnificent, as Maréchal Bosquet had remarked of the charge of the Light Brigade, but it was not war – surely? Certainly no member of the British cabinet who gave the order for the Task Force to sail thought on that day that it would ever be used. Yet, given the dimensions of the dispute and the intransigent personalities of the leading players, it is clear in hindsight that once that mighty engine was set in motion it was inevitable that it should. The moral dilemma was as poignant as it was insoluble: if permanent armed services were to be kept, what were they for if not for this? If Galtieri were not to be confronted, how could the argument for *force majeure* ever be parried? No one saw quite how high the horrendous risks were: if the Argentinians had owned six dozen Exocet missiles instead of a mere six the Falklands could have been a ghastly disaster for British arms instead of a gritty triumph.

Far from proving that aggression did not pay, as one top American official put it, the British proved that it could be ridiculously expensive to resist. It cost one million pounds to free each man, woman and child on the Falklands; and, infinitely more precious, the lives of a thousand young men. And all this, as Perez de Cuellar, UN Secretary General, remarked, for a dispute that could have been resolved with goodwill on both sides in ten minutes. The Falklanders got rid of one occupying army; but had to put up with another. The Falklands conflict was a resounding political triumph for Margaret Thatcher, whose fortunes had been wavering before the crisis; and may well have been the main factor that swept her irresistibly back to power in 1983. She told her countrymen to rejoice in the victory; but certainly the men who had fought the gutter war (as their commanding officer called it) eight thousand miles away, the last surely of all Britain's colonial wars, saw little to rejoice about. As the Duke of Wellington had remarked after the Battle of Waterloo when a lady said what a glorious thing a victory must be: 'The greatest tragedy in the world Madam, except a defeat.

Farming There have always been three ways to lose money in England, or so they say: gambling, women, and agriculture. The first is the most speedy, the second the most pleasant, and the third the most certain.

The coiner of this aphorism was probably a farmer himself, and one who farmed in the inter-war years. Today English farmers, handsomely endowed by the Common Market agricultural policy, highly mechanised and politically sophisticated, are doing very nicely thank you; though they still cry all the way to the bank.

The Fifties   The average wage in Britain in 1950 was £6 8s. Petrol was still rationed and food still on points; at one time the fresh meat allocation was eightpence-worth a week, and there was still a five-shilling limit in restaurants. Yet during the fifties the national income roughly doubled. It was, as Harold Macmillan famously remarked, the time when the island race never had it so good.

It was the era of espresso bar and rock'n'roll. The first long-playing record reached England in 1950. It was the decade of the picaresque novel and the shambling, oafish anti-hero, flotsam of the welfare state: Lucky Jim and his first cousin Joe Lampton in *Room at the Top*. Then, in May 1956, the curtain rose at the Royal Court Theatre on an attic flat somewhere in the Midlands* where Alison Porter and her husband Jimmy fought, loved, argued, suffered and made up. Playgoers nourished on the bland pabulum of Binkie Beaumont did not at first know what to make of *Look Back in Anger;* but they could not ignore it. John Osborne had brought a new passion and a new rage into the English theatre and the reverberations are still felt thirty years on.

The coronation of Elizabeth II in 1953 made England rush out and buy television sets by the million; and the coming of a commercial television channel in 1956, run by an Independent Television Authority, gave the BBC a much-needed jolt. Men who put their money in the new commercial television companies took a huge risk and lost initial fortunes. When the corner was turned and the advertising cascaded in many of those who had hung on became millionaires overnight.

Roger Bannister was the first man to run the mile in four minutes (on 6 May 1954); the barrier had evidently been psychological, for it was run inside that magic marker a further fifty times before 1960. England regained the Ashes in 1953 and held them most of the decade. It was the era of great British racing drivers – Hawthorn, Collins and Moss – though only Moss was to survive the decade. It was the era of the great traitors: Pontecorvo, the atomic physicist, defected to Russia; the renegade diplomats, Burgess and Maclean, disappeared in 1951, to resurface in Russia four years later. No one knew then that two more celebrated traitors – Blunt and Philby – still lay undetected in the bosom of the Establishment*.

Twice in the decade the world came close to war: in the Korean conflict of 1950 and again during the complex events of autumn 1956 which culminated in the Suez crisis and the Hungarian revolution. Suez was to divide fathers and sons, husbands and wives, as no issue in England had since the Boer War, and no issue since. Though now seen as an evident folly, a last spasm of the old imperial imperative, then the issue was by no means clear. A million Brits had seen service in and around Suez in the war and had no love of the wogs*; *The Guardian*, which took a strong and clear anti-Suez line, had bricks thrown through its windows for its pains. It had been a turbulent decade: but would the sixties prove any better?

Fish and Chips   Dickens* mentioned a fried-fish warehouse in *Oliver Twist* (1837-9) but in those early days the fish were cooked in open pans at the seller's home and then hawked around the streets with a piece of bread, or later baked potatoes. It was only in 1865 that chipped potatoes (an idea imported from France) began to be sold with fried fish; they were soon to be inseparable, indeed unthinkable apart. The new railways enabled fish from Grimsby, Fleetwood and Hull to be landed one day and on sale anywhere in the country the next. Soon the staple of the working class, fish and chips were the first of all convenience foods: ready cooked, needing no washing-up, eaten standing in the street, delicious, nutritious and cheap. Englishmen of middle years will recall how children could once buy a penn'orth of chips without the fish, shovelled mouth-wateringly from the sizzling fat into a small white bag; and that was when there were 240 pennies to the pound. Properly taken with rock salt and vinegar or HP sauce*, fish and chips must have an outer wrapping of newspaper to ensure the authentic olfactory and tactile experience. Though they now have to fight for their share of the market with the hamburger boom and the Chinese takeaway, fish and chips endure: they were the first thing the troops called for when they had retaken the Falklands*.

Fishing   Six million Englishmen fish and it is thus the second most popular pastime of the race after darts*. As to why they fish, perhaps only one of the fraternity can explain. One summer day during the last world war the English writer H.E. Bates went fishing and reported: 'There is something mesmeric about it. You can sit sometimes by the water when the wind is rippling it into small rapid waves and watch the float until the waves and the scarlet cap produce a queer feeling of magnetism ...

'You hear people say that fishing is a waste of time. Can time be wasted? . . . In a hundred years it will not matter much whether on a June day in 1941 I fished for perch or devoted the same time to acquiring greater learning by studying the works of Aristotle, of which, anyway, I have no copy.

'The day is very hot, and there are thousands of golden-cream roses blooming on the house wall in the sun. Perhaps someone will be glad that I described them, sitting as I am forty miles from the German lines at Calais. Perhaps someone will wonder then at the stoicism, the indifference, the laziness or the sheer lack of conscience of someone who thought roses and fish have at least as much importance as tanks and bombs.' (*The Country Heart,* 1949)

Fleet Street The Fleet was once a river; today it is a sewer: the symbolism will not be lost on Fleet Street's enemies, and they are legion. As a collective metaphor for the newspaper industry, Fleet Street looks set to have a life of about a hundred years: roughly, say, from the moment in 1888 when Alfred Harmsworth (1865-1922) founded *Answers* to the moment not far distant when the long-prophesied nemesis overtakes the Street of Shame, as it has now become.

Answers gave Harmsworth the platform from which to launch his vastly successful *Daily Mail,* the paper, as Lord Salisbury remarked, written by office boys for office boys. It made Harmsworth rich and gave him power. It made him Lord Northcliffe and ennobled *four* of his brothers: Harold (Lord Rothermore, 1868-1940), Cecil (Lord Harmsworth, 1869-1948), and the baronets Leicester (1870-1937) and Hildebrand (1872-1929).

The Harmsworths were the first bold bad press lords; but there were soon many more: Lords Beaverbrook*, Camrose, Kemsley, Iliffe, Burnham, Bracken and Thomson. They collectively caught and mirrored the aspirations of the newly literate millions; but by a combination of avarice, stupidity and cowardice created a monster riddled with malpractice, inefficiency and over-manning now swollen to bursting point.

They gave jobs to a host of aspiring scribblers but the words of most have melted with the lead in which they were set. The only hacks of genius they employed were Evelyn Waugh*, George Orwell* and, if we are to count the backroom boys on the sub-editor's table, Graham Greene.

For the last quarter of its uneasy century-long sway, Fleet Street has been hoist by its own petard: mercilessly flayed with ridicule by its incorrigible house journal *Private Eye*,* an offset-litho fortnightly begun in 1961 on a capital of £450 and a circulation of three hundred.

Fleming, Ian (1908-64) To Beaverbrook* he was 'The Chocolate Sailor'. To his colleagues on *The Sunday Times* he was Lady Rothermere's Fan (she became his first – and only – wife when he was forty-two). He began to write his first book, *Casino Royale* (1953), at Goldeneye, his house in Jamaica, as an antidote to the shock of marriage. It took him seven weeks.

Despite all his disclaimers, there are clear similarities between Ian Fleming and James Bond. Both were worldly womanisers; both were naval officers; both were *aficionados* of food, drink, cards and cars; both knew the seamier sides of the world's great cities from personal patronage. To be fair, flesh-and-blood Fleming was rather less coarse than cinematic Bond, and far more interesting to talk to; he was a noted book collector, for example, and Bond would never have had time for that.

He became a citizen of the world early, spending all his school holidays, like Richard Hillary*, at *pensions* in Austria, Germany and Switzerland. Though arithmetically successful with women, he shows little sign in his books of understanding them. 'Very poor lover', his old friend Cyril Connolly adjudicated, 'always used to get up and go home for breakfast.' And when he wrote the Atticus column for a spell on *The Sunday Times,* it was Connolly who dubbed it Attila.

Yet Fleming was never dull, and his faintly arrogant insouciance amused men as it fascinated women. 'Only call God and the King Sir' was one of his early maxims. And how he could write! The first sentence of *Casino Royale* exactly sets the tone for the entire *oeuvre:* 'The scent and smoke and sweat of a casino are nauseating at three in the morning.' The world read on.

Flowers 'When daisies pied and violets blue / And lady-smocks all silver-white / And cuckoo-buds of yellow hue / do paint the meadows with delight' wrote Shakespeare, whose *oeuvre* is strewn from end to end with a profusion of country flowers: cowslips, pansies, primroses, thyme, oxlip, eglantine, and marigolds or Mary-buds ('And winking Mary-buds begin / To ope their golden eyes').

This passion for flowers runs right through English writing, and even finds its place among the gritty imperatives of George Orwell*: 'What until twenty years ago was universally called a snapdragon is now called an antirrhinum, a word no-one can spell without consulting a dictionary. Forget-me-nots are coming more and more to be called myosotis. Many other names, Red Hot Poker, Mind Your Own Business, Love Lies Bleeding, London Pride, are disappearing in favour of flavourless Greek names out of botany textbooks . . .'

Those botany textbooks, however, have a curious hold over the island race. The Reverend William Keble Martin (1877-1969) was eighty-seven when he published his *Concise British Flora in Colour,* illustrated with his own meticulous and graceful drawings. The book encapsulated a lifetime's love and study of the flowers of England and has sold nearly a quarter of a million copies so far.

Still, the national love affair with flowers is by no means confined to literary men. Benjamin Disraeli adored primroses; Henry Royce was a devoted amateur rose-grower while not designing the world's best car; Joseph Chamberlain loved orchids and when Field Marshal Wavell published a wartime anthology of poetry he called it simply *Other Men's Flowers.*

Fog An oddity, since in its most malevolent and man-made manifestation, the pea-souper, it has ceased to be the indispensable prop of the English imagination. There have been mighty and memorable fogs in London since the sixteenth century at least; the pea-souper is an essential accoutrement of many of the greatest Sherlock Holmes* stories as well as of any self-respecting film about Jack the Ripper.

It forms the magnificent opening to *Bleak House* and was well named by Dickens* 'London particular'. In one of his most celebrated images, T.S. Eliot made fog rub its back upon the window panes, and in one of her most beguiling numbers Ella Fitzgerald sang of a foggy day in London Town that had her blue and had her down. That sort of mock-romantic fog – in truth, no more than a filthy blanket of soot suspended in the freezing air – got its marching orders after the great fog of December 1952, when it was responsible for 4,000 deaths.

A commission of inquiry into the disaster led to the Clean Air Act of 1956. It took a little time to bite – the Lewisham rail disaster a year later was directly due to fog – but since December 1962 London has been without its pea-soupers, to the distress of romantically inclined visiting Holmesians from Manhattan and Moscow, but to the relief of all Londoners.

Football The name for a whole family of games with a common ancestry. At least a dozen kinds of football are still played and six have reached national or international status. They are American, Australian, Gaelic, Rugby League, Rugby Union (or rugger) and Association football (or soccer). When an American says football he means the gigantic war-game played on a grid-iron field with an oval ball, eleven in each team, and all the showbiz bezazz of a presidential election. When an Englishman speaks of football he could mean rugby*; but he probably means soccer.

English football, so defined, is in dire straits. On the field players embrace each other after each goal, while off it (or indeed by running on it as often as not) the fans lay into each other with bricks and bottles. Football hooligans are the staple diet of the Monday papers as throughout the long season they rampage their way across Europe. Football managers have professional lives little longer than wartime bomber pilots; football clubs go bankrupt with depressing regularity. Recently the French played soccer and rugger against England in Paris on successive Saturdays. On the day of the soccer international there was a pitched battle between French police and English fans and scores of arrests. Next Saturday all passed off peaceably (except for one English rugger fan who fell in a fountain and had to spend a night in hospital being thawed out). Why should there be such a vast and embarrassing chasm between the image of the two football codes?

According to the old canard, rugger is a game for ruffians played by gentlemen, soccer a game for gentlemen played by ruffians. There may have been a kernel of truth in the distinction when rugger still clearly showed its public school provenance; but nowadays it is played by all kinds of young Englishmen from policemen to farmers and salesmen to miners. Yet there remains this central difference: in England rugger is still played for fun; soccer for money. When money comes in at one door in a sport, fun usually soon goes out of the other. It has assuredly gone out of English football.

The Forties 'Blood, toil, tears, and sweat' was all Winston Churchill* could offer on 13 May 1940; and for the next five years there was to be enough of it for the British people. Paradoxically though, it was a curiously carefree era. People were given jobs and had no choice but to get on with them. 'These are not dark days,' Churchill told the boys at Harrow* in 1941, 'these are great days.'

The man in the street had far more money in real terms than he had in the bleak thirties, and all the statistics show the health of the country dramatically improved from 1942 on. Whether this was because of better medical care, simpler food, or from some psychosomatic root has never been proved. Bombing proved a great leveller. The rich had to do without servants, clothes and travel; the whole nation, as A.J.P. Taylor* noted, lived roughly on the standard of the skilled artisan.

Besides, one day it would all be over and there would be peace. Johnny would go to sleep, as Vera Lynn crooned, in his own little cot again. The atomic bomb, which was to deny all men the taste of true peace for good, was not yet born. The word teenager was not in use. There was no drug epidemic, no drink problem, and no dieting mania. There was no unemployment; the golden handshake was not invented. The dark progeny of affluence lay in the womb of the future. Men in the services went to current affairs lectures and talked of the brave new world they would build. Perhaps, as is sometimes alleged, the Army Bureau of Current Affairs precipitated the Labour landslide of 1945; but it was probably inevitable anyway. Sir Arthur Harris, then head of Bomber Command, told Churchill that 80 per cent of the RAF would vote against him, the rest not at all. He was not that far out.

When the new House of Commons assembled the Conservatives and their allies had lost 203 seats, Labour had gained 227, and the Liberal Party was reduced to a bare dozen. In the first three months of 1946 Attlee's government brought in bills to nationalise the mines, set up a national insurance scheme, repeal the Trades Dispute Act, and establish a National Health Service. Independence for India* was to follow next year. 'We are the masters at the moment,' proclaimed the Labour Attorney-General, Sir Hartley Shawcross, in a sentence that was to haunt him and his government for many years, 'and not only for the moment, but for a very long time to come.'

One thing not even the Attlee government could master was the weather. The winter of 1946-7 was the vilest in living memory. Scotland was cut off totally; there was no power at all in the south, midlands and northwest; two million were thrown out of work; parsnips were dug out with pneumatic drills. Domestic power, where it was available, was banned five hours a day; television and the BBC Third Programme were suspended. There was less food than in the war. In one week in 1948, for instance, the average man's allowance was thirteen ounces of meat, one and a half ounces of cheese, six ounces of butter and margarine, one ounce of cooking fat, eight ounces of sugar, two pints of milk and one egg. In desperation, the government imported ten million tins of an unknown fish called snoek. The island race did not take kindly to it.

This was the heyday of the spiv and the wide boy. It took a special kind of heroism in all this compacted misery for the government to plan a Festival of Britain. One wit was to describe the plethora of new design on show in the 1951 south bank exhibition as all Heal let loose. However, eight million went along, and the Festival worked as a kind of natural watershed between the shabby deprivation of the forties and the high, wide, handsome days of the fifties which surely lay in store. Nothing, the English decided, at any rate, could be any worse than what they had been through. But each decade holds its own horrors.

Fortnum and Mason   William Fortnum was a footman in the royal household of Queen Anne; Hugh Mason, a small shopkeeper in St James's market, gave him lodgings. Being in royal service then provided useful perks; in William's case, the disposal of all the unlighted candles used by the royal family. Since fresh candles were provided every day, this proved a flourishing sideline, and in 1707 he persuaded his friend Hugh to join him in starting a grocery business – at first no more than a stall in Piccadilly on the site of the present green and gold building.

By the time Charles Fortnum, grandson of William, entered the service of Queen Charlotte in 1761 at the age of twenty-three he could command a wage of £10.5s.3d per quarter; but this was only the beginning of it; for the royal perks now extended to flogging food, coal, linen and wine. By 1788 the shop sold food with a distinctly modern flavour: game in aspic, potted meats, Scotch eggs and mince pies.

Since there was then no NAAFI Fortnum boxes were dispatched to all parts of the British Raj to feed hungry officers in the Zulu war, the Chinese rebellion, the two Boer wars; Sir William Parry took two hundredweight of Fortnums cocoa with him on his expedition to find the North West Passage; Queen Victoria sent two hundred and fifty pounds of concentrated beef tea to the troops in the Crimea.

On Derby Day* the staff would be on duty at 4 a.m. to stock the long line of coaches that queued in Piccadilly for their hampers. To this day Fortnums staff wear morning coats, thus often getting confused on the days of big society weddings with their customers. 'You shouldn't look so distinguished, my lord,' said one salesman to a nonplussed peer who had been asked for a pot of jam.

But it is not so much homely jam as exotic delicacies with which the name of Fortnums is perennially associated: a small memento from a maharajah to a lady, say, made up of half a dozen bottles of champagne, a ham, a tongue, three tins of sardines, a box of fruits, a box of chocolates and a little basket of Turkish Delight.

The real point of Fortnums is that it still represents the delights of home to thousands of Brits abroad: from India comes an order for *marrons glacés*, from Saudi Arabia another for Christmas pudding, from Zimbabwe a call for chocolate digestive biscuits.

The French   'Frogs', declared Uncle Matthew in Nancy Mitford's *The Pursuit of Love*, 'are slightly better than Huns or Wops, but abroad is unutterably bloody and all foreigners are fiends.' Time may have softened the edges of this judgment a little, but something of it still lingers in the English mind. The trouble is that the French are not merely the *first* foreign people an Englishman normally meets; they are the *most* foreign. The first and most evocative memory of France any Englishman carries in his head is her smell; that inimitable odour of mingled Gauloises and garlic. And how can a race who still make such divine food endure such deplorable plumbing?

Yet the French have many friends in sophisticated England; traditionally intellectuals, writers and the left are francophile, while business, music, and the right instinctively favour Germany. The trouble is that to the English, politically the French remain a pain in the arse. When Edward VII made his triumphal tour of France in 1903, thus paving the way for the *entente cordiale* next year, he was greeted with cries from the street of 'Vive Edouard' but also by counter-cries of 'Vive Jeanne d'Arc'. On the English side of the Channel, the man in the street still regarded France as the corrupt and traditional enemy; so much so that the leaders of the new Liberal government of December 1905 felt justified in concealing from most of the Cabinet, not to mention the Commons and the country, the fact that conversations had begun between the British and French general staffs.

Things were no better by 1940, when most Frenchmen saw, and perhaps still see, the British withdrawal at Dunkirk* as a supreme betrayal. Charles de Gaulle was to prove one of the thorniest allies any country could wish for and it was his systematic hostility which kept Britain out of the Common Market till after his death. Whether it is such a good idea to be in it now, as Britain is flooded with Golden Delicious apples and French farmers sportingly respond by blockading English lorryloads of spring lamb, is something many Englishmen are beginning to doubt. Their melancholy conclusion tends to be that while you can't live with them, you can't live without them; and so in Brussels the interminable wrangles with these intolerable and indispensable neighbours roll ever on. *Entente*, maybe; *cordiale*, not yet.

Gardens If class is the English pox, then gardens are the English passion. It runs right through the race. There is a long dull street in San Francisco which was suddenly lit one spring by a pyrotechnic display of colours: great tubs of crocuses, hyacinths and daffodils. The neighbours thought it must be a new funeral parlour; but later learned that an Englishwoman had come to live there.

England can claim not only a rich roll call of the finest professional gardeners – John Tradescant, father and son, Joseph Banks, Lancelot (Capability) Brown, Humphrey Repton, Joseph Paxton, and Gertrude Jekyll – but also some of the most celebrated amateurs. No one in this group is more remarkable than the writer Vita Sackville-West who, when she bought Sissinghurst with her husband Harold Nicolson in 1930, found a rubbish dump with a few old apple trees and in a decade had turned it into one of the most celebrated gardens in England.

There are plenty of prose poems to the glory of the garden in English literature from the grace of Francis Bacon to the guff of Compton Mackenzie; but Rudyard Kipling got closest to the truth: 'Oh Adam was a gardener, and God who made him sees / That half a proper gardener's work is done upon his knees.'

Harold Nicolson concurred. In his diary for 20 March 1932 he wrote: '. . . we weed the delphinium bed . . . It is very odd. I do not like weeding in any case. I have a cold coming on. I cannot get a job and am deeply in debt. I foresee no exit from our financial worries. Yet Vita and I are as happy as larks together.' He spoke for every English couple who have ever made a garden.

Gentleman   He has had a long innings: roughly from the moment when Chaucer's verray parfit gentil knight makes his debut (1387) till the moment when a very gallant gentleman called Captain Oates makes his exit (1912). The First World War saw the notion of the temporary gentleman born, but by then the old idealised romantic figure was already beginning to sound a touch apologetic if not downright comic. Thus Daisy Ashford gave us the magnificent Mr Salteena ('I am not quite a gentleman but you would hardly notice it'). Lord Curzon contributed to posterity the absurd if endearing observation that no gentleman eats soup at luncheon. Bernard Shaw* introduced us to the millionaire cannon king Undershaft, who offers his future son-in-law Adolphus Cusins half what he has asked to work in the factory. Cusins: 'You call yourself a gentleman and you offer me half?' Undershaft: 'I do not call myself a gentleman but I do offer you half.'

Just as in cricket the separate pavilions which, within living memory, served gentlemen and players have now been amalgamated, so in the great pavilion of life gentlemen and players now rough it together and are hard to distinguish. If there are any gentleman farmers left they are too busy driving the combine harvesters to mention it. The word lingers on in unexpected places; in saleroom catalogues, for example, where a consignment of wine will be gnomically labelled 'the property of a gentleman'. It probably survives best in the imperial Raj, where much of a lost England is enshrined. Thus, in the Second World War, Nehru, released from prison to see his wife, was asked to sign a paper saying he would not try to escape. He found this demeaning. After hours of debate, the perfect formula was found: he would make a gentleman's agreement not to cut and run, shook hands with his captors, and kept his word. Happy, vanished days!

In England now though, it is used (if at all) with increasing desperation, and often in a contrary sense; the gentlemen of the press, for instance, are manifestly nothing of the sort. We might still just speak of one of nature's gentlemen, but the word is too covered with custard to be used alone and straight.

So we shorten it and tacitly apologise for it: 'He's a real gent.' By the same token, gents' is now the most handy shorthand for the male loo and tends to be spelled out only in contexts like the famous British Rail appeal (or do they intend it as an assertion?) 'Gentlemen lift the seat'. Gentlemen adventurers like Richard Hannay have given place to right bastards like James Bond. A gentleman never willingly gives pain, said Cardinal Newman. Tell that to 007.

The Germans The English, despite two world wars, have never been able to work up any lasting antipathy towards the Germans. To this general principle there will of course be exceptions; notably among the 176,000 people now living in Britain who were born in Germany. Many, though not all, were refugees from Nazism; many, though not all, have the best of reasons to retain a bitterness to all things German for the rest of their lives.

Yet the Englishman finds the German rather more like him in his language, his religion, and even his national drink than any Frenchman. In the First World War there were the celebrated meetings between English and German soldiers in No Man's Land on Christmas Day. There was a strong sense that Fritz and Tommy were equally victims of faceless brass-hats back at GHQ. In the Second World War it was Germans themselves, Catholics, trade unionists, socialists, army officers – who were the first casualties of Nazism. Many died heroes' deaths. Besides, simple arithmetic shows that there are Germans now entering their fortieth year who had not even been born on VE Day; and to have seen any action in the Second World War a German – or Englishman for that matter – will have to be now nearing his sixtieth year.

Then again, few nations seem to have changed their spots quite so thoroughly. The Germans have given the world some unpleasant words in their time: *Blitzkrieg* (lightning war), *Herrenvolk* (master race) and *Ubermensch* (superman); but since the war have been more noted as proponents of green peace, nuclear disarmament, and economic miracles. While old war movies and newsreels still project the alarming image of disciplined, blond stormtroopers goose-stepping across Europe, modern German youth is reassuringly indistinguishable from our own; scruffy, disorganised, and bolshie. German leaders too give, on the whole, a sympathetic account of themselves now: not only decent men but able to speak fluent English into the bargain. So they must be all right.

Gilbert and Sullivan It was Lord Robert Cecil who remarked that Gilbert and Sullivan did not like each other as men; nor did either want to write operettas. There is an element of hyperbole in the epigram; certainly the two men quarrelled often enough in a collaboration that lasted nearly thirty years; certainly each had another and more serious career already behind him. Gilbert was a successful playwright (he was estimated to have made £40,000 – in Victorian money – from his play *Pygmalion and Galatea* alone) and Sullivan an accomplished composer. When Charles Dickens* went to hear his *Tempest* music at the Crystal

Palace in 1862 he said afterwards: 'I don't profess to be a musical critic, but I do know that I have listened to some very remarkable music.' The critics concurred.

W.S. Gilbert (1836-1911) and Arthur Sullivan (1842-1900) were first introduced to one another by John Holingshead, owner of the Gaiety Theatre, in 1871; the fruit of that meeting, *Thespis*, was staged at his theatre without success. Playwright and composer went their separate ways until an enterprising young manager called Richard D'Oyly Carte brought them together four years later to write *Trial by Jury*. It opened on 25 March 1875 and ran for 175 performances. This encouraged D'Oyly Carte to commission further pieces from the temperamentally ill-matched but artistically fine-meshed pair. The dramas of their long and turbulent partnership are as vivid as anything they wrote for the stage.

Sullivan wrote the carefree music for *HMS Pinafore* racked with pain from a stone in the kidney. *Pinafore* mania swept America and within months no fewer than fifty unauthorised productions were mounted there. It was performed by all-Catholic and all-black casts, and on a Mississippi paddle-boat. When they decided to give the world première of *The Pirates of Penzance* in New York, Sullivan unpacked his bags after landing and discovered he had left the score of Act One in England. He frantically rewrote it from memory, finishing the overture at 5 a.m. on the day of the opening performance, 31 December 1879. He rehearsed all morning, went to bed at 1.45 p.m. but could not sleep. He dined off a dozen oysters and a glass of champagne before taking up his position in the orchestra pit. 'Fine reception,' he recorded in his diary. 'Piece went marvellously well. Grand success.'

Five years later, though, Gilbert and Sullivan were in the doldrums. D'Oyly Carte called for a work that would revive their fortunes; Sullivan told Gilbert he was fed up with absurd plots. Gilbert, pacing his library in Harrington Gardens, was unable to come up with the answer – till a large Japanese executioner's sword mounted on his wall crashed to the floor before him. Thus was the idea for *The Mikado* born. At one point in 1886 there were 170 separate productions running in America. There was a jazz version in Berlin in 1927; while the Americans have mounted *The Swing Mikado* (1938), *The Hot Mikado* (1939) and *The Black Mikado* (1975). There was even a *Cool Mikado*, made in 1962 and starring Frankie Howerd.

Success did not make the warring collaborators any happier together. 'Another week's rehearsal with WSG and I should have gone raving mad,' declared Sullivan. 'He is like a man who sits on a stove and then complains his backside is burning,' riposted Gilbert. In the end though, their admiration for each other as artists prevailed. 'I must thank you for the magnificent work you have put into the piece,' wrote Gilbert to Sullivan on the morning after *The Gondoliers* opened on 7 December 1889. 'It gives one the chance of shining right through the twentieth century. . .' He was right.

Gin Mother's ruin is its English nickname, and though not so much in use now, reflects the Hogarthian world in which domestic gin, backed by a breathtakingly daft law made by William of Orange to discourage imports, became the favoured tipple of the working classes. Drunk for a penny, reported Tobias Smollett, dead drunk for twopence, clean straw free.

With the expansion of empire, angostura bitters were prescribed on all British navy ships as a preventive medicine; soon someone realised that by putting in a little gin an attractive drink could be made: and sailors are still renowned takers of pink gin. In the same way, tonic water containing quinine was prescribed against malaria for Brits in India; gin and tonic soon caught on.

From denoting depravity and want, gin came to convey affluence and even decadence, as in 'floating gin palace' for motor cruisers, and 'gin and Jaguar belt' to denote the terrain of stockbroker self-indulgence. What you add to your gin, though, still denotes class and age: gin and orange is thus middle-aged and downmarket; gin and French much smarter than the sweeter gin and Italian vermouth. But the gin base has a mighty pull. Pimm's No. 1, the only one of the six Pimm's drinks to have it, is the only one to survive. Besides, as all the world knows, gin has the devoted patronage of the Queen Mum, and there can be no firmer seal of approval in English eyes than that.

Golf ' "After all, golf is only a game," said Millicent. Women say these things without thinking. It does not mean there is any kink in their character. They simply don't realise what they are saying.' Thus wrote P.G. Wodehouse* in *The Clicking of Cuthbert*, the very first of his books to celebrate a magnificent obsession that was to continue for more than half a century.

It would be agreeable to report that the male chauvinism buried in the amiable observation was a mere whim of the Master, brought on by using a mashie at a moment when a light iron would have been the right answer. The truth is more shameful: for on any given Sunday in England 200,000 people are out in England playing golf, and of these 199,000 are men; for there is hardly an English golf club that allows women to play on that hallowed morning.

It is a sad record for a country that can boast the oldest golf club in the world (the Royal Blackheath – founded 1608) and a god-given profusion of clubs from the heather and gorse-strewn Sunningdale and Wentworth southwest of London, to daunting windswept seaside places like the Royal Birkdale in Lancashire, and the Royal St George's at Sandwich which has the unusual honour of starring in the *oeuvre* of Ian Fleming*.

The Good Food Guide Founded in 1951 by a socialist historian, detective novelist and classical scholar called Raymond Postgate (1896-1971). The combination of leftish politics with gourmet leanings is common enough in France; rare in England. The little guide (as it then was) from the start proved incorruptible, elegantly written and idiosyncratic. Its main drawback was that it relied on amateurs to report on restaurants; and though it is now swollen to glossy prosperity so that proper paid inspectors can be afforded, a small army of anonymous unpaid spies remains the backbone of its workforce.

The consequence is that the *Guide* sometimes seems bafflingly capricious, especially in London; though in fairness it must be conceded that a visit to a restaurant inexplicably dropped often reveals that the *Guide* is just ahead of the game. It is also now dangerously close to self-parody, being couched sometimes in a ludicrous Latin beak's lingo. At the Étoile, for instance, it recently reported that one ate 'between the Scylla of the spirit lamps and the Charybdis of customers' cigars'. Yet the *GFG* has always fought the good fight and over the years done incalculable benefit to English cooking. Besides, it is always rivetingly readable.

An entry for the Betjeman* restaurant in the Charing Cross Hotel, for example, was done in a spirited parody of the laureate's own style: 'Betjemania's in season / At this BTH hotel / Read his verse: admire (with reason) / Barry's dining room as well.' The middle falters. Betjeman could never have brought himself to rhyme Walewska with Avelsbacher. But the final quatrain is a triumph: 'Vegetables are best forgotten/ Chocolate mousse will not be missed/ Coffee's decent. Cloths are cotton / Wine's good value. Pianist.' But you will scour the pages of the 1984 *GFG* for the Betjeman restaurant in vain. Like so many other proud and vaunting hostelries, it has been given the old heave-ho.

The other principal good guy in the long battle for excellence in food is, ironically, a small, dapper, sophisticated Hungarian called Egon Ronay (born 1922). He launched his first restaurant guide in February 1959. It was a modest, pink little book priced at three shillings. His 1984 guide is ten times as thick and alas, fifty times the price. The space between the two defines the battlefield on which Ronay has fought his good fight against the compacted horrors of postwar English cooking: tinned and frozen foods; melancholy meals in trains and planes; soggy vegetables and murdered meats. Equally he has identified and celebrated the best English food that tables have to offer. Where do you go if you are spending a summer day at Stratford on Avon and are resolved to eat by the river? (The Black Dog.) Where do you head if you have been up on the Marlborough Downs and come down in the morning mist as hungry as a hunger? Ronay will guide you to that little place in the High Street (Polly's) where they lay on those sumptuous Victorian breakfasts* that will set you up or lay you out for the day.

In his early years Ronay was maligned because his English was not as urbane as it might have been and certainly dim little words like 'tasty' and 'cosy' surfaced too often. It was a curmudgeonly charge to lay against a man who came to England in 1946 with very little of its language to his credit. it is also said against him that he accepts sponsorship. Yet the name of the sponsor is in the public domain; it is not a covert influence; and it is precisely this revenue that enables him to hire and train his inspectors to make their independent and anonymous judgments. he thus avoids the trace of amateurism of the rival *Good Food Guide* and the skeletal solemnity of the new *English Michelin*.

'There is still a smirk on the newscaster's face when the subject of good eating comes up', Ronay chides. 'The sauce bottles that were fixtures on a past Prime Minister's table [see under *HP Sauce*] are still regarded as endearing signs of his British homeliness, whereas they would have lost millions of votes for President Mitterrand.' On, Egon, on!

Gooseberry Another good case of a subtle change in meaning; for whereas the *OED* identifies it from 1837 as a chaperon, the word still flourishes in a world where chaperons have long been out-moded. It now means any third person who delays the dalliance of lovers by his or her presence – very often unconsciously.

Gossip It was the thing Guy Burgess, the British diplomat who fled to Russia with Donald Maclean, missed most in his exile from England. It was what brought Somerset Maugham* home from his voluntary exile in the south of France each autumn. It is one of the great uncelebrated English obsessions.

A high-powered American woman television commentator recently returned to New York complaining that no Englishman would talk to her at dinner parties about mutually phased strategic weapons limitation. She took it as an inclination to sexism: in fact it was a preference for gossip. It is the pabulum that nourishes the House of Commons and the Inns of Court; the tack that feeds Showbiz and City. It finds its logical if ephemeral enshrinement in the gossip-column, that much denounced and much devoured department of most newspapers. Half a century ago, in an essay on English snobbery, Aldous Huxley propounded that nowhere else in Europe was gossip writing such a highly paid and creditable profession. Today it may or may not be highly paid; creditable it is not.

The watershed for the gossip-columnist came just a quarter of a century ago when John Osborne, goaded to rage by the attentions paid to his own personal life, wrote *The World of Paul Slickey,* an excoriating onslaught on the hacks of Grub Street. He dedicated the play 'To the liars and self-deceivers; to those who daily deal out treachery; to those who handle their professions as instruments of debasement; to those who, for a salary cheque and less, successfully betray my country, and those who will do it for no inducement at all.'

These are fighting words, and there is much to back them: but the average Englishman is dimly aware of some rough balance which ensures that though some deplorable men and women may sometimes waste their words on the innocent and guileless, the cynical operations of the gossip-columnist are used as often to throw a corrective shaft of clear light into dark places. Such certainly would be the general verdict on 'Grovel' of *Private Eye**, whose closely monitored column can sometimes bring down a minister, as indeed recently it brought down Cecil Parkinson, Secretary of State at the Department of Trade and Industry, because of his love affair with his secretary.

Should such private passions besmirch the public print? The debate is endless; the reality clear. Gossip-columnists in England look set to stay. As Paul Slickey sang: 'Don't think you can fool a guy like me / The best things in life are never free ... We have professional ways and means / Of getting in behind the scenes.'

Grammar School While there are those who argue that Eton* is no more than a grammar school (which in strict academic terms is the simple truth) the Englishman is not deceived. To him, 'grammar school' conjures up the image of a Tudor building with Victorian and probably thirties annexes where the abler children of local townspeople went daily to be taught an academic syllabus with a view to going on to university or into one of the professions.

The charge against the grammar school made by the left was that it was socially divisive and unjust, leaving all those children who could not jump the eleven-plus hurdle with a lifelong sense of failure, and gentrifying the clever working-class children who could jump it. It therefore became the policy of the left (and moderate right) to turn these grammar schools into comprehensives where all children, regardless of class, means or ability, could be educated together. The intention was good, but the snag was that the grammar schools fiercely resisted this submersion of their identities, and many simply opted out of the state system altogether, becoming independent if not boarding, and charging the true cost of their teaching to parents, or privately raised funds.

Thus an even greater divide has been driven between the two systems, and the left now accept that only legislation can close it again – legislation, that is, which will forcibly close the public schools. A government of the left with the votes and will to do this seems at present a long way off. If the grammar schools had been allowed to supersede the public schools naturally, as they might well have done, the comprehensive principle could have been quietly introduced later. As it is, English education is in an even worse shambles than usual.

Greenwich Mean Time   Though the meridian is of central import-ance to navigators, it is just as vital to astronomers. They need it to create a fixed line in the sky by which to measure a star's position. As each successive astronomer royal at Greenwich installed a better telescope, he moved his meridian to a fresh site slightly westwards.

Sir George Biddell Airy (1801-92) who became astronomer royal at the age of thirty-four, installed his celebrated transit circle, which defines the meridian, in 1851. A piece of cobweb in the lens fixed the exact spot. It had wandered just sixteen yards since the time of the first astronomer royal, John Flamsteed (1646-1719).

Since most navigational charts already used the Greenwich meridian, it seemed logical to make it the base line of longitude for the world at the international conference called to settle the matter at Washington in 1884. Still, logic is not always the prime mover at world parleys, and in the end Greenwich is said to have won only because the American railroad companies were already working from its time and lobbied their government to do the same.

No Englishman will be surprised to learn that the Irish* refused to recognise it altogether, while the French* accepted it only obliquely: as a line so many degrees to the west of Paris. *Plus ça change.*

Hampshire

Two English writers of genius were neighbours in eighteenth-century Hampshire. Gilbert White was curate of Selborne most of his life, refusing all offers of preferment so that he could live and die in the place where he was born, writing, without knowing it, an enduring masterpiece in his *Natural History of Selborne*. Twelve miles away the pretty daughter of the rector of Steventon was already penning the early drafts of novels that were to be read and loved two hundred years later: *Pride and Prejudice, Sense and Sensibility, Northanger Abbey*. Did they ever meet? Jane Austen* was rising eighteen when Gilbert White died; since both were clerical families it would be surprising if they did not; but we have no record of it.

White was educated at Basingstoke Grammar School; so, two centuries later, was John Arlott, wine writer and cricket commentator *nonpareil*. The slow, inimitable burr of his native Hampshire has become famous wherever cricket is played. Fifteen miles to the west of Basingstoke another local boy with an incomparable Hampshire accent, Alfred Denning, was educated at Andover grammar school to such effect that he went on to take a double first in mathematics at Magdalen College, Oxford before getting another in jurisprudence and becoming England's favourite judge.

If you subtract from Hampshire the great urban conglomerates of Southampton and Portsmouth, Winchester* and Aldershot* you are left with just on a million acres of still predominantly agricultural land and rivers like the Test and Meon where the trout-fishing is world famous. It is still possible to walk on top of the Hampshire downs all day without seeing a soul. The poet Edmund Spenser, we are assured by John Aubrey, went to live in Hampshire for its 'delicate, sweet air'. Four hundred years on, people still do.

Hardy, Thomas (1840-1928)   'Even in my life I have seen writers who made much stir in the world than ever I have sink into oblivion. When I was young George Meredith and Thomas Hardy seemed certain of survival. They have ceased to mean very much to the youth of today.' So thought Somerset Maugham* in *The Summing Up* (1938). Whatever we may think of Meredith (and there are two views about him too), it is an astonishing misjudgment of Hardy, all the more surprising in coming from Maugham, who had painted such a marvellous portrait of the older Hardy in his novel *Cakes and Ale* (1930). Even if Hardy were not read today (and he is) he would have found vast new audiences by being filmed (*Far from the Madding Crowd* and *Tess of the d'Urbervilles*) and televised (*The Mayor of Casterbridge* and *The Woodlanders*).

It is true that Hardy succeeds almost in spite of himself. He spent a great deal of time and trouble trying to prove he was of gentle birth; while what enthralls his readers is his minute and knowing recall of simple country folk. Thus in *Under the Greenwood Tree*, William Dewy 'was now about seventy; yet an ardent vitality still preserved a warm and roughened bloom upon his face, which reminded gardeners of the sunny side of a ripe ribstone-pippin; though a narrow strip of forehead, that was protected from the weather by lying above the line of his hat-brim, seemed to belong to some town man, so gentlemanly was its whiteness.'

Hardy's desire to rewrite the record before his birth extended equally to what had happened after it: he wrote his own account of his life, or what he cared to tell of it, and got his second wife to copy it page by page so that it would look as if it were hers. The ruse failed, and posterity has puzzled much about the true nature of the inner pain that caused this sombre and secretive man to dissemble so. We know that his first marriage was, or had become unhappy; but that after his first wife's death some inner spring released a great spate of marvellous poetry full of remorse.

'His subjects', wrote the poet Philip Larkin*, 'are men, the life of men, time and the passing of time, love and the fading of love.' In almost every Hardy poem, Larkin finds 'there is a little spinal cord of thought and each has a little tune of its own. . . your own inner response begins to rock in time with the poem's rhythm and I think that this is quite inimitable.' Larkin thinks that Hardy's poetry is not for young people, and is probably right; but everyone can appreciate the thrall of his fiction. The words with which Hardy ends *The Woodlanders*, for example ('You was a good man, and did good things'), are among the most simple and moving in the language. Oblivion, indeed!

Harrods Henry Charles Harrod, a tea merchant, took over a small grocer's shop in the unfashionable and indeed rough village of Knightsbridge in 1849. He had two assistants and a turnover of £20 a week. His son, Charles Digby Harrod, then aged twenty, bought it in 1861, taking three years to pay his father for it on the never-never. By 1868 turnover was £1,000 a week; two years later he had sixteen assistants, but his total wages bill was still a mere £15 a week. By 1874 there were nearly one hundred staff working from 7 a.m. till 8 p.m. and fines of 1½d were imposed for each quarter of an hour they were late in the morning.

On 6 December 1883 the store and all his Christmas stock were totally destroyed by fire. Charles Harrod wrote to his customers: 'I greatly regret to inform you that, in consequence of the above premises being burnt down, your order will be delayed a day or two. I hope in the course of Tuesday or Wednesday next, to be able to forward it.' He was. The store was rebuilt and reopened by September 1884, and a much impressed clientele flocked back to double the turnover.

The year after that Harrods gave credit for the first time. Lily Langtry and Oscar Wilde were early account customers. In 1898 the first escalator in London was installed; an assistant stood at the top with sal volatile and brandy for nervous passengers. The store's motto, *Omnia, Omnibus, Ubique* (Everything, Everyone, Everywhere) is rigorously fulfilled. Harrods has the last circulating library in London, and supplies all its own water from three underground wells. It has delivered a Persian carpet to Persia and a refrigerator to Finland; a 35p handkerchief by air to Los Angeles and a pound of sausages to a yacht in the Mediterranean.

If it has recently been nicknamed Harabs, this merely reflects the influence of one group of customers who contribute healthily and harmlessly to its half million pounds' worth of sales per day. Lit at night like the Blackpool illuminations by thousands of garish electric light bulbs (powered by its own generator), Harrods is a worldwide symbol; and this was no doubt the reason why the Irish bomb was planted at its door in December 1983 – precisely a century after the great fire. Despite the ghastly cost in life and limb, Harrods reopened for its January sale as always; and again the public flocked to buy as if nothing had happened.

Harrow When the great Victorian headmaster Vaughan came to Harrow in 1844, it had just over sixty pupils. Vaughan very quickly raised its numbers to some two hundred, but left precipitately in 1859 to avoid scandal (see under *Public Schools*). The fact is, Harrow has always struck the average Englishman as being a rather rum place. Admittedly Winston Churchill* was there, but even he was adjudged distinctly unsound for much of his political career, and John Profumo did not do the school much good when the great Christine Keeler scandal engulfed him and England in 1963. However Harrow should take heart. It can number among its old boys the immortal Captain Grimes, anti-hero of Evelyn Waugh's* *Decline and Fall* and one of the most sublime crooks in the whole panoply of English fiction.

Henley Regatta While Wimbledon*, Ascot*, and even Lord's* show signs of having been coarsened by the cash nexus, Henley remains, visually at least, what it always was: an Edwardian time-warp; Pimmsville-on-the-water. Though parties of Arab billionaires have been introduced to the delights of this perennial river-party with one eye on the business that might result, standards are still maintained. No woman is admitted to the Stewards' Enclosure in trousers or mini skirt; no man without collar and tie. Within these simple constraints anything goes, and here at least men can and do work the most shameless peacock effects in their pink caps and rainbow-striped blazers. However, the women look pretty good too and endearingly feminine; after all, it's only a hundred years since they weren't able to attend the regatta at all; it was thought unladylike, so they watched from carriages on the bridge. When the Russians first came to row they could not understand how all the stewards could be English; where was the famous English sense of fair play? It was finally put across to them that Henley stewards are incorruptible; now they race there without a single Russian steward to see fair dos.

Henley has seen many moving sights in its 145 years; none perhaps quite so touching as the sight of the 1914 Harvard crew that won the Grand Challenge Cup rowing over the same course (or part of it anyway) on the Saturday of the regatta exactly fifty years later. Fit, steady and well together, they got an ovation from the crowd: the odds against them all being there – senators, bankers, surgeons – and able to do any such thing – was worked out actuarially at 10,000:1. They gave a new Grand Challenge Cup to the regatta – the old one was so battered it no longer held champagne – as a tribute to the Leander eight they had beaten in that 1914 final: gallant fellows, they said, many of whom were destined to die in the war that began a few weeks later.

Hillary, Richard (1919-43) Ask an Englishman under forty who Richard Hillary was and he will be unlikely to know. He was killed flying in 1943, and as the war fades, so does his mythopeic role. He was perfectly cast for the part of lost hero: young (twenty-three when he died); good-looking (even after he was scarred in the Battle of Britain); athletic (he rowed in a famous Trinity boat at Oxford); and marvellously articulate.

His reputation as a writer rests on one book, *The Last Enemy,* his autobiographical account of how it felt to be one of the last of the long-haired boys, the student pilots who took to the skies in 1940 to play romantic gladiators *sans peur et sans reproche.* They were motivated not by a spirit of crude jingoism but by a sense of the ineluctability of fate and a grateful recognition that war had solved all their problems.

He had been two years at Oxford when the war came; was two days in the Battle of Britain (see *Spitfire; Hurricane*) with five kills to his credit before he was himself shot down over the North Sea but rescued badly burned. His book has sold 300,000 copies in English and been translated into every European language; it was particularly admired in postwar Germany. The scenes of straight reportage, the recall of war high in the English sky, is magisterial; if the reflective chapters do not quite measure up it is only by this exigent yardstick; and he was clearly destined to be a formidably equipped writer.

Why he insisted on going back to flying and why he was allowed to do so have never been satisfactorily explained; he probably did not know himself. In his will he wrote: 'I want no one to feel sorry for me. . . In my life I had a few friends, I learnt a little wisdom and a little patience. What more could a man ask for?'

Holmes, Sherlock Three fictional characters are known to readers all over the world, or so it is said: Hamlet, Robinson Crusoe and Holmes. Yet in that august trio Holmes has a further claim to uniqueness: neither Hamlet nor Crusoe is normally seen as a real, living, three-dimensional, flesh-and-blood human being. Holmes long ago transcended that shadowy divide. A department in the Abbey National Building Society's headquarters in Baker Street, which stands on the spot where the famed consulting rooms were sited by Conan Doyle*, deals with a daily mail bag from all over the world addressed to Sherlock Holmes and soliciting his help.

A vast and whimsical literature has grown up around the Holmesian *oeuvre*, much of it from distinguished pens. A former city editor of *The Sunday Times*, Norman Crump, once retraced Holmes's steps along the

London Underground* in the small hours of the morning, to check a point, and later published his researches under the title 'Inner or Outer Rail?' in the *Sherlock Holmes Journal.* Dorothy L. Sayers published profound research on the knotty conundrum of Holmes' university career, and was later joined in the magnificient obsession by Monsignor Ronald Knox. The best summation of all this learning suggests that Holmes was an undergraduate at Oxford from the autumn of 1872 to the start of the long vacation in 1874; and at Cambridge until 1877.

All English experts are known as Holmesians; American *cognoscenti* as Sherlockians. One noted Sherlockian, Franklin D. Roosevelt (who in his off-duty moments was president of the United States) speculated that Holmes was a foundling. Later, he changed his mind, and decided that Holmes was an American, 'brought up by his father, or foster-father, in the underground world, thus learning all the tricks of the trade in the highly developed American art of crime'.

Be that as it may, Holmes began his practice in July 1877 and met John H. Watson M.D., late of the Army Medical Department, in the chemical lab of St Bartholomew's Hospital in January 1881. Watson, recuperating from a wound sustained in the Afghan war, had bumped into Dr Stamford in the Criterion Bar. Delighted to see a familiar face, Watson took Stamford, who had been a dresser under him at Bart's, out to lunch at the Holborn. Over it, he heard about a fellow who was carrying out experiments in the laboratory. He was, Stamford declared, 'a decent enough fellow, but queer in his ideas'. He was, it seemed, also looking for someone to share digs with him. Watson asked to meet Holmes and there in the lab, beside the blue flickering flame of the Bunsen burner, the historic introduction took place – to the world's delight.

Home Counties Strictly, they were the four contiguous with the old boundaries of London: Surrey, Kent, Essex and Middlesex. Now, though, Middlesex has been finally swallowed up. Originally the land of the Middle Saxons, it lost much of its territory to the new County of London in 1888; the rest in 1965 to the Greater London Council. Today it exists only as a cricket team, a postal address and the northern station in the Boat Race*. Few Englishmen grieve deeply, for its history has long been London's.

Of the remaining three home counties, Kent probably has the greatest claim to its own identity: for centuries the paths of successive waves of invading armies lay through its smiling orchards; and its cathedral towns of Canterbury and Rochester, its medieval Cinque Ports of Dover*, Hythe, Romney, and Sandwich, its great houses and castles (Penshurst, Knole,

Hever, and Leeds) make a rich tapestry. Most Englishmen are dimly aware too of the historic distinction between a Kentish man (born west of the Medway) and a Man of Kent (east). Many, however, have to be reminded that Kent, improbably, has its own deep quarrying coal-miners; though very few need reminding that it has one of the best cricket teams and a magnificent tradition of great wicketkeepers.

Essex, on the other hand, to most Englishmen, is a flat and indistinct hinterland to the northeast of London famed for its Colchester oysters, as the *mise en scène* for many notable Constable paintings, and not much else. Frankly it has been largely subsumed by the Great Wen of London; and so has Surrey. Drive south from Hammersmith Bridge, for example, and down the Kingston by-pass, and you are still in London: Surrey now begins at Worcester Park. The distinction is perhaps logical, for the line broadly separates urban sprawl from the beginnings of the stockbroker belt (see *Stock Exchange*). The now-diminished Surrey (Box Hill, Hog's Back, Farnham, Guildford) is still beautiful if over-domesticated. One literary critic described a couple in a recent novel as being happy 'in a Surrey sort of way'. Englishmen knew what he meant.

Homesick 'Take me back to dear old Blighty'; 'God I will pack and take a train'; 'Oh to be in England, now that April's there': the island race know what it is to be homesick, though it can be argued that, being a restless and peripatetic people, they have only themselves to blame.

Just as we now know that almost anything under the sun can remind people of sex, so we now know that almost anything can remind the faraway Englishman of home. It may be the thought of kippers, faggots or liquorice; raspberries, strawberries or blackberries; frogspawn or crested newts; hedgerows, flat, full rivers, pollarded willows or simple rain. It can be draught Guinness or double-decker buses.

One antidote is to build your own simulacrum of England: hence the cricket clubs of California and the English pubs of Paris. Oddly, the sickness can strike even those not born in England: thus the erstwhile GI in Manhattan will buy his fish and chips* wrapped in English newspapers; and the Indian politician will inquire wistfully whether the little bus of his student days still runs across Hampstead Heath to Highgate (it does).

Hooray Henry He is a young man in a city suit, probably a merchant banker or wine merchant by profession, who turns up at jazz clubs with his Sloane Ranger girlfriend and applauds politely after each number, while braying 'hooray'. He knows little or nothing about jazz, but thinks he does, and to the professional jazz-man is a pain in the arse.

Henry has two close cousins. The first is the self-explanatory 'chinless wonder' (no doubt a play on the boneless wonder once heartlessly on show in Barnum's Circus). The second, a striking new coinage, is the 'young fogey'. A fogey was originally a Scottish term for an invalid or garrison soldier; hence, an old fogey was anyone with hidebound or antiquated ideas.

It was a brilliantly simple notion of a newspaper columnist to call Prince Charles a young fogey, for such he evidently is; and the breed prospers in Margaret Thatcher's England under such auspicious patronage.

Horse 'I know two things about the horse / And one of them is rather coarse', wrote our old friend Anon in *The Weekend Book*. The other thing is no doubt Robert Burton's celebrated remark that England is a paradise for women, and hell for horses. A casual intruder from another planet, picking up a paper or switching on the box, could well be forgiven for thinking that it was the other way round.

HP Sauce It stood for Houses of Parliament when first marketed by a grocer called Garton in 1896, though in truth there was no firm evidence that it was known at all in the Palace of Westminster till 1964, when a newspaper profile of Harold Wilson quoted his wife Mary as saying that he had only one fault: he would smother everything she cooked in it. HP shares at once rose by half-a-crown on the Stock Exchange*, and were ever afterwards known as Wilson's Gravy.

The much-loved sludge now sells all over the world: in Sweden it is proudly displayed on tables as a sign of breeding while in Saudi Arabia it is thought to have aphrodisiac qualities. The French legend on the label, however, owes more to poetic licence than strict logic, for HP is not a big seller over the channel; nevertheless the familiar incantation '*Cette sauce de haute qualite*' remains the first French (and sometimes the only French) that many Englishmen know. Unhappily the words as originally printed contained an unfortunate double entendre; HP was said to be free from *aucun préservatif;* not any preservative, as HP HQ had intended but, to a Frenchman, any French letter.

The slip has since been rectified, and HP continues its onward march for, with its aromatic *mélange* of malt vinegar, fruit and oriental spices, it is nothing less than the English working-class equivalent to Proust's *madeleine*.

Hurricane   It is a well-nigh universal belief among Englishmen that the Spitfire* won the Battle of Britain. That quick, lovely, and lethal plane needs no defence here. Still, it is a simple arithmetical fact that the Hurricane brought down more enemy aircraft in the Battle of Britain than all the Spitfires, Blenheims, Defiants and ground defences together.

The reason is not far to seek: there were far more Hurricanes then than Spitfires. The Air Ministry ordered one prototype high-speed monoplane from Hawker's in February 1935. It first flew in November 1935. The Hawker board decided to tool up and order material for a thousand Hurricanes in March 1936 without waiting for government support. That followed in June; but the Hawker gamble meant that the Hurricanes were that much ahead when the war in the air started.

The chief reason for the superior performance of the Spitfire was its thin wing. Hawker's had been advised by the National Physical Laboratory – wrongly as it turned out – that no advantage in speed would accrue from it. On the credit side, the thick wing could hold a fat, low-pressure tyre when retracted and this enabled the Hurricane to take off from grass when a fully loaded Spitfire sometimes could not. Moreover, the Hurricane with its tubular airframe was less vulnerable to enemy gunfire and could be repaired more easily: a distinct advantage when resources ran desperately low. In the end 14,500 Hurricanes were built: and every one was precious.

I Not a polite word in England. Should the sense allow, *we* is preferred; or even *one,* though here class turbulence may be encountered. If the ill-favoured one-letter word so mistrusted by Englishmen is unavoidable, some stout wrapping paper should go round it. Note, for example, how the Queen*, the only person in England entitled to use the royal We, in practice reserves it only for occasions of state, and in an everyday context shelters inside the self-deprecating formula 'My Husband and I'.

Idiot The village idiot of English country lore was not quite so daft as he looked. He would sit on his bench outside the village inn, ready to regale unsuspecting strangers with his rustic simplicities in return for a steady supply of free ale. With the rise of sophisticated psychiatric medicine, it has become impolite to call anyone like that an idiot, unless in the strictly defined clinical sense. Instead, the word has moved inside every living room and been assimilated in the 'idiot box' or television set. Whereas one artful poseur used to do for each village, we are all idiots now.

Inch Long used in English life as the only way to measure rainfall and waistlines, the inch has punched its weight in proverb – 'give him an inch and he'll take an ell' – and epigram – 'every other inch a gentleman'. We shall miss it when we finally go metric. Yet in this as in all else, England must not fail to millimetre forward.

India The shadow of the Raj still looms large over England. It was not only the nabobs of the East India Company who did well out of it; unnumbered soldiers and engineers, teachers and lawyers, missionaries and misfits, went east. Some, however, found the noonday sun too much for them and went west. Noël Coward* memorably transfixed the syndrome: 'They had him thrown out of a club in Bombay / For apart from his mess bills exceeding his pay / He took to pig-sticking in *quite* the wrong way / I wonder what happened to him?' What indeed.

Yet the scenes and scents of India, the interplay of culture and creed, the laminations of class and caste, the rhythms of sport and work, the code of skin and mesh of sex, the thrall of politics and the mill of money have proved a potent catalyst indeed to generations of English and Indian writers and artists: to E.M. Forster in *Passage to India,* to Somerset Maugham* in *The Razor's Edge*, to Kipling *passim.*

More recently India has inspired Richard Attenborough's majestic if faintly lead-footed film *Gandhi;* and Paul Scott's intricate, subtle and magisterial *Raj Quartet,* marvellously translated to the television screen by Granada as *The Jewel in the Crown.* Certain images of blood and horror continue to haunt the Anglo-Indian imagination; thus the mindless Amritsar massacre of 1917 is recorded unflinchingly in *Gandhi* and finds reverberations in the *Raj Quartet.* Yet there is a happier side. Though India made many Englishmen rich, England is now making many Indians as rich in return: an ironic and perhaps fitting coda to the long saga of the Raj. For details, see under *Mr Patel.*

Initials There is a curious snobbery about the use of initials in England. The number of people who still use NQOTD – Not Quite Our Type Dear – is happily fast vanishing. Even when it flourished, the code was self-defeating: those using it were self-evidently NQ all right themselves. FHB (Family Hold Back) has a prewar charm: even NSIT (Not Safe In Taxis) is dying out with the demise of the debutante.

The most celebrated codes of all were penned on the outside of wartime letters. SWALK meant Sealed With A Loving Kiss and ITALY meant I Trust And Love You. The longest in this category is probably HILTHYNBIMA (How I Long To Hold Your Naked Body In My Arms) and the most romantic BURMA (Be Undressed Ready My Angel).

The army was a fertile progenitor of initials. RAMC stood variously for Rather A Moderate Corps, Rather A Mixed Crowd or – most popular of all – Rob All My Comrades. Even more intriguing in its echoing intimations of time lost is the code for QAIMNS, properly The Queen Alexandra Imperial Military Nursing Service, but to the irreverent, on what hard evidence it is now difficult to say, Queer Assortment of Individuals Mainly Non Sexual.

The Church, however, supplies us with one of the most subtle shorthands. Candidates for the episcopate sometimes had their applications marked with three potent initials: WHM. These stood not, as many supposed, for Westcott House Man (after the distinguished theological college) but for something far more to the point: Wife Has Means.

Introductions In England they are so bad that in certain clubs men will go thirty years or more without knowing each other's names. When introductions *are* made, names are so slurred that they are nearly always lost. Besides, there is a convention in well-bred English society that no extraneous information may be given which will assist the hearer to come to grips with the person he is meeting. Let us say that Air Vice-Marshal Sir Harold Cracker DSO, DFC, is meeting Lady Georgina Farquhar. Then the only polite mode open to the English hostess is to say: 'Georgie, this is Harry Cracker. Harry, this is Georgie Farquhar.' To give people titles or job descriptions is simply not done. The only recourse open to a hyper-conscientious hostess is to say in advance: 'I so much want you to meet Harry Cracker. He's doing something frightfully important with RAF Strike Command.' Even here, though, precise ranks and definitions will not do. This, by the way, is between equals; if children are being introduced handles can and should be given.

The lacuna is particularly hard on our American cousins who not unnaturally like to get things straight thus: 'Doctor Gunge, I'd like to have you meet Professor Grockle.' Worse, the natural American reaction, 'Pleased to meet you,' still grates on well-bred English ears, though on what logical ground it would be hard to say. *How do you do* is both the only possible greeting and rather absurd response in such circles. With such ramshackle conventions, it is hardly surprising that the English go through agonies of amnesia on meeting chance acquaintances in the street. Gladstone's solution was to raise his hat and open the conversation by saying 'Gladstone,' hoping that the unidentified acquaintance would respond with his own name too. Such a device might well have helped the unfortunate gentleman who, meeting Wellington in the street, raised his hat with the words, 'Mr Jones, I believe?' 'If you can believe that,' said the Iron Duke, 'you can believe anything.'

Ireland The hate-love relationship between Ireland and England is reciprocal. Ireland has given England some of its best generals (Wellington, Alexander, Montgomery) playwrights (Sheridan, Wilde,

Shaw*) and broadcasters (Robert Kee, Terry Wogan, Frank Delaney). It has also given her the IRA.

The chasm between the quicksilver of the finest Irish minds and the lacklustre of the rest is neatly explained by Hugh Leonard's epigram: 'Ireland is a country bursting with genius but with absolutely no talent.' Still, the English role in Ireland gives no cause for comfort: from Cromwell's iron fist through the horrors of famine to the bloody Black and Tans. The young Disraeli saw the problem all too clearly: a starving population, an absentee aristocracy, an alien Church, and the weakest executive in the world.

The only answer to the Irish Question is one Ireland; but how that is to be honourably (or even practicably) achieved is a matter that has taxed some of the best minds in England: William Ewart Gladstone, Herbert Henry Asquith, and now Margaret Hilda Thatcher.

Jaeger   Though the name now stands for a certain kind of classic, natural English outdoor chic, it began as the slightly potty brainchild of a Victorian philanthropist called Lewis Tomalin. He was an accountant who had married a German girl and could speak her language well. In 1880 he came across a book called *Health Culture* written by Dr Gustav Jaeger, professor of zoology at Stuttgart. It put forward the principle that *homo sapiens* would be far better off if he – or of course she – dressed in clothes made entirely from animal hair and, in particular, wool.

So enthralled was Tomalin with this notion that he translated the book himself and published it in England at his own expense. So persuasive was his case that in 1884 *The Times* published a leader supporting the idea. Tomalin had opened the first Jaeger shop in London earlier that year, with a licence from Dr Jaeger to use his name. He intended it merely as a philanthropic hobby, and the legend over the door of that first shop was endearingly dotty: *Dr Jaeger's Sanitary Woollen System.* Soon the idea was taken up by eminent Victorians like Oscar Wilde and Bernard Shaw* (who walked about London in one of the first Jaeger suits, looking, so it was said, like a bifurcated radish).

In five years, it dawned on Tomalin that his private obsession had become a thumping success. He went into the business full-time and by 1900 had twenty Jaeger shops. Today there are sixty in the UK, forty abroad. Stanley took Jaeger with him when he went in search of Livingstone; Scott took Jaeger with him to the Antarctic. The word entered the language, gradually shifting its stance from its first slightly barmy connotation to the international *réclame* it enjoys today.

Nicholas Tomalin, a great-grandson of the founder, was killed covering the Yom Kippur war for *The Sunday Times* in 1973. He was forty-two, one of the great reporters of his time, and in his humanity, intelligence and eccentricity, a chip off the old block.

Jaguar Bill Lyons nearly went into making gramophones, but fortunately at twenty-one decided instead to join a young Blackpool pal called Bill Walmsley in making side-cars for motorbikes. Lyons senior, who ran a music shop, put in £500, Walmsley senior, a coal merchant, another £500, and that was all the capital the boys ever needed. Soon they were making bodies for cars; Standard Austin, Morris Fiat and Wolseley. They were curiously graceful, as indeed was everything Bill Lyons ever built. The Standard connection proved most durable and in 1931 the boys were involved in the launch of the new 16 h.p. Standard SS. It was known even then as a real cad's* car: two short men could shake hands over the top, though the engine tended to boil.

In 1935 the company went public; Bill Walmsley took his money; Bill Lyons became sole boss. He took over the name of an obsolete Armstrong-Siddeley aero-engine which appealed to him: the Jaguar. The first SS Jaguar appeared at the 1935 Motor Show; guests were asked to guess its price. The average answer was around £650; the true price £385. Bill then drafted in a young engineer called Harry Weslake to raise the Standard's power from 90 to 105 b.h.p. enticing him with a cash reward of £100 for each b.h.p. he squeezed out.

That still wasn't good enough and in the war, during long nights of fire-watching at the factory, Bill Lyons and his lieutenants dreamed up a totally new engine called the XK. It is still fundamentally the unit which powers all Jaguars today. The XK 120 was the sensation of the 1948 Motor Show and hugely popular with starlets and playboys, especially in America. It was followed by the Mark II, famed for its enormous acceleration and therefore popular with the underworld as a getaway car; the Mark VII, much loved by the rag trade; the E-type, favoured transport of the first highly paid pop-stars and footballers; and lastly the feline, silky, and highly refined XJS, Jaguar's final passport to respectability (the E-type had been dubbed the greatest crumpet-catcher known to man).

Jam In English usage jam is not just the stuff you spread on your bread and butter, but in a transferred sense, any good fortune, as in Lewis Carroll's* 'jam yesterday and jam tomorrow, but never jam today'. Thus, 'jammy one' since the First World War has meant the sort of minor wound which would get you out of the trenches but not seriously impair your faculties; and the man who got the jammy one became a 'jammy bastard'.

Meanwhile, the business of jam-making has acquired a highly pejorative status in the language of feminist politics; it stands for the work women have done uncomplainingly and indeed with pleasure in country kitchens for centuries and is therefore held to be a backward step in the onward march of the women's movement.

Still, while English home-made jam – strawberry, raspberry, cherry, rhubarb and ginger, greengage, blackcurrant, redcurrant, blackberry, apricot, quince, and damson – remains as good as it is, clear, pure, sweet and brilliant as stained glass, best bought in a marquee on the day of the village fête, it is unlikely to stop being made. At least, we must devoutly hope so.

Japanese The English attitude to the Japanese has undergone several radical metamorphoses. Before the war they were a comic race known principally as slavish imitators of British innovative skills. In the war, they took Singapore: probably the biggest single catastrophe to befall British arms, and an even more profound psychological trauma. The Japanese were a joke no longer. Indeed, when British prisoners were used as slave labour to build the Burma railway, the Japanese were seen, with some justification, as sadistic psychopaths.

To a new generation of young English people, however, the Japanese are neither buffoons nor bastards, but a brilliant race who have given them their Sony transistor radios, their Hitachi television sets, their Toshiba microwave ovens, and their Honda motorbikes. A young Englishman may now indeed be working for a Japanese bank or in a Japanese car plant while learning judo or karate in his spare time. Recently the Japanese invoked the law against an English manufacturer who was trying to pass off his product with a Japanese trademark. In just half a century, the wheel has come full circle.

Jeeves 'What would I do without you, Jeeves?' sang Ian Carmichael as Bertie Wooster* in the BBC TV serialisation of the immortal *oeuvre*, 'I'd be in the most awful stew, Jeeves.' He would indeed; but the need is reciprocal. Wooster and Jeeves are two halves of a single whole. One without the other would be like the sound of one hand clapping. Jeeves has quite properly entered the English language with an entry to himself in the *Supplement* to the *OED*. He is an archetypally English creation: an American Jeeves would be an absurdity, a French Jeeves a nightmare, a Japanese Jeeves a mockery, a German Jeeves a catastrophe. The relationship between the two great Englishmen is marvellously balanced. The proper distance is maintained at all times: Wooster is always sir, Jeeves never Reginald. Though Jeeves defers to Bertie's social rank with the innate gravamen of his class he is the result of some curious misalliance, for his mother was a barmaid, his father a noted philologist. He has no respect for Bertie's intellect: indeed he has been heard to speak of the young master as mentally negligible. Bertie, on the other hand, though he may bridle a bit under his man's iron tutelage, especially when his favourite banjolele or purple socks have to go, never loses his awe at Jeeves's giant brain, which he fondly (though as it happens misguidedly) believes to be fed on a steady diet of fish. He also notes, with a proper sense of wonder, that Jeeves's head sticks out at the back to accommodate the massive cerebellum. The relationship is unsentimental: Jeeves can and will give notice if thwarted or temporarily replaced by one of Bertie's girls; but he always comes back. He must. He is the perfect manservant. He does not enter Bertie's room; he shimmers in. His morning cuppa is perfect (see also *Tea*) and his pick-me-up, though it momentarily lifts Bertie's skull off, quickly restores him to his customary zing.

Though Jeeves has been variously traced back to Sancho Panza and Sam Weller, he is in truth triumphantly *sui generis:* deeply read (Spinoza, Nietzsche, Dostoevsky, Pliny the Younger – but the list of his reading is endless), naturally magisterial (he takes the chair at meetings of the Junior Ganymede, the Dover Street club for gentlemen's gentlemen), perennially discreet. 'In times of domestic crisis,' Bertie reports, 'Jeeves has the gift of creating the illusion that he is not there.'

The reason that he is so triumphantly and palpably there in the English imagination is that he has a Boswell of genius in the improbable person of Bertie Wooster: 'It was the soft cough of Jeeves's which always reminds me of a very old sheep clearing its throat on a distant mountain top.' On the other hand, we have Jeeves's word for it that 'In the presence of the unusual, Mr Wooster is too prone to smile weakly and allow his eyes to protrude.'

Occasionally other fellows have tried to snaffle Jeeves. He was with Gussie Fink-Nottle for a few days. But he always comes homing back to Bertie's bachelor rooms in Berkeley Street, where it is eternally spring, in an England that never really existed; more's the pity.

Jews To be a Jew in England does not seem a bad fate, but it will bring its challenges, as being one does everywhere. A strain of antisemitism has disfigured English writing since Chaucer. Orwell*, writing in 1945, detected it in Wells, Huxley, Shaw*, Eliot and Thackeray (and did not even bother with the notorious antisemites like Chesterton, Belloc, Buchan and Sapper). It clearly reflected the way people thought, but never approached the systematic paranoia of central Europe (in 1909 when the notably philosemite Edward VII visited the Kaiser the conversation on world politics could not proceed till cousin Wilhelm had delivered a lengthy diatribe against the Jews). Still, it is unattractive enough.

Open the most innocuous-seeming book anywhere and the words leap from the page. In *The Fifth Form at St Dominic's,* published in 1881, we have to wait no longer than the second page before Bullinger of the Fifth calls a small boy an avaricious young Jew for whistling at the terms of a £50 scholarship. 'A Jewish boy at a public school,' noted Orwell, 'almost invariably had a bad time.'

He was looking back to the pre-Hitler world, but things were no better for English writer Frederic Raphael, at Charterhouse in the 1940s, when the preacher of an antisemitic sermon in the school chapel apologised to him later, explaining that he would never have made such remarks if he had known a Jew were present. (That shows, *inter alia,* just how numerous Jews were at Charterhouse then.) The incident was translated wellnigh unadorned to Raphael's smash-hit TV serial *The Glittering Prizes.* So were things better after the last war?

As late as the fifties candidates for jobs at the Cambridge University Appointments Board were described as Jews with clammy handshakes; there was a fuss when it came out but nobody was sacked.

Among great English writers, Orwell noted, only Dickens* could be said to be positively pro-Jewish (overlooking George Eliot and *Daniel Deronda*). Since the mid-thirties and the rise of Hitler, however, it has been thought uncivilised for any serious writer to commit antisemitic sentiments to paper. Besides, Jews like Frederic Raphael, Jonathan Miller and Bernard Levin have made an increasingly attractive contribution to English life.

Jonathan Miller, for example, explained in a hilarious sketch from *Beyond The Fringe* that he was not a Jew; only Jew*ish*. What this meant, perhaps, is that Jews become accepted in England the more English they become. Thus Julius Victor in John Buchan's *The Three Hostages,* though one of the richest men in the world, is also 'the whitest Jew since Saint Paul'. He has, in effect, become an Englishman.

In a more down-to-earth context, the good done to the Jewish image by a brilliant business like Marks and Spencer*, pervading every household with its bounty, is incalculable. Paul Johnson has said that intellectual life cannot flourish in any country where the Jews are even slightly uneasy. With three Jews in the 1983 Thatcher cabinet (Lawson, Brittan and Joseph) it could be said that in modern England they are easy enough: time will tell.

Johnson, Samuel (1709-84)   We tend to think of him as old: he was, after all, fifty-four, the great dictionary already written, Boswell a callow twenty-three on that celebrated day their paths first crossed in Tom Davies's back parlour. By then, as Boswell noted in his journal (a treasure trove which came to light only in this century) he had 'the most dreadful appearance'. In his youth he had been tall and lanky; by now, Boswell noted, he had grown 'gigantick'. He was, moreover, 'troubled with sore eyes, the palsy, and the king's evil ... very slovenly in his dress with a most uncouth voice'. None of this mattered when he began to talk.

Every Johnsonian will have his favourite moment. Some will savour the night when Sam sat down to dine with his *bête noir* Jack Wilkes, radical, rationalist and rake, a meeting engineered by Boswell with dexterous cunning. It could have been a disaster; it was a triumph. True, Wilkes went out of his way to please, plying the old trencherman with fine veal; 'Pray give me leave Sir – It is better here – A little of the stuffing – Some gravy – Let me have the pleasure of giving you some butter . . .'

It worked. 'Sir, sir I am obliged to you sir,' returns Sam. A mutual taste for jokes against the Scots, and later a shared pleasure in a picture, of the curve in a woman's bosom, set the seal on their unlikely conjunction. Others will relish that carefree-evening during the tour of the Hebrides when a pretty married Highland lady sat on Johnson's knee and kissed him: 'Do it again [said he] and let us see who will tire first.'

The sound and feel of the man carry over the two centuries with a clarity and freshness denied us by the flat, glassy technology of the tape recorder and the television camera. It is the most vivid case we have of the warts-and-all portrait. 'I have not wasted my life trifling with literary fools as Johnson did when he should have been shaking England with the thunder of his spirit,' complained Bernard Shaw peevishly. Yet it is precisely the trifling in taverns that laces the vast learning with humanity and makes us all feel we would have enjoyed a jar or two with Johnson: before, that is, he gave up fomented liquors.

Boswell's father, Lord Auchinleck, could not understand what Jamie could see in 'the auld dominie', and we all know Mrs Boswell's epigram: 'I have seen many a bear led by a man: but I never before saw a man led by a bear.' No matter; we can see the point of the old bear now; and must be grateful that Boswell survived the collapse of his legal career, the extinction of his political ambitions, and the onset of his chronic drinking to complete the greatest biography in the English language. He knew he had pulled it off. 'I have Johnsonised the land,' he boasted; and he had.

Jug v Straight Glass The question of which kind of glass the Englishman should take his beer from is a complex and serious one. Very broadly, the straight glass or sleeve finds its natural home north of the Wash and in working-class hands; though there are plenty of well-heeled southrons who swear that beer tastes better from a thin straight glass and that you can assess the contents far better than you can if it is in a dimpled jug. On the other hand there are those who claim that the straight glass tends to slip from carefree fingers as the hour advances (though a slight bulge near the top of the sleeve has been introduced to obviate this design fault). The jug is most often found in saloon bars, southern rugger clubs, and air force messes where it is characteristically held with three or four fingers through the handle on the far side and the thumb pressed against the belly. It has even been argued in Scotland that the sleeve is to be preferred in a free-for-all, when the glass can be smashed on the bar and the jagged remnant brought up to the ready in one continuous movement. Here, however, we treat only of England, where such an ungentlemanly deployment of the beer glass is happily rare.

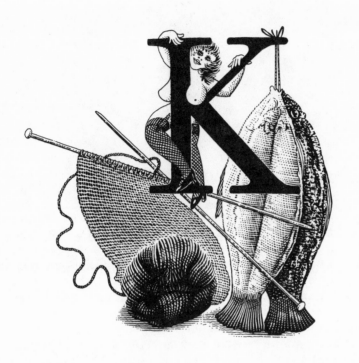

Kew Gardens They have a dream-like quality to the average Englishman, for here he enters a world of sumptuous and extravagant fantasy. With a small dose of laudanum, who knows what new Kubla Khan might not here be spun out by some latter-day Coleridge? For here are the Queen's Beasts, the Campanile, the Pagoda and the Ice-House; the Temples of Aeolus, Bellona and Arethusa; the Ruined Arch, Orangery and Japanese Gateway; within those hot and humid glasshouses where tropical rain forests are re-created, ferns and fronds, palms and pines, loofahs and lotuses, pineapples and paw-paws proliferate. All this exotica was first brought here by the colonising energy of the Victorians. It is the organised plunder of empire; and when he steps into its magical ambit the Englishman, in short, enters his ill-gotten inheritance.

Keynes, John Maynard (1883-1946) He was one of the dozen or so most influential, most original, and most able Englishmen of this century; not to beat about the bush, one of the *greatest* Englishmen. His world fame rests on his seminal book, the *General Theory of Employment, Interest, and Money* (1936), which did for economics what Einstein's General Theory of Relativity had done for physics twenty years before, that is, stood the subject on its head. There are countless economists today who can explain how Keynes is outmoded or superseded; not one of them could even put his case without the conceptual tools Keynes provided.

Still, another book, published by Keynes in 1919, may have been even more important: for *The Economic Consequences of the Peace,* written in white heat engendered by his anger at the so-called peace at Versailles that year, retails, in prose of glittering beauty, how a more generous and imaginative settlement could have prevented the Second World War. It was precisely because the botched job at Versailles left an appalling moral and material vacuum in Germany that the scum of Europe had the chance to spawn, flourish, and, for a fatal while, prevail.

Quite apart from the grandeur of its theme, *Consequences* teems with unforgettable cameos of the main actors at Versailles. The picture of Lloyd George was at first cut out because Keynes felt it disloyal to print it so soon after working for the Welsh prestidigitator; but it was restored later, and is breathtakingly savage. 'This syren,' Keynes wrote, 'this goat-footed bard, this half-human visitor to our age from the hag-ridden magic and enchanted woods of Celtic antiquity ... is rooted in nothing; he is void and without content ... he is a prism which collects light and distorts it and is most brilliant if the light comes from many quarters at once; a vampire and medium in one.'

It was Keynes's lot to do his most celebrated work for his country at the end of each world war; and if he failed in 1945 to get all the cash Britain wanted from America, he probably did all that was humanly possible; and he was a key figure in the setting up of the International Monetary Fund and the International Bank, both destined to be fundamental in the smooth transition of the world to peace. But the strain on an already weak heart proved too much; and he died in 1946.

He was a fellow of Eton, a trustee of the National Gallery, a director of the Bank of England and chairman of the Arts Council. He loved to play the stock markets; very nearly went bankrupt but came back to make substantial fortunes for himself and King's College, Cambridge, of which he was bursar. He is always remembered for one epigram – 'in the long run we are all dead' – but also coined one of the most elegant of all the definitions for inflation: 'the euthanasia of the rentier'.

He was married to the Russian ballerina Lydia Lopokova (who would be remembered, if for nothing else, then for her remark that she disliked the country in August because her legs got so bitten by barristers). They had no children, and we now know much more about Keynes's homosexual predilections (he advised his friend Lytton Strachey on which places in Tunisia provided the best bed and boy bargains). He once told a great college feast that it was a principal regret of his life that he had not drunk more champagne; but in a sense all his life was a long bottle of fizz; would we had some more like it.

Khatmandu The capital of Nepal, an independent country which usually enjoyed friendly relations with the British Raj and generally managed to get away with no more serious occupation than a British Resident. However, British troops were assuredly posted there, none more celebrated than Mad Carew, the hero of a dramatic monologue by J.Milton Hayes, once recited on the music hall with huge effect and perfect solemnity.

The Green Eye of the Little Yellow God is a morality story which celebrates the essential frivolity of womankind, the clash of deeply opposed cultures, and the ineluctable fate which awaits young Englishmen who flout the *mores* of the foreign soil on which they stand.

'He was known as Mad Carew by the subs [second lieutenants] at Khatmandu,' we are told. 'But for all his foolish pranks he was worshipped in the ranks.' This usually gets the first laugh of the evening nowadays: the ranks no longer worship anyone, and certainly not idiots like Carew.

'The Colonel's daughter smiled on him as well.' What could Mad Carew give her for her impending twenty-first? Nothing, she averred, but the green eye of the little yellow god. It would be a Buddhist idol there, probably, and to desecrate it as mortally inept as it was morally indefensible. 'He returned before the dawn with his shirt and tunic torn / And a gash across his temple dripping red.' He had with him the green eye as well; but the Colonel's daughter wouldn't take it. That night, at the height of the ball, she hastens to his room and finds a knife in his heart: 'Twas the vengeance of the little yellow god.'

So 'a broken hearted woman tends the grave of Mad Carew / And the Yellow God forever gazes down.'

The real fascination of the ludicrous doggerel lies in the unrecorded moment when it shaded from a perfectly serious, indeed solemn, morality tale into an uproarious comic turn. That moment cannot be accurately pinned down now; almost certainly the laughter began at some time between the two wars, and grew to gale force after India* got her independence and the British rule became a vast subterranean folk memory.

Today's Mad Carews (and the breed miraculously lives on) have to be content with less disputatious dares like walking from the south to the north pole or crossing the Atlantic in a bathtub. Not for nothing did Halvard Lange remark that his countrymen did not see Englishmen as foreigners: 'We look on them only as rather mad Norwegians.' Like Mad Carew.

Kippers Though the Scots have some cause to be proud of their Loch Fyne kippers, and though they are nowadays often thought of as a quintessentially Scottish dish, there is some evidence that the first kippers were made by a Northumberland fish curer called John Woodger. He knew that salmon had been kippered as long ago as the fourteenth century, and decided to try the same process on herrings. He split them down the backbone, gutted them, and soaked them in brine, then hung them over oak fires to smoke for some twelve hours. He had invented kippers and excellent ones are still made there (as well as in the Isle of Man and around Great Yarmouth). Still a sturdy runner-up on British Rail to the ubiquitous mixed grill as a breakfast dish, kippers have found favour with celebrated Englishmen like George Orwell*, and Laurence Olivier* who made a famous fuss when the kippers were taken off his Brighton-Victoria train. Though the succulent fish have attracted only a small literature, they were commandeered with splendid effect by the Labour politician Eric Heffer. The Conservative Party, he opined, were nothing but a load of kippers: two-faced with no guts.

Knighthoods The honours system in England is a shambles. The man who after the First World War called Birmingham* the City of Dreadful Knights – an enchanting verdict on the sort of people who had been honoured there for making fortunes out of the blood and agony – deserved the accolade far more than those who actually got it. Though Lloyd George's tariff for honours (knighthoods cost £25,000) was notorious, neither Harold Wilson with his resignation honours list nor Harold Macmillan with his cheerfully cynical largesse did the much overhauled system much good.

Certainly, good men are made knights, and some middling men, and some patently deplorable men. The disgrace is the chaos which pervades the honours machinery. Certainly in the imaginative world it is now more of an honour to be left out. While the truly great writers, whether by accident or design, go unknighted (Wells, Hardy*, Conrad, Eliot, Auden*, Orwell*, Waugh* and Greene) there is no shortage of such accolades for the second-rate: duffers like Henry Newbolt and John Squire.

So laughter may seem the only possible response to the solemn buff envelope. Bernard Shaw* replied that nothing less than a dukedom would do for him.

Knitting   The insidious natter of the knitting needle was once heard only in the purlieu of grannies and maiden aunts. It is now a trendy pursuit among the young, and owes its new rage to a young Englishwoman called Patricia Roberts. She took the fashion course at the renowned Leicester College of Art, and knitting, unfashionable then, as her main subsidiary subject. She now has four hundred women knitting for her and recently opened her third shop in Covent Garden*. She has had a galvanic effect on British wool, previously unbelievably awful, now as chic and svelte as her sweaters. Americans, being lousy knitters, are among her best customers.

Knocker   One of those multi-purpose English words within whose hospitable bounds new meanings jostle for space against old ones. Thus it is a goblin, and what we bang against a door to attract attention. It is also in modern parlance a denigrator, a sense which seems to have American provenance – 'don't knock the rock' – and since about 1940 it has also been an idiomatic term for the female breast. The word was most memorably used in recent times by the England rugby scrum half, Steve Smith, who complained that when a well-endowed young woman took it into her head to run across the field topless during the half-time interval at a Twickenham international, it had been impossible for his captain, the great Billy Beaumont, to secure the concentration of his players on tactics for the second half: 'They wouldn't pay attention with those great knockers whistling by.' We may deduce therefore that the colourful phrase is still in lively idiomatic use among young and active Englishmen.

Koestler, Arthur (1905-83)   He was part of that unquantifiable credit balance of talent England acquired as a result of fascism, but he was something more: an object lesson in how well English can be written by somebody not born speaking the language. The other two great exemplars are Conrad and Nabokov (though Nabokov learned English in the nursery). For Arthur Koestler it was a third language; he wrote in Hungarian till he was seventeen, in German till he was thirty-five, then in English. Though he grumbled about the alien's uphill fight, taking aboard his hard-won new idiom, only to have to discard it next day as cliché, the truth is that few Englishmen have written better English this century, and few indeed have written a greater novel than *Darkness at Noon*. Koestler graced English with the garlic of his prose.

Labour Party 'Lunched with Desmond MacCarthy at Gatti's wrote Harold Nicolson in his diary for 27 February 1930. 'He tells me a story about Keir Hardie,' (the pioneer labour leader). 'Looking down on the 1905 House of Commons a friend remarked to him how few members there were from the working classes. "Yes, it will take the British working man twenty years to learn to elect his equals to represent him. And it will take him another twenty years not to elect his equals." ' Nicolson thought this was true: 'I saw it with Ramsay MacDonald the other day – his longing to get hold of the young university men. His feeling that the *cadets de bonne famille* were the people he wanted.'

Seventeen years later, no longer a *cadet* but indisputably *de bonne famille*, Nicolson joined the Labour Party himself. The decision shocked his family. His son Nigel, Conservative candidate for Leicester, said he was 'struck dumb'. Harold's wife, the writer Vita Sackville-West, wrote to him: 'Of course I don't really like you being associated with those people. I like Ernest Bevin and Philip Noel-Baker. I have a contemptuous tolerance of Attlee, but I *loathe* Aneurin Bevan, and Shinwell is just a public menace. I do not like people who cannot speak the King's English.' Harold Nicolson later confessed it was the cardinal error of his life: 'the realities, and above all the personalities, of Labour politics really revolted me'.

The melancholy vignette illustrates graphically the headaches men of goodwill have had in trying to come to terms with this ramshackle rag-bag of a party, containing, or trying to contain, within itself intellectuals and trade unionists, Christians and atheists, pacifists and militants, lost liberals and miscast radicals, socialists and communists, Trotskyites and Marxists, pedagogues and demagogues, opportunists and idealists, bullies and ninnies, saints and sinners. It had two short periods of minority government between the wars until it was hopelessly split by Ramsay MacDonald's National coalition of 1931; three periods of real power in the post-war world, ending with the defeat of Callaghan in 1979 and the rout of Michael Foot by the triumphant Margaret Thatcher in 1983.

Racked by schism over Clause 4 (the crucial point in the party constitution calling for the common ownership of production, distribution and exchange) it finally came apart, with Roy Jenkins, Shirley Williams, David Owen and Bill Rodgers forming the new Social Democratic party. Yet even within the remaining rump of the old Labour party, left and right continue to fight a pitched battle for the soul of the movement. The plain fact is that the Labour Party is historically, fundamentally, and, it seems, irrevocably fissile. 'What a genius the Labour Party has', wrote Sir William Connor (Cassandra of the *Daily Mirror*), 'for cutting itself in half and letting the two parts writhe in public.'

Lancashire   'In the early morning the mill girls clumping down the cobbled street, all in clogs, making a curiously formidable sound, like an army hurrying into battle. I suppose this is the typical sound of Lancashire.' Thus George Orwell* wrote in his diary on 18 February 1936; the notebook from which *The Road to Wigan Pier* was later to be constructed. 'Clogs are very cheap', he continued. 'They cost about five shillings a pair and need not wear out for years because all they need is new irons underneath costing a few pence.' A vivid picture from a vanished world? The clogs have gone, and so have many of the mills. Yet the unemployment is still there, and relatively at any rate, the poverty. Today the world gets its most vivid picture of Lancashire through the lens of the television camera; twice a week the rest of England peers hypnotised into the alien civilisation portrayed in Granada TV's marathon soap opera *Coronation Street*. Perhaps over the half-century time has softened many of the sharp edges of Lancashire life; the older generation may cling to their cloth caps and hair nets; younger people in the street are indistinguishable from the young anywhere. Yet still the broad vowels and glottal stops of the whippet-fanciers, ale-suppers, and tripe-takers distinguish north from south and in times of recession the gap between them yawns dangerously wide.

There is an agricultural and beautiful Lancashire to the north; but essentially still it is a county of industrial cities: Rochdale and Preston, Wigan and Warrington, Blackburn and Burnley, Nelson and Colne. Ambitious plans and millions of pounds of venture capital are being poured into the great Lancashire cities of Manchester* and Liverpool*, but the heart of Lancashire must be won in these smaller, beleaguered, industrial towns. Disraeli said there were two nations in England, who were as ignorant of each other's habits, thoughts, and feelings as if they were on different planets. Granada TV has reduced the gap from stellar to human distances; but in Lancashire it is still there.

Landscape   Seeing the shimmer and haze of his landscape, insubstantial and dreamlike through the creamy air of any early May morning, the average Englishman tends to think of it as fortuitously given and always there. The truth is that landscapes are made by men just as much as men are made by landscapes; and in England it was the work of the great landscape gardeners – William Kent, Capability Brown, Humphry Repton – which gave England its languorous look.

They did it by a genius for following the artless lie of the land, for the seemingly casual disposition of trees, shrubs and flowers, for the apparently unintended scatter of lake, ha-ha, and folly. Today the landscape architect – as he is more grandly called now – acts not for landed proprietors but for local authorities; his workplace is no longer around the mansion but along the motorway. Even as he faces up to his new challenges, the landscape his forebears left is changing step to the music of time. The intimate patchwork quilt of small fields is disappearing as the immemorial hedgerows of England are swept away; and the land that was once thickly peopled by farmworkers is now innocent of any life except for the solitary technician chuntering by in his combine harvester.

Even the gentle pastel of traditional English crops is now shot through by the saffron blaze of the rape grown for the margarine makers. The electric pylons which caused such a furore when they first marched over the English landscape half a century ago have curiously melted into the picture now; but nothing can be done for a generation about the desolate skeletons of England's eleven million dead elms*.

Larkin, Philip (born 1922)   If writers had a work-reward unit as engines have a thermal efficiency unit, then Philip Larkin would rate the maximum score. In his sixty-two years he has published two novels: *Jill* (1946) and *A Girl in Winter* (1947); and four very slim volumes of verse. They are: *The North Ship* (1945) which contains thirty-two poems; *The*

Less Deceived (1955) with a modest twenty-nine poems; *The Whitsun Weddings* (1964; and thirty-two poems again); and in 1974 *High Windows* (a mere twenty-four poems). In recognition for this exiguous *oeuvre*, he has been made a CBE, a C. Lit and a FRSL. He has been appointed a Visiting Fellow of All Souls College, Oxford, and a Foreign Honorary Member of the American Academy. He has won the Queen's Gold Medal for Poetry and the A.C. Benson Silver Medal. He has been given the Loines Award for Poetry and the Shakespeare Prize of the FVS foundation in Hamburg. His home town has bestowed the Coventry Award of Merit on its much-medalled son. And no fewer than five universities – Belfast, Leicester, Warwick, St Andrews, and Sussex – have given him honorary doctorates. From this great plethora of palms and prizes we can draw only one of two conclusions. Either the world's honorific machinery has stripped its gears and gone into some kind of ungovernable overdrive; or Larkin's little harvest must be uncommonly ripe.

Lawns   There are eleven million lawns in England. No other nation on earth can boast the lushness and profusion of English grass. In part, this is no doubt the consequence of the wellnigh perfect weather for it: mild, damp and relatively pest-free; but it is also a reflection of the preoccupation the island race has with sport that quite so much grass is grown and tended. In cricket endless hours are devoted to the preparation of the wicket, or more accurately the stretch of turf between the two wickets; in horse racing the punter will want to know how good the going is, in other words, the state of the turf; in the relatively tranquil game of bowls each player must accept the rub of the green; in polo the chief source of social intercourse between chukkas is the quaint habit of treading the divots or restoring the turf cut up by flying hooves.

'Nothing is more pleasant to the Eye,' declared Francis Bacon in 1625, 'than green Grass kept finely shorn,' though the modes of keeping it so – grazing, trampling and scything – were far less precise than those we now have. True, some greenkeepers claimed till recent times that they could cut with a scythe to a smoothness not possible by any other means; but the invention of the lawn mower by Edwin Budding at Stroud in 1830 took much of the sweat out of tending grass; and the arrival of the motor mower around the turn of the century took the rest.

By 1902 the self-propelled forty-two-inch mower with saddle for driver was being used by Cadburys, the Quaker* chocolate firm, at their model village of Bournville, thus providing that broad striped zebra effect now so familiar throughout the land. There is no mistaking the velvet pile of a well-kept English lawn, wrought from fine-bladed bent and fescue grasses mown regularly at carpet height, nor the frequency with which such images recur in English writing. 'Close and slow, summer is ending in Hampshire,' wrote Louis MacNeice* in the great opening to his *Autumn Journal,* 'Ebbing away down ramps of shaven lawn where close-clipped yew / Insulates the lives of retired generals and admirals / And the spyglasses hung in the hall and the prayerbooks ready in the pew.'

Liberty's   There is an unexpected link between Oscar Wilde and two great Regent Street stores: Jaeger* and Liberty's. Oscar enthusiastically endorsed the characteristic products of both. Indeed, he can fairly claim to have begun the long love affair between Americans and Liberty's, for in his celebrated American lecture tour of 1881-2 he included a talk on house decoration, which turned on the cult of the new aesthetic school with the odd name. Gilbert and Sullivan's *Patience* contained the seminal lines: 'A greenery-yallery, Grosvenor Gallery / Foot-in-the grave young man.'

Greenery-yallery, though rather opaque now, made perfect sense then. In 1879 Liberty's had introduced a new cashmere, described at the time by *Queen* magazine: 'There are tints that call to mind French and English mustards, sage-greens, greens that look like curry.'

Liberty's had supplied the fabrics for costumes in Gilbert and Sullivan's *Patience,* and when D'Oyly Carte was working on *The Mikado,* sent special envoys to Japan to bring back exactly the right materials for the clothes. Not surprisingly, Arthur Liberty, founder of the firm, had a box at Gilbert and Sullivan first nights. To give the cult another helpful push forward, *Patience* was running in New York even as Wilde was sweeping America.

The link between Liberty's and Japan was not new. Young Arthur Liberty, then a sales assistant at Farmer and Rogers on the west side of Regent Street, had been inspired by the Japanese section of the International Exhibition of 1862. He ran the oriental side of Farmer and Rogers which sold these Japanese exhibits after the show closed; and when they failed to make him a partner in 1875 crossed the road and started on his own.

The fashionable world crossed Regent Street with him. Liberty had a close working friendship with Thomas Wardle, the Leek dyer and printer; together they introduced the new range of delicate pastel tints which had previously been the prerogative of the East and which were to be known worldwide as Liberty colours. To a world accustomed to harsh colours and stiff silks these soft, pretty fabrics were a revelation.

His customers included William Morris, Alma-Tadema, Burne-Jones, Rossetti and Whistler. Liberty silks make their appearance in Somerset Maugham's great novel *Cakes and Ale*; Liberty curtains are found in a thriller called *The Documents in the Case* by a young writer called Dorothy L. Sayers; a letter from Liberty's features in D.H. Lawrence's *Sons and Lovers*. A penniless Isadora Duncan danced in Liberty fabric bought with a borrowed £10 at her first London party.

Despite the handicap of its ghastly mock Tudor headquarters Liberty's continues to thrive: Mary Quant uses Liberty prints; Yves Saint-Laurent used a whole range when he dropped his skirt length to mid-calf. And while Liberty's still scour the East for new ideas, they are now, in a final irony, exporting Liberty fabrics to Japan.

Liverpool When he was Secretary of State for the Environment Michael Heseltine made it his business to pay a visit to Liverpool once a week. As an ambitious minister, he was quite right. Liverpool is a stage on which the contending views on how wealth and power should be distributed in modern England are being dramatically played out. The Toxteth riots, a series of paroxysms of rage or cries for help (depending on one's political colour), had marvellously focussed the attention of the Thatcherite government on the squalor, poverty, and despair which had ignited them. It is a city of infinite extremes and violent contrasts.

Its socialist council barely rescued itself from a collision course with the government and had elected to go bankrupt rather than toe the line about spending cuts. It harbours the Bishop of Liverpool, the Right Rev David Sheppard, who in his 1984 Dimbleby lecture on BBC TV appealed to the conscience of Britain to meet the horrors of unemployment by state intervention. It harbours Professor Patrick Minford of Liverpool University, easily the most ultramontane of all English academic economists in his call for enormous slices of the welfare state to be returned to private hands. There is, in short, nothing temperate or moderate about Liverpool.

It has been a crucible of wealth for some two centuries; and one of the principal ingredients in that vast wealth was the slave trade. It was one corner of the ghastly triangular traffic which carried cotton goods to Africa; exchanged them for black men, women and children, took them across the Atlantic to America; and came home with raw cotton, tobacco and sugar. John Gladstone, father of the great reforming and humanitarian Liberal statesman William Ewart Gladstone, was ironically a Liverpool slave-owner (along with many peers and even some bishops). He defended his moral position vehemently, and when emancipation came in 1833 received £75,000 (some £12 million today) in compensation for the 1,609 slaves he owned. Thus Liverpool has an old crime lying on its conscience; this has in no whit prevented the city from acquiring a parallel reputation for gaiety, originality, and cosmopolitan fizz. The port (still the largest exporter in the Commonwealth) was a melting pot for races; for West Indians and Chinese; for footloose Welshmen and for Irish migrants en route to the New World. It can boast two of the best twentieth-century cathedrals in England: the Anglican, begun in 1904 and finished seventy-five years later, and the Roman Catholics' ultra-modern Metropolitan Cathedral of Christ the King, completed in 1967 after just four and a half years. It contains the Lady Lever Art Gallery and Pilkington Museum, monuments to the great fortunes Liverpool made their founders in soap and glass. It has two of England's finest football teams (Liverpool and Everton). Its university can claim (from its university college days) two unexpected and improbable alumni: F.E. Smith and Lytton Strachey. It is celebrated for its racecourse (Aintree); its comedians (Tommy Handley, Arthur Askey); and of course for the Beatles, who made the Liverpool sound world famous. Liverpool has remembered its favourite sons by founding Beatle City, a permanent exhibition centre dedicated to the art of the four fabled Merseyside troubadours, and erecting a statue in their honour. There is now another of John Lennon. An over-indulgence? Hardly. Gladstone, the slave-owner's son, has two.

London But which London? The segments devised for the delivery of the mail break the great wen conveniently for us into a wide spectrum of different villages, each with its own flavour. Thus NW1 or Camden Town is Stringalong territory, though you have to be over a certain age to remember this trendy family created by Mark Boxer and sounding suspiciously like Tomalin in reverse. The Stringalongs stand for trendy, caring, intelligent bourgeois values, often rendered ridiculous in the press of everyday life. They cluster in a few substantial roads just east of Primrose Hill, patronising the same bookshops, restaurants, laundromats, boutiques and delicatessens. You could do worse than join them there; but it will cost you a few bob: NW1 is no longer cheap.

Nor is NW3, melting pot for television directors, senior civil servants, barristers and many other varieties of intelligent high-earners. The flavour of NW3 is leavened by Jewish garlic eco-concern and Liberal politics. Hampstead (for that is NW3 under another name) is still *sympathique,* but very, very pricey. So what about N1? It's central, and full of interesting, slightly seedy Georgian houses; but other people have had the same idea and for a generation now Islington has been progressively gentrified with aubergine doors and coach lamps taking the place of the broken windows and peeling paint.

We can rule out SW1 or Belgravia; home of American film actors, Arab oil sheiks and, increasingly, Japanese tycoons; while SW3 or Chelsea is now as classy as Hampstead: full of estate agents, stockbrokers, merchant bankers and advertising men. So what about St John's Wood? Again, we are a generation too late: once the favourite nesting ground for mistresses and sculptors, still charming with its Regency verandahs and secret high-walled gardens, it is increasingly the domain of brassy classy foreign money: it has little or no indigenous life left. W1 (Mayfair) is impossible, while W2 (Paddington) still has some interesting enclaves buried between the kebab and tandoori places. W8 or Bayswater may still have some bargains, especially round the Portobello Road*, but Kensington proper (SW7) is now a maze of museums and stuccoed apartments for the well-to-do.

So where should young married people go? Fulham has many adherents, it's ugly but only pricey in patches and not too far from the centre; Hammersmith has possibilities though you will be lucky indeed to find anything by the Thames*; and perhaps the best bet for those who do not mind going over the river is Clapham, where there are still rows of imposing late eighteenth-century houses facing over wide green spaces.

Much government money has gone into trying to persuade people to move east to dockland and the Isle of Dogs; geographically it's attractive (a City worker can walk to work) but no lemming rush is yet discernible. The Thames east of Tower Bridge is however increasingly in favour, in a move led by SDP leader David Owen, who lives in Lime Street, and photographer Tony Snowdon, one of the first to have a Thames-side hideaway. Perhaps the smart money should be on Battersea (SW8) where two of the best restaurants in London now flourish cheek by jowl in an otherwise uninteresting street: they are a mere seven minutes by bus from Sloane Square over Chelsea bridge. If Nico can flourish in such an unpromising milieu, so can the rest of us.

Loo A blessing to the English this last half century, for it has at last given the island race a word for 'lavatory' (itself a euphemism) that is neither wincingly genteel like 'toilet', coyly vulgar like 'lav', heartily military like 'lats', arcanely naval like 'heads', coarsely schoolboyish like 'bog', hopelessly archaic like 'closet', or ingratiatingly transatlantic like 'john'. Despite some typically intricate word play by James Joyce, and learned articles which hesitatingly relate it to Waterloo, we should credit Nancy Mitford with first giving 'loo' printed usage, so getting England out of a tight corner.

Lord's Not the House of Lords, of course, though many peers belong, but Thomas Lord's cricket ground, first opened at Dorset Square for the Marylebone Cricket Club in 1787 and moved to its present site in 1814. The headquarters of English cricket, as it now is, intermingles much of the most gratifying and exasperating that country and game have to offer.

The Long Room in the pavilion is one of the most beautiful in the land: but women are not admitted. You can have a drink at Lord's or talk to a girl, or watch the cricket; but the only way to do all three at once is to have tickets for the exclusive Warner Stand or wangle one of the scarce and costly boxes. If you are lucky enough to get one of these latter in the members' draw, it will set you back £1,250 as a private person for a five-day Test (£1,950 if you are a company).

Though the ticker tapes bringing news from the far corners of the Empire have long gone, the cavernous men's loo beneath the pavilion still contains discreet in-jokes like the Out and Not Out signs above the swing doors. Ties and jackets are still *de rigeur,* even when the temperature is up in the nineties. The food is schoolboy stuff, mainly of the buns and char variety, but Bollinger have recently introduced a champagne tent for racier *aficonados.*

Still, every cricketer worth his salt has dreamed of playing at Lord's, of seeing the massed Charters and Caldicotts* rise to applaud his century for England. The walk back to the pavilion after a duck, on the other hand, and the silence in the Long Room, which must be crossed on the way to the dressing rooms, can make it one of the loneliest places in the world.

Yet when the sun is benign and the square a blaze of perfectly kept emerald, a finer setting for a torrid spell from the Aussie pace bowler Dennis Lillee or an elegantly constructed innings from the graceful bat of David Gower cannot be had in Christendom.

Love 'Continental people have sex lives,' said that Central European cynic George Mikes, 'the English have hot water bottles.' If you can believe that, you can believe anything. The English are the only people in Europe who habitually address total strangers of the other sex as love, dear or darling. On St Valentine's Day* they go collectively and comprehensively mad in a way not approached anywhere north of the equator. They have a love literature of unparalleled richness and beauty:

ranging from the god-given sonnets of Shakespeare* to the wry lines of Larkin* and from the haunting ache of Hardy* to the comic thrall of Betjeman*. Hot water bottles indeed!

Lunch The word – and the thing itself – cause endless trouble still in England at that join in the class pyramid where it is still called dinner. Any Englishman who does call lunch dinner indicates at once and for sure to any other Englishman that he hails from somewhere below the middle of the middle class. The difficulty is relatively new in the long vista of English history, since the word till quite recently meant a snack between proper meals. There was a time when everyone in England who could afford to do so dined in the afternoon and supped in the evening. Then, with ease and affluence, lunch began its metamorphosis to a meal in its own right: an agreeable pause in the rhythm of the working day for deals and dalliance. It is now a social divider of infinite power. It distances husbands from their wives (he had roast beef in the cafeteria, she had cottage cheese salad in the kitchen). It distances bosses from their workers (grouse and claret in the boardroom, sandwiches and tea on the building site). It separates the employed from the unemployed (steak and kidney in the pub, baked beans by the telly). The proliferation of the expense account has allowed a whole clutch of restaurants to spring up serving meals customers would never dream of eating at home. Whether much business is achieved at these festivals of cholesterol is a moot point: in certain flash callings like showbiz and publishing the point is not so much what you eat but with whom you eat it. It has become a handy way for royalty to entertain foreign potentates who are not worth putting up and for government to entertain middling visiting politicians; a convenient means for business to coddle new clients and a continuing solace to underdogs for their meagre rewards. There may be no bonus at Christmas again but at least there's lunch to look forward to with old Ronnie at L'Escargot (see *Soho*). Though a socialist government did its best to discourage lunch by making meals no longer tax-deductible it has had little effect. In any event, the left seems as keen to go out to lunch as anyone else. Lunch will cease to be a problem in England when it means the same to every Englishman as *déjeuner* does to every Frenchman.

MacNeice, Louis (1907-63) Once the most junior of the thirties poets (see also under *Auden, Spender*) he could end up as the best known and loved. His attributes were a nutcracker brain, a dazzling grasp of technique, and a hard-nosed scepticism about the workaday world. He was leftish but never Marxist; a male animal who liked women and understood them; a Belfast Anglican bishop's son who perceived the English better sometimes than they did themselves; a radio playwright of the first rank whose untimely death was precipitated by his insistence on going underground with his engineers to see the sound effects were right for a programme, thus giving him a chill which turned to pneumonia.

In MacNeice the ideas may be complex, and the line fastidious; but the sense is always crystal clear. There is none of the encrusted reference that makes Eliot's work so difficult for most readers; nor the rune-like density which sometimes invades Auden even at his most magisterial. None of the other thirties poets quite equals MacNeice's sense of fun: 'It's no go the Yogi-Man, It's no go Blavatsky / All we want is a bank balance and a bit of skirt in a taxi'; and none of them writes such tender love poetry: 'Who has left a scent on my life and left my walls / Dancing over and over with her shadow / Whose hair is twined in all my waterfalls /

And all of London littered with remembered kisses.' Each admirer will have his own favourite piece of MacNeice; but the *Autumn Journal*, written in the phony peace between August and Christmas 1938, takes some beating: 'The New Year comes with bombs, it is too late / To dose the dead with honourable intentions: / If you have honour to spare, employ it on the living / The dead are as dead as Nineteen Thirty Eight.' He was in Spain twice, the first time with his Marlborough friend, Anthony Blunt, though never conned by him into treachery; in Iceland memorably with Auden (*Letters from Iceland*); he travelled for the BBC to Rome, India and Pakistan, to America, the Gold Coast, and to South Africa. He remained to the end totally without illusions: 'What will happen will happen; the whore and buffoon / Will come off best; no dreamers they cannot lose their dream / And are at least likely to be re-instated in the new regime.' He went much too soon: but his words still haunt the mind.

Madame Tussaud's One of the most intractable puzzles of modern English life is the survival of this weird anachronism. In an audio-visual age, when every public person must live in the glare of the television lights, and can be seen in colour, in sound and in motion, who needs waxworks? Some two and a half million people a year, it appears.

Perhaps the chance to gawp at the infamous, departed and mighty without having one's head cut off has something to do with it. Perhaps the macabre pull of the Chamber of Horrors still exercises its malevolent thrall (the Duke of Wellington, a regular habitué, used to ask to be told whenever they had an interesting new exhibit). Perhaps the effigy of the original Madame Tussaud, who lived nine years in the Palace of Versailles, art tutor to Louis XVI, has the strongest attraction of all. She made death masks of many victims of the Terror, some of which can still be seen in her waxworks.

The Tussaud family continued to run the business till 1967 but it is now a public company which has diversified into entertainments as disparate as Chessington Zoo, Warwick Castle and Wookey Hole. Most significant of all, perhaps, is the London Planetarium which adjoins Madame Tussaud's and is owned by the company. Future generations may prefer watching waxing stars wane to watching waning wax stars. However, while there are macabre curiosities on show like the actual blade that cut off the heads in the French Revolution, no doubt there will be those who will still derive some perverse pleasure from becoming, for one brief shining moment, vicarious *tricoteuses*.

Maidenhead Though it is still of course there, the heyday of Maidenhead was indisputably the thirties. At one time during that unpleasant decade there were ninety-seven nightclubs in and around it, ranging from the very plush places like Skindles to shabby drinking dives charging ten shillings entrance at the door. Across the river from

Skindles was the even more ritzy Hungaria with its ivy-covered walls, private pools, and lawns running down to the water's edge. Here the Prince of Wales (later Edward VIII) and Prince George (later Duke of Kent) circulated frequently on the celebrated postage-stamp glass dance floor, thus following in the footsteps of their grandfather, Edward VII, who liked to install his medium-term mistresses in the opulent riverside mansions of Maidenhead. Here people used to come on from the Astor house-parties at Cliveden just down the river (see under *Thames* for later shenanigans there). Here Ivor Novello used to drop in from his nearby house with theatrical guests; and here too came thousands of unre-corded merrymakers, speeding down the A4 in their Alvises, Lagondas and MGs (and occasionally indulging in the risky sport of having a drink at every pub on the left- or right-hand side of the road on the way). These affluent young drank beer at 6d a pint and whisky at 9d a shot; it was all right for some. At regatta time in August they took to their punts in droves with picnic baskets, cocktail shakers, cretonne-covered cushions and wind-up gramophones; and flocked at night to hear lewd but classy entertainers like Ronald Frankau. There was a fair bit of canoodling and Maidenhead vied with Brighton* for supremacy in the dirty-weekend stakes. It was all very innocent, this thirties whoopee, compared with the present equivalent, and ephemeral; the war was coming, and after it, Maidenhead would never be quite the same again.

Manchester Manchester men and Liverpool gentlemen, goes the old Lancashire saying, and there is a kernel of truth in it. Liverpool* retained for too long an unjumpable chasm between rich and poor; in Manchester, the wealth and power founded on cotton were always far more evenly spread. The Manchester School of Cobden and Bright were the apostles of free trade while conservative Birmingham remained the citadel of protection; the *Manchester Guardian* became the renowned champion of radical politics, independent ideas, high thinking and plain living (its greatest editor, C.P. Scott, appointed to the chair at twenty-five, and dying at eighty-five, cycled to the office till very nearly the end of his life). 'During the 1830s and 1840s', wrote Asa Briggs in his *Social History of England* (1983), 'Manchester was a Mecca for everyone who wished to understand what was happening to society and what would happen to it in the future.' It fascinated Engels, who lived there as a businessman and wrote his *Condition of the Working Class in England* (1887) from a Manchester vantage point. In a new sense it still reflects the condition of England, but now through the lens of the television camera; under the intelligent leadership of Sidney Bernstein, Granada Television, operating from Manchester, has given the English indelible images of themselves from the sooty saga of *Coronation Street* through the aristocratic annals of *Brideshead Revisited* to its magisterial account of the Raj in *The Jewel in the Crown*.

It was in Manchester that Miss Horniman used a Victorian tea fortune to pioneer the concept of repertory theatre; here that Sir Charles Hallé lived and worked for nearly half a century, bequeathing his name to one of the country's best orchestras. It was in Manchester that the Victorian novelist Mrs Gaskell settled with her husband, minister of Cross Street Unitarian Chapel; here that Charlotte Brontë* visited her and began *Jane Eyre*; here that her friend Charles Dickens* gave some of his greatest public readings. The university could do little for the God-intoxicated, drug-dependent poet Francis Thompson, who failed his medical examinations three times; but under L.B. Namier it acquired a world reputation for history. Manchester Grammar School has long been an intellectual power-house where clever boys could win their way, however poor (and sometimes not so poor: Michael Marks and his brother-in-law Israel Sieff, of Marks and Spencer*, were both there).

'I came to love Manchester as I have known and loved no other city,' wrote the novelist Howard Spring, for sixteen years a *Manchester Guardian* staffer. Manchester is the Dumble of Mrs Gaskell's *Cranford* and the Doomington of Louis Golding's *Magnolia Street*. Neither writer would recognise the modern city with its high-rise office blocks, swanky shopping precincts, and international airport. London is now only two hours forty minutes away by inter-city express rail: still, we must trust, not near enough to drown out the city's idiosyncratic and independent voice in England's life.

Marks and Spencer 'Don't ask the price, it's a penny' was the slogan with which Michael Marks, a Polish refugee with scant command of English, opened his stall in Leeds market just a hundred years ago. Today the wonderstore has 262 shops in the UK and eight in France, Belgium and Ireland. They pull in a net trading profit of very nearly a million each. M and S are top of the shops not just for princesses and tourists (some of whom are not as meticulous as they might be in shelling out their shekels for what they've bought) but also with housewives and teenagers. They sell a third of all the bras and nightdresses bought in the UK; half of all the slips. They are the country's largest fishmongers and sell a million chickens a week. Their Marble Arch store is listed in the *Guinness Book of Records* as having the fastest-moving stock in the world. And so on.

Just one family have guided the fortunes of M and S for their first century and one man, Simon Marks, Michael's son, was at the helm for nearly half that century. It was his innate flair that shaped the characteristic M and S strategies: tight control of costs, an insistence on quality, and a formidable control of the merchandise. Cannily, they have never actually owned a factory. Being an M and S manufacturer has never been a bed of roses; but fifty of them have been suppliers for over forty years and have their Rolls-Royces to prove it.

M and S are also renowned for being years ahead of their time as employers. During the thirties, Simon Marks and his brother-in-law Israel Sieff discovered that a salesgirl in one of their stores was working through her lunch break because she couldn't afford a meal. There and then they began subsidised lunches: today they cost the girls 30p and the chairman of M and S, Michael's grandson, Marcus Sieff, eats the going lunch at whichever store he is in that day. Indeed, the hungry shopgirl set M and S on the way to becoming a minor welfare state: doctors, dentists and chiropodists visit stores regularly; all female staff are encouraged to have cervical smears and breast screening; hairdos are done in the lunch hour with time off in lieu.

M and S mania for hygiene brought one unexpected snag when they opened in Paris. The French salesgirls were put through the usual drill: no cooking if you have a cold, rings off before you touch food, and a constant supply of fresh paper towels instead of the customary bacillus-ridden kitchen towels. The girls then went home and began to criticise their mothers. Soon M and S were inundated with furious letters, all with the same livid theme: how dare you call me a slut? M and S lived to fight another day: indeed their store in the Boulevard Haussman now holds the French record for turnover per square metre. And so on. Next stop for the gentle giant: America.

Marmalade It does not taste right on anything but toast, and at any time but breakfast*. To take it with butter as well is a comparatively modern function of affluence – see A.A. Milne's poem *The King's Breakfast,* where the dairymaid tells the Alderney cow not to forget the butter for the royal slice of bread and the animal replies sleepily: 'You'd better tell His Majesty / That many people nowadays / Like marmalade instead.' That was in 1924. Marmalade (to be truthful) began its triumphal march in Scotland, where a canny Dundee housewife called Janet Keiller boiled a consignment of bitter Seville oranges from a sheltering ship into orange jam and found it so popular that her husband launched the firm which still bears his name. Within a century two other Scottish houses followed suit: Baxter's of Speyside with their distinctive whisky marmalade; and Robertson's of Paisley with their clear jelly and fine peel which every Englishman knows as Golden Shred. In England it was Sarah Jane Cooper, wife of an Oxford grocer, who first began to make the coarse, thick, dark marmalade which undergraduates delighted to serve at their gargantuan Victorian brekkers and which were to go with Scott to the Antarctic – as well as to Buckingham Palace in consignments of twenty-four jars. Cooper's also made their marmalade in specially grand pots for VIP passengers on the old British Overseas Airways; an indulgence that has long since gone. All the same, marmalade still conveys the very faint sense of privilege at a price everyone can afford and remains the bitter-sweet début to the English day.

Marques   Originally a licence for piracy bestowed by the sovereign, marque has denoted for much of the twentieth century a make of high-performance motorcar. Any discussion of the great English marques must begin with the fabled prewar Bentleys, victors at the Le Mans twenty-four-hour race in 1927-8-9-30, driven by a small group of wealthy *aficionados* led by Woolf Barnato and known as the Bentley boys. It would also have to include the chain-driven Frazer-Nash, the Alvis Speed 20 with the famous chrome exhaust down the side, the long, elegant Lagonda, the nippy, early MGs (notably the K3 with front blower), the quick, suave Riley, and the pretty little Morgan 4-4. All these grand old marques are now collector's items and command very high prices. At Christie's recently a tiny 1932 MG Midget J-2 type two-seater, which had cost £199 when new, was knocked down for £14,000. As it sparkled from the closed-circuit television in the saleroom, everyone there cheered it to the echo. It had become a work of art. See also *Aston Martin, Jaguar, Rolls-Royce*.

Mate   In the winter of 1927-8 the young George Orwell*, only six years out of Eton* and full of an aching need to expiate the exploitation, as he saw it, practised by his class on the poor, got together with some difficulty a set of ragged clothes and sallied out into the East End to see the working class as they really were. 'Presto!' he wrote later, 'in the twinkling of an eye, so to say, I had become one of them. My frayed and out-of-elbow jacket was the badge and advertisement of my class, which was their class. It made me of like kind, and in place of the fawning and too-respectful attention I had hitherto received, I now shared with them a comradeship. The man in corduroy and dirty neckerchief no longer addressed me as "sir" or "governor". It was "mate" now, and a fine and hearty word, with a tingle to it, and a warmth and gladness which the other term does not possess.'

The fine and hearty word is still mainly working-class, but is increasingly used by disc jockeys and media people to denote a slightly jokey chum, or even, in the plural, an entire audience. Tacked on to expletives it adds derision, as in 'Up yours, mate' (see under *Up*).

Maugham, Somerset (1874-1965)   'I have noticed that when someone asks for you on the telephone and, finding you out, leaves a message begging you to call him up the moment you come in, as it's important, the matter is more often important to him than to you.' With this enchanting *aperçu* Maugham launches us into the thrall of *Cakes and Ale*, the most delicious and malicious novel in his *oeuvre*. The man on the telephone was the egregious popular novelist Alroy Kear, and the opening twelve pages of the book one of the most sustained exercises in character demolition English writing can offer.

Hugh Walpole, the fashionable thirties novelist, sat up late with an early proof copy of *Cakes and Ale* so transfixed with horror at the mirror image of himself in it that he eventually slid to the floor prostrate with cramp. Maugham denied that he had sat for Kear; but owned up when Walpole was dead. The passage catches Maugham at his most characteristic and effective: the observation is microscopic, the workmanship is scrupulous, the tone is polished, and the invitation to read on irresistible.

It is often observed of Maugham that he won all the glittering prizes except the palm the critics throw, and it is true that some ignored or dismissed him (three key books on the modern novel failed to mention him at all).

Yet he had a lifelong champion in Desmond MacCarthy; Harold Nicolson thought he had been consistently underrated, and Cyril Connolly claimed he was the greatest living short-story writer. The plays that first brought him fame (he had four running at one time in Edwardian London) are now period pieces and the mystical preoccupation of some novels like *The Razor's Edge* may no longer convince. Perhaps he did fail to push out the boundaries of technique like Joyce or to exploit the nuances of character like James; perhaps his world is dissolving and his position square. None of this matters a jot. The man was a born *storyteller*: ask the readers who bought 64 million copies of his books.

Mews   If you want a shorthand account of what has been happening to the kaleidoscope of class in England, take a walk one morning round some of the six hundred mews of London. Originally they were built for servants – specifically, for the coachmen and grooms, their wives, children, and all the tack essential to the servicing of the horses in great London houses as the city sprawled westwards. Since the land in the path of that great drive west lay in the hands of some dozen or so hugely wealthy landowners it was possible for the new squares and crescents to be laid out in coherent blocks, with the rows of mews lying to the rear and below the big houses. Teeming with life and jingling with the sounds of spit and polish, they nevertheless belied their romantic externals by an absence of light, space, drains and water that rendered them pools of pestilence. Because nobody else then wanted them much, many became small workshops or ateliers, thus reinforcing their romantic if un-hygienic charm. As the horse began to give way to the car around the turn of the century, the first garages began to appear in the mews and continue there to this day, though often now converted into extra bedrooms. Then, even before the First World War, as taxes began to bite, the idea of the tarted-up, de-loused mews as a fun place for the well-to-do to have a *pied-à-terre* began to take shape. The inter-war years saw this notion spread until today few of the gallant six hundred retain many of their original inhabitants. Instead, they have become showcases of bourgeois chic; patchworks of window boxes and avocado doors. The charms of the mews are obvious: cobbled streets, little or no passing traffic, access to fashionable London, the chance to own a small house rather than rent a flat, and the sense of slightly raffish fun they purvey. In being gentrified though, they tend to lose the children and artisans who gave them their colour and vivid social mix. Just as the poor have been dispossessed of their cottages in the village*, so they have been eased out of their mews in the city. Nevertheless, the survival of the London mews does provide a warren of secret escapes and vistas of sudden surprise to the perceptive stroller, and helps to make London still the most civilised city in the world.

The Midlands   Sodden and unkind, said Hilaire Belloc, in the only memorable intrusion they make under that name into English poetry. In English prose they are somewhat better served: George Eliot's great novel *Middlemarch* is based on her life at Coventry, much of D.H. Lawrence's fiction is set around Nottingham, where he grew up, and the work of H.E. Bates is firmly rooted in the Nene Valley of Northampton-shire.

All his life the great Samuel Johnson* pronounced 'where' like fear and 'punch' as poonch: he was born at Lichfield, twelve miles from Birmingham*. Anyone who has heard Bernard Miles read Shakespeare as he would have read it himself will remember the frisson at realising that England's greatest poet did not speak like Olivier* or Gielgud but like any other son of Warwickshire: that is, in what is to us now a broad Midland dialect.

Yet the Midlands remain too wide and vague an idea to have any clear identity in the English mind. The *OED* recognises the difficulty by awarding them one of its clumsiest and most long-winded definitions: 'The counties south of the Humber and Mersey and north of the Thames, except Norfolk, Suffolk, Essex, Middlesex, Hertfordshire, Gloucestershire, and the counties bordering on Wales.'

A simpler way to put it might be to say anywhere within commuting distance of Birmingham. But Birmingham has its own distinct life. Since the Midlands are within such easy reach of London, no separate, modern Midlands school of politics, literature or art is discernible; though there are clusters of good poets from the Potteries (John Wain, Charles Tomlinson, Philip Oakes) they really are part of a separate tradition stemming from the great novels of Arnold Bennet, born at Stoke.

Perhaps the remarkable poetry of Philip Larkin*, heir apparent to the Laureate, and a son of Coventry, will help a discernible Midlands school emerge. But it has not happened yet.

Milkman He is an ambivalent, indeed protean figure in English life, representing as he does probity, enterprise, trust, efficiency but sometimes far more *risqué* values. In the first place, the very sight of milk bottles on English doorsteps still surprises foreign visitors. Not even in great market societies like America is the daily pinta delivered daily to each door. And even if it were, would it not be stolen? And even if not stolen, would it not suggest to thieving eyes that the occupants are away and the house open for the taking? And even if the thieves were baffled by the plethora of pintas, on what trust would the milkman take it that his customers will pay later? Alas, the old verities are crumbling, and in some deprived parts of England milkmen now deliver only in return for milk tokens bought in advance. Yet the milkman remains a shining exemplar of the capitalist system, acting as a mobile retailer and nowadays diversifying into bread, biscuits, tea, coffee, cereals, orange juice, eggs, butter, potatoes and, most recently, wine. Still, the very ease and authority of the milkman's penetration into the Englishman's hearth and home does raise certain ribald questions; in the great subterranean folklore of England the milkman typically figures as the rotten sod who put the wife in the family way. While hard logic will suggest that few milkmen would have time for this kind of dalliance on their daily rounds, the sheer numbers of housewives seen each day may have laid temptation at certain doors, as it were. The upshot is that no one treats the English milkman with quite that *gravitas* which is his due.

Money Any Englishman of middling years has seen a melancholy decline in the pound. It now stands at one twentieth of its 1938 value, and though its decline may have slowed a little recently, it has by no means ceased. Any Englishman who can remember the thirties can remember when one pound equalled five dollars; and during the 1939-45 war it still equalled four. Then came the trauma of the Stafford Cripps devaluation in 1949 when overnight it was slashed to $2.80. Yet that is twice its dollar value at the time of writing and parity is clearly only just round the corner.

At the same time the Englishman has had to adjust to a world where, far from belonging to the richest nation in the world he now ranks in income terms fifteenth, trailing far behind not only the evident giants like the United States, Germany and Japan, but well behind too such comparative monetary tiddlers as Norway and Denmark. The average Englishman, in short, is now just about as well off as the average Austrian.

Such income as the English have, however, is more fairly distributed than before the war. A miner is now three times as well off in real terms, while graduate schoolmasters have just held their own, and civil servants enjoy only three quarters of their prewar purchasing power.

Yet the English still look wealthy on average in world terms, with each adult owning more than £4,000 in land and buildings, £1,700 in insurance policies, £740 in building societies and £450 in shares.

Perhaps unexpectedly, the greatest advance has been in the income of the working woman. Thus in industry her weekly earnings, though still trailing well behind those of men (£84 a week against £137) are dramatically up on 1938. In that year she earned £1.63.

Motorway Each has its own character. The M1 is a pig of a road: ugly, bad-tempered, treacherous. The M2 is a good-natured road, leading to Dover* and to the delights of abroad. The M3 is a placid, relaxed, under-used road leading to the medieval magic of Winchester* and, for those who can run to it, Southampton and the QE2 (see *The Queens*). The M4, highway to Bath* and Bristol, starts anxiously as its heavy load debouches from Hammersmith, but grows carefree once past London Airport, swinging by the Marlborough Hills into Wales* and (one day) to the Atlantic.

The M5 is a blessing, for it siphons off some of the worst of the

Gadarene rush to the west each summer, though not nearly enough; the M6 is too narrow round Birmingham* and overloaded with thundering HGVs, though it grows light-hearted and indeed beautiful as it threads its way through the Lake District. Perhaps the most exhilarating English motorway of all, though, is the M40, slicing dramatically through the Chilterns like the autoroute to the Midi and then swooping down to Oxford* and the Cotswolds*. There will be many more motorways, each establishing its distinctive mood; thus the M25, when complete, will allow the English to belt in a great liberated arc round London* without slogging through it, if they are so inclined.

Though motorway melancholia and even motorway madness have been identified, and though motorway cafés are nodal points of modern desolation, it is well to contemplate the alternative. Without motorways, old roads like the A1 and A4 would by now have become infernos. As it is they are, on the whole, pleasant options for the unhurried, restoring some sense of how it must have felt to have motored in uncluttered England before the war.

Mummy   The word used by boys up to about seven and a very few upper-class grown men in England to describe their mothers. It is also the word used by most girls from the middle of the middle class upwards, and here lies a celebrated piece of arcane English social lore; for the words 'Mummy and Daddy' do not mean just what they say but are a class indicator signifying the kind of parents who would drive a Rover, have a cottage in the country, and give dinner parties.

Mummy and Daddy may be dearly loved by their daughters, but not by playwrights like John Osborne, whose Jimmy Porter in *Look Back in Anger* vented all his pent-up social rage against Alison's Mummy, 'an overfed, overprivileged old bitch'; though when Daddy enters the action he turns out to be rather gentle and *sympathique:* 'He likes you,' Alison tells her father, 'because he can feel sorry for you.'

Mummy and Daddy will also not do in the international pop esperanto spoken by all the young, and may therefore be doomed. After all, every Englishman has a Queen Mum; a Queen Mummy would be an excruciating embarrassment. Mama and Papa are the terms used by the royals themselves and by naturalised Englishmen who started life in Central Europe, but sound affected from an indigenous Englishman. Nevertheless, he still feels a bit self-conscious just saying Mum and Dad. Here is another hole in the language (see also *Afters*) that badly needs filling.

Music *Das Land ohne Musik* was the title of a celebrated German book, branding England: the land without music. That was never true, and today, when London* is the undisputed musical capital of the world, it is evident balderdash. On any given night, more music is made in London than anywhere in the world. The South Bank alone can offer fourteen concerts during a single weekend; and this before we even consider the Royal Albert Hall, the Wigmore Hall, St John's Smith Square and, now, the Barbican. Nor should we forget the opera on offer not only in Covent Garden, but also at the Coliseum, Sadler's Wells, and now overflowing into the Dominion and Bloomsbury theatres. Then there is music in the cathedrals, the churches, the colleges and the academies – but the argument needs no further pressing; it is a musical cornucopia.

Why will any young foreign musician make London the first place in which to make his bow? Not simply because of the great spectrum of venues we have noted, but also because he is far more likely to be dealing with honest impresarios (it is hard to get a fee out of Madrid), and because he will be assessed by the best music critics in the world. Translate a review by Desmond Shawe-Taylor, David Cairns, Andrew Porter or Felix Aprahamian into French and it will make perfect sense; translate the sort of prose poem that passes for music criticism in *Le Monde* into English and it will read like gibberish. Since a new young artist wants his notices to be immediately intelligible anywhere in the world, he will rather they emanate from England.

It is a sad truth in view of all this excellence that four of the five resident orchestras in London (more than any other capital except Tokyo) are in the hands of foreign conductors, while even the BBC Orchestra under John Pritchard is conducted by a wide range of foreign visitors. Meantime, excellent conductors like Andrew Davis and Sir Colin Davis flourish abroad. It was truly said that a prophet is not without honour save in his own country.

'Extraordinary how potent cheap music is,' wrote Noël Coward* in *Private Lives*. He should have known, for he wrote much of it himself; from the hummable sentiment of 'I'll See You Again', and 'London Pride' to the astringent cynicism of 'Don't Put Your Daughter on the Stage, Mrs Worthington' and 'The Stately Homes of England'. He wrote in a rich vernacular tradition derived from the English music-hall ('Any Old Iron', 'Boiled Beef and Carrots', 'My Old Dutch'); from the vast subterranean musical lore of the services ('Bless 'em All', 'Tipperary'); and from the cognate world of sport ('You'll Never Walk Alone', 'Abide With Me'). This last song started life as a hymn, but the ecclesiastical influence on popular music is now small, and the melodies (if such they be) of the modern young in England are inspired by mega-powered pop groups like Duran Duran ('Rio', 'The Reflex') and, though they are now becoming part of pop-history, the Rolling Stones ('Brown Sugar', 'Jumping Jack Flash') and the Beatles ('Yesterday', 'Love Me Do'). Indeed, far from finding England a land without music, the average Englishman may be forgiven for feeling sometimes that his country has given birth to rather too much.

Nanny When Sebastian Flyte first takes Charles Ryder to his parents' house at the opening of *Brideshead Revisited* (see also under *Waugh*) it is, he says, to see a friend of his called Hawkins. In the upshot this turns out to be Nanny Hawkins: '. . . she was fast asleep. Long hours of work in her youth, authority in her middle years, repose and security in her age, had set their stamp on her lined and serene face.'

She has, in effect, become Sebastian's mother; the member of his family he loves most. The scene could be multiplied thousands of times; for the Nanny Hawkinses of England have gone to the ends of the earth to bring up the children of Saudi Arabian sheiks, Portuguese sherry patriarchs, Indian maharajahs and uncountably rich Texans. To all these exotic settings they brought their traditional virtues: common sense, order, cleanliness, firmness, sweetness and total dependability. A casual glance at *The Times** any morning will immediately show how that accreted, gilt-edged reputation will still earn any proper English nanny a top billet anywhere in the world.

'Other people's babies, that's my life; mother to dozens but nobody's wife,' said the old song. No longer; today's nanny may well wear jeans, drive a mini, have a bloke, and be merely filling in an agreeable few years working in *grand luxe* before marrying, and having her own children. Never mind: while she does her nannying she knows that she belongs to an unassailable elite: for, thanks to the remembered legions of Nanny Hawkinses, for people who must have nannies, nothing but an English nanny will do.

National Trust It does not win all its battles. It lost, for example, its fight to buy Land's End; someone simply bid more. Still, in its hundred years it has shown a pretty sturdy independence and formidable growth. Despite the 'national' in the title it is a private body, financed entirely by what it can earn, though with special dispensation under two Acts of Parliament to avoid alienation of the enchanted pieces of England, Wales and Northern Ireland it has acquired over the hundred years. (The Scots work separately.)

It began in 1885 when three Victorian philanthropists got together to protect the open spaces of England against the incursion of the dark satanic mills. That year it had 100 members; in 1926 still only 1,000; reached 100,000 in 1961 and the million in 1981. Now it is the country's third biggest landowner, ranking only after state and Crown.

There is one snag to such vertiginous success; you can actually have too many people coming round your stately homes: six and a half million visited National Trust properties in 1982. As long ago as 1947 it warned that too many visitors would destroy what people had come to see. Some of it had been destroyed already: in a separate campaign, Operation Neptune, the Trust estimated that of our 3,000-mile coastline, some 1,000 miles were already spoilt, another 1,000 of no special value, while the last 1,000 were of the greatest beauty and should be preserved at all cost. Today it owns nearly half of that most precious thousand miles; not to mention just on half a million acres of land, eighty-four stately homes, one hundred and five gardens, twenty-four castles, twenty-two villages, eleven barns, seventeen dovecotes and more than a thousand farms.

So much is beyond debate. However, the National Trust, besides preserving the best of our industrial archaeology, our Roman antiquities and prehistoric sites, does something else: it has devised and perfected a machinery through which the owner of a great English house can go on living in it. He must open to the public in certain agreed ways and he must, for example, see to it that bright sunlight does not get at his heirlooms; but within the civilised rules he can enjoy his inheritance in the style to which he has been accustomed; or at least a semblance of it.

The servants may be thin on the ground, but when his daughter has a twenty-first he can give it in style, with discos thumping in the ancestral courtyards and fireworks fizzing over the Adam porticos. He no longer owns the bricks and mortar; on the other hand he no longer has to worry about their upkeep. Thus the English upper class has yet again been saved by the bell.

Critics of the system will have to come up with a better one: but the stately home as museum or mausoleum frankly fails to attract most

English people of whatever political persuasion. They would rather see them lived in. Once again the English genius for compromise seems maddeningly to have carried the day.

Navy 'The royal navy of England hath ever been its greatest defence and ornament; it is its ancient and natural strength, the floating bulwark of the island.' So wrote the great lawyer William Blackstone, and in the eighteenth century there was some truth in his brave words. Through the long Pax Britannia which stretched from the Napoleonic wars to the beginning of the First World War, though, the navy developed a fatal *hubris*. It was encouraged. When the Americans began to build their own navy in the 1890s, the first of their new armoured ships, the *New York*, even had an admiral's walk at the stern, a quite unnecessary luxury and a direct compliment to the Nelsonic tradition of the Royal Navy.

When the great British fleet began its massive assault on the Dardanelles in March 1915, wrote James Morris in *Farewell the Trumpets*, the Turkish gunners saw 'the towering grey forms of sixteen capital ships. In the van was the splendid *Queen Elizabeth*, the largest warship ever to enter the Mediterranean ... around and behind her sailed a chivalry of warships ...'

But the vaulting plan turned into a nightmare shambles '...and instantly a myth was shattered. The Royal Navy was not omnipotent, and gunboat diplomacy, here carried to its ultimate expression, was no longer sufficient to discipline the natives.'

Next year at the Battle of Jutland Admiral Beatty saw two of his finest ships, the *Indefatigable* and the *Queen Mary,* sent to the bottom of the Atlantic after being blown to pieces by direct hits. 'There seems to be something wrong with our bloody ships this morning, Chatfield,' he remarked to his flag captain. A quarter of a century later the battle cruiser *Hood* blew up after a shell from the *Bismarck* had found exactly the same fault in her construction. Fifteen hundred men died; three survived.

'So roll on the *Nelson*, the *Rodney, Renown*', went the lugubrious old sweat's new verse to *Bless 'em All*, 'You can't have the *Hood* 'cos the bastard's gone down.' Seventy years later in the Falklands conflict, British ships were turned into infernos when hit; the electronic gear they carried on their decks proved to be lethally inflammable. The chaps did well; they always have. But yet again, there was something wrong with our bloody ships.

Neasden Literally a nose-shaped hill, and until 1876 a hamlet containing three or four large houses, a few cottages and a smithy. In that year houses were built for workers of the new Metropolitan Railway; then two waves of new building followed the extension of the line and the building of the North Circular road respectively. It has thus become an archetypal London suburb, faceless and formless. Perhaps, though, it was the accident of its name which led *Private Eye** to choose it as its example of, not so much suburbia, as what our American cousins would call Nowheresville. Many *Eye* readers who live outside London even now do not credit its undoubted reality. It has one unexpected claim to fame as the birthplace of Twiggy.

Neighbours To Jesus of Nazareth the term had a universal flavour, connoting all one's breathing, suffering fellow human beings; to Franklin D. Roosevelt a geo-political context, embracing as he did in his celebrated good-neighbor policy all of South America. On an everyday level, the most famous of all neighbours this century have been the Joneses, the notional people we have living next door with whom we feel obliged to keep up. They have been a powerful tool in the hands of the consumer society, compelling Englishmen and Americans to buy the new consumer durables – cars, lawn mowers, washing machines – which are the outward and visible sign that they have not fallen behind in the great race. Yet the word has a derisive undertow: for are the Joneses really worth keeping up with? The Jonesian notion is essentially a function of suburban sprawl, an unloved child of ribbon development; and needs garden fences to flourish properly; flat-dwellers on the whole feel no need to emulate their neighbours whether Joneses or anybody else; while the upper class speak rather grandly of a neighbour when they mean someone who lives in the same county ('our neighbours are coming to dinner' can involve a round trip for them of fifty miles).

Nelson In darts, according to the indispensable compendium *Hoyle's Games*, the number 111 is known as Lord Nelson. This is 'for a reason that is probably known to most darts players' and, we trust, will be equally clear to worldly readers of this companion who are familiar with his reputation both as sailor and lover.

Nosh From the Yiddish for a snack, now widely used for any sort of meal, but especially either an informal one or in deprecating description of a formal one. It entered the language suddenly in the fifties and, as with so many Yiddish words, supplanted previous idiom by its innate strength. Similarly with 'nosher' (usually a hearty eater) and 'noshery' for any place selling food, though originally a delicatessen. The Yiddish comes in turn from the German *naschen,* to nibble or eat on the sly, and an element of onomatopoeia probably contributes to the word's comedy and popularity.

Oak 'Heart of oak are our ships, heart of oak are our men.' About the ships, at least, there can be no doubt. With oak from the New Forest they built at Buckler's Hard some of the great ships that fought at Trafalgar: *Illustrious* with its seventy-four guns, *Agamemnon* with forty-four and the smaller *Swiftsure* and *Euryalus*. Long before that they had used the Forest oak for the ships that took on the Armada. Strongest, most durable and long-lived of trees, the oak stands well in the English countryside; and sometimes the sheer vastness of its age leaves the onlooker awestruck.

At Knightwood Oak, for instance, not far from Lyndhurst in the New Forest, stand three giant trees. Each is specially mentioned in the Ordnance Survey map; but the Knightwood Oak itself is by far the most stupendous of the three. It is thought to be among the oldest and largest oaks in England.

'This great tree was here, though no more than a seedling', wrote Brian Vesey-Fitzgerald in his *Hampshire,* 'when Stephen was ruling a troubled kingdom. It was here a mere boy when John was signing the Magna Carta . . . It watched its friends fall before the fury of the storm and the cold precision of the axe . . . In its old age it heard of Dunkirk and Tobruk . . . It has seen kings come and go and dictators rise and fall. It has watched year upon year men make love in just the same way and in much the same words . . . And each year in October its leaves come spinning to the ground. They have done so now maybe eight hundred times.' He concluded that it would doubtless still be there long after his own time; in which assumption he was assuredly right.

The OED *The Oxford English Dictionary* was described by Arnold Bennett as the longest sensational serial ever written. It took just on fifty years to compile. Its twelve volumes contained 414,825 words and the type in which they were set if laid end to end would have extended to 178 miles. It is not only the greatest dictionary of English both in scale and content but has few rivals in other languages. There are two American dictionaries but they deal only with the distinctively American branch of the language. American English is, so to speak, a vast dialect of English. However, there is a price to be paid for such daunting labour. One lexicographer employed by the Oxford University Press cut his throat. Another finished up describing himself as the Seer of Barras, and writing an endless epic poem in which Kenneth Sisam, his boss at the OUP, appeared as Anti-Christ.

When the *OED* was finally completed in 1928 it was £375,000 in the red and had of necessity left out all the new words that had entered the language during the half century it was in the making. So a *Supplement* was published in 1933. Another half a century on, and a torrent of further new words spawned in that tumultuous era clamoured for admission. So in 1957 a thirty-four-year-old New Zealander and former Rhodes Scholar called Robert Burchfield was given the task of editing a new *Supplement*. One of his great predecessors at the *OED* had remarked that lexicography is best done on the kitchen table. Burchfield began with not much more: a small room in a modest villa in a shabby Oxford back street, one male assistant, three young women graduates, and a secretary.

He planned to publish in 1967; at the time of writing he proposes to give the world his fourth and final volume in 1985, so he will be eighteen years late; not that this matters tuppence in the world of the lexicographer. The last full edition of the two-volume *Shorter OED* appeared in 1944; the *Compact OED,* which is the entire dictionary reduced micrographically to one volume and read with a magnifying glass, in 1971. The latest *Concise OED,* published in 1982 and containing 75,000 definitions, is thus for the moment the only complete Oxford account of modern English yet in print.

It is the work of an amazing polymath called John Sykes, a mathematician with a doctorate in astrophysics, who translates textbooks from twenty languages and has won *The Times*/Cutty Sark crossword contest four times in a row, giving away his prize of a holiday for two in Monte Carlo and half a gallon of whisky. Had he been receiving a normal author's royalties instead of a straight salary, his income from the OUP would have been some £250,000 a year. But then fleshly pleasures and the making of great dictionaries do not seem to sit well together.

Kenneth Sisam, Secretary to the Delegates of the OUP and the man who appeared as Anti-Christ in the poem, had an aversion to food. He would avoid lunch altogether and resolutely manoeuvred to avoid dining out. Travel abroad was especially hazardous for him, and in America he went in terror of hospitality. Nemesis overtook him, however, in the First World War when he was sent to the Ministry of Food and appointed Director of Bacon Contracts. It looks as if the old rule of thumb about the best dictionaries being made on kitchen tables should not be flouted with impunity.

The Old Boy Network   Not to be confused with the old school tie*, though those who wear the one may well belong to the other. Strictly, it was the name for wartime army radio communications linking squadron, regiment and brigade, and went into action whenever those using it were on close enough terms enough to call one another old boy. Then, the old boy net was used for cutting red tape and getting things done. In peace, however, it has taken on a more sinister connotation: the invisible web of connection between those who have been at the same school or university, used to ensure that those who are part of it get the best jobs.

The left see this network as a lively argument for the abolition of the public schools. Without doubt the old boy network used to work, particularly in arcane and unreconstructed areas of business like the wine trade and the Stock Exchange.* Increasingly though, proponents of the old boy network begin to sound like classic conspiracy theorists; relying as they do on the basic principle that if you are an Etonian you are more likely to give another Etonian a job. Such theorists do not know their Etonians, who must be numbered among the most ruthless and unsentimental products of English society. Network theory also works on the naive assumption that being, say, an old Harrovian will help you get – and keep – the kinds of high-voltage job that matter in modern society: video editor, say, computer programmer, or finance director. It postulates, moreover, that there are plenty of plush jobs nowadays which, once occupied by an Etonian or Harrovian backside, are permanently inviolate to threat or change. Such romantic and primitive theories of modern business take little account of the *Sturm und Drang* to which its denizens must be subjected. Nor do they allow for the fish-eye which will be bestowed on old boy arguments by our American, German, Japanese or EEC overlords. When Margaret Thatcher formed her government after the 1983 election, not a single Etonian sat on the front bench in the Commons. Can the network be on the blink?

The Old School Tie Formerly worn as a tribal badge to show where you stood in the complicated hierarchy of the English class structure. Even then, however, it was more of an insider's game than a public display system: how many Englishmen would know an Old Sedberghian from an Old Salopian by his neckwear?

The hard truth is that only certain specialised races like prep-school masters and club porters can recognise many ties beyond the Etonian blue stripe and the MCC egg and tomato, and even these celebrated ties are increasingly worn more in a spirit of larkiness than real camaraderie. Most Old Etonians who sport their school tie look increasingly bogus; most men who wear the MCC tie except on Test days at Lord's* are increasingly suspect.

Perhaps very conservative and elderly men wear the Brigade of Guards tie in the country as a tribal totem; but up in London members of the Garrick who sport the pale salmon and cucumber club stripes do so mainly for fun. It must be faced that ties, blazers and crests have filtered down to every bowls club in the land; and the upper class have therefore had to find a new uniform to distinguish themselves: dark blue blazers with no distinguishing marks at all, 'cavalwy twill twousers' and chukka boots.

Olivier, Laurence (born 1907) There will be few Englishmen who carry no image of Laurence Olivier: brimming with brooding power under his pudding-basin haircut in the film of *Hamlet*; the haunted, well-bred quarry of a dead bitch as Max de Winter in Hitchcock's *Rebecca*; paddling the stage with his splayed walk as the Moor in *Othello*; wheedling, nudging, canoodling and camping his way through the seedy title role in John Osborne's *The Entertainer*; upstaging all in sight as the wily, cagey, testy old barrister in John Mortimer's TV play *A Voyage Round My Father*. Hemingway once described courage as grace under pressure. Anyone who saw Olivier in that last role, in his seventy-fifth year, survivor of cancer, thrombosis, pneumonia, piles and gout, but still squeezing the last ounce from his part as if he were twenty-five, will know exactly what Hemingway meant.

Orwell, George (1903-50) If his name keeps recurring in this book, it is not only because it is published in 1984. His life and work reverberate, casting deeper and wider ripples as the years pass. Why? Because few Englishmen indeed have reached so hard for the truth and, every now and then, found it. No Englishman can put his hand on his heart and say that no word of Orwell reaches him, or concerns him, or describes him.

Orwell saw into the heart of England in a way that no writer had done before or has since.

He achieved this extraordinary vision by moving through the invisible barriers of English life – walls of class, income, lifestyle, time and place. There have been Etonians before who have become doctors or clergymen, politicians or lawyers; jobs that by their nature require and assume some contact with the poor and the disadvantaged. It is hard to think of another who not merely knew the outer perimeters of poverty, hunger and want, but also lived right inside them.

Orwell did not deplore poverty; he was poor; he did not simply bewail the fate of the down and out; he was a down and out. Nor was it just the question of a rough weekend in pursuit of copy: he knew what it was not to have enough for a decent meal night after night, week after week, month after month. He knew how the poor died because he had been in a hospital for down and outs and seen them horrendously die; he knew what it meant to earn eight shillings net for picking hops sixty hours a week because he had done it himself.

He had got inside the skin of his suffering brother men as few saints have succeeded in doing, and there is something of the secular saint about his denial of self and messianic vision both of a lost world of innocence and a new world to come in which our destinies will be worked out.

It has been said of Orwell that if he had died half a dozen years earlier he would have been a minor cult figure but no more. If he had died before he had written *Animal Farm*, this would undoubtedly have been true; for it is on the power of this meticulously worked out allegory on the bitter fruit of revolution, and the sombre magnificence of his minatory fable predicating one possible nightmare future, *1984*, that his world fame rests.

Nevertheless, there would remain a whole clutch of vividly etched documents: slightly polemicised reportage which makes a collective testament to the mean and nasty thirties: notably *Down and Out in Paris and London, The Road to Wigan Pier*, and *Homage to Catalonia*.

It is not the least of Orwell's claims that his wincing honesty makes him attractive to many layers of English society; never taken in by the communists, he deeply despised what he called the pansy left: English fellow-travellers who had felt no qualms in making the transition to what he saw as no more than the mirror image of fascism (he once changed places in a restaurant so as not to look at the corrupt face of Kingsley Martin, editor of the *New Statesman*, who was deeply involved in the alliance between communism and socialism).

Yet this stance lent no comfort to the right; Orwell hated too the hidebound minds, instinctive arrogance, easy clichés and braying voices of the English ruling class. He passionately believed in England, but saw it as a family with the wrong people in charge of it. Never an easy man (he drank his tea noisily out of his saucer in the BBC canteen to show his solidarity with the working class), he was self-evidently not one either who could be bent or bought.

He was to make himself adept at a plain, vivid, colloquial style so unobtrusive that it looked artless. In this simple English he wrote books that few Englishmen will be able to open anywhere without a start of recognition; among them two masterpieces that touch men everywhere.

Ovaltine   Stood (and stands) for the innocence, comfort, wholesomeness and safety of English childhood. Originally a drink marketed by a Swiss doctor called George Wander, it was (and is) known as Ovomaltine on the Continent, but the name was shortened when it was first introduced here in 1910. Advertising was always Ovaltine's forte, and the rosy-cheeked dairymaid in the ads with her basket of fresh eggs and sheaf of barley epitomised its spirit of simple purity.

. The Ovaltiney Club, founded in 1935 and broadcasting from Radio Luxembourg every Sunday evening from 5.30 to 6 p.m. became a secret society for children, with its own badges, rule books, and inside codes: by 1939 it had five million members. The programme's signature tune, 'We are the Ovaltineys', became probably the best-known jingle in the world; and was so well embedded in the national subconscious that the company was persuaded to revive it as part of its television commercial in 1975.

Though primarily a children's drink, Ovaltine was supplied to the armed forces in both world wars. Tommies sang 'we are the Ovaltineys' as they marched, in sharp contrast to the German preference for the 'Horst Wessel Song.' It has been an official drink at Olympics since 1932, went up Everest with Sir Edmund Hillary and with Freya Stark to the Arabian desert.

It figures, needless to say, in the Betjeman* *oeuvre*: 'He gives his Ovaltine a stir, and nibbles at a *petit beurre*.' Though still sold simply as a malted food drink, its actual ingredients are somewhat more banal and clinical: barley and malt extract, to be sure, but then dried skimmed milk, sugar, whey powder, glucose syrup, vegetable fat, full cream milk powder, fat reduced cocoa, caseinates, egg powder, emulsifier, stablisers, flavouring and vitamins. The Ovaltine diarymaid still smiles winsomely out from the goo at us; and her drink still conveys instant childhood.

Oxford   It is the place where the MG was born, and penicillin first given to a patient. It is the place where the first mile was run in under four minutes, and the first six-foot high jump recorded. It is also the seat of an ancient university which has been in the wars now for seven hundred years.

In its earliest centuries a place where poor scholars went to learn Latin and make good in the Church, Oxford gradually changed into a place where young gents went to booze, wench, hunt and roister. It went to sleep in the eighteenth century and woke in the nineteenth. Even in the first decade of the twentieth century it was still, as Bernard Shaw remarked, a place for making a few scholars and a great many gentlemen. Between the world wars, though Auden*, MacNeice* and Spender* had arrived, you could still read for a pass degree or even take no degree at all. The Second World War put an end to all that and Oxford is now a very large incubator for eggheads of both sexes and all classes: Alphaville-on-Thames.

The charge of élitism remains, and will never be dismissed unless some crazed future government does actually, as has been suggested, distribute places there in some kind of mad random lottery. Even this might not be noticed: Oxford is, after all, the place where the story of *Alice in Wonderland* was first told. Television accounts of books like *Brideshead Revisited*, though no more in truth than beautifully wrought baloney, do nothing to dispel the sun-dappled myth inside every Englishman's head. Oxford is loved and loathed not simply because it has ancient buildings, priceless libraries, college autonomy and tutorial teaching, but because it is thought to have magic.

Pardon   Its cringing gentility is anathema to middle-class England, and it is the thought of their children being taught to say it (along with 'toilet' and 'pleased to meet you') that still sways some parents to choose the private rather than state sector in education. Certainly one celebrated woman writer of our era told her young son that it was a worse word to use than that other one and she no doubt meant it. It is a vivid example of how certain words, like certain names (Albert, Ada) imperceptibly fall from grace because they have been taken up by the lower middle class and are therefore NQOTD (see *Initials*).

Mr Patel   There are nine pages of Patels in the London telephone directory: not yet as many as the Smiths and Browns; but as many as the Greens. The Patels come from the Gujarati region of northwest India, and have been travellers and traders since Vasco da Gama made landfall there in the fifteenth century.

One in every six London Patels is a shopkeeper*, and there is hardly an urban street corner in England now without a Patel selling papers, sweets, cigarettes or groceries till late at night seven days a week. They thus provide a notable new dimension to the amenities of English life and many have become rich doing so. There are one hundred Gujarati millionaires in London now, most of them called Patel; and they believe there could be a thousand in another decade.

The reasons for their business success are not hard to seek. Many of them were kicked out of Uganda by Amin and have a much keener incentive to succeed than the average English shopkeeper who wants to close so that he can play darts or watch telly. Then the Patels have a formidable family structure which means any new business is backed by reservoirs of capital and labour at bargain prices from an army of brothers, sisters, uncles, aunts and cousins.

Besides, official policy under Maggie Thatcher, a shopkeeper's daughter herself, is exceedingly amiable towards small business and there is a plethora of government schemes to help Mr Patel to get started. Then again, small shops do not have to face the might of organised labour. What they do have to face is the might of Sainsbury and Waitrose, W.H. Smith and Boots; and they may survive only by offering the lure of herculean hours. Meanwhile they make an attractive contribution to English life. Many Patels are qualified well beyond their calling; and it is quite possible now to be sold your eggs by an economist or your milk by a micro-biologist.

Pets   The code-name given by the English to the animal master-race which has taken them over.

Pevsner, Sir Nikolaus (1902-83)   He came to England penniless from his native Germany in 1935. He was already a distinguished art historian, but had precious little of his new country's language at his disposal. His first published work over here was therefore stylistically somewhat rough. Yet he was soon the master of a deft and elegant English which led Colin Macinnes to rank him directly after Conrad. His magisterial *Buildings of England* – forty-six volumes written over a twenty-five year span – is full of felicities. He speaks of spare buildings, wilful buildings, playful buildings. He even gets away with naughty buildings. He found England an uncharted territory as compelling as Africa had been to Burton, Livingstone and Speke. In a real sense, he discovered English architecture.

Pheasant   There is one cardinal rule for all English pheasants: stay well away from Sandringham. It has become a tradition among Princes of Wales that each shall try to outdo his predecessor in their slaughter. The record bag there for one day was the 3,114 pheasants shot on 14 November 1896. 'I love shooting more than anything else,' wrote the future Edward VIII to his father George V in 1912.

Next year at the Beaconsfield estate of Lord Burnham, all previous royal records were shattered. As Edward later recalled: 'My left arm ached from lifting my gun, my shoulder from the recoil, and I was deaf and stunned from the banging ... when in the late afternoon the carnage stopped almost 4,000 pheasants had been killed. The bright limp carcasses were laid out in rows of 100; the whole place was littered with feathers and spent cartridges.' That day, however, his father remarked that perhaps they had gone too far.

By modern standards they assuredly had. When newspaper editors were given a stiff wigging by the Palace recently for intruding on royal privacy at Sandringham, the real reason for the Queen's concern was undoubtedly the adverse publicity elicited by the sight of her elder grandson at his first shoot. This bloody slaughter might well precipitate a future rift between the Crown and the English people, most of whom are not amused by it.

Picnics On the face of it, there is something perverse in the English predilection for picnics. If the English summer were half as bad as it is made out, picnics would be a continuing and depressing series of write-offs. That great English cookery writer Jane Grigson has actually suggested that a good English picnic should contain some kind of disaster, and certainly our literature is rich in such lovingly recalled minutiae of discomfort. John Betjeman*, for example: 'Sand in the sandwiches / Wasps in the tea / Sun on our bathing dresses heavy with the wet / Squelch of the bladder-wrack waiting for the sea / Fleas round the tamarisk, an early cigarette.' The English genius is to roll with the punches thrown by the weather and to indulge the national passion with escalating recklessness. There is indeed something very slightly unhinged about the whole exercise. The most famous picnic in English literature (the Mad Hatter's tea party) did not actually take place; and the best loved (*The Teddy Bears' Picnic*), used by the BBC* because of its range to test the sound, is one to which we have only the music; though every Englishman feels he was at it.

Celebrated in England for centuries, picnics have grown distinctly more sophisticated as the years have unrolled. When the three men in a boat of Jerome K. Jerome's immortal masterpiece picnicked by the Thames*, they did so on such fundamental fare as cold meat, tea, bread, butter and jam. When Lewis Carroll* rowed the three little Liddell girls up the river on that golden day in 1862 and first told them the story of *Alice in Wonderland* they took a picnic of cold chicken, salad, cakes and tea. This may sound well enough, but on the simple side by today's elaborate standards (when crisps and coke, bangers and biscuits would certainly be required; and where were the boiled eggs?). Interestingly, even then William Harcourt, owner of the riverside land at Nuneham, allowed people to land on Tuesdays and Thursdays and use his purpose-built picnic huts, thus foreshadowing today's faceless picnic areas.

Carroll and his friends were sufficiently informal to borrow glasses, plates, knives and forks from cottages by the riverside; compare these casual preparations with the sophisticated hamper provided by that other great river-picnicker, the Water Rat for his friend Mole in *The Wind in the Willows**. ' "There's cold chicken inside it," replied the Rat briefly, "coldtonguecoldhamcoldbeefpickledgherkinssaladfrenchrollscress sand-wichespottedmeatgingerbeerlemonadesodawater –" "Oh stop," cried the Mole in ecstasies. "This is too much!" '

Today a whole industry provides picnic hampers and fills them with even more elaborate fare than Rat could command: smoked salmon for Glyndebourne, caviare for Ascot*, strawberries for Wimbledon*, Pimm's for Henley*, and so through the whole scrumptious, lunatic cycle of the English summer*. Yet, with all its elaboration, the English picnic is essentially an informal meal taken sitting on the grass. To eat at a table like a Frenchman might well be more logical and less messy; but it would not be a *picnic*.

Pint   The Englishman has been taking his pint since time immemorial; but the written testimony goes back two and a half centuries (Henry Fielding refers to the pleasant practice in 1742). It is not so much a measure of cubic capacity as a definition of ritual – 'I'm just going out for my pint'. Around it have grown such comparatively new diversions as 'poems and pints' (when poems are read between draughts of ale*). A pint is a curiously satisfying amount of beer, and will not seem quite the same when it becomes .5683 litres.

Plonk   Yet another of those handy words that have changed their meaning. Originally rhyming slang for vin *blanc* (plinkety-plonk) it has gradually shifted its load till now it conveys to most English people cheap *red* wine. Recently, though, a new subtlety has crept in. People tend to say (have some plonk' when what is on offer is, say, fair-to-middling claret; they would not say it if offering some of the really dire red ink on sale at the very bottom of the market. This trend to defensive deprecation runs through the whole language now (see for example under *Gentleman*, which is decreasingly used seriously).

Pong   Another of those words which change meaning as they cross the Atlantic; to an American, an electronic game resembling ping-pong, played on a pinball machine or a television screen; to an Englishman, an exceedingly disagreeable smell.

Porn There are three main charges against porn: it demeans women, it incites violence, and it uglifies whatever it touches. Some defence may be mounted against the first two charges; to the third there is no answer. The porn shops have rendered Soho, once the beguiling and cosmopolitan Latin Quarter of London, a desolate enclave haunted by the unhappy customers of the now ubiquitous porn-monger. Perhaps the change was inevitable. In Orwell's *1984*, porn had replaced religion as the opiate of the masses and was called, contemptuously, prole-feed.

Portobello Road Increasingly it is becoming the true Latin Quarter of London. Its exotic name is a fortunate accident: in 1739 Admiral Vernon captured the Caribbean city of Puerto Bello from the Spanish. A number of English places were named after the victory; one was Portobello Farm and another the lane which led from it down to Notting Hill Gate.

By the early 1870s the first dealers had appeared in Portobello Lane: gypsies buying and selling horses at the nearby Hippodrome and offering herbs as a sideline. By the twenties there was a flourishing market with many of its street vendors recruited from demobilised wartime troops; but it was strictly illegal till 1927 when London County Council gave it a licence.

Today it stretches two miles and is visited by a quarter of a million people a year. Many of the vendors nowadays are actors or actresses; a stall works well with the long periods of enforced rest between roles; but there are also housewives who take a stall simply for Saturday when the street antique market is open (the fruit, vegetable and flower market is open every day of the week, and so is the bric-a-brac which stretches north above that to the Grand Union Canal).

Insiders know that the best time to be at the market is very early, before the tourists have arrived and when the dealers are trading among themselves. Anything goes here: silver, maps, porcelain, linen, lace, maps, books, dolls, glass, medals. Christian's, the delicatessen, puts its stalls outside and sells salt beef sandwiches, croissants, coffee and *geffulte fisch*.

Here you will find one of the best wine bars in London ("192"), one of the best restaurants (Monsieur Thompson), a proper bookshop (Elgin Books) and, at the southern end of the market, one of the best pubs in London (The Sun in Splendour). Poet Christopher Logue, singer George Melly, playwright Christopher Hampton and politician Roy Jenkins are all locals; among celebrated former denizens was George Orwell*, thin, ill and angry from his stint as a Burma policeman, who worked on *Down and Out in Paris and London* at 10 Portobello Road.

Post Office   Like all English institutions, it is not what it was. Though a letter now costs nearly forty times what it did when Sir Rowland Hill launched the penny post, no Englishman in his right mind banks on first-class mail arriving next morning. Nor could a master sleuth like Sherlock Holmes*, who used telegrams as a principal tool of his trade, possibly operate with a post office that now only deigns to deliver them with tomorrow's mail – whenever that might arrive.

Still, we must at least grant the post office this: it acted as patron to one English novelist of genius, Anthony Trollope, who kept up a steady output of ten thousand words a week, written while working in its hospitable maw, and to one English poet of genius, W.H. Auden*, who worked for a while with John Grierson in the GPO Film Unit. Here he turned out soundtracks for documentaries which, despite the obvious constraints of the brief, have his inimitable stamp:

'This is the night mail crossing the border / Bringing the cheque and the postal order / Letters for the rich, letters for the poor / The shop at the corner and the girl next door.' The only office space they could find for him was in the corridor with the messenger boys. 'There, on that old Post Office table,' recalled his director, Harry Watt, years later, 'he wrote the most beautiful verse.'

Priestley, J.B. (born 1894)   When someone asked C.P. Snow how a Russian wishing to understand English life at every level should go about it, he suggested reading the complete works of J.B. Priestley. Between his debut in 1922 with *Brief Diversions* through *English Journey* in 1934 to his last book, *English Humour* in 1976, Priestley has chronicled England with enormous and evident scope and relish. He is the ordinary Englishman writ large: outwardly comfortable and complacent; inwardly passionate and romantic.

He is moreover a genuine, old-fashioned man of letters with a huge range: novelist, essayist, playwright, reporter, travel writer and social commentator. His most successful novel, *The Good Companions* (1929), does not reflect him quite so fully as more complex works like *Bright Day* (1946). The solid Yorkshire persona is at odds with the experimental writer of the 'time' plays inspired by the serial universe of J.W. Dunne – *Time and the Conways, I Have Been Here Before* (both 1937) – and the quasi-surrealist morality play *Johnson Over Jordan* (1939). He would be remembered, if for nothing else, for his wartime broadcasts which equalled and perhaps sometimes outdid Winston Churchill's* in formulating the feelings and aspirations of the man in the street.

He was an articulate champion of the unemployed in the thirties and a principal advocate of nuclear disarmament in the fifties. He gave up playwriting too early (in 1963) but can always console himself with the true thought that at any single minute of the twenty-four hours some company somewhere is performing *Dangerous Corner* (1932), his most popular play.

Private Eye   Sometimes at smart parties in England you will see a figure who very slightly disturbs the bonhomie of the evening. He may well be wearing a corduroy jacket when all about him are sporting their black ties. He will sip water as the company quaff their wine: not quite in the swim yet by no means out of it either. This is Richard Ingrams, embattled editor of *Private Eye,* a puritan publication that has grown uncommonly rich and powerful by playing its hunches and living on its nerves. Intolerant and indispensable, he (and it) are skeletons at any feast nowadays. He acts out a dangerous destiny: the conscience of England.

Prole   Short for proletarian. Though widely associated with George Orwell* and *1984,* it was in fact used fifty years earlier by George Bernard Shaw*, and has always been derogatory. However, it now seems to be losing ground, probably due to the rapidly shifting shape and nature of the English working class.

Proms   Literally, concerts where the audience could walk about, but now where they stand, if they so choose, to hear good music at bargain prices. Although the first English promenade concerts were held as early as 1838, the word now instantly conveys to every Englishman the image of Sir Henry Wood. His bust is ritually enwreathed by Promenaders on the last night of the Proms each year in the sight of some 200 million television viewers, and rightly so.

He launched and conducted the new series of Proms at the old Queen's Hall in 1895, aided by a gift of £2,000 from a music-lover and throat specialist called George Clark Cathcart, who offered the money on the condition that the existing high pitch, ruinous to singers' voices, should be abandoned in favour of the lower French pitch.

Wood was a tireless champion of modern music, who played the work of Tchaikovsky, Sibelius, Strauss, Scriabin and Debussy to English audiences before they were widely known, conducted the first performances in England of Mahler's First, Fourth, Seventh and Eighth Symphonies, and introduced the music of Jánáček to the English. Every major English composer of his lifetime was performed at the Proms. He was the first conductor to introduce women to an English orchestra (in 1913). In August 1944, though now seventy-five and in failing health, he achieved his ambition of conducting the first night of his fiftieth Prom season; he died later that month.

A worthy laureate then; and if the televised second half of the last night of the Proms may well strike foreign viewers as some kind of mad football celebration scored for orchestra and massed choirs, it might be remembered that this is the culmination of an eight-week feast of music, devoured by the army of Promenaders. By most measures, it is the greatest festival of music in the world, and gives the lie yet again to the old canard that England is a land without music.

Prostitution 'There is something utterly nauseating about a system of society which pays a harlot twenty-five times as much as it pays its prime minister,' said Harold Wilson during the Christine Keeler scandal. He was not the first prime minister to take an interest in the subject. William Ewart Gladstone conducted clandestine work among fallen women, no doubt with the loftiest of motives, though now that we have access to his private diaries we can see that he probably derived a vicarious kick from his good deeds.

Victorian England was the heyday of the whore, with 80,000 and perhaps more to serve a London only half the size of the modern city. It took an eminent Victorian surgeon, William Acton, to point out to his hypocritical readers that, contrary to received opinion then, a woman on the game (to use their own time-honoured euphemism) did not invariably end up ruined; her health was often quite as good as that of a working-class mother of the same age who had all the drudgery of a Victorian family to contend with; and very often the prostitute retired and took up respectable life with no one in her new milieu being any the wiser.

Mrs Warren's Profession, the play in which Bernard Shaw put the point with brutal force, was written in 1894, but refused a licence till 1925. It is the story of a woman who, weary of working in the bar of Waterloo Station fourteen hours a day for four shillings a week and someone else's profit, decides to sell herself for her own profit. What else, she asks, are girls in society taught to do but sell themselves to some rich man? It was altogether too near the truth for comfort.

With the rise of the permissive society and the coming of the age of affluence, London no longer needs 80,000 whores; but it has no more eradicated them altogether than any other civilised society has been able to do since the dawn of history. All it has been able to do is to take them off the streets and into service flats for Arabs, clubs for northern businessmen, and the so-called massage parlours for the man in the street.

The theme of the good girl what's been ruined has given rise to much lore and a couple of memorable snatches of verse. First, Thomas Hardy* at his most wry, knowing, and worldly: ' "You left us in tatters, without shoes or socks, / Tired of digging potatoes, and spudding up docks: / And now you've gay bracelets and bright feathers three!"– / "Yes: that's how we dress when we're ruined," said she.' Then, a cheery observation from our old friend Anon*: 'When Lady Jane became a tart, / It almost broke her father's heart. / But blood is blood, and race is race, / And so, to mitigate disgrace, / He bought a most expensive beat / From Asprey's up to Oxford Street.'

Public Schools In America, Scotland* and the colonies, says the *OED*, they are schools provided at public expense and managed by public authority, to provide public and usually free education. Quite so. In England, though, they are a different kettle of fish altogether: 'large boarding schools, drawing from the well-to-do classes pupils who are prepared mainly for the ancient universities or public services'. This common-sense definition probably fits the average Englishman's mental picture nearly enough. It noticeably omits, however, the newer criteria of independence, fee-paying, and selection, none of which totally fits either. Like the *OED*'s famous dictum on the English language, the English public school has a well-defined centre but no discernible circumference.

A book entitled *Our Public Schools,* published in 1881, named just seven: Eton*, Harrow*, Winchester*, Rugby, Westminster, Marlborough and Charterhouse. In 1889 the first *Public Schools Year Book* included a list drawn up by 'three Public School men' who were guided by such principles as 'Does the school possess the Public School spirit?'. By such cloudy criteria it extended the list to thirty-eight schools, including Portsmouth Grammar School, and Boston Grammar School in Lincolnshire. Clearly the task of definition was already proving a headache. Ten years later the *Year Book* abandoned its own judgement and simply listed the schools attending the Headmasters' Conference. This rule of thumb is still often used, though it omitted the two grammar schools previously listed and brought in a number of others (King Edward's, Birmingham; Lancaster; Wolverhampton).

In the beginning *all* English schools were religious foundations for clever poor boys training to enter the Church, the clerical establishment who would conduct the nation's business. The secret code for this career was *grammar*; specifically Latin grammar; the teaching of it laid down by *public* statute; herein is the seed of the perennial confusion. For many centuries aristocratic boys were educated at home or *privately*; gradually the increasing prestige of the new grammar schools like Eton encouraged their parents to send them away to be educated *publicly*.

Through a long stretch of Victoria's reign one new public school was founded every year to provide the men who would officer her armies and rule her dominions. Thomas Arnold pioneered the concept of character and the cult of muscular Christianity at Rugby; he was, it was remarked, 'among the first to see that although our Saviour taught us to turn the other cheek He did not mean that we were not to tackle our man low'. Arnold's disciples spread his message throughout Victorian England: Hart at Sedbergh, Butler at Haileybury, Cotton at Marlborough and Vaughan at Harrow. Vaughan, however, came to a sticky end. His impassioned love affair with a boy called Alfred Pretor was leaked to Alfred's friend, J.A. Symonds, who blurted it out eight years later during a reading party to John Conington, Corpus Professor of Latin. Conington advised Symonds to tell his father. He did, and Dr Symonds confronted Vaughan with his infamy. Though Mrs Vaughan threw herself at the good doctor's feet, Vaughan had to go. He finished up as Dean of Llandaff.

Little local difficulties like this did nothing to impair the onward march of the public school, nor the innate confidence of its products. When Stephen Spender* went to Oxford* in the late twenties he found his fellow Etonian undergraduates helpless with mirth at the discovery that the senior scholar of their year was the son of an Eton confectioner. The wheel has not taken too long to come full circle. There are English universities now – though perhaps not Oxford and Cambridge* – where public schoolboys are reticent about their provenance. Even at Oxford they have become the object of caricature.

Pubs In Hampshire there is a pub with no name. You have to bump up an unmarked track to get there, and, apart from having no name, it has no sign to help you find it, though once inside, you will find the barman sports a sweatshirt: The Pub with No Name it proclaims. Here there are log fires and oak settles, ancient drop-leaf tables, for masks, gazelle heads, farm tools and candle-lit country pictures.

There are some beguiling country wines: cowslip, parsnip, peach, elderberry, damson, wheat and raisin. There are moreover some handsome hand-pumped ales: not least a local brew called (but you've guessed) No Name. If you choose your day, you can buy Jersey cream over the bar ('eat in two days' says the legend on the lid) and pheasants* in season. On summer days there is a mind-smoothing view of the Hampshire Downs. It is an enchanted pub: but it is in effect a secret one.

There are still, on the other hand, rebarbative boozers in inner cities where the beer tastes of disinfectant and the ploughman's lunch of blotting paper, mousetrap cheese and margarine, and it is still a good general rule not to take wine in pubs unless well recommended.

Having said that, there is a scattering of English pubs that are a solace and a delight: riverside pubs like the Dove at Hammersmith, ritzy pubs like the Bells of Peover in Cheshire, medieval pubs like the Fleece near Evesham, alfresco pubs like the Flask at Highgate, sleepy pubs like the Lamb at Burford; smugglers' pubs like the Jolly Sailor at Orford; and beautiful pubs like the Horse and Groom at Charlton, near Malmesbury. Intruders will be treated strictly on their merits.

Pudding 'Ah, what an excellent thing is an English pudding!' exclaimed François Maximilien Misson, a French visitor to England in his memoirs of the journey published in 1698. He noted that the English made puddings 'fifty several ways' and his admiration was absolutely genuine. Slowly things went wrong after that: country people lost the old skills as they migrated into the towns; poverty made them opt for margarine instead of butter and thicken with cornflour rather than eggs; then an influx of premixed puds in packets seemed to spell *finis* to the old sweet glories. Besides, there was the undeniable toll that puds took on teeth and tums.

Now a new generation of English cooks, stirringly led by Jane Grigson, are rediscovering their lost heritage. And what a rich heritage it is! The names alone ring like a great roll of chivalry: flummeries, frumenties, fools and fritters, dumplings and crumbles, junkets, charlottes and tansies, syllabubs and whim-whams. There is the fascination of trying traditional puddings with such come-hither names as Boodle's Orange Fool and Sussex Bailiff's Bliss, Suck Cream and Tipsy Cake, Half Pay Pudding and Bedfordshire Clanger, Clipping Time Pudding and Apricot Brown Betty. So it looks as if the English pud is back to stay. As Misson roundly declared after his English odyssey: 'Blessed be he that invented pudding!' See also *Afters, Custard*.

Pudding Club To join this select body is to be expecting a baby; vernacular destined to survive, like its celebrated synonym, 'having a bun in the oven', if only because it combines mordant humour with tactile homeliness.

Quakers The Religious Society of Friends has a high standing in English life. The record speaks for itself: Quakers led the fight against slavery, pioneered prison reform, have always opposed war, are concerned about mental health, build excellent schools, and did quiet but invaluable work in bringing refugees from fascism to England. There are not many of them here – some twenty thousand arranged in about four hundred meetings – but because of the example they set, their influence is out of all proportion to their numbers.

Queen, HM The (born 1926) Anyone who attacks Elizabeth II will not be hanged, drawn and quartered; but he may well feel that he has been. Such was the experience of Malcolm Muggeridge when he ventured to suggest that the Queen's broadcasting style was ill-suited to the demands of the medium, her voice being far too high and her manner altogether too stiff. There was some truth in the charge, and the Queen did indeed work at the problem with some success. Muggeridge took a drubbing but lived to fight another day. The English people have it firmly in their heads (and here they have some support from the law) that unlike other members of her family the Queen is above the battle. Each year of her reign that passes entrenches this position more surely. She has now been on the throne longer than any English monarch since Victoria; and is already over halfway to equalling that heroic innings. It has not always been as easy as it looked. The monarchy, when she succeeded to the throne, was only fourteen years away from one of its worst nadirs: the abysmal interregnum of Edward VIII. Her father, George VI, had provided a breathing space. He was a throughly decent but hardly scintillating man, and by the time Elizabeth succeeded him the monarchy was much in need of a new sense of style and drama; of expansion and distinction. With the aid of Prince Philip, not everyone's cup of tea but no ineffectual cypher either, she has done just this. On top of all the nation's adventures and misadventures (the Suez folly, the Falklands conflict*, innumerable sterling crises, a string of traitors from Pontecorvo and Nunn May through Burgess and Maclean to Philby and Blunt) she has had her fair share of family disasters, ranging, be it remembered, from the normal divorce (Margaret) to murder (Mountbatten) and sudden death in the air (Prince William of Gloucester).

Apart from being of necessity at the centre of every national drama, she has met in the last thirty-two years far more English people than anybody else; and thus has a unique knowledge of this curious and eccentric race. In short, the Queen's own story would be one of the great publishing coups of all time: but we can rest assured that here is one diary that we shall not see in her lifetime. More's the pity.

The Queens The great Cunard liners *Queen Mary* and *Queen Elizabeth* were floating encapsulations of England at her most apocryphal. They ferried people between Southampton and New York with a style and luxury that not all of them would have enjoyed on dry land, and did it with seeming effortlessness. The American liners may have been more free and easy, the cooking a shade better on the French boats, but only the Queens conveyed the sense of travelling in a time warp. It took eight hundred staff, including six liftmen and a gardener, to serve the whims of about the same number of passengers. The impression of feudal largesse was begun with the breakfast menu, opening as it did with the chilled cantaloup melon and all the juices and cereals, then casually offering onion soup or Yarmouth bloaters before getting down to the serious business of eggs any way you liked, the three different bacons, American hash and griddle cakes with maple syrup before moving on to the nine kinds of bread and seven distinct coffees. It was as well to choose a smooth crossing. After breakfast the well-disciplined would take a few turns round the deck before settling into their deckchairs to be solicitously wrapped in a blanket by stewards and then served steaming bouillon. There would be time for a drink before lunch and then an afternoon programme of films, music or games before tea and then a swim in the ship's pool before cocktails with the captain, doctor or purser – the invitations came thick and fast. Or perhaps you felt like giving your own party in the cabin. Then Cunard would be happy to supply staff who had not noticed that their pre-war world had ended, drinks duty-free and canapés with their compliments. After dinner, the nightclub would open and the dancing would go on till dawn. On the fifth morning keen passengers would surface early to glimpse the Manhattan skyline coming up through the mist: easily the best way to see America first. This inspired form of indulgence – served up with an artistry only the island race could master – lasted into the sixties, when jet planes prevailed. There is of course the *QE2*; it is, alas, but a vast shadow of the majestic, vanished Queens.

Queue It was George Mikes who first pointed out that a man in a queue was the image of a true Englishman just as a man at a bullfight was the image of a true Spaniard. The Second World War saw the apotheosis of the queue and dramatised the bovine stickability of the island race in a rather ludicrous way.

Yet, even in an age of plenty, the English still like to queue for special treats like Wimbledon* tickets, standing room to hear Domingo sing, or the last night of the Proms*. Indeed they sometimes seem to enjoy this curious ritual more than the pleasure it is designed to achieve; bringing their sleeping bags and Primus stoves, and setting up world records by queuing for days and nights on end.

Bizarre though this English sport may seem, it probably links demand and supply with less fuss than the continental equivalent (rioting) or the American (payola).

Quite Another of those English words that has been not only changing but is now even reversing its meaning. Thus, while it originally meant 'totally' ('I was quite alone'), it also meant 'actually' ('she was quite ill'); and out of this second sense has grown the use of quite to mean 'fairly' or 'somewhat'. So when we say 'his work is quite satisfactory' do we mean it 'somewhat' or 'totally' satisfies? Americans still, and not only in this instance, tend to prefer the old sense; in England the original meaning now sounds distinctly affected – and not just quite affected.

Quotation What the English are good at is not so much quotation as misquotation. Thus, Wellington did not say 'Up Guards and at 'em'; Milton did not say 'Fresh fields and pastures new'; Congreve did not say 'Hell hath no fury like a woman scorned'; Acton did not say 'All power corrupts'. What we carry around in our heads is a vast jumble of half-remembered lines which our minds simply elide to the shape that suits them best.

It must be manfully faced that the Irish have given the English far more than their share of their best quotations. From Wellington himself – 'Publish and be damned' – through Wilde – 'Work is the curse of the drinking classes' – to Shaw* – 'Every man over forty is a scoundrel' – they have shown the English how to polish epigrams till they glitter.

True, great Englishmen like Samuel Johnson* have left a whole treasury of inimitable and enchanted lines that still chime in the mind; but he was fortunate in a Scottish amanuensis of genius. In politics, the exotic Jewish adventurer Benjamin Disraeli – 'Never complain and never explain' – is far better value than the pious Liverpool Old Etonian William Ewart Gladstone – 'Time is on our side'.

In our own century, meritocrat Harold Wilson may have shown the richer sense of metaphor – 'The gnomes of Zurich' – but it was left to patrician Alec Douglas-Home, mocked by Wilson for being the four-teenth earl, to come up with the perfect riposte: 'When you come to think about it, I suppose he is the fourteenth Mr Wilson.'

Indeed, the gift for picking precisely the right phrase out of the air does not require a great quantity of formal education. Thus nineteen-year-old Mandy Rice Davies, told in court during the Profumo scandal that Lord Astor had denied her allegations, gave a reply that has passed into the language: 'He would, wouldn't he?' Political parties and big business pay fortunes nowadays to advertising agencies to fail to come up with lines half as good as that. Yet in politics as in literature, the best lines are often the work of that prolific word-spinner Anon*.

Rabbits   'Once upon a time there were four little rabbits whose names were Flopsy, Mopsy, Cottontail and Peter,' wrote Beatrix Potter in *The Tale of Peter Rabbit*. She was not the first author to exploit the winning qualities of the common or garden Oryctolagus cuniculus, nor the last – Richard Adams made a substantial fortune from the heart-rending story of the rabbits in *Watership Down*.

Still, to the countryman the rabbit is a pest, and an exceedingly persistent one. He will shoot, wire or ferret them on a Saturday afternoon or Sunday* morning most seasons of the year; residually perhaps as a bit of a sport, but principally to keep them down, for they are a voracious menace to grass, crops, trees and gardens.

Ever since the worst epidemic of myxomatosis, they have been unpopular as a dish; and though they have grown resistant to the horrible disease, rabbits can still be found stricken down by it in the briar, when the only recourse is to dispatch them as speedily as possible. The gap between the gentle creature of fiction and the noxious vermin of reality remains unbridgeable.

Radio Times   It was born in 1923 when a hostile press refused to print BBC* programmes (ironically newspapers have since spent a fortune trying to get that right). It has always been the highest-selling magazine in the country; the Coronation issue of 29 May 1953 sold nine million copies; and over the whole year in 1955 it averaged sales of more than eight million a week. It was also profitable from the beginning and at one time in the thirties was contributing a quarter of the BBC's entire revenue. This wealth and power attracted some talented people; Maurice Gorham, editor from 1933 to 1941 went on to be head of BBC Television; Eric Maschwitz, his predecessor in the chair, went on to become not only head of BBC Variety but a playwright and lyricist who would be remembered, if for nothing else, as the author of *These Foolish Things*. It was also able to call on a wide range of gifted illustrators: Edward Ardizzone, Peter Brookes, Robin Jacques and Ralph Steadman among them. Though its circulation is now well below that great fifties peak, it remains the highest-selling magazine in the land. Radio is now squeezed into smaller type after the coloured bezazz of the television programmes each day, but the *Radio Times* remains an item in the everyday diet of English life; and is as harmless and anodyne as Ovaltine*.

The RAF They have no traditions, they only have habits, remarked a naval petty officer in a letter to *The Times** as recently as 1977. There is some truth in the thrust; but no shame either. Manifestly the RAF is the most free-and-easy of the three services simply because it does not have centuries of tradition to inhibit it. Unlike the others it cannot claim to have been in battle against most of the world at some time or other; indeed, it has effectively had only four enemy air forces to contend with, the German, the Italian, the Japanese and the Argentinian; and it has given a good account against all four.

It is hard for those not alive at the time to understand the hero-worship in which the RAF was enveloped at the time of the Battle of Britain. This was a scrap which the English saw unfolding directly above them in the great diorama of the skies; and nothing was more heart-stopping than the sight of the British fighter squadrons climbing high into the cirrus to meet the silver shoals of German bombers. No fighter pilot had to pay for his taxi back to RAF Biggin Hill; the London cabbies saw to that. Though the RAF did not shoot down quite so many German planes as it had thought (all air forces exaggerate their kills in the heat of battle) it destroyed two German aircraft for every one it lost. This ratio, if not the three to one claimed at the time, was quite enough to prove decisive, and to deter the German invasion. If it had not been for the toughness of Hugh Dowding, the supremo of Fighter Command, who steadfastly refused all blandishments from Churchill and others to squander his planes and pilots over France and particularly at Dunkirk, it might have been a different story.

Bomber Command had a much less happy war. A study made in 1941 showed that one third of RAF bombers dispatched did not attack their target and of those which did only a third got within five miles of it. The total cost to German of British bombing was one per cent of production – if that. The strategic air offensive of 1940-41 killed more members of the RAF than Germans. Still, the effect of that campaign on British morale was vast; and the bomber crews were heroes too.

The trouble with men made demi-gods by war is that they have to learn to cope with peace; not all of them did. Men who had been mythogenic had to earn their livings as schoolmasters or salesmen again. They became merely mortal; even ludicrous. Thus Group Captain Max Aitken, who was in the air the day the war started and still flying the day it ended, led the victory fly-past; but lived on to earn the mocking sobriquet Biggles (airman hero of a hundred schoolboy yarns) from *Private Eye**, none of whose staff were old enough to have any clear recollection of the war in the air and quite naturally had no especial regard for the men who had fought it. Every hero, as Ralph Waldo Emerson reminds us, becomes a bore at last.

Rain   The myth that England is a rainy country dies hard. The heaviest rainfall ever recorded here in a day (9.56 inches at Bruton, Somerset in 1917) is a mere trickle compared with the several feet in a tropical downpour.

London in January has an average monthly rainfall of two inches compared with Johannesburg's 4.5 and Jerusalem's 5.2. Nevertheless England's climate is intensely humid (not quite the same thing) and it is this which gives English grass its preternatural glory and English women their gorgeous skins.

Melancholy images of rain abound in English writing all the way from medieval Anon's 'Western wind, when wilt thou blow / The small rain down can rain? / Christ if my love were in my arms / And I in my bed again!' In modern times, though, rain is seen as principal killjoy on sporting occasions.

'Rain stopped play' is perhaps the most lowering of all sports reports in the summer papers; and it was these gloom-filled words which, on their return from their shenanigans with various Nazi bounders in the classic Hitchcock thriller *The Lady Vanishes,* greeted the silly-ass, cricket-mad, archetypal Englishmen, Charters and Caldicott*.

Redbrick   For six hundred years there were just two universities in England (Scottish education has developed quite differently. The tradition of the lad o'pairts, the poor boy who comes from his village to study at the four historic Scottish universities with his pack on his back goes deep into antiquity.) In England it was not till 1832 that Durham*

was founded; London followed four years later. By 1945 there were ten English universities. Then came the real explosion: now there are forty-five.

Six hundred years is a long lead. When David Lodge, one of the most interesting novelists under fifty now writing (and one of the most fashionable English professors now teaching), went to University College, London, soon after the last war, he did not know that any other university apart from his own and the two ancient ones even *existed.*

His close friend, Malcolm Bradbury, another distinguished novelist and professor of English, began to write *Eating People is Wrong* – already established as a modern fiction classic - while an undergraduate at what was then University College, Leicester: 'It was late redbrick, verging on white tile, and still a constituent college of the University of London; it had some seven hundred students. It was located in the old county asylum . . . ' Leicester then did not offer glittering prizes: 'What it offered was sober futures, in low or middle management or school teaching . . .' All that was to change precisely because men like Bradbury and Lodge brought their considerable gifts to the service of universities like Birmingham and East Anglia.

An informal dozen or so universities seem to be grouping themselves in the English mind as an unofficial first division rather on the lines of the American Ivy League. Oxbridge, Durham, and London are fairly obvious entries, but so too are a number of the well-dug-in, old-established redbricks. No name on this list is sacrosanct. Universities must compete for students just as students compete for places. With men like Lodge and Bradbury in them, the redbricks have everything to play for.

Rice Pudding   One of those dishes that every Englishman knows from the days of his youth, it is hated by some and adored by others, for it is redolent of English childhood and thus, according to the spin of the coin, of hell or heaven. Though the sophisticated Englishman will claim to have put it away with his toys, it mysteriously surfaces at places like the Guards Club and the ultra-chic Connaught Hotel in London, where they say there is a steady demand for it. The dish also stars in one of the most colourful and contemptuous English images of moral or physical feebleness: 'he couldn't kick the skin off a rice pudding'. But see too *Afters* and *Pudding.*

Rolls-Royce   If the Rolls-Royce owned by Lord Berners, which had a piano built in the back, has some claim to be the most glamorous of its breed, the Rolls-Royce owned by the Duke of Westminster – which he used to charge a platoon of German cavalry in the First World War – has a claim to be the most gallant. We should not be too surprised to learn that not only did Tsar Nicholas II of Russia run a Rolls but also Lenin, Stalin and Brezhnev. Yet even in these austere times, a third of all Rolls-Royces are bought by the island race; another third by Americans; and the rest of the world take the rest. It must be allowed, though, that the best customer over all the years for the Rolls has been the Scottish Co-operative Society. Images of Co-op customers quietly piling up their divvies till they can afford the £55,000 currently required for the cheapest Rolls are, however, misplaced: the Rolls is top of the pops north of the border as a hearse. Most Scots take their first ride in one horizontally.

Rose It is probably a fair comment on national proclivities that while the Welsh emblem is the unlovely leek, the Irish the uninteresting shamrock, and the Scottish the positively repulsive thistle, all three plants will be much on display in England on the national day of each small country. The Englishman, however, who boasts as his emblem the most beautiful flower in the world, does not deign to wear it on his national day, being self-conscious about such displays of naked chauvinism. He can, however, grow it rather well.

The Royal Family It has long ceased to be the seat of power and is increasingly the hub of show business. Not only is a royal presence the *sine qua non* of any grand film première; in a real sense the royals are playing in their own soap opera. No scriptwriter could wish for a better cast: a large, variegated family with everyone's favourite Mum (Lilibet), a super Gran (the Queen Mum), a wilful younger sister (Margaret), a cantankerous father (Philip), interesting children (cheerful Charlie, randy Andy, educated Edward and angular Anne), all sorts of in-laws (divine Diana, problem-girl Princess Michael), grandchildren galore – but one could go on forever. Add a string of polo ponies, helicopters, fast cars and castles, and the stage is set for a run that could well last for centuries. See also *Queen, Pheasants.*

Rude Songs and Verses This is the province of Anon* that prodigal wordsmith who has contributed so bounteously to English literature, for in the entire panoply of those rude songs and improper verses which are every Englishman's birthright, few if any can be attributed with any authority, though A.P. Herbert is often credited with the saga of 'Eskimo Nell'. It is indeed a zestful narrative that occasionally rises to great lyrical heights ('Have you seen the giant pistons / On the mighty CPR/ With the driving force of a thousand horse / Well you know what pistons are'). The theme is phallic voracity matched by uterine insatiability, and was clearly written by somebody who could string a few words together. Some improper songs are parodies ('Little boy kneels at the foot of his bed / Lily white hands are caressing his head / Oh my, couldn't be worse / Christopher Robin is screwing his nurse') and some derive from famous hymns. Thus, 'There's a Street in Cairo' goes to the tune of 'Abide with Me'. Some have political undertones, as in the famous parody of 'The Red Flag' ('The working class can kiss my arse / I've got the foreman's job at last') but many purvey a brooding sense of melancholy ('It's the same the whole world over / It's the poor wot gets the blame / It's the rich wot gets the pleasure / Ain't it all a bleeding shame?')

Though perhaps the most celebrated repository of these songs is now the rugger club, and some clearly have a rugby provenance, many had their origin in the barrack or on the mess deck in the long watches of the imperial night. Prominent in this subdivision of the great genre is 'The Good Ship Venus' ('The Captain's daughter Mabel / As soon as she was able / Would fornicate with the second mate / Upon the chart-room table'). Some are cleaned up and surface as popular songs ('Roll me over in the clover') and some improbably transmogrify to advertisements, most recently 'Ivan Skavinsky Skavar', who is now selling lager.

Many of these underground ballads are not to be underrated. Thus 'Cats on the Rooftops' contains verses of real power ('Long-legged curates grind like goats / Pale-faced spinsters shag like stoats / And the whole damn world / Stands by and gloats / As they revel in the joys of copulation') would not be unworthy of Auden* on a so-so day, while some make short self-contained poems drawing on reservoirs of true desire ('Flo, Flo, I love you so / I love you in your nightie / When the moonlight flits / Across your tits / Oh Jesus Christ Almighty'). Comic, pessimistic, ingenious and above all subversive, the improper song has been a harmless safety valve for men without women wherever the English writ ran. Today it may have little or no social role; but should be preserved and probably will, if only for its charm, eccentricity and vigour.

Rugby It is hard to believe that *all* the main varieties of football – American, Australian, Association, Gaelic, Rugby Union, Rugby League – stem from the same game. But they do.

In 1863, at the first meeting of the Football Association, every possible attempt was made to frame laws for a universal game that would satisfy both those who liked to carry the ball and those who liked to dribble it. The rugby men walked out; the games began to diverge. Yet all footballers are kin, and no boy should be taught the rules of rugger until he has mastered the basic skills of soccer.

The first clue we have to that oval shape comes in *Tom Brown's Schooldays* when there is a passage about the ball *pointing* towards the goal. The first person to catch the ball and run with it (in 1823) was a Rugby schoolboy called William Webb Ellis, later Rector of St Clement Dane's, the RAF church in the Strand. His eventual resting place was a mystery till Ross McWhirter, founder of the *Guinness Book of Records*, later to be murdered by Irish gunmen, traced his grave in 1971 to Menton in southern France. Since then the French Rugby Union have been proud to tend it. The English Rugby Union placed fifteen red roses on the grave with a card thanking him for his pioneer act of 1823.

They have reason: the game is now played by over a hundred countries. The Russians are getting useful at it; the Americans have played at Twickenham*. The Romanians recently beat France, one of the most fizzing and formidable of all modern sides. The secret of rugger is that it is a joy to play (the *furor scrumicus* or ecstasy of the scrum is said by those who have tried both to be second only to the act of love itself) and a delight to watch. A majestic try fashioned from a jewelled movement can be so perfectly timed that it conveys the illusion of being executed in slow motion.

Rupert Bear   Although shortly due to qualify for his old age pension, Rupert maintains his perennial charm for the young and is still one of the basic ingredients that keep the *Daily Express* selling. In 1920 the *succès fou* of Teddy Tail in the *Daily Mail* had the *Express* badly worried. It had searched high and low without success for a suitable counter-attraction. Finally, the night news editor at that time tentatively volunteered that his wife, Mary Tourtel, could draw, and in desperation they asked her to have a go. She came up with Rupert Bear. In the thirties Rupert, till then a bit listless, was given a shot in the arm by a brilliant artist called Alfred Bestall, who today at ninety-one still displays the enviable mental agility that put Rupert on level terms with Teddy Tail fifty years ago. He has retired now, but the continuing Rupert Bear sagas both in the paper and Christmas annual still reflect his idiosyncratic genius. For a less appealing sprig of the *Ursus arctos*, see under *Winnie-the-Pooh*.

Saint George   He was a native of Cappadocia (now part of Turkey) and died in about AD 303. It was a thousand years later that Edward III made him England's national saint, and for a while his name was actually invoked by the English in battle, as in Henry V's 'Cry, "God for Harry, England, and Saint George!" ' (note the batting order). He has since, however, become something of an embarrassment to the English, most of whom do not even know what their national flag, the Cross of St George, looks like and instead rather half-heartedly wave the Union Jack, which of course represents the amalgam of all four countries and is often as not upside down.

Salvation Army   At one moment in 1983 there were two plays running side by side at the National Theatre with the Salvation Army as their themes: in the Olivier, Frank Loesser's joyous musical *Guys and Dolls;* in the Lyttelton, Bernard Shaw's delicious comedy *Major Barbara.* Both derive gusts of belly laughter from the interaction between the Army and the sinners it is bent on saving: in New York, Runyonesque gamblers with names like Harry the Horse and Brandy Bottle Bates; in London the down and outs and drudges of the East End. In both however, the laughter is good-natured; even respectful. As Shaw points out: 'It is the army of joy, of love, of courage ... it marches to fight the devil with trumpet and drums, with music and dancing, with banner and palm ... it picks the waster from the public house and makes a man of him; it finds a worm wriggling in a back kitchen and lo! a woman.'

The movement took off when its founder, William Booth, a Nottingham evangelist, picked up a pen and struck out one word in a printer's proof. It was the 1878 Report of his Christian Mission, founded in 1865 and, till that time, doing quietly conscientious good. The proof described the Mission as a Volunteer Army. Booth made it read Salvation Army and ignited the movement.

Today the Sally Ann (as it is known among those it most helps) may seem a faintly eccentric survival of Victorian philanthropy; but not to anyone whose job it is to cope with the underside of affluent England. The old battles against, for example, child prostitution may have been largely won; but the fight to help the alcoholics and the homeless goes on. In its centenary year of 1965 a Salvation Army report found 400,000 children in need of love and care, 400,000 social misfits, and 675,000 old people who were underfed, lonely and cold. It traces 1,200 vanished husbands and 3,500 missing persons each year. Nobody else can or will do these thankless jobs.

To move with the times, the Army's eighth general, Frederick Coutts, urged that the gospel should be carried into the coffee bars and disco clubs. In four months the Sally Ann's own pop group, the Joystrings, were in the charts with their first record: 'It's an Open Secret'. The scheme illustrates perfectly the Army's knack of getting at people the Church is unable to reach. Booth refused an overture from the Archbishop of York to amalgamate. At first intent on turning his converts over to the churches, he found that churchwardens in fashionable parishes looked askance at worshippers without Sunday suits; and only one man in thirty at Booth's meetings even owned a collar.

Sausages   They range from the coarse-textured, spicy Cumberland, the veal-flavoured Oxford and the highly seasoned Cambridge to the meaty Gloucester, the herby Suffolk, and the mutton-based banger of Aberdeen. No doubt they do not seem as good as they once did; though in truth by law they must now contain 65 per cent meat if pork and at least half meat if not. There is a famous passage in Orwell* when he bites into a sausage and finds it disgustingly ersatz; it is in truth a homely index in the English subconscious of honesty; when the bangers* are off something is rotten in the state of England.

The Savoy   Though Claridge's is more discreet, the Connaught's cooking better, and the Ritz ritzier, most Englishmen asked to think of a great London hotel say the Savoy. This may be partly due to the pervasive folk memory from the days of early radio when the Savoy Orpheans under Debroy Somers and later Carroll Gibbons broadcast nightly on the pioneer station 2LO. Even if he has never crossed its threshold, your ordinary Englishman knows that the Savoy is the natural showbiz hostelry; the place where Noël Coward* sang 'Let's Do It' in cabaret and George Gershwin played for the first time in Europe his 'Rhapsody in Blue'.

Maybe it is this showbiz connection which gives the Savoy its American feel; but the times of the *QE2* sailings in the lobby help. It must also please American hearts to know that the Savoy was the first hotel in England to have electric light, the first to install lifts, the first to have air conditioning. Quite separate from the technology, though, the Savoy people are renowned flatterers who keep a famous card-index system noting each guest's personal whims and preferences.

However, certain things are still not done, even in the breezy transatlantic world of the Savoy, and one is entering the bars or restaurants without a tie. The transgressor is told, in the inspired Savoy gobbledegook, that gentlemen are not served in sporting clothes; but they keep a stock of ties to get him out of the jam.

It's not only Yanks who get the treatment. A Battle of Britain pilot left his hairbrushes there one hectic night in 1940, was shot down and taken prisoner next day. When he called for them in 1945 they were still there waiting for him – of course.

Scotland An Englishman, ruled the historian and Londoner Philip Guedalla, was a man who lived on an island in the North Sea governed by Scotsmen. There is just enough truth in the thrust to permit Englishmen a rueful laugh; and every Sassenach worth his salt knows Samuel Johnson's* celebrated crack about the noblest prospect a Scotsman ever sees being the high road that leads to England. Yet there is hard reason behind the pleasantries.

The Scots, under the inspiration of John Knox, have for centuries believed in comprehensive, compulsory, democratic and free education for all who can profit by it, and at the turn of the twentieth century, when only one English child in 1,300 was at a secondary school the corresponding figure for Scotland was one in two hundred: a ratio which only Prussia could then equal.

This great cornucopia of intelligence had no choice but to emigrate in order to be fulfilled; and Scots went to every corner of earth marked pink on the map to play key roles in servicing the British Raj. In politics the Scottish influence may not have been quite so charismatic as the Welsh, divided as it is between the great patrician Etonian Scots (Balfour, Home, Macmillan) and the working-class demagogues (Willie Gallacher, Jimmy

Maxton, Keir Hardie, Ramsay MacDonald).

Yet the Scottish middle class is neglected at our peril, and its contribution to science and technology is massive. The Napiers founded marine engineering, Nasmyth devised the steam hammer, Macadam gave his name to modern roads, Dunlop to tyres. Lord Kelvin and James Clerk Maxwell dominated physics in their time; Alexander Graham Bell gave us the telephone and John Logie Baird has the best claim to be the inventor of television. And so on.

Yet the benefit of interaction between Scotland and England only slowly became clear. At the time of the Union in 1707 the London mail bag sometimes reached Edinburgh with only one letter in it. Scots looked to their old allies the French rather than the auld enemy England; Jacobite exiles lived in Italy and France; Presbyterian clergy and lawyers went to Dutch universities; Scottish merchants dealt with Holland and Scandinavia, but were excluded from trade with the English Colonies. Not any more though. The huge bonanza of North Sea oil and gas has brought new wealth to Scotland but not noticeably thinned the legions of Scotsmen who sit high in English places.

The Englishman finds the Scots less mercurial than his Irish and Welsh neighbours; duller, perhaps, but steadier and a sight less trouble. Scottish nationalists may occasionally do something romantic and dashing like purloining the Stone of Scone from Westminster Abbey; but they do not use arson like Welsh nationalists nor murder like the Irish. Besides, they have introduced him to one of his favourite games (golf*) and favourite tipples (whisky), a gill of which even Dr Johnson had to try on his Hebridean journey to see what it was that made a Scotsman happy. In this curiosity he had reason, for as P.G. Wodehouse* observed, it is never difficult to distinguish between a Scotsman with a grievance and a ray of sunshine.

The Seventies While it is clearly too soon to attempt a proper perspective on the decade, one perceptive writer, Christopher Booker, has argued already (in his book, *The Seventies*) that it was quite different in mood and meaning from all that had gone before in the century. Certainly there was a daunting crop of world-scale disasters. There was Watergate, and the first resignation in history of an American President. There was the ignominious débâcle in Vietnam, the rape of Cambodia, and the worst economic recession since the war. In Britain inflation rose to an appalling 27 per cent and the prime minister, Harold Wilson, so recently the new hope of the new left, now warned against 'a catastrophe of unimaginable proportions'.

The British people had to cope with a series of strikes by low-paid workers who, it was noticed too late, did jobs essential to the survival of any modern civilised state. Hospitals were closed, ambulances failed to run, water was shut off, sewage was untreated and bodies unburied. It was a bitter aftermath indeed to the 'Swinging Sixties'. Yet all decades can be shown to have spawned a string of catastrophes. The difference in the seventies, Booker argues, is that for the first time *homo sapiens* lost confidence in his ability to overcome material obstacles by his own innate intelligence: 'It was the decade when our bluff was called.'

In Britain this new mood found political expression in the election of a new conservative administration led by Margaret Hilda Thatcher, which embodied the precepts of the radical right: a massive swing away from the hegemony of central government and the shelter of the welfare state, towards private enterprise and self-help. The smack of firm government was heard in the land. The British people had opted for a dramatically new direction, and they had got it. How would it work out? No one knew; except, that is, the formidable dowager in one of Osbert Lancaster's inimitable cartoons. 'Mark my words,' she opined, ramrod-straight in her high-backed chair as the decade ended, 'the eighties will be worse. They always are.'

Sex *No Sex please, We're British* is the title of a West End comedy, now, as the theatre proudly proclaims, 'in its fourteenth hysterical year'. The joke is, of course, on the legions of foreign visitors, who flock to see it; for what it means is 'Oodles of sex, please, we're British'. As we have already noted under *Love*, the Brits have some claim to be the randiest race on earth, and celebrate their partiality on St Valentine's Day* with a profusion of printed erotica unknown anywhere else. Nightly on British television sexual themes are explored, sexual references insinuated, and sexual jokes cracked that would bring on instant cardiac arrest in the higher echelons of broadcasting on the other side of the Atlantic. The raunchy end of the Sunday papers dissect the amatory follies with a gusto no other press can approach in scale; while in most newsagents now whole shelves of girlie magazines compete for favour with the still popular coloured seaside postcards, garnished with the bums and tits of yore.

The English language serves the English predilection nobly. Take, for example, 'a bit of the other', first noted in Joyce's *Ulysses* where the context perhaps explains how it arose: 'They would be just good friends like a big brother and sister without all that other.' D.H. Lawrence shows the line of thought even more clearly in *Lady Chatterley's Lover*: 'She loved me to talk to her and kiss her ... But the other, she just didn't want.' However the average Englishman has forgotten the context if he knew it and uses the phrase as a bit of humorous and arcane code. It predates the permissive society, which demolished the barricades between the one thing and the other, and may therefore be doomed; though the thrust of mocking allusion is a powerful one in modern English.

Then there is the racy phrase 'to have it away', an interesting example of a phrase changing its sense in mid-journey. Modern usage in either sense, it is first noted by the *OED Supplement* as late as 1958 as criminal slang for escaping from prison. Even more recently though, and first in 1970, the *OED* notes its use in the sense of making love. Quite possibly the term went over the points through a simple misunderstanding: Did you have it (while you were) away? In any event, the sexual use now seems to be winning. Is it, though, quite such an anonymous affair as Germaine Greer suggests in *The Female Eunuch*? 'The vocabulary of impersonal sex is peculiarly desolating,' she complains. 'Who wants to have it away?' One would have thought she would have known. Increasingly, though, the phase suggests not so much apathy as abandon.

Sometimes, though, the wholesale revolution of the English sexual behaviour leaves words stranded. 'Are yer coortin'?' Wilfred Pickles, the BBC's token northerner, used to ask on the air, thus eliciting gales of giggles. Still, that was already a long time ago, and such a query today might well be greeted by blank incomprehension: cohabiting is fast replacing courting and the old convention of the front parlour where young couples of the respectable classes got to know each other between kisses has been usurped by the galvanised gavotte of the disco. Whether this is an advance is anybody's guess. Another enchanting term from the vanished era of courtship is 'walking out': the custom by which young servant girls were allowed to take a stroll with their beaux on Sunday afternoons. The phrase has however been borrowed by the sophisticated young to mean a riotous and usually illicit affair. Their walking out now means they're having it away, like everyone else in modern England.

Shakespeare, William (1564-1616) To his contemporaries he is gentle, sweet, and honey-tongued Shakespeare. A fellow actor leaves him a ring for remembrance. 'I loved the man', says his great coeval, rival and friend Ben Jonson, 'and honour his memory this side idolatry.'

What kind of man? Someone obsessed with the fragility of life, the transience of beauty and the brevity of love. A man who found sleep elusive: night and day blurring into one fevered dream. A man, above all, haunted by the pervasive and sinister menace of Time.

He returns to the charge again and again. Time, he cries, is a bloody tyrant. Time is sluttish, devouring, thieving. He shakes his fist: 'No Time, thou shalt not boast that I do change... thy Registers and thee I both defy.' He has a sovereign remedy: his own words. 'So long as men can breathe or eyes can see/ So long lives this, and this gives life to thee.'

He speaks to us directly as the living, breathing, suffering man – I, Shakespeare – only in the Sonnets. We are compelled to listen. The finest among them reach for perfection and sometimes touch it. They contain a naked testimony of passion and loss which comes to us at white heat over the centuries. They are made in a quick forge. They hold the distillation of life and the quintessence of love.

What nightmare he was living as he poured them out we can only conjecture. We must hope that he came through the storm to calmer seas. ('Poets are tough', Auden* reminds us, 'and can profit from the most dreadful experiences.') Shakespeare had a sure sense of his own power and destiny: 'Your monument shall be my gentle verse / Which eyes not yet created shall oe'r read.' He has held his great argument with Time; and won.

Shaw, Bernard (1856-1950) In his will, Shaw stipulated that for the first twenty-one years after his death his royalties should be devoted to the new alphabet which had long obsessed him. Then they were to be divided among three institutions which had rendered him much service: the British Museum, the National Gallery of Ireland, and the Royal Academy of Dramatic Art. (He liked to say, with some truth, that he had been educated by wandering around galleries and museums in his youth.) The three residual beneficiaries took the alphabet to court on the grounds that it was not in the public interest. In the end the alphabet got £8,300. A competition was held, and *Androcles and the Lion* was duly set in the resulting version. The three were then free to split Shaw's royalties, which are now running at a whopping £525,000 a year. Such is the thrall of Shaw a third of a century after his death.

Yet it was not till he was forty-eight that he began to gain authority in the West End theatre (America had recognised his worth much earlier). He thought he was a novelist, and before turning to the stage wrote five books, which are now largely unread. He had already proved himself an elegant and incisive music and theatre critic. His correspondence with the actress Mrs Patrick Campbell, a woman who could match him line for line as a wit, is an abiding delight. 'It's too late to do anything but accept you and love you,' she wrote to him in 1912, 'but when you were a little boy somebody ought to have said hush just once.'

Though we see what she was driving at, we would not nowadays require too much hush from Shaw: the fact that the West End stage still thrives on a steady diet of Shaw plays is testimony enough not just to his genius but also to his skill as an entertainer. Plays like *Pygmalion* have been turned into films, into musicals (*My Fair Lady*) and then into filmed musicals. Despite the changing shape of society, his rapier still goes home. 'All professions are conspiracies against the laity' is as true now as it was when he first wrote it. 'Assassination is the extreme form of censorship' has a chillingly modern ring.

What distinguishes the wit in Shaw – what lends it that clean edge and sharp glitter – is his gift of verbal counter-point. 'I wouldn't have your conscience, not for all your income,' cries Peter Shirley, the down-and-out, to Undershaft, the munitions millionaire in *Major Barbara*. 'I wouldn't have your income, not for all your conscience,' returns Undershaft courteously, and there is no more to be said.

The most celebrated opportunity for this coruscating counterpoint was offered him on a plate by a mysterious lady writing from Zurich. 'You have the greatest brain in the world, and I have the most beautiful body; so we ought to produce the most perfect child,' she proposed. To this there was only one possible riposte. 'What,' inquired Shaw, 'if the child inherits my body and your brains?' The English have cause yet again to give heartfelt thanks for their Irish writers. 'He hasn't an enemy in the world, but his friends don't like him,' quipped his contemporary Oscar Wilde. Not true, actually, but the epigram sits well on Shaw's bony shoulders. He was a vegetarian most of his life. 'God help us if he would ever eat a beef-steak,' opined Mrs Patrick Campbell.

'I delighted in Shaw, the formidable man,' wrote William Butler Yeats. 'He could hit my enemies, and the enemies of those I loved, as I could never hit, as no living author that was dear to me could ever hit.' Those hits still go home, night after night, all over the civilised world, and the royalties rattle in to the museum, the gallery and the academy. Indeed, student fees at RADA would be double without Shaw's bequest. That would have delighted him. 'The trouble, Mr Goldwyn,' he wrote to the movie mogul, declining to sell him his screen rights, 'is that you are only interested in art and I am interested only in money.'

Shopkeepers A nation of shopkeepers, opined Napoleon of the English with some truth; but the jibe no longer has any force (if it ever did) in a country run by a prime minister whose father was a grocer.

True, retail trade has become socially acceptable only as the century has advanced (Raymond Asquith, himself a prime minister's son, complained bitterly about having to hob-nob with retail tobacconists at country-house parties in Edwardian England) but the right kind of shop has been a chic side-line for the upper class since after the First World War (Victoria Sackville-West's mother opened a hat shop).

Indeed, with the patina acquired by long years of affluence and patronage some stores, like Harrods* and Fortnums* have become centres of chic in themselves, while eminent shopkeepers like the Marks and Spencer* and Sainsbury families have played an attractive role in the social and artistic life of the country. Increasingly, however, with the rise of the supermarket, the small trader, satirised so memorably by Dickens* and H.G. Wells, is being driven out of business – or is selling out to a new wave of talented Indian immigrants prepared to invest time and effort on a scale no English shopkeeper would contemplate. (See *Mr Patel*.)

Sir and Madam Once in continuous use between male equals (see Boswell's *Life of Samuel Johnson* passim) 'sir' is now used in that context only in slightly obsolete mockery ('my dear sir') or emphasis ('yes SIR'). It is used by retailers soliciting custom and parliamentary candidates soliciting votes, but decreasingly now as a mark of social deference.

Professor Alan Ross, in his celebrated essay on *U and Non U*, remarked that he kept 'sir' only for men of great age and/or distinction. Even here it rather depends on the man. Thus, most Englishmen would have no great difficulty in calling Harold Macmillan, now ninety, sir, while few would find it necessary so to address the chummy Emanuel Shinwell, who is nearly ten years his senior.

It is generally thought unnecessary for women to address men as sir except in shops, and contrariwise, the language is deficient in a word with which to address great ladies. 'Ma'am' (rhyming with charm) is reserved solely now for royal females, and 'madam' too is obsolete outside shops. Thus Mrs Thatcher can be addressed only by her full name or as 'Prime Minister'. Perhaps the reluctance to use madam stems from its other meanings: as the owner of a brothel or a hoity-toity female – 'she's a proper little madam'. Similarly 'madam shops', boutiques selling ready-to-wear to older women, pre-empt the ground.

On the other hand, in informal situations (restaurants, buses, pubs) the English now increasingly address each other without the slightest embarrassment as *love* (or *luv* in the north) while a young girl can now be addressed without offence by older men in similar contexts as *dear* or even *darling*. So much for the allegedly icy island race.

The Sixties Those who say decades do not have characters of their own face a dilemma in explaining away the sixties. For nothing could be more idiosyncratic and separate, original and different than that decade. It began with the election of a charismatic new American president, John F. Kennedy, who seemed to symbolise and embody all the shining hope of a new Camelot. It was soon garnished and seasoned at home by the birth of the new satire movement: the pyrotechnic debut of the four unfairly gifted young men who brought *Beyond The Fringe* from Edinburgh to London, and placed a conceptual bomb under all the old shibboleths: patriotism, religion, monarchy.

This anarchic tidal wave was quickly transmuted into a television mode of unquantifiable power as *That Was The Week That Was;* a weekly snook cocked at the Establishment with great vim, under the benevolent aegis of the new and libertarian director general of the BBC, Hugh Carleton Greene, whose term of office in that key job ran with almost runic precision from 1960-1969. It was the decade when Rachmanism – the strong-arm eviction of slum tenants – was first revealed to an astonished nation; and when the Great Train Robbery created a new race of anti-heroes, some of whom flourish outside bars to this day.

It was the decade of Dr Strangelove and Dr Beeching. It was the era when the London Hilton was built, Mary Quant made a million, and the new liberal, concerned, middle class, affluent yet faintly absurd in their self-questioning self-deprecation, took up residence in London's NW1. It saw the launch of the colour supplement*, the birth of the drug culture, the advent of flower power, the cult of youth, the craze for the mini-skirt, and the jackpot for Carnaby Street and Kings Road. The high octane roar of the E-type Jaguar* was the most characteristic sound of the decade.

It was the era that saw Gaitskell's death and Macmillan's resignation; politically in England it was the high summer of Harold Wilson and the white-hot heat of technological advance he proclaimed from the commanding heights of the economy. It was the era that first heard the plangent minor chords of the most potent popular sound the world has ever known: the songs of four Liverpool* troubadours who called themselves the Beatles.

It was high noon for the new wave of fashion photographers, born in the East End of London, who soared to fame through the phallic power of their camera lenses. Brian Duffy, Terence Donavan, and David Bailey were earning £100,000 a year between them when the pound was a pound, and had in their *macho* tow some of the most scrumptious models in christendom. It must also be said that it was the era of the Profumo scandal and the great spy sensations – Philby, Blake, Vassall –

mirrored in the scarcely less real world of the top spy writers – Deighton, Le Carré, and Fleming*.

It was the heyday too of the psychopathic East End arch-criminals; the Krays and the Richardsons. All these seamy underworld figures moved easily and without comment in and out of polite society; there was a surrealistic feel to life that was exemplified by the launch of the Monty Python show. The slow motion death of Jack Kennedy on the Magruder movie film and the meaningless agony of Vietnam on everyone's colour television confirmed the diagnosis: the western world had suffered a collective nervous breakdown; from which even the phlegmatic English were not immune.

Soho   Now one of the most desolate parts of London. A wilderness of amusement arcades and sex shops has swallowed up the bookshops and the *ateliers*, and the *Good Food Guide** can now recommend only one of its restaurants. This not surprisingly still has its proprietor always in situ: the indestructible Victor Sassie daily presides at The Gay Hussar as the tribunes of the left conspire over their Bulgar *salata* and lemon pancakes. Further down Greek Street a young Cambridge-educated commodity broker called Nick Lander has taken over L'Escargot and transformed it into a brasserie downstairs for the young, which the Guide classifies as useful. Otherwise in inner Soho only Peter Boizot's elegant new Kettner's pizzeria rates a similar mention.

Meanwhile the Terrazza has changed hands again and may be on its way back now. It was an integral part of swinging London in the sixties when two former waiters called Mario and Franco took it over, got their friend Enzo Appicella to decorate it, and made it a must for every aspiring writer and photographer. Trattorias proliferated all over town, Mario and Franco became millionaires and sold out, and without their personal magic the place went off the boil. We shall see what the new management can do.

To be fair, you can still buy some of the best cigars in the land in Old Compton Street, and just about every newspaper in Europe opposite. There is still good pasta at Parmigiani's, though Roche, for generations of gourmets the only place to buy their cheeses, escargots, and coffee shipped direct from France, is gone forever. *Private Eye** is edited from Carlisle Street and there is still some remnant of the cinema industry in Wardour Street. All in all, though, Soho is a sad place; the focus of attention has shifted to the reborn Covent Garden*. Now a new company has bought the old Trocadero, once the flagship of Joe Lyons, and plans to make it into an urban village with twenty restaurants arranged in

French and Italian quarters. Perhaps this will put Soho back on the map: good luck to them.

Spender, Sir Stephen (born 1909)   When he was made a knight in the 1983 Birthday Honours list, it was objected by one detractor that he had not written one memorable line of poetry. This is demonstrably untrue. 'I think continually of those who were truly great' is a magnificent opening line which resurfaces constantly; as indeed does the last line of the same poem: '. . . and travelled a short while toward the sun / And left the vivid air signed with their honour.' Then for sheer erotic charge it would be hard to beat 'O Night O Trembling Night': 'Covering her body as with dews / Until I brushed her sealing sleep away / To read once more in the uncurtained day / Her naked love, my great good news.'

By outliving his contemporaries – Auden*, MacNeice*, Day Lewis – Spender had to accept a curious foreshortening in the look of his work. Broadly speaking, most of his best poetry was written by the end of the war, but since then he has done excellent work as critic and teacher. His last book, on China, was published as recently as 1982 with drawings by David Hockney. Nor should we forget that he was joint founder and co-editor with Cyril Connolly* of that required reading for the age of longing, the literary magazine *Horizon*, and fourteen years co-editor of *Encounter* too.

With his strong Liberal background, part-Jewish ancestry, doughty anti-fascist record, curiously appropriate war service (in the London fire service) and consistent decency, Spender, though perhaps not so truly great as his dead friends Wystan and Louis, has signed the vivid air with his own honour.

Spitfire   '. . . the machine was sweeter to handle than any other that I had known. I put it through every manoeuvre that I knew of and it responded beautifully. I ended with two flick rolls and turned for home. I was filled with a sudden exhilarating confidence. I could fly a Spitfire; in any position I was its master. It remained to be seen whether I could fight in one.'

So said Richard Hillary* RAF fighter pilot in the Battle of Britain, who went on to prove he could. Nearly nineteen thousand Spitfires were built; its grace, delicacy and speed were never in doubt. It owed its thoroughbred qualities to its descent from the racing aircraft designed by R.J. Mitchell for the Schneider Trophy. Just as Sidney Camm and his team at Hawker's went ahead with the Hurricane* without waiting for government blessing, so Mitchell at Supermarine first built a fighter to

Air Ministry specifications, found it mediocre, scrapped it, and built the exquisite aircraft he wanted on his own initiative.

The Spitfire began its career with a speed of 346 m.p.h. and went on to an eventual maximum of 460 m.p.h. The wing was an almost perfect ellipse; there were no excrescences. The engine was completely cowled and the radiator little more than a slot under the starboard wing. The eight guns made it as lethal as it was lovely.

The early versions were delicate and sensitive, later marques sophisticated and dangerous. The danger to the enemy came from the improved weaponry; to the pilot from the extra power in the Griffon engine which, mishandled, could turn it on its back with sometimes fatal consequences at low altitudes. Later, that problem was ironed out. The Spitfire was a triumph; and the most renowned fighter to fly in the Second World War.

Spoonerisms So called after Warden Spooner of New College, Oxford, who really did announce a hymn one day in chapel as 'Kinquering Kongs their Titles Take.' He was an albino, and suffered from a slight speech impediment which, lovingly proliferated among generations of undergraduates (he was at New College for sixty-two years), gave a new word to the language.

Almost certainly he never perpetrated any of the legions of spoonerisms coined after his initial lapse. That is, he did not, alas, really say: 'You have tasted two whole worms, you have hissed all my mystery lectures: you must leave by the town drain.' Nor did he ever propose the health of our Queer Old Dean.

Yet he has another claim to our respect and affection; for during his wardenship (1903-24), and largely at his instance, a plaque was put up in the college chapel which read: 'In memory of the men of this college who coming from a foreign land entered into the inheritance of this place and returning fought and died for their country in the war 1914-19.' Three German names follow.

Spring The most treacherous of English seasons – providing perennial short measure and dashing uncounted high hopes: April is the cruellest month. However, there is a subdivision of spring which might most properly be called the fifth English season. It is what H.E. Bates called the sudden spring: that moment when the English countryside is caught by surprise and spring breaks a month before its time. When this happens, Bates remarked, 'the English have the occasional satisfaction of gathering flowers long before people living a thousand miles to the south of them'.

On the February day (in 1941 during the bleakest stretch of the war) when he wrote that: 'The grass was luminous with rain and from daybreak there was a bright call of birdsong everywhere. Thrushes sang without rest, and even a cock chaffinch lifted a warm claret breast to the sun . . . leafless crocuses, pale mauve touched with fawn and small alpine anemones, pink and white, were pushing away the drifts of light sepia oak leaves . . . here and there a touch of vivid blue, an early grape hyacinth showed up an eye of magenta-purple, a primula pushing up from wine-veined leaves.'

He concludes that in England, spring, like summer, has no official date, as in other countries. Indeed, the seasons interweave, and he sees the winter as a series of miniature springtimes. Here, perhaps, is the true explanation of spring's persistent elusiveness in England: it is not a season in its own right, but a sport of all the others; a love-child of winter, a decoy used by summer; a *Doppelgänger* of autumn.

Squash   Just as cricket* has been called chess on grass, so squash has been called chess played fast. A descendant of rackets and fives, archetypal public schools games, squash has now spread to all classes and most countries, and is one of the most concentrated modes of taking exercise in huge dollops known to man; and yet another legacy to the pantheon of sports devised by the island race.

Stock Exchange   'A low wretch who makes money by buying and selling shares in funds', Samuel Johnson* wrote of the jobber in his Dictionary, and the broker has not done much better, being associated in the English mind principally with a certain kind of house; a large, comfortable place in the stockbroker belt or outer suburbs with manicured lawns and a name like Seven Acres, built in the Edwardian era in a style known as stockbroker Tudor.

The Stock Exchange is renowned for its chauvinism (women were not admitted till 1973, foreigners in 1971), for its cliquishness, and for being the principal source of improper stories. Orwell* predicted its abolition; instead, it has grown steadily more technical and remote, dealing increasingly with the big institutions who now account for ninety per cent of the business in gilts and two-thirds of all the trade in equities.

There are nevertheless thought to be still some two million private investors in the country, but little is heard of them until they are courted in a takeover bid, one of those moments in English life when sporting considerations are put on one side and the English businessman is seen at his most steely, ruthless, venal and greedy.

Suburbs They are the great undiscovered areas of England. They have attracted little literature, and hardly any art. Whoever wrote a symphony to a suburb? They have no real past, and no clear future. They are homogenised politically, economically, culturally and racially. Frederic Raphael put the point well in *The Glittering Prizes*: 'I come from suburbia. . . I don't ever want to go back. It's the one place in the world that's further away than anywhere else.'

So the aspiring suburban young head for the inner city, where they will find jobs, contacts, ideas, money, power; perhaps even fame; but at the very least excitement. When they have carved out their piece of pie they will move right out far beyond the suburbs, to the deep country again. The suburbs are thus the one part of England no one is proud to be coming from. It is one thing to hail from Sherborne or Smethwick, suggesting as they do tranquil rural arcadia on the one hand, or gritty northern reality on the other, and quite another to come from Surbiton or Sutton which seem to stand for nothing.

But is it quite as simple as that? Where did these suburban millions come from, thronging the mock Tudor houses along the great and ghastly ribbon developments of the thirties? From agricultural labour and domestic service, to turn the cogs of the great banks and insurance companies of the City of London just before the computers came; conventional, law-abiding, aspiring men and their wives. Unconscious exemplars of the territorial imperative, they put fences round their little plots and filled them with flowers. They lived, worked, loved, played, dreamed and died there, these New Pooters; nine million nobodys. Perhaps one day they will be noticed.

Suffolk Though it has its fair claim to poets (George Crabbe, Thomas Nashe, Edward Fitzgerald) the flat brooding landscape and wide dreaming skies of Suffolk have worked potently on the imagination of two English painters and one English musician of genius. Benjamin Britten was born at Lowestoft and died at Aldeburgh, where with his friend Peter Pears he had instituted a world-famous music festival and built a splendid concert hall in the Maltings at nearby Snape. He used local themes and characters in his work, most notably in his opera *Peter Grimes,* whose first night was a triumph in the annals of English music to rank with the début of Elgar's *Enigma Variations.* Yet the visual thrall of Suffolk has been the most remarkable of all.

John Constable, greatest English landscape painter of the nineteenth century, declared roundly that it was the Suffolk countryside in which he grew up which had made him into a painter. As the *Dictionary of*

National Biography records, he was 'the first to paint the greenness and moisture of his native country, the first to paint the noon sunshine with its white light pouring down through the leaves and sparkling in the foliage and the grass ... the first to paint truly the sun-shot clouds of a showery sky, the first to represent faithfully the rich colours of an English landscape ... the first to suggest so fully not only the sights but the sounds of nature, the gurgle of the water, the rustle of the trees.'

Gainsborough, his great precursor, bore the same testimony to the spell of that hypnotically empty landscape. Sent to his uncle's grammar school, he spent all his holidays sketching, and declared that there was not 'a picturesque clump of trees, nor even a single tree of any beauty, no, nor a hedgerow, stem or post' in or around his native town of Sudbury in Suffolk that was not from his earliest years treasured in his memory.

To this day people visiting old Suffolk market towns like Lavenham with its characteristic orange-washed half-timbered houses, and un-spoiled Suffolk fishing villages like Orford, are taken by their sense of isolation and preoccupation; not so much with time past as time lost; and the country between these dreamlike places still retains that other-worldly aura which moved Gainsborough in his time, Constable in his, and Britten in ours.

Summer 'Summer has set in with its usual severity,' wrote Samuel Taylor Coleridge, thus encapsulating what every Englishman knows: that summer's lease hath all too short a date. Indeed, there is a curious short circuit in the Englishman's mind which allows him to believe that summer does not really exist: or rather that it used to exist but has recently become extinct. Every Englishman remembers the great summers of the past and most noticeably, even if he was not alive at the time, the summers of 1914 and 1939. 'Before the war, and especially before the Boer War, it was summer all the year round,' remarked George Orwell*.

The hard reality behind this myth is that the capricious English climate dishes up vile and sweet weather with an impartial hand; in 1975 snow stopped play at a game of cricket in June, while the next year a temperature of 110 degrees Fahrenheit on the centre court at Wimble-don caused four hundred spectators to faint. Given these baffling parameters, the English have simply elected to *pretend* that summer will come and have put the Derby* and Royal Ascot* in June, Henley* and the British Open in July, Cowes Week and the Glorious Twelfth in August.

Sometimes, of course, these high festivals of alfresco England take place in torrential monsoons and sometimes in a glinting glory of summer sun. The English mind then simply erases all the former experiences from the tape of memory and joins up the others to make up one vast, collective recall of shimmering heat, strawberries and cream, and hearts at peace under an English heaven. 'Summer afternoon – summer afternoon', said Henry James, 'to me those have always been the most beautiful words in the English language.'

Sunday   It has had a bad press in England; not unnaturally, for in the racial folk memory its traditional melancholy is pervasive. 'Bugger Sunday, I say', declares George Gladwell, the forty-four-year-old blacksmith in Ronald Blythe's modern classic *Akenfield*. He did not use the words lightly: he was born in 1925, but could remember people in the village as recently as the thirties going to chapel at nine in the morning and not coming home till eight at night. 'It's a fact. They were nothing but a lot of bloody hypocrites. Suffolk used to worship Sunday, not God.'

Even among the godless, the English Sunday hardly sounded more attractive; it was the time, as Alan Bennett wrote in *Forty Years On*, for washing the car, tinned peaches and Carnation Milk. It was also, certainly in the working class, the time to send the children off to Sunday School in the afternoon and use their absence to procreate some more.

However, all these stereotypes are dissolving as religion weakens its hold and affluence seeps through the land. You have, for a start, a choice no other country can offer, of eight national newspapers delivered to the door. They range from some of the very worst to some of the very best in the world, and you will be reclusive indeed if you find nothing in any of them to interest you. At noon the pubs* will open to receive you and somehow in England it hardly seems to matter that they are not open sooner. A few jars of ale or gin and tonic will fortify you for the roast beef and Yorkshire pud* of old England and then if the garden* does not call there are museums and galleries, fishing* or football*, concerts or cricket*.

When evening comes you will be a dullard indeed if nothing can hold your interest in the four national television stations and four BBC radio channels pouring out their wares all evening. Then, thanks to the great family of Patel* you can shop all day long as if it were a weekday. If you have a rotten Sunday in England nowadays you frankly have only yourself to blame.

Tarzan   What is a healthy outdoor all-American hero like Tarzan doing in an English companion? Tarzan was, of course, an Englishman, indeed, an English aristocrat: heir to Lord Greystoke when shipwrecked as a baby and left to be brought up by the apes; later he succeeded to the title. He is not the first member of the House of Lords to swing from a rope, though we must trust he will be the last.

Taylor, A.J.P. (born 1906)   He is the epitome of an English radical. He has never appeared in a New Year or Birthday Honours List and may well have turned down the invitation. He has not been honoured by his old university of Oxford with either a chair or an honorary degree (though both his old colleges there have made him an honorary fellow). No matter. His distinction comes not from what others make of him but from being his own man: a Lancashire cotton merchant's son, born to wealth, liberalism, nonconformism and conscientious objection, who has become historian to the man in the street, the first academic to find fame on television, and still the only one to give a half-hour lecture without note or prompter.

He has written twenty-eight books, most recently a highly engaging autobiography in which he manfully interweaves the tangled story of his private life and three marriages (his first wife Margaret fell hopelessly in love with both Robert Kee and Dylan Thomas). His most notable book, though, is his volume in the Oxford History of England, *English History 1914-1945*. He very nearly gave up when he got to 1931, depressed by the bleak politics of the era, when his bosom friend Beaverbrook* simply got out of his chair one night and walked up and down, talking off the cuff so compellingly about the men and issues – Baldwin ('what a rascal'), the Hoare Laval plan, the Abdication – that Taylor, shamed, took up his pen again.

It is the only one of the fifteen Oxford volumes to tell its story through the lives of ordinary people and was well called by Max Beloff a populist history. The style is crisp, racy, idiosyncratic. The last paragraph gives a vivid taste of the whole; of great learning lightly worn: 'In the second world war the British people came of age. This was a people's war. Not only were their needs considered. They themselves wanted to win. . . The British Empire declined; the condition of the people improved. Few now sang "Land of Hope and Glory". Few even sang "England Arise". England had risen all the same.'

Tea The English national drink has evolved its own rites and myths. Thus, there is the snobbery over whether the milk goes in first or not. It makes a better mix if it does, but is not deemed quite OK socially – the point is memorably made by John Betjeman* in his celebrated poem 'How to Get On in Society' where the wretched *nouveau riche* lady, having already committed any number of howlers, asks, 'Milk and then just as it comes dear?' There is the snobbery over which tea to use, Earl Grey being decidedly upmarket and China tea smarter than Indian. There is the snobbery which says tea after lunch* or dinner is decidedly socially inferior to coffee.

Tea has been a social catalyst in England for three hundred years, though the teashop is no older than the 1880s, when an enterprising ABC manageress, finding her friends enjoyed coming to the back of her shop for a cup of tea, put the table in front, thus launching a nationwide vogue. The tea-dance of the twenties seemed to have died, but is now having a spirited revival; to meet it Lyons recently reopened one of their flagships, the old prewar Corner Houses that seemed to have gone under with 78 r.p.m. records and double-breasted suits. Indeed, up and down England, inflation has driven people back to the teashop from the restaurant; to that calorific cornucopia that ranges from Westmorland parkin, rum nicky and Bakewell tart in the north, through cream teas in the Cotswolds, cucumber sandwiches in the Thames valley, and Lincolnshire shortbread in East Anglia to the toasted crumpets, home-made scones and buttered muffins of the south.

Whatever the vagaries of fashion in English tea-drinking, however, one institution remains inviolable and rock-solid: the early morning cuppa which dissolves sleep and prepares the Englishman for the day ahead.

Traditionally and quite properly made by the man in the house, it has clarified the minds of great generals like Monty who worked out his battle plans while sipping his char, and soothed the hangovers of equally great and only slightly fictional characters like Bertie Wooster.

Team Spirit Though the principle itself clearly goes back to Arnold and the kind of public school he engendered with its aura of muscular religion, cold baths and loyalty to house, school and country, the phrase itself is curiously little chronicled. Indeed in the *OED Supplement* it is first supported by a quotation as recently as 1928, and then in an industrial context. Frank Muir was much nearer the mark when in 1976 he wrote of schools 'sending forth ... superbly fit chaps, light on imagination but strong on team spirit'.

Perhaps the most absurd yet memorable extension of team spirit to real life occurs in Sir Henry Newbolt's poem 'Vitaë Lampada' with its celebrated opening: 'There's a breathless hush in the Close tonight'. There was, that summer evening, as every Englishman knows, a bumping pitch and a blinding light, ten to make and the last man in. 'And it's not for the sake of a ribboned coat, / Or the selfish hope of a season's fame / But his Captain's hand on his shoulder smote / Play up! Play up! and play the game!'

Whether in truth a captain at Clifton, Newbolt's old school, would ever have uttered words so monumentally daft at such a moment is hard, a hundred years on, to know. What is quite certain is that the scene in the second stanza, where the action has shifted to some desperate outpost of the Raj, is simply not credible. 'The sand of the desert is sodden red / Red with the wreck of a square that broke / The Gatling's jammed and the Colonel dead / And the regiment blind with dust and smoke.'

Things look pretty grim. England's far, and Honour a name. 'But the voice of a schoolboy rallies the ranks / "Play up! Play up! and play the game!"' This is intolerable. Newbolt never heard a shot fired in anger or he would hardly have perpetrated such patent balderdash. Nevertheless the absurdity, set in the aspic of the age when it was written, was to bring him instant fame. He was made a Companion of Honour, won honorary degrees from Bristol, Glasgow, St Andrew's, Sheffield, Toronto, Oxford and Cambridge, and the esteem of such eminent contemporaries as Robert Bridges, A.J. Balfour, H.G. Wells and Sir Edward Grey. He died in 1938, full of years and honour: but would not have been so honoured in modern England.

This is not because teams have ceased to exert loyalties, but because to spell out such allegiances publicly is to invite your team's belly laugh.

When Montgomery, at an Eighth Army reunion soon after the war, urged his former troops to remember in peace the tow-ropes they had used in the desert (only owing to an unfortunate impediment he called them tow-wopes) he got a ribald response. This is not to say that no Desert Rat would never extend a tow-rope to another, only that he would not want the gesture, or the frame of mind, ratified and promulgated.

Team spirit, in short, has become a rather private matter, in England, referred to allusively, almost apologetically. The only exception to this rule of modern English life occurs in the 'team talk', a dire American importation in which international teams are worked into a state of perfervid excitement by an impassioned address just before the game. The Welsh, with their passion for the *hwl*, are past masters at the team talk and it is said that an address by the former rugby star turned BBC boss, Cliff Morgan, in which the welfare of wives and families was invoked, would cause men to try to break down the doors to get at the opposition. However, the English are shy about such naked displays of emotion, and reluctant to talk about either 'team spirit' or the 'team talk' which is said to engender it.

Tennis   Originally a game for bored monks, real – or more properly royal – tennis, an indoor cult game now played at only a handful of clubs in America and England by dedicated enthusiasts, seems to have been transmogrified into lawn tennis at Hampton Court. Here there had long been (and still is) a real tennis court; but those waiting for a game began to amuse themselves by knocking a tennis ball around on the lawns outside. Certainly a rudimentary form of lawn tennis was played in the sixteenth century, for the pleasure of Queen Elizabeth I, by servants of the Earl of Hertford in Somerset. However, as in so many sports, it was left to the Victorians to put the modern game on the map.

In 1872 two Birmingham enthusiasts called Gem and Pereira, abetted by two local doctors, set up the first lawn tennis club at the Manor House Hotel in Leamington Spa. It was two years later that a Major Wingfield applied to patent the game of lawn tennis, which he at first envisaged as being played on an hour-glass court. This curious shape was supported by the MCC who at that stage still had some parental authority over the new game. In that same year, however, the All England Croquet Club began to play lawn tennis, and the MCC's days as controllers were numbered. In 1877 the *Field* magazine put up twenty-five guineas for a new cup to be played for at the All England Club, and a sub-committee was set up to modify the rules. What they decided still governs the shape of modern tennis: a rectangular court 78 by 27 feet, with a net lowered to

3 feet 3 inches at the centre, thus giving to the fearsomely fast server the early advantage which has never really deserted him.

Wimbledon*, despite all the tantrums and rows, remains the mecca of the game; but it is played at all levels and in all parts of England by English people of all ages and kinds. It has never been more lovingly enshrined than in the poem 'A Subaltern's Love Song' by John Betjeman*, where the laureate imagines himself taking on one of those archetypal outdoor girls who is much too good for him: 'Love thirty, Love forty, Oh weakness of joy / The speed of a swallow, The grace of a boy... How mad I am, glad I am, sad that you won / I am weak from your loveliness / Joan Hunter Dunn.' Betjeman takes his beating like a man: 'Her warm-handled racket is back in its press / But my shock-headed victor / She loves me no less.'

The celebrated words 'Anyone for tennis?', stock augury for the sort of play Aunt Edna would have loved, were never uttered in that order by anybody. Amazingly, the youthful Humphrey Bogart, in his first walk-on part as a Broadway *ingénu*, may have got as close to uttering them as anyone.

The Thames The entire undergraduate population of Oxford* jumped into its waters and drowned for love of Zuleika Dobson*. The three little Liddell girls first heard the story of Alice in Wonderland as Lewis Carroll* rowed them along it one golden day in 1862. Jerome K. Jerome came paddling rather inexpertly along it often in the 1880s with his friends George Wingrave and Carl Hentschel, thus providing him with the raw material for his immortal *Three Men in a Boat*. By its banks Kenneth Grahame first told his four-year-old son Alastair the story of *The Wind in the Willows**.

The Thames *Zeitgeist* is clear enough: whimsy, romance, mystery and scandal. William Morris played out his celebrated *ménage à trois* at Kelmscott with his wife Jane and Dante Gabriel Rossetti; the eccentric and dissolute Francis Dashwood conducted his obscene rites with his debauched friends John Wilkes and the Prince of Wales at Medmenham Abbey by the Thames; while not far down the river at Cliveden, at one of Lord Astor's lavish parties in 1961, the Secretary of State for War, John Profumo, met a girl called Christine Keeler. Its hospitable banks accommodate the Palace of Westminster, St Thomas's Hospital (whose students have been able to land missiles from their side of the water on the Mother of Parliaments with a giant home-made catapult), two universities (Oxford* and Reading), three famous schools (Eton*, Radley and St Paul's), a film studio (Shepperton) and a plethora of pubs ranging from the ritzy Rose Revived at Newbridge (built *c.*1250) to the metropolitan Dove at Hammersmith, haunt of Ernest Hemingway, Sylvia Plath, Graham Greene, A.P. Herbert and many generations of rowing men. Fun is the name of the game: see also under *Maidenhead.*

Thank-you   It takes four *thank-yous* for a ticket to be bought in an English bus. First the bus conductor heaves in sight and calls out *thank-you* (I have arrived). The passenger then hands over his 30p with an answering call of *thank-you* (I note that you have arrived and here is my fare). The conductor then hands over the ticket with another *thank-you* (I acknowledge receipt of your fare and here is your ticket in return) whereupon the passenger replies *thank-you* (thank-you).

This elaborate and formal ritual amazes Americans, who can do the whole transaction with hardly a single *thank-you* being exchanged. It certainly slows life up, but oils the gears of everyday intercourse. It is also the curious custom in English pubs for the customer to say *thank-you* on receiving his beer and *thank-you* again on leaving the pub. The well-mannered publican, if he hears, will respond to each in kind.

Even on British Rail trains, the guard will thank his passengers for listening to him, as will the British Air pilot after communing with his. All this archaic ceremonial probably reflects the gradual escape of a very old feudal society from its medieval chrysalis. It also reflects another curious hole in the English language; for whereas a Frenchman can say *de rien* neatly and politely when someone says *merci* to him, the English vernacular is defective in the reciprocal.

'Don't mention it' is dated, and 'don't mensh' positively Edwardian in its masher-like larkiness. The American riposte, 'you're welcome', sounds too folksy on this side of the Atlantic. So it is 'thank-you', 'thank-you', 'thank-you', and 'thank-you'.

They   One of the most troublesome words the Englishman has to cope with; and in more than one way. It is a grammatical trap (everybody has *their* price). It is also a handy portmanteau word for the anonymous hosts of invisible authority ('they're building a new airfield down the road'). *Pace* the feminist movement, everybody has *his* price. As for that new airfield, aren't *we* building it? The latter difficulty is profound, and may have a lot to do with the fallible nature of a democratic society that is still only skin deep.

The Thirties It was a mean and shoddy time. It was the decade of the hunger marches and the Left Book Club, of gormless comedians like George Formby and guileless comediennes like Gracie Fields, of George V's silver jubilee and Edward VIII's abdication. It was the decade that Hitler came to power and Chamberlain flew to Munich; of the 1936 Olympics, when the flashing black legs of champion sprinter Jesse Owens made mincemeat of Nazi theories about race supremacy. It was the era of civil war in Spain and the ominous, distant war in China. It was the golden age of wireless and high summer for the popular press. It was vintage time for motor racing at Brooklands and joyriding at Croydon airport. It was the era of Amy Johnson, everybody's favourite girl, who took to flying too high with some guy in the sky (in this case the dissolute and cack-handed Jim Mollison). It was the heyday of the socially conscious novel: A.J. Cronin's *The Citadel* and Richard Llewellyn's *How Green Was My Valley*. It was the time when Bernard Shaw* and Julian Huxley went to Stalin's Russia and liked what they saw; or more accurately, what they were shown. It was prime time for the thirties poets Auden*, Spender* and MacNeice*: hard-nosed, unsentimental, worldly men who saw the canker in the rose. It was for every schoolboy one endless summer in which to savour the majestic batting of Donald Bradman and the bodyline bowling of Harold Larwood. It was the famous time when Tommy Farr, the boy from Tonypandy, went the distance with the previously unstoppable heavyweight champion of the world Joe Louis, and countless Englishmen sat up in the small hours to hear the epic battle on their crackling, whistling radios. It was cocktail time for those who could afford it. It saw the fight for the Blue Riband of the Atlantic, the birth of the Dorchester Hotel* and the launch of Penguin books. It was the heyday of the Reverend Dick Sheppard at St Martin in the Fields and Charles Laughton at the local Odeon as Henry VIII, or Quasimodo or Captain Bligh. It was the decade that began with the great Stock Exchange crash and ended with the Second World War. Through it all, and in ironic counterpart to the increasingly sombre scene, men like George Gershwin, Cole Porter and Noël Coward* wrote the most carefree popular music, full of fizz and wit; the music and poetry were two of the very few products of the thirties worth remembering.

The Times It is not what it was, say the Jeremiahs; but then it never has been. These prophets of woe should be asked to give a clear account of the golden period from which *The Times* has lapsed. They do not mean, surely, those early years two centuries ago when both owner and managing editor did spells in prison, and the government paid secret sweeteners to ensure favourable coverage. Nor, surely, do they mean a century ago, when *The Times* was made a laughing stock and very nearly ruined by publishing a series of palpable forgeries it alleged to be in the hand of the Irish leader Parnell. Nor can they mean surely the early twenties, when *The Times* had a proprietor, Lord Northcliffe, who had clearly lost his marbles; and most certainly of all, not, surely, the thirties, when its editor, Geoffrey Dawson wrote that night after night he did his utmost to keep out of the paper anything that might hurt the susceptibilities of the Nazis.

Yet of course there have been shafts of light and triumph between the years of gloom and folly. The brilliant despatches of William Howard Russell from the Crimean War saved an army and destroyed a government. When Russell went on to report the Civil War in America he was received in Washington by President Lincoln himself. 'Mr Russell,' said the President, 'I am very glad to make your acquaintance. The London *Times* is one of the greatest powers in the world – in fact I don't know anything which has much more power – except perhaps the Mississippi.' Yet Russell's coverage of the Battle of Bull Run incensed the North, who had lost it. He was never allowed south, and came home in 1862, to be replaced by Charles Mackay, a fanatical advocate of the South, who was to cover the war for the next three years from there in a totally partisan fashion.

Still, *The Times* played a crucial role in bringing down Asquith in 1916 and came out of the General Strike with credit: not only was it the only independent paper to continue to publish (the *British Gazette* was a government mouthpiece); it even drew praise from the left-wing *New Statesman* for the fairness and balance of its coverage.

One of its problems has been that foreigners have understood it to be the voice of the British government; in truth, as we have seen, it has been at its best in bringing down governments; and earned its nickname, 'The Thunderer', for the passion and power with which it advocated the great Reform Bill of 1832. Yet not even the most scrupulous drafting has been able to secure *The Times* a future combining editorial independence with financial viability. The Astors, who had bought it from Northcliffe, were compelled to sell it to the Thomsons, who threw their hand in when they were £70 million down. In 1979 it was shut for nigh on a year; since then it has acquired another new owner in Rupert Murdoch, and has had three editors. What it clearly needs now is a long stretch of peace: whether it will get it is anybody's guess.

Traitors Though England has had its refugee traitors like Fuchs and Pontecorvo, the names that still haunt the English imagination are the diplomats, Donald Maclean and Guy Burgess, who disappeared together one day in May 1951 and surfaced four years later in Moscow. They were upper-middle-class Englishmen, public school and Cambridge*, alcoholic and fatherless, who were traitors to their country but who, it seemed to the man in the street, had been protected by their class long past the point of reasonable doubt.

Persistent murmurs that there must have been a third man, much higher up, who had made their escape possible by warning them it was time to go, reverberated until Kim Philby (Westminster and Cambridge) was unmasked; and then came the sensational disclosure that Anthony Blunt (Marlborough and Cambridge), principal adviser on the Queen's pictures, no less, had been a traitor too. What incensed the ordinary Englishman was that all four seemed still to live within the invisible web of Establishment connection even *after* they had been rumbled; Blunt, for example, was even given an excellent lunch in *The Times** boardroom.

The notion of the well-bred traitor imprisoned in the aspic of Russian life, still loyally English in all but one crucial regard, has fascinated English writers like Cyril Connolly* (who saw Maclean on the day he disappeared and wrote a short book, *The Missing Diplomats*, on the theme) and Alan Bennett (who has written two excellent plays on it: *The Old Country* and *An Englishman Abroad*).

Bennett in particular has explored the ironies with delicate skill: in *The Old Country* the traitor Hilary is living in a nondescript country house set in a landscape which could well be Aldershot*, and is revealed only halfway through the first act as somewhere outside Moscow. He still wears his Garrick Club tie, reads *The Times*, and plays Elgar* incessantly on his gramophone. Meanwhile Burgess, in *An Englishman Abroad*, asks the actress Coral Brown (who played herself on BBC TV) to order a new suit from his London tailor and a fresh Old Etonian tie to replace his worn one.

What he misses in exile from London is the gossip* ('How is Auden? Have you seen Connolly?') and he, too, has a theme tune for his gramophone: Jack Buchanan singing over and over again 'Who Stole my Heart Away?' Bennett put into Burgess's mouth his own position: 'I can say I love London. I can say I love England. I can't say I love my country, because I don't know what that means.'

Tunbridge Wells All nine English spas, in the nature of things, symbolise the status quo, though one (Bath*), has now become so cosmopolitan that the faint aroma of reaction has been long drowned in headier scents, and two (Droitwich and Woodhall) are really too small to have impinged much on the national consciousness at all. The remaining six (Buxton, Cheltenham*, Harrogate, Malvern, Leamington and Tunbridge Wells) will all strike the average Englishman as bastions of bourgeois conformity; but of the doughty half-dozen only one has entered the language. Disgusted of Tunbridge Wells has become the notional signatory of countless cod letters (most typically to the *Daily Telegraph*) railing against the collapse of what he sees as civilisation. What Tunbridge Wells did to get lumbered with Disgusted is not totally clear; but lumbered it assuredly is.

The Twenties The grievous domestic problems that had obsessed English life before the First World War afterwards came back again unsolved and exigent: the future of Ireland; the status of women; the fate of the miners. As England knows to her cost, they have still not gone away as the century draws to its close. There were watersheds: the union with Ireland was ended in 1922, but the festering sore of Ulster remained; women over thirty got the vote in 1918 though the so-called flappers, or women in their twenties, had to wait till 1928 till they were enfranchised too; the miners were defeated when they struck in 1921 and again when they led the General Strike in 1926; they would have to wait till 1974 when they smashed the Heath government for their revenge.

Yet 1926 was the last year in which a clear class struggle was fought; after the two inconclusive minority Labour governments of the 1920s, a sizable part of the middle class threw in their lot with the working class to form the great reforming Attlee Labour government of 1945-51. Back in the twenties the fear of red revolution was real enough; returning ex-servicemen who had the training – and the motive – to precipitate revolution were bought off with generous welfare settlements until they were resettled.

Ex-officers, who were supposed to have private means, frequently spent their gratuities on businesses that went bust; and the discontented, unemployed ex-officer was to play the hero in the thrillers of Sapper and the detective stories of Dorothy L. Sayers. He was also, in the real world, to officer the brutal Black and Tans, whose appalling reign of terror in Ireland just before independence created a bitter urge to revenge that is still being worked out.

The fear of revolution remained real enough: an Oxford undergraduate and ex-officer was asked to leave Balliol, of all places, because he had passed his vacations in Russia. It was the era of the bottle party and the Bright Young Things; the Charleston and the shimmy; of swindlers like Jimmy White and Horatio Bottomley; cocktails and cigarette holders; Noël Coward* and Somerset Maugham* had four plays apiece running in the West End. It was the era of ribbon development and mock Tudor, silent films and lawn tennis.

Despite the incursion of the dreadful *nouveaux riches*, the hard-faced men who had done well out of the war, the upper class carried on as if nothing had happened; it was the age of the great society hostesses like Lady Cunard and Lady Sybil Colefax. It looked as if the Jazz Age had come to stay: but the collapse of the New York stock market on 29 October 1929 spelled goodbye to all that.

Twickenham   It was Philip Toynbee who once remarked that a bomb under the West Car Park at Twickenham would end fascism in England for a generation. The fact is that it is not the jackboot but the car boot which is the symbol of rugby football's international headquarters, and on the day of a big game it is instructive to stroll between the lines of parked Rovers and Jaguars inspecting the cornucopia on display: barbecues and *boeuf en croûte*, salmon and sandwiches, chicken and cheddar, plonk*, Scotch, bubbly and barrels of beer. A conscientious appraisal of the massed revellers would suggest that any lurking fascists are effectively drowned in the shoals of schoolmasters down from the north, Welsh miners, Scottish salesmen, Frenchmen on a weekend spree from the Dordogne, and Irish priests. Say what you will, a Twickers crowd is typically in high good humour, and despite the huge quantities of booze put away, outbreaks of fisticuffs and chauvinistic set-tos are rare indeed. As big money inexorably seeps into this traditionally amateur game, the goodwill may seep out at the other end: it usually does.

Underground   It is easy to forget how old it is. The Metropolitan, oldest underground line in the world, was opened in 1863. There is a photograph of Gladstone sitting in an open carriage wearing a top hat. These early undergrounds were served by steam trains and were only just below the surface: channels over which new buildings would later form a roof. With the coming of electric trains far deeper shafts could be dug, but only at some expense; many streams had to be channelled and the river Westbourne, for example, can still be seen carried in pipes above the station at Sloane Square. The Bakerloo line is said to have originated in the desire of City businessmen to see the last hour's cricket at Lord's without leaving their offices too early (if so, they might have placed St John's Wood station rather closer to the ground).

Today the Underground has proliferated till it thrusts deep into outer suburbia: to High Barnet and Upminster; Wimbledon, West Ruislip and most recently Heathrow. Though underground travel offers a womb-like intensity – and indeed at rush hours a well-documented adventure playground for frottage – it has not precipitated such a rich literature as the railway. Nevertheless, it floats in the Englishman's mind as the backdrop for some of Henry Moore's most memorable wartime paintings of Londoners sheltering from the bombs above.

The poet of the Underground is John Betjeman* ('Gaily into Ruislip Gardens / Runs the red electric train / With a thousand ta's and pardon's / Daintily alights Elaine.') Alas, the early innocence of the Underground has been swallowed up by bomb alerts and casual muggings; the scene for grisly suicides, inexplicable crashes, and one or two fine cops-and-robbers chases along the tunnel. It has been a political arena, as when Ken Livingstone, leader of the GLC, drastically lowered all the fares as a populist gesture; an industrial cockpit when closed by strikes; and an exhibition gallery for the display of new and bold forms of poster art.

United States When Mrs John Bull's Westclox alarm goes she puts on her Maidenform bra, Playtex girdle and Max Factor lipstick. She breakfasts on Weetabix, washes up with Fairy Liquid, and Hoovers the house. Then she goes shopping in the Ford, buys Campbell's soups in the Safeway supermarket, and in the afternoon makes a dress on her Singer sewing machine. Later she answers the children's questions from the *Encyclopedia Britannica*, pays the Diner's Club account, and watches a Columbia film on television.

Her husband comes home in a Hertz hire car. They retire to bed under their Monogram electric blanket, and her husband swears he will dream of his firm, the advertising giant J. Walter Thompson. This scenario – much scaled down here – forms the preface to a book called *The American Take Over of Britain* by James McMillan and Bernard Harris. The point they are making is that every single brand named is American. Does it matter? Would England be a better place without Fords or Hoovers? The debate can go either way; but the fact of the American domination cannot be gainsaid. It soaks through every crevice of English life.

Insofar as this American suzerainty is economic most Englishmen outside the committed left accept or even welcome it. Insofar as it is political their attitude is ambivalent. On the one hand, they know perfectly well that only American intervention won two world wars. As Winston Churchill put it after Pearl Harbor: 'To have the United States on our side was to me the greatest joy ... So we had won after all! ... England would live.' On the other, incidents like the Grenada action remind them uneasily that when the chips are down America is perfectly prepared to go it alone; and whatever the political disclaimers no English restraining hand holds a key to the horrendous American missiles now pointing into the Russian heartland from English soil.

This political collision is not new. 'The Great Republic was the chief foreign threat to the well-being of the British Empire', wrote James Morris in his imperial trilogy *Pax Britannica*. 'Time and again since Victoria's accession the two Powers had quarrelled ... over the sovereignty of Oregon, over British naval supremacy during the American Civil War, repeatedly over Newfoundland fishing rights, incessantly over Canadian frontier issues.'

Still, none of this mattered much if, like many Englishmen of the time, you saw America as hardly a foreign power at all. The *Illustrated London News*, in its Christmas issue for 1849, said that though the British race would undoubtedly continue to rule the world, it would presently be from the other side of the Atlantic. Well, it has not worked out like that, and even the romantic notion propounded by Harold Macmillan that England is playing Greece to America's Rome is as condescending as it is simplistic. The interplay between the two cultures is so intricately woven that it can no longer be disentangled, and perhaps this is the most reassuring point about it.

The Royal Shakespeare Company may slay them on Broadway; but the best modern life of Shakespeare is by a professor of English at Northwestern University (Samuel Schoenbaum) just as the best edition of Shakespeare's Sonnets is by a Berkeley professor (Stephen Booth). The *Oxford English Dictionary* remains the greatest reservoir of the English language; the *New Yorker* the most scrupulously tended mill through which it courses. Meantime the Hoovers seem destined to prevail in England, at least until Hondas go into the business: but that, thank heaven, will be for a future edition of this companion.

Up An English adverb of enormous power. It lends spectacular magnification to otherwise unremarkable words; thus to be 'beaten up' is far more comprehensive than to be merely beaten, a 'fry-up' more enticing than a fry, a 'ton-up' (100 m.p.h. for the unworldly) on a motorbike far more dashing than doing a ton, a 'balls-up' a far greater disaster than making a mere balls of something can ever be; to be 'done up' far more thoroughgoing than to be done. And note how in the Harrow* school song, 'Forty Years On', which Winston Churchill* so delighted to sing even in old age, up makes all the difference. 'Follow up, follow up, follow up' is a call to action and to arms; 'follow, follow, follow' is something you do when dreamily pursuing the merry merry pipes of Pan. Up, on its own, is moreover an expletive of great if coarse power, as in 'up yours, mate'. It is also used poignantly in the vernacular verdict, 'he can't get it up any more' or more personally, 'he can't get it up for her'.

Valentines Nothing is so calculated to overthrow a national stereotype as the behaviour of the English on St Valentine's Day. Some eight and a half million Valentine cards are dispatched, and newspapers groan under the weight of a great gallimaufry of bizarre, arcane and often unashamedly erotic messages. 'Petalbum sends nuzzles and kisses to his favourite duck', says one in the normally po-faced *Times*. 'Pin', declaims a *Guardian* troubadour, 'nibble my nose and I'll follow you anywhere.'

Even the stern comrades on the communist *Morning Star* are not immune: 'James. This is more than just a petty bourgeois, individualist, ideological construct. Your relatively autonomous Jackie.' Images of small and furry animals abound: 'Pooh Bear. Will you be my valentine. Your small, squeaky-voiced but highly intellectual piglet.' Sometimes past glories are relived: 'Wally Jumblatt Thank you for revolutionising my knicker collection. Love Pole Pole.' Sometimes a lover's lacunae are forgiven, as in 'Furry furry lovekin Love you eternally, even the wobbly bits. Hairy Bear.'

Sometimes crabbed age and youth seem to have clicked, as in 'Elaine: Love you lots. You make an old man very happy.' Sometimes the message is unfashionably romantic: 'L. May I walk out one midsummer morning with you knee deep in wild irises? Love M.' And sometimes we hear intimations of lost love calling for its own: 'Hairy Bum you matter to me. Come back soon. Love you forever Fatty.'

The point about this collective English February folly is that nothing similar is known in France or in Germany, or even in America. It is yet more evidence of the total unpredictability of the English.

Victoria Station   It was in fact two stations, one serving the Brighton* line, the other Dover*. The former was thought the smarter and in *The Importance of Being Earnest*, Oscar Wilde made a point of the fact that, though Jack Worthing had been found in a handbag at Victoria, it was at least on the Brighton side. Though all great stations have what Cyril Connolly called *angoisse des gares*, giving us that stab of anxiety as we arrive or depart, he felt it most keenly at Victoria and worst in the evenings. It was the scene for uncounted partings as the troop trains took to France thousands of men who would never come back.

In a happier context, Victoria is the symbolic gateway to the start of immeasurable adventures abroad, and Ernie Bevin spoke for all Englishmen when he defined his foreign policy as being able to buy a ticket at Victoria Station and going anywhere he damned well pleased. It was, for instance, the place from which the Golden Arrow, that magical train with the chocolate and cream Pullman cars and engines bearing names like *Excalibur* and *Tintagel*, began its daily run to Paris.

It made its last run on 30 September 1972 because too many people perversely preferred the plane. The buxom *Brighton Belle* has gone too, and with it those breakfast kippers which famously sustained Lord Olivier as he journeyed up to Victoria.

Village   It is in a sense the most interesting focus through which to study modern England: exemplar of a past which never really existed; snapshot of a present which shifts as we try to understand it; blueprint of a future which is essentially unknowable. It is a cluster of country dwellings, with something between a hundred and a thousand inhabitants: less would make it a hamlet; more, a small town. Typically, it will contain one pub*, one church, and one post office* (which may double as the village grocery). It might well be blessed with a green, a square or triangle of turf on which cricket* is played in the summer, football* in the winter. Yet, if we look a little closer, we may well see that the church is open only fitfully, if at all, its parish having been amalgamated with several neighbours* in some Church of England reshuffle; the pub may have been taken over by some giant chain, and feature juke boxes and space invaders with the fizzed beer and potato crisps; the post office may be moribund and its grocery losing ground to the supermarket in the nearest town. Things are not what they were. The village approximates to an ideal way of life the further one is away from it. Certainly to the original inhabitants, there was nothing particularly romantic or desirable about a tied cottage* where tenancy turned, more or less, on the whim of the owner and the compliance of the tenant. Who found Arcadia in a two-up, two-down hovel with no dampcourse, no heating and no running water? Love in a hut, with water and a crust, as Keats reminds us, is, love forgive us, cinders, ashes, dust. So the original denizens of the village with any get-up-and-go got up and went. The people they left behind tended to be slower and gentler; if they are still there they tend to be mavericks, quietists, misfits or fatalists; the new village dwellers have come, for a wide spectrum of reasons, from outside.

These modern inhabitants of an English village may well include (a) a sprig of the titled family who once owned all the land as far as the eye can see and still own a sizable slice of it; (b) the original villagers, much depleted by emigration to America, the Commonwealth, London, and even nearby big towns, but still in a skeletal sense, its inheritors; (c) a new meritocratic middle class: accountants, engineers, lawyers and computer experts who make their livings in the big towns within driving range; (d) a few daily commuters who do not mind the grind of the journey to London in return for the first lungful of God's good air when they get home in the evenings; (e) the neighbourhood farmers and their employees who actually still work the land round the village; (f) a number of retired admirals, colonels and air commodores who have decided that this will make a good last posting; and (g) the weekend Londoners, who like to hit the M4 or whichever motorway* it is at 4 p.m. on Fridays and recharge their batteries for a new assault on the corridors of power early Monday morning. Now of all these groups, only a, b and e have any long-term emotional rights in the village, and it is this grievance that has precipitated burnings in Wales* and bombings in Ireland* (an extension of the problem). In truth, the original villagers never owned their own cottages, and hated them when tenants; but that does not stop them resenting the arrival of the new villagers (see also under *Cottage* and *Class*). The best villagers are those who learn to get on with as many of the groups here specified as is tenable; but that is a hard trick. Meantime the contemporary English village is as much the nodal point of change, flux, tension and collision as the big city from which it is popularly supposed to be a portmanteau refuge.

VIP First noted in a 1933 novel of Compton Mackenzie (when it stood for Very Important Person*age*) VIP has come to be associated with air travel under privileged conditions and, though once taken quite seriously, is now used increasingly in a mocking context to mean a very unimportant person whose sense of his own importance greatly exceeds the truth and who is receiving favoured treatment at the expense of everyone else.

V-Sign Patented by Winston Churchill in the last war as symbolic shorthand for Victory, the V-sign is an ambiguous gesture in unworldly hands, for while it expresses the Churchillian mode right enough palm outwards, it means something quite different palm inwards; something of vast and uncharted antiquity, but to the worldly totally unambiguous in its import. Up yours mate, is what the palm inward V-sign signifies, or even more directly, get stuffed (see *Up*). Hugely popular with schoolboys and soldiers as a universal expression of derision, the palm-in V-sign does not yet seem to be used widely, despite the onset of women's lib, by women; though that, no doubt, is to come.

Wales 'This chap has a certain natural gift of rhetoric', observes Professor Higgins of the eloquent dustman Alfred Doolittle in Bernard Shaw's* *Pygmalion*. 'That's the Welsh strain in him. It also accounts for his mendacity and dishonesty.' The notion that the Welshman is a bit too quick for him is deeply ingrained in the Englishman's mind, and the edge is rationalised as a proclivity to light-fingeredness. 'Taffy was a Welshman', says the nursery rhyme, 'Taffy was a thief.' And as Evelyn Waugh* remarked in *Decline and Fall*, 'We can trace almost all the disasters of English history to the influence of the Welsh.'

Yet if the English image of the Welsh is unflattering, it is as nothing to the Welsh view of the English. The word *Sais* in Welsh does not just convey Englishman; it is also a term of profound obloquy. For generations now the Welsh have seen the Sais as a distant, po-faced tyrant who has rifled his land of its vast mineral wealth and forced him to sweat for his bread in the bowels of the earth. But Welsh revenge has been sweet.

They have sent up to Westminster* a series of wizards who have put a spell on Parliament. David Lloyd George was not only the most gifted politician of his time (perhaps of the century), he was also one of the funniest. 'The Honourable Gentleman has sat so long on the fence that the iron has entered into his soul', he famously remarked of John Simon; and less famously, but just as shatteringly, of Herbert Samuel: 'When they circumcised him they threw away the wrong bit.'

He was succeeded as chief thorn in the side of the English Establishment by Aneurin Bevan ('Fascism is not a new order of society. It is the future refusing to be born.') Still, most Englishmen will concede, there is nothing quite like a Welsh Speaker of the House of Commons (in this case George Thomas) to thunder out the lesson at a royal wedding: while the poetry of the young Dylan Thomas and the voice of the young Richard Burton still work their powerful magic on English minds.

There are only 2,807,000 Welshmen in Britain; if they sometimes seem ten times as many it is because of the passion and pride with which they push their luck. They are a classless people; and they believe in self help. Lord Elwyn Jones, for example, was Lord Chancellor of England from 1974 to 1979; he started at Llanelli Grammar School and made his way to Cambridge on scholarships; when he went away to college his father, a furnaceman, pushed his luggage to the station on a cart. His brother became a professor; his sister a headmistress.

Another example of the incidence of Welsh prestidigitators is at the BBC; while on the rugby field generations of Welsh players endowed with quicksilver have bewitched, bothered and bewildered the plodding English. It is twenty years since England beat Wales at Cardiff Arms Park, capital of Welsh rugby; the sound of sixty thousand Welsh voices singing 'Land of My Fathers' in that great cauldron is said to be worth a six-point start to them. Indeed, the Englishman ruefully concludes, being Welsh seems to give you a six-point start, not just at the Arms Park but anywhere in England.

Waugh, Evelyn (1903-66) The point about Waugh was that he got it right. He knew exactly what his target was, and hit it smack in the centre. He saw his characters with the high definition of a batsman who has thoroughly played himself in, and wrote about them in a prose of the most pleasing and elegant clarity. All the way from his sparkling début in *Decline and Fall*, through the darker chords which are heard in *A Handful of Dust*, to the plangent melancholy of *Brideshead Revisited*, there are no *longueurs* in Waugh. He never showed off, never belonged to a school, never worked for effect.

He considered that he had allowed the exigencies of wartime life in England to lead him into an extravagance in the writing of *Brideshead* which he sought to excise later; his *aficionados* were not best pleased. Even infidels who are obliged to reject in its entirety the religious basis on which *Brideshead* is predicated – in his own words, the operation of divine grace on a group of diverse but closely connected characters – are seized by its sumptuous settings, ineluctable plot and characters who walk out of the page.

When Waugh opened his notebook to record the foibles of his time and place he could draw on incomparable raw material. There was Lord Berners, who had a piano built in the back of his Rolls, and E.S.P. Haynes, solicitor in Waugh's divorce, who seldom finished lunch till 4 p.m. and died when his shirt-tails caught alight as he stood before his gas fire. Other writers and artists lived in the same *milieu* but did not have the divine grace to convey these foibles to us for all time, or at least as long as the air-conditioned vaults in the University of Texas preserve them. Waugh may not have been a saint – he could be abominably rude to the world, though he was kind in private – but he was an English writer of unquestionable genius.

The Weather In England it has taken on the anthropomorphic quality of a licensed jester whose latest caper is universally discussed daily with wry resignation. Indeed, as David Lodge observed in his novel *Changing Places*, to a visiting American, the English weather forecast sounds like nothing more than some bizarre extension of the satire industry: 'some kind of spoof, predicting every possible combination of weather for the next twenty-four hours without actually committing itself to anything specific.' Though popularly renowned for its fickleness, English weather is in truth more properly distinguished by its gentleness. The extremes of temperature observed in England (about +38°C to –27°C) are under half the world's widest; English rainfall is a quarter of the world's wettest. True, between these mild parameters, it displays an infinite capacity for surprise that means all English farmers, cricketers, builders, sailors, street vendors and holidaymakers are perforce gamblers who must accept the caprice of the weather with unflinching resignation and humour. The only answer, therefore, in England, seems to be to enjoy whatever heaven sends. 'There is really no such thing as bad weather,' observed Ruskin, 'only different kinds of good weather.' But see *Spring*, *Summer*, *Autumn*, and *Winter*.

Wessex Literally, the domain of the West Saxons who settled in Hampshire early in the sixth century and pushed north and west till, under Egbert and Alfred, they first created the Kingdom of England. Its perimeter encompassed what we now call Dorset, Wiltshire, Berkshire, Somerset and the original settlement in Hampshire. That was all it meant till 1874 when Thomas Hardy*, groping for a word to describe the stretch of England he would be celebrating in *Far from the Madding Crowd* and the series of novels that followed, hit on the idea of reviving the word.

'The region designated was known but vaguely, and I was often asked even by educated people where it lay', he recalled. 'However the press and public were kind enough to welcome the fanciful plan, and willingly joined me in the anachronism of imagining a Wessex population living under Queen Victoria – a modern Wessex of railways, the penny post, mowing and reaping machines, union work-houses, lucifer matches, labourers who could read and write, and national schoolchildren.'

It was a simple but brilliant device. The map of Wessex which decorates the endpieces of the Wessex novels blurs fact and fiction as his prose did: from the Isles of Lyonnesse (Scilly Isles) in the far west to Castle Royal (Windsor) in the east, and from Christminster (Oxford*) in the north to Sandbourne (Bournemouth*) in the south. Very big places like Bristol and Southampton stand as they are; but Melchester is of course Salisbury and Wintoncester is Winchester*.

Within this ambitious framework the wide, stark tapestries of his books are marvellously woven; and the actual texture of the Wessex landscape is central to their triumph. In the majestic opening scene of *Far from the Madding Crowd* 'the kingly brilliance of Sirius pierced the eye with a steely glitter, the star called Capella was yellow, Aldebaran and Betelgeux shone with a fiery red. To persons standing alone on a hill during a clear midnight such as this, the roll of the world eastward is almost a palpable movement.' Such is the thrall of Hardy's Wessex.

Westminster   'I have always thought that to sit in the British Parliament should be the highest object of ambition to every educated Englishman', wrote Anthony Trollope in his Autobiography. His view was not shared by his great contemporary Dickens*, probably the best and fastest shorthand reporter the Commons had ever known, who heartily despised the pandemonium beneath him. Trollope stood unsuccessfully for the first and last time when he was fifty-three, thus fortunately giving himself the time to write some of his best books: notably *Phineas Finn* and *The Prime Minister*.

'The government of your country', cries the armaments millionaire Undershaft to his son Stephen in Bernard Shaw's* *Major Barbara*, 'I am the government of your country; I and Lazarus. Do you suppose that you and half a dozen amateurs like you, sitting in a row in that foolish gabble shop, can govern Undershaft and Lazarus? No, my friend, you will do what pays us . . . Be off with you my boy, and play with your caucuses and leading articles and historic parties and great leaders and burning questions and the rest of your toys. I am going back to my counting house to pay the piper and call the tune.'

A brutal speech, and no doubt a simplistic analysis. Still, the modern House of Commons is a dull place. It contains no politician of undisputed world rank, and has not heard a truly great speech for forty years.

Who's Who It has been coming out for 136 years now, this perennially fascinating guide to the great and the good in national life. Not quite all of them: Bernard Levin, for example, declined to send back his form and for a while Tony Benn was unable to agree with the publishers about the bare and simple populist mode in which he latterly wished his entry to appear. For the rest, though, the annual invitation from Messrs Adam and Charles Black is the ticket for an agreeable and harmless ego trip during which far more is revealed about the traveller than might meet the casual eye. Some give father's name but not mother's; some give university but not school; some list current wives but drop all record of previous ones; some compress their lives into half a dozen laconic lines; others ramble on for a column of densely set type. Recreations provide one obvious opportunity for fun and games. Thus Christopher Booker offers as his pastimes Jungian psychology, music and following Somerset cricket team; Andrew Boyle, watching bad football matches from public terraces, especially at Fulham. Cartoonist Mel Calman vouchsafes that he spends his leisure hours brooding and worrying, while musician/writer Fritz Spiegl lists his hobbies as printing, cooking, inventing and several deadly sins. The Very Reverend Raymond Roberts, chaplain of the Fleet, says he is given to owning and driving very beautiful motorcars; writer Russell Hoban laconically and gnomically contributes a one-word diversion: stones. Science-fiction doyen Brian Aldiss is even more disturbingly arcane: his recreation is thinking about China. Famous entries from the past include Osbert Sitwell's ('educated Eton; mainly self-educated') while John Betjeman*, who used to describe himself as poet and hack, grew grander after he became Laureate and dignified himself as poet and author. The most manful entry in the great compendium, though, must surely be that from the poet Christopher Logue: 'Private in Black Watch, two years in Army Prison, discharged with ignominy.'

Wimbledon Within an hour of the Wimbledon Championships finishing, a small army of officials are on their knees examining every inch of the Centre Court. The scattered divots are lovingly replaced with ladies' hairpins, the grass is re-seeded at once and then again in the spring. Apart from four hand-chosen ladies who play half an hour of doubles before Wimbledon to test the turf it stands unused for all but the two frenetic weeks of the Championships. It is tender loving care like this that makes Wimbledon, even to those who continuously tour the great tennis venues of the world, still the most beautiful, traditional, and disciplined tournament there is.

The word disciplined may sound odd in the era of loudmouths like John McEnroe, but even he moderates his behaviour at the All England Lawn Tennis and Croquet Club; and in any event his famous disputations with the umpires are due as much to a change in the rules allowing for a dialogue between players and officials as anything else.

Yet as we have noted throughout this book, when the money comes in one end of the sport, the fun tends to leave by the other. The revenue from radio and television alone last year at Wimbledon was four million pounds and firms pay £10,000 each for the privilege of filling their customers with bubbly in one of the eighty-four private marquees. That prince of the ticket touts with the unimaginably apt name, Stan Flashman, was ordered to pay £3,000 damages last year to an American tennis tour organiser for selling £42 tickets at £125 each. Yet still the crowds flock to the Mecca of tennis: there are only 375 members of the All England Club, yet 360,000 come to see the tournament; 11,700 on the Centre Court alone. it is unforgivingly fast tennis, so fast that between twenty and forty of the world's top-spin players do not even bother to turn up.

The royals have taken a lively interest in the game since King George V gave a cup for the men's singles championship and his son, then Duke of York, played in the 1926 Championships: and every year the Kents are there to give the prizes on the last days.

Perhaps the escalating price of the strawberries (£1.20 per punnet last summer) and the press of humanity may deter some fans; certainly the draw for tickets seemed a little less over-subscribed this year. Besides, there are no action replays to be seen from the Centre Court seats. Yet, not to have been to Wimbledon at all is not to have known one of the key ingredients of the English summer: as maddening as it is magical.

Wimsey, Lord Peter In his youth Dorothy L. Sayers's aristocratic sleuth was oddly like Bertie Wooster*. Both were sprigs of the nobility, both affected monocles, both had manservants worth their weight in gold: the indispensable Bunter, the incomparable Jeeves. Both were at Oxford, but whereas Wimsey took a first in modern history, Wooster's exploits were confined more to taking off his clothes at Bump Suppers and diving into the college fountain. Wimsey was a real goer in bed, while Wooster never seems to have gone the whole hog with any girl; though often as near as dammit. The main difference between them would seem, on superficial analysis, to be that while Wooster looked an ass and was an ass, Wimsey looked an ass and had one of the best brains in Europe (for a fairer and truer account of Bertie's intellectual powers see under *Wooster*).

Wimsey, on the other hand, was intolerable in his accomplishments. He rode superbly, shot expertly, drove a car at grand prix level, played the piano beautifully, was a connoisseur of wine and so on. Perhaps Dorothy L. Sayers modelled him on Eric Whelpton, with whom she had been in love (like Whelpton, Wimsey had 'a long narrow face, like a melancholic adjutant stork'); perhaps on the mysterious and cosmopolitan John Cournos, whom she had loved too; perhaps on the Chaplain of Balliol, for whom she also had a soft spot. Probably, though, she should be believed when she claimed that Wimsey was a composite.

There can be no doubt, however, about Harriet Vane, heroine of many Wimsey tales, Lord Peter's mistress and eventually his wife. Harriet, like Dorothy, was tall, dark, and no great beauty. She too wrote detective stories, and she too signed herself with a middle initial: Harriet D. Vane, echoing Dorothy L. Sayers (the L stood for Leigh, her mother's name, and denoted her descent from one of the founders of *Punch*, a provenance of which she was very proud). The actual circumstances of Peter's acceptance by Harriet in *Gaudy Night* still set a high-water mark in self-indulgence which will take some beating: 'With a gesture of submission he bared his head and stood gravely, the square cap dangling in his hand. "Placetne, magistra?" "Placet." '

Whatever Wimsey's defects, there is no doubt that Harriet doted on the man. At a performance of the Bach Double Violin Concerto at Balliol 'Peter, she felt sure, could hear the whole intricate pattern, every part separately and simultaneously, each independent and equal, separate but inseparable, moving over and under and through, ravishing heart and mind together'. Perhaps Wimsey was the ideal husband Dorothy would have liked. The one she actually got was Oswald Fleming, a former captain in the Royal Army Service Corps, later motoring correspondent of the *News of the World*, a snob, a hack and a drunk. Yet if she had found a real-life Wimsey, there might well have been no need for her to write the Wimsey detective novels, and the world would have been a much poorer place.

Winchester 'The ancient city of Winchester, city of Alfred, once capital of England, perhaps even the Camelot of Arthur': so writes A.G. Macdonell in the last chapter of his flawed masterpiece *England Their England* (1933). Its hero, fledgling writer Donald Cameron, a young Scottish ex-officer and a dead ringer for Archie Macdonell himself, has nearly completed his quest for the hearts and minds of the English. The immortal cricket match at Fordende has been played, and now Donald, seduced from Lambeth by the scents and sounds of the imminent English spring, is playing truant from his book.

He has taken a train to Alton, hitched to Alresford, drunk some Hampshire beer, then hitched again until the water meads of the river Itchen lie beneath him, not to mention the city of Alfred. In truth it was never undisputed capital of England (though certainly an important royal centre and the seat of treasury in Norman times) and its claims on Camelot, if they rest on the Round Table in the Great Hall, are slim indeed: though old, maybe six hundred years old, it is nowhere old enough to have served Arthur, who flourished, if at all, a good eight hundred years before the table was made.

The book is a love letter to the auld enemy and though the last chapter simply will not do ('the muted voices of grazing sheep, and the merry click of bat upon ball, and the peaceful green fields of England') Macdonell seems to know his Winchester. He takes us into the Cathedral, to the chantry of William of Wykeham, defended by a Wykehamist captain in Cromwell's army with drawn sword against his own pillaging troops; and the memorial to Jane Austen* ('kindliest and gayest and gentlest'). He leads us through the Deanery and the Canonries and the Tithe Barn into the College itself, where the newest of new boys is called a Winchester man and the school motto is the best known of all: Manners Makyth Man. Every other motto he'd ever heard of, Macdonell remarks, called on an unspecified Supreme Power to allow the institution to flourish or prosper or to wax strong: 'In general to get on in the world.' This school, however, put kindness before power or fame.

From the College Archie Macdonell takes us on to the Abbey of St Cross, which still disposes its traditional bounty, the wayfarer's dole of bread and ale, to any who ask for it. Then we go up St Catherine's Hill, where he falls into a rather embarrassing trance in which the whole tapestry of English history rises before him out of a cloud of steam like a telly ad for Watney's Ale. What a rum place.

Winchester has turned out a handful of military men like Wavell, Dowding and Portal, politicians as disparate as Gaitskell and Mosley; mavericks like A.P. Herbert and Cecil King. In six hundred years, it could have done better. Never mind, we shall forgive Winchester for giving us Archie Macdonell, a Wykehamist himself, of course, and that immortal chapter seven of *England Their England*.

The Wind in the Willows   The Secretary of the Bank of England – for that is what Kenneth Grahame (1859-1922) was, no less, when he wrote this enchanting story, published in 1908 – had much on his side. First, he had hit on a title of spellbinding power. It sounds like an invocation. When A.A. Milne, another skilled artificer, turned it into a play, he could choose from Grahame's text a title of well nigh equal charm: *Toad of Toad Hall.*

Next, Grahame had hit on a phrase for a form of time-squandering that was always, and remains still, dear to the island race: 'messing about in boats'. The river and its thrall are central to the fascination of *The Wind in the Willows.* Again, foreshadowing *Watership Down* by more than half a century, he had seen the appeal of using anthropomorphic animals to animate his plot. 'In reading the book', wrote Milne, 'it is necessary to think of Mole, for instance, sometimes as an actual mole, sometimes as such a mole in human clothes, sometimes as a mole grown to human size, sometimes as walking on two legs, sometimes on four. He is a mole, he isn't a mole. What is he? I don't know. And, not being a matter-of-fact person, I don't mind.'

Indeed, all the animals have distinctly human foibles: naive Mole, kindly Rat, worldly Badger and capricious Toad. A visitor to the Grahame house at Cookham Dean by the Thames paused entranced outside the night nursery, hearing 'two of the most beautiful voices, one relating a wonderful story, and the other, soft as the south wind blowing, sometimes asking for an explanation, sometimes arguing a point, at others laughing like a whole chime of bells – the loveliest duet possible'.

It was his only son Alistair for whom Grahame spun the magical story of the river animals, just as on the same river Dodgson had spun his story for Alice. But Alistair was destined to die at twenty on an Oxford railway line in what may well have been suicide. The story written for him lives on, still enchanting new generations of children and grown-ups who have never quite shaken off the spell cast by the mist on the river.

Winnie-the-Pooh   The name of a rebarbative bear owned by Christopher Robin, infant son of the English writer A.A. Milne (1882-1956). Bear and boy are extensively celebrated in Milne's books, notably *When We Were Very Young, Winnie-the-Pooh, Now We Are Six,* and *The House at Pooh Corner.* These books with their illustrations by E.H. Shepard have found an enormous audience on both sides of the Atlantic and in many translations from Japanese to Bulgarian; but the applause has not been universal. Reviewing *The House at Pooh Corner* for the *New Yorker* in 1928 Dorothy Parker opened by printing the song on page five: 'The more it / Snows – tiddely – pom, / The more it Goes – tiddely pom / The more it / Goes – tiddely – pom / On / Snowing.'

Pooh explains that he put in the word pom to make the little lyric 'more hummy'. We shall concur with Dorothy Parker's verdict: 'And it is that word "hummy", my darlings, that marks the first place in *The House at Pooh Corner* at which Tonstant Weader Fwowed up.'

Winter   The English achievement was to turn it from a noun into a verb. No one in his right mind denies that an English winter at its most vile is an unencompassable horror; though even at its most unspeakable it will suddenly throw out at random days flooded with a cold and golden sunlight which are among the most casually beautiful the English year can afford.

Still, well-to-do Englishmen long ago learned the knack of heading south as the winter solstice approaches. Not for nothing did the Promenade des Anglais at Nice get its name and it was here, two centuries ago, that Tobias Smollett first amazed the locals by actually swimming for fun in the sea. For good measure, an Englishman called Arnold Lunn taught the Swiss to slalom and winter sport is now the alternative diversion that rescues tens of thousands of the island race from the horrors of an English Christmas.

For the unadventurous and the stick-a-beds, even the inspissated gloom of the English midwinter can be suddenly illumined by the miraculous winter jasmine, the innocence of the first snowdrops, the blaze of the early crocus. By February the national folly of St Valentine's Day* signals the emotional start of a thaw that may well continue to midsummer.

Wodehouse, P.G.   (1881-1975)   Perhaps the most interesting point about his enormously long working life (seventy years) is his relationship to George Orwell*. On the face of it, no two English writers could be more inimical. Wodehouse lived in an imaginary world in which politics, crime and sex hardly obtruded; Orwell in a wincingly real world where they manifestly did.

Oddly similar in their family backgrounds (Wodehouse's father was an English upper-middle-class judge who served the British Raj in Hong Kong, Orwell's father an English upper-middle-class civil servant who served the British Raj in Bengal) one made his name by celebrating the eccentricities of the English upper class; the other by dramatising the predicaments of the English working class. In the upshot, they had much more in common than either of them might have cared to admit.

When Wodehouse gave five broadcasts from Berlin in 1941 as a civilian prisoner of the Germans he aroused the fury of A.A. Milne and Duff Cooper, but the sympathy of more understanding men like Compton Mackenzie and George Orwell. Though there is nothing in the five talks now which causes the slightest offence, he was clearly unworldly to make them. However, being unworldly was his stock in trade. He belonged indeed to another world where time had stood still since the summer of 1914. Orwell, penetrating as ever, and a Wodehouse fan since the age of eight, saw that Bertie Wooster*, who made his début in 1917, was already late and really belonged to Edwardian England.

Even here though, the matter is somewhat more complicated than it appears. Was Edwardian England quite as sun-kissed and C major as all that? Of course not; it was a bitter and divided era (strikes, suffragettes, Ireland*, the Lords) and a notedly inhuman one (forced feeding, the cat, capital punishment). It was just that Wodehouse took what suited him from the golden days between the leaden ones.

Orwell argued that since Wodehouse's mental clock had stopped in 1914 it was pointless to blame him for the German gaffe; the entire *oeuvre*, he went on, was innocent of any reference to fascism. This was not quite so, for in *The Code of the Woosters*, P.G.W. specifically mentioned the Black Shorts, a farcical outfit to which the beefy lout Roderick Spode belonged; and in a spate of sudden awareness he even let in the dire word fascism. Still, it must be allowed that this is merely a dash of realism in the immense confection.

The Wodehousian world is a remarkable one; enclosed, logically quite consistent, yet at an angle to reality. It is like one of those alternative universes postulated by the theoretical physicists. Within, it is always spring, and at the Drones Club in Dover Street Bertie Wooster is harmlessly passing the noon hour with the young men in spats: Catsmeat Potter-Pirbright, Dogface Rainsby, Bingo Little, Oofy Prosser, Gussie Fink-Nottle, Pongo Twistleton-Twistleton and Barmy Fotheringay-Phipps. *Si non vero,* as the Italians so well put it, *e ben trovato.* If it didn't actually happen, it sounds as if it did.

No doubt, as Orwell complained, Wodehouse made the English aristocracy nicer than they really were. He could not have made them more odd. Besides, it was done with such glittering panache. Open the books anywhere, as Evelyn Waugh remarked, and you will find three brilliant and original similes leap at you from the page: 'He writhed like an electric fan' or 'He was uttering odd strangled noises like a man with no roof to his mouth trying to recite "Gunga Din" ' or 'Uncle Tom always looked like a pterodactyl with a secret sorrow'. With the unequalled purity of his style went a matching penchant for the delineation of character; and he would be remembered, if for nothing else, then alone by the creation of the great Jeeves*.

Wog Originally an offensive term for an Indian or Arab or anyone not white; more lately, for any European who is not British ('wogs begin at Calais'). It was popularly supposed to be the acronym for Wily Oriental Gentleman; but Egyptians working on the Suez Canal were issued with special shirts bearing the legend Working On Government Service, and this seems to be the true, or at any rate earlier acronym.

Women 'He glanced at her feet – being an old stager; she was perfectly shod.' Thus does Bulldog Drummond first appraise his future wife Phyllis in the Carlton one day in 1919. Can a woman be shod like a horse? Drummond clearly thought so, but then he was an English sportsman and a gentleman*. Whether he knew much about women is another matter.

It is an evident absurdity to take any general stance about half the race; especially when it must contain human beings as disparate as the late Diana Dors and Margaret Thatcher. Nevertheless, the formal outer framework within which women's lives are lived is clearly changing fast. In a country with a woman on the throne and another in 10 Downing Street, it might well be argued, parity has been found. Still, feminists will argue, with some force, that these are cosmetic changes which conceal the real imbalance still surviving. Apart from Maggie, who?

We do have women priests and women judges, and nobody raises an eyebrow; women members of the Stock Exchange* and women dining as of right at virtually every high table in Oxford* and Cambridge*. So a start has been made. Still, it may take a generation or so before the mental bias has been ironed out; and not least in the minds of women themselves.

They face a bewildering world. The invention of the Pill, the laws on sex equality, the gradual onset of equal pay, and the rise of militant feminism have overturned the old verities. The transient partner, the lesbian alternative, the commune and the crèche, have replaced the old certainties. Whether this has made Englishwomen any happier is a nice point; but they clearly have the right – and must have it – to choose the nature of their own happiness or unhappiness.

Meanwhile the English woman, in the eyes of the Englishman at least, seems a sight less neurotic than the American woman, far less daunting than the Russian woman, and much less of a handful than the continental woman. She remains, in short, very much his cup of tea*.

Wooster, Bertie 'As far as brain is concerned,' says the great Wodehousian scholar Richard Usborne, 'he is as near to being null and void as makes no difference.' We know that his manservant, the great and inimitable Jeeves* concurred, and Bertram seemed to have some faint inkling of his own limitations too. 'Providence looks after the chumps of this world; and personally I'm all for it,' he remarked in 1925.

Yet have we been underestimating the chump all this time? After all, he was a bit of a goer with the racquets, and had even got his half-blue in the arcane sport. Then there is his strong moral sense, the celebrated Code of the Woosters. This manifests itself in two principal rubrics: (1) Thou shalt not let down a pal and (2) Thou shalt not scorn a woman's love. It is his manful adherence to these two doctrines, his over-riding sense of *noblesse oblige*, that has landed Bertram Wooster in so many tight corners.

As that other great Wodehousian Geoffrey Jaggard has noted, Bertie has been saved by the gong from matrimony times without number. Aunt Agatha failed to marry him off to a prim, missionary type of girl who turned out to be a gangster's moll. Tough intellectuals like Honoria Glossop and Florence Craye tried to mould him for marriage only to find his clay disintegrated into sand and slipped through their fingers. And so on.

He was engaged to Pauline Stoker, and all but figured in a shotgun wedding at the hands of her father after she had found refuge in (the absent) Bertie's bed. As Jaggard observes: 'It was clearly one up to Pauline, since the only other sensate beings ever discovered in Bertie's bed were a hedgehog and a lizard (up the left pyjama leg).' He has, according to Jeeves, a pleasant light baritone voice in which he sings (in the bath or at smoking concerts) 'Sonny Boy', 'Roll Out the Barrel' and 'Every Morn I Bring You Violets'. Still, let us not damn Bertram with faint praise. The man can string a few words together when all is said and done: 'She wriggled from base to apex with girlish enthusiasm', or 'Bingo swayed like a jelly in a high wind', or his fine portrait of the dreaded Honoria, 'who read Nietzsche and had a laugh like waves breaking on a stern and rockbound coast.'

Once, alarmed at the prospect of the coming revolution, Bertie took a course in self-survival, and actually got a prize for sock darning (though to tell the truth he had smuggled an old woman in to do it for him and was expelled in consequence). Yet, come the revolution, Bertram could surely make a few bob by stringing those few words together. After all he has been doing just that for three-quarters of the century already, and shows no signs of strain yet, chump or no chump.

Xenophobia It was not that the prewar Englishman did not like foreigners: he generally did not know any. After all, he lived on an island, and unless well-heeled, holidayed at Brighton* or Blackpool*. The war, and its economic aftermath, changed all that. Your modern Englishman is a far more sophisticated citizen of the world. He has to be. His firm, most likely, is owned in America, his car is from Japan, his camera from Germany, his transistor from Hong Kong. His son has gone to seek his fortune in Saudi Arabia, his daughter is an *au pair* in Marseilles, his lunch-time pizza was cooked by an Italian, and his newspapers sold to him by an Indian. He holidays in Spain or Greece, and is beginning to think about a package to Guadeloupe. His football teams are full of Argentinians, his cricket teams of Jamaicans. The one unchanging consolation in all this flux is that all these foreigners speak his lingo, which relieves him of the necessity of speaking theirs. To this indulgence he owes the ruthless energy and greed of his forebears, who colonised a quarter of the globe and left their language behind even when their writ had ceased to run. But see under *The English Language*.

Yob Originally a back formation from 'boy', it seems likely to supersede lout and loafer as the natural term for any teenage layabout. *Private Eye** invented a character called Sid Yobbo who edits one of the more raffish daily papers. He is not over-hard to identify; though some would argue that there are many Sid Yobbos in the Street of Shame.

Yomping   The term invented by the Royal Marines to describe their disconcerting habit of marching seventy miles in a day during the Falklands* conflict, a distance thought to be well outside the ambit of possibility by the Argentinians. The practice is a vivid example of the truth that in conventional war the English military, with their much-tattooed soldiers, brass-lunged sergeants and po-faced officers, all doing the job because they feel like it, are still not to be taken on unless it is absolutely essential.

Yorkshire   'There's nowt so queer as folk' goes the Yorkshire adage; but to the Englishman there's nowt quite so queer as the folk from the dales. Yorkshire has been called the Texas of England; but in a profound sense it seems more English – more Anglo-Saxon at any rate – than any part of the country. The most celebrated characteristics of the Yorkshire-man are his bluntness, his hard-headedness, and his stubbornness; all virtues for which the English have some grudging admiration. Admittedly, there is a less attractive side to this stereotype. 'Hear all, see all, say nowt; sup all, eat all, pay nowt', is said by detractors to be the Yorkshireman's motto; in truth, the lines probably owe more to his well-developed if earthy sense of humour.

When a Yorkshireman finds fame, it seems if anything to accentuate his roots; no one in England has been left in any doubt about which county politicians like Harold Wilson and Denis Healey hail from; nor have the English ever been in the slightest doubt about the provenance of writers like J.B. Priestley* or John Braine. Yorkshire has some claim to be the home of the working-class hero, wincingly on the make in Braine's *Room at the Top* or articulating his passion in David Storey's *This Sporting Life* with a clump round his lady-love's lug-hole. Rugby League football is the improbable strand round which Storey weaves his novel, and the game is played with dedication there; but the prime Yorkshire obsession is cricket.

All England watched bemused as Yorkshire was rent in twain by the great Geoffrey Boycott controversy. Was Yorkshire's greatest and dourest batsman exacting too great a price in morale and unity from his team-mates and would he have to go? He went; but a palace revolution at Headingley, the county's cricket Mecca, brought him resoundingly back. Every Yorkshireman worth his salt, from Westminster's Roy Hattersley to television's Michael Parkinson, felt impelled to pronounce on the grave dilemma. But then, a kind of psychic steam seems to drive all Yorkshire people: from writers like the Brontës* to reformers like William Wilberforce, explorers like Captain Cook, composers like Frederick

Delius and conspirators like Guy Fawkes.

Fortunately, that dour and laconic sense of humour, laced by the inimitable dialect, never deserts your Yorkshireman for long. Thus, there is no doubt where we are when a courting couple sit long hours by the fire in the front parlour till suddenly the young man blurts out: 'Wilt th' marry me, lass?' To this she has her reply ready: 'Ay, I will lad.' After that the clock ticks away and for an hour there is a deep silence in the parlour. At length the lass inquires: 'Hast th' nowt else to tell me?' Her intended thinks this over in the way Yorkshiremen will, and at long last replies: 'Nay: I've said too much already.'

Yorkshire Pudding   'It is an exceeding good pudding; the gravy of the meat eats well with it,' wrote the Elizabeth David of her day, Hannah Glasse, in *The Art of Cookery Made Plain and Easy*, published in 1747. It still is. In a typical small English country inn, for instance, three quarters of all lunches ordered on Sunday are still roast beef and Yorkshire pudding.

The original *raison d'être* of the pud was undoubtedly frugality: the batter of eggs, flour and milk was placed under the roasting spit to catch and soak up the dripping and juices as the meat turned. In Yorkshire then and now the pudding is often served first. Here again necessity was the motive. Mother would offer most meat to whichever child ate the most pud: but when the pud had been demolished, there was that much less room left for the beef, so it went further.

George Orwell* maintained in 1945 that you were more likely to get a good rich slice of Yorkshire pudding in the poorest English home than in a restaurant. There is still a lot of truth in this, for the wretched little buns served often in restaurants with roast beef, full of air and innocent of gravy, are but pale travesties of the home-made pud.

For true delicacy, the batter should be allowed to stand after it has been mixed; and a perfectly made Yorkshire pud should be able to stand up to the most sophisticated French soufflé in lightness of texture. Every Englishman worth his salt knows that the interior of a Yorkshire pud is moist and saturated with the juices of the joint; the outside light, brown and crisp. The art of the true pud connoisseur is to be sure of being served a little of both.

Z

Zizz   A short nap or snooze, a useful word for the language, and a vivid example of the thrall of onomatopoeia. It probably derives from the z-z-z- used in balloons by cartoonists to indicate the gentle sound emitted by someone asleep and, because it acts out its sense, seems bound to prevail.

Zonked   A newish word, probably echoing the sound of a heavy blow, and used for utter exhaustion brought on by drink, drugs or even work.

Zoo   To most Englishmen it is the headquarters of the Zoological Society in Regents Park, a fashionable port of call these last one hundred and fifty years and a favourite with many celebrated Englishmen, notably Cyril Connolly*, who was given a surprise seventieth birthday luncheon there and was found hours later wandering amid the cages which housed his beloved lemurs. It was also a happy haunt for the infant Christopher Robin Milne, who used to visit a favourite polar bear there, the *fons et origo* of Winnie-the-Pooh*. In 1981 a middle-aged Christopher Robin unveiled a statue in the zoo to Winnie-the-Pooh – arguably the most famous bear in the world, though this will be disputed by adherents of Rupert Bear*.

Zuleika Dobson   The story of Max Beerbohm's divine temptress is yet another illustration of the profound truth that the Thames is a magic river, Oxford an enchanted city, and England, as may be seen throughout this book, an imaginary land inhabited by improbable people.

Index

The headings in the *Companion* are indicated by page references in **bold type**.

ARAPAHO SUMMER

ARAPAHO SUMMER

KINLEY ROBY

FIVE STAR
A part of Gale, a Cengage Company

GALE
A Cengage Company

Farmington Hills, Mich • San Francisco • New York • Waterville, Maine
Meriden, Conn • Mason, Ohio • Chicago

LIBRARY OF CONGRESS CATALOGING-IN-PUBLICATION DATA

Names: Roby, Kinley E., author.
Title: Arapaho summer / Kinley Roby.
Description: First edition. | Waterville, Maine : Five Star, a part of Gale, a Cengage Company, [2019]
Identifiers: LCCN 2019002606 (print) | ISBN 9781432857974 (hardcover : alk. paper)
Subjects: LCSH: Western stories. gsafd
Classification: LCC PS3618.O3385 A89 2019 (print) | DDC 813/.6—dc23
LC record available at https://lccn.loc.gov/2019002606

First Edition. First Printing: October 2019
Find us on Facebook—https://www.facebook.com/FiveStarCengage
Visit our website—http://www.gale.cengage.com/fivestar/
Contact Five Star Publishing at FiveStar@cengage.com

Printed in Mexico
1 2 3 4 5 6 7 23 22 21 20 19

For Mary

CHAPTER 1

It was dark now on the boulder-strewn hill, and the thunder of battle had ceased, but whiffs of burned gunpowder still drifted in the humid air. The sounds were those of crickets in the ripped and trampled grass, bull bats diving above the hill, and the groans and cries for help of the wounded. Shadowy figures with stretchers slowly worked their way up the hillside, searching for those still living.

Caleb Stone regained consciousness very slowly. More slowly still, he remembered where he was.

"Must get up," he said, his mind still at war. "Press ahead!" But the shout he'd intended was only a weak croak, and a strong hand pressed against his chest, checking his effort to rise.

"Lie still, Captain," said the man sitting on the ground beside him. "You're hurt. Lie still. Help is coming."

"Colonel Chamberlain?" Caleb managed to whisper.

"Yes."

"We were charging . . ."

"The 20th broke the Alabamians' line," Chamberlain said in an expressionless voice. "At the end, those that could run, ran. Rest now. Help is coming."

Caleb knew he should feel something, but his contact with awareness was too tenuous, and the faint tremor of relief, if that's what it was, faded as soon as felt. He tried to answer, but the words he reached for darted away like the trout in the spring on his farm back home. Above him, he saw patches of stars and

clouds, the latter gray in the intermittent moonlight.

Something is wrong with my body, he thought. *I can't make it move.* He tried to think about that, but the light above him dimmed. Giving up the struggle, he sank into the encompassing darkness.

CHAPTER 2

A musket bullet had smashed Caleb's right shoulder, and, moments after being shot, he was bayonetted between his right hip and ribs by a yelling soldier of the 15th Alabama regiment during the final Confederate attack on Little Round Top. His assailant had yanked back his rifle for a second thrust, but Colonel Joshua Chamberlain, charging after Caleb, Colt in hand, reached over the fallen captain and shot his attacker in the head.

Chamberlain had scarcely stepped over Caleb when the Alabamans' line faltered, broke, fell back from the assault by the 20th Maine, and collapsed into a full *"skedaddle,"* as a Confederate officer would later describe his corps's retreat. Colonel Chamberlain's successful charge by the remnants of his force against the Confederate assault crushed General Longstreet's flanking move to roll up the southern end of the Union line.

On the following day, General Lee, stymied by the defeat of his forces at both ends of the Union line, launched an assault against the center of the Union defenses, massed on Cemetery Ridge. In the catastrophic defeat that ensued, the Confederacy suffered a wound from which it never recovered.

When Caleb woke in the field hospital, he began once more calling on his men to charge. This time it was an orderly who held him down. His first sensory response to his surroundings

came in the gut-churning stench of blood, sweat, urine, chloroform, and vomit swirling in the tent's fetid air. Then the pain claimed him, running in channels of liquid fire from his right shoulder to his hip. His head felt as if it had been kicked by a horse.

"Your charging days are over for a while," the stout, bearded man with bloodshot eyes said, bending over him, replacing the orderly and adding stale cigar smoke to the stench. "What's your name?"

"Captain Caleb Stone." The sound of his own voice startled him. It might, he thought, belong to someone knocking at death's door.

"All right, Captain Stone, it appears your brain's working. I'm Dr. Hasten Stevens. I took a piece of lead the size of my thumb out of your shoulder, then sewed you up. That out of the way, I sewed up your belly where some Dixie mother's son ran a bayonet through you. Luckily, it missed your gut. You won't be going anywhere for a while. So, lie still. Do as you're told, and you just might walk out of here."

Patting Caleb on his left shoulder, he added, "I say *might*. So just in case, you would do well to attend to anything that needs mending between you, the Lord, and anyone else likely to have an interest in your crossing over.

"Be grateful you're in this tent. There's many in your condition that aren't. That's rain on the roof and not drums you're hearing. The battle's over, and Old Snappin' Turtle's got himself a victory." With that cheering message given, the doctor shambled off, coughing and spitting on the dirt floor as he went.

"Don't take it to heart." The speaker was a one-armed man, holding a small tin watering can with a spout on it. He stood near Caleb, having just finished dribbling water into a patient's mouth whose entire head, except for his mouth, was wrapped in

10

a bloody bandage.

"He says that to every last living soul that comes in here," the man continued. "I've been here since the shooting started, got sent down from a hospital outside Fredericksburg, and I ain't yet heard him say nothing different to anyone he cuts and stitches."

"Was he telling the truth? Has General Meade given us the victory?" Caleb asked.

"Yes, he has, but, from what I've seen, the winning is about as bad as the losing."

"Lord God," Caleb said, remembering. "Colonel Chamberlain and I must have been among the last of the 20th Maine standing when I was taken down."

"The colonel's still on his feet. You from Maine, Captain?"

"Yes, I am," Caleb said, his mind sliding again so that he was no longer sure if what he was hearing and seeing was real or more hallucinations.

"You didn't just lose your arm here, did you?" he asked, trying to keep his thinking clear.

"No, sir, it was right off I lost it." The man paused, and his gaze drifted away from Caleb for a moment. "It was Bull Run." He shook himself as if he had a chill and said, "I don't think on it. You want a drink?"

"Yes."

With great care, he bent over Caleb, rested the spout against his lips, and let the water trickle onto his tongue.

The water, Caleb thought, tasted like the tin spout.

"Thank you," he said, when he had drunk his fill. "What's your name?"

"It's Dil. I don't rightly know my real name," the man said. "Seems that hunk of iron that took off my left arm took my memory of earlier times with it."

"How did you come to be called Dil?"

"After I began nursing, there was a fella with no legs and only half his mind would call out 'Dil' when he was thirsty. I figure it was the name of someone he once knew. Anyway, it stuck like a fly to molasses. He died of the sepsis. It's what carries off the most of them."

Caleb made no answer. The pain was building again, and, as he tried to decide whether or not to ask Dil more about his injury, the pain set his thoughts flickering like moths around a candle flame, and, with a groan, he passed out.

It was still dark, except for the feeble light from the kerosene lanterns hung from the tent's ridgepole, when Dr. Stevens, with Dil trailing in his nightshirt, shook Caleb awake.

"You've got company coming, Captain Stone," the doctor said in a sour growl. "Appears we got to get you and this tent redded up in honor of the event. Get over there, Dil. We're going to have you in a half-sitting position. I doubt you'll like it, but, if it kills you, don't blame me. We've got a tight-assed colonel running this place who wouldn't know a bedpan from a ballpeen hammer."

Caleb understood some of what Stevens had said as the two men started to lift him, but not much. He was too busy dealing with the pain in his right side that felt like a red-hot poker being shoved into him. Agony brought him near to fainting, and he slumped over. Stevens swore and eased him back down. "Whiskey, Dil, and be damned quick or we'll lose him. Of all the stupid goddamned ideas . . ." Caleb felt the doctor's hand chafing his wrist. "Hang on, Captain. Hang on."

Caleb's side burned like the fires of Hell. He drifted away from the pain, was dimly aware of someone else's arrival—a woman, her voice like a foghorn that set his head pounding. He caught a few words here and there as she argued with Stevens—*not to be moved . . . miracle he's alive at all*—and the doctor giv-

ing back as good as he got. Then Dil, arriving out of nowhere, and the smell of liquor beneath Caleb's nose.

"Is that for you or the patient, Dr. Stevens?" the woman inquired.

"Hold his head," Stevens told her.

She did, gently. Whiskey spilled into Caleb's mouth. His eyes flew open, and he began coughing violently.

"Idiot!" the woman exploded. "Not you, Captain. Breathe through your nose. That's it. There we are. Much better."

"Where am I?" Caleb whispered. For a moment the smell of soap made him think of his mother. The woman holding him was handsome, with black hair worn in tight braids wrapped around her head, in a style common among the volunteer nurses.

"In a field hospital," she said. "I'm Isabel McFarlan, head nurse, doing my best to keep Dr. Stevens from killing my patients." Gently, she eased Caleb's head back on the pillow. "Doctor, why were you lifting this man?"

Stevens scowled. "Colonel Andrews sent one of his people to roust me out of bed and tell me I was to prepare the patients for a visit from Major General George Meade, who wants to speak with Captain Stone this morning. I wanted to have the captain looking as good as possible. Once that was done, I intended to move the worst of the wounded into Tent C." He took a pull on the whiskey flask, which Dil must have brought.

Isabel McFarlan folded her hands across her stomach, drew herself up, and said, loud enough to be heard from one end of the tent to the other, "Dr. Stevens, I do not care if President Lincoln is coming to pay us a visit, you are not moving these patients or their beds an inch. Is that clear?"

"I am the physician in charge of this hospital, Mrs. McFarlan," Stevens fired back, "and I will decide who will be moved and who won't."

"I am charged with their care and wellbeing, Dr. Stevens. You

sew up their torn bodies and cut off their shattered limbs. I say they stay where they are."

"Mrs. McFarlan," Caleb said through the pain, "would you ask Dil if there is any whiskey left in that flask?"

CHAPTER 3

An hour later, General George Meade, tall and gray and looking in his stained and wrinkled blue uniform as if he had given up on sleep, strode down the center aisle of the tent beside Mrs. McFarlan, upright and grim as her general. They were followed by Meade's staff, the group moving in silence, save for the jingle of the two cavalry officers' spurs.

Entering the tent, Meade had been met with a series of feeble cheers from those in the beds sufficiently aware to know what was happening. Meade had raised his hat in acknowledgement, but the cheers did nothing to shift the lines etched in the weary man's face.

"Captain Caleb Stone, General," McFarlan said to Meade, halting at the foot of Caleb's cot. "And this, Captain," she said, turning to Caleb, "is Brigadier General Meade, Commander of the Army of the Potomac, and your commanding officer, if I'm not mistaken. Do not attempt to sit up, Captain. You are in no condition to do so. The general will understand."

There was some restless shuffling of feet among the staff officers, but the expression on Meade's face did not change. He stepped past Mrs. McFarlan, bent over Caleb, and rested his hand lightly on the captain's left shoulder.

"Captain Stone," he said quietly, his face breaking briefly into something that might have been a smile, "Colonel Chamberlain wanted very much to be here this morning, but I regret to say illness has prevented it. Are you aware that your

15

and the colonel's bravery and that of your men prevented General Longstreet's corps from turning our south flank and gave the Union forces a victory?"

"The Alabamans struck five times, sir," Caleb said in a whisper. "It was the colonel who called for that charge. He deserves the credit."

"And he will have it, Captain, but I don't think you fully comprehend that you and the rest of the men of the 20th Maine are heroes."

Caleb felt himself fading again. The last thing he heard was Mrs. McFarlan's voice. "General," she said quietly, "he no longer hears you."

From a spot in the shadows two beds away, Dil watched General Meade and his entourage. The general stood for some time, staring down at Caleb Stone. After a long pause that had his officers beginning to clear their throats, he raised his head and turned to Mrs. McFarlan. "How many wounded are in this tent?"

"Fifty."

"How many will die?"

She looked shocked. "Only the Lord knows that."

"Yes, but since He's not available, I must rely on you for an answer."

She closed her eyes briefly. "God forgive me. More than half."

"And what will most of those die of?"

"Infection of one kind or another." She said it scarcely above a whisper, her hands clasped so tight her knuckles were white.

"If it were not for you and your nurses, Mrs. McFarlan, they would all die." General Meade fixed the doctor with a cold stare. "No later than tomorrow, today if possible, Captain Stone is to be moved to the Armory Square Military Hospital in Washington. He will be accompanied by a nurse with sufficient

skills to care for him as long as he draws breath. Make certain that person is furnished with enough chloroform, bandages, and soap to keep himself and the captain as clean and free from pain and infection as possible. I will arrange for an escort."

"General," Mrs. McFarlan said in a low voice, "I doubt he will survive being lifted out of this bed. He is very frail."

"Send him *in* his bed," Meade snapped, "and I will let it be known that, if the bed is dropped while he's in it, those carrying it will be stood up and shot." He turned to the nearest officer. "Is that clear?"

"Very, General," the man answered. Dil caught a slight twitching at the corners of McFarlan's mouth.

Turning back to her, General Meade said gravely, "You have the weight of men's lives on you, Nurse McFarlan, as do I. On behalf of all the men in your care and those who will be, as well as myself, I give you heartfelt thanks for your service. Good day."

With that, the general turned, and his staff opened ranks and then closed behind him as the group strode swiftly out of the tent.

Dil came up beside Mrs. McFarlan as she stood watching the soldiers leave. "Can you read, Dil?" she asked.

"Yes, ma'am. I believe I'm a very good reader. I seem to canter right along."

To Dil's astonishment, Mrs. McFarlan laughed. She paused to wipe her eyes with a handkerchief smelling of lavender that appeared almost miraculously in her hand. "Dil, you are going to accompany Captain Stone to a hospital in Washington. If he dies on the way, it will be on your head. So, keep him alive. It seems Caleb Stone is a hero, he and Colonel Chamberlain of the 20th Maine. They are a long way from home."

"Yes, ma'am," Dil said. "And, when his mind wanders, he talks about his farm and worries over it not being cared for

17

rightly. It weighs on him considerably."

"I had not thought of him as a farmer," she said, staring down at Caleb, "and he doesn't wear a ring."

"No, but I expect he reads. Also, there's a woman he calls Millie. He keeps asking after her as though she's gone missing."

Mrs. McFarlan sighed and shook her head. "This war, Dil," she said. "This wretched war. If you can, get this man home."

"If I have enough help from the Almighty, ma'am," Dil said quietly as she strode away.

CHAPTER 4

On June 9, 1865, three months to the day after Robert E. Lee's surrender of the army of northern Virginia to General Ulysses S. Grant at the Appomattox Court House, Caleb Stone and Dil, in newly laundered but faded uniforms of the Union Army, walked out of the Armory Square Hospital in Washington, D.C. It was a muggy, thinly overcast morning, and their uniforms were already sticking to their backs.

"We are civilians again, Dil," Caleb said, failing to sound as cheerful as he intended.

"We are, Captain," Dil said, "and I have a letter from the recruiting office that says my last name is Smith, and I may have come from Seviere County in Eastern Tennessee and the township of Pigeon Forge. But, since I have no memories of the place, I find I have no stomach for going there and walking around on the skinny hope somebody might recognize me."

Caleb gave a short and bitter laugh, thinking he felt much the same way about returning to his farm in Indian River.

"Fortunately," he said, "you don't have to make that journey. Neither do I. The Indian River farm is sold, the money is in the bank, along with five years of logging, hay, and pasturage income, and I appear to be done with Maine."

People hurrying past, if they glanced Caleb's way at all, would have seen a tall, broad-shouldered man in his mid-thirties, in an officer's uniform, his long, brown hair shot through with white. His face, pale and marked by the war as it was, revealed a spirit

unbroken and, in his steel-gray eyes, a will not easily deflected from its goal.

Dil, also thin as a rail and of slighter build, had a face perpetually young, but there lurked in his brown eyes shadows of suffering that time would not erase. As proof that the army had not forgotten him, he had been promoted to the rank of sergeant just three weeks before his discharge and Caleb's resignation became official. On receiving news of his promotion, he had said, "I expect I'm the only one-armed sergeant in the Union Army.

"I'm going to step onto thin ice now, Captain," Dil said, "but I can't start off for Oregon with you without finally asking you who Millie is."

Caleb's voice hardened. "I don't recall mentioning that name."

"No, Captain, you wouldn't. Your mind was always wandering when you spoke of her. I haven't heard you mention her for some time, but, at the outset, you spoke her name often."

The anger that had flashed through Caleb slid away, but the pain of hearing Millie's name was an old one, recently deepened. After a moment's reflection, Caleb decided he would answer Dil's question. Perhaps it might lessen the burden.

"She was a school teacher I knew in Indian River," he said. "Three months before I enlisted, I asked her to marry me, and she accepted. Then came the firing on Fort Sumter. In May, I decided I must go and told her. She said if that was my decision, she would not marry me."

"Then will she be waiting?"

"No. Two months ago, she wrote to say she had found me through Senator Lot Morrill and wanted me to know in advance, in case I was returning to Indian River, that she had been married for two years."

"Two years? And she never told you?"

Caleb shook his head. "For reasons she felt compelling, she refused to enter into a correspondence after I left for the battlefield. I heard nothing from her until the war's end."

He paused. His mind, trapped by his words, brought up the image of two people standing on granite steps behind a white, clapboard summer house, shaded by two tall wine-glass elms. The steps, nearly buried in moss and ferns, led down the bank from the screened porch and ended abruptly at the edge of a dark and quiet millpond. Millicent True, the woman facing him, was tall, slender, and auburn-haired, with *pince nez* on a black cord resting on the breast of her gingham dress. Her hazel eyes, usually so warm, were icy with anger.

"Captain?" Dil asked.

Recalling that moment had ripped away the scabs on all the old wounds from their quarrel, leaving him raw and sore. With effort, he banished it. "Forgive me, Dil. I seem to have drifted."

"I've raised painful memories, Captain," Dil said. "I apologize."

"You need not. I went to war, knowing I had hurt her deeply."

"Is her being married the reason you're not going home?"

"Not entirely," Caleb said. "I have no family in Maine. My parents are dead. I was running the farm alone until I enlisted."

He did not add that, whatever else the war had done to him, it had made him a different man from the one who had left Indian River four years ago. The question remaining was, *who was he now?*

"I'm ready when you are, Captain," Dil said, bracing his shoulders.

Caleb shook off the memories. "Our train awaits us, Dil," he replied.

He might have said, "Our fate."

CHAPTER 5

Ten days later, Caleb and Dil were on a huge, stern-wheeled, steam-powered flatbed ferry, easing away from the Independence shore.

"On our way at last," Dil said, gripping the ferry rail as the huge barge swung into the Missouri River's current. "Praise the Lord. There's only about two thousand miles of the Oregon Trail between us and the Willamette Valley."

Caleb grinned at his friend.

"It's not too late to change our minds," he shouted, to make himself heard over the rattle of the ferry and the hammering of the steam engine that pushed the churning paddle wheel. Except for their two riding horses, two pack horses, and two tall, black, aristocratic-looking pack mules, they had the ferry to themselves.

"Way too late, Captain," Dil said. "We have cast our bread upon the waters. All I quarrel with is those two mules. They've both been looking down their noses at me since we bought them. They don't look at all like work mules."

"Do you know why I bought them?"

"To carry our necessities."

"That, too, but if either Lady or your horse, Hiram, goes lame, we can ride one of those mules. I've ridden them both. If it weren't that I couldn't part with Lady now I've got to know her, I'd be saddling Sheba or Joshua come morning."

"Good planning, Captain," Dil said, "but they look smarter than I am, and that's embarrassing."

"Look each of them in the eye and say, 'You're a mule and I'm not.' That is, if we don't drown crossing this river," Caleb said as the barge gave another shudder that set the horses and mules tossing their heads and stamping nervously.

Luckily, the rest of the ferry trip was uneventful. Once off the boat and mounted, with the pack animals trailing Caleb on a lead, they were on their way, against the advice of all the people they had encountered, including the captain of the ferry boat. "It's too late to be setting out for Oregon," he'd told them, frowning and shaking his head. "There'll be snow in the mountains, and on the plains the wind will freeze your balls."

"Still going?" Dill asked Caleb as the captain was walking away.

"The farther I get from Indian River, the happier I'll be," Caleb said. "What about you?"

"Can't wait to start."

Caleb didn't care. Snow, mountain passes, freezing wind . . . he welcomed any challenge that might help him put Indian River more completely behind him.

On the second day, they encountered a tall, white-haired man, riding toward the ferry with two pack horses on a lead. He stopped to talk, and they learned he was a wagon master on the Oregon and California trails. He wore an Indian deerskin jacket with rawhide fringes on the sleeves, leather trousers, and well-worn boots and spurs that Caleb recognized as Union cavalry issue.

"Alder Goodnight," he said when they exchanged names with him. "You're startin' late, but I suppose you know that. Don't linger. Push hard, and keep your eyes on the pack animals; switch them off every little while to see they don't weaken. The mules usually look after themselves, but listen to what they tell you.

"One more thing, and harken to me: Don't be caught any

23

distance from your camp on foot or on horseback or anywhere without your rifle. The Indians are stirred up. They've been raiding the wagon trains all spring, in part for plunder but mostly because they're mad as hell."

"Why?" Caleb asked.

"Ever since Black Kettle's Cheyenne band lost a hundred and fifty men, women, and children killed last year by the Third Colorado Cavalry, there's been Indian trouble all over the Plains—that, and the government's not living up to its treaties. Their hunting grounds are being invaded. The buffalo are being driven away and killed."

Goodnight paused and seemed to be looking at something only he could see. "Also, there's bear and there's buffs," he said. "You can't outrun either one. Don't even go to relieve yourself without your mount and your long gun. If you see a war party approaching, shoot before they get close enough to peg you with an arrow." He pronounced it *arrar*. "Keep spare shells on you at all times."

"Much obliged for the warning." Caleb felt some alarm but quashed it. After all, they couldn't turn back. "We're going to Oregon. Will we make the mountains by September?"

"The question is, will you get over them," Goodnight replied. "Just hope there's not an early blizzard. Another thing: There's eyes watching the length of this trail, and they're looking for easy pickings. Two men are mighty tempting, and not all the bad Indians on these plains have red skin. Grow eyes in the back of your head, sleep with your rifles, build fires that have mighty little smoke, and don't camp in a wash no matter how dry it is."

"I thank you kindly," Dil said, "but Captain Stone and I have been killed two or three times already. We're kind of used to it, but we'll keep our fires small, sleep on high ground, and stake our horses close by."

"See you do that, and camp early, to give your animals time to graze on their hobbles. Then stake them out right by your bed, come dark."

With that, Goodnight shook their hands and wished them well.

Their first goal was the Platte River, three hundred-twenty miles northwest of Independence, a lot of it through the Kansas River watershed, a region notorious for thunderstorms with driving hail as often as rain. They forded the Kansas River the second day out. Luck was with them for the next several days as they went deeper into a rough, rolling country with scattered trees and grass, learning as they went that the Oregon Trail was not a trail at all but a miles-wide scattering of wagon wheel tracks. Even this close to the starting point, broken wagon wheels, pieces of furniture, and sometimes entire abandoned wagons lay scattered in the grass.

With no cattle to trail and not limited to the speed of bullocks hauling a wagon, Caleb estimated they were averaging between twenty and twenty-five miles a day. The country through which they were riding climbed toward the Platte River and, over ten days, changed from watershed to prairie. They saw their first bear and a small herd of buffalo that went thundering away at the sight of them. Caleb shot a young mule deer, and they paused long enough to dress it, saving the best cuts to eat and to dry, leaving the remainder for scavengers. The country abounded in black and white-tailed jackrabbits, prairie chickens, prairie dogs, and occasional badgers. Hawks, meadow larks, and other songbirds brightened their days. At night they learned to sleep through the occasional howling of coyotes and wolves.

The two men quickly settled into a routine they would follow all the way to Oregon. Their days were controlled by weather, the nature of the terrain, and their own as well as their animals', need to drink, which meant camping near water. They rose at

daylight, rolled their bedding, and, while Caleb watered the horses, saddled the pair they were going to ride that day, and put their packs on the rest. Dil gathered buffalo chips for a fire and cooked their breakfast of bacon and fried cornmeal. Lunch at midday was thin strips of jerky, chewed while riding. Supper, eaten at the fire, was whatever Caleb had shot during the day, most often prairie chickens. While their supply of flour lasted, Dil made biscuits in a small tin reflecting oven.

After the heat of the day, the cooling at night and the wind that blew away most of the flies made sleeping under the stars a pleasure. Except for the morning Caleb woke up with a four-foot rattlesnake draped across his chest, enjoying the warmth. Fortunately, he spotted the snake before moving. He also saw Dil, half sitting up and eying the early light.

"Dil," he said quietly, "I've got company."

Dil turned his head. His eyes widened when he saw the rattler, which chose that moment to slither off Caleb onto the grass nearby. "You lie real still, Captain," Dil said, reaching for his boots and slipping them on. "We've found our supper."

"You might shoot its head off, and we'll discuss supper later."

"Just lie still, Captain," Dil repeated. He stepped around Caleb's feet and edged toward the snake. The creature raised his head slightly, running its tongue in and out, testing the air.

"Dil," Caleb said in a tight voice, "what in hell . . ."

The snake snapped into a coil and struck, hitting Dil's boot. Dil bent and grasped the snake behind its head, set his boot on the twisting body, and with a single twist of his hand broke the rattler's neck, tossing the snake away from Caleb.

"Not too bad for a one-armed man," Dil said, looking pleased with himself.

"I'm not eating that snake," Caleb said. "Don't even think of it."

Dil drew his long face into an expression of astonishment.

"I'll gut it, skin it, put the meat into a sack, and, come evening, I'll cook some of it along with whatever you shoot and challenge you to a tasting contest. Rattlesnakes are Sunday eating, and that skin will make a mighty fine belt. You Yankees have fallen from grace on this one."

Following Alder Goodnight's advice, they camped early, this time near a cattail-rimmed pothole between two low hills. Caleb took Sheba off the lead rope and walked her to the little pond, to see if she would drink the water. She had refused to drink at the last pothole, and, in riding around the pond, Dil had found a dead elk in the pool. After that, Sheba became the company's guide to potable water. Here, she drank, and they made camp.

Once Caleb had stripped the animals of their saddles and packs, Joshua and Sheba gave themselves a good shaking and then dropped into the grass and rolled, scratching their backs on the dusty earth. The horses, less demonstrative, settled for a shake. Caleb unpacked the curry comb and brushes and gave their backs a good grooming, then checked their legs and hooves. When the mules were back on their feet, he brushed them and hobbled the animals, keeping an eye on them while they grazed. At supper time, he staked them around the fire.

He found he enjoyed learning about the grasslands, which began early in their journey. The wind, the sky, and the flowers were the things Caleb and Dil noticed first. The wind blew most of the time, a hot wind that bent the grass in great sweeps like waves, making a sighing sound as it passed. It carried the huge white clouds with flat, shadowed undersides, skimming on the sea of air, endlessly sailing out of the west in scattered ranks and files. On clear days, the blue sky was a vast inverted cup curving over their heads. Look where they would, the blue dome encompassed them.

"I believe I miss the trees," Dil said one day when they paused for a rest. He was standing in his stirrups, turning his head, to

27

gaze around him. "Not a tree in sight. I feel like I'm being watched."

"It is an odd feeling," Caleb agreed, pulling out a bandanna to mop his face. "Some shade would be welcome."

"Well, I guess I'll get accommodated to it," Dil said. "I don't really see why anyone would want to watch me."

"Alder Goodnight said there were eyes always watching on this trail," Caleb reminded him, only half joking.

And there was the wind; every day it ruffled their hair and sometimes blew the horses' tails out like flags. By the end of a month they had grown used to it and found themselves beginning to forget it. Then, in the middle of an afternoon, a different and fiercer wind announced itself with the sudden appearance of heavy black clouds to the west of them, climbing over the horizon like ominous giants.

"Captain," Dil said, "I think we'd better get out those oiled covers."

Caleb stood in his stirrups and surveyed the prairie. "I don't even see a badger set, so let's break out the hobbles and lay the saddles over the packs. We'll shelter as best we can."

They finished their tasks none too soon. Lightning was bounding around inside the thunderheads as if loosening up for what was coming. The horses, skittish as the thunder drew nearer, took some handling to get the hobbles on them, but Joshua and Sheba turned their tails to the storm and pushed up against one another once their packs were off and stood patiently while being hobbled. The two men piled their packs on the ground and covered them with the saddles, Caleb shouting to be heard over the crashing of the thunder. "We've done what we can. Get under the covers."

A tremendous roar of wind came as the storm descended on them, accompanied by jagged bolts of lightning and bellows of thunder that shook the ground. "Look there!" Dil shouted,

pointing west.

Caleb paused in his struggle with the oiled canvas and turned his head.

"Lord God," he said.

A dark wall of water, racing before the wind, bore down on them with the sound of a thousand galloping horses. Caleb had faced fifty-horse cavalry charges, but their pounding hooves had been a whisper compared to this.

Both men dove under their oiled canvas covers, clinging to them tightly. There was too much noise for conversation, so Caleb listened as the wind ripped around them, howling like a pack of demented wolves, while driving icy rain pounded them like buckshot.

The silence, when it came, was instantaneous. Caleb, chilled through, eased back the canvas over his head and sat up, watching the storm race away from them, the thunder fading as it retreated.

Dil shook the remaining water off his canvas. "Those horses must be half froze. You all right, Captain?"

"Yes," Caleb managed to say, somewhat surprised that it was true. "What about you?"

"I don't know that I believe I'm still alive. I peeked out once and saw a jagged leg of lightning not fifty feet from us. Right over there. Looks like it fried the grass where it hit."

They walked over to the blackened circle, the diameter of a corn silo. It smelled of burned hay where the lightning had torched the grass despite the avalanche of water pouring down on it.

"They told us there'd be some heavy storms," Dil said, "and I now believe them."

Both men burst out laughing, from sheer relief at having survived. Caleb walked back to the animals, feeling as though he'd been given a new lease on life. The sun was already burn-

ing away the traces of the storm and drying the animals. Caleb undid their hobbles, then threw a saddle over Joshua's back and put Lady on the lead rope. He had chosen Joshua because the mule was the largest and strongest of their small remuda. Once in the saddle, Dil passed up the lead rope. Caleb eased the mule forward.

Within moments, they came to an abrupt halt. Sheba refused to move. Caleb gave the lead rope a couple of turns around the pommel and told Joshua to move on. The larger mule did so very slowly until the rope tightened. Caleb looked back. Sheba had her four feet planted in the earth and her neck stretched and was refusing to budge.

"We can't pull her all the way to Oregon," Dil said, riding back for a closer look at the problem.

Caleb turned to find Joshua looking at him, ears pricked. "Back up," Caleb said.

Instantly, Joshua eased the tension on the rope.

"Let's try something," Caleb said. "Unhitch Sheba from the rope and see if she'll walk up here to me."

Dil did as directed. Once off the rope, Sheba walked beside Dil, ears up and sprightly.

"Give me the lead," Caleb said, and Dil passed it to him. "Walk on," he told Joshua.

The bigger mule stepped out briskly, and Sheba moved forward with him. Caleb leaned forward and stroked Joshua's neck. "Well done, Mr. Mule," he said, grinning.

Following the storm, the prairie looked as if it had been swept by a gigantic broom. The dust devils had vanished. The air was so clear, the flowers shone in the grass like yellow, white, blue, and purple jewels as far as the eye could see. Even the horses and the mules seemed in better spirits, and Dil, following at the end of their short line, was whistling.

For the first time since receiving Millicent's letter, Caleb felt

an easing of his sorrow.

That evening, they camped beside a crystal clear, spring-fed stream with a scattering of willows growing along its green banks. There was no shortage of buffalo chips, and Dil soon had a fire burning and biscuits baking. The two quail Caleb had shot were plucked and turning on spits over the fire. They ate just as the sun was setting in an orange and red blaze.

"I wonder," Dil said, "if that saying, 'Red sky at night, sailors' delight,' has any truth in it? I don't believe I ever really thought about it before."

" 'Red sky in the morning, sailors take warning,' " Caleb said, dipping his biscuit in the drippings from the roasted quail. "It probably does. It's even in the Bible. Jesus speaks of it."

"I didn't know you had read up that way on the Good Book." Dil stopped eating to express his surprise.

"My mother could quote reams of it. She loved to tease my father by quoting what she called 'The Book' against him in an argument. It made him hopping mad, but if he burst out about it, she would begin singing a hymn, usually 'Rock of Ages.' She did it just to get a rise out of him. I still miss her."

"It's your good fortune to remember her, even if you do grieve her loss."

Reminded that Dil lacked such memories of his past, Caleb felt abashed. "You're right, and I'm sorry I mentioned her. It was thoughtless of me."

"Please, Captain," Dil said. "It gives me pleasure to hear about your family. It really does."

Caleb could see he meant it. Not for the first time, he blessed the luck that had brought Dil to him as a traveling companion.

After supper, when they'd brought in the animals, staked them around the fire, kicked ashes over the glowing coals, and settled into their bedrolls, Dil fell instantly to sleep. Caleb lay awake longer, staring up at the velvet darkness of the sky,

sprinkled with stars and the Milky Way gleaming as if spread by the stroke of a giant's brush.

Speaking about his mother had dragged Caleb back into the world he was leaving behind. Flashes of memory overcame him—his mother rolling out dough on the sideboard, the sleeves of her dress rolled to her elbows; the first day he reached up and touched the pump handle in the kitchen sink without standing on his toes; sitting on the hay rake, driving the horse, the smell of the newly cut hay, the clatter of the rake. Millie, her laughter, kissing her. All gone. All of it. And so, he thought bitterly, was the boy and the man who was no longer Caleb Stone.

CHAPTER 6

It was Joshua who saw them first, or more likely smelled them. The big mule leaned back on the lead rope and snorted a warning. On a hot midafternoon of a partly overcast day, Caleb and Dil were moving through dry, deeply broken country that prevented their seeing more than a quarter of a mile ahead. A few minutes earlier Caleb had caught the scent of smoke and had thought dry lightning might have set a fire, but, when the smoke didn't thicken, Dil said, "Indians."

In the past week two small parties of warriors, riding north and moving fast, had crossed the trail in front of them. Both groups had pulled up on seeing them but paused only long enough to confer briefly, then quickly kicked their ponies into a gallop that soon took them out of sight. Where the Indians were going and what they intended, Caleb didn't know and hadn't wanted to think on. Now, he turned Lady up the nearest rocky hillock, hoping for a better view of what lay ahead.

"More of the same for at least a mile," he said, guiding Lady back down the hillock. "No sign of smoke that I could see. Can you smell it any longer? I can't."

"No," Dil said, "but the wind is going every which way in these breaks."

They forged ahead, winding their way through rock and gravel hillocks and stony gullies thinly strewn with wire grass and skimpy weeds. The terrain made it impossible to see more than thirty or forty yards in any direction. When they came out

of the breaks and into the grass again, Caleb pulled Lady up. He raised a spyglass to his face and surveyed the landscape.

"I don't like the looks of that," he said after a moment, lowering the spyglass and passing it to Dil.

"Looks like two people huddled under the brush at the bottom of that creek bank," Dil said. "And that's where the smoke's coming from."

Indeed, a thin pencil line of white smoke was rising through the willows and quickly vanishing in the wind.

Spyglass still raised to his face, Dil eyed more of the makeshift camp ahead. "There's three ponies staked behind the willows. I suppose we could just back into the breaks and come out south or north of them," he added.

Caleb took the spyglass back. "You don't sound very enthusiastic."

"The day is getting on, Captain, and this is the first water we've seen since midmorning. Also, I don't fancy going back into those breaks. It's a perfect setup for an ambush."

"Just what I was thinking." Caleb slid his Spencer rifle out of its leather scabbard and hitched the lead rope to the pommel of his saddle.

"Very carefully, Captain," Dil murmured. He wedged the reins between his teeth and drew his revolver.

The ponies, all paints, had thrown up their heads to stare at their visitors and were pulling at their stakes. "They don't like us any better than Joshua likes them," Caleb said in a low voice.

A figure dressed in deerskin clothes rose out of the brush, holding a drawn bow. Dil and Caleb checked their mounts. Joshua snorted loudly and began pushing his way up the lead rope.

"Joshua," Caleb said sharply. "Stop." Surprisingly, he did.

Dil shoved his revolver back into its holster and grasped his reins. "Captain, that's a woman." He slipped down from the

saddle and walked toward her, holding his open hand raised shoulder high.

"No," the woman said. "No closer. Go away." Her arrow was aimed squarely at Dil's chest.

Caleb slid his rifle into its scabbard and dismounted.

"Can we water our horses?" Dil asked, pulling off his hat.

Looking carefully at the makeshift camp, Caleb saw at once something was wrong. In the roughly built lean-to made of sticks and hides someone was laid out, moving feverishly.

"Stop where you are, Dil," Caleb said. "Somebody in their camp is sick. It could be smallpox."

"Not," the woman with the bow said.

She appeared to understand English well, or at least the word *smallpox*. "Where are your people?" Caleb asked.

The woman hesitated, then said, "Go away."

Dil turned to her. "I might be able to help."

"You doctor?"

"About that, I reckon," Dil replied.

Caleb studied her more closely. She was tall, with two heavy, black braids hanging down over the front of her dress, reaching to her waist. She was not young, possibly his own age, with high cheekbones, large, black eyes, and chiseled features. Her bold stance, and her bow, never wavered. It puzzled him that her deerskin dress, gathered at the waist by a length of a rawhide, was a stained and tattered remnant, torn in places and ragged at all the fringes. She wore it with dignity, he thought admiringly.

"May I look, ma'am?" Dil asked.

Slowly and with obvious distrust, the woman lowered the bow. "Yes." She gestured with her bow toward Caleb. "That one water horses and mules."

Dil stepped past the woman toward the lean-to. As he bent down to enter, the person inside sat up, knife in hand, and

35

slashed at him.

"Whoa!" he shouted, jumping back. His heel caught on a root, and he tumbled over backward.

The woman turned and grasped the knife wielder by the wrist, shaking her head, speaking swiftly in what Caleb supposed was Sioux. The sick person sank back onto the bed of furs, groaning.

Dil scrambled up. "That's a young woman, maybe the other one's sister."

"Go look," the older woman said. The corners of her mouth twitched. "She not hurt you now."

Dil gave the woman a stern look. "You think I should have taken her knife and maybe hurt her more?"

She frowned. "Look at her."

"What's her name?" Dil asked.

She kept silent a moment. Then, "Little Rain."

Dil crept into the lean-to, took the sick girl's hand, and placed it on his chest. "Dil," he said. He released her hand and placed his own on her chest. "Little Rain." He waited a few seconds and then repeated the actions, but she said nothing.

"She hears but does not speak," the older woman told him.

"Where is she hurt?"

"Her leg. Arrowhead at the top."

"Show me," Dil said.

After some tugging and struggling, the injured woman was stripped of her leggings, and the wound in her thigh exposed. Dil studied it, frowning, then backed out of the lean-to and spoke to Caleb. "The arrowhead's in there an inch deep, I'd guess, and the wound's infected." He turned back to the older woman. "If the arrowhead is not taken out, she will die. I can take it out and cleanse the wound. We have something that will make her sleep while I work."

"Whisky?" the woman asked, a sour look on her face.

"No. Chloroform."

Her frown deepened. "I do not know it. She will live?"

"Yes," Caleb said. "She will sleep and then wake after the arrowhead is removed."

The woman glared at him. "If she does not, I will kill you."

"All right," Caleb said. "My name's Caleb Stone. What is yours?"

Her eyes widened. "To have a name is to have power over a person. Is your mind broken?"

"No, but if you believe what you just said . . ."

"Captain." Dil shook his head.

Caleb took a deep breath. "Then you know something I don't," he said. "Are you going to tell me your name, or are you afraid?"

She said something to him that sounded like dry sticks breaking, and her face darkened as she spoke. They locked eyes. She gave way first, her shoulders slumping. "White Cloud."

"It's a beautiful name," Caleb said, feeling guilty for having spoken sharply to her. "When did you last eat?"

"Three days," she said. "No animals here."

"We should take that arrowhead out while the light lasts," Dil said.

"Take out the arrow from Little Rain and leave. You cannot stay here," White Cloud said sternly. "There are six of them, and all are warriors."

Six of who, Caleb wondered. "Why have they left you here alone?"

"Little Rain could not ride any further. I would not leave her."

"Are you the wife of one of the warriors?"

"I am nobody's wife," she said bitterly. "Little Rain and I are Arapaho, captured in a raid by Hawk Hand. He is a dangerous man. War chief. All fear him."

Caleb thought of the war parties they'd seen in recent days. "I'll start a fire," Dil said and went off to collect buffalo chips.

"While he does that," Caleb said, "I'll unpack the mules and water the horses."

White Cloud tensed. "Hawk Hand will kill you if you stay until he returns."

"I am also a great warrior," Caleb said, with a wry grin at his own folly.

White Cloud remained wary, watching and listening for approaching riders, while the fire burned down enough to produce coals. Dil shoved a bone-handled skinning knife into them and piled more chips around the blade. He picked up his canvas sack and walked back to the lean-to. "Captain, you and White Cloud must hold her while I put her to sleep," Dill said.

White Cloud hesitated, then knelt beside the girl and spoke rapidly to her. Caleb crawled into the lean-to and gripped Little Rain's shoulder as gently as he could, pressing his other hand against her stomach. After a moment, White Cloud did the same on the other side of Little Rain.

Dil crawled inside the lean-to, holding a canteen and a folded green bandanna. He placed the bandanna on Little Rain's chest and unscrewed the cap. "White Cloud, I'm going to sprinkle a little of this on the bandanna, put the top back on the canteen, and then press the cloth over Little Rain's nose and mouth. She will fight, but only for a minute. Hold her still."

For the first time, White Cloud looked worried. "It will not kill her?"

"No, but it must be done quickly. When she sleeps, we will take her to the fire. I will clean the wound as best I can, take out the arrowhead, and cauterize the wound. Then you wrap her leg with a clean cloth I will give you."

The injured girl fought hard, but Dil had done this to many wounded men, and within seconds she went slack in their hands.

Caleb and White Cloud carried her to the fire. Dil soaked the bandanna in whiskey and cleaned the wound. Working quickly, he cut out the arrowhead, then pulled the knife out of the fire and pressed the red-hot blade into the torn muscle. The smell of burning flesh rose around them. As intended, the cauterization stopped the bleeding. Again Dil cleansed the incision. "Now we wrap the leg," he said.

"Wait." White Cloud jumped up and ran to the lean-to. She came back carrying a small leather bag, tied with rawhide. From it, she took out several large leaves. "Put these on the wound," she said. "It is strong medicine."

Dil laid the leaves over the wound, then handed her a length of white cotton cloth. "Captain, hold up her leg. White Cloud, wrap it with the cloth."

After they finished, Dil got to his feet and looked down at the young woman. "You did not tell me, White Cloud," he said quietly, "but Little Rain is beautiful."

White Cloud scowled at him. "You have only one arm."

"And she has no tongue," Caleb replied.

She whipped around as if to strike him but settled for a fierce scowl. Caleb returned it. "Let's get her into the lean-to," he said. "She should be kept warm, and this wind is turning cold. Then we'll eat some of that venison we've been saving."

They settled the injured girl amid the furs, and White Cloud gently covered her. Dil hurried off to prepare their supper. "Her eyes are not open," White Cloud said darkly, less than a minute after he left.

"She will sleep for a while longer," Caleb said.

"How do you know this?"

"I was in an army hospital for nearly two winters, and I had chloroform used on me."

"I do not know *hospital*," she said.

He sat back on his haunches. "Do you know that my people

39

in the North fought a war with people in the South in which thousands of warriors died?"

"No. What is 'hospital'?"

"A place where those who are wounded or fall sick go to either die or get well."

"You were there?"

"Yes, Dil and I were there for two years. By then the war was ended, and the warriors went home."

Her frown was more puzzled now than angry or afraid. "Is Dil your slave?"

Shocked, Caleb gaped at her. "No. He is my friend. He saved my life."

"He lost his arm in battle?"

"Yes. I was shot and then stabbed with a spear. Where did you learn to speak English?"

She shrugged. "When I was five winters, my mother took a white man into her teepee. He taught me some of the language you speak."

Curiosity piqued, Caleb drew breath to ask more, but Dil called out to them, and they moved to the fire to eat. White Cloud had never seen a biscuit and took some persuading to bite into one. Caleb finally persuaded her by breaking off a piece of the one he was eating, dipping it in the juice from the venison and passing it to her.

"Be brave," he said.

At that, she snatched it from him and crammed it into her mouth. Both men stopped eating to watch her. For a moment she sat very still as if expecting to spit it out. Then her eyes widened and she began to chew. The next instant, the piece of biscuit was gone.

"More," she said, glancing at Caleb and then away. "Is good."

After the meal, and much arguing with White Cloud about the wisdom of staying, they brought all of the animals close to

the fire and staked them.

"You are fools," she said.

"If we weren't," Dil said, "we wouldn't be here at all."

Caleb smiled, and White Cloud planted her fists on her hips. "Is not for laughing. Your scalps will hang in Hawk Hand's lodge," she said.

"I'll take the first watch," Caleb said, getting to his feet, "and stand with Joshua."

"You will not hear him come," White Cloud warned.

"The mule will." Caleb guessed the sharpness in her voice was a cover for her fear. Of them, or of her captor?

I hope it's not me, he thought.

CHAPTER 7

Shortly before midnight, Little Rain awakened, groaning with pain. Dil gave her a few drops of morphine, allowing her to sleep, and, in the morning, she could sit up and eat. Caleb and White Cloud watched Dil dress the wound, talking away to Little Rain about the rattlesnake that had crawled onto Caleb's chest one night for warmth. Little Rain watched him but said no word in response.

"How old is she?" Caleb asked White Cloud.

"Nineteen winters."

"Is she married?"

"No."

"How was she wounded?"

Her shoulders stiffened. "We take horses, try to run away. Hawk Hand put arrow in her leg. He is a hard man. We will not try to run away again."

"White Cloud," Caleb said, "Dil and I will leave this morning. If you wish, you may come with us."

"There is no use. They will follow, kill you, and take us with them." She spoke with a mixture of resignation and bitterness not lost on Caleb.

He thought for a moment. "Do you know what hope means?"

She turned to him, two frown lines between her eyes. "It is something I lost when Hawk Hand caught me," she said evenly.

He nodded his understanding. "The way I see it, if you stay here, you have no hope. I know what that feels like. Dil and I

are going west through the country of your people. If you go with us, you will find hope again. Hawk Hand and his warriors may kill us, but they may not. Also, they may be dead."

"If I go, I will have your deaths on my head. I do not want it."

"I've read," Caleb said quietly, "that you believe in the Great Spirit who is in charge of our lives. Is that true?"

"Yes." She sounded puzzled.

"White people call the Great Spirit God. If Dil and I die, it will be because God has decided it is our time to die. Am I right?"

She bit her lip. "It may be so, but if Little Rain and I do not go with you, Hawk Hand will not follow you."

"Dil and I found you. Did you expect that to happen?"

"No."

"Perhaps the Great Spirit has other plans for you and Little Rain than to die as slaves among the Lakota. Perhaps it has been decided that you will return to your people."

White Cloud looked at Caleb long enough for the vulture circling over them in the morning sky to lose interest and drift away.

"I do not understand you, Caleb Stone," she said finally. "Why are you doing this?"

"For the same reason Dil took the arrowhead out of Little Rain's leg. He did it because he could. And because she would have died if he hadn't. Dil and I can take you and Little Rain away from the Lakota."

"Since I cannot ask the Great Spirit what his plans are for us," she said, the corners of her mouth twitching, "I will speak with Little Rain."

As she hurried away, Caleb realized with surprise that she had been laughing at him.

★ ★ ★ ★ ★

With a wolf skin wrapped around the wounded leg and an elk hide folded under her for a saddle, Little Rain could ride one of the ponies with little pain.

White Cloud had broken camp and was ready to leave well ahead of Caleb and Dil. She sat on her paint beside Little Rain, one leg crossed in front of her, saying things now and then that made Little Rain laugh. Comments about his and Dil's progress, Caleb had no doubt.

Caleb and Dil had lifted Little Rain onto her horse while White Cloud held its head by the hackamore. Pressing upward on the end of the loop under the horse's jaw, White Cloud quieted it enough for the men to work beside it without being kicked.

"How does that feel?" Dil asked Little Rain once she was astride her paint. She was shorter than White Cloud, and her face was more oval, but she had the same bright, black eyes, long, braided hair, and flashing white teeth, and a softer smile than her companion's.

Before White Cloud could translate the question, Little Rain looked down at Dil, smiled and nodded. Caleb and White Cloud looked at one another. White Cloud shrugged.

"We will be travelling north-northwest, looking for the Platte River," Caleb said, lifting himself into Lady's saddle.

"I will go in front." White Cloud raised her hackamore and turned her horse away. "Watch Little Rain closely."

"Wait," Caleb said, "I've got the compass, and I'm armed."

"My compass is in my head," she said over her shoulder, "and you do not know what you are seeing. I will tell you when I see an antelope and show you how to bring it near enough to shoot. I will cook it tonight."

Dil rode up beside Caleb and stared after White Cloud. "Looks like we've got ourselves a trail boss," he said with a

44

straight face.

"It looks that way," Caleb said. "She certainly doesn't behave like a slave."

"You've met a lot of them, Captain?"

"Had I gone back to Maine, I might have become one," Caleb said. "It makes for a bad nightmare."

Little Rain urged her horse in front of them, pointing at White Cloud, who was growing smaller in the distance every minute.

"I'll take the back end," Dil said, "behind the mules."

Caleb nodded. "Keep looking over your shoulder." He pointed at Little Rain and then back at himself, hoping she would understand she was to stay with him. She shook her head vigorously and pointed at herself and then at Dil, who was just getting the string under way.

"All right." Caleb pointed at his eyes and then at hers and made a sweeping gesture with his hand. "Keep looking around."

She repeated the gestures, finishing with a smile. Caleb found himself smiling back.

The wind rose over the next few hours. They had ridden into country with the horses belly deep in the grass, and they were constantly jumping meadow larks and quail and dozens of smaller birds into flight. On all sides of them gopher mounds rose, mostly occupied by the little animals that stood up and whistled loudly at their passing.

At midday, Caleb saw White Cloud standing on her horse's back and slowly turning in a circle. Her turn completed, she jumped to the ground and out of sight in the tall grass. They reached her near a creek with plants and scrubby trees along its bank. She had hobbled her paint and started a tiny fire. On her hands and knees, she was digging up purple flowered plants with furry stalks and cutting off their long tubers. Caleb dismounted and hunkered down beside her, curious about what

she was doing.

"Breadroot," she said curtly. "Fry some for Little Rain. Gives strength." She pointed to another pile of what looked like small potatoes. "Ground nuts. She will eat and heal better."

By the time Dil and Caleb lifted Little Rain off her horse and laid her on the spread-out furs, White Cloud had the peeled tubers in her frying pan with some fat and placed over the fire.

"Little Rain's wound is acting up," Dil told White Cloud. "I'd like to give her a few drops of morphine."

"How do you know that?" White Cloud demanded, coming to her feet and glaring at Dil.

"She told me," Dil replied calmly. "The same way she tells you things, I guess."

"She is not your woman," White Cloud snapped.

"Is she yours?"

"Dil was trained to care for injured people," Caleb said quickly. "He can tell when someone is in pain."

"Yes," White Cloud said, less sharply, "but . . ."

"She's your sister, isn't she?" Dil said.

"No. Why you think that?"

"Because you love her and protect her as much as you can, but you have not been able to protect her since you were captured. Isn't that so?"

"Give her the medicine." Scowling, White Cloud went back to her cooking.

Caleb watched Dil walk away. Then he looked down at White Cloud as she poked at the tubers, sizzling in the fat. "Why are you angry with Dil?"

"Not angry. Go away. Look after horses. Do something useful."

Caleb didn't know whether to be angry in turn, or amused. He opted for a joke. "Yes, Mother," he said, turning away.

He wasn't sure, but he thought he could sense White Cloud

raising her head to stare after him.

They ate at the fire a short while later. As soon as she finished eating, Little Rain fell asleep.

"The morphine has kicked in," Dil said, staring down at her.

" 'Kicked in'?" White Cloud looked puzzled.

"Started to work, making her sleep," Dil said.

White Cloud nodded. Then she glanced at Caleb. "Hawk Hand is coming," she said. "We go or let her rest a while?"

Caleb eyed his friend. "What do you think, Dil?"

Dil shrugged. "An hour won't matter one way or the other, will it, Captain?"

"I suppose not," Caleb replied. "Let her sleep."

He was uncomfortably aware White Cloud was probably right. Hawk Hand and his men likely would come. *We'll have one rifle and a revolver against six skilled fighters, unless . . .*

He looked over toward White Cloud, but, to his surprise, she wasn't there. She'd left the fire so soundlessly, he hadn't even noticed. Surmising she'd gone off on some project of her own, Caleb went after her.

He found her within minutes, digging up plants with her knife and sliding them into a beaded bag. "Have you ever fired a gun?" he asked her.

"No," she said. "I am busy."

He sat on his heels next to her. "If Hawk Hand comes with his men, there is only Dil and I against six. Dil can't shoot a rifle, only a handgun."

She stopped digging, swung around, and scowled at him. He thought she was a handsome woman, even when frowning. "You want me to shoot Hawk Hand for you?"

"Not for me," he said calmly. "For yourself and Little Rain."

"What is the difference if I am a slave to Hawk Hand or to you?"

The blunt question pushed Caleb into anger. "I wish I could

47

speak Arapaho. I would give you a dressing down."

Confusion crossed her face. "You want to give me a dress?"

"Do you want to find your people again?" he said, too loudly as he got to his feet, "or do you just want to go on being bad tempered with me?"

He walked away then, to keep from saying anything more.

When he reached the campfire again, Dil was sitting near Little Rain, who still slept. He was cleaning his Colt revolver with an oily cloth, holding the weapon between his knees. "I'm beginning to feel a little sorry for Hawk Hand," Caleb grumbled. "I'm not surprised he hasn't caught up with us."

"Don't worry," Dil said sourly. "He will, and we can give her back to him."

"Do you suppose she just doesn't like white men even though her stepfather was white?"

"Yes, smell bad," White Cloud said.

Caleb turned to find her standing behind him. He almost said, *You're no bed of roses* but checked himself. "You could get yourself killed doing that," he told her instead.

She straightened her spine. "I will learn the gun," she said.

"Lesson one, then we must wake Little Rain and go." He went to Lady and pulled his Spencer carbine out of its boot on the horse's saddle, then led White Cloud away from Dil and Little Rain. When he'd gone a few yards from the campfire, he stood beside White Cloud, lifted the rifle, and pressed the butt against his shoulder. "Now you do that," he said and handed her the weapon.

She did it with an ease and grace that pleased and encouraged him. From there, he went through the rudimentary steps in pointing and firing the rifle.

"Does rifle have name?" she asked.

"Yes, it's a Spencer."

"Good name."

"We will shoot it once," he said, "and it will hurt your shoulder because when the powder explodes and pushes the bullet out of the barrel, some of the push comes back against you. It comes back very fast. Stand with one foot ahead of the other so it won't knock you down." He pointed at the trunk of a willow about thirty yards away. "Try to hit that tree."

She cocked the rifle, pressed her cheek against the stock, aimed, and fired. The next instant, she was sitting on the ground.

"Next time," he said, "hold the gun harder against your shoulder and stand with one foot in front of the other."

He did not put out a hand to help her up, guessing she'd ignore it. "Your shoulder may be black and blue tomorrow, but you will learn quickly how to absorb the kick."

"You will kick me?" she demanded, rubbing her shoulder and looking angry.

He fought back laughter. "No. I meant the gun kicks you in the shoulder. By the way, you missed the tree."

"Next time I will not miss, and Spencer will not kick me down." She shoved the rifle at Caleb and stalked back to where Little Rain was sleeping.

CHAPTER 8

Three days later, they reached the Platte and crossed where the banks were low and the water was shallow. Once across, they turned west and began looking for a place with shade, to rest the horses and bathe.

"You two first," Caleb told the women when they were camped in a grove of cottonwoods, green ash, and hackberry. "Dil and I will follow."

"Has the Great Spirit told you the women should go in the water first?" White Cloud asked.

"You can go or be thrown in," Caleb said.

"It is you who needs wash most," White Cloud replied, obviously enjoying herself.

"Among palefaces," Dil put in, "it shows respect to let women go first. What about your people?"

The question killed the banter. Dil muttered to Caleb, "Quick, say something."

"Have you got soap?" Caleb asked.

The women looked at one another and then at Caleb, blank-faced.

Caleb went over to one of the mules and dug around in a pack until he found their soap supply. He fished out a bar and gave one to White Cloud. She scowled at the soap, still apparently at a loss. Little Rain appeared equally bewildered.

"Take it with you into the water," Caleb told them. "When you are wet, rub the soap on your body and wash all over. Go,

take it with you. You'll see."

Dil pointed at Little Rain's wound, made a rubbing gesture, and shook his head. "Leave that alone. Let the water clean it."

After they'd gone, Caleb and Dil waded into a section of river out of sight of the women. "Lord in heaven," Caleb said, "you never know when you're going to step on their toes."

A few minutes later they heard whoops of laughter from beyond the willows.

Dil gave his shirt and trousers a final rinse, then climbed the bank and spread his wet garments on bushes to dry. With surprising ease for a one-armed man, he tugged on a fresh pair of trousers and a shirt. "I think it's very strange, captain, that Little Rain can laugh and groan, maybe even scream, but she can't speak."

"I have a feeling something very bad happened to her." Caleb likewise spread out his wet clothes on the bushes and changed to fresh ones. "She's not at all sickly, and she's recovered from the arrow wound much faster than I would have expected."

Dil frowned. "It might be nothing, but an hour or so after we left camp this morning, Joshua got restless. He was tossing his head, dancing out from the lead rope like he was trying to look behind us."

"Have you seen anything to account for it?"

"No, but I think we should bring the animals in early and keep them close. It might be a good thing to have our camp as much in the open as possible. The trees along here give too much cover for my comfort."

Caleb glanced up at the sun. "I agree. We've got at least another hour before the light goes."

"How is White Cloud doing with the rifle?" Dil asked as they finished dressing and gathered their things.

"I've given her our second Spencer," Caleb said. "She can load and fire, and, at twenty or thirty yards, she can put a bullet

into a ten-inch circle."

Dil rested his hand on Caleb's shoulder. "It might never come to that."

Caleb hoped so. "I really don't want her having to kill one of these men."

Dil nodded grimly. "It changes a person, Lord knows."

White Cloud gave Caleb a slashing glance as they returned to the camp. "I am keeping the soap, so that Little Rain and some other person will not have to stand downwind from you."

The women's dry clothing was even more tattered than the clothes they had washed, and hung off them like a gathering of rags, but both women wore them with an erect grace that made Caleb regard them with pleasure and admiration. Their long, shining black hair, spread out over their shoulders to dry, was, he thought, their glory—that, and White Cloud's eyes.

"You know you were misnamed, don't you?" he replied. "You should have been called Dark Cloud. That said, I think you smell very good."

"Maybe Thunder Cloud," she snapped, turning her back to him. He caught a note of humor along with annoyance in her tone and guessed she didn't want him to see she was smiling. A maddening woman. But definitely interesting. A brief memory of Millicent True flitted through his mind, ghost-like and gone in an instant.

In another mile they found a place where the river bank was ten or more feet high with a nearly vertical fall to the water, and no trees or shrubs grew for nearly a hundred yards.

"Have to carry water," White Cloud said to Caleb after they had hobbled the animals and were standing at the top of the bank, looking at the surrounding country, "and no place to hide."

Little Rain was starting the fire, while Dil tried to distract her with the sign language she had been teaching him. Caleb could

see she was doing her best not to laugh and failing. Dil waved his arm wildly, which completely broke her down.

White Cloud pursed her lips. "Those two are seeing one another."

"Does that trouble you?" Caleb asked.

"She is a slave because of me."

Caleb wanted to ask how that had come about but decided not to pry. She had very little beyond her privacy . . . best wait for her to tell him when she was ready. "I think they may be falling in love."

"He cannot care for her," White Cloud said coldly. "He has only one arm. He must live on what others give him."

"Is that the only reason you object?"

"She is woman of high rank and should marry her equal. Dil is not her equal."

"Because he has one arm?"

"No. Because he is white poor man with no rank among his people."

Her answer riled Caleb. He drew breath to ask if she thought he was a man of no rank as well, but checked himself. A few days' travel together wasn't enough for him to know this woman, let alone her people or their ways of thinking. "We'll have a double watch tonight," he said.

"And I will have Spencer with me," she said, as if reciting a lesson. "I am ready. I have the way in my mind: Set the hammer at half cock, push down the lever, bring in shell, close the lever, thumb hammer to full cock, aim, and fire."

"Yes." Caleb heard his own voice in hers. "You have it memorized."

She looked offended. "You do not sound happy with me."

Without thinking about it, he took her hand in his. "White Cloud," he said, "if you fire Spencer tonight, you will be shooting at a person. I do not want you to kill anyone."

Her eyes narrowed. "Why? Are you thinking that honor is only for you?"

The question stopped him for a moment while his brain spun, trying to understand. "These men are your enemies," he said at length. "You wish to kill them."

"I wish to avenge myself and regain my honor. If I can, I will kill Hawk Hand, but I will not honor him by hanging his scalp in my lodge."

For a moment Caleb looked into a world that was not his. It was White Cloud's world, and he would have to work hard to build a bridge to it.

"If we are to live, we must kill them all," she continued, holding his gaze. "If one lives, he will tell his people, and they will hunt us down. Do you understand, Caleb Stone?"

"I understand, White Cloud," he said sadly, slowly releasing her hand.

In the last of the light, when the animals had been brought in close to the fire and staked with their hobbles off in case of the need for a quick escape, and the bull bats had begun their booming dives over the prairie, White Cloud slipped away and returned with stripes painted across her face.

"I have only black, but it is strength," she said defiantly. "Now I am ready with Spencer. I will be in first watch."

Caleb saw Dil glance at Little Rain, who nodded.

"All right," Caleb said, "but we will talk first." He looked around but met with no objections. He took another moment to gather his thoughts. "If I were Hawk Hand and knew there were only two men in this camp, and I had five other mounted men," he began, "I would ride over us, turn, come back and jump down to kill whoever survived. To do that, they must come from our right or our left."

"That is a white mind speaking," White Cloud said dismis-

sively. "They will come with first light. They will creep through the grass, making no sound. When they are very close, a bird will call, and they will run in with the dark sky behind them and axes in their fists, to strike hard and count coup. That is how it will be."

Dil was watching White Cloud. Caleb looked from them to Little Rain, who was staring at him with a strained expression. When their eyes met, she nodded.

Caleb turned back to White Cloud. "We have one advantage," he said, not ready to respond to her version of what was coming. "Joshua will warn us before we hear the bird call."

"Unless they steal the horses first," she said.

"With us here?" Dil asked.

"Maybe," White Cloud said. "At least one of them will try to touch you without dying or being wounded. That one will earn great honor. He will wear an eagle feather in his hair."

"If White Cloud is right," Caleb broke in, "Hawk Hand and his men will come in from the west, but we must still cover the north and the east. That means we have to put the animals behind us, and pile up our packs and saddles in front of us, and fire over them."

Little Rain began signing rapidly to White Cloud. "She says she will remain covered until one of them reaches for her," White Cloud told them when Little Rain finished.

Dil looked troubled. "Then what?"

White Cloud answered in a matter-of-fact voice. "She has a knife and will kill one, leaving five for us."

Caleb exchanged a glance with Dil, who was clearly struggling with the same shock Caleb felt. Neither of them was used to women who thought like soldiers.

"All right," Caleb said finally, turning to Little Rain. "I hope it won't come to that."

Little Rain signed. Dil said, "She says it will."

Silence fell for a time. "Let us put things where they should be," White Cloud said. "Then I will lie with Spencer, half-cocked, a shell in the breech."

"That is how it will be," Caleb said. His deliberate imitation of White Cloud's words brought a snort of laughter from Dil, quickly stifled.

"It is good to laugh," White Cloud said, her eyes narrowing slightly. "Even Little Rain is smiling." At that, Little Rain's smile faded.

"I want two of us sitting up until first light," Caleb said. "Let's bring in the animals, then lay out the packs and the beds."

They worked without talking, first staking out the horses. Caleb brought Joshua and Sheba as close to the beds as he could and staked them lightly. "Why do this?" White Cloud asked, putting the last pack at the head of her bed. "If frightened, they will run over us."

"They've become accustomed to you and Little Rain. Not to the men coming. Remember that advantage I mentioned? I'm hoping we'll get some help from them."

"Ride, pull travois," White Cloud said disdainfully, unrolling her bed.

"Are Joshua and Sheba the first mules you've seen?"

"Yes. They are big."

"And smart," he said. "You will ride Joshua soon and see."

"If we live," she said quietly, "I will ride the mule."

"I have been in many battles and lived, White Cloud. We will live through this one." He hoped he sounded as though he believed what he was saying. It was going to be a long night filled with threat. Dil would understand, but Caleb wasn't sure about White Cloud.

She stopped what she was doing and faced him. "Caleb

56

Stone," she said, "it is a good night to die. Help me with these packs."

CHAPTER 9

The moon had set, the night wind fallen to a fitful breeze. The morning star was low in the sky, the air redolent with the smell of the grass and damp ground. Caleb watched along with the others as a soft, pale-gray light gradually rose from the eastern horizon. Slowly, the stars faded from the eastern sky. Silent and motionless on their beds, staring into the darkness, they waited.

Joshua raised his head, stamped a foot, and snorted. Caleb turned his head to look at the mule. The animal was staring west. Then Sheba snorted and tossed her head, staring the other way. A moment later, the horses shifted uneasily. A bird whistled. Turning toward the sound, Caleb saw a dark shadow at the western perimeter of their camp. Dil's revolver cracked, and the shadow collapsed.

In the next instant, wild yells filled the air as the attackers came racing out of the dark. Rising to his knees, Caleb fired his rifle from his hip, sending the man in front of him sprawling. Drawing his revolver, he turned to the left and fired at another warrior with axe raised to throw. The warrior went down.

Beside him, White Cloud was on her feet, shooting to her right. An attacking Indian on her left had nearly reached her, his axe raised. Joshua leaped past Caleb, striking White Cloud with his shoulder and sending her flying just as her assailant brought down his axe. Joshua hit the Indian squarely with his chest, flattening the man, and then galloped over his body.

Spinning away from the mule, Caleb saw an Indian bending

58

over Little Rain's bed. He raised his revolver to shoot, but the man fell forward with a strangled cry. Little Rain rolled the man off her and lay back down.

"Captain!" Dil shouted.

Caleb turned. A tall, powerfully built Indian swung a wide-bladed chopper at his head. The painted face loomed over him as he ducked and then threw himself forward, driving his head into the man's stomach. The impact sent the attacker somer-saulting over Caleb's back. He hit the ground and regained his feet in a single bound. The clash had cost Caleb his revolver and the warrior his axe. With a shout, the Indian threw himself at Caleb, hands outstretched to grasp whatever he could. It was clear to Caleb that in sheer strength he was no match for his as-sailant—Hawk Hand, he was certain.

Caleb side-stepped and delivered a hard blow to Hawk Hand's kidney. The Indian staggered slightly, giving Caleb time to step forward and strike him squarely in the throat. The big man reeled, unable to get his breath.

White Cloud stepped up beside Caleb. "This one is mine, Caleb Stone. Mine and Spencer's." She raised the rifle and shot Hawk Hand in the heart, knocking him off his heels and onto the ground. Swiftly, she jacked a fresh shell into the chamber and set the hammer at half cock. Then she calmly turned to face Caleb. "He is the last one."

The echo of the rifle died away, and silence settled over them and the animals. Little Rain stood up, and she and Dil hurried toward one another. Satisfied that Hawk Hand was dead, Caleb turned to White Cloud and pulled her into his arms, the rifle crushed between them.

"Spencer digs into soft parts," she said in a tense whisper. "Can't breathe."

Caleb released her, and she shed the gun. "Do close again," she said, throwing her arms around him.

A cheer went up from the other side of the camp, mingled with a high-pitched warlike cry. "Did that sound to you like two people?" Caleb whispered in White Cloud's ear.

They pulled apart enough to look at one another. Her eyes were like saucers, and Caleb found himself wanting to go on looking into them.

"Two people," White Cloud murmured, still holding him. "Someone's eyes are color of the sky." Then the significance of what Caleb had said sank in, and they released one another. "Cannot be two!" White Cloud cried, looking across at Little Rain and Dil standing together, holding hands.

"Little Rain can speak," Dil shouted, wrapping his arm around her shoulders and pulling her against him. Caleb saw her slip an arm around Dil's waist, making no effort to step away. White Cloud ran to her, speaking rapidly in Arapaho.

Little Rain answered her, and White Cloud said, "She can speak Arapaho, but she has not tried to speak the Nihoothoo's tongue."

Caleb hadn't heard that word for his own language before. For the moment, he preferred not to ask exactly what it meant.

Dil bent toward her. "Little Rain, say 'nose.' " He released her and tapped a finger against his nose.

"Nose," she said shyly, clapping her hands over her face.

Dil grinned. "Now she speaks English."

The morning sun was slowly burning away the thin mist that had risen from the damp earth. Caleb and the others stood staring at one another, too overwhelmed by the aftermath of battle and victory to move.

"How are we going to dig a hole to put them in?" Dil asked, breaking the spell. "We don't have any shovels, and we can't leave them for the scavengers."

Alarm and disgust spread across White Cloud's face. "Not put them in ground!" she said. "Only Nihoothoo would bury a

person. Wrap them and put them up away from wolves, coyotes and foxes and crows and vultures."

Lacking spare blankets, the four got into a brief verbal scuffle over substitutes, Little Rain joining in with a lively mix of Arapaho and fierce signing, delivered with passionate intensity. In the end, armed with ropes, knives, and two small axes, they all rode north along the river to the nearest stand of willows. Once dismounted, the women located four willows, growing in a rough square.

"Make bed," White Cloud said, pointing to the trees.

The women went in search of cattails to wrap the bodies in. After cutting them, they pulled up other plants near the water with long roots, that Caleb guessed they would use to tie the cattails around the dead men's bodies.

It was midday before Caleb and Dil had the frame of the platform in place and the poles cut to form its bed. They paused briefly to eat a meal prepared by Little Rain and drink dried rosehip tea boiled over a tiny fire. "I'm sorry to ask this," Dil said after swallowing the last of his tea, "but how do we get these bodies up onto that contraption?"

"Three will stand on ground, lifting one body at time to Caleb Stone," White Cloud said. "He will put body on platform."

"Standing on Joshua's back." Caleb sounded doubtful.

"For Hawk Hand, I will put rope around his chest. Two will push from here, you and I pull on rope from there." White Cloud pointed up at the platform. "Start now."

Joshua took the clambering on and off his back patiently. He didn't move once, except to show interest in what was going on by turning his head and watching. They dropped Hawk Hand twice but finally rolled him onto the platform. That done, White Cloud and Little Rain covered the bodies with the cattails and bound them with the roots they'd dug, then unrolled over them two elk skins from the women's cache.

At White Cloud's direction, Caleb laid the half dozen cotton-wood poles over the hides to hold them in place. Their work finished, White Cloud and Caleb sat down on Joshua's back, legs dangling side by side, leaning on one another shoulder to shoulder.

"I feel I should be on that platform," Caleb said, sore all over.

When the burial squad was sufficiently recovered, they returned to their campsite and plunged into the river. Dressed again and back in the camp, White Cloud stopped braiding Little Rain's hair, to say that they should move.

"Too near the burial platform?" Dil asked.

Little Rain frowned up at him. "Not talk of those."

"Then we move," Caleb said, glancing at the last of the sun.

White Cloud nodded and went back to braiding. Then they broke camp. In fifteen minutes, the women had the packs on the mules and were mounted and ready to go. Along with their natural grace, both women possessed a remarkable economy of movement that Caleb and Dil had watched with admiration.

"I could get used to this," Dil told Caleb as they started off.

"Do you think you and Little Rain might make a life together?" Caleb asked.

Dil looked thoughtful, and a little sad. "I suppose they will go back to their people." He eyed Caleb. "What about you and White Cloud?"

The idea startled Caleb, as did the realization that Dil had noticed his interest in the older Arapaho woman. "White Cloud has no interest in me. To her, I'm nothing but another Nihoot-hoo." Saying that out loud made him feel bad, more so than he expected. He gave Lady a prod with his heels and rode away from Dil and the others, telling himself he needed to find something for supper. In the last of the light, he jumped a young buck deer out of a swale surrounding a spring hole and shot

and gutted it.

A short while later, he found the others making camp. Seeing the deer slung over Caleb's pommel, Little Rain clapped her hands.

"Do not be too pleased, Caleb Stone," White Cloud said, helping him drag the deer to the fire. "She already has one man who never stops looking at her."

"I'm thinking about marrying her," Caleb said, feeling lighter-hearted for no reason he could fathom and pleased to be teasing White Cloud.

She dropped the deer's leg and shoved Caleb so hard, he nearly fell down. "You will not think that!" she said. "You are hearing me?"

"Yes, yes." He backed away as she advanced on him, holding his hands out toward her as if frightened.

"Not a joke," she said, fists on her hips, stiff-faced.

He halted and let her reach him, staring at her with intense interest. "Your eyes are very beautiful," he said quietly. "They are like the night sky."

She stopped, studying his face as if she had not heard him right.

"You promise you will not marry her?" she asked softly.

"I promise," he said.

In her next words, he heard pain. "It is hard to understand you, Caleb Stone."

What could he say to console her? "Sometimes, I don't understand you, but we will learn," he replied.

"I wonder when?" she asked, regaining some of her wryness. "Now let me skin this deer."

Caleb could not sleep that night. Tired of staring at the stars, he got up quietly and walked out to the horses and mules. A few were cropping the grass within reach while the others stood

sleeping. He went to all of them except the paints, who still acted uneasy when approached by him or Dil. If they snorted or stamped, they'd wake the others, and Caleb wanted solitude just now.

He stopped longest with Joshua. There was something about the animal that calmed him. He did not consider himself an introspective man, but he did think deeply about things, and killing Hawk Hand and the other warriors had left him troubled. He knew they intended to kill him and Dil and drag the two women back into slavery, but killing still bothered him as it had in the war.

"Isn't there a better way?" he asked the mule.

The most devilish thing about the question for Caleb was he had never found an answer. He knew there might have been ways the North and South could have rationally resolved the issue of slavery. But he also knew, all too well, that men did not always act rationally.

He thought of the Indians, and the white migration flowing like a river for twenty years. Soon it would become a flood, spilling across the Plains, sweeping the Indian tribes and the buffalo before it. "Part of why we fought the Revolution was over Indian lands," he murmured to Joshua, as if the mule could understand a history lesson. "The British tried to stop the colonists from moving west into Indian country. After we won the war, settlers poured over the Allegheny Mountains and claimed every inch of land they could." He didn't care to say the rest aloud—that they'd killed any Indians who tried to stop them, even hunted Indians for sport.

Joshua pricked his ears and whickered softly. Caleb cursed himself for not having picked up his rifle. He turned to find White Cloud standing nearby, her rifle in the crook of her arm, scowling at him.

"Someone not have Spencer," she said.

64

She stepped past him, ducking under Joshua's head, and laid a hand on the mule's shoulder, speaking quietly to him in her own language and stroking his neck. To Caleb's surprise, Joshua stood still, his ears still cocked as if listening to her. When she stopped speaking, the mule lowered his head and pushed his nose against her chest.

"Mule saved my life," White Cloud said.

"He was listening to what you told him." Caleb suppressed an impulse to say *he might not understand your language.* "Putting his nose against you like that means something. Aside from me, the only other person he does that to is Sheba."

"Sheba is not person."

"In Joshua's thinking, you and I and Sheba are mules. I like to think about myself as a mule. The only way to do that is to think of Sheba as a person."

White Cloud laughed, something she almost never did, Caleb had noticed. The sound of it and the look on her face delighted him. "You have a good laugh," he said. "I wish you laughed more."

"Caleb Stone," she said, "you also saved my life." She placed a hand on his arm and spoke rapidly in her own tongue. Thanking him, maybe?

"You are welcome, White Cloud," he told her when she finished, laying a hand over hers. "You fought as a warrior."

She lifted her chin. "I and Spencer regained honor."

They stood for a while in silence. Caleb listened to the horses, some moving, cropping the grass, others breathing quietly in sleep. Then White Cloud spoke. "When you say my eyes beautiful like the night sky, are you asking me to come under the buffalo robe with you?"

Her sudden directness startled him. Rattled and uncertain of her meaning, he couldn't answer her at once. Abruptly, White

Cloud dropped her gaze. "We will not talk about the buffalo robe now."

She hurried away, leaving Caleb open mouthed and wordless, watching her go.

CHAPTER 10

Three days later while Caleb rode ahead of the others, on point and looking for game, White Cloud caught up with him. She was carrying the Spencer across her thighs, her hair spilling over her shoulders and down to the horse's back. She had tied a half-inch-wide rawhide band across her forehead, knotted at the back.

She rode as if she and the horse were one, and Caleb was delighted by the way her shining black hair rippled in the wind. It came to him that even in her ragged doeskin blouse and split skirt, she bore herself like a princess. For an instant, his vision of her was blurred by the image of another woman, auburn-haired. That picture vanished as swiftly as it had come but left him feeling as though he had been struck hard in the chest.

White Cloud searched his face. "What is wrong?"

He forced a smile. "Watching you, I remembered something."

"Something or someone?"

"Both, I suppose."

"Why did you leave her?"

"The war did it, and I don't want to say more."

He caught a flash of sympathy in her gaze. "Perhaps later you will tell me, if the hurt is not too much." She paused. "There is something I should have told you on the day you found us. I did not know you then."

"You also thought you might kill me," he reminded her.

"Yes. I had darkness in my eyes. You will listen now. The na-

tions are rising all over the land of grass, all the way from the water called Missouri, to the mountains where the sun sets. They see the buffalo are not so many, and the number of your people coming grows."

Her words recalled the warning they'd gotten from Alder Goodnight before setting out. It seemed like a lifetime ago. "Is that why Hawk Hand was here?"

"Yes, and also to steal women and horses to sell to Lakota that wanted them. The numbers of the Lakota are growing less. They need children."

"Even white or half-white children?"

White Cloud looked puzzled. "It does not matter that woman is white. She will become Indian and one of the people. Her children also. If you live among the people and do as we do, you become one of us."

Tension crept upon him as the weight of her revelations sank into his mind. "Do Little Rain and Dil know what you've told me about the tribes making ready for war?"

"No."

"Then tonight we have to tell them and decide what is to be done."

She drew herself up straighter and met his eyes. "You are angry with me?"

He shook his head. "I wish you had told me sooner, but I am not angry with you, White Cloud."

"You should be angry. I put us all in danger." Snatching her paint's head around, she kicked it into a gallop.

Caleb watched her race away, aware that he was beginning to feel more than just liking for White Cloud and equally aware it was hopeless. She and Little Rain would go back to their people. Would Dil go with Little Rain if they grew more attached to one another, or would she decide to stay with him?

As he urged Lady into a trot, the possibility that White Cloud

might stay with him if he asked her rose in his mind. Instantly, he shut the thought down by forcing himself to concentrate on the ground in front of him and was rewarded a little later when an antelope dashed across his path. He shot it, gutted it, and threw it over the pommel of his saddle, then turned back to find the others. On the way, Caleb recalled one of his doctors warning him that he couldn't run away from himself. The warning was clear enough, but the question it raised had proved more difficult. Who was he? Only if he knew that could he know what he wanted from the remainder of his life.

Later, when they had finished eating and were sitting around the fire, Caleb broke the silence. "White Cloud tells me the Indian nations are talking to one another and are rising against the whites. Too many people like Dil and me are coming into their lands, killing buffalo for food or taking only their hides, driving the Indians away from their ancestral hunting grounds. The horse people can't exist without the buffalo. They will attack all along the Oregon Trail."

Little Rain looked worried. "Must we turn back?"

"No." White Cloud stood and continued speaking in a formal voice. "What I think is, because Little Rain and I have no place to go back to and our people may be where this trail goes, we should go on."

She sat down and looked into the fire.

"Does anyone else wish to say anything?" Caleb asked.

"Yes." Little Rain rose to her feet. "I have heard White Cloud. I think is best to go on. I should learn how shoot Spencer. I think we need one more person to kill those who would harm us. That is what I think."

She sat down and, like White Cloud, stared into the fire. It dawned on Caleb that the women were recreating the way their people settled issues of importance.

"Captain?" Dil stood next, catching on. "I think White Cloud

and Little Rain have spoken well."

When Dil sat down, Caleb rose to his feet in turn. "I agree with what has been said. You have all spoken well. We will go on and Little Rain will learn how to use Spencer."

He paused to look at his companions, all sitting and staring into the fire, the flickering of the coals reflected on their faces. No one spoke, so Caleb continued. "In three or four days we should reach Fort Kearney. There we rest and buy supplies and a Spencer rifle for Little Rain and more ammunition. I will listen to the officers in the fort. They will tell me what is happening between them and Fort Laramie, which is a little over two hundred miles west of Kearney."

He sat down, stared into the fire, and allowed himself to wonder how rough the road ahead was going to be.

Within two days, Little Deer could load, work, and fire the Spencer rifle as well as White Cloud, an achievement that made her walk a little straighter and gave Dil the opportunity to tease her. Caleb and White Cloud, cutting up a deer, heard the resulting uproar and stopped working.

"Like children," White Cloud said, wiping her knife on the grass. She was trying to sound critical but failed.

Caleb was amused as much by that as by the antics of Little Rain and Dil. "Has Little Rain asked Dil to come under her buffalo robe?" he asked.

White Cloud tilted her head. "I thought you did not know what that meant."

"I still don't know." He only suspected, so technically that was true. "I thought you were going to tell me, but you have not kept your promise. I must say, you have a lovely smile."

"Stop it," she said. "I have everyday teeth, not special."

"You are extra special all over. What is being under the buffalo robe all about?"

"You know," she said quietly, avoiding his eyes. "I think yes. Little Rain has asked Dil, or will soon. They see each other and feel they should be one."

"I think so, too. I envy them."

She stared at him. "You want to feel that way with Little Rain?"

"No, just to feel that way. Have you ever?"

She shrugged, glancing away again. "Perhaps. Pick up your knife. Work now."

Fort Kearney consisted of a large parade ground, surrounded by cottonwood trees and sprawling wooden buildings. Spaced around the fort were wagons with canvas roofs, smoke rising from their fires. Further out, oxen and horses were grazing, protected by uniformed men on horseback, moving slowly among the herd, their eyes on the horizon.

White Cloud pulled up short. "This one is not going any closer."

"Not go closer," Little Rain echoed, shaking her head.

Despite frustration, Caleb managed to keep his voice down. "By my calculations, we've come over three hundred miles to get here. We've got another two hundred and more to reach Fort Laramie. Don't you both want to see the place, at least?"

"Too many Nihoothoo," White Cloud told him.

"There are a lot of Indians there, mostly Lakota, I think," Caleb said.

The two women sat straight-backed on their horses and studied the horizon in silence.

"Captain," Dil said, "can I show you something back there on the string?"

Exasperated, Caleb grudgingly agreed.

Once out of hearing, Dil said, "I don't think it's the Nihoothoo that's the problem, Captain. I'd bet a brick chimney it's their clothes."

"Lord God," Caleb said. "I never thought of it." He took off his hat and scratched his scalp. "Look, we can't camp downstream of this place. The water's running death. Take them a mile or so west, find a place to camp. If you can find a spring, so much the better, and see if Sheba will drink. I'll go into the fort and then see about the clothes. Do you think they'd wear cloth dresses?"

"I doubt it."

"So do I. Go on. I'll see what I can do."

"Good luck, Captain." Dil grinned. "If you could see your face . . ."

Caleb rode down to the fort and settled Lady comfortably, then found the main building of the First Nebraska Cavalry and climbed the splintery steps to the Headquarters Office, where he introduced himself to the bored sergeant at the desk and asked where the commissary was.

The sergeant, a lean, long-armed man with large hands, got up from his chair and answered his question, then asked, "What part of Maine are you from?"

A fellow Mainer, from his speech. "Southwest. What about you?"

"Bangor, and I doubt I'll ever see it again. Where are you headed?"

"Willamette Valley."

"You and about ten thousand other people. I hear the place is pretty well settled up. You might want to look for land a little short of there. There's some beautiful little valleys with brooks running through them, and soil you could shove a dead stick into and it would sprout."

"Thanks for the advice. What's the Indian situation west of us?"

"There's trouble," the sergeant said, frowning. "You with a wagon train?"

"No, just the four of us, two mules and five horses. We got a late start, or so a wagon master told us back in Independence."

"A mite. You've still got fifteen hundred miles and some more to reach Oregon. My advice, for what it's worth, is either winter up here or at Fort Laramie along with these wagoners you've already seen, or go like a bat out of hell for the mountains. Don't stand on no hilltops or make much smoke. The army's leaning hard on the tribes, sending out units to punish them for their raids, but their blood is up, and their warriors are demanding their chiefs fight us. I'd say you've got about a fifty percent chance of getting through. If you see you can't hold the bastards off, and you've got any women with you, shoot 'em."

"They're Arapaho," Caleb said. "They were slaves of a Lakota warrior named Hawk Hand. They helped us kill him and the other five in his war party."

"You're taking them back to their people?" the sergeant asked, his tone carefully neutral.

"That's about it, and I need to buy another rifle, ammunition and supplies, and clothes for the women."

"Well, you've come to the right place for that. We're stocked to the roof with just about anything you might need. The commissary is the biggest building at Kearney." He thrust out his hand. "Was you by any chance at Fredericksburg?"

Caleb shook it. "I was."

"With the 20th Maine under Colonel Chamberlain?"

"I was."

"God Almighty, you must be Captain Caleb Stone! Your people stopped General Longstreet's attempt to outflank our line and just about saved the day, saved the battle, and ended Lee's advance into the North. I'm proud to shake your hand. Very proud."

The man had nearly wrung it off before Caleb eased out of his grip. "Thank you, Sergeant. What's your name?"

"Nathan Brooks."

"You give us too much credit, Sergeant Brooks, but it was a near thing. Colonel Chamberlain's ordering the charge broke the Alabamans. He deserves all the praise and honor he's had. He saved my life, and I'm not likely to forget it."

The commissary was a huge, rambling building stuffed from floor to ceiling with goods of every description people crossing the country in wagons might need, from flour to oxen yokes. Caleb stood for a moment, breathing in the rich odors of wood, cloth, grain, leather, axle grease, molasses, and a dozen other smells he could not identify.

Moving on, he wound his way through the laden tables to the sales counter, where he found a white-haired clerk with a handlebar mustache and a weathered face.

"Greetings, Pilgrim," the man said. "What can I do you for?"

"These things for a start," Caleb said, passing him a list, "and head me towards the guns and ammunition."

"Down thataway." The man pointed towards the rear of the building. "Come back here after you've got the firearms. I'll have these things ready for you,"

"Something else," Caleb said. "I need to buy some women's clothes."

"I'll get you set up with the help you'll need," the man said, "although it don't speak well for your judgment. Buying clothes for a woman is a risky undertaking."

Caleb was enjoying their exchange almost as much as he was the clerk's ferocious mustache, but asking him if they carried any Indian women's clothes made him uneasy. The clerk, however, took the question as though he was asked it every day. "You'll have to go out to other side of the parade ground for that. You'll find some squaws selling that sort of thing. Just be sure you don't get cheated, and don't lay nothing down around them. They'd steal the gold out of a preacher's teeth, and he'd

never feel it happen. You be careful," he added, shaking his head and sighing. "If you've got a native woman with you, you keep her out of sight. There's a lot of people passing through here who'd shoot both of you, quick as a swallow's wing."

Half an hour later, Caleb walked out of the commissary, leaving his purchases with the clerk, who said they'd be safe with him until Caleb found a pack horse. The female assistant the clerk had found for him had helped him choose two cloaks with hoods, both red, and two blue woolen toques that could be pulled down over the ears. He also had his eyes on skirts and long-sleeved blouses, but decided to wait until he had seen what he could find in deerskin.

The women selling native dresses on the far side of the parade ground all spoke a little English, and as soon as he told one of them what he was looking for, several others flocked around, eager to help. The question of size was settled by their having him choose two of their number who most closely matched White Cloud and Little Rain.

In a few minutes they had White Cloud and Little Rain's story out of him, and only when they were satisfied they had heard it all was he able to get on with buying the dresses and leggings the Indian women thought appropriate. He also saw at once that they, not him, meant to decide what he would buy. Arriving at those choices was not a quiet negotiation. All the women insisted on being heard, and tempers flared and subsided more than once.

The woman he was buying from named a price, but when he reached for his money, a cry of alarm rose up. Those closest to him pushed his hand back into his pocket. The oldest among them, or so Caleb judged from her white hair, said something to the chosen seller, who cried out and shook her head vehemently. Someone else suggesting a price also met with ferocious objection. Finally, a compromise was reached that satis-

fied everyone.

The white-haired woman took charge of the negotiations, and Caleb paid her beaming compatriot, who passed him the deerskin garments. Caleb returned to the commissary feeling very pleased with himself. Striding across the parade ground, he turned over in his mind what he was going to tell White Cloud about buying the clothes and did not ask himself why she was the person with whom he wanted to share the story.

CHAPTER 11

For nearly half an hour after being given their clothes, accepted in silence, Little Rain and White Cloud sat cross-legged in the grass, holding up each garment for one another to look at, talking quietly but scarcely stopping for breath. Finally, they each chose a dress and a pair of leggings, put the rest among their belongings, and rode away without saying where they were going.

"Their new clothes and their rifles," Dil said with a chuckle, watching them go. Caleb recalled what Little Rain had said when he passed her the Spencer: *Now there are five of us.*

"I'd guess they're going to bathe and then put on their new dresses," Caleb said. "But I'm uneasy about their going alone."

"Those two could take on a whole division of cavalry." The pride in Dil's voice shone through. "I expect they'll wash one at a time, the other keeping watch."

Caleb was seeing to the mules when the women returned. They set about their work as if nothing had changed, but Dil would have none of it. "Captain," he shouted, "come away from that mule and look at what the cat's dragged in."

Caleb dropped Joshua's hoof and reached the camp to find Dil rounding up the two women. They both claimed to be too busy to be bothered, but finally White Cloud got up from her place by the elk hide they'd been scraping. "All right," she said, cleaning her knife on a handful of grass. "We will come."

Caleb had sat down beside the ring of stones where their fire

was set. White Cloud studiously avoided Caleb's gaze but managed to walk back and forth in front of him, showing him her outfit from every side. Little Rain was far more open about her delight and kept glancing at Dil, to see if he was looking. Their dresses had deerskin fringes running the length of the sleeves, and, when they walked, the fringes rose and fell with the swing of their arms, making their movements doubly graceful.

"You are lovely," Caleb told White Cloud when she stopped in front of him.

"It is first clothes since I was a child I not make for myself," she said, quickly and softly. Then she stepped forward, bent down, and pressed her forehead against his. The gesture surprised him—and her, to judge by her flustered look as she stepped away again.

"Night comes," she said. "There is much to do."

"You're welcome," he said to her back as she hurried off.

The next morning as they finished breakfast, Dil said, "I have an announcement to make. Last night I asked Little Rain to marry me, and she said, 'Yes.' "

Little Rain grasped Dil's hand, happiness shining in both their faces.

"Congratulations." Caleb reached over and clapped Dil on the shoulder. "I hope you both will be very happy."

White Cloud set down her tin plate. "We must get beyond the mountains before you are too far along to travel."

Startled, Caleb said, "Hold on! Little Rain, are you pregnant?"

She looked surprised at the question. "I told you we are now five."

White Cloud had picked up a stick and was fussing with the fire. "Some people are slow to understand."

"You will be next," Little Rain said. She and Dil rose and

went off together, to wash their tin plates in the nearby creek.

White Cloud stood and watched them go. Quietly, she said, "When the waters run up the hills."

The bitterness in her voice shocked Caleb. "Why do you think you will not marry until the waters run up the hills?"

She avoided his gaze. "Someone carries another woman in his heart."

Disappointment made his heart sink. She'd never mentioned any man she wanted to marry. One of her own people, no doubt. He should have expected it and felt like a fool. "I'm sorry," he said and felt worse. *What a useless thing to say to her.*

He forced himself to continue, changing the subject to everyday concerns. "Dil and I have to go back to the commissary before we leave. Are there things you and Little Rain want, or we need?"

To his relief, she followed his lead. "You did not buy salt," she said. "Also, it will be cold in one more moon. Need buffalo robes."

"We should wait 'til we reach Fort Laramie to buy them. The ones they have here look moth-eaten."

"What is *'moth-eaten'*?"

"Old and ragged. The hair is falling out. The clerk told me there's a lot of trade in buffalo robes at Laramie. You can pick out the best ones for us. We may need another mule."

She was showing more interest now. "Also, we might make teepee for the mountains," she said. "If you want, get more leggings tomorrow. Riding hard on them." As she walked away, she tossed over her shoulder, "Also, a shovel. I might have to bury you."

Since reaching the Platte, they had encountered mostly fair weather, but, after Fort Kearney, things changed. The temperature shot up, and thunderstorms became more frequent. Aside

from the inconvenience of being drenched and dealing with spooked animals when the lightning struck around them, the storms were of little consequence. The frequent downpours brought on a vast bloom of flowers, and they rode through a world bright as a painter's palette.

One particular morning broke airless and miserably humid. Even the animals were short-tempered. The rising sun only increased the heat. Caleb, circling back to check on the others, spotted a heavy line of thunderheads rising to the west.

"Storm coming," he told White Cloud, who had ridden out to meet him. "It might cool things down a little."

She nodded toward the clouds. "I do not like them. Stay with us."

Dil and Little Rain rode up beside them. "That's a mighty nasty looking storm," Dil said.

White Cloud frowned. "Air feels heavy." She turned to look at the sky around them. "Wind going other way. Have seen this before. No good."

Her anxiety was starting to annoy Caleb. "Why not? It's just a thunderstorm."

"We will keep watch and stay together," Little Rain put in.

"What's wrong?" Dil asked.

"White Cloud," Caleb said, "what do you see that I don't?"

"You have not seen wind that goes around?" she demanded.

Caleb and Dil looked at one another. "Like the dust devils we see every day?" Dil asked.

She shook her head. "Those are plant spirits dancing. They do no harm. This is big storm with tail of wind that drops to the ground. Wherever it touches, it rips up trees, eats whole villages. This one has not put down its tail yet, but its anger will grow. When it comes down, we must ride fast away to one side."

"Twister, tornado!" Dil said. "That's what she's talking about. I've heard men from Kansas speak of them lifting whole houses

80

into the air and tearing them apart."

"Thunder god angry sometimes with earth and goes on warpath," Little Rain said. "We will watch and, if tail comes down, run as White Cloud said."

"If our medicine is strong, he will not follow us," White Cloud added, but she sounded uncertain. Not what Caleb was used to from her, and it worried him.

Dil cracked a joke. "Should we make more medicine?"

"Not time for laugh," Little Rain said sternly.

"We need holy man to make medicine," White Cloud said impatiently. "Here we will go on our horses and our medicine." She glanced at Caleb. "Yours, perhaps, is very small."

"Wrong," he replied. "Joshua is a big medicine mule. Keeps me fully supplied."

"Wrong in the head, is your name," she shot back.

Little Rain was watching the sky. "Thunder cloud has found legs," she said sharply. "Watching is best now."

Caleb followed her gaze. The huge tumble of black clouds was bearing down on them, lightning within it burning across its face and leaping to the earth, while the thunder shifted from a rumble to a roar.

"The tail!" White Cloud shouted.

"Damnation!" Dil cried, as a white funnel poked down and touched the ground. Almost instantly it turned brown as it sucked up dirt and anything loose in its path. It swayed and wove like a gigantic snake as it sped toward them.

White Cloud kicked her horse into a gallop, heading away from the fearsome funnel cloud at a right angle, shouting, "Follow me!"

Caleb turned back just long enough to put himself behind the pack horses and urge them on, but they needed no prodding and ran straight out. The front of the storm was nearly over them all, blotting out the light as the rain struck. The roar

of the funnel terrified him as it ripped grass and shrubs and leaves from the larger trees and spun them up into the cloud, spewing the wreckage into the surrounding air. He fought down fear and raced after the others, wondered if the funnel would engulf him and the pack animals struggling under their loads to keep up.

The funnel missed him by a hundred yards, then veered to the south. It struck the river, wreaking havoc among the trees along the banks and sucking up water and mud until it looked like a towering water spout. White Cloud, Little Rain, and Dil had pulled up after the funnel passed by, and Caleb swiftly joined them. They sat in the last of the rain, watching the storm draw away until the sun broke free from the thinning clouds.

"Lord God," Dil shouted, standing in his stirrups, "I swear that twister scared me more than Confederate guns, but I wouldn't have missed it for all the tea in China." He dropped his reins, snatched off his hat, swung it over his head at the departing twister, and gave a long rebel yell. That broke the spell, and the others waved their hands over their heads and yelled with him.

The first to recover, White Cloud gave Caleb a dark look. "Someone might have gone up to the Thunder God."

He grinned at her. "Your medicine kept me safe."

She held his gaze for a long moment.

"Perhaps it was Joshua's medicine," she said finally, turning her head, possibly to hide her smile.

"No, it was you," he said.

She sat still without looking at him, apparently frozen.

"White Cloud," he said, "what's wrong?"

Her voice, when she answered, was softer than he'd ever heard from her. "Caleb Stone," she said, "sometimes I think you are idiot."

Little Rain prevented Caleb from answering by riding up and

calling out, "Dil says we must go on. He goes." She turned her horse and galloped away, her loosened hair flying out behind her.

"Dil asks her to let her hair go free," White Cloud said, in a tone Caleb thought carried envy. "What color hair does your woman have?"

The sudden shift threw him. "I don't have a woman, White Cloud. The one I had hoped to marry had auburn hair, dark red with gold highlights."

"What color her eyes?"

"Green."

"She was very tall?"

"She was the same height as you."

"I have seen such women. They have soft, white skin and wear hats to keep the sun away. I have black hair and black eyes, and my skin is dark."

It dawned on Caleb that she thought Millicent was more beautiful than she was. Why was she making the comparison? "You are a very beautiful woman, White Cloud," he said.

"Not enough."

"For what?"

She scowled at him. "Perhaps someone needs to be hit in head with a stick," she said and rode away.

That evening, they camped near two huge piles of rock and clay, the larger one rising three to four hundred feet out of the open prairie. After making camp and eating, Caleb and White Cloud rode out for a closer look at the huge piles. They had fallen into the habit of these evening rides, to give Dil and Little Rain some privacy.

"This big one is called Courthouse Rock and that smaller one is Jailhouse Rock," Caleb told White Cloud.

"Not like them," she said, sitting on her horse with her left leg crossed in front of her. The Spencer rested across her thigh.

He had been thinking how good she looked, her hair lifting and falling around her shoulders in the light wind and shining in the late sun. "Why not?" he asked, surprised by her response.

"Too lonely, as if someone had gone away, leaving them behind."

He eyed the giant formations again. "Now you say it, I see what you mean, but they're just dirt and rocks."

"Spirit in all things," she countered, looking sharply at him. "Mother Earth and Father Sky and all things in between."

Curious, he asked, "Is everything alive?"

She shrugged. "Perhaps," she said. "Spirit in all things. When kill something to eat it, the hunter thanks the animal for giving him its life, to feed the people. Then frees the spirit to go up there." She nodded upward, toward the sky.

"You have a heaven, a place somewhere beyond here?"

"The shamans go there sometimes in search of answer to difficult question, like, 'Will this sick child live?' "

"There's a lot of you, White Cloud, that I don't know," Caleb said. "You are a fascinating person."

"What?" she demanded, straightening her back.

"*Fascinating?* It means something or someone you cannot stop looking at or wondering about."

"Why?"

Caleb wasn't sure how to answer her, but he tried to be truthful. "Perhaps there is something that pulls you toward that person," he said, wondering where these questions were going.

"You think I am fascinating that way?" White Cloud sounded doubtful.

His answer surprised him. "Yes, I do."

"I am glad, Caleb Stone," she said quietly. "What if someone thinks that way about you?"

Another surprise. "It would make me very happy," he told her, even as it dawned on him there was no going back from

that statement.

"But you carry the woman with the auburn hair in your heart, Caleb Stone."

Her statement with its hidden question jolted him. He hadn't seen it coming, and he was far from sure he wanted to answer it.

"Her name is Millicent," he said reluctantly. Having started, he found he wanted her to know what had happened to him. "When I went away to war, I did carry her in my heart, but I was away six winters. She married another man. I had a farm and thought I would become a farmer again, but I couldn't go back."

"Because of her?" White Cloud asked in a strained voice.

"No. I was not the same person as the one who went away. The war changed me. I saw the world differently. So now I am here."

Her tone turned reflective. "We follow the buffalo. You left your farm. We cannot leave the buffalo. What will happen to your farm?"

"Another person bought it."

"You have to go back there for the money?"

"No. It's in a bank, a safe place, where it will stay until I need it."

She let out a breath. "My head is troubled thinking of Nihoothoos' way of living."

Caleb smiled. "I'm not surprised. My head is often troubled thinking about it."

"People do not own the land," she said. "We have it to live on and care for. Those who follow us will do the same. It has been that way from the beginning."

All that, he thought sadly, *is going to change.* Did she know it? She must.

White Cloud was quiet for a while but clearly had more to

say. "When care is not taken, bad things happen. My father was a trapper. He once told me the story of the . . ." She frowned as if in thought. "They eat tree bark, have flat tails, and live in water. Nihoothoo want coat."

"Beaver," Caleb said.

"Yes. Beaver. My father said the beaver once lived in all prairie waters, built houses. With mud and sticks held the water and made more water. Then the Nihoothoo came and traded things with the Nehiyaw people, who came from place where the sun rises, trapped the beaver, and white people like my father trapped them until all are gone from this place, away to mountains where the sun sleeps.

"My people and the other horse people would not trap them, my father said, because the beaver made big water to live in, and in those times when the rain did not come, there was water in those places. Now there are no beaver waters for dry times. That is what happens when people do not take care of the world. That is what I heard."

"Did your father ever call them the Cree, those people who trapped the beaver?"

"I have heard that word, yes."

"The Hudson Bay Company came to Canada nearly two hundred winters ago," Caleb told her. "They told the Cree they would give them guns and beads and blankets and knives and axes if the Cree brought back beaver fur. The beaver coats were made into hats and other things in countries across the Atlantic Ocean."

Caleb dreaded having to explain what the ocean was, but White Cloud said, "I have heard of the big salt water where the sun comes up. My father drew for me a picture of a big canoe with wings. He drew it with a stick that had black stick inside it, on a piece of white deerskin. My mother was angry because she had to wash it off, and it was not easy."

"Are your mother and father still alive?"

"No." She glanced at the earth beneath them. "When I was fourteen winters, a Nihoothoo sickness of the throat killed them. I was sick, but Death did not want me, and I stood up again."

"I'm glad you stood up," Caleb said. "It was probably diphtheria that killed your mother and father. I'm sorry."

She bit her lip. "I should not have spoken of those who have gone into the spirit world."

"So you've said." Caleb wanted to touch her, to offer some kind of comfort, but wasn't sure how she'd take it. "What did you do after that happened?"

"My mother's sister took me into her teepee, but she had five young children. I went to Chief Snow Owl and said I wanted to get married. That way I could get my mother's teepee back and the furs and everything else in it."

Shock made him sit back on his horse. "You were married at fourteen?"

She avoided his gaze. "I was an old fourteen. Snow Owl married me to a warrior no one else wanted, but there was no one to speak for me, and my aunt was glad to have me go. His name was Falling Tree. We were married two moons, and then I told him to get out of the teepee. He refused. I said I would kill him while he slept. He left. He only wanted someone to look after him while he drank whiskey with others like him."

They sat for a while without speaking. Finally, White Cloud broke the silence. "Caleb Stone, we have talked enough. It is time for you to ask me something."

Caleb almost said, "What?" but stopped himself. "Are you sure, White Cloud?" he asked. "I am a Nihoothoo. You are Arapaho, and you are going back to your people. I am going to Oregon."

"Is that all you have to say?"

"No. You are close to my heart, but I do not see how we can

be together for more than a short time."

"Did you go under blanket with Millicent True?"

Another jolt, but Caleb decided to tell her the truth. "Yes," he said, "but it was long ago. We were in one another's hearts then."

White Cloud raised her eyebrows. "But she married another man."

"Because I left her to go to war. She was very angry."

"Nihoothoo," she said, obviously disgusted with what she had just heard. "Tonight, you will be with me." She paused and then said, "Unless the Great Spirit has told you not to."

That did it. Caleb burst out laughing. He vaulted off Lady, pulled the Spencer out of White Cloud's grasp and laid it on the ground, then reached up and lifted White Cloud off her horse. When she touched the ground, he wrapped her in his arms. "I want to kiss you," he said.

She buried her face in his shoulder. "Perhaps someone doesn't know how."

"Look up," he said. She did, and Caleb pressed his lips gently against hers.

"What do you think?" he asked when she broke away.

She tightened her hold on him. "Hard to hold breath, but perhaps we will practice."

"Yes." He lowered his head. "Begin now."

CHAPTER 12

At first Caleb thought the distant rumble was thunder, but when he glanced up at the sky, there were no clouds. They were passing through an area of grass-covered, rolling hills. Since leaving Fort Kearney, they had been careful not to ride onto hilltops where they would be silhouetted against the sky. At this moment, though, pressed for an answer as to what was happening, Caleb rode Lady up the nearest rise and saw a cloud of dust rising to the west of them.

At the same time, high-pitched yips startled him. Turning, he saw White Cloud and Little Rain riding toward him at full gallop. They rode with their hair tied back, no hackamores on their mounts, holding their Spencers over their heads and giving war whoops as they sped toward him. He had no idea what they were doing, but the way they looked stole his breath away.

"Buffalo!" Little Rain shouted, as the women brought their horses to a skidding stop when they reached him. Their faces shone with excitement.

"Caleb Stone," White Cloud said, while her horse danced and flung up its head, "the buffalo are coming. You must not try to run in front of them. Ride hard until you are no longer in front. Dil is already at the river. He will be safe."

The rumble was growing louder, and Caleb had to shout to be heard. "What are you going to do?"

"We ride with you," Little Rain broke in. "Then we will kill two buffalo." She gave a loud cry and thrust her rifle over her

89

head. "They come!"

White Cloud lingered a moment. "Caleb Stone, do not ride with us. Lady does not know buffalo. Our horses have done this. We will eat buffalo tonight!"

She turned her horse and kicked it into a gallop toward the river. Caleb followed suit. Suddenly the buffalo poured over the hills a few hundred yards away, a black wave of animals thundering toward them, the pounding of hooves ending all talk. With less than a hundred yards separating the women and Caleb from the oncoming herd, the three riders swept around the south end of the river of animals and pulled up to watch them stream past.

Next to Caleb, White Cloud shouted, "We go. You follow, but not come near buffalo, not try to shoot. You are hearing?"

He nodded. She laid a hand on his arm for instant and then was gone, Little Rain following, whooping loudly. They rode straight at the herd, with only their rifles in their hands.

"God above!" Caleb said, as they slowly turned until they were riding along the churning edge of the racing animals, their horses giving their all to stay even with the buffalo.

Something stirred in Caleb, and he wanted above all things to race along beside that herd as the women were doing. He leaned forward over Lady's neck, loosened the reins, and shouted, "Go!"

Lady needed no urging. He reached down and pulled his rifle out of its boot, intending to shoot one of the buffalo, but racing beside the herd he found that feat impossible. The rifle needed two hands and the reins needed another. Before he sorted that out, a huge bull swung out from the herd and charged. With an upward heave of his massive head, he caught the mare's belly just behind her front legs.

The blow lifted Lady off her feet. Caleb felt her turn under him and kicked out of the stirrups. He went down, hitting the

ground along with her. He and the rifle parted company as he bounced over the hard ground, somersaulting and losing hide as he went. On the last bounce, he came down on his head, and the world stopped turning upside down, the thunder in his ears vanished.

Then a voice, very faint, as if reaching him from a great distance. Slowly, it grew louder. It annoyed him. He clung stubbornly to the profoundly peaceful place where he had been.

"Caleb Stone!" The voice kept saying that, while something softly stroked his face. It was a little while before he realized someone was talking to him. He opened his eyes and instantly closed them in the vain hope of shutting out the violent pain in his head.

"Come on, Captain," another voice put in, slightly louder than the first. Caleb risked opening his eyes again and found the pain had diminished slightly. A blurred oval blocked out the sky. It took him a moment to recognize the face of the woman bending over him. His head must be in her lap, he thought fuzzily.

"You are lovely," he told the face in a cracked whisper.

Dil shouted, "Hurrah!" Just beyond him, Little Rain clapped her hands and lifted her face toward the sky with a loud and celebratory shout.

"And you are idiot," White Cloud said, smiling.

"Lady . . ." he said hoarsely. "Lady . . ."

White Cloud pressed a palm to his cheek. "She is all right."

That was all he heard before closing his eyes again and letting the world slip away.

The next thing Caleb saw was a blaze of stars in a dark and cloudless sky. He could hear horses cropping grass and a night hawk diving and booming somewhere above where he lay. *How long was I out?*

A body stirred beside him. "Caleb Stone," someone whispered.

"White Cloud?"

"Yes. You will stay and not go away again. Is someone listening?"

"Someone has no wish to go away." His voice sounded as if he'd borrowed it from a hoarse crow.

She sat up and turned toward him, supporting herself with one hand on each side of his chest as she stared at him.

"I have missed you," he said.

He wasn't proud of that remark, but it was the best he could manage. At that moment, he doubted he could put his arms around her, something he wanted very much to do.

Ever so gently, she lowered her body atop his and brushed his lips with hers. The warmth and gentle weight of her pressed against him abruptly banished the fog in his brain. "More practice," he said when he could breathe properly again.

"My Nihoothoo," she murmured and kissed him again.

"That was much better," he said as she lifted herself off him.

He could hear the smile in her voice. "We will count the stars," she said.

On the second day, Dil said Caleb had recovered enough to ride. White Cloud was not convinced and fussed over him like a hen with newly hatched chicks. She would not even let him bathe alone. That, of course, led to further tests of his health, which, she said, didn't count. So it went on for a bit. She often put her legs around him in the water, and, on one occasion, approaching the top of the mountain, forgot herself and squeezed.

"Easy!" he groaned.

Later, as they clambered up the bank and sat down, he said, "My God, woman, your legs are incredibly strong."

"Ride horse, no stirrups." She wrung the water out of her

hair, glancing at him archly. "Ride you same way."

For the next week, they encountered increasingly hot days with the nights bringing a welcome cooling. No one paid much attention to the weather, finding more of interest in one another than in the world around them. Badger families waddled past them unnoticed. Coveys of quail rose and no one reached for a shotgun. Coyotes trotted beside them, ignored.

Just before they reached Scott's Bluff, the heat broke in a rip-snorting thunderstorm and rain that fell like a river. The storm left as suddenly as it had arrived, and they stopped long enough to change into dry clothes. They had just finished dressing, all of them complaining about the cold wet garments, when Dil said, "Company."

Caleb looked up. Less than a quarter of a mile away, a wagon drawn by four mules was approaching. Two men sat on the wagon seat, one driving and the other holding a rifle resting on its butt beside him.

"Buffalo hunters." White Cloud picked up her rifle and leaped onto her horse's back. "They will not like Little Rain and me," she said. "Keep guns near."

The two women drifted away, one on each side of the oncoming wagon. Caleb mounted his horse, loosened the rifle in its boot, and made certain his hand gun was free to draw.

"If they're as bad as they smell," Dil said, "we're in trouble." He and Caleb were downwind of the wagon, and the odor was rank.

"I'd guess it's the buffalo hides under that canvas adding to their stink," Caleb said.

White Cloud had picked up the lead rope and led their animals away, keeping herself between the approaching wagon and their small remuda. Caleb, watching the hunters, was not encouraged by what he saw. Both men were large and heavily bearded, wearing black hats. The rifle, he noted, was a Sharps.

The newcomers looked to him like trouble.

At talking distance, the driver checked the mules and said, "What are you two playing at?" It was more a snarl than a question. His partner sat gripping his rifle and glowering at them.

"Minding our own business," Caleb said evenly. "I suggest you do the same."

"Our first business," the second man said, "would be to shoot those damned savages on the ponies." He started to jack a shell into the chamber of his rifle.

"I'd stop right there," Dil said.

The man shifted his gaze from the women and found he was facing Dil's drawn revolver. Quicker than a snake strike, the driver snatched a derringer halfway out of his coat. The air cracked, and a bullet from White Cloud's rifle knocked him backward off the wagon seat. The second man jumped to his feet, shouldering his rifle. Dil fired, and the man spun halfway around and pitched headfirst into the grass.

A moment later, the two women galloped in, their rifles pointed at the fallen men. Caleb slid his revolver into its holster, feeling a profound disgust mingled with anger at what had happened. "Needless deaths," he said, mostly to himself.

"Don't never seem to end," Dil added.

"They stink too much to scalp." White Cloud poked the driver with the barrel of her gun. Little Rain and Dil sat looking at one another in silence.

An hour and a half later, with the two women and Caleb taking turns digging, they had the two buffalo hunters buried.

"Good you bought shovel at Fort," Little Rain said, holding her back. "Not shoot any more. Shovel not like me."

"What about mules?" White Cloud asked.

"We'll take off their harnesses and set them loose," Caleb said.

"Why not keep them?" Little Rain asked.

"We're close to Fort Laramie," Dil said quietly. "Someone would be sure to recognize the animals. We would be charged with stealing them and, probably, with killing their owners. Likely we'd be hanged."

Little Rain looked at White Cloud, who shrugged and said, "Nihoothoo."

That night, lying with Caleb, White Cloud said, "Caleb Stone, why am I seeing your back?"

He rolled over to face her. "I feel bad about killing those two men," he told her.

"They would kill us," she countered.

"Yes, and we killed them first. I am sick to death with killing."

"What is 'sick to death'?"

"The heart feels very heavy, and food does not taste good."

She put her arms around him and pulled them together. "The Great Spirit made everything," she whispered in his ear. "He hadn't made you yet, to tell him what he could have done better. Later he made you to do that, perhaps by mistake, but I am glad."

Despite his low spirits, Caleb had to chuckle. He embraced her and kissed her on the forehead.

"You missed," she complained.

"What?"

"I am now thinking it is good to kiss. Try again. Take time, aim better."

Beginning to enjoy himself, he kissed her on the nose.

"Why I have to do everything?" she demanded, and, grasping his head in her hands, she planted her lips firmly on his.

CHAPTER 13

Fort Laramie was much larger than Fort Kearney. After their experience with the buffalo hunters, White Cloud and Little Rain both said, when close enough to see the fort, "Camp far away."

"What's wrong?" Dil asked.

"Bad medicine here," White Cloud said. "As child I heard story. Long ago, white man named Jacques La Ramee come here to trap beaver. My people not want beavers killed. So, killed him and buried him in stick and mud wall to hold water beavers make."

"It's called a dam," Caleb said.

"What is it called in Arapaho?" White Cloud snapped.

Little Rain glanced at Caleb. "Someone may be angry. White Cloud and I will camp in cottonwoods. You and Dil come later and find us."

"Well, there's not much to keep us here," Caleb said.

Dil gave him a look. "Oil on troubled waters," he said.

Belatedly, Caleb recalled the dead buffalo hunters' threat to shoot "those savages" and felt ashamed of himself. White Cloud and Little Rain had every reason to be wary.

Even as they talked, two groups of mounted soldiers passed them at a gallop, heading north.

White Cloud watched them go by. "I am thinking there is trouble. Dust rising in three directions north of the river. Soldiers moving."

Some of White Cloud's uneasiness rubbed off on Caleb. "All right," he said. "Dil and I will go into the fort and see what we can learn. We'll buy the buffalo robes and warmer clothes. I'll add one or two mules as baggage animals."

"Medical supplies," Dil said.

"Those too." Caleb looked to the west and the broken foothills of the Rockies. "There's some hard riding ahead of us."

They sat on their horses without speaking for a minute or two, as though the nearness of the mountains and Caleb's comment had burdened their spirits.

"Now's as good a time as ever," Dil said, lifting his reins.

"We will go back to the river and then toward the mountains," Little Rain said, looking as concerned as White Cloud. "We will hide ourselves and the animals. We will watch for you."

The two women turned their horses and rode away, taking the pack animals with them.

Caleb watched them go. "Superstitious, both of them."

"Wonderful companions," Dil said.

"Is that a criticism?" Caleb asked, without rancor.

"That depends on you, Captain," Dil replied. "White Cloud needs a lot of encouragement. Her sharp edges hide a lot of her real feelings."

"We're approaching their country and may soon encounter their people," Caleb responded. "What if we have to shoot some of them? What if White Cloud and Little Rain decide to stay with them?" It was the first time Caleb had given voice to the fears that haunted him, admit it or no.

"I guess I'll wait for it to happen, Captain," Dil said, a little stiffly. "I'm not holding back on loving Little Rain because she might leave me. I'll love her as hard as I can, as long as I can, and I hope for your sake, as well as White Cloud's, you'll see your way clear to do the same with her."

Dil's words stung, which Caleb hadn't expected. "I hear you, but, whatever happens, we've got a lot of road ahead of us with people we love and yet still hardly know."

"Amen," Dil said. "Let's get going."

They stopped and left their horses at what passed for a livery stable, then set off down the line of animals and found the mule yard, where a grizzly-bearded man in worn buckskins with iron-gray hair hanging to his shoulders leaned on a plank of the corral.

"You the man in charge here?" Caleb asked.

"Do I look as if I'm in charge of anything?" the man said, without turning his head or taking the match out of his mouth.

"I'm looking for a good mule," Caleb said.

"You've come to the wrong place."

Dil nudged Caleb.

"My name's Caleb Stone." Caleb thrust out his hand. "What's yours?"

The man ignored the gesture. "You wouldn't be none the wiser were I to tell you."

"You'll either tell me or fight me. Which is it going to be?"

The man slowly lowered his foot to the ground and turned away from the fence. "Let's get us a drink and see what we can work out."

With Buckskins leading the way, they walked into a low-roofed barn and into a room that held a desk but no chair. Half a dozen nail kegs were scattered around the room, some upright and others tipped over.

"Grab a barrel and take a load off," Buckskins said, heading toward the desk. He pulled a half full bottle of Old Overholt whiskey out of a side drawer, along with three Mason jars. He poured a liberal charge into each of the jars, then turned toward Caleb and Dil and said, "The name's Johnson, Wolf Johnson. I did some trapping when I was younger, hence, the first name."

He passed the jars around, setting two atop Caleb and Dil's chosen barrels. Caleb and Dil each shook Johnson's hand, picked their jars up, and sat down.

Johnson raised his glass. "Here's to the girl up on the hill."

"She won't but her sister will," Dil said.

"Then here's to her sister," Johnson said with a broad grin.

Caleb chose not to go on with the toast. Johnson's eyes narrowed slightly, but he said nothing. When Caleb raised his jar, Johnson and Dil raised theirs and drank.

"This stuff would burn the rust off an iron gate," Dil said when he had caught his breath. "I hope you're not selling it to the Indians."

"I'm not, but some others are. How-some-ever, the Injuns don't need any firewater to get heated," Johnson said grimly. "I reckon there's an uprising coming. The raids are increasing. The last two wagon trains to pass through here got shot up pretty bad and half their horses and cattle run off."

"How long ago?" Caleb asked.

"A month, maybe six weeks. If you're going to Oregon, you're cutting it a mite fine."

"We're not hindered by a wagon," Dil put in.

"Thank you, Mr. Johnson, for the drink," Caleb said. "Can we look at your mules?"

"I got some good horse flesh in that corral. You sure I can't sell you one of them?"

"That might happen," Caleb said, "but I'm looking for a big mule to match one I've got. I bought him back in Independence and couldn't find another his size."

"I've got a couple of Jackstock mules might interest you."

Johnson led them back to the corral, went in, and came out with a large, black animal. "This one is a three year old. You might want to check his teeth and see if I'm right. I ain't had much to do with mules. I got him off that last wagon train I

99

told you about. Sad story, really. The wife got took off, something to do with her heart. The husband sold off everything but two horses. After grubbing up, he headed back for Kentucky. I got this mule off him. What do you think?"

Caleb eyed the animal. "Is he broken to the saddle?"

"Can't say, but he and another one pulled a wagon from somewhere East to here."

"What about the other one?"

"I sold him to a couple of buffalo hunters. You might have run into them. They were going that way the last I saw of them."

"I believe they passed us a couple of weeks ago," Dil said. "They seemed in a hurry."

"Didn't much cotton to them," Johnson said sourly. "You did well to let them pass by. Tried to cheat me."

While Dil and Johnson were talking, Caleb looked at the mule's teeth. "I'd guess the same age you did," he said, rubbing the mule's nose and stroking his neck.

The dickering began and ended with Caleb owning the mule and a bay mare named Dolly. "Has the mule got a name?" Dil asked.

"He may have had one," Johnson said, "but I don't know it."

"Then it will be Abe." Caleb laid a hand on the mule's shoulder. "Short for Abraham."

After they shook hands and Johnson pocketed his money, he said, "From here on you'll be climbing through some fairly rough country. Stay off the tops of rises as much as you can, keep your fires small, and kill your meat with one shot. Fish the creeks. That don't make no noise, and the fishing's good. You're about one quarter of the way to Oregon. In two and a half months, there'll be snow in the high places. Skip the South Pass and take the Lander Road. The cutoff will shorten the distance to Fort Hall by about eighty miles."

They talked more generally for a few minutes. Johnson said

as they were parting, "Watch yourselves here in Laramie. There's two companies of Confederate prisoners here. They figured if they couldn't fight Yanks, they might as well fight Injuns."

"Galvanized Yankees," Dil said. "Thanks for telling us. I expect that while they're wearing blue, they're still gray inside."

"And edgy as a wet cat," Johnson said.

Leaving Abe and Dolly with him, Caleb and Dil set off for the commissary. The stack of goods they piled up included two pack harnesses with leather carriers for Abe and the mare. By the time they had Abe and Dolly loaded, the sun was dropping in the western sky, and the patrols were riding back into the parade grounds. Fires were being lighted in the camps, and the smells of meat frying and coffee steaming drifted in the air.

"We may have to get by on biscuits and jerky," Dil said a bit glumly as they saddled their horses and set out to find White Cloud and Little Rain.

"Sounds right," Caleb said. "We're in Arapaho country and plunging deeper tomorrow. Are you going to talk to Little Rain about it?"

"Not sure what I'd say," Dil replied. "What about White Cloud?"

"I think something has to be said." Caleb wished it was a conversation he could avoid.

"Should we bring it up over supper?"

"That's good of you, Dil, but I think White Cloud will want to discuss it with me in private."

"I should have told you sooner, Captain," Dil said. "Little Rain is going with me to Oregon. We're tied tight."

Caleb managed a smile. "It's not a surprise, Dil. Congratulations. Have you thought about whether or not the people where we're going will welcome her?"

"Little Rain brought that up. We've decided to go ahead and if there's a problem, deal with it then."

Caleb let the matter rest, but his mind was a long way from resting.

CHAPTER 14

Wolf Johnson and Little Rain had been right about the change in the country ahead of them. By the second day, the land had begun to lift, and the trail wound its way through an increasingly hilly and broken landscape. During those two days, White Cloud avoided Caleb and scarcely spoke to him. When she couldn't avoid him, she gave single word answers to his questions without looking at him.

All too quickly, Caleb concluded that entering Arapaho country was the cause of her withdrawal and that she was preparing to leave him. Painfully aware that he had told her he would take her and Little Rain back to their people, he felt reluctant to question her. The realization that he might lose her hit him like a kick in the stomach, leaving him feeling as if the sun had lost its light.

Following a nearly sleepless night, during which he tried with little success to resign himself to his loss, he completed his morning chores as usual. Once he and the others had crossed the Platte without trouble, Caleb took point, determined to carry on as if nothing was wrong. After a couple of hours' riding, and knowing they needed meat, Caleb shot a young bull elk. Little Rain caught up with him and insisted they stop long enough to skin the animal. White Cloud had fallen a little behind to deal with a stone in her horse's hoof. The three set to work skinning the elk and were nearly finished when Little Rain bounced to her feet, grasping her rifle as she rose. "Bear."

Both men scrambled up after her. Approaching them at a lumbering run was the biggest bear Caleb had ever seen.

"It is good day to die," Little Rain said. "All shoot together."

At the first volley, the bear stumbled slightly and bellowed in rage or pain but came on at a gallop. Behind them, their horses were squealing like stuck pigs and hopping in their hobbles. The mules had moved together and stood watching the bear.

"Lord above," Dil said, "make our aim good."

"Make good blanket," Little Rain added.

Caleb dropped to one knee and put two bullets solidly in the charging animal's chest. The bear staggered again and turned away to the right. Dil and Little Rain fired together, striking the animal just behind its shoulder. Caleb's next shot slammed into its neck. The bear staggered to a stop, rose on its hind legs, then fell to the earth like a tree going down.

By this time, White Cloud had ridden up, carrying her rifle. "Not go near him," she warned. "These dead ones sometimes get up."

Finally, they walked over to the bear. It gave a deep, defiant rumble. Dil bent and shot it behind the ear.

Little Rain placed her hand on the bear's shoulder and spoke briefly in her own language. "You want to eat?" she asked. "His spirit goes now."

"I think I'll eat some of the elk," Caleb said.

"Bear put hair on you and grease muscles. I not need more," she said and grinned.

Dil chuckled. "You'll make the Captain's face burn."

"I'm way beyond that," Caleb said. "I suppose we've got to skin this beast."

"Yes," White Cloud said with a scowl. "Perhaps Little Rain make us laugh too much."

"Watch what happens when we put hide on horse or mule," Little Rain said defiantly. "Much fun."

And there was. They tried putting it on Dolly, and she fell down trying to get away. Next, they went to Abe. He whirled around, filling the air with flying rear hooves. That left Joshua. He and Caleb stood looking at one another for a while.

"All right," Caleb said. He went back to the food supplies, dug out a length of peppermint stick candy, and fed it to the mule. While Joshua chewed and moved his head up and down, Caleb, with White Cloud and Little Rain's help, threw the folded raw bear hide over the packs on the mule's back.

The fourth day they stopped early to scrape the bear skin before it could rot. Armed with the curved front leg bones from the elk, White Cloud and Little Rain staked out the bear's hide and set to work. By the time Dil had supper ready, they were finished. Caleb helped them carry the hide to the creek that ran past the camp, from which he'd taken half a dozen ten-inch trout in less than half an hour. They submerged the hide and left it to soak overnight.

"Tomorrow, we squeeze out water and maybe rub in some salt to keep fresh," White Cloud said, rinsing her hands alongside Caleb.

Surprised by the warmth in her voice, Caleb said, "Something hard as this is easier when we do it together." Maybe he'd misread her intentions, and she wasn't going to leave him after all.

The lift in his spirits was brief. Without answering him, she scrambled to her feet and hurried away. He watched her go, his hope going with her.

That night when they were in bed, White Cloud lay with her back toward Caleb, as she had for the past several nights. She drew a deep breath and said in her formal voice, "Someone must speak."

Caleb's heart thumped. He knew that voice, and it meant trouble. Nonetheless, he made himself wait for her to continue.

Only when her silence outwaited his patience did he brace himself and say, "Tell me, White Cloud. I will listen."

"Someone will not want to hear what must be said. She is sorry and full of pain but must speak."

An icy hand gripped Caleb's heart. She *was* going to leave him. Steeling himself, he said, "White Cloud, it's all right. Tell me whatever is troubling you."

Suddenly, she flung herself over and faced him. He could not see her expression clearly in the darkness, but he knew that whatever she was struggling with was giving her severe pain. He ached to take her in his arms and pull her against him but held back, giving her more time to speak.

Finally, with something close to a groan, she broke her silence. "Before I was captured, I lived alone in my mother's lodge. After two winters, I took an Arapaho man, a warrior named Elk Turns, under my blanket because I had lived alone too long. I did not speak of marrying him because he was not in my heart and is not. He is a good man, but I will not go back to him."

Pain and anger welled up in Caleb at hearing she had been with another man. "But you are going back to your people," he said.

"It is as I feared," she replied, her voice failing. "You want me to go away."

Caleb's head was swimming. "Why would I send you away?" he asked, fearing he was losing his capacity to think.

She rose up on one elbow. "Caleb Stone, I thought when you asked if I was going, I was no longer in your heart."

Silently, Caleb cursed his mistake. "White Cloud, you will be in my heart forever. Am I still in yours?"

"Yes," she cried. "Hold me."

Lying in one another's arms with the rain drumming lightly over them, Caleb felt a terrible load of grief lifting from him

and drifting away like smoke in the wind. He held her close, and they wasted no more time in talking.

When they reached Independence Rock, White Cloud and Little Rain sat on their horses and stared at it for some time. Caleb and Dil let the animals graze, giving themselves and the two women ample opportunity to contemplate this hundred-foot-high hump of granite, squatting on the prairie.

"I heard the Indians often held tribal meetings at this rock," Dil said, "and used it in their stories about their beginnings."

"It's a mile around," Caleb said, awed by its size. "The Lord knows how it got here."

"A powerful lot of people left their name on it," Dil said. "I wonder why it's called Independence Rock?"

"Most convincing account I've heard," Caleb said, "is that in 1830 the mountain man William Sublette was leading a wagon train west and reached this rock on July Fourth. He climbed to the top of it and christened it Independence Rock, whether or not with whiskey, I don't know."

Dil eyed White Cloud and Little Rain, who sat on their horses as still as the stone. "What do you suppose they're seeing? I didn't think Little Rain could sit still that long." He paused, then said carefully, "Have you and White Cloud talked about whether or not Elk Turns is likely to be looking for her?"

Caleb had briefly mentioned White Cloud's late-night revelation without giving Dil much detail, though it had never been far from his mind. Looking uneasy, Dil continued. "I asked Little Rain about him. She knew him but didn't like him. He was a good-looking man, she said, older than White Cloud and a warrior many women hoped to marry. He'd never married, possibly because he didn't own many horses. I guess that's a way the Arapaho judge a man's importance."

"White Cloud won't talk about him."

"Little Rain says he was a hard man. He'd counted coup and killed in battle but never became a leader. She doubts he's searching for White Cloud. She doesn't think anyone's looking for her, either."

That thought made Caleb feel sad, despite the blessings it had brought him and Dil. "That must be a burden for both of them."

The women rode up beside them then, having gazed their fill at the monumental rock, and Caleb said, "We're going to follow the Sweetwater River all the way to the Lander Road, where we'll pass over the continental divide on our way to Fort Hall." He wanted to ask White Cloud why Elk Turns had not come after her, but now was not a good time.

That night under their blankets, when he finally raised the subject, White Cloud pulled away from him. "How can I know?" she demanded. "Perhaps Elk Turns is dead."

In her sharp tone Caleb heard pain and uncertainty along with anger. Whether or not she believed what she'd just said, he guessed she was using it to ease the sting of abandonment. "I hadn't thought of that. I'm sorry."

She rolled back to face him, threw her arms around his neck, and pulled herself against him. "That one is not in my heart, Caleb Stone," she said, "but in my head. I ask myself why he did not try to save me from Hawk Hand. I am ashamed of my weakness."

Caleb held her tightly. "It's only human to expect those who love us will at least try to take care of us. You would not be human if you did not feel as you do."

"Little Rain and I went back into our world for a while before the rock. You knew that, didn't you?"

"I knew you had left us," he said. "I did not know why."

"We are in our country. We feel its spirit. We remember things we did in our lives here, the people we knew. Little Rain loved

her father and mother, but the spotted sickness took them and her brother. She was visiting an aunt in my band and stayed after their deaths. We became friends."

"Do you share memories of times when you were happy?"

"Yes." A softness shone in her eyes. "We were wild ones. We ran away, and people had to come after us. Sometimes we had to stand up in the middle of the village while some older person told everyone how bad we were. After that we were good for a while, but then we would do something else. We hunted like the young boys and were not supposed to. Once we were beaten with a bow, not too badly, and scolded by the chief. He said if this kept up, he would feed us to the vultures, but he couldn't keep his face hard because we had killed a deer before any boys our age, and he was proud of us."

Caleb was quiet for a few moments, picturing them as girls, laughing and playing together. The images that formed gave him the wistful feeling he had experienced as a child, looking at paintings of people long dead.

He didn't want to ask it, but felt he had to. "Are you sure you don't want to go back to your people?"

"I have nothing to go back to," she said. "You and Little Rain, her child, and Dil are my family now."

Relief settled over him. "I'd hoped you would stay with me, but I was afraid you might not."

"I will stay with you," she said, but something in her voice made him think she had not shared everything about her feelings with him. He drew breath to inquire, but the stillness with which she lay staring up at the heavens prompted him not to press her further. *Not yet.*

When Caleb got up to replace Little Rain on watch duty, he found the sky had cleared.

"Do you like the moon?" she asked, standing with him, not apparently anxious to go to bed. She had shed her hooded

mackintosh and wrapped a deerskin around her shoulders like a cape, to hold off the sharp chill in the air.

"Yes, I do," Caleb said. "I like it because it reminds me of my mother. She loved the moonlight, and when I was small she often carried me outdoors to stand in it. She would hold me until my father called her in. She was not very well, and he worried the night air was bad for her."

Little Rain kept her gaze skyward. "After my mother and father died," she said, "I was angry at them for a long time. Sometimes at night my pain comes."

"Because they left you?"

Before she could answer, the three mules all snorted and stamped their feet. "Wake the others," Caleb said, suddenly alert for danger.

She vanished without a sound. Caleb stepped into Joshua's shadow, peering into the darkness in the direction the mules were staring. He nearly jumped out of his skin at the sudden outburst of screeching, howling and yammering that exploded a little beyond the horses.

"Something sick," White Cloud said quietly, making Caleb catch his breath. He had not heard her approach. A moment later Dil and Little Rain joined them.

"Maybe wolves," White Cloud said. "Not Indians."

Caleb nodded toward their animals. "Pick a horse and put your backs against it."

The two women slipped away, and Dil followed. The mules had quieted briefly when the rest of the traveling party appeared but soon grew restless again, stamping and snorting. Caleb had almost convinced himself it was nothing to be concerned about when a large shadow detached itself from the darkness and attacked Lady. The mare squealed, reared, and struck with her hobbled front legs.

"Wolves!" Caleb shouted. As he charged forward, gun raised

to strike the beast attacking Lady, he heard the bark of a Spencer rifle, followed by a yelp and then silence, except for the other pack animals' snorting and stamping.

By the time Caleb and Dil reached the stricken mare, the marauder had vanished. Another shot cracked out. Then silence.

"Sick," White Cloud said as she ran past the men, followed by Little Rain. A moment later, she called out, "Gone, but I think Lady has bite."

Caleb ran his hand over Lady and felt the wound in the horse's side. "It's nearly a handspan long," he said. "We need a fire for the light."

CHAPTER 15

Once Dil and White Cloud had a fire burning, Caleb took the hobbles off Lady and led her to it.

"There," White Cloud said, pointing to a long gash on the mare's left side, still oozing blood, her hide ripped open by slashing teeth.

"Dil?" Caleb asked.

"First, we heat water, put in salt and wash the cut. Then we fill the wound with sugar."

"Sugar?" Caleb asked, surprised. "How does that work?"

"It's a very old way of preventing infection and allowing a wound to heal from the inside out, keeping gangrene from setting in. She should be scabbed and healing in a week, but we have to wash the wound and pack it with new sugar morning and night. Oh, and if maggots form on the wound, we need to leave them. They'll eat the dead flesh and work with the sugar to keep the wound clean."

"Nihoothoo!" Little Rain shook her head. White Cloud said nothing but looked at Dil with a new interest.

When morning came, they went out to the place where the wolf had attacked and found the beast dead, shot through the lungs. It was a large animal but so thin its ribs were showing. A white scum of dried foam rimmed its teeth.

"Only one year old, or little more," White Cloud said. "Sick. That's why attack horses."

"We haven't seen coyotes or gophers or even a badger for three days," Dil said.

"We go," White Cloud said firmly, turning away from the dead animal. "Bad medicine here."

"What sickness?" Caleb asked.

"Rabies is my guess," Dil said.

"Very bad." Little Rain sounded strained. "Everything die."

"She means," Dil said, "everything bitten by a rabid animal dies. There's no cure for it I know about."

"What about Lady?" Caleb asked.

The others stood looking at him but not speaking.

His heart sank. "How long?"

"Maybe a moon," White Cloud said. "I have seen longer." She paused, but it was clear she had more to say.

"Tell me," Caleb said.

"One day she will hang her head, not walk with strength. Then, in the sickness, kick, bite, strike. Better she die now before she go like wolf."

Caleb felt as if he'd been kicked in the stomach. For a long moment, he couldn't speak.

"Caleb." Little Rain put her hand on his chest. "White Cloud right. She cannot lose the evil spirit wolf put in her."

Dil spoke up. "Captain, I will—"

"No," Caleb said. "I'll do it."

"I will go with you," White Cloud said, and Caleb found he was relieved not to be doing this alone.

He picked up his rifle and asked Little Rain for one of the cloths she sometimes wore around her head. She ran to her bed and came back with and a red-checked bandanna.

One on each side of Lady, Caleb and White Cloud walked her away from the camp and around behind a hillock. When they stopped, White Cloud asked quietly, "You know how to do this?"

Caleb stood in front of the horse, stroking her nose and her neck. He paused and with his finger drew a line from her left ear to her right eye and then from her right ear to her left eye. He placed his finger where the two lines crossed.

"Give me gun," she said. "You cover eyes."

Caleb tied the bandanna across Lady's eyes and had just stepped back when White Cloud shot her. The dead horse fell forward, nearly taking Caleb down, but White Cloud grasped him by his shirt collar and pulled him away from the toppling animal.

"Better I should do it," she said, passing him the rifle. "Tell her she can go now and will never be sick. Then come back. We should leave here."

It had happened so fast Caleb did not begin to be angry until she had gone. Then rage blazed up in him like a prairie fire. He thought first he would kill White Cloud. Then he thought he would never speak to her again. He opened his mouth to shout after her and then remembered what she had told him to do. "Ridiculous!" he said, swearing.

Then something broke through his anger. He found himself dropping to his knees beside the fallen animal's head. Hesitantly, he began stroking her neck, his eyesight blurring.

"I'm sorry, Lady," he said. "You can go now. Your work is done here. You can go where the fields are always green and there is no sickness."

He knelt beside the dead mare a moment more, then got to his feet. An unexpected calm spread through him, wiping away the remnants of his anger. Staring down at Lady, he was suddenly certain that she *had* gone. He turned away and strode back to the camp.

The others were packing up, drawing on skills acquired from weeks of repetition to roll up their beds, load the packs, and unhobble the animals. Caleb put Lady's saddle on Joshua and

114

helped spread the extra packs among the remaining animals.

"I'm sorry, Captain," Dil said when they were under way. "She was a good horse."

"Thank you, Dil," Caleb answered. "I felt her go. White Cloud told me to tell her she could go. I did, and she went. Can't explain it."

"Don't have to, Captain."

The country was slowly growing rougher and, aside from the birds, increasingly empty. As Little Rain had noticed, the vultures were more in evidence. White Cloud rode up beside Caleb and said, "You are speaking to me?"

"I am speaking to you," Caleb said, reaching a hand toward her.

"You want to punish me?" she asked.

"Take my hand."

Tentatively, she edged her horse closer to him and slipped her hand into his.

"Thank you for shooting Lady," he said. "I'm not sure I could have done it. I told her she could go. She went."

She said something to him in Arapaho and squeezed his fingers.

"Tell me what you said just now."

"You are in my heart, Caleb Stone."

"And you are in mine."

Soon after midday, having forded the Sweetwater three times because of its meanders and snaked their way through a hot, dry, windy, boulder-strewn canyon, Caleb sighted a pair of coyotes. White Cloud, riding behind the pack train, pointed out a badger vigorously digging for mice, making the dirt fly. By the time they stopped for camp, they had seen a small herd of elk, three wolves, and a dozen prairie dogs. The two women agreed they were out of the sick zone. That evening, sitting around the

115

fire, Dil asked, "What's in front of us? I've been eying the high ground but can't make much from looking."

"Plenty water and grass," White Cloud said. "But much up and down. Easy place for horse to get careless, break leg. Also bears, like to eat horse."

"Also Mormons, maybe," Little Rain said frowning into the fire. "Bad medicine."

"I heard about that while I was nursing," Dil said. "A few years before the war, the federal government sent Colonel A. S. Johnston out to Fort Bridger, to protect it against the Mormons. Story was they had drove off Jim Bridger, who'd built a trading place there."

"That is story I also heard from my father," White Cloud added. "He said Mormons had a Nauvoo Legion. They burned Fort Bridger and a supply place near there and stole the cattle."

"A thousand," Caleb said, "but it was some years ago. The quarrel between the Mormons and the U.S. government ended when federal troops occupied Salt Lake City."

"Some Mormons not hear that," Little Rain said quietly.

"Best to watch out for black hats," White Cloud said, backing up Little Rain.

Caleb nodded. "All right. We've got something close to a hundred miles to reach South Pass, and if we take the Lander Road cutoff, we can avoid Fort Bridger."

"Let's let trouble find us and not go chasing it," Dil said, clearly trying to cheer up the group. He got scowls from the women, and Caleb rose to his feet.

"I'm on first watch," he said, avoiding any response.

The nights were growing cold, and when the remains of supper were cleared away, White Cloud brought Caleb his coat.

"Are you worried about the Mormons as much as Little Rain is?" Caleb asked, shrugging into the coat's welcome warmth. White Cloud and Little Rain had sewn a rabbit skin lining into

it, adding to its comfort.

"Some Mormons hard men," White Cloud answered. "They kill Indians, kill anyone not one of them. Mormon medicine bad medicine."

"I thought the U.S. Army took care of the problem ten years ago," Caleb said.

"Small bands still dangerous."

"Then we must be alert. We'll talk about it in the morning." He slipped an arm around her. "For now, look at the stars. Did we finish counting them?"

She leaned into his embrace. "When I was small, I was told we will go somewhere far away, in the east, near the big water where we will always have plenty to eat, not be sick, be happy."

"Do you still believe it?" he asked.

"I have heard about Nihoothoos' heaven," she answered, avoiding Caleb's question. "My father had a book he read to us sometimes. They were stories and prayers. I liked them. He said there was heaven. When I asked him where it was, he said, 'I think up above the sky somewhere, where the horse and buffalo raced, leaving dust behind, became stars.' "

"The Milky Way," he said quietly.

She fell silent for a few moments as both of them stared at the night sky.

"You didn't answer my question," he said.

"I don't know, Caleb Stone," she answered quietly. "Do you?"

"I don't think so, not anymore, but I do know I am happy to be with you. As long as I have you, I will not ask for more."

They were approaching the end of July, and Caleb figured they had almost fifty days of travel behind them. He knew that when they reached the Lander Road, they would be just about halfway to their destination. That meant they might still be in the mountains in the middle of September. It weighed on him. He

didn't share his concern with the others, but he was determined to press them to make a solid twenty miles every day without darkening their spirits.

They were two days away from the Lander Road cutoff, nearly through a narrow, dry, boulder-strewn canyon, when seventy or eighty yards in front of them a rider came at gallop from a break in the low, steep hills to their right, followed by four men, bare-chested, long hair flying from under their hats. The men gripped their rifles in one hand, yelling and yipping like Indians.

Caleb, ahead of the others, yanked Joshua around and shouted, "Go!"

The mule went. A bullet took off Caleb's hat just before he reached his companions. As he turned Joshua, he saw White Cloud and Little Rain breaking away, racing their horses to the right and left. He had pulled his rifle out of its scabbard when behind him two shots rang out. One knocked the leader of the attackers out of his saddle. He hit the ground, bounced once, and lay still.

The remaining attackers kept coming, firing as they rode, the crack of their rifles echoing against the hills. Dil sat stiffly, swearing quietly and waiting for the raiders to come within range of his revolver. Caleb placed his sights on the second rider and fired. The man dropped his rifle, slumped, lost his grip on the reins, and fell forward against his mount's neck.

"Near enough now," Dil said calmly. His shot took down another of the riders. A final round of shots, almost simultaneous from Caleb, Dil, White Cloud, and Little Rain, knocked the last two marauders off their horses. One horse stopped. The other, carrying its dead rider, bolted past them, and then halted, snorting and trampling with fear.

"Not Indians," Little Rain said, staring down at the last two men killed.

White Cloud pulled up beside her. "Mormons. Big trouble."

"How do you know they're Mormons?" Caleb asked.

She nodded at the nearest dead man. "The hats, all black, flat brims, round tops."

Caleb dismounted from Joshua for a closer look. "They even painted their faces." He glanced up at White Cloud. "What do you mean, 'Big trouble'?"

She looked grim. "Mormons have forts in these hills. Raid in daylight and go back at night. These don't go back. Someone wonder why, come find out."

"That means we should put all the miles we can between ourselves and this place by dark," Caleb said.

"What about the ones we killed?" Dil asked.

"Can't dig this ground," White Cloud said with finality.

Dil shook his head. "It's nothing but rocks and a little gravel, that's for sure."

"Put rocks on them?" Little Rain asked. "Put them together and bury them under rocks, if we can find enough?"

Caleb turned in his saddle, eying the ground for stones heavy enough to keep scavengers off the bodies. "Can you and Dil drag them together?" he asked White Cloud.

"We can do that," Dil said, "but first someone should gather our animals."

"Right," Caleb said. "That will be Little Rain and me."

Over the next hour, they covered the bodies with a pile of rocks and stripped the Mormons' horses of saddles and bridles. "We go," Little Rain said to White Cloud.

"Yes." White Cloud mounted, then paused to stare at the rock pile with the dead men's rifles and saddles leaned against it. "Bear knock that down."

"Maybe they'll be found before it happens," Dil said.

"I take the pack train," Little Rain said.

Dil caught her eye. "I'll follow."

119

"I'd like you up front with me, White Cloud," Caleb said. "Two sets of eyes are better than one."

"They come from back if it happens," she answered darkly.

"Do you want to stay back with Dil?"

"Not yet. Later, maybe." She kicked her horse into a trot.

"Everyone stay in sight of the others," Caleb said as they got under way once more.

The trail remained rough for the next hour and then opened into a west-running valley with a creek meandering in it and plenty of grass in its flood plain. They emerged into hills again just as the sun reached the mountains on their horizon. A cold wind had started up, and a few hundred yards to the north was a stand of spruce large and dense enough in Caleb's judgment to provide them with firewood and a good windbreak.

"I am hearing voice," White Cloud said, catching up with him. "Child, I think, or spirit. If spirit, we not stop here."

"I'll look," Caleb said. "I'm spirit-proof."

"Not to laugh about," she said, then turned to wave Little Rain and Dil towards them. "But I will go with you. Someone who thinks there are no spirits should not go anywhere alone."

They crossed a narrow creek that bubbled down from the stand of spruce and rode at an easy gallop across the open area in front of them, the grass standing knee high to the animals. As they pulled up within shooting distance from the trees, someone shouted, "Git!" The order was followed by a short, sharp yip.

"Not sound like dog," White Cloud said, jacking a shell into her carbine's chamber.

Caleb slid his rifle out of its scabbard and eased Joshua forward. They were fifteen yards into the trees when White Cloud, putting some space between herself and Caleb, suddenly pulled up and raised a hand. Caleb eased the mule over to her and saw ahead of them what looked like half a tent set up in a small clearing.

120

The trees had lessened the wind, and what there was carried a faint smell of wood smoke. White Cloud looked at Caleb. He nodded and touched his heels to Joshua's belly. Head raised and ears pricked, the mule refused to budge.

"Hold up," Caleb said softly to White Cloud.

She pulled up again and eased herself onto her feet on the horse's back, looking around. A moment later, she let herself down.

"Wolves," she said to Caleb.

"Let's take a look."

What they found hunkered under the canvas was a thin-faced boy, with narrowed blue eyes and a tangle of hair that might once have been blond, bent over a tiny fire with a pile of small rocks beside him. At their appearance, three wolves melted away into the dark trees. The boy looked at his visitors, showing no sign of being glad to see them. There was bedding behind the boy, and Caleb counted six places. At one end of the tent, a partially skinned deer haunch hung from a post.

"They was after the meat," the boy said. "You'd better go on. I'm expecting my people back. You won't last two minutes should they find you here. 'Specially that Injun."

The boy was dressed in a man's shirt and trousers that looked as if the shirt sleeves and trouser legs had been hacked off with a knife. He had rags tied around his feet and for a coat, a square of elk skin with holes cut for his arms.

Caleb dismounted. "What's your name?"

"Foster," the boy said. "Foster Wiggins."

"Where your parents?" White Cloud asked.

The boy eyed her, then Caleb. "What you doin' with an Injun?"

"Her name is White Cloud. Mine is Caleb. Can you answer White Cloud's question?"

The boy dropped his gaze. "Daid."

Pity shot through Caleb. "Cholera?"

"Raiders, stealing cattle. They didn't see me. I was fetching wood." He nodded toward the empty bed rolls. "These ones found me, walking east on the trail."

White Cloud dropped off her horse and came to stand beside Caleb. "How long have you been with them?"

"Don't rightly know. Since early summer." He caught Caleb's eye again. "She your woman?"

White Cloud bent forward, bringing her face close to his. "We have promised to care for one another and to be with one another. Do you understand, Foster Wiggins?"

Foster met her eyes and, after a long pause, nodded. "I ain't never spoke with an Injun person before," he said. "Do you take people's scalps?"

"Not yours," she said. "I am Arapaho. Can you say that?"

"Arapaho."

"Good. How old are you?"

"Nine, I reckon."

She opened her arms. "Come here," she said.

He took a few steps toward her and she swept him up, lifting him off his feet and holding him tight. Caleb was surprised to see the boy relax against her, burying his face in her shoulder and putting his arms around her.

After a while she set him back down. Holding his gaze, she said with a smile, "I like you, Foster Wiggins. I might hug you more."

He turned red faced. "I guess it's all right if there ain't too many around."

"Is good," she said, straightening up. Behind them, Caleb heard familiar hoofbeats approaching. "What you call me?"

"White Cloud. It's been a spell since I had any huggin'. I ain't used to it."

"Here's somebody else might hug you," White Cloud said,

stepping aside as Little Rain and Dil joined them.

Foster glanced at Little Rain. "She Arapaho, like you?"

"Yes," Little Rain said, and gave her name. "This is Dil."

"I'm Foster Wiggins," he told her. "You're as pretty as White Cloud." Turning to Dil, he said, "How come you ain't got but one arm?"

"I lost the other one and never did find it," Dil said, shaking the boy's hand. "Pleased to meet you, Foster Wiggins. What are you doing here all alone?"

"I'm supposed to keep the fire going and the wolves off, but they're getting mighty darin', and my store of rocks is runnin' low."

Little Rain held out her arms. "Come here, Foster Wiggins."

When she put him down, the boy turned to Dil and asked, "Does she hug you like that?"

"Not as much as I'd like," Dil said.

"How many men are here?" Caleb asked the boy.

"There's five right now. They come from a Mormon fort over yonder," he said, pointing south. "I ain't never bin there, and I ain't in no hurry to go, neither. Some of that bunch is rougher than a cob and meaner'n a bear with a sore tooth."

"Where did you come from, Foster?" Dil asked.

He frowned as if in thought. "I believe it was the Cumberland," he said.

"Tennessee." Dil laid his hand on the boy's head. "I knew it. How did I know that?"

Caleb and the women looked at Dil, with varying expressions of surprise. White Cloud spoke first. "Maybe this boy has good medicine. You remember when you put hand on his head."

"I had some medicine once," Foster said. "I ain't never drunk no horse piss, but I reckon it'd taste a good deal like that medicine."

"Somebody needs to learn what is good to say and what

123

not," White Cloud said, trying not to laugh.

"You got any leftover food?" Foster asked.

"When did you last eat?" Caleb said.

"I believe it was yesterday. It warn't today."

Caleb and Dil foraged in their pockets and came up with three sticks of pemmican. Caleb passed them to Foster, who grabbed them and began chewing eagerly.

"You will eat with us tonight," Little Rain said firmly. "Have good meal."

"They'll come for me," the boy said, his mouth half full. "They're aiming to sell me."

"Foster, can you ride a horse?" Dil asked.

"I ain't been throwed yet."

"They won't be coming for you." Caleb looked around the lean-to. "You're coming with us." He glanced at his traveling companions. "Are we agreed?"

They all answered yes without hesitating.

Caleb turned his attention to the boy. "Do you want to come with us, Foster? Would you like to go to Oregon?"

"I've heard of it." The boy had finished the pemmican and dusted his hands together. "Can't be any worse than here."

When the travelers made camp, Little Rain and Dil made up a bed for the boy next to theirs. They washed him and scrubbed his head until his hair was light as young corn, then checked him for lice and wrapped him in a blanket while Caleb burned his clothes. They rubbed him all over with tea tree oil and kept putting food into his plate until he couldn't eat any more. Before bedtime the two women made him a new shirt and trousers. Little Rain cut down a pair of her moccasins for him, and White Cloud turned half a blanket into a coat.

"Next rabbit we shoot, make you a hat," she said.

He scowled, suspicion clear in his face. "You-all cleaning me up to sell me?"

124

"No," she said, "not unless you act bad."

Tears welled up and ran down Foster's face, though the boy didn't make a sound. When White Cloud saw what she'd done, she pulled him close. "We never sell you, Foster Wiggins. Not ever, and we not let anyone take you away from us. You hear me?"

The boy nodded and threw his arms around her neck, clinging to her as if she were the last stick floating in a raging river.

Caleb came over and pulled both of them to him. "Foster, you're safe with us," he said. "You're one of us now. Would you like that?"

The boy nodded, but it was several minutes before he released his hold on White Cloud. When he did, she pressed her forehead against his and said, "Caleb Stone speaks truth. All of us want you with us."

"I might stay," he said to her, wiping his eyes with the backs of his hands, "if you was to make me that rabbit-skin hat."

Chapter 16

The morning after finding Foster, Caleb got up in the dark and said to White Cloud, already up, "I'm taking Joshua and going back to where we left those horses. I'll try to rope one of them and bring it back here for Foster to ride."

"If you wait for light to go. Not good, riding in the dark."

He agreed, and they set about building a fire and preparing breakfast. Dil came in from his watch and told them everything was quiet. "When you woke me up for my turn," he said to White Cloud, "did you see where Foster was sleeping?"

"Between you and Little Rain," White Cloud said.

"That's right." Dil grinned. "I may have been kicked out of Little Rain's tepee."

"Not let that happen," White Cloud said, sounding very serious. "Little Rain pregnant and thinks whole world is her child. Tonight, put Foster Wiggins back in own bed."

"Now we have him, what do you think about our taking him with us?" Dil asked her.

"It is all right, but we not know him yet. We should take good care of him but also watch. That is all I have to say." She turned away from the men and walked off.

"I think maybe she's jealous," Dil said to Caleb, keeping his voice low. "Little Rain is pregnant, and now she's laid claim to Foster."

"Hadn't thought of that," Caleb said. "I'd better bring Joshua in."

With his ride on his mind, he let slip away what Dil had told him. Having eaten and saddled Joshua, he threw a coil of rope and a halter over his pommel and set off at a gallop to find the horses they had turned loose after dealing with the attack. Alone and with Joshua's long stride under him, Caleb cut in half the time it had taken them the day before to cover the same distance. He found the horses grazing in a small valley with a creek in it. They paid Caleb little attention until he stopped beside a bay mare and emptied a small sack of oats close to the animal's head. As soon as she began eating the oats, the other horses came in, crowding their heads together for the treat. Caleb studied them briefly and chose a chestnut mare, the smallest of the five, dropped a loop of his lasso over her head and led her out of the group. He had a little trouble getting the bridle on her, but he had knotted the lead rope to the pommel, and Joshua snubbed her attempts to bolt. With the halter on, she quieted, falling in next to Joshua and running beside the mule with no further resistance.

When Caleb overtook the others, a loud whoop from Foster greeted him. "That there horse for me?" the boy shouted.

Foster was sitting on Sheba's back between the sacks, an added weight she scarcely noticed. The trail had been climbing gradually, taking the travelers into thicker stands of evergreens and aspens. The sun was still hot, but the air had a drier, sharper smell with a tinge of pitch in it. The grass was shorter and greener, and the granite punching up through the uneven earth bore the gray, unyielding look of age, reminding Caleb of the pastures in Indian River.

"Come over here and meet her," Caleb said, dismounting and letting the horse walk towards Foster as the boy slithered off Sheba.

"She's a pretty one," Foster said, bouncing up and down with excitement.

White Cloud, leading her horse, walked over to stand beside Caleb. "Someone is glad to see you," she said, watching Foster rubbing the horse's nose.

"Someone is glad to see you," Caleb answered, bringing a smile to her face.

When the horse reached Foster, Dil gave the boy his hand to step up on and hoisted him onto the chestnut's back. He took the rope off the mare's neck, and Little Rain began leading the horse to give the boy a ride, turning to watch him and asking him how he liked it, while Dil made them laugh with his comments.

"Foster will become part of Little Rain's family," White Cloud said stiffly.

Caleb knew at once White Cloud was not happy. "Did you want to take Foster with us?"

"I want a family," she said in her stony-resignation voice, her gaze on the trail ahead, "but cannot have one."

"Aren't you and I a family?"

"What will someone do with me in Oregon with all white people?"

Her swift change of subject caught Caleb off guard, but he rallied and turned her to face him. "The first thing I will do is marry you, White Cloud. The next thing I will do is build two houses, one for us and one for Dil and Little Rain, and then we will have ten children."

Finally, she raised her eyes and said, "You and Foster Wiggins both have nine years," but she pressed her face into his shoulder. He held her tightly and felt her tears soaking through his shirt.

After a few lessons in bareback riding, with White Cloud for his teacher, Foster had learned the rudiments for staying on the chestnut, starting, stopping, turning, and galloping, all the while cheered on by Dil and Caleb. Little Rain refused to watch and

busied herself with other tasks during the lessons.

"She's sure he'll fall off," Dil told Caleb, "land head first on a granite ledge, and die. I don't seem able to get her mind off it. I woke up last night to find her crying."

They were camped in a level, grass-covered area at the bottom of three partially wooded hills. A spring-fed stream clear as air and finger-numbing cold ran through it. The mountains to the west of them were drenched in the flaming reds of a blazing sunset that had set the entire range on fire. Overhead, two golden eagles, basking in the sunset, circled slowly in the updrafts of warm air still rising from the slopes below. Caleb and Dil had paused from gathering wood for the evening fire, buffalo chips having run out, to watch them.

"Would it help if White Cloud talked to her?" Caleb asked.

"She and White Cloud are staying away from one another." Dil rested on his hatchet. "I don't think you and I know those two as well as we hoped."

"No," Caleb said. "White Cloud doesn't think I'll marry her once we get to Oregon. My saying I will doesn't seem enough. When I insisted, she said Foster and I were both nine year olds."

"A day at a time, Captain," Dil said.

The next day, having concluded the Mormons were not following them, they began to enjoy their slow, steady climb through a rough, rock-strewn country that took them to the South Pass area a little after noon.

"I'm surprised to see how open it is," Caleb said to White Cloud, who had been keeping him company for the past hour, riding close to him but apparently absorbed in her own thoughts. Before them lay a wide stretch of grassland leading to a low saddle between two hills, marking the pass. To the north lay an imposing range of snowcapped mountains, and in the distance beyond the pass the jagged outline of more mountains.

"Cold up there." White Cloud stared at the snow-covered peaks, seemingly lost in them.

"According to my map it's the Wind River Range," Caleb said. "They look close, don't they?"

She nodded. "Air is like it is not there."

"We're seven thousand feet above sea level here," he said.

"How do you know that?" she demanded, looking at him as if he had been lying to her.

"Because men called engineers know how to measure the height of things and then the heights are put on maps and in books. We are soon going to pass over the Continental Divide. On this side of it, all the water flows east into the Mississippi River. On the other side, all the water flows west into the Pacific Ocean."

"My father saw that big water," she said.

"Would you like to see it?"

She pulled her horse's head around. "I will not see it," she said and galloped back toward the others.

Caleb watched her go, sadness settling in him along with dread that he would not be able to lift the burden crushing her spirits. He pressed onward until he reached the pass and sat waiting for the others while Joshua grazed, brooding on White Cloud's frame of mind without finding the cause of her depression.

When the others reached him, and the dust the animals stirred up had blown away, Caleb rallied himself and said, "Foster, come over here."

The boy for once made no remark, silenced, perhaps, by the fact no one was smiling.

"We're turning onto the Lander Road in a little while," Caleb said to him, speaking loud enough for the rest to hear. "We're a thousand miles from where we started and halfway to Oregon. Also, we will soon be crossing the backbone of the country. It's

called the Continental Divide."

He repeated what he had told White Cloud about the water flowing west from the divide and east from where they had come. "We're sitting seven thousand, four hundred and eleven feet above the sea level," he concluded. "And those mountains with snow on them are the Wind River Range."

"How come it doesn't feel like we're high up in the air?" Foster asked, looking as doubtful as White Cloud had.

"Because we're so small and the earth is so big, and you can't see the Pacific Ocean. If you could, you'd see we're more than a mile above it. Don't you notice how clear the air is?"

"I'm hungry," Foster said.

"Goes with being nine," Dil said to Caleb. "Cheer up, Foster, nooning is ahead."

"Cain't come too soon," Foster said, grinning.

"I am not seeing good place to make camp," White Cloud said as she overtook them. "No water. No wood. No buffalo chips."

"Let's go," Caleb said, a bit soured by the lack of interest his companions had shown in his geography lesson. Foster was occupied with a jackrabbit that had sprinted across their track, and White Cloud stared stone faced ahead of them. Caleb said, "I'll take the lead rope. Foster, with me. Dil and Little Rain, go on up ahead. The next turn you come to will be the Lander Road cutoff. Wait for us there."

White Cloud shook herself out of her lethargy and turned her horse. "I will ride after us."

With Dil and Little Rain in the lead they went through the saddle and were soon moving downhill through dry, open country with bunch grass, and increasing scattered scrub growth, replacing the lush grass of the approach to the pass. Foster, impatient with the pack animals' slower pace, rode ahead of Caleb until he was about halfway caught up with Dil and

Little Rain. Caleb could see them all clearly, though Little Rain and Dil were some distance ahead. A quick glance over his shoulder showed him White Cloud lagging, a smaller figure and further behind than he liked. *She'll hate it if I wait for her, tell me she's not a child or some such.* Irritated and worried in equal measure, he kept going.

Time passed. Lulled by the steady motion of riding, Caleb belatedly noticed that Dil and Little Rain had stopped and were waiting up ahead. They must have reached the Lander Road. As he watched, Foster spurred his horse to join them. Caleb picked up his pace, eager for the next stage of their journey. He glanced back but saw no sign of White Cloud amid the softly rolling landscape behind. *She can handle herself. She'll turn up.*

The pack animals were kicking up dust as he reached the other three at a divide in the trail, one leg of which turned sharply north. Foster had slid off his chestnut, whom he'd named Dakota, and was grazing the mare on a patch of grass that looked thicker than others close by. From the subdued expression on his face and a sharpness in Little Rain's, Caleb surmised she'd scolded the boy over something. He chose not to ask.

"We go north now and should find some water and decent grazing," he said, pulling off his hat and knocking some of the dust off his clothes.

"Looks like we go to the snow mountains," Little Rain replied, resting on her horse with one leg crossed over its shoulders.

He nodded. "I haven't seen White Cloud for the past hour."

Dil stood up in his stirrups, looking back at where they'd been. "She's coming and raising some dust herself."

White Cloud slowed and within a few minutes came up to them at a trot. "Someone following us," she said. "We get to those trees and wait to see who." She pointed to a line of trees

about a mile from where they were gathered.

"Did you get a look at whoever it is?" Caleb asked.

"No, but not people with wagons, not enough dust, and when I stopped, that one stopped."

"One person?" Little Rain asked and then told Foster to get on his horse.

"I think so and not want me to see him."

"We don't want to make a dry camp," Caleb said, "so let's get to those trees and hope for water."

Putting Foster beside Little Rain and Dil in front, Caleb fell back as White Cloud took up the lead rope. Dil moved them off at a trot that ate up the ground at an encouraging rate. Moving Joshua to the right, to avoid eating the dust the riders and pack animals were raising, Caleb brought up the rear. He kept looking back, hoping to catch a glimpse of whoever was tracking them, but he saw nothing other than a flock of crows suddenly taking flight a quarter of a mile to the east of the road.

They reached the woods without incident and saw the Sweetwater River below. They soon had the packs stacked, a fire started, and the animals watered and staked out. Foster insisted on going with the men to chop wood and, oddly, didn't once complain about being hungry.

"I reckon he's been hungry a lot in his life," Dil remarked to Caleb as they walked behind Joshua with the boy on his back, dragging in the extra wood White Cloud had asked for. She had also insisted they take Caleb's rifle with them. Both she and Little Rain had their Spencers close at hand as they worked preparing supper. Caleb had told White Cloud about the flight of the crows, and she had said, "Just how Indians would follow—off to one side and maybe come in from front to make surprise."

"And maybe with the sun at their backs," Caleb said. "Have you told Little Rain?"

"Only that camped we will be more safe. She not want Foster to go for firewood, but I tell her it better if he be with you and Dil. She still worried, not happy."

Camped close to the river, they took turns washing off the dust of the trail. It was Foster's first time river wading, and, after finding the current wasn't going to sweep him away, he began to splash and play like any other child. Little Rain had to drag him out when she and White Cloud finished bathing. The women had undressed him and themselves, and all three bathed together naked. Caleb, guarding them, wasn't sure how he felt about that or about the fact that the women were apparently not in the least self-conscious about undressing in front of Foster.

Later, while the women worked around the fire, and the two men were still stacking the packs, Foster asked Little Rain if she "had a bun in the oven."

Caleb and Dil nearly choked trying not to laugh. The two women looked at Foster with blank expressions. Foster looked from the men to the women, not understanding the reaction of either pair. "Little Rain," Caleb said, recovering slightly before Dil, " 'bun in the oven' is an expression meaning you're going to have a baby."

The two women spoke briefly to one another in Arapaho. Then Little Rain spoke to Foster. "Yes, I have bun in oven. Dil is father. I am mother."

"I thought so when I seen your belly," the boy said, unfazed. "My ma, she done that." He went back to tending the fire, leaving the adults to sit looking at one another.

White Cloud broke the silence. "It is as I said. This one is old person in young skin."

Joshua suddenly snorted loudly. The adults grasped their guns. Little Rain jacked a shell into the chamber of her Spencer and stepped over Foster. "Sit," she said, "and not speak."

Approaching them on the trail, perhaps fifty yards to the north, were three Indians on horseback. They were dressed formally, with feathers in their hair, but they were not wearing war paint. The riders closed the distance to about thirty yards, then slid off their horses and walked toward Caleb and the others. One of the three, a tall, slender man in leggings and a white deerskin shirt, had an axe and a bone-handled knife in his belt and a bow and quiver slung over his back. The other two men were shorter and stockier, armed in the same way. They stopped within speaking distance, and the tall man addressed White Cloud in Arapaho.

She kept her eyes fixed on him as she translated. "Elk Turns says he comes in peace."

The name struck Caleb like a blow. "Why is he here?" He knew why, or thought he did, but felt it necessary to ask.

Elk Turns spoke again, his voice lowered. White Cloud pressed her lips together, but otherwise seemed made of stone.

"He says he has not come to fight," Little Rain said. "He wants to talk to White Cloud alone."

Caleb felt as if ice water ran through his veins. "White Cloud," he said, "do you want to talk with Elk Turns?"

Dull voiced, she answered, "I will talk with him."

"Only if you want to."

"I must do this," she said.

"Little Rain," Caleb said, forcing the words out, "please translate for me. Elk Turns, you will stand where you are. We will step back, give you space. If you touch her, we will shoot you. Do you understand?"

Little Rain repeated Caleb's words in Arapaho, and Elk Turns nodded.

Caleb and the rest backed away, spreading out as they retreated. Little Rain kept herself between Elk Turns and Foster. A few yards away, Caleb stopped. "Far enough," he said, watch-

ing closely Elk Turns and the other two Indians.

Elk Turns began speaking, his voice little more than a murmur to Caleb. White Cloud replied more loudly, sounding angry enough to make Caleb watch her instead of the interlopers. He caught himself and looked away, spotting Elk Turns's two companions. They were mounted and moving their horses away from one another, starting to circle the camp.

Fear and anger sent his heart pumping. "Arrows coming!" Caleb shouted.

At his warning, Little Rain and White Cloud both swung on the attacker to their left. Across the fire from them, Caleb turned and aimed at the rider drawing a bow on him.

Four shots rang out. The Indian horsemen toppled to the grass. Screaming with pain, Elk Turns was spun off his feet as Dil's shot struck him in the right shoulder. His belt axe fell from his grip.

"He lied," Dil shouted. "He tried to kill her."

White Cloud spun around and saw Elk Turns on the ground, writhing in agony. The axe lay nearby. Caleb, checking that the Indian he'd shot was dead, came back at a run to the fire. White Cloud was standing over Elk Turns, staring down at him. Slowly, she raised her Spencer and rested its butt against her shoulder. She was lifting the barrel when Caleb shouted, "No, White Cloud! No!"

She paused—only for an instant, but long enough for Caleb to reach her. "Don't do it," he said. "Don't!"

"He tried bury axe in my head. I will kill him."

"Did you tell him you would not go with him?"

"Yes."

With effort, Caleb lowered his voice. "He tried to kill you out of jealousy. If he couldn't have you, nobody could."

"He left me with Hawk Hand," she said. "He did not want me then."

She swung the barrel of the carbine just enough to point at the fallen man's head, her finger on the trigger.

"White Cloud," Caleb said desperately, "if you kill him, you will have him with you forever." Dimly, he noted that Dil and Little Rain had drifted up behind White Cloud and were standing absolutely still. Even Foster stood frozen in place. For several seconds, the only sound was the snapping of the fire and the wind in the trees.

White Cloud looked up from Elk Turns, who lay insensible. Unconscious, Caleb hoped. "Once," Caleb said quietly, as if beginning a story, "you and Elk Turns shared a blanket. Perhaps you didn't take him all the way into your heart, but he gave himself to you. Also, you thought he should have come after you because of what you had shared. Now you're both very angry and maybe not thinking very well. Perhaps Little Rain and Dil think as I do. That you should wait, talk about it. Then, if you want to, you can kill him." He held her gaze and thought he'd spoken long enough for some of the seething rage in White Cloud to boil off, but he was far from being sure enough had gone.

"I have heard you both," Little Rain said in a reflective tone. "Yes, you could shoot Elk Turns." She paused, then went on. "He did try to kill you, but first he wanted you to go away with him. Maybe even some little part of you was glad he wanted you. Perhaps you want to say something now."

"Yes." White Cloud stepped away from Elk Turns and lowered the hammer on the Spencer. Elk Turns groaned. White Cloud looked down at him. "If I am not going to kill him, I think we will have to keep him from dying."

"Foster," Caleb said, "listen to me. First, put three more pieces of wood on the fire. Then tie Elk Turns's horse to a tree and don't try to get on him. After that, see if you can bring in

the other two Indians' horses. And don't try to get on them, either."

"Why not?"

Little Rain said, "Because they don't like the smell of Ni-hoothoos."

CHAPTER 17

Three days later, Elk Turns was on his feet, his arm in a sling. Since waking from the anesthetic, he had not spoken. But on the fourth morning, when he had mounted his horse with a week's supply of meat in deerskin sacks slung over the horse's withers and the lead rope for the other two Indians' horses in his hand, he broke his silence. He addressed White Cloud, and Little Rain began translating.

"I have gained no honor from this," he said. "You should have killed me. The Nihoothoo have no honor, so they will not understand. I leave alive but less than I was. The two who died will be honored. I will be scorned."

He paused and turned to Dil. "Was it to humiliate me, you did not kill me?"

"I didn't do it for you, Elk Turns. I did it for White Cloud."

Elk Turns made no response to that other than shaking his head as if confused or disgusted. When he turned to Caleb, his face hardened. "If we meet again, Caleb Stone, one of us will die."

Rankled by having been told he had no honor, Caleb started to reply, but Dil interrupted. "Go in peace, Elk Turns," he said in a loud voice. "Thank your lucky stars Caleb Stone has White Cloud in his heart." He stepped up and slapped the man's horse hard on its rump. Startled, it threw up its head and leaped forward. Elk Turns struggled to rein it in, but the animal fought the rein and carried Elk Turns off at a gallop.

White Cloud walked away from the others and stood still long enough to see him out of sight. Then she broke into a run past their staked horses and into the woods. Caleb turned to run after her, but Little Rain caught his arm. "No, Caleb. She does not want you to see her crying."

He stared after White Cloud, then asked softly, "Is she still in love with him, Little Rain?"

She took a moment to answer. "Perhaps how you still love Millicent True. It is as you said. Now she can let him go, but they once shared her blanket. We cry for ourselves sometimes."

Foster shouted, "Dil says to get a move on. We've got three days to make up, and it ain't getting no warmer."

"Get Dakota," Caleb said. "Little Rain and I will follow you."

Foster ran off. Caleb turned back to Little Rain. "Thank you. You're right, and so is Dil. We do have time to make up."

They broke camp quickly, even without White Cloud. When they were nearly ready, Caleb called Foster, telling him to whistle. The boy obliged. Leading Joshua and White Cloud's horse and carrying her saddle blanket and her Spencer, Caleb walked towards the trees where she had vanished and found her sitting on a fallen trunk, elbows braced on her knees and resting her head in her hands.

"We missed the train," Caleb said, "but I brought a mule and a horse."

She sat up straight but avoided his eyes. "You go without me," she said.

"I thought of doing that. I really did, but the nights are getting cold. I have become used to whatever it is that keeps my back warm."

It wasn't fair because he knew if he said that, she would laugh. She gave a sputtering one, but it was genuine, and it brought her to her feet. Still not looking at him, she said, "You think now I still have Elk Turns in my heart."

He shrugged. "Little Rain reminded me that I still had Milli-cent in my heart, sort of, and that you have him in yours in the same way. There is room for others in our hearts. Soon Foster will be there, the way Dil and Little Rain are."

She snapped her head around, her braids flying out. "I not like Millicent True in your heart," she said. "Why you not angry if Elk Turns in mine?"

"Because I'm a better person than you are."

"You are largest idiot," she shouted, glaring at him. Then she flung her arms around his neck and hid her face against him.

"You're right," he told her. "Let's go to Oregon anyway."

"If things go well, we should be at Fort Hall in a bit under two weeks," Caleb said.

They had been following the Sweetwater River north for two days, and now the towering Wind River Mountains lay to the north of them and loomed closer. Looking at the others, resting on their horses, gave Caleb a strange feeling.

The women, dressed in leggings and deerskin jackets with fringes on all the seams, their hair in braids, looked a part of the land through which they were passing. Foster, browned by wind and sun, looked almost half again the size of the starved boy they had found in the Mormon camp. *And Dil and I*, Caleb reflected, *look just as wild as the women*. Both men had long since ceased trimming their hair and wore similar clothing on the trail—a mixture of dark wool and elk-hide trousers and jackets and moccasins. He wasn't sure whether to be amused or alarmed, but for a few moments he felt a lightness of heart he had not known for years.

"We ain't going over the Wind River Mountains, are we?" Foster sounded concerned. He was sitting on Dakota in perfect imitation of White Cloud on her horse, one leg crossed in front of him with an elbow on his knee and his chin resting on the

heel of his hand.

"Nope," Dil said, "we're going thataway." He pointed west.

Foster scowled. "Don't look much better."

"It's not," Caleb said. "We're north of South Pass now and sitting on the Continental Divide."

"How many moons have we been on the trail?" Little Rain asked.

"About two months . . ." Caleb began.

"In three suns, it will be two moons," White Cloud put in.

"Right," Caleb said, impressed with White Cloud's quick response. "A moon is twenty-nine and a half days," he added. "That makes two months, give or take. We've made fairly good time, but we need to press hard. In another moon, we'll have snow in the mountains."

"Those mountains in front of us look cold," Little Rain said. "When we go over the passes, maybe we will sleep under buffalo robes."

White Cloud gave her a look. "Some people should not think so much of going under robes."

"Pot," Little Rain observed, sounding like Dil, "should not call kettle black."

Dil and Caleb laughed, but White Cloud stared blankly at Little Rain.

"Dil told me that," Little Rain said smugly. "Pot and kettle both sit on fire, get black."

"Oh!" White Cloud sat up straight. "I am understanding. Someone may find flea in her bed one night."

When the threats and laughter ended, Caleb said, "The biggest challenge for us between here and Fort Hall will be Thompson Pass in the Salt River Range. It's eight thousand-eight hundred feet high. Then come the Caribou Mountains, which we can hope to reach in ten to fifteen days, depending on how difficult the going is."

"We ain't runnin' and whoopin' on what's in front of us, or I ain't no judge of trails," Foster put in, his eyes fixed on the broken, high country the Lander Road was leading them into.

"You're right, Foster," Dil said, "but I think we're good for it. Anybody want to add anything to that?"

"Why are we still here?" White Cloud demanded. "Some men rather talk than do something."

Dil chuckled. "This man knows when someone steps on his tail. Let's go."

"About time," White Cloud said. "I learn that from Caleb."

They had been averaging twenty miles a day, and Caleb was counting on the Lander Road, despite its height, to let them better their average. Things started off well—the road descended from the Continental Divide to the Green River Valley with no obstacles and plenty of water and grazing for the animals. The weather held fine, and the scattered stands of pine, juniper, aspen, and ash alternating with grass and scrub openings provided plenty of game, especially elk, mule deer, rabbits, grouse, and an occasional moose.

There were also bears. Except for mothers with cubs, black bears were not a serious problem, but grizzlies, from yearlings on up, were dangerous. In three encounters, involving first Dil and then White Cloud and Little Rain, their horses took one glance at what was coming around a bend in the trail, turned on their hind legs with a squeal of fear, and bolted. All three animals got their hindquarters raked with the grizzlies' claws before the bears gave up the chase.

They dealt with the problem by fashioning wooden bells to hang around the necks of the lead horses that clattered loudly enough to give the bears warning. Caleb and Dil were skeptical, but White Cloud and Little Rain ignored their protests, and the trouble with the bears ended. Mostly.

One night, they came to the end of the evening meal with

most of the boned meat of an elk's hindquarter left over. As usual, the women wrapped it in a square of oilskin and laid it aside for the next day. White Cloud had the second watch, and just before first light her yells brought everyone else in camp out of their beds and scrambling for their rifles, Little Rain shouting at Foster to stay where he was.

The next instant White Cloud split the night with her Spencer, firing as fast as she could jack in shells while yelling in Arapaho. Whatever she was saying, Caleb thought, it was probably good that Foster's language lessons hadn't gotten that far. A sudden yodel of pain erupted that didn't sound quite human. It was followed by White Cloud's whoops of laughter.

The shooting stopped. One by one, the rest of the little band gathered around the remains of the fire that lay scattered as if something had kicked it.

"Bears," White Cloud said as she joined the group, her face relaxed in a broad smile. "Four bears, not one. I am standing beside Dakota horse, thinking about the day coming. Then three middle-size black bears hurry past me. At first, in moonlight, not sure what I am seeing. Then come she bear. Horses go on eating grass, but I am seeing large bear. The first ones find elk meat and begin fight over it. Mother bear get there, swat right then left and grab meat. I run at them, shouting. All run every way. I shoot. One small bear run away, not look where going and jump into fire, burn feet, and yell loud. I am laughing too hard to hit anything, so I stop shooting. After now, we put meat in tree."

In the gray pre-dawn light, the group set about their morning tasks. Foster picked up his hatchet and started away to fetch firewood, but Little Rain stopped him. "Wait for more light," she told him. "Take Dakota to drink."

Caleb, returning with White Cloud to roll up their bed, asked, "Do you think Little Rain and Dil will keep Foster with them?"

She stopped what she was doing, dropped to sit cross-legged, and looked at him. All traces of laughter had drained from her face. "Would you like to have Foster for child?"

He was awake enough to grasp that her question hid another one. To buy time to consider his answer, he pulled on his moccasins. "I would like you to have our child," he said.

She stopped pulling at the bedding and looked at him with hard eyes. "I am Arapaho. You are white. If we have child it will not be one or other, not among Nihoothoos."

"How do you feel about Foster?"

"He is good child. I like him."

"Would you like to have him for a child?"

"He not want me for mother."

"Haven't you noticed that everything you do with your horse, he does with Dakota? He even sits on her at rest with one leg crossed, chin on his hand, like you, not like Little Rain or Dil or me."

She did not answer but sat, head bent, staring at the bedding in her lap.

"You taught him to ride, how to put the hackamore in Dakota's mouth," Caleb continued quietly. "He even uses Arapaho words to give her commands."

"You want me to say Arapaho or white not matter?"

"Foster has all of us in his heart," Caleb replied, "but it is you he has taken into it most deeply. He goes to Little Rain to be hugged because he knows she wants to hug him, but when he needs help in knowing what to do, he goes to you."

Her face softened a bit. "He is good little boy, makes me laugh sometimes when I don't want to," she said. "Even you laugh."

"Yes," Caleb said. "Now tell me why you are unhappy."

She rose to her knees. "Elk Turns will come again," she said in an unsteady voice. "If he kills you, it will be my fault. It is my

fault he is coming."

"Before his wound heals," Caleb said, "we will be far away."

"He follows us now. He will not go to his people. He has lost his honor."

"He can't hunt. How will he eat?"

"He will trap rabbits, maybe ptarmigan. Make spear and kill deer. He knows how to live as I do."

"He must know one of us will shoot him if he comes after me," Caleb said.

"Dying will restore his honor."

Caleb held out his hand to her, but she wouldn't take it. He got up and went to her, lifted her to her feet and put his arms around her. She turned her head away.

"White Cloud," he said. "Look at me."

She did as he asked, but he saw that she was in pain. Her black eyes, so full of fire less than an hour ago, had lost all their life. Looking into them sent a chill through Caleb and left him with no road to follow. He pulled her against him and held her, still without an idea of what he needed to say, and decided to just start talking. "What did you think of me when Dil and I first found you and Little Rain?"

She leaned back from the waist to look at him, surprise animating her face. "I thought, I will kill him. You don't remember I had a bow?"

"Oh, yes," Caleb said. "When did you decide not to?"

"A little at first, then more later. Why you are asking me this?"

"Do you know what I thought when I first saw you?"

"What?"

"That you were a person of great dignity."

She frowned as if puzzled. "Dignity?"

"*Honor* is perhaps better. Even in the rags you wore then, you were someone I wanted to look at."

146

"You never say that before."
"Maybe I forgot until now."
"You are teasing?"
"A little."
"You are wanting me to feel better."
"What I want is some breakfast."
"I am not thinking that is all."
"Now that you mention it . . ."

CHAPTER 18

Their conversation remained unfinished, but it had ended on a happier note than it began. Caleb decided to call it at least a partial victory, though he did not mislead himself into thinking their problem had been solved. He thought White Cloud was probably right about Elk Turns but saw no way to prevent its happening.

They made good time on the Green River Valley road. The sun stayed with them. The air was dry and tinted with the smell of grass and junipers with something of the mountains in it that lifted their spirits, and they grew more cheerful as they rode. It was a green country with the cold, clear water of Piney Creek flowing through it. Hawks and the occasional golden eagle swung over their heads, and pronghorns, mule deer, and elk moved away without haste as they passed.

That evening after supper, as they sat around the fire, Little Rain got to her feet and said in her formal voice, "Something may happen."

"What?" Dil asked, showing surprise.

"Someone may come in the dark."

"Who?" Dil demanded.

"Elk Turns." White Cloud fixed Little Rain with a hard stare. "Little Rain is right. We should talk about it. Suns have passed. Soon, he will heal enough to come."

Little Rain remained standing. "It is not easy. Perhaps someone knows what to do."

Caleb eased to his feet and addressed Little Rain. "I have thought about this. I think it is best for us to do as we did when we waited for Hawk Hand."

A moment of silence fell. Then Little Rain said, "Elk Turns wants to kill you and take White Cloud."

White Cloud stood. "Perhaps someone does not want to be with us."

Dil jumped up. "Hold on. Little Rain didn't say that."

Little Rain ignored Dil's protest. "I have four to think of. Maybe Elk Turns bring others, kill all of us. That's all I have to say."

The silence stretched out as the fire crackled. Somewhere in the woods, an owl hooted. Throughout, Foster had sat in silence. Now, he rose and went to stand between White Cloud and Caleb.

"Little Rain," he said, "we will protect you. I don't want anyone to go away."

Out of the mouths of babes, Caleb thought, pulling Foster against him. "Don't worry, youngster," he said firmly. "No one's going to leave you."

In the end, they all sat down, and Dil called for coffee. Little Rain made it, and gradually the tension eased and they talked about the trail ahead. Once in bed, Caleb asked White Cloud what she made of Little Rain's pronouncement.

"She is afraid," White Cloud said, sadness coloring her voice. "Dil say she not mean what we heard, but I think she did."

"Does she really want to take Foster and Dil and leave?"

"She Arapaho woman. Not making joke."

"White Cloud," he demanded, rising on an elbow to look at her, "is she really going to leave us?"

"She and Dil will talk. Lie down; you letting in cold."

"There it is," Caleb said.

It was midmorning, and they had come to the end of the valley and were looking up at the Salt River Range and the approach to Thompson Pass, the highest peaks soaring nearly nine thousand feet in front of them.

"Goodbye easy living," Dil said, shoving his hat back on his head as he slowly took in the mountains facing them. The higher ground was dotted with clumps of aspen and juniper and lodgepole pine.

"Bear country," White Cloud said. "Soon will look for winter place."

Caleb felt glad to hear her voice. She had scarcely spoken for days. Although she wouldn't talk to him about it, Caleb was sure she was brooding over Little Rain's comments at the fire. He had wormed one response out of her, and it had done little to settle his mind.

"Little Rain has said we should leave them," she told him the morning after Little Rain's speech at the fire. "She is Arapaho and will wait to see what we do."

"If we don't go, will she?"

"Perhaps. Also, Dil and Foster."

And that was all Caleb had persuaded her to say.

Later, when he asked her if she thought they should go, she replied, "You should decide, but I say no" and went back to putting the riding blanket on her horse.

That had been days ago, and now they were at the foot of the climb to the pass that had been on Caleb's mind for many days. He found seeing it a relief. The encounter could begin.

"Let's stay together," he told them, "and move at a steady walk. Let the animals pick their way. If one of us needs to stop, call out. We'll all stop."

Foster had been studying the rock-strewn trail ahead. "Not a good place to get sleepy."

That produced laughter. Two days earlier, he had gone to

sleep and fallen off Dakota.

"Maybe keep Spencers close," White Cloud said. "Lots of place to hide and wait."

Little Rain sat stony faced, not looking at White Cloud.

Caleb snapped a lead rope onto Dakota's rein, taking a couple of turns of the lead around his own pommel before leading the group off. The influence of the mountains on Foster became clear when the boy made no complaint at being attached to Caleb.

They had been climbing for a half hour when Foster said, "I'm having some strange feelings."

"It's the mountain," Caleb said. "You'll notice it more the higher we get."

"You ever been in these mountains?" Foster asked.

"No, but I climbed Mount Katahdin in Maine some years ago, and I remember the feeling you just mentioned."

"Should I be scared?"

"No, it's just the feeling mountains waken in us."

"Mountain spirits very powerful," White Cloud said. "They should be honored."

She was riding close behind them, leading the pack animals. Little Rain and Dil were following the string.

"How do you do that?" Foster asked.

"When we stop, Little Rain and I will show you. For now, we should be quiet and watch for signs."

"What are they?"

To Caleb's surprise, White Cloud did not tell him to use his eyes and ears and not his mouth. Instead, she answered patiently. "If you see water run uphill, that is a sign to stop, perhaps go back. Now we will go quietly and watch and listen."

"If that ain't a ring dinger," Foster muttered.

As they climbed, the cottonwood, alders, and willows gradually gave way to juniper and pinyon pines and a scattering of fir

and low-growing spruce. The ground between the ledges and rocks was overgrown with grass and dense, low brush. Over and through it all, a chilling wind passed with a cold, whistling sound that turned to humming and groaning in the pines and juniper.

"Listen, Foster," White Cloud told him. "You will hear what the wind says."

"You're jawing me," the boy said.

"Listen. It has much to tell."

The sun climbed higher, driving out the morning chill. Soon the vultures, hawks, and eagles found the updrafts and appeared above them, riding the rising towers of newly warmed air. As Caleb and the others climbed, more mountain peaks revealed themselves as if rising out of the land.

"I sure ain't never seen such a thing as this," Foster said in an awed voice, swinging his head around like a weather vane in a shifting wind in an attempt to see every inch of the landscape.

"Keep eyes and ears open, Foster," White Cloud told him quietly. "It is powerful medicine. Open your eyes and your heart."

A sharp whistle behind them brought the three lead riders to a stop. White Cloud swung her horse around and gripped her rifle. "I go back."

"Dil don't usually whistle 'lest there's something wrong," Foster said, his eyes wide.

Caleb caught his eye. "We'll just wait, and remember, son, most things that go wrong can be put right."

Foster gave him a puzzled look. "I ain't your son."

"You are and you aren't, Foster," Caleb answered, drawing closer to the boy. "I'm not your father, but to all of us you're our son if *son* also means a boy we care for and are looking after. Is that all right?"

"Does that go for White Cloud and Little Rain?"

"Yes, it does."

White Cloud came back at as close to a run as the footing for her horse would allow. "Something up there," she said, pointing up the mountain with her rifle. "We have not seen this one before."

"I can't see nothing but rocks," Foster said, staring at the vast arc of rocks and ledges and sparse scattering of green growth above them.

Little Rain and Dil joined them, both looking a little troubled. "Whatever's up there," Dil said, "keeps slipping in and out of sight."

Caleb fished his telescope out of a saddlebag and began slowly scanning the side of the mountain.

"There it is," he said, grinning as he lowered the telescope. "Have a look, Foster."

"Them there's sheep!" the boy shouted, "and one of 'em's got almighty big horns."

One after another they all had a look at the sheep. Foster, of course, wanted to go up to where the sheep were and was temporarily crushed by not getting his way.

"Bighorn sheep," Caleb said, "and they're working their way down the mountain, probably coming down to graze."

Having spotted them with the spyglass they were all able to make out the herd, made up of lambs, ewes, and one very large ram, followed by two or three younger males. A large, gray-coated ewe appeared to be leading the way, with the rest grazing and moving steadily in her wake.

"One of them make good eating," White Cloud said.

"Hide make good coat for Foster and blanket for baby," Little Rain added.

"Why does that lead sheep keep stopping and looking around?" Foster asked.

"Many animals like to eat them," White Cloud said. "My

153

father told me lynx, bobcat, coyotes eat small ones. Cougar, bears, wolves eat the rest."

"Uh-oh," Dil said. "They have company, and that ewe is looking the wrong way. It's behind them, up among the rocks."

Caleb brought out the telescope again and scanned the place just above the sheep. "It's a big cat, and it knows what it's doing, waiting until the herd moves before trying to get closer."

"I see it," White Cloud said.

"Is big," Little Rain said.

"I don't want no goddamned mountain lion killing none of them sheep," Foster said loudly.

Their attempts to clean up Foster's English had been making very slow progress. Dil might have tried right then, but he saw the two women raising their rifles. "Hold on," he said sharply.

Caleb looked away from his telescope and echoed Dil with a loud, "Whoa!"

"Cat have good hide," Little Rain protested.

"Claws make necklace, strong medicine," White Cloud said in support.

"Look up there." Caleb pointed to a large, bare area immediately above them, covered with loose rocks and broken shale. "That's a slide just waiting to happen."

"The Captain's right," Dil said. "This is no place to bang away with guns."

"What if we go up there and 'bang away'?" White Cloud asked, her eyes narrowing.

Dil exchanged a quick look with Caleb and said, "Fine idea. I'm sure the Captain thinks so, too."

"Oh, yes," Caleb said on cue. "Dil and Foster and I will wait here. How does that sound, Foster?"

"Don't shoot none of them sheep," the boy said, scowling at Little Rain and then White Cloud.

"If we did, you would eat most of it," White Cloud replied.

The two women dropped off their horses and soon vanished into the brush and rocks, popping up at intervals as they clambered over ledges they couldn't find a way around.

"They'd rather hunt than eat," Foster said. "I never seen the like of them. They're kind of wild, ain't they?"

"Don't ever say that to either of them," Dil said. "They'd skin you alive."

"I reckon they would," Foster said, shaking his head. Caleb couldn't help laughing.

"Foster," he said, "we've got to find some children for you to play with. You carry around the weight of the world. Do you know that?"

Just then, Dil's hat blew off his head, accompanied by the sharp crack of a gun. Caleb pulled his rifle from its scabbard and swept Foster off Dakota. Dil had already drawn his revolver and was on the ground. "There's cover behind you," he said calmly. "I'll have my back to yours."

They did not lose time asking themselves what to do. Their years in the war had taught them all they needed to know. Find cover, locate the shooter, and set about killing him, preferably without being winged.

"The shot came from downhill," Dil said when they were crouched in a jumble of large boulders, which gave them cover but prevented them from seeing where their assailant was.

"Foster," Caleb said, pulling him closer. "You've got to do what I tell you. Understand?"

"I reckon."

A bullet struck one of the rocks where they were hiding and ricocheted over their heads with a nasty whine.

"You're not going to like it, but Dil and I have to find this man and stop him." As he spoke, Caleb drew his derringer from his boot and passed it to the boy. "I'm going to show you how to shoot this, and if someone other than any of us comes in

155

here, shoot him."

"I know," Foster said. "I cock it, point it, and pull the trigger. It'll kick like a mule. I know that 'cause I've done it a couple of times."

Two more bullets knocked chips of stone out of the boulders. Dil and Caleb slipped out, separating as they scrambled around the rocks. Caleb got into a position that gave him a view of the trail. A dozen feet from him, an Indian appeared and bent over to pick up the pack train's lead rope where Caleb had dropped it. Joshua reared, striking at the man with his front feet.

"Get out of here!" Caleb shouted.

The man whirled, pulling a hatchet from his belt as he turned and raised it to throw at Caleb. A rifle cracked, and the hatchet flew out of his hand. With a yell of pain, he grasped his injured wrist and fled up the trail. A second Indian, carrying a rifle, dashed onto the trail and tried to grasp the lead rope, but a second bullet bounced a handful of gravel into his face. Leaping back, the man looked up to his left and raised his rifle.

"Wrong move," Caleb said, but, before he could fire, a bullet struck the magazine of the man's rifle, slamming the gun butt into his jaw as it flew out of his hands and knocking him out, stone cold.

A tense silence fell over the trail as if that little piece of the earth was holding its breath. Caleb counted under his breath. Reaching fifty, he shifted carefully to a new position but saw no one. The shooting had not resumed. The birds were beginning to call, and a very pregnant rabbit hopped past him, pausing to eat in a small patch of grass before hopping heavily off.

Dil whistled. Caleb stood and slowly edged his way onto the trail. The fallen Indian had not moved. White Cloud and Little Rain joined him.

"Where's Foster?" Little Rain asked.

"Right here," the boy said, handing Caleb his derringer. "I

didn't have to shoot nobody. Is that Injun dead?"

"Snakes," White Cloud said, bending over the fallen warrior.

"Where?" Foster shouted, jumping and turning around to see where they were. "I don't have no truck with snakes."

"Name of tribe," White Cloud said, nudging the man with her foot and producing a groan from him. "Bad medicine."

"What we goin' to do with him?" Foster demanded.

"Get him onto his feet and send him packing." Dil moved toward the man, who was showing more signs of life. "White Cloud, perhaps you might step back from him. He's going to be mad when he wakes up."

"Little Rain say not kill them," White Cloud said. "Maybe I should have."

"That was outstanding shooting," Dil told her. "Caleb, let's stand him up and see what shape he's in."

The two men dragged the Indian to his feet and steadied him until he could focus his eyes. An immense bruise darkened the right side of his face, and his right eye was bloodshot. White Cloud and Little Rain held their Spencers on him. He was in his forties, Caleb guessed, scruffily dressed with greasy, chopped-off hair and in serious need of a bath.

He said something and tried to shake himself loose. When they released him, he reached for the knife in his belt, but White Cloud thrust the barrel of her rifle into his solar plexus, knocking out what little wind he had. Caleb and Dil caught him as he was falling, and Caleb grabbed his knife away.

When the strange Indian could stand alone again, Little Rain spoke rapidly to him. He glared at her but answered, waving a hand in the direction they had come.

"He says there are many of them and will kill us," Little Rain said scornfully. "He is a liar and a man of no consequence. They are thieves and not warriors. He wears no paint and has no feathers in his hair."

"Ask him if he has seen Elk Turns," Caleb said.

White Cloud spoke. The man thrust out his chest and replied loudly.

Little Rain translated. "Elk Turns would kill us when he caught up with us. He said he could kill any two Arapahos. He does not know Elk Turns."

"Foster," Caleb said. "Find the hatchet the other man lost."

The boy was back with it in less than a minute.

"I'd like to have that," he said, passing the weapon to Caleb, who shoved the handle into the Indian's belt and put the knife back in its sheath. Foster groaned.

"Little Rain, translate what I'm going to tell him," Caleb said. "Go. If we see either of you again, we will kill you."

Rapidly, Little Rain relayed the words. The man turned without speaking and set off past their string of animals, making good time but wobbling a little and occasionally staggering as if he were drunk.

"That blow to his head unhooked his balance," Dil said. "I'm surprised he can walk at all."

"I could have used that tomahawk," Foster complained.

Caleb set him on Dakota. "Maybe we'll find one," he said, "but now let's think about making up for lost time."

CHAPTER 19

They didn't reach the pass before darkness overtook them. As they climbed, pines gradually replaced the other trees, and the scrub growth was shorter and dense as a wire brush. Perhaps an hour short of the pass they came on a large opening in the pines with a spring emerging from under a long granite ledge and grass enough for the animals.

"Stop here," White Cloud said. "Two are tired."

She tilted her head towards Little Rain and Foster, nodding on Dakota. After the steep and rough climb, the animals were starting to lag.

"I'd hoped to get through the pass before dark," Caleb said, "but I'm willing to call it a day."

Dil and Little Rain showed their approval by instantly dropping off their mounts. While the adults unsaddled and unpacked the animals, Foster quickly found the spring and began building a dam with stones and moss that spurted water in a dozen places. Nevertheless, it soon created a pool large enough for the animals to drink from.

Once the animals were watered and picketed, Dil and Caleb, led by Foster, went in search of firewood. Since the attack by Elk Turns, Little Rain had refused to allow the boy to leave the camp site alone. White Cloud had supported her.

"We're outnumbered," Dil said to Caleb. "We'd better surrender."

"You ain't!" Foster protested. "There ain't but two of them,

159

and I'll throw in with you."

"Foster," Dil asked, "have you ever won an argument with Little Rain or White Cloud?"

The boy's mouth turned down. "Well . . . no."

"Neither have I, and Caleb won't argue So, we might as well go fetch the wood."

Foster looked up at Caleb. "Why don't you argue?"

"I always lose," he answered. "Here, carry this hatchet."

Later that evening, after Foster fell asleep and the others were preparing for bed, Little Rain said in her formal voice, "I will speak."

The other three stopped what they were doing and turned toward her.

"Somewhere in front of us is Elk Turns," she said, facing White Cloud and Caleb. "He waits for you. The mountain tells me he will kill Caleb, perhaps others."

She paused, folding her hands in front of her, waiting.

White Cloud stood. "Little Rain has spoken from her heart. She fears Elk Turns. Perhaps others also fear him. We must discuss this, to find what we are to do."

Caleb had listened carefully in an effort to understand the structure of their exchange and what needed to follow. The others were looking at him. Reluctantly, he put aside the pack he had been repairing and stood. "Perhaps it's best for me to begin by saying I do not fear Elk Turns. I do not speak boastfully. Perhaps Little Rain is right. He may wait for us. He may have turned and ridden ahead. He was angry and felt he had lost honor in our fight, but we need not fear him."

"Little Rain," Dil said, having risen while Caleb was speaking. "I do not fear Elk Turns. He may come, but he may not. He was badly wounded. He will not have full use of his arm at least for another moon. Perhaps you are mistaken about what the mountain told you. Sometimes dreams are mistaken. I agree

with Caleb. We are safer together."

"I will speak again," White Cloud said. "No one can tell Little Rain what to do. No one can tell another what to do. Perhaps it might be good now to think about what has been said and later talk again about it. It is important to think carefully. That is all I have to say."

But it wasn't, because she spoke briefly in Arapaho to Little Rain and then left the group. Little Rain made no response but stood staring into the fire for some time.

"What did you say to Little Rain?" Caleb asked White Cloud later, when they lay together under a buffalo hide. The night was cold, and their blanket was not thick enough to keep them warm.

"I told her we would take care of her and that we care for her deeply," White Cloud said. "I know you care for her."

Caleb did not answer at once, unsure whether or not she had given him a jab. The subject of Little Rain was a fraught one between them. Her pregnancy had sharpened all the edges. That White Cloud lay with her back to Caleb was a sure sign of trouble, and he didn't want to make it worse.

"Do you love her?" he asked, hoping to avoid angering White Cloud.

"A pregnant woman worth more than a barren one," she replied. "Go to sleep."

"Didn't you say you can't tell another person what to do?"

White Cloud flung herself around to face him. "This all my fault," she said in a choked voice. "Everyone knows this, but no one says it. I should be the one to go, but I can't, and I have lost my honor."

Her grief made his heart hurt. "I will go with you, if that is what you want."

"You cannot leave them," she said. "They would not live long."

That's probably true, Caleb thought. "What, then?"

"Perhaps someone would hold me so I feel his heart beat."

Caleb did as she asked. When he woke, she was gone.

"She had the last watch," Dil said. "I think she waited for the light and then left." He, Caleb, Little Rain, and Foster were standing around the morning fire.

"She waited, to be sure we were safe," Caleb said.

Foster looked frightened. "Where has she gone?"

"To find Elk Turns," Little Rain told him.

"We don't know that," Dil said with a trace of sharpness.

Caleb turned to her. "Little Rain, would you get me three days' supply of meat, and one of the small frying pans? I will get some things together and saddle Joshua."

"Take your spyglass and plenty of shells for both guns," Dil said. "We'll come behind you as fast as we can."

"All right. Keep going, press hard. Keep a sharp lookout. Foster, stay close to Little Rain and Dil. No chasing rabbits. Do you hear me?"

"Yes. I'll look after them best as I can."

"Good." Caleb clapped a hand on the boy's shoulder.

When he was mounted with his bedroll, food and medical supplies behind him, Little Rain came up and laid a hand on his leg. "Caleb, if you find them, if she has not killed him, you must. With him she will die inside in small pieces, one by one. Do you understand?"

"Yes. Sleep with your Spencer beside you."

"I'll take care of her and Dil," Foster repeated.

"Good man. Stay close to them. Promise?"

"Yes. You come back, all right?"

"All right."

It was noon by the time he reached the pass. A shower had

162

swept over the area in the night, but the tracks of White Cloud's horse were still sharp and clear in the places on the trail where the earth had softened enough for the horse's hooves to leave an impression.

He rested Joshua midway through the pass, despite the chill north wind scouring the sparse, twisted brush pushing up between the rocks. He sat there for several minutes, forcing himself to look at his surroundings in an effort to master the tangle of anger, fear, and anguish that roiled his mind. Tumbled gray and white-streaked clouds, looking close enough to touch, raced over his head. Glancing at them, he imagined grimly that they mirrored his thoughts.

To the west, the Salt River Range loomed. *Somewhere in there,* he thought, *I'll find White Cloud.* That assertion brought him up short. What if she did not want to be found? What if she had run away to find Elk Turns? The possibility that she had finally admitted it was Elk Turns she loved nearly froze Caleb's ability to think at all.

"I will believe that when I hear her say it," he told the wind.

Fighting down the remnants of doubt, he saw that from here on, he would have to ride with a lot more care. She couldn't be more than a few hours ahead of him, he reminded himself. He had ridden Joshua hard, and the big mule would have gained steadily on her horse.

"Let's find them, Josh," he said, sitting up in the saddle and lifting the reins.

The Lander Road had been built with federal money in 1858 and cleared of trees and other large obstacles to accommodate wagons, but it was still a rough road, running through a lot of high country. Their descent from the pass was winding and difficult, and, until they reached heavier tree growth, what wasn't gravel was a loose mix of stones and thin dirt that did not show tracks Caleb could follow from the saddle. Nevertheless, he

pressed on, convinced she was still ahead of him and equally certain that when he found her, he would find Elk Turns.

An hour later on softer ground, he came upon the fresh tracks of two horses, neither shod. The horses were moving at a trot and then walking, which confused him. He pulled up Joshua and sat still, searching his mind for an explanation as to why Elk Turns wasn't trying to get White Cloud as far from him as fast as possible. The most logical answer was the one he liked least: she had joined Elk Turns willingly, and the Indian had no reason to hurry.

It had also occurred to Caleb that Elk Turns was setting a trap for him. That was the answer he chose as the reason for what he did next. Like it or not, it was clear that to overtake them, he had to press ahead, and he had no intention of giving up on White Cloud. He felt all the more determined when he recalled what Little Rain had told him just before he left: "If you do not kill him, she will die inside in small pieces, one by one."

With her words burned into his memory, Caleb turned Joshua off the high side of the road. Two hours later they came out on a wooded ridge overlooking the road a hundred yards below. Caleb backed Joshua into a clump of junipers and dismounted. He pulled his telescope out of his waistband and moved into a position where he could observe the stretch of road beneath him without being seen. At first, he saw only patches of empty trail through openings in the trees. Then, shifting the glass more slowly, he caught movement through a thin stand of pines.

It was a horse, swishing its tail. Caleb edged slowly along the ridge, staying low in the brush, pausing at short intervals to use the telescope. A minute or so later he spotted White Cloud, sitting on her horse. He swore silently as he saw her hands were bound in front of her. Much worse was the leather lead fastened

around her neck. He could not see where the other end was tied.

"That's the bait," he murmured. "Where's the trap?"

He could not see Elk Turns from where he was, but he felt sure the man was there somewhere. Caleb edged back to Joshua and led the mule back around the ridge in a half circle, returning them to the road a little west of where he had seen White Cloud.

"He's expecting us to come from the east," Caleb told Joshua, standing beside the mule's head and wondering what to do next. Then he knew. "Find Elk Turns," he said, "and don't spook that horse she's on. That means going in on foot. You stand, Josh. I won't tie you. If I don't come back, you head back to camp."

The mule blew softly and Caleb tied the reins over his neck. He glanced at the sun, already slipping down the western sky, and pulled his rifle out of its scabbard. Feeling the pressure of time, he set off through a dense stand of pine and aspen. The ground under the pines was carpeted with needles, making it easy for Caleb to slip almost silently between the trees. The aspen leaves were turning yellow but had not yet begun to fall, which gave him cover and left the ground under them padded with soft, damp mulch from past years' leaves.

When he reached a point parallel to White Cloud, he found he still couldn't see where the strap on her neck was fastened, but he assumed Elk Turns would be counting on Caleb going straight to her. He stopped and studied as much of the trail as he could see to the east of White Cloud, certain that within twenty-five yards or less of her, hidden in the trees bordering the trail, Elk Turns was waiting to kill him.

Caleb looked back at White Cloud. Her horse stood almost parallel to the road, and she was facing west. Keeping that in mind, he moved slowly toward her. He made it up the trail

about fifty yards without finding any trace of ambush, so he knew Elk Turns was on the other side. He retraced his steps, then eased out of the sheltering trees and stepped up beside White Cloud's horse.

"White Cloud, don't move," he said quietly. "I'm going to cut the lead on your neck and free your hands."

She remained motionless. The horse neither shied nor snorted, a gamble that paid off. He had also gambled that Elk Turns, wherever he was, was looking east.

"Where is he?" he asked as he cut her free.

"Across from us. He has my Spencer."

"I'll step back into the trees. When I say, 'Go,' go. The others are coming." He eased back into the woods and raised his rifle. "Go."

White Cloud gave a loud yell and drove her heels into the mare. The mare sprang forward.

Elk Turns leapt out of the trees, shouting, but White Cloud did not stop. He was raising her rifle when Caleb shot him. The bullet struck the man under his right arm, knocking him off his feet, sending the Spencer flying. Elk Turns dragged himself onto his knees, fell again and did not move.

At the sound of the gunshot, White Cloud turned her horse saw Caleb standing in the road and raced back. She pulled up near him, and he lifted her down from the horse.

For the next few moments they stood embracing one another.

"You came for me," she said, her face pressed against his.

"You're safe now," he said, wanting to ask her why she went to Elk Turns, but held back, thinking, *There was time enough for that later.*

The sun was nearly down. The air was cooling rapidly, the shadows lengthening. "I have food," he said as he released her. "We should make camp." He moved toward Elk Turns's fallen

166

body and picked up White Cloud's rifle. White Cloud bent over him, pulled a knife from his belt, and put it in her own.

"Not here," she said. "Bad place."

He stood. "All right. I'll fetch Joshua."

"He is behind you," White Cloud said. "I watch him come, making no noise. Like a ghost mule."

Caleb turned and greeted the animal. "Well done, Josh," he said, stroking the mule's neck. "Looking after me, weren't you?"

White Cloud pointed at the rising ground to the west of them. "Clearing at top. Go there."

"What about him?" Caleb nodded toward the dead man.

"Raise body up, like Hawk Hand." She shivered. "Not now. Too late, and cold. Camp and sleep first."

Caleb took a minute to move the dead man to the edge of the trees, and then they rode in uneasy silence to the wide grassy opening on the north side of the road. When they reached it, Caleb spoke. "There's a small creek over there. We won't have a dry camp."

White Cloud looked worried. "Should others be here by now?"

"Probably not," Caleb said. "I pushed Joshua fairly hard. They might be here by noon tomorrow."

Still not addressing what had happened with Elk Turns, they hobbled the animals, leaving them to graze, and began making camp. Carrying his rifle and a hatchet, Caleb walked up the sloping green space, stepped over the small rill running quietly out of the woods, entered the stand of spruce that crowded around a large granite ledge, and began chopping off dry branches from the base of the trees. Casting about, he soon found a fallen tree and quickly added larger branches to the pile. White Cloud appeared and helped him carry the wood back to their camp, where she had laid a small circle of stones to hold their fire.

Many of the peaks to the west were even higher than the pass, and the sun was soon lost behind them. While Caleb laid out their bedroll beside the fire, White Cloud fried the meat Caleb had brought. They worked in silence except for the wind dragging through the spruces and the hooting of a great horned owl calling from somewhere in the woods. After a while, further down the mountain, coyotes began serenading the new moon.

When their supper was ready, Caleb sat on their bedding, but White Cloud did not sit down beside him. Instead, she stood very straight, looking past rather than at him, and said, "Someone must speak. Will Caleb Stone hear me?"

A chill ran through Caleb that owed nothing to the evening air.

"Of course I will."

She paused a moment as if gathering courage. "In another time, I thought Elk Turns and I would marry, but I found I did not love him," she began. "Then I gave my heart to you for as long as the wind blows. Do you hear me?"

"Yes."

"Later, someone came for me, but I did not want him. He was shamed and went away. I was certain he would return, to kill anyone who stood against him. I thought day and night about that and those who were with me. It was a bad feeling, and I decided it was my fault the person had come."

She paused again. Caleb could see the pain the account was causing her.

"I left to end the bad medicine growing," she went on. "I said to the person, 'Take me, but do not harm the others.' He said, 'Sit down. We will talk.' I sat down and laid Spencer across my legs. He leaned forward as if to sit and threw ashes from dead fire in my face. He took Spencer, knocked me backward, and pulled my knife from my belt. He said he would kill all the others but not Foster. He would sell Foster and me."

Caleb stood and grasped one of her hands. "If you want to tell me more, White Cloud, I will listen. You do not have to. I know what you did and why."

Still she wouldn't look at him. "When sun rise this morning . . ." She broke off, then began again in an increasingly choked voice. "He put me on horse, put leather lead around neck and tie end to tree. I was sure you would ride down road and die, and I knew it would be my fault. I wanted to die."

He touched her cheek, then turned her face toward him so their eyes met. "I'm here," he said. "So are you. That's all that matters. I was angry at first that you ran away, but it didn't stay."

"Do you still love me?" she asked.

"Will the grass grow?" he answered, taking her into his arms.

CHAPTER 20

Dil, Little Rain, and Foster reached them half an hour after the sun broke over the jagged eastern horizon. Caleb was at the high end of the clearing, taking the hobbles off Joshua and White Cloud's horse. White Cloud was crouched over the fire, turning on a spit two grouse she had shot. The moment he saw her, Foster dropped off his horse, ran full out toward her, and threw himself on her back, nearly knocking both of them into the fire. White Cloud gave a wild yell and fought her way to her feet, drawing her knife as she rose. Foster landed on the ground, the wind knocked out of him.

Caleb sprinted around Joshua, drawing his revolver. Seeing Foster on his back and not moving, Little Rain screamed. Dil stood in his stirrups and shouted, "No, White Cloud! No!"

White Cloud sheathed her knife. She grabbed Foster by his arms, pulled him upright, and shook him, calling his name.

"He's all right," Caleb said, reaching them. He eased the boy out of White Cloud's grip before she shook Foster's teeth loose. Whether because of the shaking or despite it, Foster gasped and croaked, "Am I dead?"

"No, but you should be," White Cloud snapped, in anger born of relief. "Don't you know someone might have killed you?"

Foster rushed at her again and threw his arms around her. "I was scared we lost you," he said.

She sank to her knees, pulled him down, and pressed her

forehead against his.

"Foster Wiggins, I am sorry I frighten you. Not do that again," she said in a rare display of emotion, wrapping the boy in her arms.

After White Cloud told Little Rain and Dil what had happened with Elk Turns, the two women finished preparing breakfast while the men, having talked themselves out, watered the animals. Eating breakfast, seeing to packs, and lifting Elk Turns onto a platform high enough to keep the scavengers off him took nearly until noon. Finally, they set off.

"This road is supposed to be going down, but it seems to me to be going up," Dil said an hour later.

"We've got another pass ahead of us," Caleb said. "It's in the Salt River Range, and it's about as high as Thompson Pass." He turned Joshua, going back to relieve White Cloud leading their string, leaving Dil to ponder. He passed Little Rain, who was shepherding Foster. She did not like having him out of her sight.

"Talk to White Cloud," Little Rain said, and immediately went back to teaching Foster Arapaho names of the trees and plants growing around them.

White Cloud passed Caleb the lead without speaking and started to urge her horse forward. "Hold on," Caleb said. "Little Rain said I should talk to you. What's wrong?"

She reined in her horse and sat, her back straight, looking ahead. "Little Rain has mouth like hurrying water."

"Don't change the subject." Caleb urged Joshua around to stop beside her. "Tell me what's wrong."

She had plaited her hair and wore the braids down the front of her deerskin shirt. He liked her best that way, possibly because it was how she looked the first time he saw her. Now, with the sun on her and her black eyes shining with life, he forgot about everything but her.

171

"You are beautiful, White Cloud," he told her. "You fill my heart with happiness. Do you know that?"

Unexpectedly, her eyes filled. "I have made your heart dark with pain. You will not forget that. I have dragged myself out of your heart, and now mine, as is right, is broken." Her face was wet with tears, but she stoically refused to wipe them away and kept her gaze on his.

Caleb threw a leg over the pommel of his saddle and dropped to the ground. He reached up, grasped her by the waist, and pulled her off her horse and into his arms. His face pressed close to hers, he asked, "Is this because when Foster said he felt funny inside when you were gone, and you said the sun lost some of its brightness, I said that was how I felt when I found you gone?"

"Not know," she said.

She stood stiff as a board in his embrace, leading him to think he was losing on all fronts. "Sit down," he said abruptly and dropped to his knees, taking her with him.

The animals began drifting as they grazed on the skimpy grass. Caleb ignored them. White Cloud shifted to sit cross legged, staring down at her hands cupped in her lap. Tears kept streaming down her face, but she made no sounds at all.

"I'm going to talk." He imitated her sitting position as well as he could, but his knees did not go down the way hers did. "I am also going to ask you some questions. Is that all right?"

She nodded.

"Do you believe me when I say you and I are going to be married?"

She shook her head.

He thought her response probably laid bare the roots of her misery. "Would you still like to marry me?"

She nodded.

"Do you think I want to marry you?"

She shook her head.

"Why don't I want to marry you?"

"I am Arapaho. You know you cannot live among your people with Indian wife."

Caleb sat looking at her without speaking so long that she finally sneaked a glance at him.

"You know I speak what is true," she said, suddenly sounding angry.

Progress, Caleb thought and went on sitting silently.

"Ground cold," she said, getting to her feet. "Not good. Get up."

Caleb stayed seated, even when familiar hoofbeats sounded, and Little Rain approached at a full gallop, rifle in hand. "What wrong?" she demanded, reining in her horse so hard it nearly sat down. "We worried."

"Someone won't get up," White Cloud said.

"Caleb," Little Rain demanded. "You sick?"

Caleb said nothing.

"He not speaking?" she asked.

"No," White Cloud said.

Little Rain glanced around. "Perhaps we camp here," she suggested doubtfully, even though there was no water, no grass to speak of, and no piece of ground flat enough for a bed.

"No," Caleb said, "you go on. I will sit here until White Cloud figures out why I'm sitting here. Then she can tell me, and I will get up and talk. Not before. Go."

By now Dil and Foster had come back as well. Foster, hearing what Caleb said, went over and sat down beside him.

"I'm setting here," he said in a loud voice, "so Caleb won't be alone."

"No." Little Rain grasped Foster by his arms and snapped him onto his feet. "One foolish person at once is all I can do." She marched him to his horse and heaved him onto it, all the

time talking fiercely in Arapaho. Meanwhile, White Cloud stared at Caleb, apparently at a loss. Little Rain shook her out of her trance.

"Come," she said. "We must find camp site. Dark comes soon."

"I can't leave him," White Cloud said. "Something broken in his head."

"No, is not," Little Rain said loudly. "Is your doing. Come now; we find place to camp. Maybe the wolves get him. Problem go away. Get on horse."

Dil took White Cloud gently by the arm. "Come along. We need your help with the animals."

It was a measure of White Cloud's confusion, Caleb thought, that she didn't snatch her arm away and threaten to take Dil's life. Instead, she allowed herself to be led away, looking back at Caleb over her shoulder.

"I'm going to tell you something," Dil said as she mounted her horse. "That man's stubborn as an oak stump. You'd better put on your thinking cap."

She gave him a wide-eyed look. "What is that?" she asked, sounding desperate.

"If you don't want the wolves to get him, or the Shoshones, you'd better figure out why he's sitting there."

A quarter of an hour later they found a small creek with grazing around it and a patch of level ground for their beds that wasn't quite all rock. White Cloud went through the tasks of hobbling the horses, starting the fire, and, because Caleb wasn't there, gathering the wood. She did all this in a haze of confused dread and grief. Her mind was filled with the picture of Caleb sitting on the cold ground and refusing to speak to her. That it was her fault made her feel sick to her stomach and terribly guilty. Tears welled in her eyes, but she dashed them away, dreading the mo-

ment when she would run out of work to do.

To her surprise, once the chores were finished and the fire started, Dill drew her away from Foster and Little Rain. "I know I'm not supposed to interfere in your and Caleb's business, but maybe you better tell me why you were quarreling."

"Get married," she said. She felt desperate for help but also furious with herself for being frightened. Even telling him that much made her feel the words might choke her.

"Go on," Dil said calmly. "Spit it out. You're the only one who can get him on his feet."

"He ask if I believe he will marry me."

"And you said no."

"Yes. White man can't have squaw for wife in place where Nihoothoos live."

"Lord God!" Dil exploded. "I thought you were a smart woman!"

Anger sparked through her fear. "What you mean?" White Cloud demanded.

"One, White Cloud, you are not a *squaw*! If you told the Captain you were, it's no wonder he won't speak to you. If he said he'd marry you, he will marry you, come hell or high water."

Puzzlement brought her up short. "What is hell?"

"A very hot place where you will go when you die if you don't stop this damned foolishness you've been indulging in."

She folded her arms and looked away from him. "Not understand."

"All right. I'll speak more plainly. You've been saying Caleb won't marry you when you know he will, and you're too afraid of something else to admit it."

That hit home. White Cloud's arms fell to her sides, and she bowed her head. "He still has Millicent woman in his heart," she whispered.

"No, he doesn't," Dil replied forcefully. "He loves *you*. It's so

obvious a blind man could see it."

Giving words to one fear made it hard to stop. "I don't know what to do in house, how to sleep in bed, cook in stove," White Cloud said, still staring at the ground. Despair engulfed her as she went on, her voice breaking. "Millicent knows those things. He expect me to do as she does. I can't ride horse in house, carry Spencer, shoot deer. I not have reddish hair." That last came out close to a wail.

"Look at me, White Cloud," Dil said, quietly but firmly. "You are frightening yourself over things that have nothing to do with what Caleb Stone wants from you. Do you love him?"

"Yes."

"Does he love you?"

"I think so."

"White Cloud!"

"Yes, he does."

"Do you want to break his heart?"

She looked up, shocked. "No! Why you ask that?"

"Good. Get your horse, take the Spencer. Go and tell him you believe him when he says he will marry you, and stop being an idiot."

"What is idiot?"

"Someone whose head is broken."

She stared at him for a moment longer, then ran to grab Spencer. Rifle in hand, she threw herself onto her horse and galloped out of camp.

As she neared the place where they had left Caleb, fear knotted White Cloud's stomach that he wouldn't be there. *Bear, Wolf, Shoshone. All could have killed him.* She was also afraid something had gone wrong in his head. She had never seen a man do what Caleb had done. He had not beaten her and told her she would do as she was told. He had not ridden off and killed something, brought back its scalp or its meat, and gone

on as if nothing had happened between them. To her relief, she picked out his dark figure from other shapes caught in the moonlight.

"Someone is coming to talk," she called, her heart pounding as she reined in her horse.

Caleb had waited for what felt like more hours than it could have been. Twilight came on and darkness fell, and still there was no sign of White Cloud. On the edge of losing faith, he heard an Indian pony's hoofbeats from the direction Dil and the others had gone to make camp. A minute later, White Cloud moved into view. She pulled up some distance away from him and called out that someone had come to talk.

He tried hard to mask his relief as he answered. "If someone is not White Cloud, go away."

"I am someone coming to speak with Caleb Stone."

"Speak from where you are," he said. "Then I will decide if I want you to come closer."

She raised her voice. "Someone wants to tell Caleb Stone she believes he wants to marry her."

"What?" he said. "I can't hear you."

"Someone wants to tell Caleb Stone she believes he wants to marry her."

"Louder. I can't hear you."

She lifted her head, closed her eyes, and shouted, "Someone wants to tell Caleb Stone she believes he wants to marry her!"

He shot to his feet and dashed toward her, grasped her waist, and pulled her off her horse. "But does White Cloud want to marry him?" he said close to her ear as he held her, struggling hard against him. He loosened his grip just enough to let her spin around and embrace him with one arm. Her knife glinted in her other hand.

"Yes, after she cut out his liver for frightening her," she told him.

"I'm glad," he said, nearly bursting with relief and laughter, "but she will have to make up for taking so long to get here."

"Now?"

As they went deeper into the mountains, the fair weather and infrequent storms that had so far marked their journey gradually gave way to turbulent skies and bursts of driving rain, whipped over them by groaning, swirling winds. Although they wore their foul-weather gear, the fierce wind pushed the rain up their sleeves and into their boots and down their necks. Adding to their discomfort, the temperature was inching down, and more and more frequently the rain was shot through with pellets of ice and wet snow.

"We're not making the distance we need to," Caleb told them one evening as they sat around a fire finally coaxed into burning by the half-dry kindling they had taken from the dead, brittle bottom branches of the surrounding spruce trees. They had spent a week on the road since crossing the Thompson Pass. "I don't think we're making more than fifteen miles a day." He stared into the flames. "It's not enough."

A light snow was falling, hissing as it touched the flames, which flickered in the gusts of a cold, restless north wind.

"If we go more," Little Rain said, also as though talking to the fire, "we will lose horse for sure. Trail is bad. If freezes, be worse."

"Cannot winter here," White Cloud said. "Elk already moving down mountain, look for valley. Deer also. Bear go uphill."

"Why?" Foster asked.

Little Rain pulled him against her. "Looking for place to sleep in for winter."

"How far are we from Fort Hall, Captain?" Dil asked.

"I'm not sure exactly. We'll come down out of the Salt River Range into the Star Valley, where the animals should get some good grazing, and follow that to the Caribou Mountains. Once over them, we pass the south end of Grays Lake and go west to Fort Hall and join up with the trail again. Then we follow the Snake River to Fort Boise. After that, we have the Blue Mountains to cross."

"It will be Moon of Drying Grass, before we get there," Little Rain said glumly.

"September," Dil said.

"Snow in mountains," White Cloud said. "May need snow-shoes. Maybe buy in Fort Hall. Take too long to make now."

"I remember sliding on snow," Foster put in.

Little Rain smiled. "Sometimes as child I slide down hill on old deer skin."

"In snow, people use travois," White Cloud said. "Where horse can go, travois go, too."

"Our horses scrape away snow with front feet, to find grass," Little Rain added. "Not know if other mules and horses know how."

Dil rubbed his chin. "If the snow comes early, and we can't cross the Blue Mountains, we might winter at Fort Boise."

White Cloud shivered. "Not easy to winter in teepee. Snow and cold come in the smoke hole. Never be warm until spring."

Later, while Caleb pulled on extra clothes for his stint as watchman, White Cloud said from beneath their blankets, "I saw smoke today. Someone send message."

He paused and looked at her. "Could you read it?" he asked.

"Not sure. Think it say, 'Come.' "

He resumed dressing. "When are smoke signals used?"

"War parties, sometimes talk."

"We heard at Fort Hall the Shoshones were rising," he said. "Was the smoke behind us or ahead?"

"Across that small valley we saw from ridge we cross before stopping here. Perhaps good idea to stay close tomorrow."

"Very good idea," he said, picking up his rifle.

White Cloud's tale worried Caleb, but his watch proved uneventful. The morning broke fair, and the dusting of snow that had settled was soon gone. Their spirits rose with the increasing warmth of the sun, but they stayed in sight of one another throughout the day. Shortly after breaking camp, White Cloud killed a young mule buck with her bow. It had been thrashing a small spruce with its spike horns, and she had crept within a dozen yards of it.

"Better not to make noise," she said, "but also must eat."

No one disagreed with that. Little Rain used the deer's dying to teach Foster the ritual of thanking the animal for giving its body to feed the people. He said the words after her, placing his hand on the deer's neck.

"It's still warm," he said when he had finished. "Does that mean it's not dead yet?"

"No," White Cloud said. "By the time we have let blood run out, skinned, and cut it up, the heat will have gone back to the Great Spirit that gave it."

"Does the deer have a spirit?"

"Yes," Little Rain said, "and it has also gone to the place of the Great Spirit."

The two women were kneeling beside Foster, knives in their hands. "Now we work," White Cloud said to him. "Watch and learn."

Caleb and Dil had long since given the women the task of dressing out game they had shot because White Cloud and Little Rain could do the work in half the time the men took. Once the skin came off, it became the table on which they dismembered the carcass. Then they wrapped the meat and hung it on the pack animals. Caleb had seen them do this dozens of times, but

this time he listened to what they said to Foster. For a moment, he wondered if it was right to let the boy be taught Indian beliefs. Then Caleb realized that honoring the animal's sacrifice, and understanding that its death provided food, insured, probably, he would never kill an animal for sport.

Dil stepped up beside Caleb. "You thinking what I'm thinking?"

"Are we turning the boy into a heathen?"

"Yes."

"I can't think of a better way of teaching him that he's part of this world and how to live in it."

"I'm with you, Captain," Dil said quietly.

The dressing done, White Cloud got to her feet and looked up at the vultures coasting in and descending. "If they are watching," she said, nodding toward the scavenger birds, "painted ones may be getting on their horses."

181

Chapter 21

On a blustery, gray day, they came down from the high country exhausted and battered by the weather and the trail, itself damaged by washouts, tree falls, and landslides. Emerging from the woods was a relief, and it pleased Foster most of all.

"I'd begun to miss that sky," he said, wearing a grin, the first of the day.

The north end of Star Valley spread out before them, still dense with green grass, belly high on the horses. The animals wanted to graze and took a lot of urging to go forward.

"A beautiful place," Caleb said, glancing west and then south. "I think we're looking at the breadth of it to the west, but south of us it seems to stretch forever."

As soon as the women settled on a place by a small river with a stand of spruce and aspen close by, they set up camp, watered and hobbled the animals, and left them to graze, which they did eagerly. The two mules lay down and rolled, rubbing their backs with obvious pleasure.

"Tonight, we eat fish," White Cloud said when she returned from the stream. "Big fish there."

"Shall I get out the lines?" Caleb asked.

"No," Little Rain said, "we catch with hands. Foster will come with us. We teach him how to catch fish."

"You and Dil bring wood," White Cloud told Caleb. "These trees not big enough."

The women set off with a rabbit skin sack and their rifles,

Foster between them.

"How, Captain, did we get along before we took on those two women?" Dil asked, watching them go.

Caleb watched them as well. "Correction, Dil," he said. "They took us on, gradually reducing us to beasts of burden. I'm surprised we're not carrying packs."

Dil grinned. "And wasn't we lucky."

"Wouldn't have missed a day of it," Caleb agreed. "Well, nearly every day."

Talking about the remainder of their journey while they walked, the two men reached the stand of aspen and pines and set to work. By the time they got back with heaping bundles of cut wood on their backs, two small fires were burned down to coals with two frying pans sitting on them and four thick, gutted cutthroat trout, each more than a foot long, sizzling.

"I did it!" Foster shouted, jumping up and down with excitement. "They showed me how, and I caught one and throwed him right onto the bank."

"We are impressed," Caleb said, lowering his load to the ground. "How did you do it?"

"You got to lay right on the edge of the bank," Foster said, still too excited to stand still, "and slide your hand into the water, slick as a snake, feel under the bank until you find a fish and startin' at the tail, run your fingers real light up its belly, then grab it and throw it."

"Well done, Foster." Dil sat on his heels and joined Caleb in stacking the wood. "And that fish smells good enough to eat. What do you think?"

"I like to catch 'em better'n to eat 'em," Foster said. "I'm a meat man myself."

That made everybody laugh, but Foster scowled. "I don't see nothing funny about being a meat man."

They made short work of the fish, Foster eating his share,

and both women remarked on the number of fish in the stream. "We have fresh ones for breakfast," White Cloud said.

It was still light when they built a single night fire out of the two cooking fires. Foster fell asleep over the last of his dinner, and Caleb carried him to his bed and laid a blanket and an elk robe over him. "That boy is growing like a weed and getting heavier every day," Caleb said, returning to the fire.

"I not trying to carry him now," Little Rain said, then added, "We not go down as far as we come up. I am feel cold even near fire."

"From the looks of the trees, I would judge we're still up about a mile," Caleb said. "Mostly aspen, spruce, and lodgepole pines."

"If Shoshones come, it is from there"—White Cloud pointed at the area where Dil and Caleb had cut the wood—"or straight across water, which is up to here." She held her hands up to her armpits. "Maybe tonight we stake Joshua between us and water, Sheba between us and pine trees."

"Are we making a mistake, sleeping so close to the river?" Dil asked.

"Is deeper below us," Little Rain said. "Horse has to swim. Maybe camp there?"

"Might help a little," Caleb agreed, "but I don't think enough to change places this late." Turning his attention to White Cloud, he said, "What makes you think we're in any more danger here than we've been in the mountains?"

"This valley, maybe Shoshone hunting ground from the beginning," she answered. "Also, Indians not like the high places at night. Bad medicine."

"All right," Caleb said. "We'll double the watch just before daylight. Everyone agreed?"

"Would like to stay here for one more day," Little Rain said. "Animals and Foster need rest. All too tired."

White Cloud agreed. "Foster falls asleep on Dakota's back. Pack horses begin stumble."

Caleb poked the fire with a stick to make the sparks rise. "It doubles our risk, but we haven't had a rest for some time. What do you say, Dil?"

Dil looked thoughtful. "If we get through the night, we might build us a redoubt. Wouldn't have to be more than three or four logs high. Just something to lay down behind and shoot from. That done, we might give ourselves a real rest. Enjoy eating fish and dry some meat. Little Rain could use some time off a horse."

"Done," Caleb said, blaming himself for forgetting Little Rain's condition. "All right with all of us?"

It was, and Caleb said, "White Cloud and I will take first watch. Then Dil and I will take the dawn one."

"I will watch with Dil," Little Rain said, "not just sleep and get fat."

That made White Cloud laugh. "You not get thin standing up," she said.

"Wait until you have bun in oven," Little Rain protested. "I will talk all times and say, 'Have seen White Cloud with huge belly? Never see such big belly.' "

The joking went on for a few more minutes, but, as the fire died, they gradually grew quiet and finally went to bed. The sky had cleared, and the stars drew nearer and sharper as the temperature dropped. Two owls in the woods called intermittently, their hooting softened by distance. A half moon swung up, crisp and clear. Somewhere back on the trail a lone wolf howled. The blustery wind slowed and died, and a dreaming silence slowly settled over the valley.

Caleb decided to watch from the shadows of the aspen grove. With help of the moonlight, he had a good view of the animals, all still grazing eagerly. The hair on the back of his neck lifted

185

briefly when White Cloud spoke quietly from behind him. "Is me."

"Damn," he said softly, loosening his grip on his rifle. "I wish you wouldn't sneak up on me like that."

"Lucky for you I good Arapaho," she said. "I have worry."

"About being a good Arapaho?"

"Smartass."

He raised his eyebrows. "Where did you learn to say that?"

"Foster told me it. He said when someone is know-everything, say *smartass* back." She tilted her head, apparently reading his expression. "Is something wrong?"

"Well, your ass is what you sit on, and 'smartass' means you think with what you sit on and not your brain."

"English a pain in what you sit on," she said. "Very strange language. Too many words." She shifted her grip on her Spencer. "I have worry."

"Tell me."

"How I cook in stove?"

Her question amused him, though he was careful not to show it. "Have you ever seen one?"

"No," she said.

"The stove is an iron box on short legs. Its top is flat so that skillets and pots can be placed on it. Inside the box there is a place where the wood burns to heat the top of the stove and the oven box beside the fire where things can be put to bake or roast. At the back of the stove there is a hole. A pipe goes from that hole to the chimney to take the smoke away."

"What is chimney?" she asked.

Before Caleb could answer, an arrow whizzed between them waist high and sank with a solid *thunk* into the trunk of the aspen under which they were standing. At the same moment one of the mules squealed in anger, the sound followed by a yell of pain.

Caleb and White Cloud dropped to their knees, staring over the low brush, rifles at the ready. Two dark figures rose out of the grass and ran towards the horses. Both mules were squealing now. Caleb and White Cloud fired, and the shadows vanished.

"I'll try to get between them and the woods. Shoot a little high," Caleb whispered and crept away.

A raider rose out of the grass and flung himself onto one of the Indian horses. The horse sprang forward, but White Cloud shot the thief off the animal. Four more figures jumped up and sprinted for the pines. Caleb raised himself in the grass just high enough to see the men running, but he held his fire.

Dil's voice rang out. "Heads down!" he shouted as he and Little Rain raced between the horses. By the time they were clear of the animals, the runners had vanished into the darkness. Caleb gathered the horses while the others stood facing the woods, guns at the ready. They fell back together and picketed the animals between the night fire and the stream. After Little Rain stoked up the fire and Foster, woken by the shooting, had joined them, White Cloud stood to speak.

"They will come again," she said solemnly, "maybe at daylight, maybe later. They try steal horses first, stop us running away. At daylight if they not come, we must gather the dead ones. Little Rain and I will say something to ease their journey."

"Where are they going?" Foster asked.

"To the next place," Little Rain told him.

"Where's that?"

"No one knows. It is going that is important."

"I've heard something about heaven," Foster said. "Somebody in a black coat talked about that once, but it seemed like you had an awful lot to do to get there."

"Not hard at all," White Cloud said. "Just die. Everything else is already done. Living and dying are like two sounds that

go together in a good way."

"Harmony," Dil said. "All the notes in harmony."

"Nobody comes back from heaven," Foster said.

"Nihoothoo book sometimes say one warrior did," White Cloud countered. "That's what my father told me."

Caleb had heard all he wanted to hear about the hereafter and getting there. He knew all he wanted to know about the *dying* part, and he was willing to go on waiting for the second part. "What can we do to ready ourselves for the next attack?"

The silence following his question lasted until he broke it. "I suggest we establish a perimeter a little closer to the water," he said, "using our packs and saddles to lie behind. Do you agree with that?"

"Well, we can't build a redoubt in the dark," Foster said.

"Good," Little Rain said, ruffling the boy's hair. "We will take all of the animals into the trees."

The sun had been up for some time before it reached the valley, but the group in the aspen grove had been awake since first light, lying behind the line of saddles and gear, rifles resting on the piles. They had taken turns cat napping until the light brought them to their feet. Foster was still asleep.

"He will sleep until sun over heads," Little Rain said with a smile, looking down at the boy.

"You could lie down again and sleep," Dil said, his concern obvious.

She tried to look irritated but did a poor job of it. "You worse than mother grouse. Fuss, fuss, fussing all times. Is all right, Dil. Is hokay."

"*Okay*," Dil said. "The word is *okay*."

"Let's water the animals," Caleb said. "We'll take them down two at a time. The rest of us will keep watch. Who wants the first go?"

"I'll take them," Dil said. "That leaves three active rifles."

"Remember to take Sheba and Joshua down together or Sheba may dunk you in the river—almost certainly if you take Joshua down with one of the mares."

Dil led the animals down two at a time and brought them back, leaving White Cloud to tie them to the trees again.

"What do you think?" Caleb asked, turning to her after she had tied the last animal. "Are they coming, or aren't they?"

"Not easy to know. They may have seen bad sign. If so, they go. Maybe they had whiskey and got drunk last night."

"Or maybe they are coming now," Caleb said sharply. "I don't like it. Perhaps we should pull stakes and get out of here. Would they follow us?"

Little Rain broke in, clearly annoyed. "You ask question with no answer."

"We can't keep the horses and mules tied all day to these trees with nothing to eat," Dil said. "I suggest we let them graze for an hour or so. Then pack up and leave."

"We look first for dead warriors," White Cloud said. "Cannot leave them on ground."

"Let's have a look, then," Caleb said.

Little Rain stayed with the sleeping Foster. The rest spread out and crisscrossed the area where the encounter took place. They found four dead men, one little more than a boy and one with gray hair. The sight of them roiled Caleb's insides, but he set his teeth and helped drag them to the edge of the aspen grove.

"We put them on raised place, like with others," White Cloud said quietly, glancing up at the trees. Caleb and Dil had brought axes with them, and White Cloud had brought elk hide straps that she and Little Rain had cut, stretched, and dried.

"We can't climb these trees. The limbs aren't strong enough to support us."

"Use Joshua," White Cloud said.

"We've got that block and tackle I bought at Fort Laramie," Caleb said. "I could stand on Josh's back, strap the top block to the tree, and haul the bodies up to where I can roll them onto the platform."

Dil nodded. "I'll go get it and bring it and Joshua back with me."

Caleb and White Cloud set at once to cutting down aspens. With Joshua to stand on, they soon had the frame in place. Once the dead men were hoisted even with the platform, Caleb lifted their legs and rolled them onto it. White Cloud began a low singing prayer. That ended, she turned and slid back to the ground.

Caleb recovered the block and tackle and followed suit. "I hope we don't have to do this again."

White Cloud said, "My father told me there will be no end to it ' 'til Kingdom Come.' I asked what *Kingdom Come* was, and he told me, 'Don't worry your head about it.' Do you know what it is?"

Caleb glanced at Dil, who looked as reluctant as he did to answer. Then Dil shrugged. "All right," he said, "let's see if I can explain it. Among the white people there's an idea that sometime the son of the Great Spirit will come down to earth, put an end to time, and take all the good people up to heaven with him."

"What about the rest?" White Cloud asked.

Dil sighed. "They are sent to another place called Hell where they are burned in fire forever."

Her eyes widened. "What kind of Great Spirit would do such a thing?"

"It's just a story," Caleb told her. "Not everybody believes it."

"Caleb Stone!" She pressed her palms to the sides of her

head. "Do you believe that?"

"No. Now, can we get on with what we're doing? And one thing more; if Foster hears this story from any of us, that person is in trouble with me."

"Too late, Captain," Dil said. "Some hell-fire preacher already got hold of him a couple of years back and gave him the whole shebang. The good news is Little Rain has been working on him and pretty well replaced it with the harmony idea."

Caleb opened his mouth to shout it was all damned foolishness, then clamped his jaws shut instead and strode away, pulling Joshua with him. Behind him, he heard White Cloud ask Dil, "Why he angry?"

"The war," Dil said. "It burned off any beliefs about hell, heaven, and harmony with it."

Chapter 22

The Shoshone war party found them two days later deep in the Webster Mountains, where they encountered some of the most difficult road conditions of the journey. White Cloud, riding rear guard, had turned her horse on the top of a saddle to look down at their back trail and saw a swirl of vultures rising from a bear carcass near the road, probably the same ones they had disturbed when they passed earlier. Within moments a group of horsemen rode hard around the turn in the road. White Cloud heeled her mare into a gallop.

"They are coming," she told Dil when she caught up with him.

"How many?"

"Eight. All in war paint."

Dil gave a shrill whistle that brought Caleb and Little Rain racing back from scout position. When White Cloud told them what she had seen, Caleb stood in his stirrups, taking in their options.

"Into those rocks," he said, pointing to the north side of the road, where a tumble of rocks lay. "Horses with us. White Cloud, make sure our friends don't get above us. Foster, you're with Dil and me."

They drove the pack animals around the rocks, likely from a landslide, that had left a crevice into which they chivvied the animals.

"Spread out. Pick your station," Caleb said. "Take your time

when the shooting starts. Put your sights on your target. Squeeze off the shot. Aim again, but don't come up in the same place twice. On my call, start shooting. Foster, down here beside me, and don't move until I tell you."

The words were hardly out of his mouth when eight riders in war paint came over the lip of the saddle at a scrambling run. They were hardened fighters armed with rifles, grim faced, with eagle feathers in their hair. Once over the saddle, they halted and took in their surroundings. One of them barked an order. All eight warriors dropped off their mounts and hit the ground running.

"Now!" Caleb shouted.

The first volley took two of the men down. The others, using their horses as cover, raced off the road and disappeared among the rocks and low evergreens.

"White Cloud," Caleb said quietly, "turn your back to the road. Keep your eyes on what's above us."

She carefully worked herself into a place that gave her the most open view of the brush and rocks above them, reloaded, and settled to watch.

"You want I shoot their horses?" Little Rain asked.

"No," Caleb said. "I'm hoping they'll break for them in an effort to get away. If they do, don't shoot them."

A bullet whined and knocked a chip out of the rock about a foot from Caleb's head, showering him with rock dust. "White Cloud," he said. "That came from behind me."

She laughed. "He mistake your head for rock."

Then rifles cracked, and bullets ricocheted all around them.

"They will come fast," White Cloud said.

The words had barely left her mouth when the remaining six fighters sprang out of their hiding places, yelling, and ran at Caleb and the others. Clambering over the rocks slowed them down, as did the loose scree that gave poor footing and made it

impossible for the attackers to aim and fire their weapons. Caleb, White Cloud, Little Rain, and Dil let loose withering fire, downing another warrior as four more dove for cover. *That's only five,* Caleb thought with a jolt of panic, just as the sixth man jumped down from above them. He landed a stride away from White Cloud, his knife raised to strike. She swung her rifle barrel at him, too late.

A shot rang out and the attacker's head exploded. The bullet slammed him sideways into the rock wall and spattered White Cloud with blood and brains. He bounced off the rocks and sprawled dead at White Cloud's feet. Next to Caleb, breathing hard, Little Rain lowered her Spencer.

The few warriors remaining slipped from sight, and an ominous silence fell.

Caleb swallowed hard. "White Cloud, Little Rain, put your backs together and keep looking. Make sure they don't come back at us."

He and Dil did the same. Caleb was never sure how long they waited, but then came a clatter of hooves on gravel and a series of sharp, brief yells. They sprang up and saw four riders, guns raised in defiance, plunge over the edge of the saddle. White Cloud ran to her mare, leaped on her back, and galloped out onto the road. She pulled up at the edge of the saddle and watched for several minutes, then nodded sharply as if satisfied.

"They are gone," she told the others when she returned to the rock pile. "The vultures fly up and go down again."

They found two dead Indians and one shot in the leg who had tried to hide under a shelf of rocks. The two women kicked his gun out of his hands, grabbed him by his feet, and dragged him out from under the rock shelf. Coming up to them, Dil looked at the man's wound and said, "Unless the bleeding is stopped, he will die."

194

White Cloud grabbed her rifle. "I will shoot him."

"No," Caleb said. "Dil, let's see how badly he's hurt."

Little Rain bent over the injured man. "Who are you?" she asked in Arapaho.

His hands flew up, and he grabbed her by the throat. White Cloud whipped her knife out of her belt and flung her full weight down on him, knocking Little Rain aside and driving the knife into his heart. She scrambled to her feet and helped Little Rain, who was choking and coughing, to sit.

"Lord A'mighty!" Foster cried. "I ain't never seen the equal of that!"

"If you're lucky, you won't again." Dil swept the boy up in his arm and carried him to the horses. "Get on Dakota. I'll pass up the lead rope. Take the string onto the road. And don't say anything to White Cloud about what just happened. Best if you forgot about it. If you want to talk about it, come to me. Understood?"

"Yes, but I reckon she saved Little Rain's life," Foster said as he climbed onto Dakota.

"She did. Here's the rope." Dil followed the pack animals out of the crevice and made sure Foster got them safely to the road.

Caleb followed in Dil's wake. "White Cloud is with her," he said. "She may have a sore throat for a while, but I'm fairly certain there's no permanent damage."

"Did you notice that you and I had to stop to think? White Cloud didn't. How do you figure?"

"I don't," Caleb said, "beyond guessing we would have had to live her life to do what she did."

"I told Foster not to talk to her about it."

"Just as well. How is he?"

"I think White Cloud is fast getting to be his hero."

"He could choose worse."

Gathered in the road, with Little Rain a bit hoarse and sore

195

around the neck but otherwise mostly over the experience, White Cloud broke the silence that had settled over them. "Cannot make platform for the dead ones from low brush," she said, then turned to Little Rain. "Can lay them out on rock or ledge?"

Little Rain nodded, as if it hurt to speak.

"Start with last one," White Cloud said. "Work fast; leave this place. Bad medicine here."

Caleb turned to Little Rain as well. "Why would you want to help the man who tried to throttle you get to heaven?"

"Ask White Cloud," she replied in a rough whisper.

"Warrior fought to last breath," White Cloud answered, as if any idiot should know that. "Is honorable to attack enemy with last breath. Little Rain is honored by his action. He shows he regards her as worthy of killing."

Realizing he had stumbled into a thorn bush, Caleb backed away quickly. It didn't help that Dil was grinning. "Then let's get to work," Caleb said, hoping to regain some face. "Little Rain, you and Foster stay with the animals."

After they finished the exhausting task of carrying the bodies through the jumble of rocks and lifting them onto the ledge they had chosen for the bier, White Cloud and Dil left. A short while later, White Cloud returned with Foster and Little Rain. Not pleased to see Foster exposed to the dead again, Caleb picked up the boy and would have turned him away from the ledge, but Little Rain shook her head. "There is life and there is death," she insisted, speaking with effort. "He must see."

Not fully convinced but unwilling to risk a quarrel, Caleb turned so that the boy could see the dead men and what the two women were doing. The ceremony was brief and conducted in Arapaho, the women taking turns speaking.

"Them wasn't Arapaho," Foster said when they all were moving away from the ledge.

"Not matter," White Cloud told him. "They are now free to

go to next place."

"What happens if someone dies alone?"

"Maybe his spirit will wander here for a while. Bad medicine."

"What's that mean?"

"Means not talk about it."

Foster subsided, grumbling.

"Boy never stops asking questions," White Cloud complained once they were under way again.

"It's one of the ways children learn," Caleb said. "By having questions answered, they gain knowledge and the confidence to go on asking more questions and learning about more things."

"I think Arapaho children are taught the things they need to know," White Cloud said. "That is enough."

Caleb almost said Arapaho children were born into a world much less complicated than a white child's world but stopped himself and said instead, "White children are taught for a long time. All can go for eight years and many for longer. Some will go for sixteen years."

Surprise widened White Cloud's eyes. "Foster does not seem slow as that."

"They're not slow. They have reading, writing, arithmetic, and geography to learn first. Later, they have history and more difficult arithmetic." Seeing her puzzled frown deepen, he decided to stop there.

"Did you go for a long time?" she asked.

"Yes, eighteen years in all. After that, I returned to work the farm until I joined the army to fight in the war."

He fell silent, absorbed in his own thoughts. Then White Cloud spoke. "Little Rain is helping Dil and Foster to talk in Arapaho. Foster is going fastest."

"Children learn languages faster than those who are grown up."

"Why?"

"I don't know; perhaps because they are still learning their own language. Can you remember learning to speak Arapaho?"

"No."

"I can't remember learning to speak English."

They were riding side by side through a narrow valley buried in pines and spruce. The air was redolent with the sharp, cleansing smell of pitch and pine needles. The sun was already behind the mountain in front of them. A soft wind drifted into the valley, and a fading golden light lit the road.

"Would someone want to learn Arapaho?" White Cloud asked after another long silence.

"Yes, someone would if he had a teacher."

She said something in Arapaho and translated, "That means, 'I ride horse.' "

And so, Caleb's lessons began. She turned out to be a tough teacher, not above poking him when he made a mistake. "You sound like idiot," she would say and was parsimonious in doling out praise. There were days when he decided he would quit, but White Cloud met that suggestion with steely-eyed rejection. "No talk, no blanket," was one of her responses. Others included, "Someone is much slower than Foster and Dil," and "Someone behaves like child needs whacking," dished out with a dressing of scorn that invariably made Caleb's face burn.

The mountains, although less daunting in appearance, tested them every day. Frequent rain showers turned low places in the clay and gravel road into a heavy, sticking mud that wearied the animals, softened their hooves, and made them short tempered. Within three wet days all the horses and mules bore kick and bite marks. The rough travel didn't improve the humans' dispositions either. Even the irrepressible Foster rode with his head hanging, refusing to be cheered up. A few times Dil snapped at Little Rain. White Cloud acquired a permanent scowl and a tongue like a razor. Caleb, under the burden of

language study, found a defense in refusing to speak to White Cloud, a strategy that temporarily put an end to her harassment.

CHAPTER 23

When a fair day came, it eased their stress, allowing them to travel with the sun all day long in its steady, spirit-lifting westward journey. Another balm was the mountain air and the sheer beauty of the land. More than once, the travelers came out of the many small valleys smothered in trees and climbed again, then emerged suddenly into the vast open vistas of the scrub-dotted mountains.

"Sometimes," Little Rain said to Caleb one morning as they took the lead, "someone wish we never get there but go on forever through mountains that never stop."

They were fording a shallow stream that flashed in the sunlight over a bed of multicolored stones. A small herd of elk that had paused to drink moved away slowly, showing little fear of the two people. A golden eagle hunted over their heads, and earlier they had seen two herds of mountain sheep on the high ridges north of the road.

"Your people moved a lot. Did you like that?" Caleb asked.

"Followed buffalo, but not so much now. Stay more to trap and trade, drink whiskey. Buffalo not so many. Nihoothoo hunt too many for their hides, leave rest to rot. Coyotes and vultures like, not the people."

"How do you feel about living on a ranch, living in a house? Does it trouble you?"

"Not if I have Dil," she said, then paused. "Well," she began again, "perhaps not know how to live in house. White Cloud is

afraid of stove."

"You will both learn in a week all there is to learn about living in a house," Caleb said. "And if you don't like it, Dil and I will have to move into a teepee. But it is much warmer in a house in winter."

"There is a word for what you are doing," she answered.

"Teasing," Caleb said, "to take away your fear."

She sighed. "I am having fear for other things more. I am having child and no women with children to tell me what to do. White Cloud knows only what I know. Not much."

"If things go well, Little Rain, we should be in Oregon in three moons, plenty of time before the baby comes. There will be women and doctors there."

She threw him a skeptical look. "Do not know about *doctors.*"

"They are men who are trained to help women have babies. There are also women, called midwives, who know how to help a woman have her baby. There are doctors and midwives where we are going."

"But I am Arapaho woman."

"All women have babies the same way, just as we all make babies the same way." He felt pleased to have thought of that.

"Do not want man helping me have baby," she said with finality.

"Doctor is better when you are sick and need medicine," Caleb said, responding to her unease. "You can have a midwife to help you when the baby comes."

Her face darkened. "Much strange thing to talk to man about having babies."

Caleb pretended he had misunderstood. "I'm not much help," he agreed. "But perhaps someone will think about what has been said."

"I will think about it. If someone has more to say I will listen."

A little ahead of them and up the mountain slope to their

right, a small herd of mule deer burst out of a stand of lodge-pole pine and sprang down the scree and across the road, closely followed by a mountain lion. The big cat slid to a stop in the scree, snarling in disgust as its faster prey retreated, its tail slashing.

"Shirt for Foster." Little Rain raised her rifle to her shoulder and shot the beast through its neck, killing it instantly.

He marveled at the swiftness of her reaction to the sudden appearance of the deer herd and the mountain lion. White Cloud would have done the same things, Caleb realized. He watched Little Rain drop to the ground, her knife already in her hand to skin her kill, and thought the two Indian women were perfectly integrated with the endless flow of life.

They made camp late that afternoon and let the animals graze while they busied themselves with various tasks. Little Rain's cougar skin had to be scraped to rid it of traces of fat and everything else, then washed thoroughly and left to dry. Caleb was mending harness by the campfire when Dil's shout broke the gathering twilight calm. "Don't move!"

Startled, Caleb looked up. Foster knelt at the edge of the clearing, a wolf crouched in front of him as if ready to spring.

As Dil ran toward him, gun drawn, Foster jumped up and faced Dil, arms outspread. "Don't shoot!" he cried. "It ain't a wolf. He's some new kind of critter."

The wolf, or dog, or whatever it was, vanished into the woods.

Dil holstered his revolver. "Lord in Heaven, Foster! You looking to get yourself killed?"

By this time, the women had come at a run, weapons in hand. Foster wore a look of stubborn resolve that would have done credit to Horatio. "I ain't done nothing," he protested as the adults surrounded him. "I was only giving him chunks of pemmican. He was looking peckish."

"That critter weighed a hundred pounds if he weighed an ounce," Dil said. "It looked like a wolf to me."

"He don't act like no wolf," the boy insisted. "Him and me been getting to know one another ever since that dust-up with the war party. He's been trailing us for days. I think he's lonely."

White Cloud gripped her rifle tighter. "I will shoot it."

Foster drew himself up to his full height. "Nobody ain't going to shoot him, y'all hear me? That there's my friend. He's gentle as a kitten. I ain't seen no bad in him, aside from being a mite people-shy."

The grown-ups looked at Foster, then at one another. "Look after the fire," Little Rain told him. "Go."

The boy hesitated for a moment and then went.

Caleb felt guilty and wanted to be angry. "I thought we were looking after this child."

"Too many cooks spoil the broth," Dil said.

"What this have to do with cooks?" White Cloud demanded.

"All of us were responsible for Foster, and none of us was watching him," Caleb told her.

Little Rain looked like she might cry. "When we not see him, we ask where he is."

Caleb sighed. "What about the wolf—if it is a wolf?"

"Too big for a coyote, that's for sure. Maybe a wolf/dog cross breed," Dil said. "Now I think about it, the thing's coat was gray all right, but it looked thicker than the usual wolf pelt."

"I mean, what are we going to do about it?"

"This one has not had much for himself," Little Rain said. "I say we make sure we near him when he meets wild dog."

"Dogs around camp are good at warning if something comes at night," White Cloud added, though she didn't exactly sound enthusiastic.

"Let's sleep on it," Dil said.

Little Rain glared at him. "I not want to sleep on dog!"

"My father used to say that," White Cloud told her. "It means he hope something would go away."

For the next two nights, the animal did not appear, perhaps because Foster was never allowed out of the sight of one of the adults. Not seeing the animal was a serious letdown for the boy, and while he was too stoic to cry, he looked glum as a rain cloud.

"His chin drag on ground," Little Rain told White Cloud, who told it to Caleb, who asked Dil what he thought they should do but got no satisfactory answer. In an effort to cheer him up, Caleb asked what he might like to name the beast. With a defiant set to his jaw, Foster said, "I like Wolf for a name."

"Sounds right," Caleb answered, all the while hoping they never saw the thing again.

On the third night they camped in a small valley with a cheerfully bubbling stream running through it. It had been a bright, cool day with a scattering of clouds, but the trail was washed out in spots, making the going slow and treacherous for the animals. In many places, past storms had blown shallow-rooted lodgepole pines across their path. By the time they camped, the adults were worn out. Foster had a chance to practice his fishing skills, and finding he could catch nearly every fish he tickled cheered him considerably, much to the grown-ups' relief. Despite their fatigue, everyone went to bed in better spirits than they had enjoyed since seeing Foster's wolf.

A half moon made its appearance over the dark peaks and had not yet climbed high when the silence of the camp was ripped apart by snarling and growling, mingled with the roar of an angry grizzly that had followed its nose into their camp, seeking horse steak and left-over fried elk. In varying degrees of undress and struggling to full wakefulness, Caleb and the other three adults scrambled out of their blankets and into the open,

carrying their guns. The grizzly was facing off with Foster's wolf, and both animals bore the marks of combat.

Little Rain grabbed Foster as he tried to run toward the battle. The hobbled pack animals were hopping away, striving to put as much distance as possible between themselves and the melee as it made its loud and bloody way toward the campfire. The wolf appeared equally determined to stop the bear and was taking the fight to the larger animal, despite the odds against him.

"Where's everybody?" Caleb called, as his eyes adjusted to the meager light of the moon and he tried to make sense of what was happening. White Cloud and Dil answered "Here," a few yards to Caleb's left. Caleb had thought to get between the bear and the mules and horses, but clearly that was not where the wolf-and-bear fight was headed.

"I can't get in a shot," Dil shouted. "That dog thing's circling the bear and rushing it too fast."

White Cloud and Caleb started toward the animals, just as Little Rain screamed, "No, Foster, no!"

The boy had broken free and was racing toward the grizzly, shouting the wolf's name. He was less than twenty-five yards from the battling animals, and both had seen him coming. With a bellow of anger, the bear turned toward Foster. The wolf, catching sight of the boy, plunged between him and the grizzly and spun around to meet it. The grizzly rose and swung one of its massive paws, striking the wolf a raking blow just in back of a shoulder. The bear's claws ripped through flesh and sent the wolf flying, end over end, giving White Cloud time to snatch Foster out of danger.

The bear, finding its new target gone, swung away toward the remains of the campfire. An instant later three guns barked. The bear crumpled and then lifted its front quarters off the ground, roaring with pain and rage. Dil thrust his revolver at arm's

length a foot from the bear's ear and shot it in the head. The huge animal collapsed.

"Too bad we shoot so many times," White Cloud said, setting the safety on her rifle. "Much work sewing up holes."

Foster would not be comforted until he had seen the wolf and made sure it was not dead. They all trooped over to where it lay in a bloody, crumpled heap.

"Wolf," Foster said quietly.

The wolf, or dog, or whatever raised its head a bit, then dropped it.

"You ain't dead!" the boy shouted. "I knowed no bear could lick him." He grabbed Little Rain by the arm, and she let him pull her closer to the fallen hero. The wolf greeted her with a deep-chest growl.

"He's a mite shy," Foster said, pulling free from Little Rain's grip. He stepped nearer the animal, which gave a soft whine of welcome.

"Too bad," White Cloud said. "Have not eaten dog for long time."

Her comment made Little Rain laugh, but not the men and certainly not Foster, who threatened to walk clear back to the Missouri if there was any more talk of eating Wolf.

White Cloud and Little Rain drew together and began talking in Arapaho—about how to patch up the dog, Caleb guessed. "You know what's going to happen don't you," he said quietly to Dil. "We're adding that thing to the company."

"That's right, and I've learned enough to know those two"— Dil nodded at the women—"are discussing how to go about it."

Foster sat on his heels close to the dog's head, telling him he was going to be all right, that Dil was one almighty fine sawbones. A few minutes later, Little Rain hurried off toward the fire and began restoring it to life. White Cloud walked up to Dil and Caleb. "Caleb Stone, bring buffalo robe. Dil, bring

ether, medicines. I will bring needles and thread. Be quick. Wolf soon bleed out."

When they had all gathered near the beast, Little Rain said to Foster, "Keep talking to him. We will throw robe over him, put him to sleep, stop bleeding, sew cuts."

"Will Wolf die?"

"Not know," she said. "Wolf hurt bad. You be brave and not shout. Yes?"

"Yes," the boy said. "Can I stay near him?"

"If you be quiet," White Cloud told him.

The fire had blazed up and was casting its flickering light across them. Turning to the men, White Cloud said, "Unroll buffalo robe. Little Rain and Caleb, throw over wolf, then hold down. I will hold jaw. Dil give ether on nose. Then Little Rain, Dil, and I work fast. Caleb, you hold ether, give more if wolf wake."

"I don't—" Caleb began.

"Not hear about, 'I don't.' Nobody else to do it. Start now."

Easier said than done. As damaged as he was, Wolf did not go down easily. A hundred and thirty pounds of bone and muscle did not want the robe on him, and the animal tried with every ounce of his strength to stand up and slash Caleb and Little Rain into ribbons. Wolf growled and snarled, and, despite his promise, Foster screamed, "Don't hurt him! Don't hurt him!"

White Cloud had fashioned a loop from a leather strap, intending to slip it over the dog's muzzle and pull it tight. She saw her chance and took it, shouting Dil's name as she threw an arm around the muzzled animal's head. Dil pressed the rag over the dog's nose, and the next moment Wolf collapsed like a deflated balloon.

"Now carry him to the fire," Dil said. "We need more light."

The bear had raked Wolf's side cruelly, exposing his ribs in places along with the shoulder bones. When the animal was laid

out, Dil said, "Now we wash the wounds with soap and water and hope."

"Then we sew, and hope he has hide enough to cover holes," White Cloud said.

Dil swiftly finished examining his patient. "No broken bones, and no arteries severed. Wolf might live."

Silence fell as they went to work, first tying off the torn veins at Dil's direction. Then the patching began. They threw the last of the wood on the fire before they were done, and Foster had long since stopped shouting. He lay on the ground near the fire, his head on an outstretched arm, exhausted. Caleb had given the dog ether four times to keep him sedated. Toward the end, the horses and mules worked themselves closer to the fire as if attracted to the warmth and light. They stood on the outskirts, alternately dozing and watching, ears pricked.

"We're going to have to tie him up," Dil said when they were finished. "He'll drag himself into the woods otherwise, first chance he gets." He and the women were bloody to their elbows. Caleb walked them to the stream, carrying his rifle. When they returned, Little Rain shook Foster awake, told him that Wolf would live, and sent him to bed.

"Must also make travois if we take Wolf with us," White Cloud said.

"Anyone think we shouldn't?" Dil asked. The others all said no, emphatically.

"Plenty trees," White Cloud said. "Will make one in morning. Which horse will pull?"

Everyone looked at Caleb. "It should be one of the pack horses," he said quickly.

They kept looking at him.

"You want Joshua to do it," he said.

Dil guessed at the source of Caleb's reluctance and addressed the women. "Could he still ride the mule?"

"I could. Little Rain could," White Cloud said. "We ride one leg crossed most times."

"I gather that's a no," Caleb said, "because of the poles."

"You ride my horse," Little Rain said. "I ride Joshua."

"Your horse has never been broken to a bridle," Caleb said. "I'll have to ride Sheba, and your horse will carry Sheba's packs."

Little Rain looked worried. "She not strong as Sheba."

"Also, cannot put her on lead rope," White Cloud added. "She fight bridle."

"Use the hackamore," Dil suggested.

"Never had a strap over back and around belly," White Cloud said.

Caleb fought to suppress his impatience. "We'll put the straps and bags on her, and let's see what happens. Now let's get some sleep."

Once they were alone together, unrolling their bedding, White Cloud said, "Someone, maybe, is angry."

Caleb had learned that when the word *someone* appeared in her speech, she was being serious, and he should tread carefully. "Someone thinks he had reason to be. Perhaps someone else was making trouble when she didn't have to."

"I am worrying about horse. I am only one to ride her. Frightens easy if I not there. Also, bad temper."

"You and the horse," he said, trying to make her smile.

She halted in her task. "You see any difference?"

"Yes. You are the first thing I look for when I wake up. Not your horse. I would rather kiss you than the horse. You have no tail. I don't love your horse. Horse never asks mean questions."

"I worry horse buck, kick, try to throw off packs. Hurt herself." Abruptly, White Cloud collapsed on the half-opened bedroll, her shoulders shaking as she wept without sound.

Caleb had seldom seen her cry. For a few moments, he stood

frozen in place, unable to think what to do. Then he dropped to his knees and gathered her in his arms. "White Cloud, you will ride your horse. I will ride one of the Fort Laramie horses. We will spread its packs among all of us. You will take something small for Daisy."

Surprise made her raise her wet face from her hands. "Who Daisy?"

"Your horse. She has markings like a daisy, a flower. I always think of one when I see her. You love her, don't you?"

She wiped her cheeks. "Can't love a horse," she said.

"But you do love her. Would you like her to be called Daisy?"

She stood very straight, but Caleb could tell when she spoke that she was barely holding back more tears. "Arapaho call horse, horse," she said flatly.

"What if you *want* to call her Daisy?"

She stared into the darkness and then turned to look at Caleb. "I will call her *Notoone*," she said. "My daughter."

"A beautiful name." Caleb laid his hands on her arms. "It is all right for you to love her."

"It feel very strange, Caleb Stone, to give horse a name and say, 'I love her.' It might be like putting one foot in your world. Perhaps I lose my world."

"You will never lose your world, White Cloud. I love you, and you are Arapaho, and you love me. We have already stepped into one another's worlds. We now have two worlds to travel in."

"You are strange man, Caleb Stone. Not like any I have known, not even my father."

"And I have never known a woman like you, White Cloud. I am very lucky to have found you."

Before getting started the next morning, Caleb and Dil cut down and limbed two young lodgepole pines, each about fifteen feet long.

"Should have willow for poles," Little Rain said, "or maybe from stronger tree with leaves."

"This will do," White Cloud said, "but sticky water no help."

"It's pitch," Dil said, "and hard to get off your hands and clothes."

Fortunately, there were only a few places near the tops of the poles where pitch oozed from cut-off limbs. The women crossed the poles about four feet from their thinner ends and tied them in place with rawhide straps. At the thicker bottom ends, White Cloud pulled the poles apart about three feet, and Little Rain snapped a cross-piece of aspen into place.

"Now we tie elk hide above aspen wood and make place to fasten Wolf," White Cloud said. "Not easy to do, I think."

No one else did either, having seen earlier the animal's snarling, growling efforts to free himself from his restraints. But eventually they broke camp and slung the packs on the animals, and Joshua was hitched to the travois. He did not like the looks of the poles, but with Caleb's coaxing, he finally stood still and allowed Little Rain to attach them to the saddle's pommel. The women then strapped a buffalo hide between the poles and the mule's back.

Loading Wolf onto the travois was only accomplished after White Cloud strapped his jaws shut. That done, Foster gave instructions, and the four adults hoisted Wolf, growling like a thunderhead, onto the travois and tied him down. Turning his head to examine his passenger, Joshua snorted in obvious disgust but appeared to regard it as beneath him to do anything about it.

Caleb came in for a lot of ribbing by the women when he demanded they put together a substitute saddle and strap it around his horse's middle. Calling him something he didn't recognize in Arapaho, they threw a rectangle of bearskin over the horse's back and strapped it down. Foster, serving as transla-

tor, broke out laughing. "That there's *old man* they're calling you, Captain. Saying, 'Old man need something soft for his ass.' They didn't know I know that word, but I do."

"Shame on you," Caleb said, turning toward White Cloud and Little Rain, "talking like that in front of this boy."

That got the women and Dil laughing, too, and even Caleb couldn't keep his face straight.

"I'm going to get on this horse," he said bravely, standing beside the big bay with no stirrups, "and anyone laughing at me gets double watch duty tonight."

"You just go right ahead, Captain," Foster said. "We won't even be looking."

"Go," White Cloud said. "Nobody sees."

Caleb grasped the belly strap over the bear skin and started to pull himself up, ready to throw his right leg over the animal's back. "No do!" White Cloud called, too late. A moment later Caleb was sitting on the ground.

"Strap slide around," White Cloud said.

"Strap slide around," Caleb repeated between his teeth.

This time he grasped the reins and the bay's mane in his left hand, rested his right hand on the bear skin, and vaulted onto the improvised saddle.

White Cloud passed him his rifle, a wide grin on her face. "You do that better by and by."

And with that, they got under way.

The day had broken fair, and a pair of bald eagles circled overhead as they left the camp, which the two women agreed was good medicine. The winds that had hampered them on previous days were quiet, and as they climbed out of the small valley, mountain quail and flocks of migrating songbirds rose around them. Elk and deer trotted away from them, and, after an hour's ride or so, White Cloud shot a yearling elk.

"Wolf need raw meat," she said when Caleb complained that

they had plenty of dried meat.

Being tied down and covered with a mountain lion skin had a mollifying effect on Wolf. Foster took on the job of watering and feeding him. When the going was slow, the rest of the group took turns walking beside the travois, talking to Wolf and putting their hands on the cat skin. The effects of the treatment were better than they had hoped. On the first day, Wolf had snarled and growled at anyone but Foster who came near him. On the second day, he only growled a little. By the third day, he greeted them all with the soft whining he used to welcome Foster.

That evening during dinner, Foster asked when they could take Wolf off the travois.

"I think in the morning," Caleb said, "but Foster, if he's put on his feet, he will most likely head for the woods."

"There's also the problem of his stitches," Dil said. "He can't get at them, tied down as he is, but soon as he can, he'll start gnawing at them and the bandages."

"Put strap around his neck and tie him to mule's pommel," White Cloud suggested. "As for chewing, I think Wolf is like dog. Let him lick and chew."

In the morning, they gathered at the travois, Dil with his gun drawn. It had taken a while, but Foster finally gave in and agreed that if Wolf attacked one of them, Dil would shoot him.

Things got off to a good start when Wolf greeted them with a whine instead of a snarl. The women began undoing the straps holding him, pausing after each was removed to see what Wolf might do. He did nothing even when the last one came off.

"Now we see," White Cloud said, preparing to lift away the cougar skin. The sound of Dil cocking his revolver sounded loud in the morning air.

Slowly, White Cloud slid the cat skin off. "Wolf," Foster said,

stepping nearer the big animal, "we're getting you off there. You hear me?"

Little Rain caught her breath and put her hand over her mouth. "I always say that to him when scolding."

Wolf cocked an ear and watched the boy out of the corner of his eye. "Y'all come and do it," Foster said, turning to the group behind him. No one rushed forward.

"Caleb Stone," White Cloud said, "it is a good day to die. Come."

Wondering why on earth he was doing it, Caleb stepped up beside her. As they drew closer, taking Foster's place, Wolf lifted his head enough to look at them.

"Wolf," Caleb said quietly, "we're not going to hurt you any more than we have to."

He bent over and began pushing his hand under the dog's shoulders. White Cloud did the same with its hindquarters. Wolf made no protest, gave no warning growl.

"Maybe we can't lift him very high," White Cloud said. "I think get on knees."

They arranged themselves so they could lift Wolf just enough to clear the sides of the travois and laid him on the ground.

"What now?" Caleb asked.

"Water and meat, I think," Dil said.

Little Rain stepped away and came back with a hunk of elk in a tin pan. "Can't believe we give you meat," she said. Foster arrived in her wake, another pan in hand.

"Water," Foster said.

Dil kept his revolver leveled at the huge animal as Foster and Little Rain placed the pans in front of Wolf. The beast struggled to his feet as soon as the water and meat arrived, but it was clearly a painful undertaking. Several times he paused, back arched and head down, uttering half-choked yelps. Once upright, however, he forced himself forward and drank thirstily.

The meat went down in large chunks, and he licked the blood out of the pan.

"That there's some critter," Foster said in admiration.

Walking proved less of a success than feeding. Wolf could only hitch along in small steps, head down and in obvious pain. He defecated but had trouble kicking back gravel to bury his leavings.

Dil gave voice to the obvious. "He's not going to be able to keep up on his feet."

"I'll bring in Joshua," Caleb said. "White Cloud, Little Rain, get the travois ready. Foster, tell Wolf we've got to pick him up."

No one thought Caleb was joking. When the travois was ready, Caleb, White Cloud, and Little Rain picked up Wolf and eased him back onto the elk hide bed, putting Wolf's head about level with the mule's belly.

"You get some rest, you hear me?" Foster told the animal in an authoritative voice, resting a hand on his head. "And, Lord above, don't make no move to jump out of there."

For the next four days, Wolf rode in his elk-hide sling and practiced walking during the evenings. He seemed also to have lost whatever fear or loathing he had initially for people, because he now ate with them, sat down beside Foster at the fire before the boy was sent to bed, and stayed up most of the night, moving around the camp and the horses and mules as if he'd taken on the job of watchman.

"First night I not very easy to have that wolf watching with me," White Cloud told Caleb the fourth morning. "Now I like. He is good company. Is quiet, not like someone."

"Someone may just stop talking to someone. I agree about Wolf. Nothing can sneak up on you when he's there."

On the fifth day, they came out of the mountains and stopped to camp near a bright stream and open area of grass. Wolf stood up in the travois, leaped down, gave himself a vigorous shake,

and trotted off to the stream to drink with Foster running along beside him.

"Well," Caleb said to White Cloud as he dismounted from the bay, "he'll either take to the woods or not. If he goes, Foster's going to be broken up."

"I think it stay," she answered, looking toward the boy and the wolf. "Sometimes, two want to be one even if different."

"Yes," Caleb said. "Look at us."

CHAPTER 24

Wolf did not run off. In fact, he seemed to feel very close to Foster and whenever he wasn't on lead point, a post he treated as his responsibility, he was at Foster's side. His relationship with the others was a matter of conjecture and a frequent subject of discussion over evening meals.

"He's a one-man wolf," was Dil's assessment.

It was true that while Wolf allowed Foster to ride on him, wrestle with him, and even go to sleep with his head on the animal's side, fully healed now, he avoided attempts by the others to touch him. If one of them bent to stroke him, he would move just enough to avoid the contact when the hand came down.

"Is strange," White Cloud said. "One moment he there, next moment he not."

Neither would he accept food from any hand but Foster's, a trait that annoyed Little Rain. Unlike the others, she did not stop trying to feed him. If she dropped meat on the ground, he would take it at once, swallow it, and look up to see if any more was coming. If not, he would drift away.

On the march, he trotted beside whoever was in the lead position, alert and observant. He always knew when other animals were near, well ahead of his human companion. He ignored most of the animals they encountered, but, if he scented bear, the hair on the back of his neck flared, and no amount of calling him back could stop him from seeing the bear off no

matter how big it was. Even the grizzlies picked up their pace with Wolf at their heels, not wanting to waste time and energy swatting him.

"One of these days," White Cloud said darkly, "comes she bear with cubs. Then we will see who runs."

It happened the next day in the middle of a cloudburst. Caleb, wrapped in his waterproof with the rain pouring off the brim of his hat, came around a corner and saw a black bear with two cubs crossing the track twenty yards in front of them. The mother bear saw Caleb at the same time and was hurrying her cubs along when she looked again and spotted Wolf. With a bellow, she raced toward him. Caleb, swearing a blue streak at having to get wet, yanked his rifle out of its scabbard.

"Run, Wolf!" he shouted, but he could have saved his breath. Wolf had already read the situation and was belting back the way they'd come with the bear in roaring pursuit.

Caleb pulled Joshua around and hurried him back along the trail. As he rounded the corner he heard everyone shouting, and the pack horses squealing. Little Rain was picking herself out of a puddle, rifle in hand, turning the air blue in Arapaho. Wolf had run straight through the pack train, the bear crowding him hard. White Cloud had her rifle out, but Daughter had decided anywhere was better than here and was twisting and bucking and fighting her hackamore in an effort to run.

The bear, apparently deciding she had rid herself and the cubs of the wolf, turned and ran back to reach them. She loped through the pack train again, muttering and woofing as she went. Joshua almost ran into her but saved the day by jumping right over the bear, who was so focused on reaching her cubs, she didn't even pause to take a swipe at him.

"I have been to war and back," Dil said when they had settled the animals and were sitting on their horses—Little Rain had remounted, muddy and soaked to the skin—talking over what

had happened. "But I never saw anything to beat that."

"I ain't been to war," Foster piped, "but I've seen some things, and I got to agree with Dil. That was a Slippity Sam Patch of a thing going and coming. Where's Wolf?"

"He will come back or he won't," White Cloud said.

"He will come back, Foster," Little Rain told him. Caleb rummaged a blanket and waterproof out of the baggage and helped her wrap herself in them. They got under way again, the rain still with them. Caleb returned to the lead and had gone less than a mile when Wolf appeared beside him. The big animal stopped to give himself a short, sharp shake and resumed his point position, glancing up with his tongue lolling out rakishly, as if to say, "That was fun, wasn't it?"

The rain lifted early in the afternoon while they were crossing a short, grassy plateau half a dozen acres in size, giving Caleb the excuse he was looking for to call a halt and bringing a shaky cheer from the group. While they set up camp and hobbled the animals, Wolf led Foster to a large spring bubbling up cheerfully from the foot of a mossy granite outcrop at the north end of the plateau. The flow was strong enough to support a small stream that ran close to the rock wall for fifty yards before veering toward the granite face and plunging into a deep fissure in the stone.

"Me first," Little Rain cried when Foster came back with his report. "I am mud in all places."

She went off with soap and a change of clothes, followed by ribald calls from White Cloud. When Caleb said White Cloud might hurt Little Rain's feelings, she waved him away with a shout of laughter. "All things are part of life, Caleb Stone. You know this. Do not make long face."

To everyone's surprise, Wolf loped after Little Rain, and it soon became clear that no one could leave the group alone without him accompanying them.

219

Towards sunset, two men on mules with three pack mules in tow came up the track, travelling east. They pulled off the road and dismounted, then headed towards the camp on foot. Both were large and bearded, wearing tall-crowned, wide-brimmed hats, shirts and leggings of tanned hide, and open wolf-skin jackets.

"Howdy," the older stranger said. "My name's Dawson Ring." He jerked his thumb toward the other man. "This here's Birchard McBride. We're trappers, heading for the Green River country. Come spring we'll cross on towards Independence. You come from that way?"

"That's right," Caleb said. He had gotten to his feet, holding his rifle. The two strangers each carried Sharps rifles. Dil and the women were likewise on their feet, guns in hand, not yet leveled but ready for any trouble.

McBride eyed them. "I'd gather," he said, "you've had some unsociable encounters with strangers as you've come along." Caleb spotted a wide grin amid the fellow's wiry, red beard.

"You could say that," Dil replied. "My name is Dil, he's Captain Caleb Stone, the boy is Foster Wiggins, the woman to my left is Little Rain, and the other woman is White Cloud. I would have thought the Green River country was pretty well trapped out."

"There's scarcely a beaver left in the whole place," Ring agreed, "but we'll collect some buffalo hides before the snows get too deep. Then we'll lay out lines for otter, mink, bobcat, fox, and wolf. Come spring, we'll load up on more buff hides and then head for the Missouri."

"We both got families," McBride added, "but the wandering bug bit us years back. We stick to this life even if it don't do much more than keep us from starving." He turned toward the mules and saw Wolf standing close, guarding the pack animals. "Lord Jesus and Mother Mary," he said and swung up his rifle.

"That there's my dog!" Foster shouted, darting past the men and running to Wolf. McBride and Ring both looked at Caleb.

"If that's not a wolf, I never seen one," Ring said, a trace of aggression in his voice. McBride's rifle was on its way to shoulder height.

"Stop!" White Cloud said.

The men turned to look at her and saw the business end of her Spencer.

McBride scowled. "I don't take to being told that by a red Indian, especially a squaw."

"Lower rifle or we bury you where you fall," she said in a steely voice. Caleb, Dil, and Little Rain each leveled their guns at the strangers.

"All right," McBride said, taking one hand off his rifle, "but you can't make a pet of a wolf. He'll kill that boy one of these days."

"We think there's a lot of dog in him," Dil said, attempting to calm the waters.

"We'll move on," Ring said, still scowling. "This ain't the place for us."

The two men went back to their mules, making a wide detour around Wolf and Foster. Wolf never took his eyes off them. White Cloud dropped her rifle into the crook of her left arm and watched them out of sight.

"Why ain't it the place for 'em?" Foster asked.

"They follow different trail," Little Rain said.

Caleb and Dil looked at one another. "Hadn't occurred to me," Caleb said. "Do you think so?"

"It happens," Dil said. "I saw a lot of it in the hospitals. It got so it didn't even seem strange to me."

"In villages, not all men follow the warrior way. They are not sent away," Little Rain said.

Caleb found it hard to talk about the subject. "Among our

221

people, men and women try to hide it. Often, they go as young people to cities to find others like them."

"Nihoothoos," White Cloud said in disgust. "Always make easy things not easy."

Three days later, they came out of the Webster Mountains into a high, open, semi-arid country where the grassland was dotted with cactus, sagebrush, tumbleweeds, pinyon pine, and juniper. Over this open, rolling land, they made good time. Almost fully healed now, Wolf trotted happily ahead, his long strides eating up the miles and setting a stiff pace for the horses.

Every evening, they camped by streams where Foster was in fisherman's heaven, and they ate fried trout every night. Little Rain's waist was expanding, and she had to make regular adjustments in her clothes, a visible sign of the child's presence that made Dil a happy man. Unfortunately, White Cloud did not share in the general upwelling of good spirits.

On their second night out of the mountains, Caleb tentatively approached the issue. "Are you feeling at all ill?"

"No," was her answer.

"Someone thinks something is not all right," he said.

"Some other person thinks others should mind their own business," she snapped back.

So much for the circuitous route. "I think it is my business. Lying with your back to me isn't going to solve this problem. Besides, I like looking at your face."

"Sometimes you have said other side looks nice."

He found that an encouraging response. "Roll over," he said. "Don't be a coward."

Saying that was taking advantage and probably unfair. Nothing bothered her as much as having her bravery questioned. She flew around, kicking off the buffalo robe and sitting up, shoulders squared.

"I not afraid," she said, her eyes boring into his.

"That's better." He lay back and folded his hands behind his head. "Now we can talk."

"Not want to talk. Want to sleep."

"What's wrong? Stop saying *nothing.*"

"Why I not have bun in oven?"

"Pregnant," Caleb responded. "The word is *pregnant.*"

He was stalling and knew it, but he was at a loss. He had wondered why the other men she'd been with had not made her pregnant but didn't want to bring that up.

"Why I not pregnant?" she asked.

"Have you ever been pregnant?"

Her shoulders slumped. "One time, but went to old woman who gave me something that made me very sick. Bleed and no longer pregnant."

He sat up and put her arms around her. "This is something I don't know much about. I remember hearing it said a few times that when a woman wants a baby very much, sometimes it is very hard for her to become pregnant. Do you want a baby very much?"

"I want us to have baby. Yes. Little Rain is pregnant. Millicent True will have baby. Only I don't. What if I can't?"

"It's much too soon to ask that," Caleb said. "But if you couldn't, I would love you just as much. You are the person I want to be with. If you have a child, I would love it. But I have seen too much for too long to wish for a child to come into this world. I want to live in peace and happiness with you. That's all."

She pulled away enough to cup his face in both hands and gaze into his eyes. "Are you sure you speak truth, Caleb Stone?"

"Yes, I am certain."

A few days later they reached Fort Hall only to find it deserted, except for a few yapping dogs and an ancient Indian woman wrapped in a faded red blanket, sitting in front of her

teepee door, smoking a pipe. The dogs took one look at Wolf and vanished. White Cloud and Little Rain got off their horses, took a large slab of elk meat out of the packs, and went to talk with the old woman.

"Three days back on trail," White Cloud said when she returned to Caleb. "There is trading place in Camp Connor, near place of bubbling water."

"It's called Soda Springs," Caleb said. "Indians have gone there forever to drink the warm waters and bathe. The springs have minerals in them that make them bubble and fizz."

"What's fizz?" Foster asked.

"Bubbles of air form in the water, rise to the top, and make a hissing sound when they pop," Dil said.

"I like have a warm bath," Little Rain said.

White Cloud sighed. "Probably too many Nihoothoos."

"We should talk more about this," Caleb said, "but I don't want to camp here. The Snake River is in front of us, and it will have smaller streams feeding it. I suggest we go on a few miles."

Foster looked disappointed. "Why can't we just camp here and start for Soda Springs in the morning?"

"Cholera, for a start," Dil said. "Any water around here is not likely to be fit to drink or even wash in."

"It sounds like fun, I know," Caleb said to Foster but also thinking about White Cloud and Little Rain. "But there are things we need to discuss." He could tell the women wanted to see the springs, and the possibility of a warm bath exerted a powerful pull. Nevertheless, they bit their tongues and put heels to their horses. Foster sulked for a bit, but a couple of miles on Wolf rousted a bull moose out of a stand of spruce trees and ran him across the trail right in front of Foster, who whooped in delight.

For a moment, it looked as if Wolf might overtake the moose, but then the huge animal laid its antlers back on its shoulders,

lengthened its stride, and ran away from its pursuer. Wolf loped back with his tongue out, looking exceedingly pleased with himself. The episode lifted everyone's spirits, and, soon after, they found a grassy area with a small stream. Once off Dakota, Foster grabbed his fishing sack and set off to catch some trout.

"Time to talk," White Cloud said, when their supper of elk steaks and fish was ready and everyone was gathered around the fire.

Caleb looked at each person in turn. "Here's how I see it. It's around sixty miles to Soda Springs. That means three days out and three back. Counting the two days we'll probably stay there, we'll lose nearly a week of traveling time."

"How far is it to Fort Boise?" Dil asked.

"From Fort Hall, it's around two hundred and forty or fifty miles."

"That is fourteen suns," White Cloud said.

"How far to the valley where we go from Fort Boise?" Little Rain asked.

"Much further; a day or two over four hundred miles," Caleb replied.

"Twenty more days and fourteen. More than a moon. Do we have more mountains?"

"After Fort Boise, we have the Blue Mountains."

"Snow," Dil said.

"Cannot spare a week to see bubbling waters," Little Rain said quietly.

"Are we agreed?" Caleb asked.

White Cloud frowned. "There is more to say now."

"Let's hear it," Caleb said, knowing the *it* would not be good.

"What if, as we heard from old woman, the Shoshone and Bannock warriors have put on war paint and are raiding wagon trains along the Snake River valley?"

"What is our trail to Fort Hall?" Little Rain asked.

"It's difficult even without raids," Caleb said, weighing White Cloud's question. "Crossing the Snake River, as we must, more than once. Judging from what I have read, it will be difficult."

"We will swim horses. Have done that," White Cloud said.

"Little Rain, how are you feeling?" Caleb asked. "Dil says you're all right, but your temper isn't getting any better."

"Someone may feel sick in morning again," she said, sounding glad to be asked. "Have to get off horse more often and wake more at night for same thing. Tired more. Belly and others getting bigger."

"I can't see you fording rivers and running from an attack," Caleb said. "We can avoid the Snake River by taking Goodale's Cutoff. It runs north of the Snake and is about the same distance to Fort Boise. It goes through some harsh country, dry and rough, but there's also the Camas Prairie with plenty of water and feed for the animals."

"Camas root!" both women cried. "Blue flower, root very good to eat. Best to dig up in spring, but root still there," Little Rain added. "Harder to find when no flower, just leaf."

"We'll find them," Foster said, turning to Little Rain. "If you get one and let Wolf smell it, he'll find more."

The women burst out laughing. "Give wolf digging stick," White Cloud said, sending Little Rain into another paroxysm of mirth.

"What's funny?" Foster asked. Caleb wondered that, too.

"Only women dig camas roots, not men, not wolves," Little Rain said weakly, wiping her eyes.

"Back to the question," Caleb said. "Are we agreed? Do we take the cutoff?"

The others nodded. They would go north and then west.

"What would you say if I asked you to ride Sheba?" Caleb said to Little Rain. "She is much more sure-footed than your horse, and with a saddle you would not be bumped so much."

"Not know how to ride saddle way," she answered stiffly.

"It's not hard," Dil told her. "I could show you in five minutes."

"We not have saddle for Sheba."

"We make one in morning," White Cloud said. "Have extra buckles. Easy to cut straps. Use buffalo robe for saddle seat."

"We have awls of different sizes," Caleb said, "and yards of sinews you and White Cloud have collected for sewing the straps."

"What about my horse?" Little Rain still sounded doubtful.

"He will carry packs and have a neck rope," Dil said.

"What if Sheba not like me?"

"She will," Caleb said. "She knows you are pregnant and will be very careful with you. Just trust her, and you will soon find you hardly have to tell her what to do. She will probably know before you do."

"She tall," Little Rain said. "Can't jump on back now."

"We'll make you a stirrup," Caleb assured her.

"Soon I be Nihoothoo woman," she groaned.

"My horse now has name," White Cloud said, surrendering her secret to the cause.

"What is it?" Little Rain demanded, wide-eyed.

"Notoone," White Cloud told her, looking defiant and sheepish simultaneously.

"Daughter," Little Rain said quietly. "Is very good name. Maybe sometime I will give my horse a name. Now I ride mule named Sheba, who knows what will happen next?"

She didn't add, *If you and I go on living with these Nihoothoos,* but Caleb knew what she meant. He said quickly, "More likely Dil and I will become Arapahos."

Both women gave him skeptical looks but said nothing.

CHAPTER 25

The following morning, two miles from their camp, they reached the river, the first of only a few fords on the Snake between the place where they were and Fort Boise. They stared at the ford with marked misgivings. The day had broken overcast and cold, and the dark water surging past them looked decidedly uninviting.

"If this is what the Snake looks like in early fall," Dil said, "what must it look like in the spring snow melt?"

Foster leaned forward and gazed between Dakota's ears at the roiling river. "I ain't going to try swimming that."

Although the river wasn't more than thirty yards wide where they stood, it was deep and moving with obvious power. The banks were ten or fifteen feet high, but sufficiently slanted to allow their mounts to enter the Snake slowly and reach the top of the opposite bank safely. The problem was getting from one bank to the other.

"We've got to cross it," Caleb said, trying to sound confident. "Our gear is wrapped as tight as we can make it. The packs should float and give the horses some lift."

No one said anything in response.

"Up here with me, Foster," Caleb said, aware that the worst moments were those before the charge. "Hold onto Dakota's reins."

Looking grim, the boy dropped to the ground and came around to Caleb's stirrup, leading Dakota. Caleb reached down

and swung Foster up behind him. "Give me the reins," he said. "Now wrap your arms around my middle, and you hang there no matter what happens. You hear me?"

"Yup," Foster said, hugging Caleb, the side of his face pressing into Caleb's back.

"Go," Caleb said to Joshua.

The big mule strode into the water, followed by Dakota and the pack horses Caleb was leading. Joshua had scarcely waded his length into the water before he was swimming, quickly followed by the horses plunging in behind him.

"Wolf's right here with us, swimming like a fish, and that water's cold," Foster said loudly as his legs plunged beneath the surface.

"Hang tight," Caleb said.

The mule was a powerful swimmer, but, before his hooves found ground under him, the water had swept them twenty yards downstream. Wolf was on the shore waiting for them, giving himself a good shake. Joshua, Dakota, and the pack horses came out of the river without mishap.

Once up the bank and back opposite their starting point, Caleb said, "Foster, take this pack rope and get on Dakota. I'm going back to bring Little Rain over. Wolf will stay with you."

Foster slid off the mule. "I'll do it, but I'm shaking like an aspen leaf," he said.

When Caleb reached the other bank, he said to Little Rain, "Give me Sheba's reins. You hold tight to Sheba. White Cloud, when I start, make sure Sheba is moving."

"I'll cross last," Dil said.

"Cross with me," White Cloud countered. "That way we have three arms."

"I'll race you," he said, coaxing a grin from White Cloud.

Caleb took Sheba's reins. "Hold on," he said and started Joshua forward. They entered the water quickly, and he found

he need not have worried about Sheba. With Joshua in front of her, she would have swum an ocean. Soon, Caleb and Little Rain were with Foster and Wolf and the pack animals.

On the opposite bank, Dil and White Cloud readied themselves. "Go!" Dil called out. Notoone started into the water, and White Cloud sprang up to stand on her horse's back.

"Look a'there!" Foster shouted. "Look at White Cloud."

"We do that when children," Little Rain told him. "Come along, we will start fire for us and those not yet grown up."

Caleb, at first alarmed by what White Cloud was doing, felt his fear ebb as he watched her. She was truly enjoying herself, a rare experience for her. Effortlessly balanced on Notoone's back, the wind fluttering her white deerskin dress and swirling her long, unbraided hair, she looked happy and proud. He turned back to the shore with a swelling heart, a new happiness pouring through him.

It took until midday to dry their clothes, except for White Cloud. Fortunately, none of the tightly wrapped packs soaked through, and, once the elk-skin covers had dried, they were ready to leave.

Caleb dug out his map and consulted it. "We go north from here for a while and then turn west," he said when they had the pack animals lined up and everyone mounted. "There are some rivers to cross on the cutoff but none like the Snake."

Foster pointed northwest. "What's that mountain up there all by itself?"

"Big Southern Butte," Caleb told him. "I guess it was a volcano once, long ago."

"How long will we be on cutoff?" Little Rain asked.

"Twelve to fifteen days?" Dil guessed.

"Sounds right," Caleb replied. "It's about two hundred and thirty miles."

A few hours after they resumed their journey, Caleb rode

back to Little Rain and asked how she was getting along with Sheba and the buffalo robe saddle.

"Is good," she told him with a modest smile. "I am liking Sheba. I begin to be with her. Is a good place. She is careful with me. One thing hard. I have not learn to move with her."

"I think you will soon. She will help you. She is very strong but gentle."

"That is what I think."

As they rode north away from the Snake, the land became much drier, the grazing, sparser, the trees shorter and growing in smaller stands, while the brush was thicker. The wind felt more like it had on the prairie, blowing with more voice and strength, as if glad to be free of the mountains. Eagles and hawks and vultures wheeled in the pale-blue sky. Quail exploded out of the brush like blue rockets and sailed away. Foster loved to see them and always shouted after them. Late-summer flowers dotted the land, and the air smelled sweet and clean, lifting the travelers' spirits. Even White Cloud often laughed at small things.

Sometimes Little Rain sang, joined now and then by White Cloud. Caleb, usually on point well ahead of the rest, heard it faintly but clearly and found it strangely haunting, evoking feelings he could not describe. To everyone's surprise, Foster learned the songs just from hearing them. He loved to sing with the two women, and his high, pure voice sometimes evoked in Caleb feelings he had not experienced since coming under fire in the war.

"Have not heard voice like that," White Cloud told Caleb. "He has been touched by Great Spirit. If Arapaho boy have such a voice, he would be raised as holy man."

"In churches we have choirs, people who sing in the church services. Sometimes in large churches with a lot of people, boys like Foster are trained to sing that way. Later, the best of them

231

sometimes make their living singing or playing a musical instrument."

"My father spoke of that," White Cloud said. "My people have drums and rattles, and whistles and instrument with strings—also songs for love and war and all the ceremonies of life. Songs now mostly of sadness because of the Nihoothoos that never stop coming into the land. When I was a child, the people sang often, were more happy, and there was peace. The young men becoming warriors went out, stole horses, counted coup, sometimes were wounded. Not very often died."

She fell quiet.

"Have I made you feel sad?" Caleb asked after a moment.

"No," she replied, "you make me happy, but your people are too many, and the life that was for Arapahos cannot last, maybe already gone."

There was not a trace of self-pity in her voice, Caleb noted, only a resignation and certainty that made him see her in a new way. It saddened him, probably because he could not tell her she was wrong. Neither, he admitted with regret, could he do anything to lessen the threats to her people.

The further they went on the cutoff, the drier the land became. Tumbleweed and steppe growth increased, and trees were fewer in number. They still found streams and occasional springs, but day after day there were fluffy cumulus clouds drifting over their heads from west to east and a dry wind whistling through the faded grass and weeds.

"This here air's got an edge on it like the prairie and clear as one of those mountain creeks," Dil said one morning as they were finishing breakfast. "It's a change, that's for sure."

"I kind of like it," Foster said, "but this air smells like dirt and grass, and it's drier than a rock. Have you noticed the grass ain't wet in the morning for longer than it takes a crow to caw?"

"This boy will be teller of stories at the fire when he is older," Little Rain observed to Caleb as she watched Foster run off with Wolf to begin watering the horses. "What he says is full of pictures."

"You're right," Caleb replied. "His mind is waking up to the world around him, and I think he is healing from whatever put him among those Mormons, if that's what they were."

"In the beginning, I did not know I would take him into my heart," she said. "It is so with Dil, too."

Caleb felt uneasy, knowing they had strayed into a potentially explosive subject. "Are you telling me you would like to take Foster into your family?"

"Dil and I have asked one another this. Are you and White Cloud speaking of it?"

"I think we should talk about this more, Little Rain, when the four of us are together and Foster is asleep."

With that, he took himself off, relieved that more had not been said.

Caleb pushed them hard all day, and the sun had nearly reached the distant blue mountains when he finally called a halt. Foster was nearly asleep when Caleb set his feet on the ground. Even Wolf flopped down with his tongue out when the horses stopped. When Little Rain returned to the fire after seeing Foster to bed, she remained standing. "Someone thinks it is time to talk about Foster."

White Cloud and Dil looked up, surprise on both their faces. Caleb groaned silently and got to his feet.

"This morning," he said, forcing himself to sound at ease, "Little Rain and I spoke briefly about what is to be done with Foster when we reach Oregon."

Dil frowned at Little Rain. "Why now?"

"Perhaps it should not be left to the end."

"Decide what?" White Cloud made no effort to conceal the steel in her voice.

Little Rain answered with equal firmness. "Where Foster will go."

"Perhaps it would be better to wait, Little Rain," Caleb said, "and then ask Foster to decide."

Dil got to his feet. "No, Captain. That would be an awful mistake. However he chose, he'd be riddled with guilt because he didn't pick the other two."

By now White Cloud was standing. She, Caleb, and Little Rain stared at Dil as though he had lost his mind. "All right," Dil said after the silence grew uncomfortable, "I'll explain. Foster goes to the Captain to learn about the trail and Oregon. He goes to White Cloud to learn about horses and hear stories of her father. He goes to Little Rain when he needs comforting or affection, and he comes to me to hear stories about the war. I never tell him about the killing but about the country we saw, the singing at night around the camp fires, the things that make him laugh. How is the boy supposed to choose between us?"

"This won't be easy," Caleb said. "Both White Cloud and Little Rain feel strongly about this. I think we should wait. See how things go for us. Make sure Foster doesn't think he is the cause of any of our troubles. Dil is right—I was wrong. It would be cruel to ask him to choose between us. Like it or not, we are all his family."

White Cloud glared at Little Rain. "Some people think they should have everything."

Little Rain bristled. "And some people do not want to listen to what others have to say."

"Little Rain," Caleb said, "we know you love the boy, but perhaps White Cloud also loves him."

"Then someone should say it, if Foster is in her heart." Little Rain folded her arms across her chest. "Someone else has said

it. Caleb Stone has heard."

"I remember a story from when I was young," Dil said. "It's in the Bible, a book about the Great Spirit. A king had two wives and each wife had a child. One of the children died, and the women quarrel over who gets the remaining child. They take their quarrel to King Solomon. The king calls for his knife and tells the women he will cut the baby in half, so they can each have half of it. One woman agrees. The other, weeping, tells the king she will not see the child die and surrenders her claim. The king then gives her the child, saying she had proven her love."

"Only a fool would agree to cut child in half," White Cloud said, "and only a man would make up such a story."

It was all going wrong, and Caleb had no idea how to salvage things except by delay. "White Cloud, Little Rain, will you agree to wait longer before trying to make this decision? In that time, we can all think about it."

Neither woman answered, but both turned and stalked away.

CHAPTER 26

"Captain," Dil said the next morning, having ridden ahead to join Caleb on point, "we'll be lucky if we don't wake up someday soon to find one of those women with a knife in her back."

Anger flared in Caleb, but he pushed it back down. "I hope that's not prophecy."

"I haven't heard him say it for a while," Dil replied, "but Foster sometimes calls one or the other of them wild. I used to laugh and warn him not to say that where White Cloud or Little Rain could hear him."

"Your point?" Caleb asked.

"It's easy to forget, but they're not like us, Captain, in lots of ways. They're not deep into forgiveness. Patience isn't their longest suit, and they don't like being crossed. Also, it must have struck you that they took to killing like ducks take to water. I recall seeing grown men break down weeping after shooting a man in battle. These two have never so much as flinched."

"I think that has to do with the warrior code they were raised in," Caleb said. He knew what Dil was moving toward and had been there before as well.

"They have their own code of honor, Captain. It's tougher than an eye for an eye. It's more like a head for an eye. Losing is not something to shrug off, is what I'm saying."

"And you're saying that if there's a struggle over Foster, one of them loses."

"That's about it, Captain."

"What do you suggest?"

"Don't let it happen. You and I best make sure neither of us takes a side, and we mustn't let either of them lay claim to the boy."

They rode in silence, while Caleb struggled to find a hole in Dil's argument.

"Here's what I think," he said at last, "and I don't much like your proposal, because I don't know what the outcome will be. That said, I can't think of anything better. We follow your plan but add something to it. We tell them in a fire talk that as long as we are on the trail, none of us is going to lay claim to the boy, and he is not ever going to be asked to choose."

It was Dil's turn to think, but his pondering was short. "It's risky, but I'm with you. We'll do it, and we'll wear hats to bed."

"Why?" Caleb asked, puzzled.

"So we won't get scalped. 'That there's two wild women.' " His imitation of Foster's voice was good, and it relieved Caleb to laugh.

That night after Foster was asleep, Caleb stood by the fire. "Dil and I have something to say. As long as we are on the trail, none of us will say Foster is ours. None of us will ask him who he wants most to be with. We are his family. That's all Dil and I have to say."

He sat down. After a moment he said, "Perhaps someone else wishes to speak."

A few minutes passed with no sounds but the crackling of the fire and the howling of coyotes somewhere to the south of them. Wolf acknowledged the coyotes with a half-hearted growl as he moved closer to the fire, the night having turned cold.

Little Rain rose, folding her hands in front of her. "Someone has something to say. There is much to think about, but Caleb Stone and Dil have spoken to keep peace among us. That is

good. I do not see how it can work in Oregon, but I am satisfied now."

White Cloud rose slowly, perhaps reluctantly.

"Little Rain has spoken wisely," she said quietly. "Caleb Stone and Dil have spoken well but perhaps not seen far enough. Yes, we are his family; that is true. But the suns will bring us to the place where we will not be doing what we are doing now. It is known that people can change how they think about something but perhaps not who they are. Also, what is in their hearts may not change. That is all I have to say."

She sat down. They all stared into the fire, unable or unwilling to respond to White Cloud's warning. Then Wolf lurched to his feet with a rumbling growl, the hair on his shoulders rising.

"Bear!" Caleb shot upright and dashed for his rifle. By the time they all had weapons in their hands, Wolf had raced into the darkness toward the horses. An instant later Joshua squealed, and Wolf snarled. The grass was thin and clumps of it scattered, so the horses had spread out. The new moon was not much help, but, once their eyes adjusted enough away from the campfire, they could make out the animals. Caleb listened for a bear's roar, but none came. Was Wolf tangling with a mountain lion?

"Wolf!" he called out. The volume of Wolf's snarling suddenly shot up. A rifle cracked, followed by a howl of fear.

"Over here!" Dil shouted, waving toward the muzzle flash.

They all rushed forward and found Wolf pinning a man to the ground, his teeth bared inches from the man's throat.

Caleb dropped his hand onto the wolf's head. "Wolf, let him up. It's all right."

Wolf slowly backed off. The pale moonlight still glinted on his teeth, and his gaze never left whoever was on the ground.

"Grab an arm, Dil," Caleb said, "and let's get him on his feet."

The stranger stayed silent as they pulled him off the ground. On the way up, the man lost his hat, and a dense tumble of hair fell around his shoulders.

"Lord above," Dil said, "it's a woman."

The stranger shook herself loose. "I wondered when you'd notice."

White Cloud appeared out of the darkness. "Maybe best to stick knife in her now. Save us much trouble."

"Keep her," Little Rain countered. "Make her work."

"Let's get some light on this." Caleb took the woman's arm again, more gently this time, and started towards the fire.

"Hold it." The woman pulled back. "Somebody pick up my rifle and the sack I dropped."

White Cloud picked up the gun, and Dil found the sack.

"I have been wandering in this godforsaken wilderness for a while," their prisoner said on reaching the fire. "Don't expect too much." She shook out her hair and made a stab at straightening her clothes. She was almost as tall as Caleb, green-eyed, full bodied, and possessed of a glorious head of thick, auburn hair. She had a generous mouth and a ready smile. A full set of teeth showed when she grinned at them, displaying no fear at all.

"I was right." White Cloud stared across the fire at the strange woman. "Should have stuck a knife in her."

"Why you are out here alone?" Little Rain asked in a cold voice.

The woman shrugged. "I got lost from a wagon train."

"What's your name?" Caleb asked.

"Augusta O'Neill."

"Where were you going?" Dil asked, as he dumped the sack out and began sifting through its contents.

"As far as the Pacific Ocean."

"Did you reach Soda Springs?"

"I did."

"Not possible you are here," White Cloud told her.

"I had a horse until two days ago. I swam her across the Snake River and headed for Goodale's Cutoff."

"What happened to your horse?" Caleb asked.

"A large bear got her. I didn't dare shoot the bear. I was pretty sure one shot wouldn't kill it."

"Old gun," White Cloud said, holding up the stranger's flintlock.

Foster appeared in the firelight, roused by the commotion. "Who is this?"

"Hello, who is this handsome young man?" Augusta bent over him and put out her hand. "My name is Augusta O'Neill, but you can call me Gussie."

"I'm Foster Wiggins," he said, grasping her hand and shaking it vigorously. "You're a mighty good-looking woman, Gussie."

"Leave boy alone," Little Rain snapped. Her ferocious glare matched White Cloud's.

Foster glanced at them, wide-eyed, but Augusta ignored them. "Well, thank you, Foss. That's a fine compliment. Will you be my beau?"

"I don't rightly know what a *beau* is, but if you tell me, I reckon I'll be it."

"It's a special friend, Foss. I need one real bad. What do you say?"

Foster spat on his hand, thrust it out, and said, "Done."

Augusta spat on her own hand without hesitation and grasped his. "Done, Foss. I feel better already."

Wariness of this odd woman fought with amusement in Caleb's mind. "Let's see," he said when Gussie straightened up, "you got lost on a horse while carrying a flintlock rifle, a knife, a powder horn and bullets, extra clothes, flint and steel, and about ten dollars in silver. How about going over your story

again, and tell us the truth this time?"

"I never was a good liar," she said, throwing up her hands. "I don't know why. I practiced hard enough all the time I was growing up and got caught every time. I can't tell you how many meals I lost over it."

Dil grinned at her. "Have a go."

"First, how about you tell me your names. It would make me feel more at home."

"All right," Caleb said. "I'm Caleb Stone."

From there he went around the circle. After he finished, Augusta beamed at them all. "Ladies, I envy you your names. They are lovely, and I hope one day soon you will tell me the story behind them. As for you, Dil, I assume you started out with two names and two arms? I would love to hear about that. Caleb, I heard Dil call you 'captain.' That and your accent could only mean one thing. You were in the Union Army. Your last name's appropriate for a Yankee. Which state?"

"Maine," Caleb said. He couldn't help smiling at Augusta's manner. Her streams of words and touch of a brogue reminded him of a stage show.

"White Cloud, Little Rain, put your knives back in your belts," Augusta said. "Foss is my beau, and I only ever have one at a time. Is there any chance of my getting something to eat? I'm near fading away with hunger."

Dil got up and fetched some dried meat from the nearest pack animal. Augusta took it with thanks and wolfed it down. How long since she'd had a decent meal, Caleb wondered.

"Were you trying to steal one of our horses, Gussie?" Foster asked her after she had eaten. He'd stayed close to her ever since they shook hands, scarcely taking his eyes off her. Little Rain watched the pair of them with a thundercloud on her forehead, shooting glances at Augusta that were sharper than any knife.

241

"My Lord, no!" Augusta wiped her mouth with a corner of her skirt that was beyond dirty. "I was only going to borrow it until I could get to Fort Boise, because, if I had to walk, I wouldn't arrive before Christmas. Foss, can you read and write?"

"I can read middling well, but my writing's a mite scratchy."

"I was a school teacher before setting out for the West," she said. "Would you like me to get you started writing?"

"We ain't got no pencils nor paper, I don't think. We was going to lay in some at Fort Hall, but there wasn't nothing there in the way of a store."

"The boy came to us after we left Fort Laramie," White Cloud said coldly. "No trading post since then to buy paper and pencil."

"Can you and Little Rain read and write English?" Augusta asked.

Caleb looked up from the fire, half expecting to have to dive in and keep White Cloud from cutting Augusta's throat.

"My second father was white man," she said, to his relief. "He taught me some. Little Rain, no."

"I won't ask her, White Cloud," Augusta said quietly, "but if you think she would like to learn, I will gladly teach her."

"It's late," Caleb said. "Let's hear your story in the morning."

White Cloud gave Augusta a waterproof cloth and two blankets from their store and took away her rifle. All seemed in order to Caleb, except for two things, or so he told White Cloud: What to do about her attempt to steal one of their horses, and Wolf's refusal to make friends with her.

"I watched Foster trying to bring them together," he said. "Wolf wasn't having it. When she tried to put her hand on him, the hair on his neck stood up, and he showed her all his teeth. I think if Foster hadn't pushed between them, Wolf might have gone for her."

"Dil is taking first watch," White Cloud replied. "I told him take Wolf and stand in shadows."

"Any special reason?"

"Something wrong," she told him. "I think also she tried to shoot Wolf. He not forget."

An hour later, they found out what *something wrong* was.

It began with the crack of a rifle, followed by a shout of "Hold!" from Dil and a louder scream from a woman. Caleb and White Cloud scrambled out of bed and upright, rifles in hand, to find Augusta's bedding rolled up beside her canvas sack. In the pale light of the sickle moon, they saw Augusta and Little Rain fighting over something, Augusta swearing like a drill sergeant.

White Cloud flew into the fray, knocking Augusta onto her back. At the same time, Dil appeared with three men, herded along by Wolf. "Keep moving," Dil ordered.

One of the men caught sight of Augusta. "There she is!" he shouted.

"Stop right there," Caleb said, bringing the men up short.

White Cloud swung her rifle away from Augusta and toward the men. Little Rain scrambled to her feet, her own rifle in hand.

Augusta got up more slowly, cradling the arm White Cloud had twisted in knocking her down. "These are the people I've been trying to get away from," she said in an accusing voice.

"She's a thief and a liar," another of the men countered. He looked to be in his thirties, with a head of curly blond hair and a week's growth of beard. "We been chasing her nearly a week."

"Where are your weapons?" Caleb demanded.

"Our rifles are with the horses. We don't carry side arms."

"Foster," Caleb said as the boy appeared, rubbing his eyes, "get over here."

The boy looked startled as he took in the scene. "Gussie!" he

called. "Are you hurt?"

"No, Foss. I'm all right."

"She run off with what money we had," the blond man said.

"I never. You know why I left, and more's your shame."

"Did she come in with a canvas sack?" another man asked, moving toward her.

White Cloud cocked her rifle. "One more step."

"Now just hold on," the man said, backing up.

"The three of you sit down," Caleb said. "Wolf and Dil and White Cloud will keep you company. Little Rain, you and I will take Augusta with us and uncover the fire."

Once they had moved out of earshot, Caleb said, "Augusta, why were you fighting with Little Rain?"

"She said I was trying to take Foster away from her, and she was going to kill me. So I decided to take her gun away from her."

"My God." Caleb's voice rose. "Don't you know every Indian woman you will ever see carries a razor-sharp knife in her belt and has spent her life using it to cut up large animals? It's a miracle your innards aren't lying back there on the ground."

"I was doing pretty well until White Cloud hit me in the head, which wasn't fair," Augusta protested.

By this time, they had reached the fire. Little Rain fed it twigs until it was burning brightly. "Little Rain," Caleb said, "did you threaten to kill Augusta?"

"Is true. I say, you try take away that boy, I kill you."

"Oh," Augusta said. "I thought you said 'if you try to talk to that boy, I kill you.' "

This woman can't tell a straight story about anything. Desperation took root in Caleb's stomach. "You will tell Little Rain you're sorry," he said. "Little Rain, after Augusta says she's sorry, you will shake her hand."

They did as he told them, but Caleb saw a glint in Little

Rain's eye that troubled him.

Dil and the three men arrived at the fire, led by Wolf, and nobody held a gun on anyone. "These men are Ben Larkin, Horace Fisher, and Tom Bailey," Dil said. "They say Augusta took all their money and a horse and ran away."

"Gussie, why did you do that?" Larkin, the blond man and the oldest of the three, demanded in a hurt voice. The other two looked to be brothers, Caleb thought—dark haired, the younger not more than fifteen and the elder possibly twenty. All three were dressed in ragged cloth coats and worn boots.

"The lot of them are poorer than church mice," Dil said quietly to Caleb.

"What did you expect me to do, Ben Larkin, after you tried to rape me?" Augusta said.

"I never tried to rape you. God A'mighty, Augusta, I was kissing you because I love you and wanted to sweep you off your feet. You needn't worry about the horse; we found it."

She looked abashed. "I didn't spend any of the ten dollars," she said. "Do you really love me?"

"Yes, I do. I'm sorry if I frightened you."

"I misunderstood your intentions. Why didn't you tell me?"

" 'Cause you did the knee thing, and I couldn't talk."

Caleb and Dil nearly choked trying not to laugh. Augusta glanced at them, maintaining her wide-eyed expression, but the corners of her mouth quivered.

"Ben," she said, looking back at him, "if you wanted to kiss me again that would be all right."

Larkin did. His companions gave a ragged cheer, with Caleb, Dil, and Foster joining in. Fists on their hips, White Cloud and Little Rain stared at the scene in obvious disgust.

"*Nihoothoos,*" White Cloud said with finality.

Little Rain dug out the last of their coffee and served it in cups and bowls for everyone but Wolf and Foster, who didn't

want any. When the newcomers had hobbled their horses and were bedded down, and Dil, White Cloud, and Little Rain had cleared away and spread ashes on the coals, Caleb called Wolf and took the rest of the watch. The night passed without further disruptions, and an hour before dawn he gratefully gave the watch over to White Cloud and crawled into bed.

At first light, White Cloud slipped out of camp with Noto-one. She returned half an hour later with a young elk, gutted and bled, thrown over the mare's back. She woke Caleb and said, "We will talk."

He sat up and pulled on his shirt. The day was breaking cold. "I'm listening," he said.

"Ben's people die at first snow in the mountains. No clothes. No money."

"What do you want to do?"

"I look at their packs. Nothing in them—only rags, salt, more rags, some powder and bullets for old guns. They have four horses. How they find horse bear has eaten?"

"The bear changed its mind?"

"Is early for joke. You have red hair in your eyes?"

"Here's my guess: the bear rushed the horse. Augusta"—he carefully did not call her Gussie—"fell off the horse and ran. The horse got away, and she assumed it had been killed."

"To say she is liar takes fewer words. Do not mind that. I have more to say. You will listen."

"If it's this bad now, what will it be like when we are married?"

"Just as bad. We will send these children ahead of us. If they get into trouble, we will find them. When we get to Fort Boise, you will buy them warm clothes for the mountains."

"I thought you wanted to stick a knife in her," Caleb said in surprise.

She looked away from him. "Maybe still do," she said, "but

she is brave person and told us she was taking Foster into her heart where was room for only one. I think she very lonely and has honor, even if lie about horse. It may be the Great Spirit has touched her. She not get things right. Not know difference between *I love you* and rape. Not understand Little Rain. She must be cared for, and Ben and two young ones not warriors. She will have to be warrior. You teach her shoot straight before she leaves. Show her how to aim like you show Little Rain and this one. Go, there is much to do."

Caleb pulled her to him. "Come here, black-eyed warrior."

She made a pretense of resisting but soon had her arms around him.

"You are a fine person, White Cloud," he told her. "I love you with all my heart."

"Does Augusta look like Millicent True?" White Cloud asked, pressing her face against his.

"A little."

"Do you miss her, Caleb Stone?"

"Do you miss anyone you loved in your past life?"

"I think you tell me you do."

"No, I'm telling you I remember her and being in love with her. But I am not in love with her anymore. I am deeply in love with you."

"I have memories sometimes of others, but my heart is filled with you, Caleb Stone."

For a short time, they lay in one another's arms with the morning expanding around them, birds singing, and the smell of cooking on the fire. Then they rose and continued their day.

CHAPTER 27

Caleb found that Augusta's .45-caliber flintlock was fitted with a rifled barrel, guaranteeing accuracy. Aimed properly, it would dependably hit its target at fifty yards and, Caleb was confident, much farther. He also found her a quick learner and more than strong enough to hold the rifle steady. He cut a fat pad off a prickly pear cactus and stuck it on a spruce tree twenty yards away. "Try your luck," he told her.

She raised the gun in a single smooth movement, aimed, and fired. The cactus pad exploded.

"Use your rod to keep the barrel clean," he told her, "and you'll be able to keep your men in meat."

"I lied about the horse," she said, squinting at the target. "I jumped off when the bear charged and ran away. I didn't want you and the others to think I was a coward."

Touched by the Great Spirit, Caleb thought wryly. "It's all right," he told her, half amused and a little angry with her, "but jumping off the horse is the last thing you should have done. You're almighty lucky the bear didn't take after you. You can't run as fast as a horse."

"Why, Mr. Stone, are you scolding me?" she asked archly, with a sideways slashing glance that went straight through him.

"Perhaps a little," he said, feeling his face burn and his heart pick up some speed. "Let's go back. Your people will be ready to get under way."

"Thank you for blushing, Caleb," she said as they began

walking. "I needed some encouragement."

"Augusta O'Neill," he said with a wide smile, "you're being wicked again. I'll wager you know that when you walk into a room full of people, there won't be a man who's not looking at you."

She took his arm and matched his stride. "If our situations were different, Caleb, I think we might become friends."

"I'm sure of it," Caleb said, feeling several years younger.

He and the others agreed to give the four visitors a day's start. Dil had suggested asking them to join their group, but the two women told him loudly what a bad idea that was. Caleb felt considerable pleasure that he hadn't given in to his impulse to suggest the same thing.

"I don't see any need for you two to get all het up," Dil protested, sounding insulted. "It was a just a suggestion."

"Don't have more like that," Little Rain snapped.

"I'll miss Gussie," Foster put in. "I liked her. She said I was her beau, and I was looking to be a good one."

"Wood, Foster. Go." White Cloud shooed him toward the trees.

"When you reach the lava fields," Caleb told Ben the next morning, "you stick to the trail like a burr. Camp near a spring, and don't think you can improve on that map I drew for you."

"I'm much obliged for the help," Ben said. "Thank you for taking Gussie in. She can get confused about what's happening and what she should do, but I will look after her. The boys and I were about sick from losing her."

Instead of saying it was a miracle Wolf didn't tear her throat out, Caleb shook the man's hand and told him he could understand how they felt. "Be sure to wait for us at Fort Boise and good luck," he added.

The four visitors left, laden with elk meat, a sack of flour and a frying pan, and information regarding the trail. "I wonder

how much money she took?" Dil said as they watched Augusta and her escorts round the first turn in the trail.

"Ten dollars," White Cloud said, "to take them to Oregon."

"Lord God." Dil gave a long sigh. "Maybe we were selfish in not taking them with us."

"Trouble will follow her like wolves follow buffalo," White Cloud said. "The Great Spirit has touched her."

"What does that mean?" Foster asked.

"It means her way is only her way, and she must walk it alone."

"Ain't she and Ben going to be together?"

"Yes," Little Rain said, pulling the boy against her, "anyway, for now."

"She and Ben are together," Caleb said, seeing the pain on Foster's face. "Let's hope they will be happy." Even as he spoke, he felt his assertion was the triumph of hope over probability.

The good weather held for the next several days. The country was generally flat or rolling and dry, making it possible for them to travel twenty miles a day despite their midday rests without exhausting Little Rain. In fact, she insisted that riding Sheba was a pleasure, especially with the buffalo-skin saddle. Foster got over missing Augusta enough to begin singing again, and White Cloud, using Caleb's shotgun, varied their deer and elk meat diet with quail and grouse.

Wolf found a small spring around noon, hidden in a cluster of junipers. Caleb chose the site as their midday halt, something he now insisted on, to give Little Rain time to rest. Despite her denials, it was clear to the other three adults that in the past few weeks, she had begun tiring more easily. Caleb had held off sharing what he knew about the Craters of the Moon, the rough country ahead of them, in part not to upset her.

Caleb and Foster built a small rock dam, creating a pool

large enough to enable the animals to drink. There was nothing much in the way of trees where they were, but with Foster and Dil pitching in, they soon gathered enough dead wood in the junipers and surrounding brush for the women to cook dinner.

"Did not expect to miss trees," White Cloud said when they sat down to eat, "but this sun and wind are too much."

"Mountains ahead," Dil said cheerfully.

Once they began to eat, Caleb stood. "I have something to say. I've been keeping it from you. It concerns what's ahead of us. I haven't said anything about it because I didn't want to worry you."

"Is it bears?" Foster asked. Their encounter with the bear that nearly killed Wolf, followed by the one that attacked Augusta's horse, had given the boy nightmares that began the night Augusta left them.

"No bears," Caleb told him firmly. "It's about a place that doesn't look like anything we've seen before. Something happened to it a long, long time ago. The name of the place is Craters of the Moon. It will take some time to cross over."

"Why we have to be told before we get there?" White Cloud asked. "If we can't go around it, we have to go through it or stop."

"You don't like surprises," Caleb said.

"Will it be safe to go there?" Little Rain asked.

"Yes," Caleb answered, "but it might look scary. Long ago, there were mountains called volcanoes there. When the volcanoes exploded, the insides of the mountains became so hot they melted and their tops blew off. The melted rock inside them poured out, spreading over the land for miles around, killing everything it touched."

He paused to see what effect he was having on his audience. It was not what he had hoped. After Little Rain's brief interest, the only person listening was Foster. Dil already knew the story.

The two women regarded Caleb with suspicion.

"At first," he said, determined to finish what he had started, "the lava ran everywhere, fiery red as burning coals. As it cooled, it flowed slower and slower until it stopped, and the more it cooled, the blacker and harder it became. And nothing grew there. Not much grows there now. Our trail will follow the outer edge of the lava flow."

"Bad medicine," White Cloud said.

Little Rain nodded.

Caleb drew breath to speak, but White Cloud interrupted him. "What is lava?" she asked sourly. "There will be bad spirits."

"Oh no, White Cloud," Dil said, turning to face her. "Lava is just the name of the molten rock that came from the mountain— like honey, only very hot. It is cold now. It can't do us harm."

"Why nothing grows on it?" Little Rain sounded sour as White Cloud.

"Because there is no dirt for plants to grow in."

Little Rain frowned. "Great Spirit stays away all this time. Bad medicine."

Caleb took a deep breath and counted silently to ten. "Think of it this way. Great Spirit blew up the mountain and told the inside to melt and run out as far as it could and then grow cold and black and hard. Then he went away after saying, 'Nothing grow here until I say so.' He still hasn't said so."

"Why did he do that?" Foster asked.

"Because he wanted to."

That struck the women as hilarious. White Cloud laughed so hard, tears streamed down her face.

"Stone age hears why things are as they are," Dil said, looking delighted with the spectacle.

"When you are old," White Cloud told Caleb, rubbing her face with both hands, "I will take you to all the villages. You will go into the chief's lodge, and all the people will come to listen

to the old Nihoothoo. You will tell them what the Great Spirit has done in the world."

She paused to catch her breath. Caleb started to say something, but she interrupted him. "Someone will ask why the Great Spirit did all these things, and Caleb Stone will say, 'Because he wanted to.' People will fall over laughing, and Caleb Stone will become a great man, welcome wherever he goes, because no one on earth ever said such a thing before."

For the rest of the day, the women sometimes burst out laughing again, and Foster told Caleb not to tell any more Great Spirit stories because it made White Cloud and Little Rain silly. The laughter stopped three days later when they came to the place where nothing grew. They stopped and gazed at the dry, barren land covered with broken black rocks, stretching away in front of them as far as they could see. Even Wolf stood and stared.

For several minutes, no one spoke. Then Little Rain broke the silence. "Even coyote could not live there."

"No birds singing, no vultures in the sky," White Cloud added. "No antelope staring at us. It is like end of world."

Wolf started to walk toward the cinders, but Caleb called him back. Not waiting for Foster to ask why, he said, "Those chunks of cinder are sharp as razors and will cut his feet."

"What we do?" White Cloud asked.

"We sew leather moccasins for feet," Little Rain said.

"We will," White Cloud agreed, "but what we do to get past this?" She waved an arm at the landscape facing them.

"We will turn north and follow the edge of the lava until we can turn west again," Caleb said. "This is why we filled our water bags this morning at the river."

"No rivers here is my guess," Dil said.

"It will be a while before we see another river." Caleb turned Joshua away from the cinders, heading him north.

That night as they sat around the fire, Foster said, "I wonder how Gussie and her folks are getting along."

"If we not see them, then all right," White Cloud said. "I think more if animals have enough to eat."

"Mules will do better than the horses," Dil said.

They had reason for concern. The areas bordering the lava lands were dry, and the best grazing available was the scattered clumps of buffalo grass. The mules did do better because they browsed where they couldn't graze, but the horses wouldn't eat the leaves on the brush.

"There'll be no problem if the springs hold out," Caleb said. He hoped to strike an optimistic note but lifted no one's spirits.

The following day, they found the first evidence of the price the wagon trains paid for taking Goodale's Cutoff. What appeared to be perfectly good wagons stood abandoned, sometimes with bureaus and dressers under the canvas, their drawers pulled open and their contents taken or strewn by pillagers, and mirrors often smashed, standing in the wagon beds. Having examined the first few wagons they came to, Caleb and Dil solved the mystery to their satisfaction and shared their findings with the others.

"It comes to this," Caleb said. "The dry weather shrunk the wood in the wheels, and the iron rims fell off. The wooden wheels broke after that. So their owners just left them."

"Why don't it rain more in this place?" Foster asked.

"Great Spirit mad with it," White Cloud said, ruffling his hair.

"Don't start!" Dil begged. "You saw those mountains in front of us?"

Both women agreed they had, and Foster chimed in as well, giving Dil their mock attention. "We're approaching the Pacific Ocean," Dil said, "and whatever rain comes this way has to come from it on a wind blowing toward the mountains. The

clouds carry the rain. The wind blows the clouds this way. When the clouds get to the mountains, they drop the rain on the west side. So this side is dry."

"Why does it drop the rain on the mountains and not here?" Foster asked.

"The clouds get pushed up by the wind. The air up there is colder, and the clouds can't hold the water."

"I like White Cloud's answer better."

"Best answer," White Cloud said.

Caleb recognized the futility of arguing. "I'm going to bed. Dil, wake me when your watch is over."

The next day they reached the open lava fields and were stunned into silence by what looked like a vast black lake, frozen in place. Wolf gave it a tentative sniff, then shrank back from it, his hackles rising.

"Now then," Caleb said. "We follow the edge of this west until we run out of lava."

CHAPTER 28

Trouble hit them the next day in mid-afternoon. It began with traces of dust rising somewhere ahead of them. They had made good time, despite having to follow the winding edge of the lava. Sometimes they rode northwest half an hour only to have to turn southwest for nearly as long.

"It's devilish hard judging how far we're actually going west," Dil complained after they had completed one such long loop and were starting on another.

"Dust," White Cloud called from the head of the line.

Wolf was with her, while Caleb led the pack train, and Little Rain took her turn bringing up the rear. They were passing through a particularly dry and flat area with the tallest shrubs not reaching ten feet. The earth was a dusty tan and the sparse grass a tangle of pale brown and dull green that matched the color of the leaves and spills on the scattered scrub. Every step the animals took stirred a small cloud of dust, quickly whipped away by the wind.

Dil rode ahead to join White Cloud. Foster, helping Caleb with the pack animals, asked, "Could it be buffalo?"

"I haven't seen any buffalo chips," Caleb replied. "It might be too dry here for them. Could be riders."

"Indians?"

"Maybe," Caleb said, not wanting to tell Foster that if it was, they were likely a war party. He glanced around for a place to make a stand if they were attacked. White Cloud stood on her

256

horse's back. Turning, she waved Caleb forward. Passing the lead rope to Foster, Caleb reminded him to drop it if the pack animals bolted and urged Joshua into a gallop.

"It's riders, not cavalry," Dil told him. "No flags, no lines."

White Cloud dropped to her seat. "They move fast. Come this way. Not look good. Could be someone looking through spyglass saw us. Raiders maybe."

Caleb stood in his stirrups, straining to see what lay ahead. "We can't outrun them and keep the pack animals." He made a swift decision. "We'll put the lava field at our backs. They won't run their horses on the lava. How long have we got?"

"Judging from the dust, I'd give us fifteen minutes at most," Dil said.

"Put horses behind us?" White Cloud suggested.

"Yes," Caleb said, "and the packs piled in front of us to shoot over. White Cloud, any idea who they are?"

"War party," she said, face set in a scowl. "Do not allow self to be caught. I will not be slave again."

"How many?"

"Don't know yet."

Caleb stared at the rising dust. "I've seen a lot of cavalry charges. There aren't many in this group. Not over a dozen. Let's do it. Dil, picket the horses to the right of the firing line. They'll shoot high, and we don't want to lose any animals."

Little Rain and Foster had caught up with them and already dismounted. Working swiftly, they stripped the packs off the animals and piled them in a line with the lava behind them, their ammunition spaced between them to allow them to reload without getting up. Dil and Foster picketed the animals beside the line.

"Foster," Caleb said, when they were ready, "you're going to lie between Dil and me. This will be very bad, but you can be of

greatest help if you just lie flat and don't even think of getting up."

"What about Wolf?"

"I'll put him at your feet, but don't call to him. He may try to charge them. If he does, you must let him go. Understand?"

"Yes. Maybe he won't."

"Maybe not."

By now the pounding of the oncoming horses' hooves and the raiders' yells filled their ears.

"Eight in war paint. Have guns!" White Cloud shouted. "Shoshones and Bannocks, I think. Renegades."

The riders, wearing headbands with eagle feathers trailing in their hair, their clothing a mix of Indian and American, fell into a line. They pressed within ten yards of the travelers' defenses and rode across the front of the line of packs, yelling and firing.

"All together!" Caleb shouted. "Aim! Fire!"

Their salvo took down one raider. The rest galloped past and regrouped.

"We all here?" Caleb asked.

"Except one water bag," White Cloud answered.

It was clear to Caleb that facing eight guns, they were outmatched. Unless he thought of something, one by one they would be killed. "Take your time," he said, loudly but calmly. "Shoot the horses. Reload. Shoot anyone moving."

The renegades had circled and came on again in a line, yelling as they whipped their horses into a faster gallop. Caleb and the others fired. The first four horses went down, forcing those following to pull to the right or left instead of shooting. "Up!" Caleb shouted. "Keep firing and don't stop."

White Cloud was singing as she rose and squeezed off a shot. Caleb fired at almost the same time. Dil was shooting slowly but with deadly effect, taking down two of the fallen riders who had jumped to their feet. The four still in their saddles whirled

their mounts, crouched over their ponies' necks, and rode away. Still singing, White Cloud swung her rifle after them and fired. One escaping raider dropped off his horse and did not move.

"Little Rain ain't on her feet!" Foster shouted.

When they reached her, she was spread-eagled on her face, her head soaked in blood. Dil dropped to his knees and called her name. White Cloud knelt on the other side and slowly lifted her head, wiping the blood away with her hand.

"She has breath," she said.

"Her pulse is strong," Dil said. "It looks like a bullet grazed her head."

"Captain!" Foster shouted. He and Wolf were behind Caleb, trying to reach Little Rain. In their rush to get to her, they had taken their eyes off the fallen men in front of them. A tall, one-eyed raider, bare to the waist, his stomach smeared with blood, had risen and was charging toward them.

Caleb turned to face the attacker, too late to pick up a gun. Dil drew his weapon but lost his balance turning and fell onto his left side. The raider ran straight at Foster, knife hand raised to strike.

Wolf growled deep in his chest. He hurled himself over the packs, landed with his feet bunched under him and sprang at the oncoming warrior. The man tried to dodge, too late. With a slashing snap of his jaws, Wolf tore the man's throat out. Blood spurted from the wound as the raider fell. He thrashed for a moment and died with Wolf standing over him.

"Lord above," Dil said, on his feet again. "To think we once thought of shooting that animal."

"You lost some hair," White Cloud said as Little Rain opened her eyes. "New shirt all blood."

Dil knelt by her again and carefully cleaned and bandaged the wound. "The bullet creased your skull," he told her. "How does your head feel?"

"It hurts, but I am most mad about shirt," she said in a weak voice. "Finish sewing last night."

"We need find water and camp there," White Cloud said. "Little Rain not ride far. I will find water."

"Wait," Caleb said. "Is there any chance those three raiders we didn't kill will come back?"

"No. Their medicine bad. They ride far away."

"We can't put these men on a platform," Caleb said.

"And we cannot camp here," she replied. "I will find us water and then say what must be said for them."

"You can't go out there alone. Stay here and keep your gun with you. I'll take Wolf with me. He'll find water faster than we can."

White Cloud nodded. "Foster and I will put packs on the animals. Look, listen, smell," she added, not being ironic for once. "Come back, Caleb Stone."

That, Caleb thought later, was the only indication she ever gave that she was shaken by their encounter with the renegades. That night, they camped a mile and a half to the west. Little Rain could not ride Sheba, so Caleb had mounted Joshua while White Cloud and Dil lifted Little Rain, silent except for oc- casional half-suppressed groans squeezed out of her, high enough for Caleb to get his hands under her arms and drag her onto his lap. Joshua watched the struggle, and when it was time to go he set off at a gentle walk without Caleb touching the reins.

Once at the site, they made Little Rain comfortable on a temporary bed and left Foster with her, making conversation to keep her awake, while they set up camp. When supper was ready they carried it to her, propped her up, sat with her, and ate together. She managed to eat a little, but her headache had taken away most of her appetite.

"Little Rain," Foster said, leaning over her, "has the cat got

your tongue?"

"What cat?" she whispered, making a noise that might have been a laugh.

"The house cat," he answered. "We'll have one in Oregon."

"What I do with cat?"

"Sit in a rocking chair with it in your lap, rocking and stroking it to make it purr," Foster said. "I once seen a woman doing that."

"She'd better rest now, Foster," Dil said. He took another look at the wound. "I'll give you a touch of laudanum," he told her. "It should ease the pain and let you sleep through the night."

"It is time to put head down." Little Rain spoke as if from a distance. "Buffalo robe now."

Caleb carried her to where she and Dil slept. Dil gave her the laudanum. "I will stay with you until you sleep. I will be here when you wake."

Eyes already shut, she did not reply.

"Will she be all right?" Foster asked once they were back at the fire.

White Cloud pulled him close and hugged him. "She will walk tomorrow."

He looked doubtful. "Is that a straight answer?"

"Straight as arrow," White Cloud said, "to talk like you."

"Okay."

"You don't sound very certain," Caleb said to Foster.

"I'm thinking them renegades might have come on Gussie and her people," he answered. "If they did, Gussie and them've all been kilt."

"I looked at all of the dead ones," White Cloud said. "No one wearing anything from Augusta. If she was dead or made slave, someone would tie something on belt or on head."

"I'm thinking they're travelling faster than we are," Dil added.

"The renegades might have just come down to the trail and not seen them."

"Caleb?" Foster asked.

"I hope they're all right." His answer didn't seem to help, so Caleb gave it another try. He crouched on his heels to bring his face closer to the boy's. "White Cloud and Dil gave good reasons for thinking Gussie and her folk weren't killed. Are there any reasons for thinking they were?"

Foster looked up at him. "Until you found me, I hadn't much reason for looking on the bright side. And I had a feeling about those four that for some time they'd been trying to fill an inside straight with their luck running the wrong way."

White Cloud frowned in puzzlement. "What is inside straight?"

"It's something in a card game you shouldn't try to do," Dil said, "especially if a lot of money is riding on it."

"Foster, why you talk about card game?"

Foster turned to White Cloud, a strained look on his face. "I'm trying tell you what the pictures in my head say. Soon as I was around Ben and the others a little while, I started seeing bad luck hanging off them like bark on a dead tree."

"No help," White Cloud said, clearly irritated.

"It's a metaphor," Caleb said. "In English, that means one thing is standing for another. If I say, 'When she runs she's a deer,' I mean she runs fast as a deer, not that she turns into a deer. When Foster says he saw bad luck hanging off them like bark on a dying tree, he's painting a word picture of people out of luck."

"You two like Village Explainer, use five words instead of one to hear own words. How we help this boy if we not understand what is hurting inside?"

"What do you think he means?" Dil asked.

"For long time, he went without good things happening to

him. Even now, after something good happened, he does not think that means more good things happen than bad. As for Augusta and her people, I think he right."

"Go to the head of the class," Caleb said.

"Winter always comes," she replied, getting to her feet. "So does morning. Come, Foster. I put you to bed."

The two men watched her walk away, holding Foster's hand.

"She and that boy have a lot in common," Dil said.

"I wonder why she's so impatient with him."

Dil hesitated a moment. "I think you'll take my meaning when I say it frightens her hearing Foster talk the way he does. She probably thinks those pictures his mind calls up are what she would call bad medicine."

"Sounds reasonable," Caleb said. "Her own mind's a dark enough place."

Later, in bed, Caleb asked White Cloud, "Why were you singing while those raiders attacked us?"

"I was saying it was all right to die," she said. "All my people have a song to sing if they see death put out hand to them. It makes the leaving and going to the next place easier."

The notion surprised Caleb but made a certain sense when he thought about it. "I was trying too hard to keep us alive to think of dying," he said.

CHAPTER 29

Four days later they left the lava beds. North of the Sawtooths Range, they crossed a river and began climbing, leaving the dust and the dry country behind them. Slowly, they climbed into timber and then, surprisingly, broke out onto green grass, stretching away to the west as far as the eye could see.

"The Camas Prairie," Caleb said. "We've got fifty miles of this if my map is right."

Little Rain pointed off to one side. "Antelope." As White Cloud predicted, she had made a swift recovery and after two days of rest was riding as if nothing had happened to her. Her wound healed well, but, although she tried to hide it, she did not fully recover her endurance. The wide bandage wrapped around her head gave he a rakish look that fascinated Foster.

"You look like one of them renegades," he told her, and she threatened to beat him with a stick, but he didn't let up on her, and the attention obviously pleased her.

"Supper," White Cloud said, pulling her rifle out of its scabbard. "I catch up." She set off at an angle that would bring her within firing range of the antelope without spooking it.

"How high are we?" Dil asked.

"From what I've read, about five thousand feet," Caleb replied, urging Joshua forward. The animals had taken full advantage of the pause to start grazing and walked on with their mouths full of grass. They had not gone far when they heard the crack of a rifle.

"Steaks for supper," Foster said, standing up on Dakota, looking for White Cloud.

They moved forward at an easy pace, and Caleb reveled in the simple pleasure of being in a place that contrasted so sharply with what had surrounded them in the earlier part of the cutoff. His reverie was interrupted by White Cloud's yodeling call and swift arrival with a dressed antelope across her horse's withers.

"Indians here, hunting parties, not war parties," she said excitedly. "I met one woman digging camas, had basket nearly full. She said they come from south, hunting elk for winter meat. Also, most come in spring when blue flowers show where camas grows. Whole prairie blue then."

"Must be a beautiful sight," Dil said.

Foster grinned. "It looks mighty good right now."

In less than a mile, they came on a creek and followed it north for a while until they reached a shallow widening of the stream, shaded by willows. Drawing closer, they sent ducks and Canada geese exploding out of the reeds in a clatter of wings and wild honking.

"Roast goose," Little Rain said enthusiastically. "Tomorrow morning, shoot one."

"Two," Caleb said. "I'll go with you."

"Three," White Cloud said sardonically.

"Four," Dil said, laughing.

Foster just shook his head and looked puzzled.

During their second day, they saw sage hens, prairie chickens, ducks, and geese in the small marshes along the creeks, and a pair of foxes hunting them. The sky was clear and the day warmed by the sun. Nightfall, however, dropped the temperature swiftly. There was no frost, but it was cold enough by sunset to make them take refuge in their Fort Laramie clothes.

"In Blue Mountains," White Cloud said one morning as they

ate breakfast, looking up at the peaks surrounding them, "water will freeze at night. Maybe us, too."

Foster slid more fish onto his tin plate. "If you're joshing us, White Cloud, I'd just as lief you didn't."

"I won't let you freeze to death," Little Rain assured him. "White Cloud like to joke and keep face straight."

White Cloud made no response, but Caleb, watching her, thought she had not been joking. He suspected her remarks had more to do with her own concerns over what was facing them in the Blue Mountains than she would admit. If pressed, he would have to say he shared her worries.

"We *are* likely to run into snow in those mountains," Dil said. "We were pretty close to a frost here this morning, and we've got some distance to cover to reach them."

"Another week, if all goes well, should see us in Fort Boise," Caleb said. "Then another week to ten days should see us through the mountains, and, yes, they are higher in places than we are here."

But while they were crossing the prairie, they enjoyed clear skies and cool, sunny days. Frequently, they encountered herds of mule deer, elk, antelope, and often a lone moose feeding in the marshy places. One morning when Foster was riding with Caleb, the boy suddenly climbed to stand on Dakota's back. "Look there, Caleb! There's a bird yonder 'most nearly as tall as you."

Caleb stood in his stirrups. "I believe it's a sandhill crane," he said, pleased by the sighting. "There's more with their heads down, feeding."

"White Cloud will want to shoot one of them for supper," Foster said, still excited, "and we'll need a six-log fire to cook it."

Just then, the flock took wing. They didn't fly away but rose into the air as a black bear loped through the water and reeds.

"He ain't paying them or us no heed," Foster said, laughing. "Where do you suppose he's going?"

The bear splashed out of the marsh and picked up speed and was quickly out of sight with no more than a dismissive glance toward Wolf. Wolf limited his response to a single rumble at the bear. The cranes dropped back into the marsh before the bear had reached dry land, paying the humans no more attention than the bear had.

White Cloud rode up and pulled her horse to a stop beside them. "Never saw bird so tall," she said.

"Them's sandhill cranes," Foster told her proudly. "A bear just ran through them, and they flew up but dropped back down again. Nothing here seems to notice us."

Little Rain and Dil arrived with the pack train, and Foster introduced them to the cranes and told them about the bear. "We're chewing over whether or not to shoot one of them cranes for supper," he said. "White Cloud ain't made up her mind, and Caleb's holding back until he hears from her."

"This child was born with feather in his hair," White Cloud said, a smile twitching at the corners of her mouth.

"I ain't heard of that happening," Foster protested through the laughter of the adults.

"She means you were born all grown up," Dil told him. "I guess you started talking like an adult right from the get-go."

"How am I supposed to be talking?" Foster demanded, frowning.

"Just the way you are," Caleb told him. "We all like the way you talk. Isn't that true, White Cloud?"

"Yes, Foster, and I have locked you in my heart."

"Also mine," Little Rain told him.

"I'm glad we found you, Foster," Dil said.

The boy brightened. "I hope we don't eat one of them cranes. They look like they'd be tough as a boiled owl."

"I think we eat goose," White Cloud replied, getting nods of approval.

Later that morning, they saw a pair of coyotes kill a young mule deer too lame to run with the herd the coyotes had spooked into flight. Just as swiftly, they lost their meal to three gray wolves that tore into the coyotes and sent them racing away.

"Lucky wolves not kill them," White Cloud said. "Wolf not like coyote. Kill, lots of times."

The wolves had just settled down to feed on the carcass when a large brown bear appeared. The wolves tackled the bear together, which met them roaring, its paws swinging. After the bear got bitten hard enough to bleed, it settled down to fighting seriously and dealt one wolf a blow that sent it flying end over end. The remaining two wolves slowly fell back, keeping the bear occupied until the third was on its feet again, giving itself a good shake. Then, their honor intact, they abandoned the fight and loped away, looking none the worse for the encounter, their tails straight out behind them.

"Bye and bye," Little Rain said, sitting cross-legged on Sheba, "coyote come back, eat what bear left. Coyote always gets plenty to eat."

"Will the wolves come back?" Foster asked.

"No," she said, "not with fresh meat close by."

Overhead, vultures were already swinging in wide arcs, waiting. "Nature's clean-up crew," Dil said, watching them.

"They are the Patient Ones," White Cloud said. "Know they have only to wait."

The subject of vultures and their wisdom reminded Caleb of sights on the battlefield he'd as soon forget. "We have miles to go yet."

"Maybe should stop here," Little Rain said. "Build lodges, make snowshoes, hunt for meat. Dig camas before freeze. Have

fat winter." They already had two large sacks of camas bulbs, dug by the women and Foster earlier.

"We would have much company," White Cloud said with a sigh. "Many with guns."

"This pilgrim has seen enough of that. Let's go!" Foster urged.

The next day, to general sorrow, they came to the end of the prairie. Soon after, they reached Fort Boise, built two years earlier and housing companies of infantry and cavalry. White Cloud and Little Rain were astonished by the officers' quarters at the fort. It was made of stone blocks and sported two large stone chimneys, a tall window on each side of the front door, and a portico over the door with white painted columns supporting the roof. They sat on their horses and stared in wonder.

"Chimneys?" White Cloud asked.

"That's right," Caleb said.

"Chiefs live there?" Little Rain asked finally.

"Men who are officers in the army," Caleb said. "The soldiers live in the barracks."

Those were built of wood, and less impressive in the women's view. Infantrymen were drilling on the parade ground, and cavalry units came and went. Fort Boise was a sprawling place, dusty and noisy with Indian lodges raised on its perimeter, their pony herds grazing under the eyes of boys, who appeared to spend most of their time gambling and racing their ponies around the fort. After a short time, the women grew uneasy. "Not like it here," White Cloud said. "Smells bad. Bad medicine."

"The soldiers or the Indians?" Foster asked.

"Both," the women said together. Little Rain went on, "We make camp up the river away from here."

"All right," Caleb said, "but don't you want to have a look at the commissary?"

269

"Buy snowshoes, salt, flour, coffee, maybe more waterproof cloths," White Cloud said.

"And ammunition," Little Rain added.

"I'd like some of that hard rock candy," Foster said.

"Done," Dil said. "I'd like some of that myself."

"You want to go careful," the man in the commissary said upon learning where they were headed.

He was stout and red-faced, with a bald pate and a large, white handlebar mustache. He wore a collarless striped shirt and held up his black trousers with wide, gray galluses. "The Bannocks and the Snakes are restless. They've been buying whiskey from the traders and are holding pow-wows in all the villages."

"What's gotten them riled?" Caleb asked.

"Some of it may be the crowding in of people, passing through to Oregon," the man said, "but north of us there's mines, and a bunch of toughs up there want the Indians driven out of here and the Camas Prairie as well. There's been some killings. The army's trying to keep things calm, but I wouldn't bet on their being able to do it."

"Anything else?" Dil asked.

"Well, yes." The man slid his thumbs under the galluses and gave them a snap. "You look like you know what you're doing, but were you to ask me, which you ain't, in my view you're cutting things a mite thin."

"You mean the Blue Mountains?" Caleb asked.

"That's it. The army's still moving their people through there and back, but any week now it's going to snow three feet in the passes and more, higher, and that will shut things down 'til spring. So you might get to use these snowshoes."

"Thank you for the warning," Caleb said. "Fortunately, we're not burdened with a wagon."

"You got a snow shovel?"

"No."

"I'll get you one. If you are blizzarded in, you can use it to build a house of snow blocks. Might save your lives."

"Eskimos live in them," Dil said to Caleb while the man was gone. "At least, that's what I recall having heard. Why I remember these things and not the rest is a trial."

"I can believe it." Caleb wondered how one would go about building a snow house. With luck, they wouldn't need to find out.

They left the commissary with two large baskets filled with their purchases and the snowshoes slung across their backs. In addition, Caleb carried the shovel. As they walked out of the building, six tall Indian men with feathers in their hair were racing their ponies straight at the commissary. The riders wore leggings and had bows and quivers slung over their shoulders. Four of them held rifles as well.

Caleb caught Dil's eye. "Don't flinch."

"Makes a good picture, Captain," Dil said. "Let's set these baskets down so I can reach my gun should I need to."

They had just straightened up when the men yanked their horses back on their heels and spun them around, without taking their eyes off Caleb and Dil. "Squaw men!" one rider shouted. "Where are women?"

"They getting drunk," said another, with a long white scar down the right side of his face.

"They're drunk and spoiling for a fight," Caleb murmured. "Don't give it to them."

"Right, Captain," Dil muttered. "Let's get out of here."

A cavalry unit came around the building at a trot. The officer took in the scene and shouted an order. His men broke away by ranks and fanned out around the Indians, carbines at ready.

The officer trotted his mount toward the scarred Indian.

"Bear Claw, is there meat in your lodges?"

Bear Claw looked at the odds and apparently did not like them. "There is meat," he growled in reply.

"That is good. Perhaps it is time to go there. Let the firewater bring sleep. There is nothing here for a warrior to do."

Bear Claw's scowl deepened. "The next time I come, Bent Leg, I will not leave so soon. Think about that." He raised his rifle over his head, dug his heels into his pony's side, yelled, and rode straight at the arc of cavalry facing him, followed by his companions, all howling their war cries.

"Hold your fire!" the cavalry officer shouted, wheeling his horse to face his men. The Indians poured through the line and raced away.

The officer watched them go, then dismounted and limped toward Caleb and Dil. "Thank you for getting us out of a sticky situation," Caleb said when the officer reached them.

"Heaven be praised!" Dil shouted. "Captain John Bryce. You came through."

Bryce's sharp, gray eyes lit with recognition. He was a stocky man, his beard laced with white and his face and hands weathered brown. "Indeed I did, Dil, and I can thank you for most of it." Bryce wrung Dil's hand with both of his.

"Did you marry that nurse?" Dil asked. "What was her name?"

"Susan Lockard, and, yes, I did. By my last count we've got three children."

"Congratulations. I want you to meet Captain Caleb Stone, from the 20th Maine."

"Were you at Little Round Top with Colonel Joshua Chamberlain?" Bryce asked.

"He was there and then some," Dil said. "Colonel Chamberlain saved his life, but not before they broke the assault of the 15th Alabama."

"The colonel and I had a little help," Caleb said, reaching for Bryce's hand.

"There weren't that many of you." Bryce gripped Caleb's palm briefly, with a grim smile. "Were you in that charge?"

"Yes, he was," Dil said before Caleb could diminish his own role. "And when it was over, he had more holes in him than a colander."

"Then I suspect that, like me, your being above ground is due to this one-armed miracle maker," Bryce said, clapping a hand on Dil's shoulder.

"That's right; he certainly kept me walking the earth. How long have you been here in the West?"

"I was sent out here when Dil kicked me out of the field hospital. I wouldn't let them discharge me, and they wouldn't put me back on the lines. So here I am. The family's in Oregon City. Oregon City, Salem, and Portland are full-blown cities now. They don't look like the frontier any longer."

"I guess we'll get a look at them," Dil said. "We're going that way. That is, if the Indians don't get us. We've heard the tribes are rising."

"They're being crowded out of their hunting lands," Bryce said. "The miners north of here are forming posses to hunt Indians and kill them, and demanding the army drive them out of this part of the country. Good men like Bear Claw are taking up drinking, and whiskey is poison to them. I'm afraid real trouble is coming."

"How far west is this a danger?" Caleb asked.

"If you make it into the Blue Mountains, you should be all right, but you're running late. There can be big snows anytime now. Last year the passes were closed by mid-September."

"How many days to get through the mountains?" Caleb asked.

"Depends on the weather. You got a wagon?"

"Mules and horses," Caleb replied.

273

Bryce looked a little uneasy. "Going up the Boise, my sergeant saw two Indian women and a boy. Any chance they're with you?"

"Yes, they're ours," Dil said. "Is there a problem?"

"Let me answer the first question before getting to that one," Bryce said. "The weather will have a lot to do with it. The trail's rough, and there's a lot of sharp up and down in it. But if the weather holds like this, I think you should be through the passes in three days and into the Umatilla River valley. Then it's about ninety miles, give or take, to the Columbia."

"What about the Indian women?" Dil asked.

"Don't let the Snakes or the Bannocks or any other tribes take them," Bryce said solemnly. "You follow me?"

"We hear you," Dil said. "Up to now they faced slavery if captured. Is that what you mean?"

Bryce shook his head. "It won't stop there. The tribes have lost a lot of their women to white men out here. They don't like it."

"Well, Bryce," Caleb said, bracing his shoulders and speaking with forced cheer, "it's been a pleasure meeting you. Dil and I had better be moving."

He shook Bryce's hand again and started to gather his basket and the shovel.

"Hold on a bit," Bryce said. "I'll send a couple of men to give you a hand with your gear. Good luck, Captain Stone. Good luck, Dil. I'd like to send a dozen of my men to escort you to the Umatilla, but we're pretty much on alert here, and I can't do it."

"We don't expect it, Captain Bryce," Caleb said. "You've done more than enough giving us a hand with these purchases. The pack animals are going to groan out loud when they see us."

Bryce laughed, then turned away. A second later he turned

back and seemed about to say something but mounted instead. "Good luck on your journey, and get over the Blues as soon as you can."

Dil watched him ride off. "I had the feeling he had something more to say to us and changed his mind."

"It couldn't have mattered, or he would have told us, and here comes our help."

They reached the camp site a short while later. Once Foster and the women had sorted through what Dil and Caleb had brought and wrapped the snowshoes in deerskin before stowing them in the packs, White Cloud and Little Rain put on all the bead necklaces and colored glass bracelets the men had bought them and broke out singing and dancing, to Foster's delight.

"White Cloud!" he shouted when they stopped, "you and Little Rain could go into one of them saloons in a town and dance on the tables. I seen a saloon once. You could make a slew of money."

"Whoa, Foster!" Dil sounded shaken as he glanced at the two women. "They wouldn't want to do that. No, sir! That's not the kind of thing they would do."

Fists on their hips, White Cloud and Little Rain exchanged glances. Then they nodded and faced once another, eyes locked, and broke into a different kind of dance, clapping their hands above their heads while they swiveled their hips and shoulders. Finally they broke out laughing and turned to face their audience. Dil whistled and Caleb applauded while Foster stood looking at the women as if they were people he had never seen before.

"Foster," Little Rain asked, "would that be better dance for saloons?"

Amused and slightly shaken, Caleb asked, "Where did you learn to dance like that?"

"Is dance for night before wedding," White Cloud said.

"Should have man partner. You want to try?"

Caleb felt his face burn while the women and Dil laughed at him.

"I surely do wish someone would tell me what's going on here," Foster complained.

CHAPTER 30

After leaving Fort Boise, they came to a point in the trail called the Farewell Bend. Here, they veered away from the river and set off west toward the Blue Mountains, rising dark and forbidding in their path.

The good weather held, but the days were growing noticeably colder and shorter, and the travelers became increasingly subdued. Caleb tried to raise their spirits by reminding them that this was the last mountain range they would have to confront and that, with good fortune, they should be through the Blues in three or four days.

"Frost every night now," White Cloud said finally.

"Snow for sure," Little Rain added.

Dil said, "Give it up, Captain. We'll just hope for the best."

"I wonder," Caleb replied, "if our getting toward the end of our journey might be making us feel a little depressed?"

"Or what comes after," White Cloud said.

Caleb started to say something encouraging, then remembered Dil's comment and changed his mind.

During the evenings they sat around the fires longer than usual, recalling incidents from their journey together and reviewing what they would do if the snow caught up with them. The crests of the highest mountains were dusted with white, but Caleb reminded them that the snowcaps were at seven or eight thousand feet of elevation. "The final pass won't be over

thirty-five hundred feet, and I think it's the highest one," he added.

"What's it called?" Foster asked.

"Crawford Hill," Caleb said, "and if we're going to have any trouble with the local Indians, it will probably be there."

"Then we will stay close," Little Rain said. "I not want to be alone."

"I agree," Dil said.

Caleb nodded. "We'll stay together all through the mountains."

"Indians not like make war in the snow or in dark," White Cloud said. "Maybe we hope for snow."

Everyone laughed, but only Foster truly thought it was funny.

"We begin the climb here," Caleb said.

They were mounted and gathered at the foot of the trail that would take them up and into the Blue Mountains. The dark wall of forested slopes rose sharply before them, imposing a short silence on the small company.

White Cloud broke it. "Frost last night. Clouds on the mountains today."

A brief murmur of agreement followed, but Caleb rallied them. "Let's start. The sooner we do, the sooner this is behind us."

"We done this before," Foster said, sounding triple his age. "We can do her again."

The two women spluttered with laughter at the boy's choice of words, soon joined by the men, and the travelers started forward with spirits raised.

"Someone would like to have sheep for supper," White Cloud said. She was scanning the heights above them, but wherever she looked, she saw vast stands of larch, spruce, fir, and the towering ponderosa pines, broken here and there with lighter

green meadows. "Not easy to get there," she added.

"We're more likely to see elk and deer in the openings," Caleb said. "We'll eat. Don't worry. Will the harder riding bother Little Rain?"

"Not worrying." She scowled. "Perhaps if pregnant, someone might like talking to me."

"Whoa, White Cloud. I'm sorry. Haven't I been talking to you?"

"Tongue making words. Mind somewhere else."

"You aren't used to this yet, are you?"

She did not have to ask what he meant. "No."

As they rode along, the horses picking their way over a steep, rock-strewn section of the trail, Caleb studied her face. It was something he never tired of doing. She had the strong, high cheek-boned structure of her people, full lips, and large, dark eyes he never looked into without a tingle of excitement running through him. For no particular reason, he thought of Foster saying she was wild.

"Are you?" he asked.

"What?" She turned her head sharply toward him, the movement pulling her white deerskin shirt tight across her breasts. A slight frown furrowed her brow.

"Wild," he said.

"If joke, not funny."

Her dark eyes settled on his for an instant. The beginning of a smile pulling at the corners of her mouth vanished as quickly as it had appeared.

"Tell me what's troubling you," he said.

"There is bad medicine," she replied. "Someone can feel it."

"Who is in danger?"

"All of us."

He knew asking her how she knew would be futile. Probably,

she couldn't tell him. "Is something or someone trying to harm us?"

"It is what I have feared from the beginning," she said.

"I thought you had put those fears behind you."

She shook her head. Caleb felt a cold dread enter his mind, followed by a flash of anger he quickly suppressed.

"When did it come back?" he asked.

"Fort Boise."

He reflected on her answer for a moment. "White Cloud, I'm going to repeat myself and say I think our coming close to the end of our journey, and your not knowing just what will happen, is causing this."

"We will go among your people, whole villages of your people," she told him, her voice strained. "Many will say, 'You are here now. See how we live. Some of our women need men in their lodges. Take one of them. Let this one go back to her people. Your children will not be her or you.' "

She fell silent, and the chill in Caleb's heart deepened. She had seen it so clearly. He gathered his thoughts, pulling them back from what she had said.

"White Cloud, you see what is true," he began. "There will be white people. Some of them will say what you have said, but you have not asked me what I will say."

She was watching him, listening and observing closely. "Here on this mountain, perhaps you will say one thing," she replied, her voice devoid of joy. "With your people, it will be different."

"Does Little Rain feel the way you do, about Dil?"

"She thinks only about her child."

The answer wasn't what Caleb expected. He reached out and grasped her wrist. "I love you. I will not leave you. Believe me."

"I believe you love me as I love you, Caleb Stone," she told him with a wintery smile. He realized with a heaviness in his heart that, at least for now, he would gain nothing by arguing.

They made camp in a small, sloping meadow, with grass for the animals and a quick-flowing stream, running brightly over a gravelly bed and bubbling loudly around the tumble of rocks between the deeper pools. Dense growths of spruce and lodge-pole pines surrounded the meadow, providing easy access to firewood.

As soon as the wood was collected, Foster ran off to the stream and shortly returned with five fat cutthroat trout.

"Looka here," he shouted, running toward the fire. "I got these out of just three pools."

Little Rain's knife came out of her belt, and a few moments later the gutted fish were in the frying pan, to cheers from Caleb and Dil.

"Where are we now?" White Cloud asked as they settled down to eat.

"Oregon since we left Fort Boise," Caleb said. "Does it seem a long time since we were in Fort Kearny?"

"It is not a time I like to see in the flames of the campfire," Little Rain said quietly. "Bad times went before. But we found us," she added after a pause, smiling at Dil. "That is good to remember."

"I remember when you found me," Foster said. "I was just a kid then."

White Cloud looked amused. "You are grown up now?"

"Yup," Foster said. "I growed up when I met Gussie O'Neill. I wonder where she is? We was supposed to meet them at Fort Boise."

"One of these days, we've got to do something about that boy's English," Dil said.

"You're free to try." Caleb was only half listening, his attention still on a newly arrived thought. "White Cloud, Little Rain," he said, "I know we talked about this back around Fort Hall, but are either of you having second thoughts about not going

back to your people?"

"First answer Foster's question," White Cloud said. "Foster, we see no sign of them. Perhaps they are all right. What does Caleb think?"

"He thinks the way White Cloud thinks. They're probably all right, Foster."

She nodded. "Now, White Cloud will answer Caleb. Little Rain and this person spoke of returning to our people when the old moon slept. There is nothing for us to return to. No one there to welcome us. That is all I have to say. Perhaps Little Rain wishes to speak."

"I think as White Cloud does," Little Rain said quickly.

White Cloud stared hard at Caleb. "If Caleb wants to know if meeting him made all right what was before, perhaps he should ask someone when there are just two."

"You could go ahead and tell, White Cloud," Foster said. "I won't mind."

"Neither will Little Rain and I," Dil said.

"Some people not as funny as they think," White Cloud said sharply. She rose to her feet and walked away from the fire.

Caleb sighed. "I'll take first watch. Just give me a few minutes."

He stood, and, as he walked away in the direction White Cloud had gone, he heard Foster say, "Maybe being growed ain't all it's cracked up to be."

The second day broke cold with sullen dark clouds shrouding the peaks and dripping occasional spots of fine rain that felt like tiny needles of ice striking the face. They ate breakfast in silence. Even the animals looked depressed. Sheba rejected Little Rain's attempts to stroke her nose and sing her a morning song, something that had become a ritual with them. One of the pack horses launched a half-hearted kick at Dil, being careful to miss

him, and even Joshua pulled his saddle blanket off twice and threw it on the ground before he let Caleb saddle him.

"I wonder if he knows what's coming?" Caleb asked.

"Not like the smell of the wind," White Cloud said and mounted her horse. "Snow," she added darkly.

She was right. Less than an hour after they started off, it rode in on a sharpened wind and a fall in temperature.

"It could be worse," Caleb said, tightening his coat collar and pulling his hat lower on his forehead. "It could be freezing rain." But he had Little Rain on his mind, and the worrisome fact that even Sheba could not see through snow to pick her way easily around the large rocks and chunks of ledge jutting up from the road bed. Only Foster was pleased by the snow. He danced around in it whenever they stopped, making patterns in it and calling on everyone to see what he had done.

Once they were past midday, the trail turned up at a sharper angle. The snow thickened, and soon the animals were wading through half a foot of it. One of the pack horses stumbled, shifting his load to one side and forcing a stop. Caleb and White Cloud quickly resettled the packs, and then Caleb examined the horse's legs and hooves. To his relief, he found no injuries.

The snow accumulated more quickly the higher they went. By mid-afternoon, White Cloud rode back from point and said, "Time to camp. Cannot see far enough to know what comes."

"We'll stop at the next meadow," Caleb said, "and camp close to the woods and hope it breaks the wind."

"Indian ponies scrape snow to eat. Others not know how," she said. "Maybe have to use shovel and uncover grass."

"If we have to," he said, squinting at the sky. "How long is this going to last?" He didn't expect an answer, but voicing the question was a way of easing his concern.

"Maybe all night," she said without hesitation. "Maybe longer."

"Then let's hope we make Crawford Hill tomorrow and get down out of these mountains."

"Make camp as if for longer," White Cloud countered. "Need to be warm and dry."

"Yes," Caleb agreed, "before the light goes."

They soon reached a meadow, and Wolf found water. By then, the snow had deepened another six inches. The meadow was smaller than the one they had chosen the day before, but it was nearly level and backed into a mixed stand of lodgepole pines and spruce.

Where the overflow of a spring crossed the western corner of the meadow, White Cloud and Foster kicked the snow away and built a small dam to create a drinking pool for the horses. By the time they finished, Little Rain had a fire burning, and the two men were putting up a lean-to frame. Wolf had accompanied the women to the spring, but once they reached the camp site, he loped into the woods.

"Where's he going?" Foster asked, looking up from the fire as the wolf raced away.

"Hunting," White Cloud replied. She picked up her rifle, leaned against the packs, and jacked a shell into the chamber.

"You sure? He ain't running away, is he?" the boy asked with a worried frown.

"No," Little Rain told him, picking up her rifle as well.

The snow had not let up, and, despite the trees behind the lean-to, gusts of wind occasionally swirled the snowflakes around them in frigid circles, bending the flames and making them hiss as the snow struck them.

"Foster," Caleb called, "hold this post while I tie the cross piece."

White Cloud and Little Rain had been speaking quietly and stepped away from the fire to stand, rifles in their hands, watching the woods. Before long there was a snow-muffled snapping

of branches, and five does burst out of the woods with two yearlings close by, followed by a buck. Wolf loped easily in their wake.

"The female with no young one," White Cloud said, raising her rifle. Her gun and Little Rain's barked together. The largest doe in the herd pitched head over heels and lay still. Wolf, looking pleased, trotted up to the fallen deer, sniffed her head, and sat down, waiting for the women. As always, they made quick work of skinning and dressing the carcass.

"Why didn't you shoot the buck?" Foster asked while the women piled the best cuts of meat onto the deer's hide.

"More fat on female with no fawn," White Cloud replied. "Now help Little Rain pull meat to the fire, and put more wood on."

The snow was falling heavily now, fine, wind-driven flakes that swiftly dimmed the bloody patches around the butchered animal. The shifting sounds of the wind blowing through the spruce trees caught White Cloud's attention, and she glanced up from the plundered deer's carcass.

"Snow spirits speaking," she said, holding out the deer's heart to Wolf. To her surprise, with great care, he took it from her hand and settled down to eat. For a few moments, White Cloud sat on her heels, watching him. When he finished the heart, she reached into the deer again, cut out the liver, and laid it in front of Wolf.

"We are glad you with us," she told him. "Maybe sometime you will let me hug you."

She stood and squinted up at the snow-filled sky. "We use snowshoes tomorrow," she said, still talking to Wolf, then finished cleaning her hands and her knife in the snow and strode off to the fire.

With help from Foster, Caleb and Dil had finished the lean-to by rolling a heavy log onto the base of the roof poles and driv-

ing pegs into the ground behind the log, locking it in place. Once they had laid the waterproof sheets over the roof poles, they placed more poles over the sheets, to prevent the wind from blowing them off. Finally, Caleb took the snow shovel and scraped snow from under the lean-to.

"It may not be home," he said, "but it will keep the snow off."

Foster, stoking the fire, jumped up and cheered. The air around the lean-to, blown hither and thither, was heavy with the odor of sizzling steaks.

"We eat," Little Rain said.

Sitting on saddles and folded blankets under the lean-to and wrapped in their coats, they all ate supper, facing the fire in surprising warmth while the wind groaned in the trees behind them and the snow swirled and deepened on the meadow under a coal-black sky. As White Cloud had predicted, the Indian ponies pawed away the snow until they uncovered the grass and grazed. The mules, seeing what the ponies were doing, began pawing as well and were soon feeding. The other horses simply stood with their tails to the wind, their heads down, enduring.

Wolf appeared, licking blood off his jaws, and stood between the fire and the lean-to.

"Come in here," Foster said.

Wolf grinned with pleasure and came in.

"No!" Little Rain shouted. "He shake!"

Too late. The wolf shook himself. Melted snow rose around him in a glistening corona, showering everyone. Nearly finished eating and reveling in the warmth of the fire captured by the lean-to, everyone shouted with laughter, even Little Rain. Wolf squeezed between Foster and Dil and sat down, his head higher than Dil's.

"Wet dog!" Little Rain protested, holding her nose.

At that remark, Wolf slid his paws forward and collapsed onto

the ground with a long sigh, dropping his chin onto his paws.

"He'll dry out pretty fast," Foster said, finishing the last piece of steak.

"Someone ate whole heart and liver," White Cloud said, reaching across Foster and wiping her fingers on the wolf's back. "Needs to lie down."

"He ain't no floor rag," Foster protested.

"Better," White Cloud said, smiling at him.

CHAPTER 31

Caleb and Dil alternated standing guard and keeping the fire burning. The lean-to proved strong enough to hold the increasing load of snow, which insulated the inside from the cold even more, and the sleepers under the buffalo robes had only cold noses.

At some point in the first half of the night, snarling and snapping of teeth sounded from the deer's carcass several yards away. Caleb had started toward the deer when Wolf appeared and stepped in front of him, forcing Caleb to stop. He bent down and rested his hand on the animal's head, then told him to move. At that moment, deep-throated snarls smothered the yipping and snapping of the coyotes.

"Wolves?" Caleb asked quietly, realizing there was more than one of whatever had driven off the coyotes.

Wolf remained planted firmly against Caleb's thighs.

"Good thinking," Caleb said. "Let's look at the horses."

Wolf set off at once, breaking a trail for Caleb. The mules and horses were bunched together, stoically facing away from the wind and driving snow.

"They going to be safe?" Caleb asked as he walked among them, checking every one. He wore high-top boots, woolen trousers, a sheepskin coat, and a scarf tied over his hat and ears and wound around his neck and face. Even so, his back and his feet were cold. Wolf moved with him, lifting his head to test the wind at frequent intervals. Caleb watched him carefully, but saw

in his movements no sign of unease.

"Back to the fire," he said.

Wolf set off without hesitation, and Caleb slogged after him through the knee-deep snow. When they reached the fire again, Dil was already on his feet, dressed like Caleb, except for a shawl of elk hide Little Rain had laid out for him to throw over his shoulders.

"Horses all right?" he asked.

"Seem to be," Caleb said, "but there's wolves on the mule deer carcass. I'm hoping it will keep them off the horses."

"I heard the coyotes. Then I didn't."

"The wolves drove them off. Wolf kept me from going for a closer look."

"Probably just as well."

"I saw his point."

The wind died sometime before daylight, and the storm gradually passed over them, leaving behind a foot and a half of dry snow, deeper in the drifts.

"I ain't going to walk in that very fast," Foster said, staring out from the lean-to at the white world surrounding them.

"We will let the horses walk for us," White Cloud told him, sounding happier than she usually had of late.

Caleb reached for the shovel and said, "I better dig some places clear of snow so the horses can get something to eat."

"Maybe dig around fire," Little Rain suggested. "Make place to cook breakfast."

"Anybody but Caleb and me hear the coyotes and wolves last night?" Dil asked.

Neither of the women had and having missed the wolves nearly brought Foster to tears. "Somebody should of told me," he complained.

"Dil and I couldn't see them, but we both heard the coyotes that were on the deer first," Caleb said. "Then Wolf and I heard

them drive away the coyotes. I'd guess there were at least three of them, possibly more. I wanted to try for a closer look, but Wolf planted himself in front of me and wouldn't let me go."

"Some children," White Cloud said, frowning at Caleb, "probably know not to walk over when wolves eating deer—unless want to become part of meal."

"I'll go ahead and do the shoveling," Caleb said, grinning at being chastised. Even Wolf looked as if he was laughing.

The day had broken nearly clear except for a scattering of clouds hovering around the tallest peaks, glistening white snow tails blowing off their tops. It took the travelers a little longer than usual to get under way, partly from having to deal with the snow, but also from reluctance to leave their lean-to, which had started out as a shelter and grown into something more. A roof over their heads for the first time in months, Caleb thought. *A good sign?*

Mounted on Sheba and looking back at the remnants of the lean-to, Little Rain said a bit ruefully, "Hang elk hides on sides and front, make lodge."

"We'll do better in Oregon," Dil told her, laying a hand on her thigh. He had helped her into the saddle and was standing beside her.

"Already there, cold welcome," White Cloud said, swinging onto her mare.

"Let's move out," Caleb called from the front of the line, not wanting White Cloud to get started on that subject.

Fortunately, the trail was well enough cleared of trees to allow them to follow easily the twisting ribbon of white marking it. They went along slowly, the horses making good passage through the light, dry snow, but now and then where the woods opened, the wind had piled the trail with drifts four and five feet deep. In one place, Caleb had to shovel a narrow path through a drift over six feet high.

Wolf, at the head of the line as usual, moved along at a tireless lope and soon outdistanced the rest. He had just crested a sharp rise when a small herd of elk heading down the mountain, having stayed too long on high country pastures, poured across the trail in front of him. They were running full out with half a dozen wolves pressing them hard. Wolf lengthened his stride and raced back along his trail, followed by two of the largest animals in the pack.

"Wolves!" Caleb shouted, whipping his rifle out of its scabbard as he came up in his stirrups. He fired over Wolf's back, bringing down the huge black animal less than ten feet behind.

He fired again, missed, and jacked in a third shell. The second pursuing wolf, without pausing, flung himself off the trail and bolted into the trees. Wolf skidded to a stop under Joshua's nose and spun around to face whatever else was coming.

"Wolf!" shouted Foster, urging Dakota up beside Caleb. "What was you thinking? Them fellers would of eaten your guts."

"We will skin this one," White Cloud said happily as she flung herself off her mare, followed by Little Rain moving more slowly.

"I know," Foster said, dropping down from Dakota as both women sank to their knees in the snow, their knives flashing in the sunlight. "Watch and learn."

"Will we make Crawford Hill in time to cross it today?" Dil asked.

"We might if we don't have to skin any more wolves," Caleb said, resigned to the pause but eager to be moving. "You know, Dil, Wolf is a source of surprises," he added. "Given his grit, who would have guessed he would bolt rather than fight?"

Dil looked down at Wolf, whose neck hair still bristled. "In about a split second, he must have weighed up the odds and seen they leaned away from him. Smart animal. Do you think

he'll stay with us when we stop moving?"

"I think I'm more concerned how our neighbors will take to him," Caleb replied. "People out here don't have what you'd call warm feelings toward wolves."

"Wolves and Indians," Dil added quietly, moving his gaze to the women, who were working at full speed and telling Foster what they were doing. The three of them occasionally broke out in laughter.

Caleb looked at White Cloud, half buried in the snow, her black hair lifting in the wind, her voice rising and falling, her hands moving swiftly and steadily as though the flashing knives were skinning the wolf by themselves.

How wonderful she is, he thought, his heart swelling, *how absolutely herself and a part of what she is doing. What a blessing I found her.* At that moment she looked up at him, catching his eyes. For an instant, they stared at one another. Slowly, a smile brightened her face.

"Caleb Stone," she said, laughter in her voice. "I see someone."

"White Cloud," he replied, returning her smile, "I see you."

The sun was within an hour of sinking behind Crawford Hill when they reached its foot. To their relief, the snow depth lessened as they moved west until here it was only shin deep.

"There it is," Caleb said. "We've got about an hour and a half of light left. The animals are tired, and so are we. What do you want to do?"

Dil looked up. "My guess is, it would take about that long to reach the summit. What's beyond?"

"A fairly sharp descent into a valley with the Umatilla River in it."

"Maybe no snow?" White Cloud asked.

"Possibly not. It's the mountains that caught the snow. Little Rain, how are you feeling?"

"Go," she said. "Maybe camp where no snow."

"I'm with Little Rain, Captain," Foster put in, raising chuckles and spirits.

"Dil?" Caleb asked.

"Lead on, Captain," he said cheerfully.

Wolf was already moving, as freely as if it were morning.

"Spirit wolf," White Cloud said, watching the animal start off at a lope. "Knows what people think."

The sun had been gone half an hour when they reached the summit. The last of the light was fading out of the western sky, and below them a soft mist had cast a veil over the valley. To their surprise, the pass was nearly free of snow.

"Shall we go on until we find the river and camp there?" Caleb asked as they gathered and stared down into the new land.

"Moon rise soon," White Cloud said.

"How about you?" Dil asked Little Rain. "Do you need a rest?"

"This one would like to go on," she answered. "Animals need grazing, also water."

"It's going to be a mite steep, but I'd sure like to see the moonlight on that mist," Foster said, still staring down the trail.

"All right then," Caleb said, "we'll go down. Stick together and go slow. Foster, ride with me. We'll see the moon on the mist together."

The descent was steep and the footing loose in places, but the pack animals were tired enough to walk slowly, and all of the horses and mules had learned from long experience on the trail how to pick their way safely. A three-quarter moon rose behind them, its light falling on the softly rolling mist as if it shone on a pale and restless sea.

"Ain't that something, Captain?" Foster asked. He sounded awed. "We'd go a long way to see the likes of that."

"It is beautiful, Foster," Caleb said. He turned in his saddle

to look for White Cloud, wanting to share the moment with her, but she and Little Rain had dropped back to watch the pack animals, leaving the lead rope with Dil. All of those behind him were shadows, and Caleb turned away with a sudden, cold sense of foreboding.

"We're at least halfway down this hill," he said to Foster, shaking off the gloom. "How are you doing?"

"All right. My tail's a mite sore is all. We're going to ride into that mist, ain't we?"

"We certainly are," Caleb said.

"I ain't never done that before."

"Well, we'll probably get a little wet."

The line of people and animals made a slow, silent dive into its gray dampness, filling Foster with delight. Very soon after that, they found themselves on level ground with dirt instead of rocks under their feet. The mist diffused the moonlight, but it was bright enough to see grass on either side of them. They did not have to search for the river because the animals, not having drunk for several hours, set off when given their heads and took them to the Umatilla.

Once they reached the river, they set up camp close to a stand of cottonwood and willow trees. In a short time, the pack animals were stripped of their packs and saddles. Dil and Foster accompanied the thirsty animals to the river while Caleb went in search of wood.

"Eat and then sleep," White Cloud announced as soon as the animals were hobbled and grazing.

Caleb stared into the fire, the uneasiness he had experienced on the mountain creeping up on him again. After they had eaten, Little Rain and Dil took Foster and went to their beds. White Cloud said to Caleb, "Our bed is ready. I will take first watch." She patted his shoulder. "Someone needs to sleep."

"Let's both take it," he said, bracing himself. "There's some

bad stories about renegade Cayuse and Umatillas attacking travelers in this area."

They moved off, neither speaking until they were alone.

"What are the dark thoughts you carry to the fire?" White Cloud asked.

"No single thing," Caleb answered as they walked slowly among the grazing animals. "Perhaps it has something to do with the weight of the mountains lifting off us."

"Sick?"

"No."

"You worry about us?"

"No. When I have slept, it will probably be gone. It feels as though the air is stirring. Am I right?"

"Yes, I think there will be a wind, and the mist will soon be gone."

She was right. The wind slowly rose, tumbling the mist and bearing it away, leaving a sparkling sky and the moon sailing slowly among the stars. White Cloud stared up at them. "My father knew names of some stars."

"Do you know where your father came from?" he asked, gazing upward with her.

"It was near big water. His father was whale hunter and sometimes was away two winters. He threw spear at whales. Once, he went away and ship did not come back."

"He probably came from New Bedford or Nantucket, Massachusetts, places on the Atlantic Ocean. I came from the same part of the country."

"He said he never wanted to see the big water again, but he had seen the big water we would see if we went west far enough."

"Would you like to see it?" Caleb asked.

"It can't happen, can it?"

"Yes. If you want to see it, one day we will see it."

She turned to look at him. "It is hard to believe, Caleb Stone."

"I know, but, God willing, we're going to do what we came to do."

CHAPTER 32

"Them's Indian ponies," Foster said, standing on Dakota's back and staring at the horses scattered across the expanse of grassland surrounding them.

"Wild horses," Dil said. "See how they're gathered in small herds with a stallion guarding each one."

"Why?" Foster asked.

"Making babies takes two, mare and stallion," White Cloud said, riding up beside them. "Stallion not satisfied have one mare, must have more. Stallions fight over mares. Sometimes kill one another."

"I'll be hornswoggled," Foster said. "Don't seem too smart."

"No," White Cloud answered, then burst into laughter.

"On the whole, Foster," Caleb said, "women don't have a high regard for male intelligence."

"More worse than that," White Cloud called as she rode back along the pack train.

Travel along the river was much easier and the temperature milder than they had experienced for the past few weeks. For White Cloud, however, as Caleb saw, the generally better mood was tinged with an unease that never left her. She was, he noted with pain, doing her best to hide her worry, and Caleb tried to keep her with Little Rain and Foster, to distract her, as well as talking to her whenever he could of their new life in the Willamette Valley.

For his part, Caleb had begun to shed the uneasiness he'd

297

felt by Crawford Hill. On point late one morning, he figured they had about a day's more travel to reach the Fort Walla Walla turnoff from the main trail. It was nearly noon, and he felt encouraged as he looked for a place to stop for their break. The weather had turned warm, and the abrupt shift in temperature from the cold in the mountains affected all of them, even slowing Wolf. The heat led Caleb to cast around for shade, which was proving hard to come by.

He was about to settle for a small stand of willows on the banks of a feeder to the Umatilla River when Wolf stopped suddenly, ears cocked, staring ahead of them, a low rumble forming in his chest. Perhaps a quarter of a mile away the unstable outline of three riders emerged from the rising heat. Almost certainly men with rifles across their saddles, Caleb thought.

He turned Joshua and kicked him into a run. "We've got company," he told Dil when he reached him. "Pull the string together and tell the women."

By the time the riders were within hailing distance, Caleb and Dil were in front with White Cloud and Little Rain on each side of the pack animals, rifles in their hands. Foster was between the animals and Little Rain, holding the lead string.

The oncoming riders, pack horse in tow, slowed their mounts to a walk. All three men were bearded and wore long-sleeved, gray shirts and dark trousers and boots. Their hats were dark and wide-brimmed with tall crowns, and each man carried a Henry rifle.

"I don't like this," Caleb said to Dil.

He watched their approach, and, when they were within speaking distance, he said, "That's close enough. What can we do for you?"

The oldest rider, his beard graying, scowled at Caleb, Dil, and the rest. "What are those squaws doing with rifles?" He spoke harshly, as if used to being obeyed.

Caleb bristled at the tone and the slur. "We have no intention of causing you or anyone else any trouble," he said evenly. "But this is how things stand. Those women could shoot a fly off the top of your tall hats, or they could aim a little lower. My friend here and I would have a hard time missing you blindfolded. The first one of you to reach for a sidearm or points a rifle at us will die. That will leave two of you and four of us."

A second man, much younger than the first, asked, "Where did you come from?"

"East," Dil answered.

The older man spoke again. "The boy belong to either of you?"

"Where are these questions leading?" Caleb asked.

"Is the boy's mother one of those women?"

"No," Dil answered. "Though that's none of your business."

The third man stepped his horse forward. "I'm afraid it is, gentlemen," he said. "Seeing as you're in the state of Oregon."

He slid his rifle into its scabbard and dismounted, then walked toward Caleb and Dil. He was better dressed than the other two and, judging from how he spoke, Caleb thought, educated. He stopped beside Caleb and extended his hand. "Jason Faulkner, of the Oregon Legislative Assembly. My *bona fides* are in my saddlebag, should you wish to see them. The other two gentlemen are my guides and guardians. This area is plagued with renegades of all stripes. Where are you headed?"

"Caleb Stone." Caleb bent to shake the man's hand but didn't linger over it any longer than necessary. "Our destination is the Willamette Valley. Were you to step back, Mr. Faulkner, I'll join you on the ground. Perhaps you would tell me what you're doing here."

"Gladly." Faulkner stepped away. When Caleb joined him, he said, "The assembly has called for a report on the state of affairs in the state, and I was assigned to the Umatilla region,

which is where we are." For a moment he looked uncomfortable. "I am also obliged to ask what your relationship is with the two native women. What I have to say next will be framed by your answer."

From the corner of his eye, Caleb saw White Cloud tense. He gave her a sideways glance and saw she was watching his exchange with Faulkner. How much had she heard? *Don't say a word*, he thought, willing her to hear him. *We don't know where things stand yet.*

To buy time, he gestured toward Dil. "First, let me introduce you to my friend Dil Smith," he said, belatedly recalling his friend's surname. Dil nodded, giving Faulkner a glance, but his hand rested on the butt of his revolver, and his eyes went back instantly to Faulkner's companions. "As to our intentions, we're looking to acquire title to some land and settle on it."

"And the women?"

He chose his words carefully. "Are with us. And will stay so."

Faulkner moved a few paces off, nodding toward Caleb to follow. Dil, ever alert, sidled his horse to keep within earshot. "Well now, that's a problem," Faulkner said, low voiced. "You two and the boy are welcome here. The Indian women aren't. Oregon is a whites-only state, and they will have to leave."

Shock made Caleb gape at him. "What the hell—?"

"I'm afraid it's the truth," Faulkner told him. "Slavery is banned in Oregon, but so are black people and Indians. When found, they're arrested and given a certain number of days to leave the state. If they don't leave, they're whipped and sent off. Or worse. Half-breeds go to a reservation."

"Lord God!" Dil said. "How do you sleep nights?"

Faulkner lowered his voice further. "Mr. Smith, it's extremely dangerous to express your feelings in that way hereabouts. My guides would draw down and challenge you if they heard what you just said."

Caleb laid a hand on Dil's leg. "Let it go, Dil. We need to learn what we can." What he'd heard already made him feel sick, and God only knew how much White Cloud was understanding of all this. Her worst fear, realized. He couldn't stand to think of it. "It's too late to retrace our steps over the mountains," he said to Faulkner.

"Are you looking to farm?"

"Those are our plans."

"May I make a suggestion?"

"We would welcome it."

"There's some risk involved, because quite a few locals are fully in support of the whites-only law and will not hesitate to enforce it," Faulkner said. "Indian troubles have hardened their position. I'd advise you to stay on the trail to the Whitman Mission Cutoff and follow it all the way to Fort Walla Walla. Once there, you'll be in the Washington Territory, where you will find no legal hindrances to your claiming land or"—he glanced at White Cloud and Little Rain—"whatever else you intend. Avoid contact with anyone until you're out of Oregon, and get to Washington as fast as you can."

Caleb took a moment to absorb this. Faulkner seemed a decent man, in spite of his companions. Yet he accepted the state of affairs in Oregon as if he could do nothing about it. Perhaps he couldn't. *Then what did Dil and I, and all our dead, fight for,* Caleb thought. Weary beyond words all of a sudden, he thanked Faulkner with what grace he could manage. They talked a few more minutes, Caleb gleaning every detail he could about what to do when they reached Washington Territory. Then Faulkner rejoined his men, and they rode away.

Caleb walked back to where Joshua stood patiently and mounted up. "What happen?" White Cloud demanded. "What did man tell you who got off horse? Something bad. Your face say so."

He wasn't yet up to telling her the whole truth, and, to judge from his expression, neither was Dil. "The man we talked to is Jason Faulkner, a member of the Oregon Assembly," Caleb said, loud enough so Little Rain and Foster could hear as well. "He was sent out by the government to get an idea of conditions in the Umatilla Valley. So far, the few people he's found are trying hard to get out of here. He hasn't found anyone wanting to settle and said he didn't expect to—it being too isolated and with the Indian troubles to boot."

Little Rain seemed satisfied, as did Foster, who was disappointed there wasn't more to the story. White Cloud was another matter. Her black eyes bored into him as he finished speaking, with that glint that always made him feel guilty even when he wasn't. "There's a little more," he said, "but the gist of it was that we should get a move on and stay moving until we're well on the way to Fort Walla Walla in the Washington Territory."

White Cloud wasn't having it, as her flat tone made clear when she spoke. "Perhaps someone will have more to say tonight."

A little later, riding next to Dil, Caleb said, "It's uncanny. I swear that woman can see into my head."

Dil grinned. He, at least, seemed to have recovered some cheer. "Were you ever to take on an outside woman, your life wouldn't be worth a plugged nickel."

For the next few hours Caleb pressed them hard, until Little Rain finally called for a halt. Finding themselves close to a stand of larch and fir trees and a small creek, they made camp.

"How come we've got these trees now?" Foster asked while he and Caleb gathered wood.

"We're climbing again, and their being here means there's more rain. Have you noticed how it cooled as the sun went down?"

"I guess so," Foster said. He lowered his hatchet. "You hold-

ing out on us, Captain?"

Caleb sighed. "Let's get this wood hauled in and get some food inside us and then see where we are. How's that?"

"I guess so." The boy sounded let down. *Another one,* Caleb thought, suppressing a frown of concern.

The night was cool and crisp with the stars glittering like ice crystals and the moon sailing on a cloudless, indigo sea. The animals grazed close by, and the tearing sound of them munching grass made a peaceful accompaniment to their supper talk. Despite all that, uneasiness lay heavy in the air. With the meal behind them, Caleb rose and said, "I have something to tell you. It's going to sound worse than it is." *And it's bad enough,* he thought as four faces turned to him, their expressions frozen in the firelight.

"We will not be going to the Willamette Valley," he said, "or anywhere else in Oregon, and I want you to listen carefully to what I have to say about that. Are you ready?"

"We listen," Little Rain said, pulling Foster against her.

White Cloud turned her gaze to the fire.

"Go ahead, Captain," Dil said. He knew what was coming, which helped, though Caleb hadn't made up his mind to reveal every grim detail of their encounter with Faulkner and his "guides." "Tell the worst, then give the good news."

Caleb had mulled over what to say and drew breath to start on the speech he had prepared, but, looking at Foster and the two women, he changed his mind.

"We're going to Fort Walla Walla," he began. "That's in Washington Territory. From there, we'll travel north to the Spokane Valley, stake our claims, and set about making a life together. Dil and I can each claim 167 acres of land and buy more if needed. How does that sound?"

White Cloud looked sharply at him. "Why we not go to Willamette?"

Caleb could not tell whether she was angry or frightened. Maybe both. "It's good land. We'll farm it, keep cattle and horses, maybe some sheep. The country is full of deer, elk, bears, cougars, beavers, muskrats, all kinds of critters. We'll eat well."

"Why?" White Cloud repeated.

Caleb bit his lip. He'd hoped to avoid saying this but should have known better. He walked around the fire to White Cloud and sat between her and Little Rain. Then he grasped one of their hands in each of his. "Dil and I can't marry you in Oregon."

The silence that settled over the little group was profound. White Cloud stared at Caleb, while Little Rain turned her head to meet Dil's gaze. Foster looked back and forth at the women. Then Little Rain slipped her hand from Caleb's grip and stood, gave her hand to Foster, and with Dil moved away from the fire, taking Wolf with them.

White Cloud broke the silence, her gaze falling to her own hand joined with Caleb's. "Caleb Stone, you have travelled for almost four moons to come to Oregon," she said, speaking quietly. "It was in your heart from the beginning."

Her voice broke, and for a moment she couldn't speak. Struggling, she burst out, "Now, because of me, you cannot do what you have tried so hard to do. It is not right this should happen. I not let it. I go away."

She squeezed her eyes shut to hide the tears, but they slipped out and wet her cheeks, shining in the flickering light of the fire.

Caleb grabbed her by her shoulders. "White Cloud, look at me. Look at me," he said, his voice rising. "You will not leave me."

She looked at him, her eyes flooded with tears. He pulled her against his chest and wrapped her in his arms. "Nothing short of death itself will take you from me," he said, dropping his

voice but not its intensity. "Nothing, White Cloud. Do you hear me? In Washington Territory we will be married."

She stiffened in his grasp, every muscle proclaiming resistance. Then, abruptly, she flung her arms around him and held tight.

"I stay with you, Caleb Stone," she cried, her resistance bursting like a dam in a flood. "I stay with you. Hurts too much to leave. I have lost my honor. I am sorry. I cannot go. I ruin your life."

"No, White Cloud," he said, unable to choke back tears of his own, "you have saved my life, and I promise never, ever to stop loving you."

CHAPTER 33

Five days later, full of forced marches under constant vigilance and scrambling to avoid other travelers, they reached Fort Walla Walla. A huge weight lifted off them, except perhaps Foster, who looked forward with nothing but eager anticipation to their new world.

"I didn't tell Little Rain what would have happened to her had we been arrested," Dil said once they were out of Oregon. "Does White Cloud know?"

"No." Caleb glanced over his shoulder, still not entirely easy in his mind. "I decided knowing she and Little Rain couldn't marry us in Oregon was about all she could bear."

"Little Rain went quiet after she heard what you said, but it didn't last more than a few hours. The next morning, I tried to talk to her about it, but she said, 'No, Dil, not trouble child.' That was that."

"Foster asked me if Faulkner had said anything else," Caleb added. "I said Oregon only wants white people living in the state. He told me anyone who didn't want White Cloud and Little Rain around them needed to have his ass kicked. I wanted to tell him not to talk that way but found I agreed with him."

As at the other forts they'd encountered, White Cloud and Little Rain refused to camp near Fort Walla Walla, with its constant movement of mounted soldiers and the straggle of camp followers and Indian women selling beaded moccasins and deerskin shirts and leggings. Indian ponies wandered among

the straggle of teepees or were ridden at a gallop by drunken warriors whooping and shouting.

Caleb didn't much like what he saw there either, and after some discussion they all decided to go north. In addition to wanting the women camped in a place where they might rest for a few days, his mind began shaping another plan. The land where the fort lay was mostly open, dry country, dotted with sagebrush and other low-growing shrubs, but wherever water was permanent there were stands of willow and spruce and cedar, and plenty of grass as well.

"Looks like a short-grass prairie," Dil said when they had followed a creek to a low hillside, heavily wooded and dotted with small stands of trees whose leaves had begun to turn.

"Let's ask the women what they think. If they're satisfied, we'll settle in," Caleb said.

"How long we stay?" White Cloud asked, eying the creek and the area Caleb and Dil had settled on for the camp.

"Two or three days," Caleb said. "I've got some things to attend to at the fort."

"Someone might like a lean-to," she said, looking at Little Rain.

"Right," Dil said. "Someone might be willing to rest for a couple of days and catch up on sleep."

"I might like to do some fishing," Foster said, "just to keep my hand in."

"Good idea," Caleb said. "We've missed those fish fries. Little Rain, what about you?"

"Winter comes," she said quietly.

With the possible exception of Foster, they all understood at once what she meant.

"We haven't forgotten," Caleb said. "I estimate we're a week away from the Spokane Valley. Give us another two weeks to stake our claims, and we'll be into October. That's when we

build to have a roof over our heads before it snows. You will have another three or four months to go, warm and dry."

Little Rain frowned slightly, as if figuring things out in her head. "Will work."

"I'll beat you with a stick if you don't," Dil said, putting his arm around her shoulders.

She elbowed him in the ribs. "Two children here already."

Dil groaned theatrically and fell to the ground. Despite the cloud still hovering over them all, White Cloud and Little Rain burst into laughter.

The lean-to was finished well before sunset. Foster had caught half a dozen trout, which were added to the brace of grouse White Cloud shot shortly after reaching camp. Wolf cleaned up the guts of fish and fowl, finishing off with a slab of two-day-old venison.

Supper over, Caleb rose and addressed the two women. "Dil and I have discussed this and are in agreement. So now we are bringing it to you. We considered whether each of us should speak to you separately but in the end thought, we are five people with lives so close that we should talk about it together."

"Someone sounds not so sure," White Cloud said to Little Rain, "and is slow to say what is on his mind."

"Yes," she replied, "some people have too many words at the council fire."

"Some people should keep their knives in their belts," Dil said, raising a laugh from the others.

"I'm going to bed," Foster said, sounding disgusted. He left, taking Wolf with him.

When the boy was beyond the firelight, Caleb resumed speaking. "We both had thought we would marry you, like we promised, as soon as we got to the Willamette Valley," he said with increasing seriousness. "There would be towns with churches and ministers there. Where we're going, most likely

there won't be any churches or ministers. So we would like to get married to you here. Would you want to do that?"

The women stared at Caleb in silence, and he found looking at their faces told him nothing about what they were thinking. Finally, they looked at one another, their expressions unchanged. Little Rain nodded, and White Cloud stood.

"What we have heard is important," she said quietly, holding herself straight and tall, the flickering light from the fire shining in her dark eyes, which were focused on Caleb. "We have thought about it and talked about it for long time."

She looked at Little Rain, who rose and said, "White Cloud has spoken well."

Following her lead, both men nodded agreement.

"It is in my mind," Little Rain continued, looking from Dil to Caleb and speaking with more gravity than usual, "that you may not have thought what this means. Perhaps we should go on as we are with you in our hearts."

Dil answered before Caleb could, matching Little Rain's seriousness. "Little Rain fears we do not see what it means for us to marry one another, but we also have given it careful thought. We want you to become our wives and make your lives with us. Little Rain, you carry our child. I have no doubt that White Cloud will soon carry the Captain's child. We wish to be their fathers and for them to carry our names, and for you to add our names to yours and yours to ours."

"White Cloud, Little Rain," Caleb added, "together we will be making a new world in a new place for all of us. We will have a Christian minister marry us, and, if you wish, we will gladly be married by a holy man of your people also. In marrying you we will honor both the Christian God and the Great Spirit. There is one more thing that should be said. By marrying us, by the laws of the land, should anything happen to me or to Dil, all that we had will pass to you and our children and cannot be

taken away from you."

After a long moment's silence except for the crackle of the fire, Little Rain said, "Dil, we will talk now."

"Caleb Stone?" White Cloud asked.

"Yes?" He extended his hand to her.

The four of them left the fire together, walking in the moonlight toward the tethered horses and mules, where Caleb and White Cloud drew apart from Dil and Little Rain. There was no frost, but the temperature had dropped into the low forties, and Caleb knew the sharp wind would make the lean-to a welcome retreat. But first, private things must be said and heard and understood.

Caleb stopped and faced his love. "Will you marry me, White Cloud?" he asked, holding her hands.

"I will ask you once more," she answered. "You are sure you want me as a wife?"

"I have never been more sure of anything."

"Then I will be your wife, Caleb Stone. I love you, and I hold you in my heart. Now hold me or tears will come."

He held her and kissed her, and they stood joined in the moonlight. On a nearby hill, coyotes yipped at the moon. The animals cropped grass, and near the lean-to an owl interrogated the night. A shooting star glittered briefly across the night sky, and Caleb took it as a blessing.

The following morning, Caleb left for the fort with a list of things to buy at the commissary as well as a list of tasks he had set himself. Dil remained in camp to protect the women and Foster, a move that seemed prudent, although they had seen no one since leaving the fort. The fair weather was holding, and Caleb could see from the short grass and frequent, large stretches of open ground that this was a dry country at least at this time of year.

After visiting the commissary and leaving the clerk with his list of needed goods, Caleb asked where the headquarters were of the Washington Territorial Volunteer Infantry. Once in the headquarters building, he was directed to the commanding officers' wing. "You'll need to talk with Colonel Horace Braceworth, sir," the sergeant said after Caleb introduced himself and explained why he was there. "I'll see if he's free."

He was, and the sergeant led Caleb into a sparsely appointed office where a large, red-faced and red-haired officer whose thick, red beard was streaked with silver greeted him.

"Is there any chance I'm speaking with Captain Caleb Stone of the 20th Maine that broke the Confederacy at Gettysburg and may have won us the war?" Braceworth demanded in a booming voice as he strode around his desk. He grasped Caleb's hand and nearly shook his arm out of its socket.

"I am," Caleb said, trying to free his hand.

Braceworth beamed and let go of him. "It's an honor, Captain Stone, and what can I do for you? What do you need?"

"I'm planning to settle in the Spokane Valley and will need to file a homestead claim at a general land office, Colonel," Caleb said. "Is there one in the Spokane Valley region?"

Braceworth scratched his beard and frowned in concentration. "No, but there's one in Walla Walla."

"How do you suggest I go on from here, sir?" Caleb asked.

"Stake your claim to . . . what is it?"

"A hundred and sixty acres."

"Ah, good. Can you measure that amount of land?"

"I can, Colonel. Any farmer's son can do that a week after being weaned."

That produced a roar of laughter from the big man. "Then I'd say, Captain, you're in business."

"I'll need to buy some farming equipment. Can I buy these things in the town?"

311

"Yes. The presence of the fort has enabled stores to open and farms to sell cattle and produce to us. You'll have no trouble there."

"Is there any way of getting things to where we're going other than taking them ourselves?"

Braceworth nodded. "John Dawson's got a haulage business, taking in his wagons whatever the miners in the Colville River region need and anyone else in between. The Coleville River settlements are some distance north of where you're going. Dawson's on the post, probably at the commissary. I'll send my desk sergeant to track him down if you want to talk with him."

"I'd be obliged."

"A word of caution, Captain Stone," Braceworth said, his voice hardening. "There's tribal unrest all over the eastern part of the territory. It will only get worse. The tribes see what's coming, their hunting grounds being plowed or turned into pastures for cattle. Isolated homesteads will be easy pickings. Are you alone?"

"No, there's five of us. One's a child, nine or so, but we are armed and capable. Thank you for the warning. Let's hope we don't have to go to war again."

"Amen, Captain. Godspeed and, if you need help, I'm here."

The two men shook hands, and the sergeant took Caleb to find Dawson. The wagoner was in the commissary, negotiating with the quartermaster over a dozen bullocks he was selling to the army. Caleb stood apart and watched the exchange, finding himself being drawn back to his army years and feeling, oddly enough, a touch of nostalgia. The shaking of heads and rising and falling of their voices ended in a handshake and both men signing some papers. Caleb took his chance to step up and introduce himself.

"What can I do for you, Captain Stone?" Dawson asked when the introductions were over. He was a heavyset man of medium

height, his skin darkened by the sun, with thick eyebrows and thick gray hair. He wore a deerskin shirt, worn woolen trousers, and scuffed black boots. He possessed the powerful handshake of a man who had grappled with the reins of work horses for many years. It was a reassuring grip that reminded Caleb of the farmers of Indian River.

"We're heading north from Walla Walla in search of good arable land to homestead, and that means finding a way of buying farming equipment and getting it to where we're going."

"You got oxen?" Dawson asked.

"No, we came with riding horses and a pair of mules I'll break to harness. That should get us started."

"You a farmer?"

"I was and can also work a forge if necessary."

"Good. You can buy just about anything you're likely to need here in town," Dawson told him. "Are you heading for the Spokane Valley?"

"We had that in mind."

"There's plenty of land available," Dawson said, "but a lot of it's dry country. I'd go northeast of the Spokane River. Find yourself a sizeable pond, there's a lot of them up there, and stake out both pond and headwater. That way you'll be guaranteed water year round. Later, you can dig a well. Where are you from?"

"Maine."

"All right, you know about winter. I came from Vermont. It's not nearly that bad here, but you will see three or four feet of snow and most of it will come in December. Summers are on the dry side, but the country will grow alfalfa and I suspect wheat. You can also run cattle."

"What about Indian trouble?" Caleb asked, wanting a second opinion. He knew army men tended to think war was always just over the hill, or, if it wasn't, it ought to be.

313

"I go heavily armed and have two armed men on every wagon," Dawson said. "There's smoldering resentment in places. Chiefs see their people's hunting grounds being occupied by miners or cattlemen or farmers or people like me. Makes 'em mad. We had a big shootout here two years ago. Indians were hit hard. A lot of them died. They been quiet since, but they're stirring again, and I expect things to get worse."

Not what he'd hoped to hear, but it was good to know. Caleb and Dawson talked for a while longer and made arrangements to haul Caleb's purchases up to Spokane Bridge, the settlement on the Spokane River that Dawson passed through on his way north to the mining settlements.

That attended to, Caleb had one more task on his list—find the fort's chaplain. Colonel Jeffrey Smollet turned out to be a tall, thin, balding, slightly stooped man old enough to make Caleb wonder why he wasn't retired. He wore gold-rimmed glasses and a cavalry uniform with regiment insignias. His office was bare of furniture except for two chairs, an ancient desk, and three floor-to-ceiling bookcases, stuffed to overflowing with books, pamphlets, and stacked notebooks. The room had the dry, dusty smell of old wood and books and the added odor of the chaplain's pipe, smoldering in an ashtray.

"News travels fast here, Captain Stone," Smollet said, laying down his nib pen and rising from his office chair. "How can I help you?"

"It's a pleasure to meet you," Caleb said, shaking the man's hand. "A friend and I would like you to marry us."

A slight smile lightened the man's long, solemn, deeply lined face. "I hope you and she are more than friends."

"Well said," Caleb responded, pleased at the riposte. "There are two women my friend and I are hoping to marry." He hesitated, then broke through the unexpected lock on his

tongue. "The women are Arapaho," he said. "We are on our way north in search of homestead land. We were going to the Willamette Valley but found the women were not welcome in Oregon." Try as he might, he couldn't keep the bitterness out of his voice on those last words.

Smollet motioned Caleb into the chair in front of the desk and picked up his pipe while settling into his own seat. "I know of that. It's a disgrace to the flag, a terrible mistake on Washington's part in letting it happen, but one we must live with, at least for the present. Are you willing to tell me how your situation came about? How did you come to travel with these Arapaho women?"

Caleb rested his elbows on his knees. "We weren't long out of Independence when we found them in a hut of sorts. A Sioux warrior had captured them in a raid and made them his slaves. One woman, Little Rain, had an arrowhead in her leg. She was shot while trying to escape. The wound was turning gangrenous, but my friend Dil was a nurse in the late rebellion and knew what to do." He described the operation on Little Rain's leg and the fight some days later with Hawk Hand and his war party. "By the time we'd been through all that together . . . well, let's just say one kind of bond can lead to another."

Smollet leaned forward to look more closely at Caleb. "I will risk overstepping good manners by asking if a woman figured in your leaving Maine?"

"Yes," Caleb said, finding to his surprise that answering gave him relief. "There was a woman I intended to marry, but she married someone else while I was gone."

"You've heard of rebound marriages," Smollet said quietly.

It took Caleb a moment to understand the chaplain's meaning. Spurred by anger, he replied with steel in his voice. "White Cloud and I have known each other going on four months, and in that short time have traveled nearly the breadth of this

315

country, fought off Indian and renegade attacks, and gone to some effort to keep each other alive. The four of us adopted a boy after killing the men who kidnapped him. We have traveled in rain and snow, cared for each other since then, all five of us. White Cloud is an extremely intelligent, honorable person, and it was not easy to convince her I had fallen in love with her, and that I wanted her for a wife. For her sake, I lied about why we had to leave Oregon. I told her it was against the law in that state for us to marry, but not why. I did it to spare her from knowing that all the time we were in Oregon Territory, she and Little Rain were at risk of being arrested, whipped, and thrown out, or worse."

He fell silent for a moment, then gathered himself. "No, Colonel Smollet, I'm not on the rebound."

Smollet sighed again and studied his pipe for a moment. Then he broke his silence. "I must say one more thing to you, Captain, and I must say it to your friend as well. It is brutal and it pains me, but it's the truth. For the rest of your married lives, your wives will be excluded from white female fellowship, and you will live on the fringe of whatever white community grows up around you. If you have children, they will be excluded from many of the opportunities afforded to white children and will endure many indignities. Their best hope will be to find schooling far away from the place in which they grew up."

Although Caleb knew what was facing them, to hear it from this man, whom he judged to be a man of honor, was a hard blow. After a long and painful pause, he rose from his chair. "I don't have it in me to thank you for your description of what's before us," he said, "but I do understand why you had to say it. Nothing in it was new to me. It's just hard to hear it from someone else. Now then, sir, will you marry us?"

He half expected a *no*, but Smollet's answer sent relief flooding through him. "I will be honored to marry you, Captain

Stone. Will you come to the chapel?"

"No, everything we own is at our encampment."

"Then I will marry you there. I take it you would like that to happen now."

"I would."

CHAPTER 34

Wolf was the first to see them coming. He sprang to his feet and ran to the edge of the camp, stopped, lifted his head, and gave a soft, welcoming howl. Dil and Foster unfastened Sheba from the skid on which they had been hauling wood, picketed her, and came to greet the arrivals. The two women fled into the lean-to, and, when Caleb and the Rev. Smollet dismounted, they emerged and hurried forward, dressed in their finest white deerskin dresses, braided belts, and bead necklaces.

White Cloud and Little Rain were tall for Indian women, but Colonel Smollet towered over them. "We keep him for teepee pole," White Cloud said to Little Rain in Arapaho.

"And both of you are lovely as spring flowers," Smollet said in the same tongue, bending to catch their hands in his. "Tell me your names and how you made such beautiful dresses."

Both women's faces darkened, but White Cloud recovered first.

"I am White Cloud," she said in English. "We are honored to have you at this fire, and I am ashamed. You much too tall for teepee pole. Where you learn Arapaho?"

Smollet beamed and said, "I lived for a while among your people when I was a young man, just having joined the army. They were good years among good folk."

White Cloud turned to her companion. "This is Little Rain."

"It is a pleasure to meet you," Smollet said, smiling down on her. Switching to Arapaho, he inquired how far along her

318

pregnancy was. Little Rain replied, smiling in pleasure at being asked. When they finished talking, Smollet turned to Foster, who was listening closely. He gripped the boy's shoulders by way of a greeting, then placed a large hand on Wolf's head. Everyone caught their breath, too late to stop him.

Wolf remained docile. He even seemed to enjoy this stranger's attention.

"Do you talk with animals?" Dil asked, wide-eyed.

"Sometimes," Smollet answered, "but I'm running a distant second to Solomon if that was who you were thinking of."

"Well," Dil said, "you just put your hand on the head of a gray wolf who usually takes a stranger's hand off at the elbow for even reaching to touch him."

"Why," Smollet gave Wolf's head another rub, "he's mild as cottage cheese. What's his name?"

"Wolf," Foster said, "and I'm mighty partial to him."

"I'm sure he's equally partial to you, Foster. I noticed how close he keeps to you. Dil, could I have a word with you before we do anything else?"

The two men walked to where the animals were grazing. The Indian ponies raised their heads but a moment later went back to grazing.

"Why he talk to Dil?" Little Rain asked, frowning.

Before Caleb could respond, White Cloud said angrily, "He will ask if Dil is certain he wants to marry a squaw."

"No," Caleb replied sharply. "He never called either of you squaws. From what he said to me, I know he is just as concerned about you and Little Rain as he is about Dil and me."

"What he know about it?" she demanded.

"Didn't he say he lived among the Arapaho once? He's an army chaplain, White Cloud. He's been dealing with mixed marriages for years, and he made no effort to prevent us from

marrying. He only wanted to be sure we knew what we were doing."

"And what is that?" White Cloud asked, not mollified.

"He asked if you realized what it meant to live away from your people," Caleb said. "If you knew that our children, if we have any, will face difficulties growing up in a white community. If you and Little Rain knew how hard it will be for us all to live in a white community. I said we were aware of all that. Then he said he would be honored to marry us."

"Why?"

"Because he knows we love one another, and Little Rain and Dil love one another, and that is what makes a marriage a joyous thing."

"I love Dil," Little Rain said quietly. "We will love our children. They will grow up and be good people."

White Cloud listened to her with a strained expression on her face. Turning to Caleb, she said, "I am not a good person like Little Rain. I cannot keep bad medicine out of my mind. You should not marry me."

"I wouldn't," he answered, grasping her around the waist and lifting her off her feet, "but winter is coming, and I have no other woman to keep me warm nights under the buffalo robe."

He set her back down just as Dil and the chaplain returned. "Not need to have a child, Chaplain Smollet," White Cloud said, straightening her dress. "I already have this one."

A few minutes later, following more light talk, Smollet asked if they were ready to take their vows. Caleb and Dil looked at their brides to be, who looked at one another and said, "Yes." Dil and Caleb followed suit.

Smollet placed the couples together, men on the right and women on the left, Foster and Wolf between them. He took a book from his satchel, opened it, and, without looking at the pages, began speaking. "Dearly beloved, we are gathered

together here in the sight of God, and in the face of this company, to join together these men and these women in holy matrimony . . ."

CHAPTER 35

A week later, they crossed the Spokane River bridge and stopped briefly at Charlie Kendall's store. The women were fascinated by the inside of the store and its shelves along the walls piled with goods and barrels of molasses and rum, salted fish, flour, and cracked corn. There were also traps and rifles, black powder in DuPont packaging, shovels, picks, and black kitchen stoves.

On seeing the stove, White Cloud jumped back as if it were alive. "Oh!" Then in a whisper, grasping Caleb's arm, "Stove to cook with? Where does fire go?"

Caleb showed her. Soon she and Little Rain had lifted all the lids, stared inside and peered into the oven. The clerk watched them with narrowed eyes, as if he thought they might make off with a stove lid or other moveable part. He'd already followed every move the women made throughout the small store, costing Caleb's self-control dearly. They needed supplies, so Caleb couldn't afford to throw the man into a wall.

"Will we have one of those in house?" White Cloud asked when they were outside the store and preparing to leave.

"Yes, we will, and you're not afraid of it now, are you?"

"Perhaps someone won't be, but cannot watch the fire, and perhaps someone won't cook in it all the time."

"No," Little Rain put in, "and this person does not see how to put meat over the fire."

While in the store, Caleb had arranged with Isaak Whitney, Kendall's manager, to put the goods Dawson would be hauling

into a dry, locked shed. Whitney was an elderly, white-haired man in a striped shirt with the habit of nodding while listening to anyone talking to him.

"We'll look after the shipment, Mr. Stone," Whitney said, "and settle when you pick them up. Can you give me an idea of when that will be?"

"I hope it will be less, but let's say two months at the agreed upon rent."

"Done," the man said, and the two shook hands. Then Whitney leaned in. "A word of warning. Not everyone you meet here will respect your marriages. We have miners from Oregon and immigrants from the late Confederacy who despise Indians and blacks and regard miscegenation as the work of the Devil. I don't, and most people around here don't, but I thought you should be aware of what to expect."

"And I thank you," Caleb said, shaking Whitney's hand again. "Perhaps the next time we are in your store, your clerks will not find it necessary to follow our wives around as if they were likely to steal something."

"That won't happen again, Mr. Stone," Whitney said. "Please accept my apologies. But there's your proof that for some, prejudices run deep."

It was early afternoon when they left Spokane Bridge. Taking Dawson's advice, Caleb turned them north, and the next day they came upon a small river.

"This is the Little Spokane," he said.

"Let's put some distance between us and Spokane Bridge," Dil said. "Little Rain is hopping mad, and White Cloud looks the way she does when someone is going to lose some hide."

Caleb turned to Dil in surprise. "The last I saw of them, they were talking about the wood stove and seemed fine. I thought they hadn't paid that clerk any heed."

"That's because they didn't want to get you into any trouble."

"I gave Whitney an earful. He said it wouldn't happen again."

They rode in silence for a while, and then Caleb said, "We're newly married men, Dil. Aren't we supposed to be happy?"

"We're not young enough to be happy," Dil said, "but I will admit to being very glad to be married to Little Rain."

"And I'm glad to be married to White Cloud," Caleb responded. "There were times when I came very near believing it would never happen."

He paused to watch Wolf lope back to them with a rabbit in his jaws. Wolf glanced up at them, acknowledging their presence, and went back to give Little Rain his contribution to supper.

"Last night, I asked White Cloud how it felt being married," Caleb continued. "Her answer was, 'Mrs. Caleb Stone is content. Not sure about White Cloud.' That set me back a bit."

"I asked Little Rain the same question. She told me not to behave like Foster any more than I had to," Dil said, grinning, "and to keep my mind on finding us a place to raise our lodge before winter."

"I have the feeling," Caleb said, "that being married to those two will be a learning experience. Summer may be coming to an end in more ways than one."

Dil laughed. "Well, Foster's happy we're married. 'About time,' was the first thing he said to me about it. Claimed it makes him feel more respectable."

Later that day, a brief shower brought out the smell of the earth, cheering all of them. They made camp briefly on the south side of a sizeable creek that fed into the Little Spokane. The creek ran west and reached them from the northeast. The horizon in that direction showed foothills and at least one mountain that Caleb judged to be four or five thousand feet high.

"Braceworth suggested we turn east after leaving Spokane

Bridge. What do you say we follow this creek?" he asked the others when they were mounted up again.

"It looks more green up there than this land," White Cloud said.

"More trees," Little Rain added. "Build lodge."

"Wolf likes it," Foster said.

"How can you tell?" Dil asked.

"Look at his ears."

Caleb looked down at Wolf, standing beside Joshua. "Foster's right—his ears are pricked, and he's staring hard."

"Then, let's high tail it up there," Foster crowed.

They followed the creek for two hours, slowly climbing and winding through hilly grasslands with ever-thickening stands of trees until they reached the mouth of a wide valley, carpeted with hay and scatterings of late-blooming asters.

Caleb took out his spyglass and studied the landscape ahead of them. "It's deep and it's wide, and the hay is heavy," he said. "And I can see a glimmer on the northeast corner that may be water."

A hush fell over them as they rode slowly into the valley, still following the creek. Quail and occasional families of sage grouse exploded out of the belt-high grass, flushed by Wolf in most cases, who dashed off at intervals and occasionally leaped into the air in failed attempts to catch slow-rising birds.

"He's just having fun," Foster said, watching Wolf racing again. "He ain't aiming to grab one of them. If he was, he would."

Caleb thought the boy was right and wondered as he often did at the link between Wolf and Foster. He half believed they talked to one another. Halfway into the valley, he joined White Cloud, feeling a sudden and strong urge to share the experience with her.

"There is good medicine in this place," she told him as soon

as he was beside her.

He returned her smile. "I feel it," he told her, noting with pleasure that she seemed free of the worry that had dogged her so long.

The sparkle of silver his glass had caught was a large pond at the northeast corner of the valley, drained by a swift-flowing creek. At its northernmost end, a tumbling fall of water flowed into it from the heavily wooded hill rising above.

"This feeder seems to be coming out of that high country up there," Dil said, staring at the jumble of hills to the east with a mountain behind them.

"Water running now runs all year," White Cloud said, looking from the stream to the hills. "Mean flow all year."

"Trout." Foster grinned in expectation.

"Plenty of wood for lodge," Little Rain said. White Cloud looked at Caleb, which made him grin.

Indeed, all the slopes at the head of the valley were dense with pine, Douglass fir, spruce, aspen, and a scattering of white oak along the creek below the pond. Caleb dismounted and went back to the pack animals, freed a shovel, and came back to the others. "Time to give it a try," he said. "Anyone got a place they like?"

White Cloud was standing on her horse's back, her right fist on her hip. "Nice place," she said. "Can see all round. Try where you are."

They were on a wide rise of land with the lake a few hundred yards to the north. To the east, a wall of conifers, stretching for at least half a mile, marked the eastern boundary of the valley.

"Right," Caleb said. He plunged the pointed shovel into the ground, placed his right boot on the blade and stepped down hard. There was a tearing sound of grass roots being severed and the blade slid into the dirt down to its hilt. Caleb pulled it out, stepped over the cut, and turned, then drove the shovel in

again and lifted out a thick, dark-brown slice of grass roots and earth. Dil bent and grasped a handful of soil, watched it dribble through his fingers, opened them, and said with a smile, "Loam, Captain. Good, heavy loam."

"I'd wager the whole valley has it," Caleb said. "The grass and other plants are the same height its whole length."

"Grow beans and pumpkins," Little Rain said.

"Corn, squash, potatoes, radishes," Foster added. "I seen a garden one time. There was other things in it I can't remember."

"Carrots and onions and radishes," White Cloud said, her voice rising into laughter. "My father had garden. My mother complained she had to pull all the weeds because he wouldn't."

"Are we staying?" Foster asked, hope in his voice.

"There's everything we need here," Caleb conceded, looking around again. "Between us, under the Homestead Act we can claim three hundred and twenty acres of land. For a dollar and twenty-five cents an acre, I can buy enough to give us four hundred acres. That will include the valley, the pond, the creek, and plenty of woods besides."

"How we do this?" White Cloud asked.

"Dil and I will go into the Walla Walla General Land Office and register our claims." Caleb wanted both women to fully understand what had to be done, should they decide to settle here. "Then, after a wait, we'll be issued pieces of writing called deeds, which means the land described in the deed is legally ours."

"I reckon there's a catch in there somewhere. Is that so?" Foster asked.

"Old man Foster," Dil said, dropping his hand on the boy's shoulder.

"Well, you're right," Caleb said. "In order to keep the homestead land, we have to improve it. That means grow crops, build houses, put up fences, pasture cattle, and such."

"Nihoothoos," White Cloud said in disgust. "Land already improved. Why all work that not needed? We are here, graze our horses, build a lodge. Plenty of land for people."

Little Rain nodded in agreement.

"There will soon be more people here than land for them to settle on," Dil said. "Having the deeds will stop other people from trying to take our land away from us."

The women looked at one another and shook their heads.

"Let's go to the pond," Foster said.

Everyone thought that was a good idea, and they rode down the slope to the water. There were lilies floating on the far side of the pond, and shoulder deep feeding on them was a bull moose. As they watched, he plunged his entire head under the surface and came up chewing on green lily stems while water poured off his antlers. He showed no interest in his audience.

"Lord, look at those antlers," Foster said, standing on Dakota's back.

"Good medicine," Little Rain said. "The spirits of the lake welcome us. Look down there—ducks not fly away."

It was true. At the south end of the pond, a family of mallards near a stand of tall cattails were busily dipping their heads and feeding, displaying no uneasiness. A fish rose twenty feet off shore and snapped an insect off the surface, leaving a foot-wide swirl in the water.

"That warn't no shiner," Foster said.

"A bass, maybe," Dil said.

"Can eat?" Little Rain asked.

"Best cooked with skin on, but yes," Dil replied. "They're a misery to scale."

Wolf suddenly emerged from cover onto the edge of the pond a few yards from the moose. No one had seen him slip away.

"Look yonder!" Foster shouted. "Wolf's got the drop on that moose."

The moose stopped eating and stared at Wolf for a few moments, lily fronds hanging from his antlers. Suddenly he lunged toward his visitor, making the water fly.

"Run, Wolf!" Foster shouted, but the animal seemed unafraid of what was bearing down on him.

The moose, big as he was, swiftly closed the distance between them. Wolf watched his charging attacker with apparent interest. The moose lowered his head, swinging his antlers like a scythe. Frozen by the drama, Foster groaned out loud when the moose struck, and a horror-struck Caleb was sure Wolf's demise was imminent. But when the antlers swept through the place where Wolf stood, he was no longer there. The moose tossed his head and swung around in search of his adversary, to find Wolf sitting nearby, looking up at him.

A ragged cheer went up from Caleb and the others, but no one was prepared for what followed. The moose stared at Wolf for a bit, then looked across the pond at his audience. Swinging his head back, he thrust his nose down toward Wolf. Afterward, no one could say whether or not the two animals touched noses, but, a moment later, the moose laid his rack back on his shoulders, broke into a trot, and vanished into the woods. Wolf sat still, gazing after him.

"Did you ever?" Foster said, wide-eyed.

Perhaps it was the sudden relief, but they all burst out laughing. When they had run down and wiped their eyes, Dil said, "Captain, I think we may have found the place we've been looking for."

"Shall we take a vote?" Caleb asked and got a unanimous yes. "All right, all in favor of staying here say, 'Aye.' "

Everyone, including Caleb, shouted, "Aye!" Foster shouted loudest.

The group drew together a bit more closely, giving themselves time to adjust to what they had just done.

"If we're going to live here," Foster said, looking around again, "things got to have names. What say we call this Moose Pond?"

"I like name," Little Rain said, smiling.

"Vote," White Cloud said, to Caleb's surprise.

When there was unanimous agreement, White Cloud said, "This is *Niihonkoo*, the month of yellow leaves. I think the water that runs out of the trees with yellow leaves and through Moose Pond and out again should be Yellow Leaf Creek."

"Those trees are aspens," Caleb said. "I like the name Yellow Leaf."

"Vote," Dil said loudly.

Yellow Leaf Creek it became, though Caleb privately chose to call it Yellow Leaf Brook. As that thought went through his head, for a moment he felt a stinging behind his nose and eyes, seeing for a fleeting instant his mother standing with him in the dooryard of the farm, watching geese fly across a full moon, their faint honks breaking the silence of the night.

"Caleb Stone," White Cloud asked quietly, smiling. "Where are you?"

"Thinking of brooks," he said, as his mind cleared of the vision. "In Maine, creeks are called brooks."

She glanced at the sky. "We must make camp. Tonight, we will have rain."

The weather was mild, and, because the afternoon was slipping away, they threw up a lean-to of firs, those trees being closest at hand. The lean-to consisted of a roof and corner posts, the wood strong and workable.

"I think when we get to putting together a house," Caleb said when they were done, "this Douglass fir is what we should use."

"And the logs are straight as a die," Dil said in agreement.

It rained lightly that night, and for once everyone but Wolf overslept. The sun was well over the hill behind them when

Little Rain stepped out of the lean-to and was greeted by Wolf, just returning with a fat spruce grouse in his mouth.

"Wolf catch breakfast," Little Rain called, rousing the others.

Foster came out, rubbing his eyes, and Little Rain had to pull the robes off Dil to get him onto his feet.

"Little Rain!" White Cloud called. "We have bath, and so will you," she said to the men. "But we go first."

Off the two women ran toward the pond, armed with soap and fresh clothes.

"That there water's cold," Foster said, sounding worried.

"Only for a minute," Dil said, though he didn't sound very convincing.

Caleb watched the women. "We're next."

The new day, bright with sun and a gentle westerly wind bringing with it the warm field smells of the valley, shot through with the scent of pines and spruce and fir, buoyed all of their spirits. After everyone had bathed, Foster ran off with Wolf and came back a short time later with five rainbow trout. "I caught these right there where the creek leaves the pond. There's all kinds of fish in that creek. They don't know nothing about being tickled right out from under the bank. I could of filled a basket."

"Stop talking, use knife, cut out guts," White Cloud told him, bending down to examine his catch.

At Fort Walla Walla, Caleb had bought him a bone-handled knife in a rawhide sheath. White Cloud taught him how to sharpen the blade on a smooth, flat stone she had taken from one of the mountain streams. "Women's work," Little Rain had protested at first, but watching Dil and Caleb often clean fish and gut rabbits and other animals they had killed, she became resigned to the alteration in male and female tasks.

"Is different with these men," White Cloud had told her. "Sometimes they not make decisions until they ask us if we

agree. Very strange, but also feels good to be asked."

By the second week in October, Caleb and Dil had filed their homestead claims, and Caleb had bought the additional acreage. Dawson had delivered Caleb's purchases in Walla Walla to Isaak Whitney in Spokane Bridge. Joshua and Sheba were broken to the harness easily and were soon hauling fir logs out of the woods.

They had decided to build two cabins end to end, with a roofed breezeway between them. From the sawmill in Spokane Bridge, they bought enough milled lumber to frame the doors and windows and lay the floors and roofs. They split shingles from pine and built the chimneys with stones and clay mortar.

With all of them working, they had the buildings framed, the floors in, and the roofs shingled by mid-November, just ahead of the second snowfall. Each building had two rooms, and, in Dil and Little Rain's, they added a small third bedroom with a slanted roof for Foster, who had carried the shingles for it to White Cloud as fast as Caleb split them off the pine blocks. Little Rain managed all the cooking during the cabin raising as well as dressing and cutting up the game that came in, including Foster's contribution of trout.

She was a bit over five months pregnant when they finished the cabins, and the work clearly exhausted her, but she neither spoke of her troubles nor let up on her own tasks, telling the others that once the building was over she would rest and recover. The days passed, mostly fair. With the cabins finished, they turned to digging a ten-foot square and five foot deep hole into the low, grass-covered knoll a dozen yards behind the cabins, in preparation for sinking the meat locker. The shed, built of logs a foot in diameter with a slightly slanting roof of equally large logs, was mortared with clay and weather proofed with foot-wide pine shingles.

"Pig tight and bull strong," Dil said as Caleb dropped the

hand hewn four-by-four oak beam into place across the heavy locker door and shoved home the thick oak peg, locking the beam in place.

"Now we begin to fill this locker with meat," Caleb said, stepping back to look at it. "I think it will keep the bears out." Standing next to Dil, looking at their handiwork, Caleb said, "I know she wouldn't like my asking, but how is Little Rain feeling? I thought she looked a little under the weather this morning."

Dil's frown showed worry. "She flies off the handle at me if I ask her if anything's wrong. She's so determined to go on pulling her weight and a little more. The thing is, she's tiring sooner and is taking longer to recover. I think it frightens her. I know it makes her mad."

"Then she's not in pain or ill?"

"I don't think so, Captain, but you remember how she was when I took that arrowhead out of her. I nearly had to hog-tie her to make her take anything to lessen the pain."

"I remember. If it's all right with you, I'll ask White Cloud to pry a little."

"All right, but tell her to ease in. Foster asked Little Rain if she was sick, and she snapped back so sharp he nearly lost his head. Even Wolf is stepping softly around her after she chased him with the poker for pissing near the doorstep."

"How does she like the cabin?"

His expression eased. "She's in heaven over it and can't wait for the stove to come."

Caleb grinned. "I'm glad to hear it. White Cloud won't admit she's worried that she won't be able to learn how to cook on the stove. Instead, she keeps praising the fireplace as the perfect place to cook with the swing bars and grates we installed."

They'd left much unsaid about Little Rain's condition, but Caleb decided not to press Dil further. If something were seri-

ously wrong with her, he would soon learn about it. The two men stood for a while longer looking at the locker until Foster ran up to Dil, saying either he was to get in to lunch or Wolf would eat his share.

Chapter 36

In the following weeks, there were occasional snow squalls, but the snow melted within a few days, in part because the ground had not frozen. Nevertheless, there were frosts nearly every night, and the mountain tops turned white. Elk and deer drifting down from the upper slopes began appearing in the five settlers' open land, the elk pawing away the snow and the deer browsing at the edge of the woods. The appearance of the deer and elk was accompanied by a sudden and sharp drop in the temperature.

"Meat will freeze now," White Cloud said the day the ice on Moose Pond did not melt. Within a week, the larder was filled with deer and elk, quartered and hung. Caleb stacked the animals' neck meat to use for mincemeat. He recalled eating mincemeat pies and tarts as a boy and had found a recipe for it in a cookbook in Kendall's store. The women grudgingly agreed to make it but remained deeply doubtful about the raisins. That same day, Little Rain said to Dil, "Perhaps is time to stock up for winter before we are snowed in."

Two days later, in the crackling cold before sunup with moonlight turning the snow into a sea of sparkling diamonds, Caleb harnessed Joshua and Sheba, fastened them to the logging skid, sporting a new bed of planks, and stepped aboard.

"Come back, Caleb Stone," White Cloud called from the cabin door, where she stood wrapped in a black and red Hudson Bay blanket. "Keep Spencer near."

Caleb waved and patted the rifle's scabbard, strapped to the wooden post in front of him. The mules, glad to be working, took Caleb along at a steady trot, despite the snow, that put them in Spokane Bridge by mid-afternoon. It was dark when he returned home, and, amid a lot of talk and laughter, he and the others rolled their flour barrels and carried the rest of the sacks and boxes and crates into the cabins. The supplies shrank their living space but filled them all, especially Little Rain and White Cloud, with a deep sense of security.

That done, the animals were taken to the lake for water—it was one of Foster's chores to keep a hole chopped in the ice, a task he took very seriously—and they all sat down in Caleb and White Cloud's cabin for supper. At a quiet point in the meal, Foster said, "I almost forgot. This morning I saw a man on a horse. He followed the skid tracks up toward the cabins for a little ways, then turned and galloped off."

A tense silence settled around the table. Caleb set down his fork. "What did he look like?"

"He had on one of them tall hats and a heavy, dark coat," Foster replied, digging into his meat again. "He lit out in a hurry, like he'd remembered something he was supposed to do."

"We going to have company?" Dil asked quietly.

Little Rain frowned. "Why one man making us afraid?"

"Where is one tall hat, is more," White Cloud replied grimly. "Like ants."

"Tomorrow morning early," Caleb said, "we'll hobble the animals behind the cabins. Those we ride we'll keep by the door. Also, our rifles. If they come, my guess is they'll come straight up the valley."

Little Rain's hand drifted to her belly. "I hoped we not have shooting anymore."

"Who could they be?" Foster asked.

"Maybe claim jumpers," Caleb said. "Renegades looking for easy pickings."

White Cloud caught his eye. "We take same places?"

"Yes."

Dil brushed Little Rain's cheek. "Maybe nothing will happen," he said, "but it's best to be ready if trouble's coming."

"Someone is thinking," White Cloud said, "in this world, trouble always coming."

They finished their supper and made efforts to talk of cheerful things, but even Foster was subdued. Later, when Dil and Little Rain and Foster had left, Caleb came back from the cabin door and put his arms around White Cloud, who stood at the end of the table, staring at the remains of their meal in silence.

"We have each other," Caleb said quietly into her ear. "Try not to worry."

"On the trail," she replied, turning in his arms to face him, "we had little, and losing it was not much. Now there is very much, and the fear is stronger."

"We will not lose this place," he said. "The claim is filed and safely in the government's hands, the money paid."

"When you hold me," she said, "I think you are right. When not, not so sure."

They stood for a while in the circle of light beside the table, her head resting against his shoulder.

"Table not clear itself," she said after a while, giving him a gentle shake.

Caleb released her, and they began cleaning up. As they worked, he thought about what she had said. He remembered how, as a boy, he often saw his father sitting at the kitchen table, the books containing all the farm's records open in front of him, adding columns of figures, worry lines etched deeply in his weathered face.

"Were you happier on the trail, White Cloud?" he asked,

hanging the dish cloth on its rack to dry.

She gave him one of her rare smiles. "No. Am happier now as Mrs. Caleb Stone."

"And I am happier that someone is my wife," Caleb said, "and I intend to keep her safe."

The next morning, they were up while the stars and a sickle moon were still the brightest things in the sky. With first light breaking over the mountains, and with Wolf for company, Foster watered the animals. While the women made breakfast, the men put hackamores on the Indian ponies and saddles on their own mounts.

Standing with the others on the deck between the cabins, Caleb said, "Foster, you and Wolf will watch from here. We'll rest you often enough to keep you from getting cold. The rest of us will get on with the animal shed."

"Perhaps this one will watch," Little Rain said. "Foster may go with others."

Caleb started to ask if she was not feeling good, but White Cloud elbowed him in the ribs. "All right," he said in a quick save, "keep Wolf with you. He will know before you if anyone is coming."

Wrapped in a blanket, Little Rain settled herself cross-legged on the deer skin Dil spread for her. She laid her rifle across her lap as White Cloud draped an elk hide over her shoulders for warmth. Wolf sat beside her and looked down the valley, his head towering over hers.

"If that's not a sight for sore eyes," Foster said, "I ain't never seen one."

White Cloud stifled a laugh and gave him a gentle push. "Go. There is work."

Dil dropped back to walk with them, leaving Foster to trudge ahead, practicing his whistle. After they left the breezeway, Ca-

leb said to White Cloud, "Little Rain's hardly spoken. What's wrong?"

"Morning sickness back. That is all she would say. Dil, has Little Rain told you more?"

He shook his head. "No, but she's not sleeping as well as I'd like, and her appetite has failed some. I asked if she would go to Spokane Bridge and talk with Doctor Haley, but she got mad with me for suggesting it."

Worry settled in Caleb's chest. "What should we do?"

"Wait for someone to tell us," White Cloud said.

"Ain't nobody here but us," Foster called back over his shoulder.

White Cloud made a dive for him. The boy jumped but not fast enough, and a moment later she had him down in the snow, sitting on him.

"I can't breathe," Foster yelled.

"Maybe someone will sit here until she hears something."

"I'm sorry!" the boy shouted.

White Cloud rose, grabbed Foster by his shoulders, and yanked him onto his feet and began knocking the snow off him. "Stop!" he yelled. "You'll break all the bones in my body."

"Maybe someone will hug you to death," she said, wrapping him in her arms and pulling him close. He squirmed like a worm on a hook for a moment and then collapsed against her and clung as if she were the last stick floating.

When White Cloud released the boy, Caleb saw Foster's face was wet with tears. He and Dil stopped laughing.

"I'm sorry," Foster said, wiping his eyes. "I warn't prepared for that, and something let go."

White Cloud pulled him to her again and kissed the top of his head. "Perhaps someone will have a hug every day."

Wolf had trotted up to them, and, when White Cloud released Foster the second time, he gave Foster's face a giant lick.

"Git away!" Foster shouted, smacking the wolf's head. Wolf bumped the boy gently with his shoulder, knocking him onto his back in the snow, then straddled him and licked his face again.

This time, Caleb lifted Foster back onto his feet. "I'll wager there's not another boy between here and the Pacific Ocean who's got a wolf for a friend."

"Plus a war hero, a one-armed man and two beautiful Arapaho women," Dil said, picking up Foster's hat, knocking the snow off it against his leg, and passing it to the boy. "And the whole shooting match loves you. Wolf, get back to Little Rain."

Wolf loped back to his post. Half an hour later, Dil went to see if Little Rain was all right and signaled the others that she was with a shrill whistle. The sun had broken over the mountains behind them, shining in a clear sky.

"Everyone knows what to do," Caleb said when Dil returned, and they took their positions. Some distance away four riders, one in front with three others following, were coming at a trot up the valley. Caleb raised his spyglass.

"What kind of hat is that little man in the lead wearing?" Dil asked.

"Looks like an English deerstalker," Caleb answered as he lowered the glass and tucked it away. "English saddle, too."

"It's got a visor front and back," Dil said. "I wonder how you'd know which way to put it on?" The other three riders, carrying rifles, wore tall hats and long coats, the bottom halves draped over their horses' hips.

Caleb and Dil met them halfway up the valley. White Cloud and Little Rain stayed about fifteen yards behind, placed to the right and the left. Once within speaking distance, Caleb drew breath, but the lead rider spoke first. "I'm Langton Meriwether," he said loudly, "owner of the Two Stars Ranch, and you're trespassing on my grazing land."

Meriwether was a compact man, the oldest of the four, dressed in a dark tweed suit under a heavy coat with a cape. He had a neat, grizzled beard, heavy eyebrows, and a scowling, weathered face and spoke with a clipped English accent. Clearly, he was accustomed to giving orders and having them obeyed.

Caleb straightened in his saddle. "I am Caleb Stone, and this is Dil Smith. The land in this valley, and a large area surrounding it, are registered with the federal government and the territory of Washington in our names. The land is legally ours, and you will graze your stock on it only with our permission. I hope by next summer to have it fenced."

One of Meriwether's companions, a gaunt fellow with longish hair and a turned eye, said, "Around here we don't take to squaw men." That drew a chuckle from the others.

Dil stiffened. "Are you referring to our wives?"

"I was *referrin'* to them squaws back there," the man said, grinning.

"If I had a face like a pig's arse," Dil said evenly, "I don't believe I'd make remarks like that."

The man swore and reached for his gun. The crack of White Cloud's rifle ricocheted around the hills, and the man's hat flew off his head. At the same moment he found himself looking into the barrel of Dil's .45.

Caleb urged Joshua up by Meriwether's horse. "If anyone else reaches for a gun, it will be his head, not his hat, that comes off."

"Do you know who you're talking to?" Meriwether demanded, in a squeal of rage.

"Yes, I do." Caleb pointed his rifle at the man's chest. "I am speaking with someone making a damned fool of himself and within an inch of being buried in those woods behind us."

"I'll come back," Meriwether shouted, his jowls trembling. "I'll bring a dozen men and burn you out, kill you and those

341

damned squaws . . ."

Caleb swung the barrel of his gun, striking Meriwether on the shoulder and knocking him out of his saddle. Meriwether tried to get up but got entangled in his coat and fell again. Another of his men, red-faced and fat, grabbed Meriwether's horse by its bridle. With danger suddenly turned to spectacle, Caleb regretted what he'd done. "Get him up," he said to the fat man.

The fellow gaped at him. The third rider, a tow-haired youngster looking scarcely out of his teens, sprang down and helped Meriwether back into the saddle. The Englishman sat whey-faced and gasping for breath, holding his arm as if Caleb's blow had injured it. "You'll regret this," he said.

"Mr. Meriwether," Caleb replied, "your men will see you home. I advise you to stay there. If your men have any sense, they'll refuse to be part of any further attempt you make to separate us from our land."

Dil dismounted, holstered his gun, picked the gaunt fellow's fallen hat out of the snow, and handed it up to its owner. "Do you have anything else you want to say about my wife?"

The gaunt man locked eyes with him. Then the fellow shrugged. "Much obliged," he said, examining the holes in his hat and then putting it on. "And no, except to say I hope I marry a woman who can shoot like that."

"Shut your mouth," Meriwether snapped.

"You've given me my last order, Meriwether," the man said. "I'm done with you." He pulled his horse around and rode back down the valley at a trot. A moment later, the fat man touched the brim of his hat at Caleb and nodded, then spurred his horse into a gallop and followed his compatriot.

"Can you see Mr. Meriwether home?" Caleb asked the youngster, the only rider left other than Meriwether himself.

The boy was standing in his stirrups, staring after his depart-

ing companions. "I don't reckon I can," he said. He backed his horse and winged away, shouting, "Wait up!" as he went. Meriwether watched him go, bluster turned to bewilderment as it dawned on him that he was alone.

Quietly, Caleb addressed him. "Mr. Meriwether, my wife, White Cloud, and I offer you the hospitality of our home. Come and rest, have something hot to drink. Dil will look at that arm. He's the closest thing to a doctor this side of Walla Walla. By the way, do you know Colonel Horace Braceworth at the fort? He and I are on friendly terms."

Meriwether managed a nod. He looked forlorn now, almost pathetic. With Caleb on one side and Dil on the other, they guided Meriwether's horse up to the cabins, where Wolf showed his teeth in welcome. There was no sign of the women, and Caleb guessed they'd gone inside.

Meriwether paled. "My God is that a . . . ?"

"It is," Dil said. "He adopted us a few months ago after he was mauled by a grizzly that wanted our dinners. Wolf held the bear off long enough for us to gather our wits and shoot it."

They entered the cabin, while Foster saw to the horses. The women had been busy—a kettle swung over the fire, and the table was laid out and the lantern lit. Dil introduced Meriwether to White Cloud and Little Rain.

"Maybe someone is tired and cold," Little Rain said, peeling Meriwether out of his coat and leading him to a chair beside the fire.

Seated, he looked much older and paler than he had on horseback. Caleb felt another stab of guilt for having struck this old man. Within a few minutes the women had a mug of tea in Meriwether's hands, a blanket over his shoulders and a bowl of steaming venison stew, dipped from the iron pot, on the stool beside him.

Meriwether put down the tea and started to lift the bowl with

343

its spoon, but his hand shook too much to manage it. Little Rain and White Cloud conferred briefly in Arapaho, then Little Rain knelt close to him and studied his face closely while White Cloud restored the bowl to the stool. He thanked them, but having both women so close seemed to startle him. Perhaps it was the intensity of their gaze, their black eyes searching his face. Or, more likely, the power of their presence. Watching them, Caleb thought they carried with them the aura of another world.

Beside Caleb, Foster looked up at him with a knowing grin. Caleb shook his head and frowned slightly. Foster shrugged but stifled his amusement.

"Mr. Meriwether," Caleb said, stepping forward and signaling Dil to join him, "I think our wives forgot for a moment they weren't speaking English. Would you like to lie down?"

"No, I would like to eat some of that stew. It smells delicious." Meriwether appeared to have gathered himself. "But first, I want to know why you're showing such concern for me, Mr. Stone. Had I been you, I would almost certainly have shot me."

"You're not the only one at fault for our getting off to such a harsh and unproductive start," Caleb said. "Dil and I allowed our emotions to get the best of us. I want to apologize for that."

White Cloud stood and rested her fists on her hips. "Perhaps now you want to talk someone to death, instead of looking at arm," she said briskly. Meriwether looked startled, then glanced around. Everyone, Caleb included, was grinning. Meriwether gave way and laughed.

"Mrs. Stone," he said, "I see you possess a sharp wit and do not mince your words. May I thank you for your concern as well? Also, please assure yourself that my arm is not broken, only sore."

"You are English person?" she asked.

"I am, or was. I can't be sure quite what I am now," Meriwether said, obviously enjoying the conversation.

"Someone is Arapaho, and now knows English use more words than Caleb Stone. Dil will look at arm."

The two women helped Meriwether out of his suit jacket and pulled his shirtsleeve up to his shoulder. Then they moved his arm up and down and back and forth, ignoring his complaints.

"You'll have a bruise," Dil said as he examined the injured area, "but your heavy jacket and coat prevented you from being seriously hurt. Are you up to having another go at that stew?"

Meriwether said he was and also proved up to drinking the whiskey Caleb passed him. Everyone arranged themselves around the table, and soon they were deep in stew and corn-bread.

"I've been eating bunk-house food so long, I'd almost forgotten what good cooking tastes like," Meriwether said, with a groan of satisfaction.

During the meal, Meriwether told them about himself. He was the youngest son of an English clergyman, who saw at an early age that if he meant to eat regularly after leaving school, he had better prepare himself for some form of employment. Through his father's connections, he was hired by the Hudson Bay Company and sent to Canada, where he finally rose to the position of factor and constantly moved west until he reached the coast.

"By fifty I knew this was where I wanted to live," he said, "and what I wanted to do was raise cattle. Nearly twenty years ago, my wife and I settled here and began raising and selling cattle for beef to the mining towns that sprang up to the north of us. I lost my wife ten years ago and have remained a bachelor ever since." He glanced around, taking in the pleasant dinner table and the food they were still enjoying. "Until today, I've never thought seriously about remarrying."

"Not too late," Little Rain said. "Lots of women marry you. I might if I not marry Dil and have bun in my oven."

White Cloud exploded with laughter, taking the others with her. Meriwether looked completely confused.

"It's my wife's way of making you laugh," Dil said quickly. "She's pregnant, and Foster here started it by saying she had a bun in the oven. He was brought up without much of a family and picked up some blunt language as he went along."

Meriwether gave Little Rain a broad smile. "I congratulate you," he said. "And I am flattered to think you would consider me for your husband."

That afternoon, Caleb rode with Meriwether to his ranch through open and thinly wooded country north and west of them. Within an hour of leaving the cabins, they began encountering small herds of cattle, some short-horned and others clearly of longhorn stock.

"The dark, short-legged animals are Dexters," Meriwether said, "bred up from a small number I had shipped from the west coast of England. The longhorns are a Texas breed. I'm crossing most of them, but I've fenced some pasturage for purebred Dexters. They're a good beef animal and good milkers as well. The longhorns are dangerous, but the bulls and the bullocks will fight wolves to a standstill. Only the grizzlies kill them, and that doesn't happen very often. When one of the big bears becomes a nuisance, we shoot it."

"You can buy this land for a dollar and a quarter an acre," Caleb said. "There are a lot more people like me claiming land here. You may want to get deeds for your holdings."

"I'm still an English citizen," Meriwether answered. "Never saw any reason to change. I suppose I could buy the land, but I've thought for the past year or so of going home, and what happened earlier today has only strengthened that inclination. I'm getting too old for fights over land and paying strangers to

take my side. I have enough money invested in London to keep me comfortably. Regarding our earlier encounter, I feel disappointed with myself. I acted badly. You behaved like a gentleman. I did not."

"Come to that, I'm not very pleased with my own behavior," Caleb said.

They were approaching the house, a sprawling, single story log building set on a low hill, backed by a large stand of aspen trees. "Will you come in?" Meriwether asked.

"Thank you, but I won't," Caleb answered. "I want to get back before the daylight goes. Colonel Braceworth told me the local tribes are restless, and that's something you may not have heard about."

"Oh, I have. I have contacts with some of the chiefs, and the unrest is one of the things urging me back toward the mother country. I've lived through a couple of uprisings and don't relish facing another. Despite my behavior this morning, I'm a peace-loving man."

"Are there any more men here with you?"

"Good of you to ask. Yes, half a dozen. They're good men, quite unlike those I brought with me this morning. Those three, I chose because I didn't trust them enough to leave on their own. Troublemakers. Good riddance to bad rubbish."

"Come spring," Caleb said, "I'll be in the market for cattle. Please keep me in mind if you have any you want to move. I especially like the looks of those Dexters."

"I will remember your request, Mr. Stone, and I would be honored if you and your families would be my guests a bit later in the year."

They parted with a handshake and Caleb's assurance that both families would be pleased to pay him a visit. Caleb left in good spirits, but twice on the way home he found tracks of unshod ponies crossing those left by his and Meriwether's

horses. A small band of Indians, clearly on the move. Peaceful, or a war party?

It worried him not to know the answer.

CHAPTER 37

Caleb reached home to hear a disturbing story of four strange Indians in war paint who had ridden twice around the cabins, holding rifles over their heads and whooping, then disappearing into the woods. "Lucky thing Wolf was off hunting," Foster said. "He might have taken a leg off one of them."

"He might be dead now," White Cloud said, checking the boy's flight of fancy.

"What did the rest of you do?" Caleb asked.

"Watched, with our Spencers and handgun," Little Rain said. She spoke clearly and strongly, but Caleb saw her face was drawn and sallow.

"Didn't look serious," Dil added. "More like hell-raising. Maybe they got hold of some whiskey."

White Cloud agreed, at least in words. "Young warriors, maybe looking to steal horses. Not thinking much boasting come from stealing from Nihoothoos."

Caleb had learned to read her fairly well by now, and he sensed she'd left things unsaid. Later, after dinner, he asked White Cloud what she really thought about the raid.

"Is warning," she said. "Not want to worry Little Rain."

Fresh anxiety jolted him. "How sick is she?"

"Perhaps not sick, just carrying child."

"Is Dil concerned?"

"Not telling me." She looked somber. "Not saying many funny things, either."

"I've noticed." The subject of the strange Indians was easier to deal with. "What kind of warning? Are they angry because we settled here?"

"Colonel Braceworth say too many white people coming here, killing animals, putting feet on hunting grounds. Animals leave. Tribes may rise as one, to drive everyone out."

"I hope they don't try," he said. "The army will kill them and burn their villages. There are too many of us, but I suppose they can't know that."

"Perhaps the time of our people is over," she replied stoically.

They sat looking at one another across the table. Feeling a wrench in his stomach, Caleb reached out and laid his hand over hers but refused to insult her by saying she was wrong.

Winter settled in with no further trouble from the Indians. A week before Christmas, responding to an invitation from Meriwether to spend the holiday at his place, they loaded the sled on a cold but sunny afternoon with baked goods, elk steaks, roasts, and the cured hide of a grizzly bear it had taken White Cloud and Little Rain a month to prepare. Once Sheba and Joshua were harnessed and hitched to the sled's evener, the pack animals were brought in and fastened to the lead rope. White Cloud put a saddle blanket on her mare and mounted, carrying her Spencer. Dil, also armed, mounted up as well. Gripping her Spencer, Little Rain settled herself on the sled. Caleb picked up the reins, checked his rifle in its scabbard, and spoke to the mules.

"Hold on!" Foster shouted from his seat on Dakota's back. "Where's Wolf?"

The adults all looked at one another. Finally, Caleb said, "He decided not to come. As soon as he saw us bring out the sled, he ran off into the woods."

"Has he left us?" the boy asked, looking downcast.

"No, he just doesn't want to spend Christmas with Mr. Meriwether," Dil said quickly. "You know how picky he is about people."

"Well, what's he gonna eat with us gone?"

"Foster Wiggins," White Cloud said, "what did Wolf drag onto our porch five suns ago?"

"That yearling deer he killed up on the hill."

"Perhaps someone won't starve."

"I forgot about the deer," Foster said, "but I don't like to think about him being here all alone."

"Wolf not alone now," Little Rain said, surprising all of them. "Two times I see him playing in moonlight with young female wolf."

Foster turned toward Caleb. "Is that why he won't go with us?"

"Probably," Caleb said. "Let's go."

They set off on a foot of fresh snow that made the going easy for the mules. In the last of the short day's light, they reached Meriwether's ranch house.

"Welcome to Two Stars," Meriwether called out, coming down the steps.

Two men emerged from the bunkhouse and hurried toward them. After shaking hands with everyone and speaking briefly with Caleb, the men took charge of the animals and the sled. Meriwether came over and greeted everyone, Little Rain last. He stepped onto the sled, tucked her hand under his arm, and guided her off the sled and up the stairs to the main cabin.

"Is this being gentleman?" White Cloud asked Caleb quietly, taking his arm when they reached the stairs.

"Yes," Caleb said, "it is showing respect for her and giving her help because she is pregnant."

"I never saw Little Rain hold someone's arm to walk." White Cloud sounded troubled. "Is bad medicine. Maybe also more

foolishness," she added, adopting one of Dil's expressions. "Come along." She gripped Caleb's arm just above the elbow and started pushing him up the stairs.

"Stop," he said. "You're supposed to let me help you."

She muttered something in Arapaho along the lines of, "All idiots" but adjusted her speed to his. Dil, grinning, appeared on the other side of her and took her arm, pinning her between them.

She scowled at him. "Perhaps some time, someone will lose skin," she said.

Foster had never seen a Christmas tree, and the eight-foot-tall spruce standing between the two front windows, decorated with tinsel, small bright figurines, apples, gingerbread, brightly colored curls of paper, and burning candles so astonished him, he sat down cross-legged on the floor in front of it, staring in awed silence. The two women stared at the tree, then at one another, in astonishment almost as total as Foster's.

"My wife had a German governess," Meriwether told them. "The Germans always had trees at Christmas, no doubt a holdover from pagan times but adapted to the Christian holiday."

"While my mother was alive," Caleb said, "we always had a tree, but not as tall as this. I recall my father saying many of the families in town would not allow a Christmas tree in their houses. They claimed it was bringing back paganism. Their ministers preached against it."

"Well, I don't know whether my people did or not," Dil said, "but this sure looks nice."

Meriwether ended their gazing at the tree by directing them to a hall leading to bedrooms. Foster's was beside Dil and Little Rain's. The boy ran into his room and dashed out again, excitement clear in his face. "I ain't never slept this fancy."

"And there's dinner to come," Meriwether called after him as

he disappeared into Dil and Little Rain's room for a look around.

The week they spent with Meriwether went by very quickly. He was an excellent host, and, because the weather continued fair, they all spent part of each day riding with him, looking at cattle on the open range and in fenced pastures. From the first day, Meriwether insisted Little Rain ride in a sleigh with him. Her host outfitted her in a mink coat and a fox-skin scarf, both of which had belonged to his wife, a buffalo robe to cover her legs, and red mittens and a red wool hat, also his wife's, the hat pulled down over Little Rain's ears.

"I believe the old bird is courting my wife," Dil said to Caleb, leaning over in his saddle to speak past White Cloud. Caleb could tell he was only half joking.

"He's happy and no mistake," Caleb said with a chuckle, diplomatically choosing not to say, *so is Little Rain.*

"Someone may not like wash dishes soon," White Cloud observed with a sour note in her voice.

On this morning, they were moving at a trot through a scattered herd of mixed-breed cattle. The beasts were pawing away the snow and feeding, paying no attention to the people. The cattle were of particular interest to Caleb, who'd spent an hour the previous evening learning from Meriwether all he could about the Englishman's methods of breeding and culling the animals.

The peace of the scene shattered when a large, red bull, short-horned and thick-necked and bellowing a challenge, trotted past them, heading straight for the herd bull. Meriwether pulled his bay to a stop. "Give them some space."

The huge, black herd bull, with downward-curling horns, responded with a roar. He shook his giant head and pawed the ground, sending snow and clods of earth flying. The two beasts closed the distance between them at a gallop and smashed head

to head with immense force. Grunting and bellowing, they strove to shove one another back, ripping up dirt and snow as they struggled.

White Cloud looked unimpressed. "Horses fight better. Cattle push, make lots of noise." She was wrapped in a wolfskin jacket and wearing elk-hide leggings and boots that Caleb thought suited her to a *T*, and he said so. She didn't respond to the compliment, but before Caleb could say another word, the battle in front of them abruptly ceased. The red bull gave way to his rival, disengaged his horns, turned, and raced away. The herd bull followed briefly, then trotted back to the cows and began grazing again as if nothing had happened.

As they resumed their ride, White Cloud said to Caleb, "Perhaps someone will dress me in mink coat, wool hat, and save breath."

Caleb thought it best not to respond to that suggestion.

On returning to the lodge, they found dinner, prepared by three of the ranch hands' wives, laid out on the long dining room table. As they ate, Caleb asked Meriwether if he'd made any plans for the ranch.

"Not yet," Meriwether said. "I haven't really gotten that far. I'm still deciding whether to leave for England or stay a while longer."

Though they all enjoyed the visit, Caleb found he was eager to return to their homestead. On the way home, he had time to talk with Little Rain about her experiences at the ranch. She had been unusually quiet in Meriwether's presence, and he wondered how much she understood of his fussing over her. Also, he felt certain she was not well, and it worried him that she wouldn't share with Dil or even White Cloud what was wrong.

"What did you think of Meriwether?" he asked her.

"He made me feel safe," she said in a quiet but certain voice

from the depths of blankets and furs that White Cloud had buried her in for the journey. Meriwether had insisted she keep the red wool hat, and she wore it pulled down over her ears, so that not much besides her eyes, her nose, and her mouth were in sight. The weather had thickened, and the sky was piled with heavy, dark clouds, driven by a sharp north wind that had dropped the temperature below freezing.

"Something about you reminded him of his wife," Caleb said. "Was it his dressing you in her clothes that made you feel safe?"

"Maybe. Dil not like it very much. I too tired to explain it was all right. Am tired most of time now."

"Perhaps it would be best if you didn't work so hard," Caleb said quietly. "Did you notice the two Dexter cows tied to the sled? They're following along quite peacefully."

"I never eat cow."

"We'll keep these for their milk, and you are going to drink the cream from it. It will help you feel less tired."

"Never drink milk before," she said, as if she was not looking forward to the experience.

"It's best warm. I'll teach you and White Cloud how to milk them."

"Have heard before about *learn to do something*," she said, narrowing her eyes at him. "Then you have to do it."

"We'll make White Cloud do it," he said, which made her smile.

CHAPTER 38

The winter deepened. By January the snow was falling more often but never accumulated enough to put the animals in danger, except for the cows, whose milk production began to fall off. White Cloud was the first to notice the change because she dealt with the milk after it came in from the shelter. Caleb knew at once the cows needed grain to eat or they would dry up.

He made a trip to Spokane Bridge and returned with ten bags of whole oats. To everyone's surprise, Dil had found he knew how to milk, and with his forehead against the cow's side and a pail between his feet, he could milk very effectively one-handed. Before long Foster was clamoring to learn how to milk, and the two men took turns teaching him.

Little Rain stopped losing weight and regained a little strength soon after she began drinking milk mixed with cream, but White Cloud told Caleb she was still not very strong.

"Does she need a doctor?" Caleb asked.

"If gets any worse, yes," White Cloud replied. "Yesterday, someone found her crying because she could not sew leggings. Fingers too weak. Dil said she would not see doctor. Perhaps, time comes when doctor is here without asking Little Rain."

Caleb agreed.

With deeper snows threatening, it was clear the cows needed more shelter. They had been milking them in the lean-to during bad weather, but that wasn't satisfactory. Caleb and Dil, with

Foster and White Cloud helping, soon had enclosed one end of the lean-to and added small wooden mangers for the oats. White Cloud cut and stitched an elk hide for a drop-down door over the entrance, and Dil hung an oil lamp from the roof.

They persuaded Little Rain to come out to the cow shed for its christening. Foster led the two cows into the structure. White Cloud had poured oats into their grain boxes, a treat that quickly overcame their uneasiness at being in the enclosed space.

"I guess we can call ourselves farmers," Foster said, standing between the cows, stroking their backs as they ate.

Once the milking was finished, the men left the cows to finish their oats. Then, at White Cloud's invitation, they all went into her and Caleb's cabin for dinner. When the meal was over, Caleb and Wolf led the cows to the pond. While they drank, Caleb stared at the star-filled sky.

Wolf gave a soft growl. From the corner of his eye, Caleb glimpsed a dark shadow flickering through the trees on the hillside above the pond. *Wolves,* he thought, drawing his revolver and taking a tighter grip on the cows' lead ropes. Wolf sprang away and bolted into the woods. Caleb watched, wondering what he was up to. A few moments later he slipped out of the trees, closely followed by a smaller wolf. The newcomer crowded as close to Wolf as she could, apparently unnerved by the sight of a man. Wolf and his companion trotted along the edge of the trees for a short distance, Wolf glancing at Caleb frequently as if to be sure he was watching. Finally, Wolf turned into the trees again, and the two animals vanished.

Well. Caleb found himself grinning as he led the cows back to their tie-up.

"Thanks for introducing her," he said when Wolf rejoined him. "Now I know who's been leaving that extra pair of tracks in the snow around the pond."

Foster's first response at Caleb's confirmation of their

suspicions was to insist they find a name for Wolf's lady friend.

"Maybe *hooxei*. Means wolf in Arapaho. Is strong medicine," Little Rain said.

Everyone looked at Foster. He frowned a bit and then said, "I like it."

As the days passed, her name gradually became "Hookee," because, as White Cloud told Caleb, "Foster sure she would think it sound more like girl name. This one in few years will have young women giving him moccasins."

In the last week of February, Little Rain went into labor. It began in the early afternoon, and Caleb saddled Joshua and rode into town to fetch Doctor Haley. Against all her protests, Haley had visited three times and provided her with medications and tonics, none of which effected the desired change. Her strength had not returned.

"Her heart is not strong," Haley had told the other three adults on an early visit, well out of Little Rain's and Foster's hearing. "Without improvement there, she will not grow any stronger."

When Caleb returned with the doctor, Haley examined Little Rain. "She's weaker than she was at my last visit," Haley told them. "The only thing we can hope for is an easy delivery."

"Cold comfort," Dil said grimly.

The delivery was not easy. By midnight the baby's advance had been slow, and Little Rain was exhausted. The struggle lasted until a bit before first light, when she delivered a baby girl. White Cloud washed the infant and placed her on her mother's breast. Little Rain remained awake long enough to look at her child and then fell asleep.

At that point, Dil left the room. Caleb followed, and they walked out into the dim light of a new day. Dil fixed his gaze on

the morning star, shining brightly in the cold, clear sky to the east.

"We'll call her Morning Star," he said.

"It's a beautiful name," Caleb said quickly, to fill the silence.

Shortly after, Haley came out with White Cloud and spoke in a low voice to Dil. "She is very weak, and there's nothing I can tell you to do that will help, except keep her comfortable and encourage her to eat and drink." He laid a hand on Dil's shoulder. "If you give any credence to prayer, now is the time to send up your best one. I wish I had better news for you."

"Seems to me you did all that could be done," Dil said. "You saved the child, and I thank you." The exhaustion in his face and voice made Caleb hurt for him. *We won't let her go,* he thought. *We can't.*

Dil and Harley shook hands, and White Cloud offered to make breakfast for the doctor, but he declined. "There will be patients waiting," he said. "I'm sorry I couldn't do more."

Once Haley had mounted up, Caleb said, "We thank you. There's a beautiful new child with us, and Little Rain is still here. We will give both of them all the care we can."

In the growing light, they watched him ride down the snow-white valley, accompanied part of the way by Wolf running beside him like an outrider. Haley turned once and waved. Caleb and the others returned the gesture. A few moments later, Wolf turned and loped back to them, his breath rising like puffs of white smoke in the air.

"Spirit wolf," White Cloud said as though to herself, watching him approach.

"What do you mean?" Caleb asked.

"Not sure. He is powerful medicine. That's all."

"The baby is crying," Foster called from the landing between the cabins.

They hurried toward him, White Cloud in the lead.

"Is Little Rain sleeping because of what the doctor gave her?" Foster asked.

"Yes." White Cloud pushed him in front of her, into the cabin. "Get dressed. Cows need water. Someone will milk. Then we eat."

They found Little Rain lying in bed, one hand rocking the cradle next to her.

"Can't pick up," she said weakly when White Cloud came into the room, followed by the two men.

"Baby hungry." White Cloud lifted the tightly wrapped infant. "Dil, help her with pillows to sit up to nurse."

Dil bent to the task and then asked Little Rain, "How do you feel?"

She looked pale and washed-out. "Want to sleep," she said.

"Can you feed the baby first?" Dil asked but got no answer.

When White Cloud passed the baby to Little Rain, Caleb went across the landing to his cabin and pulled on his barn coat, then picked up an axe from the wood pile and went down to the pond. A few swings of the axe broke through the new ice that had formed overnight in the water hole. Foster came along, leading the cows. The horses and mules, having learned the routine, drifted in behind them.

"I should of done that first," the boy said.

"You're doing fine. We'll get this done quickly," Caleb replied, trying to sound cheerful.

"What's wrong with Little Rain, aside from having had a baby? I know something is." Foster's face looked pinched, as if he were fighting to hold fear at bay.

Caleb saw it was time to be truthful. "Dr. Haley says her heart is weak, but there's nothing to be done for it," he replied as they started back toward the shed, each leading a cow. "You must have noticed. For the past six weeks or so, she's grown more and more feeble and spent more and more time sleeping."

Foster stopped so quickly Bess bumped into him. Caleb stopped with him. "She's going to die, ain't she?"

Caleb knew the question was coming, but it still shook him. Hearing Foster ask it somehow made it real.

"I don't know." He hoped to God his own words weren't making things harder for the boy. "It may have been that carrying the baby was the cause of it, and now she's had her child, she may get better."

"You ain't got to make this easier for me, Captain," Foster said. "I'll be all right. It's just that it don't seem right. She ain't done nothing to deserve this."

"No, she hasn't, Foster, but people don't usually die because they deserve it."

"I heard a preacher say once that God had called them home. If that's so, I don't have a high opinion of how he goes about fetching them. And Little Rain ain't been bothering him, and she ain't been asking to go anywhere."

"No, she hasn't, but let's get these cows to the shed. If we're late to breakfast, White Cloud will tell us about it."

Foster gave Bess a push, and she started walking again. "Is it all right for me to talk with you about this?"

Caleb laid a hand on the boy's head. "It's just what you should do. Any time you want to."

Three days later, Dil helped Little Rain sit up, tucked pillows behind her, laid Morning Star in her arms, and helped place her in a nursing position. "Can you hold her?" he asked, concerned.

Pale, sunken faced, and shadow-eyed, Little Rain looked up at Dil and smiled. She had not spoken since waking that morning, nor eaten or drunk.

"I'll get the diaper cloths White Cloud brought over," he said.

White Cloud had trouble locating them and then insisted on showing Dil how they should be folded to put on the baby. Four or five minutes later, when Dil returned to their bedroom, Morning Star had slipped onto her mother's lap and was beginning to fuss. Little Rain made no response when he spoke to her.

Moments later, Dil gathered the baby in his arms and crossed the breezeway.

Caleb, White Cloud, and Foster were eating lunch when he came in. One look at his face told them all what had happened. White Cloud ran to Dil, took the baby out of his arms, and led him to the table. Caleb pulled out a chair, and he slumped into it.

"She was there, and then she wasn't," Dil said. His face was blank with shock, his body limp as if he lacked strength to sit fully upright.

"Is she . . ." Foster couldn't finish the question.

Caleb gripped his friend's shoulder. "I'm sorry, Dil."

"There was no struggle, no sign of pain." Dil spoke haltingly, as if scarcely able to find the words. "I couldn't find a pulse. I closed her eyes."

White Cloud said quietly, "I will care for Morning Star."

As she went to the door, Foster started to follow her.

"No, Foster," she said. "Not now. Stay with Dil and Caleb." Then she went out quickly.

"I don't know what to do next," Dil said to Caleb. "I can't seem to focus. There's Morning Star . . ."

He leaned forward, elbows on the table, and pressed his forehead into his palms.

Caleb sat down beside him. "There's nothing you have to do now. Tell us what you want done, and White Cloud and I will do it. If you want to talk, talk. If not, you don't have to. But

please stay here with us." He rose and went to Foster, who had gone to sit on the bench in front of the fireplace.

"Are you all right, Foss?" he asked the boy quietly.

"I ain't sure," he said, dry eyed but white as a sheet.

"None of us is, but our first responsibility here is Dil. He mustn't be left alone."

"What about Morning Star?" the boy asked. "How's she going to eat? Will she die, too?"

He gave the boy a gentle shake. "No, she won't. White Cloud knows what to do. Morning Star's going to be all right." He wished he was as sure as he sounded.

"The ground's froze," Foster said, as if suddenly remembering. "How are we going to bury her?"

"I don't think we'll do that, but that will be up to White Cloud and Dil. Don't worry about it. I've got to help White Cloud now. Can you go over to the table and sit beside Dil? Just sit? If he wants to talk, he will, and then you can answer. Don't ask him questions. Just sit with him."

"I can do that," the boy said.

By the time Caleb reached her, White Cloud had dressed Little Rain in her best deerskin dress and was spreading a blanket on the floor beside the bed. "Get other blanket and help put it on this one," White Cloud said. "Then we lift her onto blankets and roll her."

Caleb guessed what this meant. As he unfolded the second blanket he asked, "Will you speak with Dil about this?"

White Cloud dropped to her knees and sat back on her feet. "First, someone must be prepared for journey."

"Little Rain was Dil's wife," Caleb began, but White Cloud stopped him.

"It is very bad medicine to speak of the dead by name," she said. "Someone must begin her journey and not be called back."

Caleb checked a flash of anger. "We are not to talk about her?"

"No. Not call her back. Very bad medicine. Is best to let dead go." White Cloud spoke with such intensity, Caleb knew how much she meant it.

He knelt beside her and looked her in the eye. "Dil and Foster and I do not believe the dead can be called back, nor do we believe the dead can harm us. Dil will not understand why he must not speak her name."

They crouched on opposite sides of the blanket, staring at one another.

White Cloud frowned, then said, "Perhaps, I will not hear others speaking her name."

"Perhaps you will not." Caleb felt relieved and proud of her for having found a way to go forward. "I'll tell Dil and Foster what you said."

"Lift her onto the blankets now," White Cloud said.

After it was done, Dil came in to sit beside Little Rain. Caleb sat with him. Then White Cloud brought a buffalo robe, and all of them, including Foster, rolled Little Rain's body into it. They tied the ends of the robe with rawhide and then tied the robe twice more.

"Tomorrow," Dil said when they were finished, "we will build a platform for her to rest on."

That evening, before Caleb and Foster went out to tend to the cows, Caleb took Foster's hand and led him inside the shed to where Dil sat beside Little Rain. "Little Rain's burial will not be like ours," he began, uncomfortable with what he was about to say. "Now she is gone. We must not speak of her or mention her name in front of White Cloud."

"Why not?" Foster demanded. Dil stiffened, looking away from them both.

"The Arapaho believe the dead begin a journey when they

die," Caleb said quietly, hoping to bring Dil along with what followed. "They believe speaking of the dead or speaking their name calls them back. To respect White Cloud's needs as well as ours, I'm asking that we don't mention Little Rain in her presence. Among ourselves, it's all right. What do you think, Dil?"

Dil turned to look at Caleb, his face strained in the shed's lamplight.

"I want to be angry, to feel sorry for myself and say I'll speak about her whenever I want to, but I understand White Cloud's thinking and Little Rain's. If White Cloud had died, I suppose she would not want to hear her own name mentioned—or mine, for that matter, if it was me."

"Foster?" Caleb asked. After a long moment, the boy nodded.

"Then let's get these cows attended to, Foss," Caleb said. "Morning Star needs milk for her supper."

CHAPTER 39

When Caleb and Foster brought in the day's milk still warm, White Cloud mixed it with ground wheat and malt flour and poured it into a china pot with an extra long spout, designed for feeding babies when their mothers couldn't nurse them. Dr. Haley had told them of the feeding pot, and the special flour mixture, when it first became clear Little Rain might not recover. Caleb had purchased it two weeks ago, while praying they'd never have to use it.

With a needle, White Cloud poked a tiny hole in a piece of pounded deerskin intended for a shirt, then tied it over the spout of the feeding pot so the baby could suck on the leather and draw the milk into her mouth. Morning Star ate greedily, and Caleb cautiously allowed himself to hope they wouldn't lose her along with her mother.

The cold weather broke in March, and the remainder of the snow vanished from their valley. The ice in the pond melted, and the trees budded. Raising fences and other tasks kept them working from daylight to dark, but nothing broke through the grief that held Dil in its grip. Every day, sometimes before daylight—because he slept so little—he walked up the hill behind the cabins and stood, or lay face down, forehead resting on his arms, under the raised platform where Little Rain's body rested. Rain or shine he spent an hour or more, talking to her or just sitting with her.

One night, as they lay in bed a few weeks after Little Rain's

death, White Cloud spoke to Caleb of what Dil was doing. "Is bad," she said, putting a hand on his arm. "Dil cannot heal. A bad spirit is in him. No good comes from not letting dead go. Someone should tell him."

Caleb leaned back on his pillow. "I've tried."

"What does he say?"

"Nothing. He seems to listen, but, when I stop speaking, he turns back to whatever he was doing."

She sighed. "He does not hold Morning Star. Bad spirit tells him baby was cause of someone's death."

"Yes," Caleb agreed, "it is bad, but if he doesn't want to let her go, there's nothing we can do."

"We will go on keeping Morning Star and Foster here with us. That is all I have to say."

Caleb wondered what it meant that she said *we* and *us*, words he could not remember hearing her use before.

"We will do as you wish with Morning Star," he said, "but don't tell Dil what you are doing or say anything about taking her away. Let's wait to see if he objects."

Dil ignored the child, never spoke of her, never picked her up, and, if he could manage it, he did not look at her. It troubled White Cloud, but Caleb convinced her no good would come of confronting Dil with her concern.

The spring unfolded around them. The sun-filled days grew longer. Newly arriving birds filled the woods and fields with their songs. Caleb plowed and harrowed the land for their vegetable garden, and all of them worked on the snake fences. With Foster's help White Cloud planted the garden and put up a scarecrow to keep off the crows, only to find a crow perched on its head a few days later.

Their routines were disrupted a few days after that by the arrival of Meriwether, with half a dozen men, all heavily armed. When he dismounted, followed by his men, he greeted White

Cloud and Caleb and then shook hands with Foster, introducing him to each of the others. Foster was particularly taken by the Mexican with a huge, black sombrero and two cartridge belts crossing his chest.

Finally, Meriwether turned to Dil. "I heard of your loss and want to say how sorry I am."

Dil made no response, but the resulting awkwardness was broken when White Cloud brought out Morning Star, thriving on her cow's milk and malt flour, to show their guests. Meriwether was delighted with her.

"She is going to be a beauty," he said, beaming over her. "Look at those eyes."

She was a beautiful child with large, dark eyes, pink cheeks, and black hair. The other men crowded around her and clamored to hold her—not what Caleb would have expected from hired guns, and he was delighted. Morning Star kicked and wriggled with pleasure as she was passed from one to another of the mostly bearded, rough-handed men, who held her as if she were made of glass. "This one will break many hearts," the Mexican said when she reached him, causing a burst of laughter.

"Perhaps some people are hungry and will eat with us," White Cloud said to Meriwether when she had the baby in her arms again.

"I wish you would," Caleb said. "I'd like to talk about buying cattle from you."

"It would be a pleasure, but we can't stay. Sorry to say, I've come as a bearer of bad news. Some of the Umatilla, Cayuse, and a few villages of the Nez Perce have risen. We've fought off two raids already. They've been within a mile of Spokane Bridge, burned some houses, run off horses and cows. It won't be long before they find you."

"How bad has it been for you?" Caleb asked.

"We lost about fifty head, all carrying my brand, but the chiefs of most of the villages will buy them anyway. More will find their way north to the mining towns."

"Young ones seeking to become warriors?" White Cloud asked.

"I'm afraid not. These were braves in full regalia with war paint and feathers."

A chill settled over Caleb. "How many?"

"Twelve or fifteen." He turned to Caleb. "I want all of you to come back to the ranch until things quiet down. You'll be safer there. If you and Dil don't feel you can go, let me take White Cloud, Foster, and the infant back with us."

"Not leave them here alone," White Cloud said quickly.

"They have rifles?" Caleb asked.

"All of them," Meriwether answered.

Caleb and Dil looked at one another and then shook their heads.

"They'll burn you out," a tall, gray-bearded man said. "You've got pine shingles on your roofs. They'll stand back there in the woods and shoot burning arrows into them, and they'll go up like gunpowder."

"And once they have you in the open, it will be all over," another man added.

"I agree with what's been said," Caleb responded after a moment's pause. He turned to Dil, White Cloud, and Foster. "It's probable they'll burn us out whether we're here or not. Do you agree, Mr. Meriwether?"

"I'm afraid there's no doubt about it," the Englishman replied.

Caleb looked at White Cloud. "We'll have to start over. What do you think?"

"Cannot start over dead," she said.

That remark was met with quickly smothered chuckles, fol-

lowed by murmurs of approval from Meriwether's men.

"Dil?" Caleb asked.

"Little Rain," Dil said, his face strained.

"Not touch her," White Cloud said instantly. "Will not go near her. Very bad medicine."

"She's right," the older man said.

"Then I'll go with you," Dil said in a dull voice.

"We must go as soon as possible," Meriwether said. "What can we do to help?"

"There's ammunition in the cabins that shouldn't fall into their hands. Foster, show them where it's stored."

"Take all clothes we can and Morning Star's food," White Cloud said.

Meriwether spoke to the gray-bearded man and the Mexican. Leading their horses, they went off with Foster.

"I'll harness the mules and hitch them to the scoot," Caleb said. "White Cloud, start with the clothes. Perhaps a couple of these men could bring in the animals and get them on a lead, and saddle those we'll be riding. The saddles and harnesses are in that shed over there. There's two milking cows in the far end of the horse shelter, if someone would get leads onto them. They're the baby's wet nurses. Mr. Meriwether, there's a fire burning in the cabin behind me if you'd like to sit by it while we get this organized."

Meriwether nodded. "I can see this move is in good hands, Captain, and I will take you up on the offer."

In very little time, the sled was heaped with all the hides, ammunition, clothes, blankets, robes, guns, and harnesses it could carry. Morning Star was wrapped in a blanket and tucked in her bassinette, then fitted snugly among the buffalo robes where Caleb could see her. The milk cows and the pack animals, loaded with more things from the camps, were hitched to a lead, fastened to the sled's rear.

After settling the last load, White Cloud went to Caleb, who stood by their cabin door. "Someone's eyes sting," she said in a choked voice as he shut the door behind them for the last time.

He pulled her to him and kissed her forehead. "They can't burn the stove," he told her. "We will dig it out of the ashes, dust it off, and it will be good as new."

"Perhaps I will bake more pies," she said.

"I'm sure you will," he said. His comment meant one thing to him and quite another to White Cloud, who managed to return his smile.

"Is Dill where I think he is?" he asked as they walked toward the sled.

"Yes. Left a while ago," she said. "Nothing good will come of it."

With a heavy heart, Caleb agreed. Pride and sadness mingled in him as he watched her mount up. She waited until the mules had leaned into their breast straps and set off with long strides, then fell in at the rear of the pack animals, her rifle across her thighs.

Until nearly noon, the journey through the rocky hills and patches of woods and fields went without incident. They passed a knoll with a shattered ledge jutting out of its top, surrounded by broken boulders. A hundred yards beyond stood a stand of dark spruce. Caleb barely had time to think *ambush* when out of it exploded more than a dozen Indians in war paint, rifles in their hands, whooping and yelling.

"The rocks!" Caleb shouted. "Follow me!" He tugged the mules to the right, slackened the reins, and shouted, "Go!"

The animals bulled up the knoll, twisting their way through the scattered rocks. When they reached the top, Caleb reined them in. He swung down, grabbed the bassinette from its nest on the sled, and ran into the broken ledges, where he set Morning Star down, then ran back for his rifle and a box of ammuni-

tion. Around him Meriwether's men scattered for cover among the rocks while their horses, trailing their reins, milled around the sled. A moment later, White Cloud, Dil, and Foster found Caleb.

White Cloud yanked the lid off the ammunition box. "Foster, sit by Morning Star. Not stand up." While she was speaking, the Indians made their first charge past the knoll, firing as they rode. Bullets whined as they ricocheted among the rocks.

Caleb, White Cloud, Dil, and Meriwether's men returned fire almost simultaneously, knocking five of their attackers off their horses and shooting them again once they were down. The marauders regrouped out of carbine range, but the Mexican had a Sharps. He stood, resting rifle on top of a boulder, and took down another of the Indians.

"Cease firing," Meriwether said sharply. "Let them go." He went on watching as the survivors, yipping and waving their rifles, kicked their horses into a gallop and rode away.

"There go the cabins," Dil said.

"I'm afraid so," Meriwether replied. "They'll follow our trail straight to your holdings. I'm glad you're here and not there."

"Dead ones died a good death," White Cloud said. "People will sing and celebrate their bravery."

Meriwether looked at her. "Will they be given a burial?"

"Perhaps, if they are men of importance," she replied. "The women will make platform, say what must be said, and put them on it, to hasten their journey."

"I know some of those men," the Mexican said. "I have bought horses from them. They are Cayuse. Their village is east of here, just over the border."

Meriwether nodded toward him. "Manuel was a trader before hiring on with me."

"Until he got one of their women in trouble, and they put a price on his head," another of the men said, to hoots of laughter.

"Not true," Manuel protested, addressing White Cloud and pulling off his sombrero. "I caught their chief trying to cheat me in a horse trade and cheated him instead. Then I had to stop trading."

"Maybe better to be cheated once than lose all trade," she observed.

Meriwether cut off Manuel's response. "Let's get under way. There may be more of these raiding parties on the loose, and I want to get home."

Caleb had noticed that, during the brief encounter, Meriwether had not fired his rifle. He had not taken cover either but stood beside a boulder, watching the Indians. It was odd behavior, but at the moment he could spare it no more thought.

CHAPTER 40

They reached Meriwether's ranch without more trouble. To everyone's relief, ten days later, after repulsing two more raids with none of the defenders being killed, Colonel Braceworth arrived with a cavalry unit of fifty men and a train of supply wagons.

The colonel rode up to the veranda and greeted Meriwether. "May we cross your ranch and set up camp on the Black Horse River? I expect it will take us at least two weeks to put an end to these raids."

"The water and grazing are good there," Meriwether said. "Stay as long as necessary. I suppose you know Captain Stone and Sergeant Dil. We fear they may have lost their cabins."

Braceworth turned to Caleb. "I'm sorry to be the one to tell you, but, according to one of our scouts, your buildings were burned to the ground. What can you tell us about the new Indian burial on the hill behind where your cabins stood?"

"That's Sergeant Dil's wife's burial place," Caleb said quickly. "She died three days after giving birth to their child."

Sadness crossed the man's weathered face as he turned to Dil. "My condolences, Sergeant. It is some consolation, I hope, that you have the child."

He waited briefly for Dil's response. Seeing he wasn't going to get one, he said, "I must go. From now until this is over, our speed will dictate the degree of our success, or lack thereof."

"You and your officers are welcome here whenever it is pos-

sible for you to come," Meriwether said.

"Thank you, Mr. Meriwether, but it must be another time." The colonel whirled his big roan and galloped away, with his officers scrambling to catch up. Caleb stood with Meriwether and the others on the veranda for a while, watching the jingling passage of the bluecoat cavalry, followed by the creaking, lumbering wagons filing by, the mule drivers shouting and the dust rising around them in a pale-gray cloud.

"Very colorful," Meriwether said, a marked bitterness in his voice. "They are bringing death and destruction to a people who want nothing more than to live as they have always lived."

"That is no more," White Cloud said. She stood beside Caleb, her arms folded, staring stoically at the passing stream of men, horses, mules, and wagons.

"It's the women who'll suffer most," Dil said, breaking a long silence.

"I'm afraid you're right," Meriwether said. "This must be difficult for you, Mrs. Stone."

"My second father told me once, 'Even oldest tree dies.' It was a long time I did not know what he meant."

"But you do now," Meriwether said.

"I'd like to think they will learn to live another way," Caleb said.

"Not in my lifetime." Meriwether moved away to speak with his foreman.

That evening, when they'd eaten supper in the dying light of a glorious sunset, Meriwether leaned back in his chair. "Could I have a word with you, Caleb, in private?"

"If you can give us a minute, Mr. Meriwether," Dil put in, "I have something to tell Mrs. Stone and Captain Stone."

"Certainly, Dil." Meriwether rose from his seat.

"Can Foster go with you?" White Cloud asked.

"Come along, young man," Meriwether said. "You can help

me look at some horses."

Foster shot out of his chair and left with their host. Dil waited, silent, until they were out of earshot.

"We're listening," Caleb said, afraid he knew what was coming.

White Cloud looked as if she knew, too. "Is someone sure?" she asked, with a slight frown at Dil.

"Yes, White Cloud, I am," he replied, grim faced. "You both may have guessed what I'm going to say, but I must say it. I owe you that, and there's a request in it."

Caleb settled back into his chair. "All right."

"I can't stay here," Dil said, clearly struggling to get the words out. "I would not be able to stay away from Little Rain. I'd have to go to her every day, and I know it's not right."

"Maybe with time . . ." Caleb said, trying to ease Dil's pain.

"That's not the whole of it," Dil went on, his voice rising.

White Cloud laid a hand on Caleb's arm. "We will listen," she said calmly.

"I want you and the Captain to raise Morning Star," Dil said in a rush. "I can't raise her even if I wanted to, and I don't because I can't look at her without thinking of Little Rain and how she died."

"We will care for her," White Cloud replied without hesitation.

Caleb floundered with the suddenness and sorrow of it all. "Where will you go, Dil?"

For the first time, a hint of life colored Dil's voice. "When Dr. Haley was treating Little Rain, he told me he and some other doctors were setting up a hospital in Walla Walla. He's offered me the job of managing the nursing end of it and stepping in to work myself when called on. I'm going down there. Maybe I can make a life out of it."

Walla Walla. A long way from here. Caleb fought not to show

how hard Dil's words had hit him. "Will you want to stay in touch with us and Morning Star and Foster?"

"Not for a while," Dil said. "This is the hardest thing I've ever done, and it's going to take all the help the Lord can give to make me stick it out."

"When you are ready," White Cloud said briskly, "you will come back. We will be glad."

"Yes, when you're ready," Caleb said, still struggling with Dil's decision. "You will always have a home with us."

"I guess I knew that," Dil said, "but I'm much obliged to you for saying it. Now comes the rest." He focused on Caleb. "What I'm doing is selfish, I know, and to ease my conscience a sliver, I'm giving my land to you and White Cloud." He thrust his hand into his trouser pocket and pulled out a sheaf of papers. "It's all made over to you. I've left you with Morning Star and Foster, too. All legal like."

He broke off abruptly, as if unable to go on.

Caleb took the papers and gripped Dil's hand harder. "White Cloud and I will keep these papers, and we'll improve all the land. When the day comes you want your share back, it's yours again. How's that?"

"All right," Dil said, in a steadier voice. "I'm leaving first thing in the morning. I'll find the cavalry encampment and have a talk with Colonel Braceworth. He'll be sending reports south, and I'll ride with the men carrying them. That will get me where I'm going safely."

"Perhaps Foster should hear you go away only for a while?" White Cloud asked.

The message in the question was not lost on Dil.

"That's just what I'll say," he replied. "Thank you."

Thinking Dil would soon be coming back, Foster took his leaving without much grief. For White Cloud and Caleb, it was

more difficult. Caleb, in particular, couldn't shake off the conviction that Dil's departure was his fault.

"I should have taken his grief more seriously and done more to assuage it," he told White Cloud as they prepared for bed.

She was sitting cross legged on the bed, brushing her hair. "That is Captain Stone talking," she said, watching him closely.

Caleb halted halfway through taking off his boots. "What does that mean?"

"Captains responsible for other people."

"Are responsible," he said.

"If I leave *are* out, you listen," she replied. "If not, not pay attention."

He dropped his second boot and faced her. "I'm listening."

"Dil is grown man, almost old as you, and good friend. Also, is sergeant with only one arm. What you think I mean?"

"If he wanted my help, he would have asked for it."

"Yes." She held out the brush to him. "And now perhaps someone might finish brushing hair."

He finished undressing, then climbed onto the bed and took the brush. Brushing White Cloud's hair at bedtime was a way they had found to talk more intimately.

"Two children will be ours," White Cloud said. "Baby daughter, son half grown already. Not easy, to be mother and father so fast. But love is there, has been for a long time. Is enough, I think. I hope."

She fell silent. He set the brush down and pulled her back against him. "Have you told me all the ways you feel about everything that's happened?"

She looked thoughtful. "When I knew cabins would burn, I wanted to lie down beside someone and never get up. Then I said, but if we had not been told what would happen, all of us would have died. I was ashamed for not being grateful that we saw into the future and escaped. Before, I did not tell you all

the truth. Now I think of all we will do, Caleb Stone, and I am happy deep down and also sad about Dil and someone else on a journey."

"I love you, White Cloud," he said. "You are in my heart, and in my arms, thank the Lord. There will be another, larger cabin with a stove in it, and you will bake more pies."

"And I love you," she said, snuggling back against him. "But now, all at once, you and I must also make room in our hearts for Foster and Morning Star."

"Our son and our daughter." Caleb held her tighter as the reality of what he had said sunk in. "If Dil marries again, he might take Morning Star back."

"Until the day trees grow upside down, she is our daughter," White Cloud told him.

Eleven days later, shortly after daylight, the returning cavalry troops and wagons began passing Meriwether's ranch house. Colonel Braceworth and his officers appeared out of the dust and rode up to the veranda steps, where Meriwether and the rest waited to greet him. White Cloud carried Morning Star.

"The uprising is over," Braceworth said. "Seven villages have been burned and the chiefs either killed or no longer making war. It is not work I'm especially proud of, but my men carried out their task with remarkable courage and restraint, and I am proud of them."

He shifted uneasily in his saddle before continuing. "A lot of their warriors were killed or wounded," he said. "Their families are scattered, the ringleaders shot, but I suppose others will take their place. It will be years before they can send more raiding parties to burn and loot and kill, though."

"Thank you and your men for your help," Caleb said. "Now we will sleep more easily. Did Sergeant Dil reach Spokane Bridge with your couriers?"

"I believe he's gone all the way to Walla Walla," Braceworth said, sounding relieved to change the subject. "I'm told he stopped in Spokane Bridge, and the doctor there sent him on. They had a couple of brief encounters with small bands of Cayuse raiders en route but shot their way out and outran their assailants."

"I'm glad to hear it." The depth of Caleb's relief made him realize how much he had worried about Dil.

Colonel Braceworth straightened himself in the saddle. "You'll have to put up with our dust and clatter for a bit, but then things should settle down. Good luck to you all. You know where we are should you need us."

With a pull on the brim of his hat, he and his officers, save one, rode away. A young lieutenant lingered briefly and said, "My orders are to tell you, Captain Stone, there are tents and supplies being left for you, and that if you need any further help now or later, you're to let the colonel know. And I can tell you, he means what he says."

"Please convey my thanks to him," Caleb said, pleased.

They watched the lieutenant gallop after his companions until he was lost in the column's dust.

"I 'spect I'll be in the cavalry when I get growed," Foster said as the group on the veranda began to break up.

"It is my sincere hope, Foster," Meriwether said seriously, "that you never have to put on a military uniform. Perhaps Captain Stone feels differently."

"I do not," Caleb said. "I most sincerely do not."

"Captain, could you spare me a few minutes?" Meriwether asked.

Caleb nodded, and Meriwether led him inside the barn. The two men sat down in Meriwether's office, a small pine-finished room with two dusty windows, smelling of wood, hay, and horses. It also had a creaking plank floor, several ancient

spindle-backed chairs, a black pot-bellied stove, and a large roll-top desk with two oil lamps, one on each side of the writing surface.

"In the last few weeks," Meriwether began, "I have made up my mind about something that may affect you. If it's acceptable, I would like to lay it out for you."

"I'm happy to listen," Caleb replied, wondering where the conversation was going.

"It began in earnest when I learned Little Rain had died. That young woman captured my heart. My wife was Welsh, with heavy, black hair like Little Rain's, and, although Alice had blue eyes rather than black, they shared a brilliance and intensity I recognized."

Meriwether paused as if lost in thought, then continued. "You'll recall I told you I was considering returning to England, but I had not been able to either go ahead with the plan or cast it aside. Little Rain's death struck me as more than the death of one young, beautiful woman. It was, I saw, the death in miniature of her people."

"You mean all the Indian nations."

"Yes. Then the raids began. When the warriors attacked us coming back here from your place, I watched how you assessed the situation, saw a strategy for saving us, took us into the rocks, and led us through to a safe conclusion. Most admirable, Captain Stone."

"You didn't fire your rifle. Why?"

Meriwether shrugged. "I couldn't bring myself to. Instead of seeing our attackers as threats to our lives, I saw only their vulnerability and the certainty of their destruction. Then Colonel Braceworth with his cavalry unit arrived, with the inevitable outcome of their assault on the tribes. At that point I made up my mind I'd had enough."

"You're selling out and going back," Caleb said, not at all surprised.

"That's partially right."

"Meaning?"

"I can't sell this place. I have no deed to the land or the buildings on it."

"You could hire a manager, I suppose," Caleb said.

Meriwether gave a wry grin. "How well do you think that would work?"

"Then what are you proposing?"

"I'd like to sell you the cattle and give you the buildings. You live here and run the place, do whatever you want with it to keep it profitable, and give me ten percent of the proceeds until I die."

Caleb's surprise did not prevent him from thinking. "What's your outlay, and what's your income now?"

"Depending on the severity of the winters," Meriwether said, "the ranch brings in from one to two thousand a year, more than enough to meet the costs of running it. The sale of beef is steady—twenty-five to thirty dollars a head in mining towns north of us and across the border. They're worth a lot less here, so I've been selling them to herders who take them north. I didn't want the task of getting the animals to market in fit condition."

"I believe you can walk steers about fifteen miles a day without their losing weight, if the grazing is half decent," Caleb said.

Meriwether shook his head. "Not a task I would relish. What do you say to my proposal?"

"I doubt I could buy the cattle," Caleb said. "I've been drawing heavily on my cash reserves since leaving Maine. Buying the land I did and outfitting the farm cost a considerable sum. And there's another thing: one of these days, people like me are go-

ing to come along and begin claiming the land that makes up this ranch."

"Good point." Meriwether made a sour face. "Well, it was worth a try."

"How much will you get for the cattle if you can't sell them to me?"

Meriwether stared at the floor. "Damned little."

"If I can get them for that, we've got a deal."

The Englishman brightened and thrust out a hand. "Done."

Within two weeks, counting a trip to a bank in Walla Walla, Meriwether concluded all the business of transferring his claim on the buildings and cattle to Caleb. A week earlier, he'd sent two wagons piled high with his possessions on their way to the coast. Caleb spent whatever time he could riding over the ranch with Ben Starks, the foreman, and putting their heads together over the ranch books.

When their surveys were done, Caleb leaned back in the squeaking swivel chair at Meriwether's rolltop desk. "Is it doable, Ben?"

Starks scratched his beard. "This is the first time I've seen the books, Captain Stone, and I'm obliged to you for showing them to me. That said, my guess is yes. There are some changes I'd recommend, but, on the whole, this ranch is a going concern."

"What changes?"

"First, build the beef stock and breed toward heft. Mr. Meriwether's Dexters are fine farm animals, but they're not heavy enough to make it worth crossbreeding with the longhorns. There's some red cattle coming up here from California that outweigh the Dexters and are a tougher breed. Also, come late spring when the calving, castrating, and branding is over, we should put together a drive and take the animals we're selling

north to the mining towns. It will double or triple our income."

"Where can we get our hands on some of that red stock?" Caleb asked.

"There's a few in those holdings around Spokane Bridge."

Caleb nodded. "Let's look into it."

The next day, Meriwether said goodbye. He embraced White Cloud, held Morning Star briefly, then put his arms around Foster after shaking the boy's hand. Finally, he turned to Caleb.

"I wish you and your family health and happiness," he said, taking Caleb's hand in both of his. "Don't feel offended, but I find now that I am actually leaving, I'm happier than I've been for years."

"I'm not offended, Mr. Meriwether, and Godspeed."

The Englishman left with three of what were now Caleb's men, to see him safely onto a ship in Seattle. After supper that evening, Caleb and White Cloud left Foster poring over an illustrated copy of *Grimm's Fairy Tales* he had found in Meriwether's well-stocked library and went outside with Wolf beside them. White Cloud cradled Morning Star in her arms. They walked out beyond the barns and stood on the end of the grassy bluff overlooking their rolling grassland, dotted in the evening light with cattle spread out on both sides of the winding, tree-lined Otter River that ran west toward distant hills.

"What will we do with our first place where stove is?" she asked.

Caleb slid an arm around her shoulders. "What if we were to build a proper house on it and turn our place into the farm we had planned? Would you like that?"

She leaned against him. "Yes. And perhaps someday, one of our children might live there."

"It would make me very happy," Caleb said. As he pulled her closer, he doubted it was possible to be happier than he was at that moment.

ABOUT THE AUTHOR

Kinley Roby lives with his wife, author and editor, Mary Linn Roby, in Southwest Florida.

The employees of Five Star Publishing hope you have enjoyed this book.

Our Five Star novels explore little-known chapters from America's history, stories told from unique perspectives that will entertain a broad range of readers.

Other Five Star books are available at your local library, bookstore, all major book distributors, and directly from Five Star/Gale.

Connect with Five Star Publishing

Visit us on Facebook:
   https://www.facebook.com/FiveStarCengage

Email:
   FiveStar@cengage.com

For information about titles and placing orders:
   (800) 223-1244
   gale.orders@cengage.com

To share your comments, write to us:
   Five Star Publishing
   Attn: Publisher
   10 Water St., Suite 310
   Waterville, ME 04901